www.hudsonhousemysteries.com

The Iron Beast

Alan McKee

CAST OF CHARACTERS

Charles Wilney
- a former navvy who ministered in the camps-
owner of the cottage in Higher Woodsford .Wilney was also a friend,
educator and spiritual advisor to the Darrows

Richard Darrow-
an orphaned child who lived in the navvy camps under
the tutelage of Mr. Wilney. Later, he is employed as a teacher of the Classics
in Miss Reade's Academy in London

Fanny Darrow
- Richard's orphaned sister who was also brought up in the navvy camps .
Later, she becomes a coster in Convent Garden in London

Sally Howard
- She is the focus of Richard Darrow intentions.
Her family is in the engraving business in London

Pamela Blackwood
- a young lady of exceptional talent as a pianist. Her ancestral home,
Blackdale, is in the highlands north of Manchester

Edward Blackwood
- father of Pamela and a wealthy collier who made his initial
fortune colleries and then by investing in the Stockton & Darlington Railway

Gregory Barnes, esq
- Edward Blackwood's solicitor in Manchester -appreciates Classical Literature

Joseph Barnes
- son of Gregory Barnes who recently returned from reading law
at Oxford with a special interest in contract law

Emily
- an orphaned child who is taken in by the Blackwoods to be educated

Elizabeth Peevy
- a governess to Pamela and Emily at Blackdale

John Bradley
- a solicitor who is elected MP for the Borough of Pilkington.
He is married to Elspeth.

John Samuelson
- self-taught engineer who is head man in the navvy work camps and as known
as "Punching Jack" and "Mighty Jack". He becomes a leading railway contractor

THE IRON BEAST

Paul Samuelson
- son of John Samuelson

John Booth
- Samuelson's confidential secreatary

Michael Vaughn
-a banker who helped fund new railway lines. Together with his
wife, Miriam they gave business and social dinner parties

Collins
- a spy from the Napoleonic wars and a former calvary officer, who now works
as a spy for Samuelson

Charles Fisk
- a carpenter and a neighbour of the Darrow's. He is a visionary Chartist

Cynthia Hackworth
- a skilled seamstress from the sweat shops of London who becomes a
companion to Fisk

Maudie
- a mudlark who knows Fanny Darrow

Arthur Rowells
- a MP for Beasley known for his oratorical skills

Anne
- a young pre-adolescent prostitute

Hans Bruckner
- a German concert pianist and teacher

Lord and Lady Thornsby
- owners of Rivington Hall which is near Blackdale - Lady Thornsby
is a music patron and a chaperone to Pamela

Wilson
- head clerk at Barnes and Cameron in Manchester

Simon Oakley
- a violent revolutionary Chartist who is befriended by Charles Fisk

Vicar Franklyn
-friend of Charles Wilney of Higher Woodsford

Annabelle Samuelson
- wife of John Samuelson and mother of Paul

*And I stood upon the sand of the sea, and saw a beast rise
up out of the sea., having seven heads and ten horns, and
upon his horns ten crowns, and upon his heads the name
of blasphemy.*

—Revelations 13

Prologue

If, on a certain evening in the year 1845, an observer had stood on the
hill just outside the village of Higher Woodsford, Dorsetshire, he might
have just been able to discern a lone figure walking along one of the
ancient roads built by the legions of Claudius. These venerable footprints
of a vanished Mediterranean empire had, in many places, been transformed
into the straight, macadam covered roads known as carriageways, proud new
thoroughfares of the 1820s, which allowed coaches to reach their destinations
at comfortable speeds of ten miles an hour. Imagine, London to Bristol in
only fourteen hours! Yet, only a short time later, the carriageways themselves
would have fallen into desuetude and become country lanes used only by
local residents, the edges of the pavement cracked and overgrown with Queen
Ann's lace and furze, no longer the lifeline of England but merely rural arter-
ies, displaced by the railways, which would bind the country together with
thousands of miles of shining iron roads. No corner of Britain would remain
untouched by the new railways. The squire in his library would not be able
to shut out the roar of their engines, the collier who shipped coal by water
would break the grip of titled canal owners as fuel came hurtling southward
on the Birmingham line; fashionable London drawing rooms would be ablaze
with the latest railway stock speculation, and even the lowest day labourer on
a poor tenant's farm would find himself touched by the new system of smoking engines, mighty embankments, tunnels and tracks.

This age of railways was to be the best and worst of times, but on
the night of which I write, the old unpaved road knew nothing of the coming
fury that would disrupt its slow, meandering progress through a lonely country of moors and meadows, a rustic, agricultural corner of southern Dorset.
On this particular evening, the stars and the moon were pale ghosts above the
twilit hills and hollows which the road followed to the few and modest habi-
tations of Higher Woodsford. There, for perhaps thirty rods, the road became
the high street of the village before passing into the thickets and woods of a

once great forest. Just before it entered the village, the road climbed one of the steepest inclines for many miles around. An observer looking out from a vantage point at the crest of this hill would have had the prospect of a small steep valley, and would have seen that as the previously mentioned pedestrian began to descend into the hollow, walking toward the village, the sun sent its last rays in long orange spikes above the horizon so that the declivity which lay between the village and the fiery crown of the distant hills was in almost total darkness. The only reason the human figure would have been visible at all was that the white dust of the road was luminous in the twilight.

Though much has been said about the road and its eventual fate, little can be said about the figure who moved along it, beyond the fact that it walked at a slow, deliberate pace and that its shadow, cast before it like a long dark veil by the rising moon, was two heads longer than that of any woman was likely to be. The sudden flight of a family of partridge out of the uncut furze did nothing to startle or even distract the figure, which marked the owner of our twilit adumbration as a person who knew and understood the country, fearing nothing it could produce even on a lonely road after sunset. But if these observations seem to argue for the pedestrian being of local origin, its next action argued the contrary: as it reached the cross road at the crest of the hill, the figure paused and looked in several directions with the movement of one who tries to get his bearings or recall the way in a strange place. Close to the road on the figure's left were some lights, which in point of fact were the bright cheerful windows of an old coach house, The Pilgrim's Inn, named after its ancient cousin, The George and Pilgrims Inn of Glastonbury. It was the one drinking establishment permitted by the squire of the parish, a countrified, elderly baronet who owned all the land around the village. On the right, the road turned away into the village proper and was canopied in darkness by the arching branches of ancient oaks that had been spared by the woodlanders during the age of the great forest clearances. Rising into the darkness of the trees with a darkness greater still, the church's steeple at the far end of the high street loomed across the road. Beyond it, in the distance, surrounded by a large park of magnificent timber were the faint lights of the squire's home. Turning into the stygian road, away from the cheerful coach house, the unknown pedestrian may have noticed the sudden drop in temperature beneath the vast trees, for the figure seemed to pause momentarily and shiver before being swallowed by the darkness of the way it had chosen.

Moments after the pedestrian had passed into the concealment of night, the sound of a wagon could be heard creaking along the road we have lately traversed. Soon after, a team of huge, Clydesdale cart horses breasted the hill. The driver guided them into the large crescent of cinders which lay in front of the inn, and then expertly drew the wagon around the back of the rambling white building. As the team came to rest, a boy sprang out of the crooked mouth of the barn, obviously waiting for the wagon and its driver. Without exchanging a word, man and boy went about their separate business:

the boy to the horses and the man to the back door of the inn. As the boy began unbuckling the traces, the man knocked at the door. A moment later light spilled into the stable yard and the carter was admitted by a thin dried-out looking man whose quick, terse movements displayed a vigour that had survived old age.

"So Benjamin Dowd, you look to be sound in all your limbs," the oldster said.

"That may be as it looks, Mr. Cantle, but it was a journey I'd not make again. Not for a year's worth of your best ale. And if the squire know'd, I'd lose my place."

"Well, calm yourself now, Benjamin," the old man said as he unlocked a wooden cupboard dark with age, which was so large as to be almost a room within the storage room where the two men stood. From close behind the cupboard door, the old man reached in and brought out a clumsy looking clay bottle and two large mugs. "This will put a spark back into ye."

Benjamin watched with close attention as the amber coloured liquid was poured. He was a big, hulking man with unevenly cropped hair and a round, beefy face whose dullness was brightened only by the interest with which he applied himself to watching Cantle pour his potation.

"Now, Benjamin," Cantle said as he finished filling a large cup, I'll have my money before you drink."

Benjamin's sluggish movements matched his appearance as he reached under his canvas smock and drew out a fist of coins which he spilled onto the table. Dull as the carter was, everyone in the county knew that Benjamin Dowd could drive a team of horses down nearly any road, so much did the dumb beasts trust him. As the thickset giant drew off his ale, Cantle quickly counted the silver coins into his own hand. One might almost have thought the two men racing to see which of them could take possession of his reward more quickly.

"'Tis a large sum the navvies paid for their beer," Benjamin said as he banged his cup down after a single long swallow.

"Yes, but no one near the line wants to sell to them. They're all afraid of what would happen if the men go on a drunken randy. So if not for me, the navvies would have to get by on what the contractor allows. And that is only a gallon a day for a man. Not enough for a navvy to get drunk on. Now, tell me about your visit to the camp."

"Oh, t'was a terrible place, Mr. Cantle. Makes my throat go dry just to think o't," he said looking down at his empty cup mournfully.

"I'll not stint your thirst, Benjamin, only give me a good tale of it. Don't be in a rush now." So saying, he filled the cup again and watched it drawn off as quickly as the first.

"Now to it, Benjamin."

"Well, I come directly on the camp from the right o' way at Melbury's and out on to Giddy Green. A good name for the place with the tenants it now has. I can tell'ee that the old wet meadow there is already white wi' tents. Some shanties is going up, besides. The navvies was only part clothed, many of them. Even the women. Mr. Cantle. One had her beesoms hanging out with no covering at all. Near the tents the smell was bad seeing as no one had dug any privies. And that was the only clear place to stop the wagon. Right away the men closed about me," and here Benjamin illustrated his narrative by throwing his thick arms around himself.

"They had spades and picks in hand and other digging tools. They was a-squinting at me like I was Satan himself. I thought they was going to kill me, the way they come on. One big lad asked me what my business was. And I think if I baint said the word "beer" they'd have struck me down dead. Yes, I believe it."

"Well, navvies is a bad lot, tis true," Cantle put in. "They've torn up more than one parish. But they're free with their money, so that makes up for some of the damage. Though I am glad they're as far as Giddy Green. That way we can take their money and leave their fights and curses."

" I bain't taking any more of their money fer ye. Drink's no good to a man with a broken head."

The wiry old man slapped the carter on the shoulder. "Your head won't break so easily, I'll wager. Have another pull."

Once more the stone jar was tipped into the cup.

Benjamin's thick face softened as he watched Cantle pour, but then a sudden frown took possession of his low heavy brow.
"Tis part of my pay or not, Mr. Cantle?"

"Not, Benjamin. Three full barrels you were promised and three full barrels you shall get."

"Ye always was a generous man, Mr. Cantle."

"And you are the best carter in the parish, Benjamin. So if you won't carry my beer, who'll I get? Some young fool who'll turn my wagon and lose my money?"

"Ah, that's fair of you to say, Mr. Cantle. But I don't fancy them navvies."

"Well, you and I may not fancy them but squire says the navvies are building everywhere. They'll be tracks that will take you right from London to Land's End. That's what he told me."

Benjamin shook his head. "The squire's wits is weak. That's what it is. Him being an old man and losing both his sons so sudden. It'd drive any man off his head."

"His wits ain't weak. But he's not young, that's truth and I wonder who we'll have in the great house when he's gone," Cantle mused.

The great house of which Benjamin Dowd and Grandfather Cantle spoke lay amid a thick growth of dark cedars, oak and alder trees that grew up like a great wall along one side of the old Roman road as it left the village of Higher Woodsford. Here, the pedestrian we followed earlier, left the road altogether and stepped into the heavy darkness of the trees where only a few patches of moonlight found its way through the late summer foliage. The only sounds were the calls of night birds and the remarkably light tread of the interloper passing through the underbrush.

The figure might have walked for half an hour without once breaking its stride or being encumbered by the branches and undergrowth. Eventually, it slipped from the deep, almost liquid, darkness of the woods into the brilliant unshaded moonlight to stand at the edge of a cleared patch of poor land where a modest stone cottage was built. Then, suddenly realizing its visibility to anyone within the cottage, the figure ducked down, and through the deepest shadows it could discover, crept toward the dwelling, until it was squatting under one of two windows which pierced the front of the building. Peering into the distorting lens of uneven green glass window panes, the watcher could see that the fire had been banked to keep it going for some hours, when, presumably, the owner of the house would return. The one room of the interior held only a rude bed, the poorest furnishings and a table that supported a book so massive it could only be a family Bible. But the lens also focused the glow of the banked fire within and shone upon the face of the dark figure itself revealing, at last, a man's high browed face in which the intelligence of the eyes was made more formidable by the strong jaw and grim expression of the mouth. Dropping back into the shelter of darkness, the figure sat down and set its back against the stone to wait.

At precisely the moment the dark figure set its back against the outer wall of the cottage, the owner of that habitation entered the smoke, convivial interior of the Pilgrims Inn on the other side of Higher Woodsford. He was a small broad man, not too far on the wrong side of forty, with a pock-marked face and still possessing a good head of black hair. The familiar sweet smell of fermenting apples and tobacco greeted him even before the hoarse voice of Benjamin Dowd cried out, "Charles, Charles Wilney."

Benjamin was obviously much deeper in his cups than he had been earlier that evening, having now started to drink up some of his actual payment for his delivery to the navvy camp. From behind the elegant brass rail and polished wood of the bar, a testament to the occasional elegant passerby on the rustic turnpike, Grandfather Cantle's black eyes watched Benjamin Dowd hail the newcomer. He decided not to intercept the carter, even though he could guess why Benjamin was so eager to talk to the other man. Charles Wilney was known to have worked on some of the earlier railway diggings in the north and was reputed to have been a navvy and even a ganger himself. Cantle had seen Wilney lift a wagon off of a man in a mud slide, a feat only a navvy could perform. Benjamin would be eager to tell of his fearsome encounter with the navvies who had invaded the neighbourhood. But Wilney was liked by all for his honesty, lack of malice and gossip. The secret of Cantle's trade with the navvies was safe with him.

As the evening advanced there was more and more talk of the navvies who had just arrived so near at hand. Mostly, the talk was speculation about what the navvies were doing in the neighbourhood and how their stay might affect the village. It was well known, even in Higher Woodsford, that there were many instances of navvy gangs destroying a town on a drunken randy. The degree of damage they did usually depended chiefly on the contractor in charge of the diggings. Men like Morton Peto and John Samuelson always kept their crews in good order, unless there was a direct profit for the railway company or unless they wanted to intimidate a land owner into giving the navvies and their work a right of way across ancestral properties. It was late in the evening when the name of the contractor began to be guessed at by the men assembled at the inn. They also speculated on whether or not the presence of the navvies meant that Higher Woodsford was to have one of the iron beasts actually rage through it, belching fire and smoke.

'Tis Samuelson's men out by Giddy Green," Benjamin Dowd proclaimed in a loud hoarse voice that badly slurred his words.

Charles Wilney looked up, jogged out of the track of his own thoughts that had clearly preoccupied him all evening. He had sat, only half listening to Benjamin's first recital of his encounter with the navvies. But at the loud mention of Samuelson's name, he was stirred into animation.

"Samuelson?" "How do you know that, Benjamin?" Wilney asked softly.

Apparently, observed Grandfer Cantle, the drunken carter was going to tell his tale again. The old man did not want it told so publicly.

Cantle broke in "Would some of you youngsters give me lend of your strong backs and help me move some barrels around back. There's a generous draft for each man who helps."

Before Wilney could get an answer to his question, every man in the room,including Benjamin, had risen and lurched to the back of the tavern where they all knew the stores were kept. When the men returned to the tables with their free beer, Charles Wilney was gone.

"Now I would have given him some too," Cantle said heartily.

"I doubt that's why he left, grandfather," Arlen Melbury opined. He was a hulking rawboned man with just a few patches of his white hair left, the only one in the tavern within a decade of Cantle's age. "He's not overgreedy about drink. Truth told, Charles Wilney is less likely to wake up with a sour tongue than any man in village."

"'Tis, true," several voices said as others murmured their assent.

"It may have been the talk about railroading," grandfather Cantle said with a shrewd glance of his dark eyes. "Terrible things are said to go on in those camps. I wouldn't be surprised if Charles was glad to forget about his days of building railways. Him being such a quiet and peaceful sort of man at this time in his life."

While he was being spoken of at the inn, Wilney made his way at a brisk pace down the road that entered the village under the arching branches of the great trees, but unlike the dark figure whose way we traced earlier, Wilney took paths directly through his neighbour's fields and yards to reach his cottage by the shortest way. He had no need to conceal himself from the people among whom he lived. The eyes he wished to avoid would not be blinded by the pendulous shadows. He knew that if he did have reason to hide this night, no shadow or darkness would be deep enough to conceal him, and he was right.

Charles Wilney was found the next morning with his head brutally injured, dead on the threshold of his own cottage. The only things that had been taken were the few front pages of his family bible. These had been savagely ripped from the binding. The brutal crime baffled and horrified the people of the sleepy village. Eventually, the murder would touch some of the highest and the lowest in the empire.

Chapter 1

Six months before Charles Wilney's murder, far away from the cries of owls, the rustle of furze and the moonbright woodlands, a dense oily fog hung over the crooked warehouses and patched together quays of east London, deepening the already sinister, secretive look of the narrow lanes and alleys near the foul smelling river. Buildings on the very edge of collapse hunched over the water, but somehow remained standing on frail, ancient crutches of wood, like a huddle of broken, crippled beggars whose uprightness defied imagination as they seemed to weave in and out of the shifting pall of the London day. Out-of-work dockers loitered on corners. Seamen on leave for a brief time slipped silently through shoals of fog, bobbing, floating, as detached from the earth as their own ships at sea, searching for drink, girls or even more exotic pleasures. Smeared, luminous patches could be seen, hovering mysteriously over a fluid as dark and impenetrable as any Chiron ever plied, the lanterns of barges and small craft getting their living among the dead, as men and women searched the pockets of drowned corpses for pennies to keep the nearly dead, alive—for a little longer. Occasionally, rising out of nowhere, loomed mountains of darkness, coal barges from the north carrying enormous piles of dirty, soft fuel that would become the very essence of the London air. Proud-masted ships filled with spices and cotton from India, —some, it was believed, even loaded with precious gems— touched the sky with their elegant masts and sails, while along the shore, the mudlarks, starving children and old people, foraged for anything that might be found lying in the oozing river bank, or stolen from unguarded, stationary craft.

Richard Darrow was no stranger to the river or the life around it, though his carefully sponged,cheap black suit and worn white shirt proclaimed his desire to reach beyond the alleys and twisted streets to a greater respectability than he had yet known. He was a tall, sandy haired, loose-limbed man of about twenty who would have been handsome if he hadn't seemed to be peering at life, apparently not quite certain whether he wanted to be a spectator or a participant. There was something crane-like about him, a certain care and deliberation in his movements which would have seemed more usual in a man much older. But in spite of the cautious bias of his character, he, like many of his time, sensed the excitement of a great transition in society which could provide new opportunities to rise in station. None had started at a lower point than he, but he was close to earning what he thought of as a secure, respectable position as a school master in a privately funded school for the children of more ambitious crafts people and artisans. While he did not believe all the homilies of Dr. Watts, he had no qualms about imparting the values of respectable society to his students with such rhymes as "though I am but poor and mean, I will move the rich to love me; if I'm modest, meek and clean and submit when they reprove me." Richard was not naive about the value of such verses to factory owners who wanted to control juvenile workers, but he believed that such control was necessary and right. He knew what life was like if the dangerous classes were not properly kept in hand. That he could now dissociate himself from those classes of casual labourers, the ignorant poor and downright felons was a measure of how far he had already risen. He would probably never again have to get his hands dirty to earn his wages; he would never fear that his speech would mark him as one of the huge mass of Victorian society who laboured for mere survival. For in 1845, the line that divided the criminal class and the working poor was very fine indeed, and often went unrecognized by those of the middle and upper classes. Richard's excellent Latin and Greek, good English grammar, fine handwriting and teaching experience was a bulwark against the muck of his beginnings.

From slatternly lodgings on Green Bank near the river, Richard and his sister, Fanny, picked their way through the bleary morning whose thick air made the close streets near the water seem even more narrow and dark, especially at 5 a.m., the hour brother and sister set out for work. Fanny was a very attractive young woman with a crown of auburn hair, very fair complexion and a willowy body that we would describe today as "sexy," but in 1845 was usually judged "too lean."

They walked first south along Wapping, before turning north into Nightingale Lane and away from the river. They then passed on through Cheapside where some of the City's rising merchants lived. Though here the streets were wider, they were still messy with drizzle and manure. The damp morning was pungent with the smell of sulphur, distilled into the moist air from coal, but in spite of the dirt and smells that wrapped the London morning in a noxious cloak, brother and sister enjoyed their next passage, up through the fashionable part of the city along the Strand. The smart clothing, the gas lit shops and their beautiful displays were windows into another world. On Whitehall, they separated.

Fanny drew off to Convent Garden to get the bruised fruit and vegetables she would sell from her coster's barrow. Richard's way took him sharply north, out into the suburbs where new homes were being built for those who were gaining in prosperity: printers, map makers and other skilled tradesmen. The wasteland of the half-built homes and squares was ugly in a different way than the old crooked streets near the river where Richard lived and so, to him, they were more attractive.

He plodded on through the suburban wasteland until at last he arrived in front of a new row of brick houses, high narrow chested buildings less than twelve feet wide. He entered the walk of the most attractive garden on the street, walked up to the door and knocked softly. A discreet brass plate announced that Richard stood on the threshold of: "Miss Reade's Academy". A moment later the patroness of the establishment, Miss Reade herself, opened the door.

In 1845, progress toward public elementary education was stuck in the middle of the furious political tug of war between clerics who wanted their own sectarian ideas to be a central part of schooling and a handful of MPs and far-sighted philanthropists who tried to put education under state control. One of the most notable educators of the era, Dr. Kay-Shuttleworth, founded London's first teacher training establishment, the Battersea Training School. Curiously, Dickens, who had a strong interest in education, first seems to have admired Kay-Shuttleworth's ideas but afterwards attacked them by creating Bradley Headstone, the murderous schoolmaster in *Our Mutual Friend,* who is described as a dull pedant, probably the product of a school like the one at Battersea. Later, in *Hard Times,* Dickens draws the pedagogy of Pestolozzi, the Swiss educational reformer who influenced Kay-Shuttlworth, as a grotesque and inaccurate caricature, personified by Thomas Gradgrind. Actually, many modern theories of education are built on Pestolozzi's remarkably far-sighted work.

The two groups who actually ran most free schools for children were the British and Foreign School Society and The National Society for the Propagation of the Faith. The schools of both groups had grown out of "charity schools" whose primary purpose was to act as a bulwark against popery. Many people, especially people who were rising in station, did not want to send their children to what was still regarded as a "charity school." On the other hand, many felt that any school connected with government or the established Church would simply try to make their children willing slaves for wealthy factory owners. There was no agreed upon basis for the content of elementary education until the National Education Act of the 1870s. In addition to the schools run by these two societies were the "ragged schools," warehouses and other donated spaces where a loose network of overworked teachers taught the very poorest children. In these recycled industrial buildings, all ages were herded together in a single room, with pupils often teaching other pupils, according to the ideas of an untrained educational zealot, Joseph Lancaster. This system of Lancaster's, which gained great popularity due to the low cost of using pupil teachers, became a pernicious problem that true educators had to stamp out of the school system in later years. Occasionally, a very bright student could actually learn something among the screaming children of all ages who were packed together in the single room of a ragged school. A prodigy just might piece together something coherent out of the fragmentary lessons often taught by students only slightly older than those being taught. Miss Reade's, the school where Richard taught, was a great step above any of the ragged or charity schools. Miss Reades' teachers were actually paid regularly and the school made a good profit.

Richard had been hired primarily because of his excellent Latin and Greek, attainments which were viewed as particularly upper class by the well-to-do tradespeople who sent their children to private schools like Miss Reades'.

The large, cheerfully papered room where Richard taught was empty. His pupils would not arrive for another half hour. He sat down at his desk and looked around with a distinct feeling of pride. To Richard the contrast between the cavernous warehouse where he had begun to teach with fifty yelling children of all ages for his pupils couldn't have been more significant. This room and its sense of peace and order were the tangible proofs of his progress in society, and if Richard seems priggish to the reader, it must be remembered that he lived in a priggish time--and there was good cause for that priggishness. The horror that Dickens experienced as a child when his family was taken to the Marshalsea debtors prison and he was forced to work in a boot blacking factory was amplified by the fact that his experience was the very essence of middle class opprobrium and horror. When one realizes that thousands of children died each year on the London streets and that once a family or individual had slipped across the line of respectability, disease, homelessness and even death were often the result, it is easy to understand that "respectability" had implications far beyond today's meaning of the word.

The only relief for the poor came in 1838 with the creation of parish workhouses, an institution which Dickens and many of his characters, such as the redoubtable Betty Higden, regarded as providing a fate worse than death itself. The vast, pent up store of suffering among multitudes of poor labouring people was the underpinning of Victorian society. It was upon this slippery foundation of misery that the grasping for money and respectability of the new middle class was based, grasping which was so pronounced that it horrified Marx and Engels into constructing a new kind of utopian economic model. It was this degraded, blood-soaked and entirely miserable multitude that made Disraeli, himself, speculate on the possibility of revolution in Great Britain.

Richard had seen this paradox of the lowest supporting the highest at its very source: he had been born in one of the earliest navvy camps. The fact that he was alive at all was a victory against great odds. The fact that he had become a teacher at Miss Reade's was a tremendous accomplishment. Further, that he had managed to help and protect a sister was heroic. It was a literal rising from the mud and the drunken ignorance of the sod shanties to a height that he could never have even envisaged if Charles Wilney had not taught him to read and opened his mind to the power and greatness of learning.

From Wilney, and from his books, Richard developed a world view that would not otherwise have been available to him, and whether through temperament or through reading, or a combination of the two, Richard formed an almost mystical belief in the importance of respectable society. Even as a child, he knew that the camp in which he and his sister lived was a world outside society, a place of lost souls who would never have the capacity to participate in the higher spheres of society, or be spiritually eligible even for baptism. At the age of thirteen, when his sister was only eleven, Richard decided that they must leave the camp or Fanny would be "ruined" as soon as she passed into puberty. Females in a railway camp were used as a form of cheap entertainment, the price of a "wife" being a day's allotment of beer, one bucket, from the truck shop. Richard's own mother had passed into a state where she little knew or cared what happened to her children. Her indifference had allowed Wilney, a self-taught minister to the railway crew, a chance to protect the children and look after them for nearly eight years.

"Remember," Wilney said to Richard as they said their farewells, standing on the dusty turnpike that the two youngsters would take to London, "don't seek a surplus in life. Seek only your modest needs and give the rest to others. This way you will be rich in friends and in goodness. Bend your knee to no man but salute what is holy in all men and keep as sacred the laws of God and society. I can't think of anything better I can give you to protect you from the dangers of the road and of London itself."

The boy's eyes were full of unshed tears,"Thank you, Sir. I, we, we'll never forget your kindness."

Diminutive Fanny, wrapped in a clean print dress, said nothing. Her delicate well-formed brow was furrowed. She looked away and grasped her brother's hand tightly.

"We'll meet again, Richard. You are young and I am not old. We shall write to each other and be good friends always. Give me your hand on it."

This was the last time Richard ever saw Charles Wilney. The difficulty and expense of travel put them beyond each others reach, but they did write frequently, especially after 1840 when the penny post came into being. Richard often sought the advice of the older man. With this help, his own good judgment and determination, Richard had built a life for himself and his sister among the working masses of the city. He had assiduously added to the store of learning that Wilney had given him, prudently spending a portion of his small wage as a student teacher to study with a law writer and an elderly Catholic priest who added to Richard's knowledge of the classics. By the time at which we meet him, Richard had established a home for himself and Fanny in rented lodgings near the river. He had also given Fanny a modest start as a costermonger by putting six months savings into her small stall in one of the poor markets where working people usually did their food shopping.

In Richard's mind, it was unfortunate that Fanny had taken so well to the life of a street seller. She had picked up the brash patter with which stall owners caught the attention of passers-by as though born to it. Her blooming figure, dark hair and eyes and remarkably white skin, especially when seen in the gaslit street, caught the notice of nearly every man who passed, Her stall made her a constant attraction on the street. Though realizing the danger, Richard could offer little else with his limited capital. Fanny had no head for learning beyond the rudiments of reading and writing. The thing he feared most was that she might take to displaying herself as an actress on a stage. He had so far managed to turn aside the attentions of men toward her, but he recognized that his power as a guardian grew less each day.

Richard's time in the classroom at Miss Reade's passed quickly, as it usually did. He taught with great concentration and interest, believing that learning was the most important activity of mankind. The way learning had provided for himself and his sister, and the great scientific discoveries of the age gave his intellectual conviction great force of feeling which communicated itself to his pupils. Even the dullest student in his class left with a great respect for learning in general, even if, through no fault of Richard's, he acquired little knowledge in particular. Richard had gotten the best things Charles Wilney had to offer: a genuine concern for his fellows and a profound belief in the value of learning and teaching. These qualities, together with his thoroughness made his somewhat pedantic air seem not at all ridiculous to his students. He was respected by them all.

Miss Reade, a faded but well-turned out, attractive blonde widow, who claimed to be under forty, had made it known to Richard that his attentions would be seriously entertained and could result in his having more than a simple teaching post at her school. However, Richard's ambitions were to have Fanny well married and for himself to attend one of the colleges open to able students of low rank. In Richard's mind, such study would place him among an aristocracy of merit whose reward was the right to participate in shaping the great thoughts of his times. Richard knew that Charles Wilney was in whole-hearted support of his goal and was proud to have a student who could aim so high. So, tempting as Miss Reade's unspoken offer was, the lure of higher education was far greater. More recently, another impediment to Miss Reade had arisen, and one nearer at hand: Sally Howard, a daughter of an engraver whom Richard had met at a lecture on natural science. She had been the only pretty bonnet in the hall, but Sally Howard listened with a high seriousness that impressed Richard enough to approach her and ask to accompany her home. This had been just a few weeks before the March day on which we've met Richard. Sally had been often in his thoughts since. In fact, in every spare moment, he could do nothing but think of her.

Before meeting Sally, Richard had not known any young women who were educated and interested in ideas. He had never been teased or laughed at by a young woman. He was quite out of his depth and knew it. Sally turned aside any serious conversation with a jest, but it was always a jest that showed she understood the real subject under discussion better than he did. Her heart shaped face was always smiling when she addressed him, her brilliant smile set off by a thick mane of blonde hair that often flowed loosely over her back and shoulders. She moved among people with an ease and assurance that made Richard feel even more awkward. Perhaps worst of all, he was never sure whether Sally wanted to encourage his visits on the family's day at home, or whether she was simply laughing at him. Though Richard had theories about society and class, he had not experienced anything like a middle-class social life. Sally had lived for years in the atmosphere of her father's gatherings of artists, designers and literary people. Even Dickens had visited in their house once or twice.

Richard immediately told Sally of his early life in the navvy camp. If she was going to reject him for his background, he wanted to know it right away. Instead of rejection, Sally invited him to her family's next day at home. The freedom and irreverence of Sally's household baffled him, refusing to fit into any of the few categories of life he had known. He felt both embarrassed and superior to the Bohemian life at the Howards'. He recognized learning and attainments that were beyond his own, but missed the belief in purposes greater than those of the individual. It was as if these people had many of the accomplishments he wished for, but little idea of how to use them wisely. He did not understand how people who were so gifted could be so cynical and jeer at so much that he regarded as sacred. Feeling off balance whenever he was with Sally, Richard thought of her constantly when she was not present. Such was the subject of Richard's storm-tossed thoughts and feelings, in any idle moments, from sun up, when he and Fanny walked to their employment, to sun down as he walked from Miss Reade's to Fanny's stall in the poor market on the Ratcliffe Highway.

Rows of stalls lined the Highway. Everything from writing paper to eel soup was being retailed. There were coffee vendors with elaborate metal canisters and poor girls with simple trays tied around their necks with string. Some of these only had matches to sell. Oysters were offered with free vinegar and salt on trestle tables. Some costmongers displayed fruits and vegetables from brilliantly Japanned donkey carts while others had only a few apples on a clean clothe. A dirty, ill dressed man was selling groundsel and chickweed from baskets slung on his shoulders, wares which had probably only cost him a long walk at dawn to the Chalk Farm on the edge of the city. Each of the many merchants shouted the value and quality of their wares as loudly as possible. The resulting din was fearsome. Shrill noises emanating from young boys pierced the lower pitched cacophony of the street with shrieks that were like the blasts of a steam calliope. Merchants often employed boys to cry their wares because of the penetrating power of their voices. Darting through the clogged pandemonium like predatory sparrows, who could find their way around every obstacle, the half-dressed, filthy street arabs dove in and out of the crowd, as they watched every movement, alert for any opportunity to steal and escape.

The sun went down over this rag tag sea of humanity, and then the glowing gas lights were lit, casting shadows that seemed to multiply the writhing forms on the already crowded street. As he neared Fanny's stall, Richard saw a tall, foppishly dressed man talking to Fanny, who in turn was smiling archly at the stranger. Richard recognized Fanny's behaviour as a form of provocation not unlike that which he had been receiving from Sally Howard. He made the comparison unconsciously but it irritated him and he neatly shifted the frustration he'd been feeling with Sally onto his sister. He acted next as he would have liked to act with Sally.

"Fanny, is this man bothering you? He asked in his most ponderous classroom voice.

Fanny's handsome dark eyes were sparkling, her white skin was flushed. Her guilty look goaded Richard into even more brotherly sententiousness.

"Look here my good fellow, are you a customer or are you giving the lady unwanted attentions?"

The young man looked straight at Richard with a superior stare which the schoolmaster recognized from some of the visitors at Sally Howard's. The man's face was narrow but with a wide brow and a handsome head of chestnut hair. His lips were pursed in a sneer petulant as he spoke. He held a beautiful new top hat in his hand which by its very smartness made Richard aware that his own head was bare.

"And who might you be, sir?" the fop rejoined, "The young lady's suitor? A knight errant? A gentleman who has lost his way and," he paused meaningfully, "his hat?" The last phrase he accompanied with a sweeping look at Richard which pointed to his poor clothing.

"No. I, sir, am the lady's brother and if you've no purchases to make, I suggest you be on your way."

Out of the corner of his eye, while he looked fixedly at the elegantly attired young man, he saw Fanny nod quickly, a communication that told Richard there was already some kind of understanding between the two.

Fanny had developed a kind of beauty closer to the ideal of our century than that of her own, that is, her hips were slender and elastic rather than plump and full, her arms and shoulders slim and muscular, and the sharp high planes of her face gave her an exotic, almost a foreign look. She was very sexy in a modern sense, rather than rounded and womanly in the Victorian manner. She spoke little, but when she did, it was usually to laugh and joke. Her appearance drew people to her. At rare times, when she wanted something from Richard, she would pretend to be a little girl and sit on his lap, speaking in a lisping voice. Rarely now, but more when she was younger, she would weep bitter tears about how hard their lives were.

After watching Fanny with the young toff at her stall, Richard realized he had never seen her so animated. His own relationship with Sally made him more sensitive than he'd ever been to his sister's behavior as a woman. In each one of her teasing intonations to the young man, Richard recognized an echo from his own recent experiences with Sally. What made it more confusing for him was that he had only thought of Fanny as someone he must protect and teach, a duty, not as an individual with her own life. He recalled how Sally had shocked him by commenting on his ideas about women.

"You are a very polite young man, Richard," she said as he held her coat one day. "But you think of women as appliances, objects without life in them, something to be picked up, put down, or patronized. Whether you know it or not, you think we are something that is only supposed to react to men. Trim their cigars, sleep in their beds but without our own consciousness. You say you respect me because of my intellect," she had said as she nearly rested her head on his shoulder, "but actually I don't think my mind interests you in the least."

He could still picture her arch smile as she'd looked up at him. It was this kind of maddening, even immoral, behavior that kept him constantly off balance with her. The truth was that even if Sally had not been a very unusual young woman for her time, from a remarkable family, Richard's peculiar history would have still left him at a disadvantage when it came to understanding any relationship that did not fit into a Victorian stereotype. All he had to guide him in social matters was the barbarity of the navvy camp for which he had substituted the more acceptable and reliable rules of public society. These two extremes of behavior left out the stock and trade of daily life, the great middle of human behavior where compromises were made between the ideal and the most basic instincts. In a sense, however, Richard's difficulty was also the difficulty of his time: a society with the most appalling human abuses and an idealized code that had to be lived up to in public, but was often experienced by Victorians as a suffocating weight. Dickens, the most celebrated man of his age had great inner and outer difficulties in taking a lover, even when he was no longer living with his wife. Even after his feelings for a young actress overcame his own Victorian prudery--a prudery that still permitted him to visit French whorehouses with Wilkie Collins--he tried to hide his affair with Ellen Ternan for fear that his public would reject him for his immorality.

As Fanny closed her stall, it began to rain in earnest. The street began to churn as rain swept the crowd.

"Hurry, Fanny," Richard said. "We have a long, wet walk ahead of us."

"I'll be home later, Richard. I have something to do first."

"Fanny, have you lost your senses? Are you meeting that man? Think of what we've been through and think again. That road will only take you in one direction, back where we came from."

Fanny pulled her bonnet more tightly around her head.

"Oh, Richard, don't tug and worry at me. I am not a good girl, I know. Please take my barrow home with the stock."

"Fanny, I beseech you..."

Even as Richard's last plea left his lips, Fanny turned and hurried off into the fast-moving knots of people and the thickening darkness. The gaslights, diffused into large luminous ovals by the moisture in the air, were reflected by the shiny fabric of her dress as she ran.

Chapter 2

It was raining again and Pamela was so dreadfully bored. Why her father couldn't let her go to London to visit Hannah must be the most vexing piece of parental foolishness ever perpetrated on a young lady. It was only just over two hundred miles by rail. She tugged at a lock of her dark red-gold hair and glanced restlessly at the book on her lap. She posed her full lips into a pout, but there was no one to see, no one to see her long slender neck, retrouvé nose and violet coloured eyes or her beautiful hair.

She could do so much in London! If it were not for her pianoforte, she would lose her mind in this awful weather. She sighed and turned back to the window. From her second storey room she could see for miles across the moors, all the way up to the rippling Yorkshire mountains. Being on the eastern side of the Winter Hill, the house had been built to make the most of the view of the moors and mountains in the distance. The long green hills rippled across the red sandstone bones of the earth like the muscles of a great beast running beneath a huge weeping sky of gray. Beautiful as it was, Pamela looked out and wondered why they had to live near her father's dreary mines and his even more dreary miners. It made no sense to her. What was the good of making money and rising in society if one lived where there was no society? Oh, some of the Manchester shops were quite elegant. Hyams in Market Street with its fifty foot long plate glass window and six crystal chandeliers was elegant enough to satisfy even Pamela. But the people! The best pianoforte teacher in the county was still mediocre. Pamela was already the best young pianist in Lancashire and Yorkshire. Worst of all, the suitable young men she met at the Manchester balls seemed oafish and crude to her after Hannah's male acquaintances in London. She rarely went into Manchester anyway, except, of course, when there was a subscription for the orchestra. Her presence then was absolutely de rigeur. She and Lady Thornsby were the two most important subscribers to the orchestra, giving twice as much support as anyone else in the county. A concert without them would be unthinkable to Mancunian society. She turned back to the window restlessly.

She had to admit that the country around Blackdale, her father's house near the ancient village of Rivington, was very green and beautiful when the sun shone. Manchester was black and ugly all the time, except for some of the better shops and the beautiful old Collegiate Church on Fennel Street. But even the Cathedral's ancient tower had been painted black by the smoke of the mills. How glad she was that her father was not in the cotton trade. But what good did it do her if her father was one of the richest men in the north? London was the hub of the world, and she was trapped here. Pamela felt she could do anything to gain her release to London.

Her enumeration of reasons why she had to go to London was interrupted by a knock at the door.

"Pamela?" Her father's soft voice reached her. She thought of the article she'd read that called him the "gentle lion of northern industry". His voice did sound like the purr of a great cat. She was very fond of him, even when she was out of sorts.

She went to her door immediately and opened it.

"Yes, Papa."

"How are you feeling today, my dear?"

Pamela threw her arms around his neck and clung to him in a pose reminiscent of a maiden fainting against the breast of her knight. "Oh, Papa I am so dreadfully bored. Can I not go to London? You know the only company I have here is Miss Peevey."

"We've been through that, Pamela. But I came to offer you a trip into Manchester with me. I have to go there today."

"Oh, it's such a sooty old place."

"Come, child, answer me seriously. I have to leave within the hour." Edward Blackwood spoke with a soft authority which told Pamela that in his present mood he would not bend to her caresses or teasing. He was a compactly built man of middle height still trim and powerful, though in his mid fifties. He had a strong, open, square-jawed face that women thought ruggedly handsome and men thought authoritative. When Pamela was angry with him, she thought he looked a little too common but at other times, when her great fondness for him was in the ascendant, she thought him very manly and handsome. Manchester would have to do.

"If you ask me nicely, Papa, I shall be your feminine escort. I'll befuddle all the other men of business so you shall gain the advantage."

For a moment the proud father got the better of the industrialist. Blackwood looked at his beautiful daughter and smiled.

"Then meet me in the hall in half an hour." He kissed her on the cheek.

"Yes, Papa."

Blackwood's fortune was exemplary of the riches to be made from the new inventions and industry of the early Victorian era. The inheritor of a small colliery, Blackwood had the opportunity and shrewdness to invest in the Stockton & Darlington Railway line, and for a time made more money carrying his competitors' coal to Liverpool than mining his own. Edward Pease, the wealthy Darlington Quaker and mill owner, who came up with the shortfall of funds needed to get the Stockton & Darlington Bill tabled in Parliament, owed a personal debt to Blackwood. Blackwood had rescued Pease from drowning when the prominent mill owner had been knocked unconscious and pushed off of a quay into the filthy River Irk by a careless Manchester carter. The fact that Blackwood had been willing to jump into the horribly polluted black river to rescue him had made a great impression on Pease. Afterwards, the men became good friends, in spite of the fact that Blackwood was not, himself, a Quaker. So, Pease gave Blackwood a chance to invest some of his own money when more funds were needed to satisfy a Standing Order that four fifths of the capital required to build the railway line be deposited with the tabling of the Bill. With profits from the Stockton & Darlington Line, Blackwood increased his mine holdings and went on to invest in the Manchester&Liverpool railway, a much more ambitious line of thirty-three miles, whose primary purpose was to break the monopoly of the Bridgewater Canal, owned and operated by the dictatorial and greedy Robert Bradshaw. Until the Manchester & Liverpool, Bradshaw's canal was the only commercially viable route between the coal fields and the city of Liverpool.

With this second railway investment, Blackwood gained substantial holdings in the two great early railways. He supplemented his good fortune with good sense: His own colliery was well-run and had fewer than the usual number of accidents. He was one of the first mine owners to use George Stephenson's safety lamps, which helped prevent underground explosions of volatile coal dust. By the standards of the times, he treated his people well and they repaid him with loyalty and high productivity, even at a time when the industrial north was seething with social unrest. Some people predicted outright insurrection in Lancashire and York if the Chartists' demands for universal suffrage were not met. There had been some local riots when the Chartist petition was defeated in Parliament, but the trouble had settled down, though political and labour problems still smouldered and could rise to a flashpoint for almost any reason. Blackwood kept a cool head throughout the troubles, but he also counselled his fellow industrialists to be vigilant, for he felt that there was more trouble to come. Fortunately, most of the trouble in the northeast was with the older industries like cotton in Lancashire and woolen production in York. There was unrest in the mines, too, but Black-wood's humane management had minimized the problems at his own collieries.

But it was a precarious time, when men like Blackwood were changing the old rules about a landholding aristocracy having unquestioned authority. It was no wonder the dangerous classes were sniffing for scraps from the tables of those who were making new fortunes. Partly to forestall labour unrest, partly out of genuine kindness, and partly because of the tenor of the times, Blackwood also practiced a limited philanthropy among his workers. Early in his career, Blackwood started a banking system for workers to help them save money. He encouraged them to hold very small investments in his companies. He had opened three schools for working children before the Factory Act was passed, schools which actually taught the children how to read, instead of forcing them to recite moralistic verses. He would not allow anyone younger than twelve to go down into his pits and limited shifts to ten hours a day, all this at a time when mining labour was still largely unregulated. In other mines, children under ten often worked twelve hours a day and more in nearly total darkness, heat and soot. But Blackwood was also a merciless competitor who would use sharp business practices when expedient and would think nothing of ruining a business opponent. He was not as visionary as some men of his type, but neither was he ignorant of the way self-interest and public interest could be made to serve one another.

As might be expected, his thoughts about his daughter were less well-defined than those about his businesses and social responsibilities. Father and daughter had become unusually close in the seven years since Mrs. Blackwood had died. Each relied on the other in different ways. Blackwood found in Pamela a handsome feminine companion who was not calculating how much a wife could spend out of his income. He enjoyed buying her new dresses and baubles, taking her out and showing her off, and hoped that one day she would marry well. Like any Victorian father with ambitions, he knew that the hand of his beautiful and accomplished daughter would be a trump card in an important business alliance. He saw no reason why Pamela's inclination and such a marriage would have to conflict. He would never force her to marry someone for whom she felt no inclination, but she would have to marry a man who was right for the Blackwood holdings. Fortunately, her genuine interest in music had provided her with some real discipline in an otherwise spoiled and petted existence. However, in relation to things other than music, he knew his daughter was a headstrong child.

As Blackwood's handsome barouche bounced father and daughter toward Manchester, the financier sighed. He would have to start thinking about a husband for Pamela soon. She was already nineteen. Then, the somewhat lonely man, for whom the girl was a warm-hearted companion, told himself that he didn't have to resolve the question at just that moment, and put it aside.

"What shall we do, my dear, once I've finished my business?" he asked. "Didn't you tell me there was one milliner in Manchester who wasn't entirely beneath your notice?"

"Oh, Papa, I should so like to do something besides go to the shops."

"Would that extend to paying a visit to some of my more unfortunate workers? I've told you how much that sort of thing means to them."

Pamela looked thoughtful, then she hugged her father's arm.

"You're such an old dear. I suppose I must help you out if you're in trouble, but let us not go where anyone is sick."

"No. I would never risk you in a sick house. There has been a collapse in one of the pits and a man was killed. I should like to visit his family. Even though you're a woman, I'd like you to understand what it means to have the responsibility of large business interests."

"Why I know my responsibility, Papa," she said with a wide-eyed look of mock surprise on her pretty face. "My responsibility to your businesses is to make certain my expenditures outstrip your profits."

Blackwood put his arms around his daughter and gave her a hug as if she were still a child. "You silly goose."

"I am not a goose, father, and it is most undignified to tickle a young lady in that manner."

The very spoiled child and the very indulgent father said hardly a serious word during the rest of the trip into Manchester, until they approached the suburbs of the world's greatest industrial city. Rising high above the green plain, the soot coated chimneys and giant buildings momentarily dashed the humour from their faces. In the distance they saw a canopy of soot- blackened air which hovered over the shrouded city like its own evil spirit. The giant brick smokestacks were black with coal smoke and reached upward into the sickened air like enormous columns, as if supporting the weight of the massive darkness exhaled from the mills. Everything within the city was covered by the great pall. The darkness of the giant buildings and the black sky which lay over them were of one substance and seemed to shut out all else, a completely alien presence obtruding itself onto the surrounding green plain and the white-tipped mountains of Yorkshire in the distance. At the edge of the city, mankind had drawn a line upon the earth and said, "beyond this point there shall be nothing God has created, only what mankind creates." Manchester did not benefit from the stark comparison. As they drove from north to south, skirting the city's edge, on either side of the road were laid out the gardens and suburban villas of the wealthier mill owners and shop keepers and other prosperous business people of the town. The prevailing winds kept the exhaust of the mills away from these handsome homes, but the closer the barouche came to the city, the smaller the houses became until the Blackwoods passed into Manchester itself and were engulfed in its smell and the wheeze and throb of its mighty steam engines.

The Blackwood's home, styled Blackdale by its owner, near the ancient Saxon village of Rivington lay far beyond suburban Manchester and was considered very far north of town at fifteen miles distance. But the vast open moors and rolling hills had bewitched Blackwood and his young, athletic wife with their beauty. So there they had built Blackdale, a large, very comfortable gray stone house with an impressive park around it. The beauty of Blackdale always made the grimness of Manchester that much more of a contrast.

"Must industry and business be so ugly, father?" the spoiled child asked as they began their progress up Piccadilly into the smoke and cinders of town. "The poor people who live here will never see anything beautiful or fine except in one of these shops where they can not afford to buy. Or during the rare times when they are free to gather on the moor."

Pamela was commenting on the fact that the only buildings fronting the road were fine stores. Hidden behind them, she knew, were the terrible hovels of the mill operatives, places she had never even seen, though occasionally a factory cripple shuffling along a public street gave her a horrifying glimpse of the ugliness and deformity that lay just beyond the elegant establishments where she bought her dresses. The houses her father provided for his miners near Worsley were small and plain, but at least they were clean and well-made.

The indulgent father stole a surprised glance at his daughter's intent face as she looked out at the handsome shops along Market Street. She had never, in his memory, seen beyond the apparent beauty displayed in the windows.

* * *

Several hours later, Blackwood's business having been concluded, his solicitor, Barnes, offered father and daughter some tea. Once they were comfortably settled in the deep leather chairs of the chamber's inner office, Barnes addressed his patron.

"Sir, there is someone whom I should like you to meet. My son is newly qualified for the bar and may at times, with your permission, do some of the simpler tasks that you may require. I should be very much obliged if you could learn to trust him as a member of the firm. May I present him now?"

"Of course, Barnes. I didn't even know you had a son. That's a comment on your closeness, Barnes, considering our fifteen years of association."

"Well, sir, it is part of our calling not to be familiar with clients except as it might touch on their business."

Barnes stood up and reached for a velvet bell pull. Pamela's only impression of him was that he was tall, stooped and gray. The room smelled of old paper, dust and leather. But a moment later the door was opened by an extremely handsome young man. His dark hair was brushed low over his forehead and his dark eyes matched his hair. He was dressed fashionably but in conservative colours. Like his father he was also tall, but he stood straight. Pamela had not counted on such an example of the male sex being presented and immediately re-arranged the way she sat.

"Mr. Blackwood and Miss Blackwood, this is my son, Joseph, recently returned from reading law at Oxford."

The young man bent his supple waist, first to the man then to his daughter.

"A great honour, sir, miss."

"Tell me, Joseph," Blackwood said, "did you have a special interest in your reading?"

"Oh, yes sir. I have made a special study of contract law, especially as it might pertain to some of the new sciences that are now being used in business."

"Such as what?" the financier prompted.

The young man flushed slightly.

"Well sir, considering your long patronage of our firm, my father thought it wise to become well acquainted with any laws that would touch on the building of railways. I also have made a special study of some of the new technology being used in the mining industries."

Blackwood looked pleased. "This is very good of you, Barnes. I see that this was more than an introduction. It is a profound statement of your loyalty to my interests. And you know that I am a man to appreciate such a gesture."

Barnes acknowledged Blackwood with a stiff bow.

Pamela had been watching the younger Barnes with some interest as he spoke.

She did not herself feel any attraction to young men, except as a prizes to be won by young women. That is, she only wanted men to be drawn to her, because it demonstrated her superiority among other women. Affection between the sexes was, to Pamela, a kind of drawing room game in which the winners were to make brilliant marriages. She merely wanted to prove her power by catching this young man's interest in some way before he left the room.

"Tell me, sir," Pamela said, addressing her remarks to the younger Barnes, "do you think the law of great benefit to society? Is it not merely a tool that the strong can use to win their points."

"Why, not at all miss. The law is the basis of society. There could be no coherent interaction between men if there were no law."

"Perhaps, sir, you hold that opinion because it adds lustre and importance to your occupation and yourself."

"Not at all, miss."

"Well, let me hear you argue your point, then," Pamela pursued.

"Miss, I have no desire to disagree with you, I..."

"Speak plainly, sir," Pamela pressed.

"Sir," the young man turned to Blackwood. His uncertainty about what to do was written on his face.

"Joseph, my daughter has taken up an intellectual battle with you. You are free to speak as you think fit. I believe that is what she wants. Am I right, dear?" The industrialist was smiling, obviously enjoying the skirmish taking place in front of him.

"Yes, Papa. Defend yourself, sir."

"Very well, then, Miss. The law defines the specific possibilities for interactions between men. Things defined as permissible are legal and have been judged over many centuries in the common law to be fair and good. Things which are defined as criminal, have, over the centuries, been found to be against the interests of society as a whole. The law is actually the patient codification of what has been found to be practicable by many people living over a vast distance of time. Without it, we would have the rule of might making right."

"And is that not what we have anyway in our courts?"

"To some degree, perhaps. But certainly not in the same degree as would otherwise be the case." The young man turned to Mr. Blackwood and said, "I think if Miss Blackwood would consult some good history texts, what I am saying would be obvious."

This appeal to her father made Pamela angry.

"Are you calling me ignorant, sir?" Pamela's face was quite red. She had not really thought about what she was saying and her interest in baiting the young man had been dilatory. Her discourse had been prompted by pure idleness and boredom and the desire to be the cynosure of the gathering. She had never felt the slightest passionate regard for any man, and, in her heart, believed she never would.

"No, miss. Of course not. But I think that we have taken our discussion far enough. And I know there is work waiting for me at my desk. Excuse me."

With that the young man bolted from the room before another word could be said.

Pamela smouldered in silence until she and her father were alone once more in the carriage.

"Well, Pamela?" Blackwood said in an interrogative tone.

"Well, Papa?" Pamela said.

"I think you rather liked that young lawyer."

"Liked him? He was an impertinent oaf. Did you think his remarks to me were just?"

"You are the one who insisted he speak, my dear."

"But to say I had not thought my position through. Talking to me as though I were a weak minded school girl, who had not studied her texts well enough."

"Come, Pamela. You made an ill-considered remark about the value of the law and he, at your prompting, told you very politely why it was ill-considered. In any case," he went on, "I, at least, must go to visit the family of my dead miner. It is particularly important in these times to pay attention to such things. You may come and add to the their appreciation of the visit, or you may have the carriage."

Pamela still felt the sting of trying to defend an indefensible position under the sharp eyes of her father and the solicitors. Her dignity felt ruffled and she was glad to have the chance to recover it.

"Would it really do you good if I came, Papa?"

"These people appreciate such gestures. Family and relationships are the things most important to them. Bringing my daughter to express her sympathy would touch a strong chord in them, I know. It would be talked about throughout my diggings."

"Well, then, of course I shall come, Papa."

The ways in which people can use each other, without knowing it, for their own ends is a particularly twentieth century point of view. So Edward Blackwood did not think about how he had used his knowledge of Pamela's vanity to get her to do something he wished her to do. He did not berate himself when, for a brief instant, he had a glimpse of a future where Pamela could support his work and participate in it, instead of leaving him to marry.

The rain had started again as their carriage plodded through the cobbled streets, the horses' hooves made sharp, percussive clicks against the stones. They had turned off the main thoroughfares and were somewhere in what was called, "the new town," somewhere between any landmarks Pamela had ever seen. The ground sloped upward and the poorly built three-story row houses were already starting to crumble into the clay of the soggy ground. Instead of lawns, each house had a gray bare patch in front where nothing would grow. To Pamela it seemed that they had become lost in a maze of grimy brick row houses, each row looking exactly like the last and the next. It was an area many mill owners spoke of with pride, asserting that the new town provided excellent
homes for their factory hands.

"We'll not be going to the miner's house which is out near Worsely," Blackwood remarked, " but to some relations of his here in Manchester,"

Pamela's lassitude was too overwhelming to say anything.
The bad smell of the Rivers Irk and Irwell mixed with the exhaust of the looming chimneys. The slowness of their progress through the streets, the bad air, the rain and most of all the intolerable grayness and sameness of one narrow ugly street after another, lay on Pamela like a weight. She found the streets so depressing to her spirits that for once, she could briefly share the awareness of another's misfortune.

"What a terrible place to live, she thought. How could anything good come from such a place?"

The universal grime, the twisting lanes and the thick, palpable air pressed her down into her seat. It was one of the first experiences of sympathetic understanding that had ever come to her. She slipped into an a kind of waking trance so that when the carriage stopped, she was little aware of anything except the grayness all around them. The next thing she knew, they were standing briefly in the rain as light spilled out from an open door. The unfamiliar smells of sweat, onions and coal tar from the badly cleaned chimney assailed her as she entered what was actually a relatively clean and pleasant working class cottage for the Manchester area. There was no strong smell of sewage, or unhealthy dampness in the building. Still, Pamela felt lost and helpless in the frightening reality of the miners' lives. Everything was gray and alien. The small room was crowded with worn, tired-looking people, of a sort whom she usually saw only from a distance.

"So sorry for your loss," she heard her father's voice say to a bent old woman. As she listened to the unfamiliar accents of her father's voice speaking to an employee, offering sympathy to the miner's family, her eyes wandered through the grayness of the room, which seemed of a piece with the grayness outside. No matter where these people looked, it would always be gray and ugly. The thought made her feel almost faint. Then, in the shadows of one corner of the crowded room, she suddenly saw a beautiful child sitting on a wooden crate. In spite of her dirt-streaked face and soiled clothes, the little girl was so beautiful that Pamela almost thought for a moment that she couldn't be real. In all this grayness, the half-naked child shone with health and beauty. Her golden hair and creamy skin were caked with coal dust but still the child seemed to glow.

"Oh, what a beautiful child," Pamela said.

"Thank you, miss," the bent gray woman of the house said. "But she's not ours. She just narrowly missed dying herself the other day when there was a collapse in the pit."

"She goes into the mining pit? Pamela exclaimed."

"Yes, miss. Every day to get her living. She boards with us, now her parents are dead."

"Oh, no. Such a beautiful child. She can't be more than eight. She mustn't go into the pit anymore. Papa!"

"She doesn't work for me, my dear. I don't allow children her age into my mines. But many others do."

The subject under discussion had gotten off of her crate and walked up to Pamela. She very gently patted Pamela's leg. When Pamela looked down, the little girl spoke.

"Please, miss. Don't send me out of the mine. Mrs. Kelsey needs my wages for food. Please miss. Don't do it."

The childish self-pity that Pamela had been feeling for a large part of the day suddenly burst out of her and found an object outside herself: she picked up the little girl.

"Papa, this can't be right. She sniffed back her tears, expressive of genuine sympathy for the child but mixed with her own sense of personal oppression. Can we not find a lighter service for this child?"

Edward Blackwood was a man who was rarely caught off guard or whose response to any proposal was uncertain or indefinite, but Pamela's ill-considered words now put him in a difficult position. If he refused to do something for the orphaned child, he would seem heartless and cruel in the face of his daughter's own appeal. On the other hand, if he acceded to Pamela's request, it would be an obligation whose fulfillment he knew these people would observe closely.

"This is not to be done lightly, Pamela."

"Papa, I am not a child. I feel it is our duty to do something."

A long silence passed in the close air of the low-ceilinged room. A wooden chair scraped against the floor. Someone coughed and finally, Blackwood answered his daughter.

"Would you and Miss. Peevey make her your ward and take responsibility for her if we found her a place at Blackdale? I can think of no other service which we could offer one so young."

"Oh, yes."

Holding the child in her arms with all eyes upon her, Pamela felt she could rise above all the unpleasant things of the day. No one could say she was thoughtless, now. And if her visit was useful and noteworthy before, now it would be even more so. She also felt a spark of genuine affection for this lovely child whose oppression she had felt sympathetically. The emotions of an adult woman were struggling to find a way through the shell of a child's vanity.

"You say the child is an orphan, Mrs. Kelsey?" Blackwood asked.

"Yes sir. Not a soul that I know of. Though we are glad to share with her, sir."

"Well, you shall not lose by letting her go, either, Mrs. Kelsey. You've just had your own misfortune. I shall instruct Mr. Barnes to pay you your husband's salary as well as your own for the next three months."

"Oh, thank you, sir. My John always said you were the best master hereabouts."

"And John was a fine worker. We shall all miss him." Then he turned to his daughter.

"Pamela, are you certain about doing this?"

'Well, of course, Papa. Why should it seem so strange?"

"Very well. We shall send a carriage for her after I've had Barnes look into it."

"We can't take her now, Papa?"

"No. There are things to be considered first, Pamela. I will talk to Barnes before we leave today."

"Papa, I shall not leave without this child. She must not go down into that mine again. Child, what is your name?"

"Emily, Miss. But if you take my wages away..."

"Do not worry, Emily. We will give Mrs. Kelsey money," Pamela said. She turned to Blackwood. "What could such a child do in a mine, father?"

"I mind the doors, miss." The child answered for herself.

"The doors?" Pamela echoed.

"That control the air flow in and out of the mine," Blackwood said. "Too much air and the fire in the smelting furnace at the bottom of the pit will explode. Too little, and the miners will suffocate," Blackwood explained.

"And this child has that responsibility?" Pamela said.

"In many of the mines it is so," her father answered.

"Well, that is more reason than ever why she must come now," Pamela said.

Having discovered something new in herself as well as a new cause that others would applaud, Pamela was not about to give it up easily. She also knew that her father would not be anxious to dispute with her in the presence of his workers.

Blackwood, for his part, quickly weighed things and decided that formalities could wait. If a guardian did turn up, Barnes could simply return the child with some money and the offer of above ground work for her. He was not angry with Pamela, for one of the peculiarities and strengths of his character was that he never got angry with anyone. He thought it pointless. Things were what they were. Solve the problem and move on was his philosophy.

"Very well, Pamela. But do not you think you should ask your young friend what she would like?"

"Emily, my little bird," Pamela said, craning her neck so she could look into the eyes of the child she held against her breast, in the cradle of her arms. "Would you like to come home with me, and not go into the pit anymore? Eat nice cakes and jellies and live in a big house?"
Emily squirmed in Pamela's arms.

"But Miss, what about Mrs. Kelsey?"

"We'll see that she gets nice cakes and jellies to eat too."

The child looked thunderstruck at the thought of all these cakes and jellies suddenly raining down on her and her friends.

"Oh, Miss," was all the child could manage.

A short time later the Blackwoods with Emily wrapped in a the coachman's waterproof stumbled out into the rain.

On the way home, Pamela wanted to play with the child but she had not counted on the girl's fatigue from the long day of labour which she had already worked. For, Emily went to work in the pit at four-thirty in the morning every day but Sunday——when her employer had made her go to school where she was taught nothing but religious homilies. Pamela was a bit put out at the child's inability to stay awake. The leaden weight of her exhausted body was heavy on Pamela's lap, but the young woman looked forward to the amazement of all the house servants, especially Mrs. Peevey, her governess, when she came home with the beautiful child. Then, following Emily's example, and tired from an eventful day Pamela, too, slept, even in the lurching carriage.

Blackwood watched his sleeping daughter and the lovely child she held. Not a man given to presentiments, he still had an uneasy feeling about the day's last transaction. Then, he let the truly astonishing beauty of the child and his daughter's own impassioned demand for her soothe away his unease. Perhaps, he told himself, Pamela is growing up at last. Her comments about the polluting nature of industry showed a new kind of awareness in her, he told himself. Still, on the edge of sleep, some intuition he could not quite grasp cautioned him about taking in the child.

In spite of the carriage's jolting ride, they were all lulled to sleep and none woke until the bright lights of their own home shone in through the door the footman had opened.

The overt response to Emily from the staff was all that Pamela could have desired.

"I am truly astonished, Pamela, " Miss. Peevey said after she had heard the story.

Elizabeth Peevey was that rare thing before the twentieth century, a woman with really extensive learning and culture. One of three daughters of a clergyman, she had spent nearly half her life reading and studying in her home, following a true vocation for learning. But when her father died, the two sisters still surviving had to leave the home that went with her father's curacy. Miss Peevey had decided that being a governess was the most appropriate and useful thing she could do. Fortunately, a friend of Miss Peevey's who ran an excellent boarding school connected her with Edward Black-wood's family.

The governess and Pamela were standing in what had been Pamela's nursery on the top floor of the house. Miss. Peevey, still had her room next door.

"It is like a fairy tale, isn't it, Miss Peevey?" Pamela remarked as she looked at the beautiful sleeping child on the nursery bed. "And I am right inside of it."

"Well, let us hope that her nature is a beautiful as her face," the older woman replied.

Later that night as Pamela lay in bed, pictures of herself and Emily together flooded her mind. She imagined introducing that dreadful young solicitor to her new ward the next time they were in Manchester. She pictured taking Emily shopping, buying her clothes worthy of her beauty. They would catch everyone's eyes. The beautiful young woman and her beautiful ward.

As self-centered as all her fantasies were, there was a small part of Pamela that was trying to wake out of her adolescent self-absorption. That she had even thought of how others might find the blackened streets of Manchester and their oppressive dirt and sameness was a great step forward for her, but in the role of an only, spoiled child of a wealthy father, she had developed few of the resources necessary for managing the situation she had taken upon herself. That lack of resource was to cause real suffering for her and have even worse consequences for others.

The next morning, the trouble began almost immediately. Just before dawn, Emily was found wandering about the house exploring various drawers and cabinets.

Miss Peevey came to Pamela's room and told her that the butler had discovered lice in Emily's hair. The little girl would have to be thoroughly cleansed. Miss Peevy also suggested a visit from the doctor, a suggestion that Pamela tried to veto but which Blackwood himself insisted upon. In the meantime, the little girl was made uneasy by the strangers and her unfamiliar surroundings. Would Pamela come to the stables where she was being held and help quiet her until the required ablutions and examinations had taken place? Such was the proposition that greeted Pamela on rising. Had she responded to the pricks of her conscience that morning and sacrificed her vanity by sending Emily home, the child's history would have been very different, but Emily was too much of a novelty to be discarded, yet.

Pamela had conceived of Emily as a beautiful doll, a doll who had given her owner new experiences and feelings. It had not occurred to the spoiled child that the doll might have its own thoughts and feelings. She naturally assumed that her stronger will would prevail over the less formed mind of the child, and that the child would do as Pamela wished. What she had not counted on, however, was the fact that in many ways Emily's will was much more developed than her own. The early discipline of going to work at dawn, of having to do many things that were not pleasant, had already formed a character that could endure many frustrations and hardships much more easily than could Pamela. So while Emily always agreed to anything Pamela wanted, she most often did it with the air of a servant carrying out a command. Pamela wanted her doll to adore her, to fawn on her like a dog. She knew not that love and loyalty can only be purchased with it's own coin and she mistook her superior position in society for a true superiority. Many things about the little girl baffled her. The older child could not understand: how the younger could sit still for long periods and quickly soak up Miss Peevey's lessons. Emily was soon reading and would spend hours at it if allowed.

Without knowing it, Pamela had wanted a playmate, one who could be picked up and put down as her own mood dictated. Instead, she found herself the guardian of a person more self-possessed than she, someone who was always obedient but never loving in the way Pamela would have liked. So it is not surprising that in a few short weeks, Emily lost her novelty and Pamela returned to her usual preoccupation with music.

Miss Peevey kept the child busy with lessons for several hours a day, but the rest of the time, Emily had to stay out of the way of the other indoor servants, who watched the petted favourite fall from the preferential position she had enjoyed. The lower Emily sank in her mistresses' notice, the worse was her treatment by the other servants. Only Miss Peevy was aware of the little girl's plight. However, her motive was to teach Pamela the error of taking the little girl away from her class. So the governess watched and waited for some kind of real trouble to present itself to Pamela. She would then step in and have Pamela send the beautiful child back where she belonged.

Chapter 3

"There are always three good courses of meat served at the Vaughns' dinners, my dear. That by itself would be enough reason to attend. But every so often Vaughn picks up something good in the City. And several of his flutters on the 'Change have enriched us modestly. That is an even better reason for going. Together, they are incontestable. So leave your headache at home and get dressed."

With these words, John Bradley ordered his wife, Elspeth, to prepare for an evening out. As he spoke, he admired his new waistcoat and smirked at himself in the mirror.

Elspeth was the kind of wife whose docility was so dependable that her husband would have been shocked beyond measure if she ever really did not do as she had been told. She might murmur a little at times about things she didn't' understand, but in the end, she always carried out her husband's orders to the letter. John Bradley was the kind of man who would only marry such a woman. He was a rotund, self-satisfied solicitor with a rising practice whose face and hands were as pink and soft as a baby's. In his own estimation, the series of small successes he had in life were attributable to the operations of a brilliant and subtle mind without sufficient scope to have had enormous successes. He thought himself eloquent and handsome, but was actually dull and fat. He possessed a small gift of repartee and thought himself a great wit. To put it shortly: he was a solicitor who would be a prime minister. The extraordinary thing about this type of man is that through his own foolish but dogged beliefs in his gifts, he often convinces others to raise him up. Worse, once he reaches these heights he is often able to continue the farce until he dies, nobly enriched and eulogized by none other than his own bombast. One could almost say that this type of character is the pattern for most politicians.

What Bradley did not know about himself was that he had at the bottom of his soul a very vicious and mean creature who enjoyed the pain of others. Since he had very little opportunity to express this aspect of his character in ways deemed permissible by society, he knew it not. His wife might have enlightened him, describing all the little ways he hurt her. His horse would have talked of unnecessary lashes, if he could have talked. Fortunately, Bradley had no children. So, Bradley had no way of knowing what he really was.

Elegantly attired, with Elspeth's headache apparently left at home, the Bradleys set off in their own carriage to dine with the Vaughns. The elegant closed carriage with driver and footman cost more than the Bradleys could really afford, but it was the one extravagance John allowed.

"One has to have one's own carriage if one wants to know the best people," he told Elspeth.

The Vaughns were, as John would put it to Elspeth, "on the next rung up" from themselves. Michael Vaughn worked for a successful City banking firm that was often involved in underwriting new offerings on the 'Change. The firm had helped put the financing together for several railway lines and were always on the look out for a "good thing."

Michael hinted at connections with several noble sources of capital, but none of these unnamed, well-born capitalists had ever graced his table. Actually, most of the people who appeared as guests and friends of the Vaughn's were on the next rung down from them, people who would gratefully scramble for the crumbs Vaughn dropped from the rarified heights of the City's financial world.

The night was thick with what Victorians called fog and what we, a century later, would call pollution. Between the coal burning fireplaces, which were London's primary source of heat, and the new gas lights of the 1830s, the greenhouse effect in the town made it more humid and six or seven degrees warmer than the surrounding countryside. Londoners felt that the more efficient Continental stove made rooms "close" and cheerless. The smoke from fireplaces, mixed with caustic exhausts from coal gas works and the miasmas emanating from polluted watercourses. These sources of pollution sent powerful toxins into the air and caused chronic respiratory ailments among London's less fortunate denizens. London pollution was so severe that it blocked out perhaps three-quarters of the sunshine normally enjoyed by country towns. So while wonderfully atmospheric, the fogs of Victorian London, such as the one the Bradley's drove through on their way to the Vaughns, were poisonous in the literal sense of the word. When nineteenth century writers referred to the "bad night air," this is what they meant.

The Vaughns' house was new but not so new that it would have been considered in poor taste. It was just large enough, and just old enough to be considered "solid" and "respectable," without being ostentatious. Working for a well-known City firm, it was important that the Vaughns avoided the look of people like the Veneerings, the nouveau riche family Dickens' would lampoon in his last completed novel. During the Victorian era, new stock issues often succeeded or not based on which firm, or even which individual, was connected with the enterprise being capitalized. Since most commercial, industrial and construction companies were operated as partnerships or sole proprietorships, purchasing stock could be extremely risky. Before 1855, the liability of shareholders was not limited and if a company had sudden need of additional funds to meet obligations, shareholders were expected to meet these calls and could be sued for non-payment. Imagine what could, and did, happen in the case of railway construction if a crew of hundreds of men and wagons was held up for days. The calls on stockholders could then be enormous. Yet, it was the fantastic wealth generated by the railways that had the greatest impact on how Victorians invested their money. Because railway stocks could offer returns in the neighbourhood of eight percent, several points higher than most other domestic investments, people became used to the idea of investing. Because of the railway stocks, more venture capital flowed into new stock issues. The 'Change became the focus of life for many of the new middle class. Of course, not all railways delivered on their promise and during the railway mania of the 1840s there were many railway stocks that went bust. However, the name of one of the major railway contractors such as Brassey, Peto or Samuelson was usually sufficient to make a stock bring even higher returns. At one time, these three men had railway building crews that numbered in the hundreds of thousands, more than the entire British armed forces. These great contractors were, in every sense, emperors in their own right, and in time, Brassey, particularly, became a close associate of the British Royal Family. Morton Peto laid out and constructed some of London's grandest public buildings. Samuelson's fate will be recorded elsewhere in this story. No one could stand against the interests of any of these three men. If land was wanted, they would get it with a private member's bill which legally bound the landowners to sell. If a right of way was wanted, they would get it by fair means or foul. If a bill authorizing a stock issue in parliament was wanted, they would get it even if they had to elect their own MPs. Their methods could range from parliamentary manipulations to threatening landholders with the fearsome violence of navvy gangs. There was no armed force in the country during the 1830s and 40s that could stand against large navvy gangs, who were often assembled in crews of over one thousand men. The great contractors themselves never feared the navvies for they could always threaten to cut off salaries and food. The navvies were then reduced to what they really were: isolated gangs of mostly illiterate, itinerant workers who had to follow any chance of work.

In short, the power of the great railway contractors was beyond calculation. They stood at the top of the pyramid of explosive industrial growth, the pyramid whose base rested squarely on the backs of the navvies, some of the most miserable men among the working poor. Whether you regarded the contractors as heroes to be emulated, or villains to be reviled depended on where you stood in Victorian society. Their true power can be understood when one realizes that though these men built vast fortunes and had a major hand in shaping the country, they were never attacked in word or deed by anyone. George Hudson, the shifty linen draper turned railway stock manipulator was eventually publicly reviled, but none of the great railway contractors ever had hard words said against them publicly. The radical press reserved most of its spleen for the factory owners of the older clothe producing industries. Many of the railway builders had a virtual Midas touch and were the greatest source of new money during the Victorian age. The power of this money was truly imperial. To this day, the full story of the attempted suppression of the Chartists by one of the great railway contractors has never been told as it will be told in these pages

All who frequented the Vaughns' dinners longed to be initiated into the mysteries of railway technology, so they could profit by understanding the Arcana of track gauges, degrees of inclines, soil types and other factors which could affect construction costs and timing. Because of the paucity of accurate information regarding new railway lines, and because of the very real technical issues involved in railway building, the closer one could get to those at the centre of the enterprise, the more likely were one's profits. Consequently, many aspirants, such as the Vaughns and their guests, saw the financial world as a spiral of ever deepening information and intelligence, with the giant railway contractors, Peto, Samuelson or Brassey at the golden centre.

Eventually, during the Victorian era, the railway companies of Great Britain became the largest and richest corporations in the history of the world. In comparison to other businesses of the time, they were colossal, and were much larger in relative size to the overall Victorian economy than any business of our own age. Imagine, then, John Bradley's feelings when Vaughn welcomed him and quickly whispered, "Samuelson's secretary is upstairs in the library. Forego the port and I will bring you up after dinner."

Bradley's pink face turned crimson. The excitement he felt at even hearing the name, "Samuelson" was almost paralyzing. If he'd been told he was going to be presented to the Queen, he could not have been more moved. He gave a curt nod of his head to hide his overwhelming feelings and to show he understood.

The Vaughns were a good looking couple. In spite of hosting innumerable dinner parties, they both still had waistlines though they were well into their forties. Vaughn's thick black hair was of medium length with a handsome touch of silver at the temples and in his sideburns. Miriam Vaughn was slender, a richly coloured brunette whose hair and skin had a hint of mahogany in them. They had both learned the modern art of careful grooming, washing everyday with mild soaps, which gave them a sleekness and glow possessed by no one else in the room. They looked like, and were, in a sense, career diplomats.

The dinners to which the Bradleys were invited had a number of uses for Vaughn. He called them "dinners just for friends" and made it known he was forced to give many other "business dinners." The truth is that Bradley had been placed in a group of the duller people who might be useful to Vaughn and his principles one day. These were men with more capital than intelligence, but who were not extremely wealthy and so didn't move at the highest levels of society. After enjoying several years of free dinners, Bradley was going to be recruited into the higher mysteries of finance. For reasons of vanity alone, Vaughn knew the ambitious solicitor would not refuse his induction.

There were an even number of ladies and gentlemen at the table, twenty in all, and the preposterously long dinner (by modern standards) was chewed and digested during a gastronomic marathon of fifteen courses. The propensity for overeating and drinking among monied Victorians is one of the reasons for the frequent mention of gout and stomach problems in nineteenth century literature. As Dickens said of Richard Carstone's solicitor in Bleak House, "I am sure his digestion is impaired, and that is most respectable."

The dining room at the Vaughns' was a temple to the act of gustation: a handsome space with high ceilings and two enormous glass doors that let into the garden at the back of the house. Guests at the Vaughns always felt so "right" in this room. The thickly upholstered dining chairs, the high ceilings and generous proportions of the room all contributed to a feeling of well-being, even when the company was dull. The food was always excellent and the solid silver and gold serving dishes and utensils emphasized the wealth of the establishment just by their very weight.

Bradley sat dumbly through the meal. He picked at his food, but could not eat. An exotic looking Brazilian gentleman across from him was saying something about harvesting jungles in a thickly accented speech, which Bradley could not understand. Every so often Bradley glanced at Vaughn, who seemed bent on not letting him catch his eye. Bradley could not imagine what momentous step he was about to take, but a man of his talent being introduced to Samuelson's secretary certainly would mean something momentous.

The dinner seemed interminable to the fat solicitor. One of Vaughn's regular guests, the aging niece of a minor, but very wealthy, aristocrat from York, Dorothea Fry, was surprised after dinner with a birthday cake. She seemed nearly to lose her wits with the surprise and had great trouble blowing out the cake's few candles, whose numbers had been thoughtfully reduced by the expedient of allowing each candle to represent a decade instead of a year. Actually, the lady was just extremely shy. The result of this additional festivity was that it was near eleven o'clock before Vaughn finally steered Bradley out of the dining room and up the handsomely proportioned staircase to the library.

"I have never been up these stairs before," Bradley said to himself with the awe of a true votary. He had never seen anyone else so favoured, either.

"I say," he tried to murmur smoothly to Vaughn, "What's all this mystery about?"

"I think, Bradley," Vaughn said clapping his man on the shoulder, "that I can finally offer you something really worthy of you." Vaughn spoke in a perfectly natural way.

Bradley forced himself to be calm. "Vaughn, you've entertained me many times, and I hope I never implied that something more than your hospitality was needed."

"Not at all. But I know a superior man when I see him. And I've long thought that one day I might, through my connexions, offer you an opportunity to improve your situation in a truly meaningful way."

The large mahogany door of the library swung open and Bradley knew his presentiment had been correct: something momentous was about to happen.

Standing with his back to the fire, facing the door was the person Bradley supposed was Samuelson's confidential secretary. He was an impressive man. Tall, large-boned and obviously strong. A thick but well-trimmed, drooping ginger mustache added to the man's imposing presence. He remained perfectly still until Bradley got within arm's reach and then he suddenly offered a huge hand to the much shorter man.

"John Booth, Mr. Bradley," he said in a thick north Scots accent, "And very glad to meet you, Sir. Vaughn tells me you are a man to be relied upon. A man of judgment."

"Well, thank you, Sir. I certainly hope that is so. Will Mr. Samuelson be joining us?"

"Oh no. That wouldn't do," the Scotsman answered. "Of course," the big man said, sounding almost reluctant to speak. "His interests are involved. But he knows nothing of our meeting,.You understand?"

"Oh, yes. I see. Of course." Bradley felt a little disappointed that the great man himself wasn't directly involved. But at least, he had been singled out by Vaughn and someone associated closely with one of the railway kings.

"But there are great interests at stake here, Mr. Bradley," Booth went on. "Interests not only of Mr. Samuelson but of the whole country. The development of our national railways and consequently the good of England may turn to some degree on the results of our conversation. You understand."
"Yes, of course," Bradley said, understanding nothing as yet.

"You are interested in helping, then?"

"I would certainly do anything in my power for the good of England, sir."

"Even if it meant a sacrifice?"

Ah, Bradley thought, going suddenly cold. They are going to ask for money for some cause of theirs. They will find they are not dealing with a child. I won't give them a shilling, he told himself.

"Within reason," Bradley said, feeling much more poised now that he had reduced his interlocutor's interest to a common and easily understood motive.

"Would you sacrifice your time and energy to help us, Mr. Bradley?"
"Time and energy that is not already committed, sir."
"I'm afraid we want more than that from you, Mr. Bradley."
The bite, thought Bradley, starting to smirk.

"Sir, we would like you to stand for Parliament for the Borough of Pilkington. You would have our unqualified support and complete financial backing."

Bradley was literally staggered. He stepped sideways into a large library chair. Only the size and weight of the chair kept him from falling. Even in his most vainglorious moments, he had never dreamt of anything like this happening. The next though the had was that the costs of running would be immense. In a moment, he had regained his balance and was, once more, firmly on his legs.

"When you say, 'complete financial backing,' sir, what does that signify?"

"I am not trifling with you, sir," Booth said. "We are not afraid to invest in good men. All your expenses of running shall be paid."

Bradley was now truly stunned.

"A brandy for the Member, Mr. Vaughn," Booth cried.

The next thing Bradley knew, he was seated in the armchair with both his friends huddled around him as he sipped the very old cognac Vaughn had given him.

"So, you will stand for Pilkington, Mr. Bradley?" Booth asked.

"Under the terms you describe, sir, who would not be honoured?"

"Your business will not suffer, either, Bradley." Vaughn said in a confidential tone. "We have some good legal minds on retainer who will handle the details of your practice when necessary. Leave everything to us."

"The one thing we must always be clear about is that none of this is known to Mr. Samuelson," Booth said. "Mr. Vaughn and his firm and myself are acting as private citizens, doing what we think right for England."

"Of course, gentlemen." Bradley murmured. He was quiet for a few moments, then he said, in an almost mournful tone, "But can I actually win?"

"Rest assured, Mr. Bradley," Booth said, "we shall win. You may have a few unpleasant moments. What man in public life does not? But we shall win the seat. You shall be the Member for Pilkington."

Bradley sprang to his feet, suddenly accepting his new role wholeheartedly. He raised his glass. "To England." His face was flushed. He had never been so stirred in his life.

Vaughn poured two more brandies. "Hip,hip, hoorah." Booth added his voice on the last syllables. As if by magic, one of the footmen appeared, framed in the door. Booth reached into his breast pocket and handed a letter to the man.

"He is to destroy this after he's read it" Booth told the footman. "He will know it but tell him anyway." The footman left and the door was closed.

Bradley was transfixed with curiosity, but somehow he knew he must not refer to what had just happened.

"Your victory has just been set in motion, Mr. Bradley. Your opponent, Mr. Atherton, shall not have a chance of winning."

"Atherton? But he's a terrifying orator. I have heard him speak, myself. I speak well but how can I win against such a man? He will say anything for effect."

"I told you, sir, your victory has just been set in motion."

"My victory? Set in motion? That letter?" Bradley said, forgetting himself.

"There never was any letter, was there Mr. Bradley?"

"No, no, of course not."

We shall now follow the non-existent letter as the footman rides on horseback through the broad avenues where Vaughn lived off of Portland Place, down into the heart of the city, then even further south and east, and eventually across the Iron Bridge and into a suburban slum filled with insects, pestilence and undrained sewers. Many of the streets here became alleys which twisted and turned into ever darker, ever more hidden courts and evil rookeries where every example of the lowest London life was to be found. Like a bird flying to its nest, the rider, even in darkness, unerringly followed the prolix way to his destination: a crumbling building propped up with posts at the heart of a dark, evil smelling court, hedged in by rotting buildings where rivulets of foul water eddied slowly across what remained of the pavement. Before he could reach this destination, the rider had to dismount and continue on foot through a foul smelling labyrinth of twisting, covered passages which lay between the dilapidated buildings. Finally, he stepped suddenly into a miserable yard with no apparent entry or exit other than the dark passage through which he had just come. He could barely see the darkness within darkness of a man dressed in black who stood in the doorway of the falling down house, framed by two of the building's crutches. To this shade, the rider handed the letter and fled without saying a word.

When the sound of horses hooves had died into the distance, the black-garbed man raised the cover on his bull's-eye lantern and opened the letter. It was a short missive. He folded it, put it back in his pocket and masked the lantern.

If the footman had seen the shade's face he would have been surprised by the gray hair and beard, an elderly face, but seamed and tough as the leather of a cavalry saddle. In fact, the spy was a relic of the Napoleonic wars, a former calvary officer and confidential agent of the Emperor, himself. With M. de Narbonne, he had penetrated the secrets of the highest council chambers of Napoleon's aristocratic enemies and aided materially in their undoing. He was an agent who had since worked for other masters and whose skills were now used only by the very few men with enough ambition and money to hire such a finely honed tool. No British policeman of the time, none of the nine-man team of detectives working out of Scotland yard, had the skills that this man possessed. He was a solicitor, as well as a soldier and had even appeared on stage, acting professionally in many dramas that required complete personal transformation. He had many names, many occupations and many identities. He rarely appeared in daylight or under gaslight.

Darkness was his element and in darkness he preferred to work. I shall call him Collins.

After reading the letter, his gaunt figure walked unconcernedly through the ugly lanes, patiently following the dark ways back into the London occupied by people with names, addresses, professions and bank accounts.

By the time Collins reached the small fashionable hotel where he was registered under the name, Boulanger, Bradley was having his fourth cognac in Vaughn's library. He wasn't yet drunk but the cognac certainly helped erase the existence of the man we have just met. If Bradley had known about Collins, he would still have been sober enough to be frightened. For, while Bradley thought of himself as a rough and ready legal warrior, Collins would have appeared to him as a child's nightmare who had come to life, an ugly shadow that Booth's letter had sewn permanently to his flesh.

"Really, you know," Vaughn said. "I think some champagne is in order. And let's introduce the other guests to the new Member for Pilkington. The two conspirators bundled Bradley out of the library and down the stairs.

The remains of tea, coffee, cakes and biscuits lay on the table..

"Ladies and gentlemen," Vaughn called to the room. "First, I must apologize for leaving my guests. But I have an announcement to make. John Bradley, our John Bradley," he repeated clasping the man's shoulders, "has agreed to stand as MP for Pilkington. And stand against the nefarious Mr. Atherton who wants to reform absolutely everything."

Elspeth, the entirely forgotten wife, just looked down at the table in front of her. She hoped that perhaps this would mean that John would have other people to whom he could give orders. She did, however, have the presence of mind to lead the applause.

"You're going to have to be a jolly fine talker, sir, to go up against Atherton on the hustings," one man called out as the applause subsided. He was a fat banker who wore very expensive clothes and gold jewelry. He always kept an unlit cigar in his mouth. On this occasion, he removed it and looked around at the room to see how his remarks had been taken by the company. He was so chagrined by the lack of interest, he actually lit his cigar.

"Speech," someone cried. "Speech," another echoed.

John Bradley, looking dazed, was passed to the head of the table. Someone poured a glass of champagne for him. He raised it and said, "To England." Everyone in the room rose with a glass in hand and echoed the toast, and then, much to everyone's amazement, including his own, John Bradley gave the most brilliant speech of his life. The peculiar combination of brandy, champagne, and having his heart's desire made actual, unleashed every good idea that had ever passed through Bradley's mind. He was even genuinely witty, poking fun at those who would block progress, likening them to a cow in a rural district that had never seen a locomotive and didn't know enough to get off the railway tracks when the train is coming.

Atherton, it was well-known, wanted more parliamentary regulation of the railways.

"How my opponent can think that a group of sleepy middle-aged men trying to stay awake in the Houses of Parliament" the room tittered, "could improve upon the visionary, the brilliant way, in which our railway-men are transforming our country is beyond me. I know I wouldn't know a narrow gauge track from another type. How could I tell our most brilliant capitalists how to run their businesses?"

He shook his head and continued shaking it as he sat down. It was a remarkable performance, especially for John Bradley. Vaughn even wondered if they had chosen someone too intelligent for the job they wanted done. He looked over at Booth and they caught each other's eye.

Once he sat down, the man of the hour had gone limp, as though his excitement and all his energy induced by the alcohol had been spent in his speech. Like all men who know at bottom they are undeserving, Bradley was beginning to feel that something was wrong with what had happened during the evening. There was even a touch of fear about the depths of the water in which he now swam. How deep were they? He didn't know. He had no specific idea of what standing for Parliament would be like. There was also the dim sense that he was now in the power of men so much bigger than himself that they could crush him in an instant. The very real non-existent letter bothered him. He wondered what kind of bargain he had made.

Chapter 4

It was the second night since Fanny had run away and left Richard standing at her stall in the poor market on the Ratcliffe Highway. By talking to other stall owners, he knew she had not been back to her place of business since. She had not picked up her barrow at home. What this meant, he could easily guess. There was nothing he could do to repair the damage done in the two nights she had been away. She had cast herself back into the pit from which they had climbed, and her choice was irrevocable. The navvy camp had shown them both unbridled lewdness from their earliest childhood. Perhaps, Richard thought, that early exposure would have a permanent effect on a female child, degrading her in a way that males might be proof against. His own sexual impulses had been consciously channeled into the hard work of learning his trade and caring for his sister. Fanny had no such centre outside herself. Personal adornment and laughter were her favourite pastimes. The emptiness of their poorly furnished rooms oppressed him with sadness for the little girl he had carried much of the way to London on his shoulders. They had both been mere children then. He thought of Fanny in her best moments, which had been usually her moments of humour, though she was affectionate, too. She had truly loved the little cat he brought home, until it disappeared somewhere on the waterfront. But she had a profound gift for laughter, he thought. At moments, it seemed, he could again hear her peals of mirth ringing through the empty rooms, echoing off the bare wooden walls and floor.

He remembered how excited she had been when he took her to Smithfield on a Friday morning, when the place was filled with everything necessary to carry on a coster's trade— from the barrows to the weights used for measurement to the donkeys and the whip. Donkeys, the favoured beast of burden among costers had been everywhere. Some had bright japanned cart saddles with new red pads, others a mouldy trace covered with buckle marks. Some had only rope halters. But nearly all the animals were healthy,

for costers love their animals and treat them well. Fanny would have liked to have one of the strong little beasts so she could have gone all over London with her vegetables. But Richard could only afford a hand-barrow and trestles for a stationary
stand. Fanny had made a brave effort to show her brother that she was not disappointed with the creaking old barrow he could afford, but she could not altogether hide her fondness for a small white donkey who brayed loudly when she stroked his face.

Richard's sorrow was not just for Fanny, he admitted to himself, it was for himself, too. His sister had helped give purpose and direction to his life. The necessity of caring for her had kept him working when he was tired or discouraged. Now, there was no one to care for but himself and it made the very young man feel painfully lonely. He thought of writing to Charles Wilney, who had always helped him with his simple, direct wisdom yet, he did not want to tell Charles about Fanny. He did not want him to think ill of her, nor of himself, that he had failed his sister. Against his own wishes, he kept thinking of Sally Howard, seeing her face. Unfortunately, it was always laughing at him, and it was hard to reconcile her pertness with his own image of a wife who sat by the hearth's glowing coals, talking with him in a sooth-ing voice, taking care of their little household necessities. Besides, her father and their friends were way above the struggling schoolmaster. If he were even to mention the idea of marriage as a remote possibility, he would probably just provoke more laughter from Sally. The images of Sally made him feel his loneliness even more acutely. It was this loneliness and the insistent ticking of his open pocket watch on the table, reminding him that Fanny was not coming home, which finally drove him out of their rooms and onto the street with no specific destination.

The district in which Richard lived was close to the river but it was largely made up of honest working people. There were many skilled trades-men: shipwrights, carpenters, a few puddlers who worked in small waterfront ironworks and the like. Most were connected in some way with maritime trades but many were not. Of course there were some of the very very poor, the watercress girls whose bare feet turned blue on the cold paving stones in the winter, the poorest flower girls who would sell themselves when they were starving or to keep a younger brother or sister, the turf cutters who could get their wares for nothing if they were willing to walk to outskirts of the city.

The waterside streets were often unpaved but they were wide enough to allow people and wagons to pass comfortably. No gaslights lit the way at night here, but there were no fetid, dangerous rookeries close by, such as those off of Rosemary Lane where the unwary pedestrian could find himself trapped in a series of dangerous twisting alleys and courts. However, London's criminals always intermixed with the working poor. There were many street arabs always on the look out for elderly pedlars who would be easy to rob when the boys came out of their hiding places at dusk. A poor class of pick pockets worked the area because they dared not venture into the better parts of town. Mudlarks waded in the polluted river to pull coal, copper and rope off the barges. It was a lively area as Gerard Manley Hopkins would say one hundred years hence: "all trades, their gear and tackle and trim."

Richard felt at home on these streets. Their noise and activity helped take him away from his sorrow and his feelings of uncertainty about the future. He had told himself that sitting for examinations at Cambridge would wait until after Fanny married. Now that she had put herself beyond his help, he was free to act as he would. Then, there was Sally, or was there? If he were prudent, Mrs. Reade should be considered carefully, as well. He would have to get a good character from her, no matter what he did next.

Richard wandered aimlessly while these thoughts ran through his mind, until at some distance from home, he was hailed by a man with a large box of tools slung over his broad shoulder. This was Charles Fisk, a carpenter who had been away at sea for some considerable time. He was a bluff, friendly man with curly graying black hair, who lived in his shop directly across the road from the Darrows. He had always been helpful to his two younger neighbours.

"Darrow, do things go well for you? How's the handsome Miss Darrow?"

"Well enough, Fisk."

"If that's so, why are you sweeping the crossings with your chin? Have you dined?"

"No."

"Come along then. I have just been paid for a commission. The older man put his powerful arm across Richard's shoulders. "There's a new chop house that's opened near the Ratcliff Stairs. Its fine joints are sure to lift your spirits."

Since it was easier to follow than give an explanation for a refusal, Richard allowed the burly carpenter to tow him through the streets.

The chop house was loud, smoky and redolent of cooking meat. Once they were settled in a high-backed wooden booth with a mug of warm cider in front of them, Fisk asked again for news of Fanny, shouting over the din of voices and clinking plates.

Finally, telling himself that Fisk would soon realize Fanny was no longer with him, Richard began to tell his sister's tale.

When Richard told of the upper class young man at her booth, Fisk's face settled into a hard tough mask of anger.

"His class misuses us all, Fisk said in a tone of bitterness Richard had never heard before."

"What do you mean?"

"The Charter, Darrow. Why should we not have our rights when it's our backs that they ride upon?"

"I know nothing about this kind of thing, Fisk. I have enough to get our living."

"Think, my friend, if this scoundrel who took your sister were poor, do you think he would dare do as he has if the Charter were law? Do you know how many laws would stand against him if he didn't have a fleet of solicitors to hide behind--and if the courts didn't regard your sister as just another trollop from the gutter?"

Until this moment, Richard had not even thought of blaming any-one but Fanny for what had happened.

"But, it was her choice."

"And what kind of a choice do you think it was? He with money and fine things, you working night and day to make ends meet. Her poor little stall where all the men stop to make lewd suggestions. He took advantage of her low position to get what he wanted. She may even think she is helping you by freeing you of her dependency."

"I really hadn't seen it that way. You think him the most culpable of the two?"

"I would say it all rested on his head. Your sister's a gentle girl with a handsome appearance who could not stand against the sweet poisons he had to offer. How many girls of her class would?"

"Poor Fanny," Richard sighed. "But tell me then, Fisk. What can I do now?"

"Oh, you can do nothing with him. You don't stand as equals before the law. And your sister is just a girl from the gutter. But you can help make yourself his equal. Then you could act."

"You mean..."

"Support the Charter. We need men with your learning, Darrow."

Richard was quiet for a moment, looking down into his glass. "No. It won't help Fanny. It will be too late. So far, all of this talk about a Charter of Rights has gotten us nothing. "

"Don't be so certain. Signatures are being collected the length and breadth of England. But in any case, if you supported the Charter, you would know you were helping to keep other girls from Fanny's fate."

Richard was silent for a time and then said, "No, Fisk. I have a career to make. With or without Fanny."

"Richard, I'm going to a meeting soon. Come with me. It will cost you nothing to attend."

"No, Fisk. But you've made me realize that I still have a duty to Fanny. I must try to find out how and where she is. And if I can strike a blow against this cad, I will do it. Now, you will have to excuse me."

Fisk watched his friend leave the restaurant and thought, By taking direct action, he will just get himself into trouble. We must act together. We must act as principled men. In violence, we are no different than our enemies. He finished his meal, paid the bill and left, walking quickly, glancing carefully around the street. Their spies could be anywhere, he thought. They begin to fear for their lives and will do anything to protect their indecent wealth.

Like an animal who knows its forest, Fisk took a labyrinthine way to his meeting. He went into basements of one building and came out another, he squeezed into narrow alleys where most would not know there was an alley, under quays, around the pilings of waterfront buildings, he sought to make his way too obscure for any to follow. How well he succeeded, we shall see.

Finally, after many twistings and turnings, Fisk entered a coffee house not five streets away from the chop house where he had counselled Richard.

The large smoky room was filled with men, talking and drinking in varying states of sobriety. Fisk passed through this room quickly and found a narrow set of stairs at the back of the building. A small dark landing awaited him at the top. He knocked three times quickly and then added two slower blows on the ancient door.

A crack of light appeared.

"Fisk," the carpenter said.

The door opened wider to allow enough light to make the landing visible. Then, "Good to have your company, Charles," said a voice from within and he was admitted.

The room was filled with men who typified the earlier Chartists meetings in the late 30s. Most were skilled artisans who were political philosophers and idealists. Here in London where the movement had been born, a few radicals of the classic mould of the eighteenth century radical movements still remained. Fisk was one of these. He read avidly, Bunyan, the Bible, Swedenborg and other religious and political thinkers who had influenced William Blake, the obscure Lambeth engraver and poet whom Fisk had stumbled across and now admired so much. He was especially fond of Blake's nearly forgotten imagery of spiritual revolution. The carpenter believed that the People's Charter must be adopted by Parliament before England would be a free and just country, and London become the New Jerusalem Blake had believed it to be. Fisk had been meeting with some of the original members of the London Working Man's Association to keep alive the spirit of Tom Paine and focus it into a Charter of Rights for all Englishmen.

The debate for the evening was over the use of force, an issue that they all recognized had never been clarified sufficiently. Some felt that the poor results of earlier risings proved that force would be ineffectual. Others in the group believed that physical violence had not been pursued vigorously enough, and never in unison with Parliamentary efforts.

As Fisk listened to the discussion, he was disappointed to hear the same arguments and disagreements that had been voiced repeatedly at earlier meetings. How can we progress, he wondered when we seem able to do nothing more than go over the same ground, again and again.

The room began to buzz with the sound of voices in disagreement. Then a rough cracked voice called out, "Brothers, brothers, do you not see?"

"See what?" Some one asked.

"The chair recognizes the senior brother visiting from Manchester. I introduce a member who comes all the way from the north to speak with us."

The chairman was a small bent man, a tailor with small black eyes sharp as needles. His name was Thomas.

"I don't know that man," someone said.

"Nor, I."

"Nor, I."

"His bone fides come from the Manchester Association. He has traveled a long way. I will vouch for him. Let him speak."

"Aye," someone said, and a general murmur of assent swept through the room.

The old man was bent with long years of hard labour. His voice was rough with age and probably the black dust of the mines.

"Forget Parliament. You have a new and greater opponent. Do you not understand that Parliament is owned now by men whose principles are reduced to percentages of profit?"

"You mean you believe that parliamentary efforts are useless?" Fisk asked.

"I mean," the old man rumbled in a voice caked with dust, "that Parliament is bought and sold by men like Morton Peto, Samuelson and their like. They care nothing for government or nation, let alone our welfare. They are your true enemies. You cannot fight them with arms or words. You can only fight them with money, money for solicitors, money for bribes, money to buy votes in government. Money is today the only measure of power. I tell you, it is the great railwaymen and factory owners who rule the country today. Not the people, not parliament. Money, money rules England. Every delicately scented drawing room wants the profit being bred by the railways. All anyone cares for is the extra two percents the railways can bring. None care for anything else."

"That sounds like the counsel of despair," Fisk said. "What can we do if you are right?"

"I am only here to speak the truth," the old man said. "I would not see you exhaust yourselves in fruitless argument. Nor would you want to be arrested for actions that accomplish nothing."

"Then what, what would you have us do?"

"Do you know about the store of arms that the men of Newcastle have hidden in the north?"

The general murmuring and conversation in the room continued for some moments before anyone could be heard clearly.

"Listen, listen," the old man from Manchester said, "Does anyone have any information about this store of weapons?"

There was silence.

"Well," the visitor went on, "it is probably just a myth. But if it were true, the money to be made from selling the arms abroad could help our cause. We could buy at least two seats in Parliament."

"You want us to use the same low weapons our enemies use?" an older man said.

"I tell you there are no other weapons worth while. Money, money sits on the throne of England today."

After this damning and treasonous statement little was said. The group broke up into small knots of men who were well acquainted with each other. The man from Manchester found himself left out of the intimate discussions and so took his leave of Thomas.

"You will keep us informed of anything you may hear," he said to the tailor.

"Yes. We understand that the N.C.A. is now our strongest arm. I will telegraph you at once if any of our members learn anything."

The two men shook hands and the elderly man from Manchester slipped from the room.

If we now trace this elderly workman from the meeting, we shall see he follows a strange course. First, he travels south instead of north. He crosses the river and as the dark evening shades close in, we see him threading what must be a familiar way through a series of dirty lanes, dark covered alleys and treacherous yards. Once again we see the falling down house held up by timbers. And if we are not yet certain of the man, we are when he re-emerges after some little time from the dark doorway, dressed in his black cloak, hat and fine suit. He walks quickly through the east end of the city and then hails a hansom and rides northwest toward the neighbourhood of the richest and most illustrious names in the realm. In that neighbourhood, high fences surround great houses. Carefully pruned trees droop luxuriantly across ornamental paths. Gravel drives lit with their own gaslights push night itself back from the homes of the wealthiest, while beautiful fish swim in ponds cleaner than the public fountains of the east end. These are the homes of the princes of the new Xanadu, for London is already so thick with buildings that only the very wealthiest can afford to have extensive grounds around their homes.

Collins slips a large key into a small gate cut into one of these walled villas and lets himself into the grand property belonging to John Samuelson, Railway King.

Passing quickly through the artfully trimmed shrubs, Collins soon stands at the french doors of a room which we can see is a magnificent library. The sharp tap of metal against the glass is sufficient to bring the King to the door. It is late, he is wearing a rich smoking jacket of burgundy brocade. He is a huge, powerful man with shoulders that tell of his years as a navvy, a well-known chapter in the tale of his rise to kingship. A cognac sits on a small table near the fire, which gives off the only light in the vast three-storey, domed room. Books line the walls and the smell of leather and fine cigars hangs in the air. Without a word the two men walk over to the fire and their shadows spring up across the high curving walls. Samuelson pours a cognac and hands it to the older man.

"Well?"

"They are not the ones we seek. They are fools and know nothing."

"Did you tell them about the weapons?"

"It was the quickest, easiest and surest way to get a definite answer. They are a group of intellectuals who spend their time spinning social theories mixed with uncertain theology."

"As are most of the men connected with that so-called movement."

"Except for the ones we seek." Collins put in as he raised his snifter. "I still say they are in the north. Probably in Manchester, Perhaps Durham or Newcastle."

"Well, I am not foolish enough to ignore the instincts of so old a warrior as you, Collins. But as you know, we have business here in London until a certain election takes place. Until then, you are needed here. We will know if there is any imminent danger of the weapons being used. It is too vast a munitions to be moved without our people knowing that something is afoot."

The enormous shadow of Samuelson towered over that of the elderly spy, almost blotting it out.

"Tell me, Collins, did you let them know that you are on their side?"

Collins gave a dry cough that might have been a chuckle. "You like reminding me that you gain my services by coercion as well as by remuneration."

"Perhaps you are right, Collins. That was unnecessary on my part. Pray excuse me."

"The Prime Minister will be disappointed with my night's work, or won't you tell him?" Collins said.

"You know it is to our advantage to have the government as worried as possible about the Chartists. It makes our resources that much more valuable."

"But we do search in earnest." Collins said.

"Oh, yes. There is no telling what these louts could do with a store of weapons like the one we are looking for."

"Perhaps even get the right to vote," Collins replied. as he tossed off the rest of his brandy and moved toward the door.

"Good night, Collins."

"Good night," the spy said as he slipped into the darkness once more.

* * *

After his conversation with Fisk, Richard wanted less than ever to go home. Unconsciously, he steps led him to Fanny's booth in the market. The evening rush was on. People packed the street. Under the glowing lights the poor market was a whirl of colour and noise, it was also the hour of the street arabs, the pick pockets and other petty practitioners of crime among the working classes.

Richard pushed his way through the crowd as quickly as possible, hoping, somehow that Fanny would be at her post. But her place was empty. It was a conspicuous gap in the thickly strewn wares of the other vendors.

The important thing now, he suddenly thought, is to find out where she is. God knows what the man might do with her. He could see that Fisk was right, now. How could a girl like Fanny resist the temptations of a man like the one he saw her with? He looked around the noisy market, at the dirty streets and poor quality of the goods displayed. How could Fanny choose this over what that man's wealth could offer, even if it was only for a short time? If he had been less severe with her, perhaps she wouldn't have acted so independently, without seeking his advice about what she was contemplating. He watched two other market girls accosted by toffs in fine clothes, obviously looking for an evening's entertainment. He could see how they enjoyed drawing in the girls. It was part of their fun, he thought bitterly, hunting these easily caught butterflies. Surely, there was truth in what Fisk said. Those with wealth and power did use the poor in immoral ways. And people of the rising new classes who were neither rich or poor, wanted no part in the conflict between the top and bottom of society. It was too easy to lose one's own grip and slide down. He knew that and couldn't blame those who wanted to increase their wealth and rise. But the lessons of Charles Wilney still held his heart. Surely, a man's neighbours should be lifted out of poverty before a man sought more than sufficiency for himself. "You're looking for your sister, ain't ye?" a raucous voice, harsh as a crow's laugh broke in on his thoughts.

Richard turned and there was an old woman standing at his elbow. She was a mudlark, whom he had seen before standing at Fanny's stall. He had seen Fanny give her spoiled goods. She wore a stovepipe hat tied with rope over her head and a soiled man's overcoat also tied closed with rope. Her odour was very strong.

"Your sister was good to me. Feed's me. Winter's are going to be harder for old Maudie without her."

"I am looking for her, Maudie. Do you know where she is?"

"Wait a minute, who are you? Oh, that's right, you're t'other one. Have you got a bit of something for old Maudie? I don't remember meeting you before." And she began to mumble incomprehensibly to herself.

Richard's heart sank. The old woman was insane. He turned and began to walk away.

He felt a strong grip on his arm. "No, no. I don't know where she is, but I know'd her young man's lay. Give Maudie a little ready, and she'll show you."

"I will give you plenty, Maudie, If you'll show me the young man's lay."

"You will?"

"Yes."

"Do you promise? So many lie to old Maudie and think she don't know."

"I promise. What do you want?"

"I wants that bright red scarf your sister has…and..and I want a new coat. Is it worth a new coat?" the old lady asked herself, questioningly, suddenly uncertain if she were asking too much.

"Yes,yes, I'll get you a new coat," Richard said somewhat impatiently.

"When?" the old woman said with a crafty glance at Richard. "I don't think you have the price of a new coat." Her sharp, bony, weather-beaten face gave him an appraising look. With her thin body wrapped in the loose coat she looked like an aged stork.

"Yes, I have it." Richard said, pulling a pound note out of his coat and showing it to the old woman. He thanked providence that he had been paid by Mrs. Reade that afternoon.

"Hide it, hide it, don't let anyone see," Maudie croaked, pressing close to Richard to screen him and his money from the crowd that hemmed them in on all sides.

"Come now," Richard said. "Show me where his lay is."

They squeezed their way through the noisy street and struck out to the north. In a block or two the crowd thinned. Every few minutes the old lady stopped, mumbled to herself and then set off again. Hours passed as the old woman shuffled along the streets, sometimes seeming dazed at other times alert as a hound on a track. Richard's hopes rose and fell with her state of mind. The one thing that gave him hope was that her way was ever westward and north, into the fashionable neighbourhoods. Once in these elegant regions, his fear was that at the last moment the old lady would forget where she was or that someone would stop them as trespassers

How long they wandered past the villas and gardens all around them, some walled like palaces, Richard wasn't sure. These are the castles of the rich, he thought, which shut us out and make them feel protected.

The full moon tried to send its rays into the relatively clean air of the neighbourhood with some success. The vast, wooded area of Regent's Park and the zoological gardens was not far away. Patches of fog drifted through the large trees overhanging the wide streets. Richard could have enjoyed the night ramble had it not been for the constant anxiety that the old woman would mislay her own thoughts at a critical moment. Then, suddenly, out of the darkness, Richard seemed to see a man walking through a wall, a very tall wall.

As Richard and Maudie drew closer, he could see the man walking away and realized there was a very small locked gate in the wall.

"That's the place. That's it," the old lady cried, seeming to rouse herself from a somnambulistic trance to point at the wall. "Maudie knew the way. Maudie knew the way," and her cackling laugh sounded strangely in the wide, elegant streets, her raucous voice like an outcry of all the misery of the east-end riverside. It was a foreign and threatening sound amid the grand homes, an ugly cry that had somehow found its way to the very gates of an enchanted palace. Richard wrote down the street number he saw above the gate.

As Maudie and Richard came nearer the gate, Collins looked back briefly, roused by the old woman's cackle. The gaslight above the gate fell on Richard's face. The spy saw the schoolmaster and immediately turned away, and strode off briskly into the night.

Chapter 5

Fisk was the only person Richard could think of who might be able to help discover who lived in the grand villa to which Maudie had guided him. So the day following his night out with the old woman, Richard sought out his friend after finishing his own work at Miss Reades. He found him in his little workshed near the docks. The walls were lined with drying pieces of domestic hard woods: oak, cherry, walnut and hickory. His well-sharpened hand tools were neatly hung from the wall with loops of heavy wire.

"Darrow, what brings you here?" the burly carpenter said looking up from a pile of woodshavings.

"Do I disturb you, Fisk?"

"No. I'm just cleaning up the day's mess so I can make a new mess tomorrow."

"I have a tale to tell and you are the only one I know who may know how to get to the end of it, Fisk. It began when I left you yesterday."

"Sit down. I'll smoke a pipe while you talk."

Richard took his friend through each step of his evening, leaving out no detail, no matter how small. The two men were burning a small tallow candle in the twilit workshop before Richard had finished. Fisk had sat silent and unmoving through the entire narrative, except to blow out gales of tobacco smoke. When Richard finished he said, "It sounds as though Miss Darrow may have made some dangerous friends. This is how wealth uses poverty when there is something that wealth desires."

"Yes, I realize it, now. You've made me frightened for her. Is there any way you can help me learn who lives in that great villa?"

"Perhaps. I have an acquaintance who acts as informer for the police sometimes down near the London dock. He also alerts some of us about the movements of the police, when it is in our interest. He may know how to get the information. Give me the address again. I shall write it down and take it to him."

Richard smiled for what seemed to him the first time in days. "I knew you could help. God bless you, Fisk."

"That's premature, Darrow. I may not learn anything. People who live in places like the one you describe have many ways to hide themselves if they wish. You might as well wait here. I may be some time, and we are close to the places I shall go. Make yourself comfortable. You can rest on those clean pieces of sailcloth."

"Thank you, thank you, Fisk. I'll be here."

How long he waited in the little shop that night, Richard couldn't tell. Once the candle had burned out, his wait was in darkness. He could not see the face of his watch in the moonless night. There was no fire in the stove. Finally, in spite of his anxiety to hear Fisk's report, Richard threw himself down on the thick rough cloths and slept.

***

Piles of huge fiery clouds, hanging over the water, clothed the new day in a mantle of light and moisture which Turner might have painted. The livid sky was visible through the small window of the shop when Richard lifted his eyes from sleep. The sound of heavy boots scraping on the wood floor echoed into his dream of Fanny's childhood. Richard sat up and was greeted by Fisk, who wore a troubled look on his face. The carpenter's broad brow was furrowed, his usually wide open eyes squinted at the floor, and he tugged at his lower lip thoughtfully as he sat down.

"Well, Darrow, I am not sure if I have hurt or helped you this night."

"What do you mean, Fisk?"

"The man I knew insisted that the only way we could learn anything was to make an official inquiry at the police station. When I gave the address, I could see at once that it was known to the sergeant on duty, though he would say nothing, of course. I gave your name instead of my own and gave your sister's name as the object of the inquiry. They would not take a less complete statement from me. I only hope there is not some conspiracy between those who have Miss Darrow and the police."

"You think such a thing possible!"

"When you deal with wealth such as you describe, there is no piece of treachery that is impossible. I listened to a man yesterday say that money and money alone sits on the throne itself. Parliament, ministers, police, all may be for sale. The fact that the address was known to the sergeant gives me great cause for concern."

"Poor, dear little Fanny," Richard murmured.

"Well, we actually know nothing, so our dark imaginings may come to nothing." Fisk said. "Go back to sleep and I, too, will lie down for a bit of rest."

Some hours later, Richard woke with a sudden shock of anxiety until he remembered that the day was Sunday and that he did not teach. Still, he was now wide awake. The sky was gray, featureless and weeping softly, so it could have been morning or dusk.

Upon consulting his watch, Richard found the time was eleven o'clock. A few moments later Fisk came through the door from outside, carrying a bag which proved to contain a breakfast of beer, cheese and bread.

After finishing their meal, Fisk lit his pipe thoughtfully.

"I suppose there is nothing to do but wait," Richard said.

"Well, you might do something more," Fisk said.

"Tell, me, Fisk. What do you suggest? I am entirely out of my depth."

"I think you should leave some money in a safe place where you can get it quickly. I would also leave a change of clothes there as well."

"What are you thinking of, Fisk?"

"Well, if I am right about the police knowing that address, I may have done nothing more last night than to have stirred a nest of vipers. I'm not sure what they will do. I would certainly sleep with one eye open. My suggestions are only to give yourself a better chance if the time comes. I'd offer this place but they probably know it."

"Why would they know it?"

"Possibly from my Chartist activities. Possibly I was followed last night in the moonless hours. And your lodgings are close by."

"All this, they would do all this because of a poor little coster?"

"Not because of her, Darrow. But because they are protecting the wealthy and powerful man who has taken her. Kidnapping is still a crime."

"But Fanny went willingly."

"She went to him willingly. But is she being held? At any chance, these people do not want to have attention called to themselves in a matter like this."

"I wonder at you, Fisk. Are you sure that your own political ideas are not painting this whole thing in lurid colours?"

"Darrow, you have never been in trouble with the law, what you call society, have you?"

"No."

"But surely you've seen what happens to other working people when they merely brush against someone wealthy, or even merely well-off?"

"Well, I've also seen the navvies give other people a pretty good fright.   Have you ever seen what a gang of them can do?"

"I have. I worked briefly on the new railway station."

"Well, my point is that authority and law are not all bad."

"The navvies live by the idea that might makes right, is it not so, Darrow?"

"Yes."

"Well, so do the wealthy. But their might will reach much farther than a navvy's burley arm. In fact, they may even command the navvy's arm."

Richard was silent for a long time. "But then, what can we believe in if not a lawful society?"

"Believe what all good men have believed in, at all times and in all places. Believe in yourself, in your own judgment. Believe that there is a spirit of goodness in the world, but know also that there is a spirit of opposition. Those who pursue wealth without regard for their fellows live in darkness and feed upon themselves until they become insatiable beasts. In my opinion, so called men of capital grow more and more like the steam powered iron beasts in their own factories. Let me show you something."

Fisk went to a dark corner of the room and from some old oil clothes pulled out a sturdy folio.

"This is my greatest treasure."

Fisk opened the folio and there, to Richard's eye, was the picture of a man who had lost all things that make a man, human. It was beautiful and horrible at the same time.

"Nebuchadnezzar by William Blake," Fisk said. "It came into my hands by chance. Now I keep it near me to remember what we are fighting. Whatever face you may look upon in your search for your sister, remember that this is his true face."

Richard looked at the terrible visage for a long time and finally said, "Put it away, Fisk. I have seen that face in the faces of the poor as well. The drunken navvies where we lived as children often looked like that. All reason and fine feeling struck from their minds."

"Still," Fisk, went on, "they are merely the tools, the lower manifestations of Opposition. The ones you seek are the Incarnation of it. I will not try to convince you Darrow, but remember this: anyone you meet on your search will believe you are nothing more than an insect to be crushed, excrement to be thrown into the gutter. Do not give him the chance, Darrow. Strike first and save your sister," Fisk urged as he walked Richard to the door.

"Leave some clothes and money with the landlord of the chop house where we went yesterday. A large fat man with a bald head. Riverton, by name. He is a friend of mine. I will go there now and tell him you will be leaving things with him. Do it soon."

Shaken by the conviction of Fisk's black, all-consuming beliefs, Richard took his leave and walked back to his own rooms. He knew that much of what Fisk said was true. The wealthy cared nothing for the suffering of the poor who laboured for them. He and Fanny had been clods of earth to most who met them as children, with the notable exception of Charles Wilney. Wilney had taught that the laws of society are good. There could be no order without them, but Richard had to admit that in the ever faster race for wealth that griped his age, the rich perverted and bent the laws. No man had the right to ill-use another. Richard gritted his teeth: No man would ill use his sister and hide behind a perverted law, either, he told himself.

At home, he gathered some clothes together, the poorest, roughest things he had, entirely unlike those of a schoolteacher, and tied them into a bundle along with the remains of his week's salary. Then he made his way to the chop house. The fat proprietor took him back to a storeroom behind the kitchen. Here Richard handed him the bundle. He was about to turn and go when the fat man stopped him.

"There is a key to the rear door of this building under the step at the back. Your bundle will always be just inside that door. You are a friend of Fisk's. I know I can trust you."

Richard nodded and left. He had the strange feeling that he was already preparing to go on a journey without knowing where or why he would go. It made him think of saying good bye to people he knew, particularly Sally Howard. Fortunately, it was the Howard's day at home.

The rooms above the engraver's shop in Cheapside were already full of people when he arrived. He was determined to talk to Sally alone and anticipated difficulty getting her to come outside with him, but almost as soon as he entered, she walked up to him with a very serious expression on her face and said, "I shall get my bonnet and meet you on the front stairs."

As he waited for her, he could not guess what had changed her so. As if in answer, she came outside and said, "I can see something has changed you. Something has happened." It was not a question.

"Yes. I may have to go away very suddenly."

She didn't ask him where or why but simply slipped her hand into his.

"It's hard to say this Richard. But I see something in your face tonight that has been lacking. I feel a man's strength in you, tonight. I hope it will help you meet whatever has come."

"Sally, I hardly know what to say. You have laughed at me so often and now you greet me as I have often wished."

"I have liked you Richard but tonight I can respect you as well. Do you understand?"

"Perhaps. I think so. But how can you know all this? Even I don't know really where or when I am going, yet. But my sister is missing and I must find her. There are other people involved and I don't know what might happen. So..."He trailed off, uncertain how to finish.

"So, you quite properly came to warn me and say adieu." The light from the shop window fell on the smooth curve of her cheek as she looked up at him without a trace of mockery in her face. Her long golden hair seemed to catch a thousand brilliant highlights from the glowing mantle of the street lamp.

"Sally, it is hard to speak now. So much is uncertain but.."

"I understand, Richard. I'll be here when you return."

"Thank goodness," he muttered as he pulled her to him in a quick, sudden embrace of goodbye. Then he turned and left without even looking at her face again.

The emotional force of the last twenty-four hours left Richard feeling curiously light headed as he walked home, almost the way a fever might affect him, though he knew he was not sick. To meet such openness and warmth in

Sally with so little effort was itself enough to make him giddy, but there was something more. He felt that he had not been the same since he met the old mudlark at Fanny's booth, he had somehow been forced to see that his simple upward climb to a meritorious end was not enough. Just as he couldn't leave Fanny to her fate because what she had done was wrong, he couldn't leave other wrong-doings of his age unaddressed. He could not remain a watcher of his own life and time. How all of this had become clear to him, he could not have explained. He only knew that it was clear and he could even see himself with Sally's eyes: as he was before and as he was now. In that moment, he longed for a friend with whom he could share his realization, but Fisk was too one-sided to understand what he was feeling. He would see everything through the words and images of his prophet, William Blake and the fervour of his political beliefs. Richard felt instinctively that this was wrong but could not say why or what belief was more correct. Charles Wilney would have been the interlocutor he would have chosen, but as far as Richard knew, Charles was far away in the southwest. Richard again told himself that he must write to him, once he had found Fanny. At the thought of her, his jaw set even more firmly. He would bring her home no matter what stood in the way, he promised himself. There was a new energy in him that carried him along the streets, the energy he had gained from Sally's upturned face, regarding him with gentle tenderness. The advantages of Miss Reade no longer existed for him.

It was rare to see stars in London's night sky in the 1840s, but Richard caught glimpses of one or two that night he walked home, walking east and toward the river from Cheapside. He did not know what lay ahead, he only knew that he would meet it and return to woo Sally. He felt a buoyancy that was new to him. The narrow track he had labouriously cut for mere survival now opened up to show him a broader perspective of his life. Where, he wondered, as he turned south into Nightingale Lane, could Fanny be?

When he got home, he paid no attention to the fact that the door of his lodging was ajar. He often left it that way. He had nothing to take and poor lodgings like his had no locks that would keep out a determined thief anyway. Though Robert Barron had invented the first patented lock in 1778, it was not widely used among the poor.

Before he could turn around to close the door, Richard felt a sharp prick on his left shoulder.

"Turn around very slowly," a voice said. "If you make any sudden movements, I shall kill you. Do you understand?"

Richard nodded and slowly turned to meet the voice. It was the man he had seen outside the house to which Maudie had led him. He held a naked sword stick in his hand and Richard had no doubt about his ability and willingness to use it.

"You have been making enquiries about a certain house. Why? What do you want with the man who lives there? Why, most particularly, did you follow me?"

"I didn't follow you. I saw you for the first time as you came through the gate. I am searching for my sister. I was told that the man she was with lived in that house."

"A woman? A young one, I take it?"

"Yes."

"She never came to that house, I can assure you."

"Why should I take your assurance?"

"Since I am holding the sword, why don't you answer my questions? You say, you did not follow me?"

"No."

"How then, were you there?"

"An old woman saw a young man with my sister. She told me he lived in that house."

"The old woman you were with?"

"Yes."

"I begin, I think, to comprehend. Your sister is a whore?"

Richard almost ran into the point of the man's sword in his fury at the accusation.

So sudden and fierce had he been that even Collins was for a moment thrown off balance. Richard pressed him to the wall, but then in spite of his age, the veteran spy twisted around and threw Richard into the corner and covered him once more with the point of his sword.

"Once more, I will ask, who is your sister?"

"My sister is a coster with a stall on the Ratcliffe Highway. A young man was seen with her. She has since disappeared. My friend went to the police to make an enquiry."

"You should be more careful with whom you associate. Your friend is a known Chartist with criminal alliances."

"Where is Fanny, then, if not in that house?"

"I do not know. But were I you, I should try Manchester."

"Manchester? Why?"

"I believe the man you seek is probably there. I also believe that you would be safer away from London."

"Who is he? And why would you help me?" Richard asked as he got to his feet.

"I cannot tell you who he is."

"Cannot or will not?"

"Will not. But I shall tell you that your sister, too, has made an unfortunate choice of association. That young man is protected by powers beyond your imagining. Your enquiry has made those powers aware that you exist. Since the man you seek has probably gone north, I suggest you do the same."

"Are you the agent of that power? If so, why are you giving me advice?"

"In this instance, I am a disinterested party. But I warn you, if you venture into areas where I do have an interest, I shall cut you down without further warning."

"And how do I know what those interests are if you do not tell me?"

"You will best serve yourself by pursuing your ends in Manchester. More than that I shall not say. You cannot know how charitable I have been tonight. Take what I have offered."

Richard bowed ironically to the man.

"Goodbye then. I hope we shall not meet again. If we do, I am likely to kill you. Following my guidance is your best chance of reaching your ends and preserving your life. Do not speak to anyone of this visit. I shall know. Do as I have told you."

The man slipped his sword back into the wooden stick that housed it, turned to the door and was gone before Richard could say another word. Once he realized he was alone, a spasm of trembling took possession of him for a moment. It passed in a wave and was gone. He thought of Fisk's words, 'anyone you meet on your search will believe you are nothing more than an insect to be struck down.' Would it be true of Fanny as well, once her lover was tired of her? How much time did he have to find her and hide her from such malevolent power? Though, there was some other reason that the power behind his visitor did not want to be watched.

Richard was confused about the motives of the man who had threatened him. The old man had also offered help by giving him a vague idea of Fanny's whereabouts and warning Richard of being watched in London. Richard was certain that the old man's interest had nothing to do with Fanny, but he felt there were hidden purposes behind his visit. However, there was no choice but to take his advice. It was Richard's only connection, however tenuous, with Fanny's lover. Staying in London offered him nothing but danger. Going to Manchester was the slimmest of hopes, but it had to be tried.

Richard was awake by the time the darkness of night had become the gray of morning. He dressed hurriedly and set off for the chop house where his clothes and money had been secreted. There was no chance to say goodbye to Fisk, who would understand the urgency of his departure. He tried to watch carefully for anyone following him but saw no one. The key was where the fat man had said it would be;. Richard let himself into the building and saw his bundle near the door. Quickly, he changed into the working man's clothes and tied his teacher's suit into the bundle. His costume should now help him blend into the mass of men on the road seeking work.

Richard had not been on the tramp for many years, not since he and Fanny had walked to London. Whether as children, their innocence had kept them from molestation he did not know, but he did realize that a young, single man who was not a peddler would be viewed with suspicion and distrust by most poor travelers and by the authorities. He would have to beware himself of the many destitute he would meet. He had too little money to stay even in the poorest road houses. An open parish might take him into the workhouse as a casual, but he did not want to get entangled with Union authorities. Besides, he had as much chance of getting robbed or beaten in many of the Union establishments as in the cheap lodging houses that the tramping criminal used as ports of call. The open country was cleaner, safer and would feel much more wholesome.

Even with the reform of the poor laws, the misery of the workhouse was well known to the destitute, and many chose to die on the roadside rather than seek the protection of indoor relief offered by the parish system. The predators who frequented poor lodging houses could be even more dangerous to a lone traveler. Now that Richard was a simple vagrant and once again had no work or place of residence, he had slipped back across the line that divided the poor from the criminal. Many people of the rising classes made no distinction between people who wanted work and those who preferred crime. Both groups looked similar and were the largest portion of the population. Not until 1849 when Henry Mayhew began publishing articles in the Morning Chronicle that would become his masterpiece, "London Labour and the London Poor," did anyone even try to distinguish between the criminal and non-criminal elements among the huge mass of Victorian disadvantaged. To the comfortably settled, vagrants, criminals and the poor seeking work all belonged to the "dangerous classes." On the road, the dangerous classes were victimized by parish authorities and by each other. The small, safe life that Richard had built for himself and Fanny was gone, for a time at least. Richard's first week on the road passed uneventfully. In fact, he enjoyed the freedom of his new life. He almost forgot his status as a member of society's lowest class until one day, he had stopped in the square of a village and was drinking from what he thought was a public fountain. A few moments after his lips touched the water, he felt a numbing blow on his upper back. He rolled away from the direction of the attack and saw a stout yeoman in a leather apron standing over him with a thick broom in his hands.

"Trying to steal water, are you?"

"No, I thought it was a public fountain," Richard said standing up.

"Ain't no public for you." get out of here before I take you to the magistrate."

Richard's next brush with what it meant to be homeless was much more pathetic. One night, after finding a quiet spot where he thought he could sleep undisturbed, he heard the muffled sobs of a woman coming from a distance not far away from where he lay. He got up, and though the night was moonless, the stars were bright and the sky vibrantly clear. After circling his own camp for a few minutes, he saw someone wrapped in a cloak of indeterminate colour. She was trying to hide herself under a hedgerow but apparently could not contain her sorrow.

"Here," he said as gently as possible, "I won't hurt you. Are you injured, can you move?"

For an answer the poor woman held out her arms which Richard now saw held an infant.

"De-dead," the woman sobbed."Ca-ca-can't bury. Not this Parish.

No help. Say, say, say," the woman gasped trying to control herself, "I killed her. Not true, not true, not true," she repeated in a keening wail. "My baby," she said holding out the child again.

Recognizing the truth of the woman's statement about the reception she would get from the authorities, Richard felt he had no recourse but to say, "I shall help you bury her."

He would never forget the next two hours of looking for a place in the grass of the roadside meadow where the ground would be soft enough to dig a shallow grave with bare hands and a stick. Finally, it was done and the child lay in it's forlorn resting place. When Richard stood up from his labour, the woman was gone, the stars were shimmering and very beautiful. He knelt down again and prayed for the soul of the tiny stranger he had buried and then prayed for the safe return of his sister. He slept fitfully in the unaccustomed brilliance of a dawn undimmed by coal smoke. Later in the morning, he continued on his road.

Richard's childhood recollection of the grimy, ugly streets of the northern industrial towns he had seen years before on their way to London, made his immediate future appear very bleak indeed. However, he was young, his love for Fanny had been tested and made stronger, and his hope for a future with Sally had also been strengthened. But if Pamela felt depressed the day she rode in her father's carriage and looked out at Manchester, it may be imagined how Richard felt when he saw the huge blackened smokestacks looming ahead, the thickened air and blackened, befouled landscape after weeks on the tramp in the clean countryside. Somewhere in the mass of soiled brick stacks reaching to the sullen skies, he might find Fanny. When he did, no power on earth would keep him from reclaiming his sister and making a new home for her.

He had realized, during his tramp, that the way he had searched for the identity of the grand house owner in London had been wrong. He had approached it as a poor person would, asking the police. He should have taken his money and retained a respectable solicitor to make the inquiries for him. He resolved to find such a man in Manchester and earn the money to pay him. That much of the mystery, he would solve.

He would find out who stood behind the man who threatened him and sent him here; that knowledge might help bring him closer to Fanny and her lover, even if she never had been inside the grand house to which Maudie had led him.

Chapter 6

"Did you hear about Atherton," Elspeth said in a confidential tone to her new friend, Mrs. Wells.

"Oh, do you mean that very young, ah, creature they found with him? I have not been really following it. But how did they know? Wasn't it the middle of the night?"

"The member for Beasley sent a messenger to the Commissioner of police right from the houses of Parliament," Elspeth said.

"Well, it certainly made Bradley the new member for Pilkington, did it not?"

Bradley looked across the supper table at his wife, as she gossiped with another parliamentary wife. The change that had been wrought in her still baffled him. He was the MP, but somehow Elspeth was the one who had been transformed by his achievement. She was so much more confident. She seemed to be reading a great deal. She had all kinds of information, facts and figures, at hand whenever he or anyone else asked a question regarding the railways. Since everything she did was helpful to his position, he was glad. Yet, the new Elspeth added to the general unease he had been feeling ever since the Atherton scandal had broken and Bradley had swept to victory on the wave of the public's condemnation of his opponent. He could not help but remember the letter that was sent the night he had his first meeting with Booth and the words: "Your victory has just been set in motion." But perhaps he was just imagining things. Booth had never said a word about the Atherton business. He had appeared just as surprised and shocked as everyone else. You certainly couldn't send someone to Parliament who was actually caught fornicating with a young child. It was one thing to indulge in such pleasures, many in the House of Commons did, but being caught. Atherton had fallen so low, he would never again appear in society, let alone public life . Bradley's own practice was flourishing. Booth and Vaughn had been more than helpful in that regard. He had to admit that Mason, the man Vaughn sent over from his office, was helping him make more money than when he himself had been handling clients by himself, and Mason was doing all the hard work. Of course, he, Bradley, had built the practice. Mason had just made sure that it operated at the top of its form. Everything was going along superbly. He had even lost some weight and Elspeth said he looked very smart in the new clothes that Booth had made him order from Vaughn's tailor. Everything was as exactly as he could wish it, yet...he had the feeling that he was no longer the one who was making things happen.

"I tell you, my dear, I wouldn't touch that stock issue," Elspeth's voice was sharp with certainty. "They are planning to use Mr. Brunel's wide gauge track on that line. Mr. Stephenson's narrow gauge tracks are sure to remain the standard. Even though the wide gauge tracks are in some ways superior, there is too much of the other track already in place. The two types are not compatible. I feel sure that the cost of introducing a new track standard will prove prohibitive. And the wide gauge is more expensive to build with as well. Putting seven feet between the rails instead of four requires larger sleepers and wider embankments or tunnels. I feel sure the wide gauge will lose out. Who knows what will happen to your dividends? We wouldn't risk our percents on wide gauge. Would we, Bradley?"

"No, no. Quite right my dear." How, he wondered, did she get up on these things so quickly? But his speculations were cut short by hearing Booth announced. He had told Bradley that he was going to pay him an important visit tonight and introduce him to another MP.

"Bradley," Booth said cordially in his thick scots burr. "Allow me to present the Member for Beasley, Arthur Rowells."

"Delighted," Rowells said, holding out his hand to Bradley. "Charmed," to Elspeth.

The fellow is demned good-looking, Bradley thought. Looks like a stage actor. Doesn't seem fitting for Parliament.

Rowells was well over six feet, athletic in build with perfectly cut jet black hair. His features were symmetrical enough for a statue from those ancient places in Italy everyone was talking about. His voice was deep and penetrating at the same time.

"Gentlemen," said Booth. "Shall we adjourn to the library?" It was as though it was his house, Bradley thought. He caught himself in that criticism and thought, What do I have to complain of? Booth and his master have been the making of me. Every change they have made in my life has been for the better. Bradley had always liked comfort, so his library was a richly appointed room. A thick turkey rug lay on the floor. The ruddy leather chairs gleamed but were soft as butter when one sat upon them. His desk and bookshelves were good English Walnut rubbed to a glowing finish. A beautifully wrought brass tray from the subcontinent sat on a stand of inlaid wood and held the gasogene, brandy, scotch and port. The glasses were handsomely cut crystal. Bradley felt good here. It was his room. It reflected him and no one else. He had selected everything himself. He did the honours with drinks and then sat down, feeling very much in possession of himself.

"Now gentlemen," Booth said, "I know we are all batting for the same team. We all want what is good for England."

"Here, here," Rowells said tipping his glass steeply.

"And like any team, we all have our parts to play. I wanted us to meet tonight to be clear about what those parts are."

"Jolly well said," Rowells spoke as he raised his glass again. Bradley suddenly realized that Rowells was a complete ass. The thought made him smile.

"Thank you, Rowells" Booth said. "Now be quiet."

"Quite, quite."

"This is how I see us being most effective," Booth went on." He was looking straight at Bradley.

"Bradley is our strategist, our general. Rowells is the infantry that goes out into the field and leads the charge. Am I being clear?"

"Oh, quite," Rowells said.

"Could you elaborate," Bradley asked.

"I'd be happy to do so," Booth replied. "Rowells will make our formal speeches, table our bills and so on. Bradley will answer questions from the Floor. You, Bradley, will have the burden of all the hard work. You must memorize the technical details of each bill we put forward and know them better than anyone else in the House. You must have answers for any possible objection to each bill that Rowells will present for us. At the same time, no one is to guess that you are Samuelson's man. No one is to guess that the two of you are working together."

"You mean I won't be speaking at all?" Bradley said, feeling both relieved and annoyed.

"No. You will speak, and at the most crucial junctures. Any time a difficult question is asked from the floor or our proposals are attacked, you will take it up. But you must do it in a way that does not make you sound partisan. I think by now we all recognize that thinking extemporaneously is not Mr. Rowells' strength. But, Bradley, you can take it from me that he can memorize and recite a speech, beautifully. Between you, Parliament will not be able to resist us. I particularly want you, Bradley, to make friends with other members. You will take peculiar care to cultivate the most provincial, the dullest and the poorest new members. Give sumptuous dinners and interest them in your own points of view. Entertain lavishly. Make them feel like real City men. Find them decent tailors. Get them into good clubs. Hint that you will let them in on really excellent railway investments. Once we toss them a few bones and let them make a few hundreds, they will hang on your every word. This will be an important part of your role, Bradley, since you have an establishment here in town. You will dun it into them that if you all pledge yourselves to always vote together, you will be a power in Parliament. As far as railway bills are concerned, you will warn them not to believe what they read in the press. Point out that newspapers can be aligned with certain capitalists who may be hidden in the background. Emphasize that vested interests exist at every turn. Interests in a certain track gauge, interests reflected in information furnished by a certain engineer, interests exercised by Boards of Directors whose connection with a stock issue is deliberately cloaked. Scare them with the dangers of speculating in railway shares and then sing them the siren song of recent railway stock earnings, such as those of the well-known City Police Commissioner William Whittle Harvey. Tell them how Harvey realized 30,000 pounds in a fortnight. This will have all but the richest Members ready to do anything for you. Don't let them forget for an instant that even if they are poor they can become rich. Remind them often that by the increases possible when passing on shares at ever higher prices, they can leave Parliament wealthy men. Teach them about the extreme danger of trading in letters of allotment. Explain the ins and outs of the 'Change. In short, make them afraid to do anything without you. Then, you will easily lead your goslings in whatever direction we want. And, here is our first Parliamentary objective."

Booth reached into his inner pocket and pulled out a document written in a bold, beautiful but unusual hand. Bradley wondered for a moment whose hand it was.

"What is it?" Bradley asked.

"This is a private members bill proposing that an amount of fourteen millions be raised by stock issue to fund a much needed railway line. I have two copies here. Rowells, I want you to read it for form. Bradley, I want you to get a good grasp of the contents. I shall be back tomorrow to go over the fine points with you, Bradley.

"Shouldn't I go over the fine points as well?" Rowells asked.

"No, Rowells. Just learn the speech I have written for you."

Bradley smiled discreetly into his hand. He was already starting to enjoy his generalship and Rowells's subservience.

"Go away now, Rowells," Booth ordered.

"Do you mean,.."

"Leave. I will see you back here on Monday next to hear you present the speech."

Even a man as limited as Rowells, Bradley thought, must feel that keenly. But the handsome member from Beasley gave no sign of offense or anger. He simply got up and left.

When the door of the library was closed Bradley observed, "What an extraordinary fellow."

"He is not quite as much a fool as he appears. But I should not trust him on his own. But his appearance, voice, connections and manner will get us many votes less expensively than they might otherwise be gotten."

Bradley had never been what we would call today, "an insider." Somehow he had always been left out when important decisions were being made. At school, and even in his practice, where most of his work was based on cut and dried things like conveying property, he rarely felt like the authority he wanted to be. He had never admitted this to himself, but Booth's manner with him and Rowells soothed a great wound that Bradley didn't even know he had. It convinced him of Booth's penetration and power as nothing else had, not even the name of Samuelson, a name which the scotsman still used very sparingly.

After Rowells had gone Booth asked him, "Now, are you ready for some real work?"

At that moment Bradley would have walked on hot iron if Booth had asked him. He felt he could build the railway himself. Some hours later, however, Bradley felt quite differently. After swotting on all the technical aspects of the line, he felt quite dizzy. Track would have to be laid across a vast boggy area, similar to Chat Moss, which had been crossed in eighteen twenty-six and twenty-seven by the builders of the Liverpool&Manchester Line. Like Chat Moss, it would be an engineering feat which many believed would be too expensive. George Stephenson had nearly lost his position as Chief Engineer of the Liverpool& Manchester Line over Chat Moss. This time, the costs and timing needed to be more predictable. To make the bill viable, Bradley had to convince other members, using the solutions Samuelson himself had provided, that it could be done with greater predictability. Members must feel that the line would get built in a specified time. There was something so powerful about the physical impression of the weight of a locomotive, track and cars sinking into a bog that the complexities of Samuelson's brilliant engineering solution still seemed unconvincing to Bradley. He said as much to Booth.

"Well, we must go over it again until you believe it. The force of argument is mostly in the conviction of the speaker. Rowells can be convinced about anything. It is you, you, who will have to answer the difficult questions, who must sound thoroughly convinced and convincing."

"Perhaps it would help if I heard Mr. Samuelson himself explain his ideas?" Booth was quiet for a moment. He leaned back in his chair.

"Hmm. Perhaps it would. That would look like nothing more than thoroughness on your part if you were to meet with him and discuss it. All right, let's go. There is nothing he loves more than talking about the details of railway building."

"Now?"

"Why not? Nothing stands higher in Mr. Samuelson's interest right now. He is in town. Which means he is at home. He almost never accepts invitations."

Such intimate knowledge of Samuelson's interests and behaviour overawed Bradley for a moment. Then he recovered himself, tossed off his drink and stood up. Inwardly, he was vibrating with excitement.

Bradley's mind was in a riotous state as they dashed through the west-end in the scotsman's beautiful carriage. Even Elspeth looked at him differently when he told her he was going out to meet with Samuelson. She was surprised for once, and Bradley was very pleased that she would have no equivalent access to the great railwayman. It helped restore his sense of power in his own house. The breathless ride through the streets and the extensive grounds of the railwayman's mansion made Bradley feel that he was now truly taking part in great affairs. His true value had been recognized.

A double row of gaslights highlighted the curving drive in front of the large, white stone mansion where they stopped. The servants treated Booth with great deference. It was clear to Bradley that the scotsman was an important and frequent visitor to the house.

Booth led Bradley through the palatial home as though it were his own. Finally, he knocked on a pair of huge double doors at the end of a long corridor.

"Come," was heard softly through the doors.

Samuelson was in his shirtsleeves, obviously not expecting callers. He wore gray trousers and a finely patterned waistcoat. Bradley's clearest impression was one of physical power. Samuelson loomed over both himself and even Booth. He was broadly made but looked hard as granite. His face was high browed, his eyes heavy-lidded but watchful.

"Oh, Booth," I wasn't expecting you tonight.

"Well, Bradley suggested that you explain the engineering behind the Westerfall passage to him. He felt he might be able to be more convincing when the time comes to defend it in Parliament."

"Good to meet you, Mr. Bradley. A very intelligent suggestion. It is a bit of scientific magic to those who don't understand the engineering principles. Let's see if I can bring you up to snuff on it. Have a seat. Brandy?"

Like George Stephenson, Samuelson was a very brilliant, self-taught engineer, but unlike Stephenson, who often sounded unconvincing and obscure when he spoke to people who did not understand engineering, Samuelson also had the gift of making his ideas clear. It was one of the reasons for his great success. He had an instinct for clarity and directness and eschewed any of the specialist's jargon.

Bradley felt flattered by the attention and after a while even felt his clear grasp was the result of his own intelligence rather than Samuelson's gift. This was another of the railwayman's great abilities: he made others feel that his achievements were their own. Whether Samuelson spoke with a navvy, an engineer, a banker, or a footman, he made each one feel that his own penetrating and original grasp of a situation belonged to the other person.

Booth spoke little. He watched his master and Bradley closely. He could see Samuelson, making another loyal follower out of the new MP.

For Bradley, these hours with one of the greatest men of the age flew by. He felt that by his attendance on Samuelson, his own superiority had finally been acknowledged. He was finally moving in a circle appropriate to his own abilities. By the time the evening ended, stale smoke hung in the air and a stack of neatly drawn engineering details, highlighted in Samuelson's memorable handwriting, lay scattered on the floor. Bradley was not only convinced but understood enough to really admire the genius of the way the bog would be crossed by heavy rails and railway cars. He had even come up with a sensational way to present it to Parliament, using a lead brick, a piece of paper and a wooden grid that he would have made up.

"Very good," the great railwayman had exclaimed when he heard the idea. "There is nothing like doing a magic trick and then explaining it. It entertains and answers all argument at the same time. You have a real feeling for this, Mr. Bradley."

Bradley flushed with pleasure. "Thank you, Sir. I believe it shall be most effective."

"And so from your disbelief," Booth said, "we have created a presentation that will strengthen rather than weaken us."

Samuelson stood up. "Gentlemen, it is late. I am tired so I must ask you to say good night."

"Oh, yes, of course," Bradley stood up quickly. "I enjoyed myself so much I quite lost track of the time."

"You are a man of sense, Mr. Bradley. I'm sure we'll have many other interesting conversations."

"Thank you, sir."

"Booth will meet you in the carriage, Mr. Bradley. There were just one or two little confidential matters we have to discuss before you leave."

"Oh, yes, of course."

Bradley continued to be so pleased with himself and his reception by Samuelson that he sat comfortably waiting in the carriage for a quarter of an hour.

Inside the library, the scotsman looked at his master and asked, "Well?"

"Excellent, I had actually expected much less intelligence. He could be dangerous later on."

"That is being seen to, sir. He is intelligent but his desire for recognition makes him very easy to steer. It takes a very small bone to make him fetch. I hope you don't mind my bringing him tonight? I felt the visit could easily be defended if need be."

"Yes, of course. No. That's fine, Booth."

"You have some letters for me?" Samuelson walked from his sitting area in front of the fire to his huge mahogany desk.

"Here," he said.

Booth tucked them into his coat.

"Well, all the players are on the stage for our new Parliamentary drama," Booth commented.

"Yes. We should do well."

"I concur."

By the time Bradley got home, it was two o'clock in the morning. He felt so elated, he didn't think he could sleep. In spite of the lateness of the hour, he went through to the library picked up a brandy and a cigar and went out into the back garden where he wandered around in a state of exaltation.

No one, he thought, could have risen faster than I. I have spent the entire evening with one of the greatest men of our age and he has complimented me on my intelligence. What higher praise could there be then that? I work hand and glove with him to help realize a great vision of England's future. Together we are making history. I always felt it would happen. But to rise so fast, so high. It is remarkable even for a superior person. Such was the tenor of his thoughts when he heard his wife in the garden.

"How was it, Bradley?"

"He told me I was a man of sense and intelligence. He told me that we would have many interesting conversations together."

"Well, my goodness. That is wonderful. What did you talk about?"

But this last question, Bradley was not inclined to answer. He did not want to admit Elspeth to the highest levels of railway arcana. This was to be his domain and his alone. Her place was at home, serving tea and biscuits. She should know her place.

"It was a very complex discussion of engineering problems and solutions, my dear. Highly specialized. Couldn't possibly repeat it all at this hour. Rather like a patent, in any case. Confidential. The only thing you need know is that tonight your husband made history with one of the greatest men of the age." He drawled his last words to underscore their importance. From the look on Elspeth's face, he could see he had carried his point.

In fact, Elspeth was annoyed as she returned to her bedroom. The more she and Bradley were out in the world together, the more she saw what fool he was, and more important, what her own gifts of understanding were. She found all the ins and outs of railway building and speculation truly fascinating, and she even suspected that she understood them better than her husband. This genuine interest and the appreciation for herself that it had engendered, had begun to work on her to create a kind of dissatisfaction she had never before felt. Like most women of her class and time, she had been content to live in society through the role of her husband. Now, she wanted something else. She had not yet worked out what it was that she wanted, but the quiescent wife had begun to feel something entirely new. Elspeth had begun to be personally ambitious.

In her quiet way, Elspeth, too, would help change society.

Chapter 7

The parliamentary election of Peter J. Bradley was well staged. When he spoke on the hustings, there were even some hecklers whose jibes he easily put by. He wondered if they were genuine or if they were of Booth's manufacture. At any rate, Bradley was cheered and lauded for a full day. His house was filled with guests. Oil lamps, artfully placed, dotted the garden. Elspeth looked lovely, having spent the entire day in some secret place of female enhancement. One of her new friends, another parliamentary wife, had taken her there. The Vaughns actually came to pay court. Vaughn brought Bradley a manly gift of a box of fine cigars. Booth, though present, remained in the background. It was Bradley's day and his alone.

Bradley would have been shocked if he had known how many people thought Atherton had been brought low by conspiracy and fraud. Of course none of these people were of Bradley's acquaintance, being largely limited to those dangerous classes who populated the rookeries, waterfront and other unsavoury parts of London. Atherton had been popular with this class, something that was cited now by better people to confirm his guilt and unworthiness. None of the poor would have mattered to Bradley, in any case. He would have laughed if he had known that he had made an enemy of a ship's carpenter named Fisk.

When Fisk had read of Atherton's downfall, he had thrown down his paper with the conviction that peaceful conversations about the Charter were no longer enough. The corruption of the Babylon of London was more than the honest and forthright carpenter could abide. He was ready to take the rotten regime apart brick by brick. He felt that all the supporters of Bradley were truly marked with the Number of the Beast. The Member for Beasley, who had denounced Atherton's alleged crime, was certainly working hand in glove with Bradley's backers. The words of the old man at the meeting came back to him: "Money, money sits on the throne of England." Fisk had been tempted to tell the visitor from Manchester what he knew about the weapon makers of Newcastle, but something had held him back, even in an Association meeting. Now he was doubly glad he had not spoken out. He would use what he knew. The arms would be used, not sold. With weapons in their hands, when the Charter was brought before Parliament again, they could make Tom Paine's arguments with a language the corrupt politicians and capitalists could not mistake. Fisk had at once proceeded to take steps to secure the weapons. Through friends he had in Manchester, he had contacted the weapon makers in Newcastle. He had arranged to use a large portion of his life savings to purchase a sizeable number of guns and a large amount of powder and shot. If the Charter was not passed by peaceful means, he thought, by the Lord Harry, it would be passed with violence. It was too much to bear that good men were falsely proven guilty in the public's mind of crimes invented by the true corrupters of the nation. Fisk had even gone to hear Bradley speak on the hustings and it seemed to him obscene that this little, doll-like man, who mouthed the platitudes of capitol and privilege, should displace a reformer like Atherton.

These were the reasons why, several weeks after Bradley's election, Fisk stood alone, after midnight, at the river's edge, on a remote quay near the marshy tip of the Isle of Dogs, awaiting delivery of the weapons from Newcastle. They might not arrive that night, nor the next, nor the next. How many nights he would have to wait depended in large part on any problems encountered down through the canals west of London. In spite of his thick felt coat, he shivered in the damp night. It was hard to see the people's inaction, he thought as he waited, when great men like Blake and Tom Paine pointed the way so clearly. But Fisk understood that it was the struggle for survival that kept the multitudes from striking down those who used iron and steam, the factory bell and railways to coin money and oppress them. He thought of Richard's personal struggle with corruption. Most people were like the lad, he thought. They were simply trying to protect their loved ones and get an honest living. They were often too busy and too tired to turn aside to attack their oppressors. Fisk felt powerfully called to do it for them. What those with families were too busy and frightened to do, he would do for them. He felt almost feverishly impatient as he waited in the darkness.

The oily water that formed the carpenter's prospect as he waited was black and opaque. The few distant lights put white edges on the shallow waves breaking the surface of the turbid water. To the carpenter, the story of Richard and Fanny was a parable of the complete degeneracy of the rich, the whores of Babylon. What was the young man facing now because of that degeneracy? Fisk wondered. What violation had been visited upon lovely Fanny? Who pursued Richard and what would his fate be when he found his sister or was found by those who had her? Where were the true prophets now? Who would actually be able to see the New Jerusalem beneath the ugly scab of poor, begrimed London? Blake implied that complete self-trust was the true way to God. That supreme inner trust had been the touchstone of the prophetic artist who had made images and poems that would outlast the kingdoms of the earth. But how was he, Fisk, to see into the spiritual realm which, he felt certain, underlay the world of nature? How was he to see with the eyes of Swedenborg or Blake? Fisk felt certain that if the Charter were to become law, men's understanding must come from the realm of Spirit, not the World. At the same time, Fisk was angry, and couldn't help but feel that a ball of lead must pierce the rotten heart of Bradley and all his friends if England were to be cleansed and free.

While he waited, caught in the opposition of his desire for revenge and desire for spiritual understanding, a wall of fog blacker than the night sky rolled across the river; the dark exhalations of the City covered the oily water and all who sailed upon it. The darkness would hide those for whom he waited, Fisk thought. Even something the size of a coal barge could not be seen without some light.

He peered into the darkness, straining his eyes to see, and that was when he saw a point of light suddenly appear in the blackest part of the darkness, just above the water. At first it was a tiny spark in almost total darkness. Then, it grew into a small ball of light, the size of a child's toy. Its size increased until Fisk could see a large ball of glowing brilliance that drew closer and closer to him. The surface of the river now reflected a fiery beauty, as though fire and water could be the same substance. Out of the surface of this strange substance, there swelled up a column of whirling fire which lit the firmament.

As Fisk watched, breathlessly, the column began to spin, like a piece of stock in a lathe, with showers of sparks flying outward into the darkness. Gradually the pillar of fire formed itself into a tall, beautiful, luminous figure who pointed to the glowing ball of light as it continued to approach. The figure had long, exquisitely chiseled wings which were light as air and heavy as stone at the same time. Neither male nor female, the face of the being wore an expression of great solemnity. Fisk thought the glowing ball would consume him and everything in its path but instead, the tall figure spoke to him and said,

"Behold the Lord."

The ball of light broke open and Fisk saw the Lord revealed just as the Master had painted him. He was sad as he looked upon the City like a loving but fretful father. The Lord told Fisk, that the carpenter was his child. He must do as he was commanded. The beauty of the presence was so great that it shot through Fisk like pain, and he fell on his knees and wept for joy. Thus he stayed, bowed down on the rough wood that smelled of tar, for a long time. Finally, he rose to his feet, and began walking back to the City.

All was now transformed. Fisk could see angels playing around the steeples of the highest buildings. Demons and spirits of pestilence were running in and out of factories and the homes of the wealthy. All things appeared in their true character. He was somehow able to see the houses of Parliament. They were lit with a red, dusky light, a light from hell. Suddenly, behind the whole panaroma of his vision, a huge thing rose up. It was shaped like a beast with four legs, and had long, many toothed jaws which protruded from each of its seven heads. On its tail was a stinger like a scorpion and its body was made of iron. It reached into the homes of the poor and devoured them and their children. Their blood ran down its many jaws as it gorged itself. In the higher air, the angels wept. Fisk knew he was seeing the Beast who would destroy the world if it wasn't kept from its ghastly feast. Yet, in the upper air, he could also see the New Jerusalem in all its shining wonder and beauty. From this height an angel descended, the same fiery figure who had appeared over the water.

He said to Fisk, "Know that in two centuries, the Iron Beast will devour the world if it is not killed now. Act in righteousness and slay this Beast in its infancy. The New Jerusalem is here, now. For all the righteous poor who shall rise up, slay the Beast and claim their birthright."

As he walked, Fisk had visions of such beauty and joy that they could not be described, yet each thing he saw was real and ordinary, available to all. The angel, who was named Gabriel, walked beside him and called him, "brother."

When he reached home, Fisk sat down and wrote an account of his vision. He had it printed for all who might want to see the spiritual city. He called the booklet: *The New Jerusalem Found: A Vision Had By An Ordinary Working Man.* It rapidly found its way into circulation through all the radical booksellers in London, the same men who had secretly sold copies of Tom Paine's Rights of Man, slipped between the covers of innocuous used books. But Fisk felt he must do more to share his vision with others, even after his Pamphlet was being widely read. He needed to take direct action to relieve the fullness of his heart. The proximity and tangible reality of the New Jerusalem made him realize how absurd the political arguments and procedural details of corresponding societies really were. The New Jerusalem was more than just a metaphor for a future state of bliss, it was a place, an experience that could be seen with the inner eye, now. Blake had understood this. He had understood that one could not separate the inner from the outer. Those who grasped after wealth with machines were torturing the outer lives of the poor with the darkness and noise of the factories. More important, the capitalists obscured the inner vision of the New Jerusalem by darkening the luminous inner world of spirit. Factory owners wanted to turn inner fire into a cold mechanical wheel that turned to the beat of a factory clock. How could the mere words of a pamphlet work against this darkness?

All who laboured, Fisk thought, now had to keep pace with the panting, tireless beast of the new age. The machines enforced a hideous kind of slavery and loss of dignity. No longer was there any pride in craft. No longer did a man or woman's skill count for anything when a child could operate a machine for less pay. The masters were engaged in an unprecedented race for wealth, a race that moved at the pace set by the iron beast itself. The haste and greed of the age was made manifest in the speed and the vast capitalization of the railways. More than any other single aspect of the times, Fisk realized, the money to be made from railway speculation fed the iron beast.

While "society" congratulated itself on progress, the iron beast crushed the poor into appalling degradation. Religion, too, had betrayed the poor and conspired with the masters: The Methodists had twisted worship itself to bind people to the iron beast. Their dry, joyless doctrine of submission that was spread among the hopeless poor like a plague of the soul was a dark cloud that choked breath and life away, and at the same time fed the greed of the factory owners and speculators. Obedience, submission and uniformity were the laws of the religion of the iron beast. It was drilled into children at factory schools. Children who should be running in the fields under clear skies were broken by religion, having to attend a full day of Sunday school after an exhausting 80-hour week of labour. Joy and ecstasy were only expressed in morbid images of death. Be ready to die for the sake of obedience and submission, but do not live in fullness, celebrating God's gifts. In this dark world, it was almost something holy when a child died from overwork or from the very terror of being late for work at the factory.

How different from Fisk's ecstatic vision. In the New Jerusalem, Fisk knew, the divinity of each creature would shine forth in a joyful life for all. How true were Blake's words: "I went to the garden of love, and saw what I never had seen...priests in black gowns were walking their rounds and binding with briars my joys and desires."

The iron beast, created as a servant, had become the master, and consumed the very souls of the working poor. Could philosophical arguments undo this monstrous combination?

No, Fisk thought. Action, carefully planned and ruthless in its destructiveness of the monster was the only way. He would need help, and he was determined to get it.

* * *

He began by making an address in Hyde Park, between two of the trails at the eastern end of the park. He chose a Sunday in the late afternoon, when the poor would not have to work or be forced into bonds of worship. The weather was fresh and mild. The many coloured birds who paddled in the Serpentine flew overhead. He saw an angel sitting in one of the trees, looking at him with eyes like stars.

"I speak today to anyone who is enslaved to a machine in a factory," Fisk began. "What would you do to gain your freedom?"

Two people stopped and began listening. The angel Gabriel flew down over their heads and Fisk knew that these two would follow him. The woman was dark, strong featured and almost pretty, or would have been if she had been not been prematurely worn in appearance. The man was young, slender and also dark. He clutched his arms around himself and swayed back and forth as Fisk spoke. He looked to Fisk like a flame starving for fuel.

"I tell you," Fisk said, "there is a great beauty available to us all, if we throw off the bonds of the iron beast. The New Jerusalem is here, all around us. We only have to realize that Christ has freed us forever. All we need to do is accept that freedom."

"What is the iron beast?" a second man who was passing called out.

"It is the idol of our age," Fisk answered. "A mightier incarnation of the golden calf, and if we who stand here today do not topple it, it will destroy us all in time. It is a precursor to the Beast of the apocalypse, it is the true Antichrist. We are made to worship it in the factories, in our new mode of travel, in our slavery to the clock, in the holiness of uniformity."

"We are truly slaves to the factory clock," one man called out. "I lost a day's wages because the master's clock said I was three minutes late."

"How many others have had to bow down to the clock?" Fisk asked. "Sometimes they don't even pay us in any case but offer shoddy goods in exchange for wages."

"That's right," Fisk said.

"I tried to improve some of the factory machines and lost my place for it," another man said. "Then, the belt of one of the machines took a man's arm and now he is a factory cripple, a beggar."

"Let there be nothing individual about you," Fisk said in a thundering voice. "That is the first commandment of the iron beast. Child, man, woman, all shall do the same and act the same according, not to our needs, but to the needs of the machines and those who coin money with them. Give up yourself, the unique beauty given you by God, and instead obey the laws of the iron beast. In the factory, does the exhausted child lie down to enjoy the sweetness of rest when he is exhausted? No. He does not rest or sleep until the iron beast says he may. Does the skilled man look to his brothers to see the praise in their eyes? No. The iron beast shall tell him if he has still any value, or if he may be altogether discarded. All of you who work in factories, is what I am saying true?

"Yes, yes," a ragged chorus of perhaps ten voices now replied.

"Then let me tell you of the New Jerusalem I have seen and can see here and now with my own eyes. I see in that tree behind you, a beautiful angel," he said pointing upward. Heads turned around to look. "It is a tall, noble figure who watches us closely and hopes that we shall take our freedom, the freedom already purchased for us by the Saviour. We do not need the laws of the religion that the greed of the masters would impose on us, we need only accept Christ's treasure. His love is our weapon against the iron beast and the owners who would enslave us. If you could only see as I do, you would see the exquisite beauty that is here, now. It is only our own beliefs that keep us chained to the iron beast. Belief in our own sinfulness and the need for obedience to the beast's law keeps us enslaved. There are no other chains. They exist only in your minds and hearts."

"And how do you say we should kill this iron beast and still feed ourselves?" the dark woman asked. "If we hurt a machine, we go to prison. It is more serious than killing a child with overwork. How shall we be free of the machines and their masters? Tell me that."

"The answer to your question is not for the open air, Miss. How many will come with me now?"

Thus, Fisk began by leading eight people to his shop and speaking privately, out of the earshot of police spies.

Chapter 8

In the weeks that followed this first address, Fisk spoke many times, drawing larger and larger crowds. He always stopped short of advocating violence in public, but in private conversations with people the angel Gabriel helped him select, he spoke of the weapons that had finally arrived and lay hidden in the far east end of the city, and of the need for a large coordinated effort when their army was large enough and spiritually ready.

"The reason the Chartist movement has failed," he said in these private meetings, "is that it is made up of many little people, each concerned to lead. Then they beg from others for what is rightfully ours already. Christ should be our leader. His is the power that cannot be resisted. Through his love we shall be inspired. Through love of him we shall form our plans to release all those in bondage."

One young man who had stopped to listen to Fisk on the first day, Simon Oakley, had been a student of engineering and been planning to work for the railways. His father, a linen draper and devout Methodist had terrified Simon from an early age with visions of Hell and the imagery of Christ's bleeding wounds. When his mother had died, the nine-year-old Simon had been forced to repeat each night for a year these words from one of Wesley's hymns:

"Ah, lovely Appearance of Death! No sight upon Earth is so fair, Not all the gay Pageants that breathe Can with a dead Body compare."

Simon was finally released from this religious terrorism when his father died, leaving Simon financially independent, though by then, the young man was unable to continue with his railway plans for he found the navvy camp he once visited a terrifying place that called up all the darkest visions of his early religious training. When he first heard Fisk speak, he was spending his time drifting through the days, reading engineering books and visiting with the elderly ladies in the respectable rooming house where he lived. Fisk gave him Blake's *Jerusalem* to read, and without being able to accept the notion of man's utter lack of sin, it relieved Simon that Blake had believed it and that Fisk, whose visions the young man admired and believed in, also thought that Christ had redeemed all men for all time. The young man even tried to induce visions like those which visited Fisk by fasting until the carpenter ordered him to stop.

"If God has not given you the gift of vision, if it is not in your nature, do not starve your body. Be whole, not divided against yourself," Fisk told him. "Use the gifts you do have."

Fisk's group of dedicated followers grew slowly, but each one accepted his idea of carefully planned violent action that would one day be prepared by them to strike at the iron beast.

"Our actions must be completely hidden and not undertaken in anger," Fisk would say. "When we strike we must amaze and cripple the masters and show our brothers that the iron beast is vulnerable," he told them. "We must not be like those who followed General Ludd. Their acts were small and were exposed, often as acts of simple vandalism and petty conspiracy. We shall become a holy army of avengers, taking back the power of our uniqueness and using it to claim self-governance. Once we have ignited our imagination and harnessed that power, we shall terrify the high and mighty and win in a few ruthless strokes what the Chartist movement has failed to do during long years of suffering. But we must be disciplined and patient and know that we are dedicating our lives to help our brothers and sisters in Christ's name. We must have faith and patience. We shall give ourselves justice in our wages, not beg from factory owners. We shall set our own just working conditions."

"By what means is this to be achieved?" one man asked.

"Through faith," Fisk said, "that knows each person possesses his or her own genius of imagination that can conquer all adversaries, that has more wisdom than all traditions and laws. Our inner vision, our unique minds, are more potent than gunpowder. It is this genius that I know will direct all of us to our goal if we but open ourselves to it. You will not doubt once you have walked with angels as I have."

It was a vague program, but Fisk's conviction and faith in his visions had their effect. The promise of violent action and the fact of the weapons drew many angry listeners. At the same time, Fisk's visions appealed to the many devout non-conformists among the working poor. Fisk might have become another working class prophet like the ones who had come and gone before: Joanna Southcott, Richard Brothers and their ilk, but six months after he started building his group of followers, he met John Cary.

Cary was the son of a wealthy Colonial merchant who had inherited huge wealth in the Indies, acquired before the South Sea bubble burst in the 1700s. With this wealth at his disposal, Fisk really had the funds to take action against the iron beast. Feeling that the wealthy Cary might supplant him as Fisk's apostle, Simon began to work on specific steps for the kind of planned violence Fisk advocated. He chose the steam driven factory machines as a starting place for action. He understood their technology and there were enough accidents that would disguise his deliberate acts of destruction, until they were ready for a really vast attack. He would hide his plans from Fisk, for now. After he had successfully destroyed a factory, he would tell Fisk and earn his praise. None would know the accidents were man-made. No one could be punished for them, as some of the Luddites had been. As Simon laid his plans, John Cary and Fisk made several long trips together to northern England. so Fisk could buy more guns from the radical armorers in Newcastle.

The woman whom the angel had pointed out to Fisk would also became a central part of the carpenter's life. Cynthia Hackworth was a skilled seamstress who had seen her means of livelihood diminish as the London sweatshops flourished. At the time she first heard Fisk speak, Cynthia worked in a small room with fifty other woman. Some, like Cynthia had done fine hand work, sewing handkerchiefs and men's shirts in their homes or in the homes of the wealthy. Now they spent a ninety-six hour work week in a cramped, poorly ventilated room, earning barely enough to feed themselves. Cynthia's husband had gone north on a tramp looking for work and never returned. She was a Dissenter and something of a free thinker. Her relationship to God was important to her. She was at first skeptical of Fisk's visions, but curious, too, so she stayed to talk to him about William Blake, of whom she had never before heard. She liked Fisk because he looked like a man who would do something instead of just talk. His strong brown hands, burley shoulders and thoughtful gray eyes appealed to her. When the other people who had come to Fisk's shop after his first speech left, Cynthia had stayed.

"You are fortunate to have such a large airy place to work, Mr. Fisk," she said after the others had left.

"Where do you work, Miss..."

"Hackworth, Cynthia Hackworth."

"What sort of a place do you work in, Miss Hackworth?"

"A sweat shop. Fifty women packed together like a heap of dried fish at the market.

Below the attic where we work are printing presses. The clatter of the machines never stops. It is so quiet here by comparison." She began coughing uncontrollably. Her inhalations were long and rasping.

"Miss Hackworth, are you all right? Let me give you some water." He went to a large bottle that he kept on one of his worktables, poured a drink into a clean glass and handed it to Cynthia, who was still coughing. The sound was abrasive and dry. Fisk thought it must be painful.

"Thank you, sir." Cynthia said hoarsely. "I shall be all right now. It is the effect of the closeness of the place I work. The fumes from the printing ink downstairs sometimes make us dizzy. That is why I commented on how airy your workshop is."

"Yes, I am fortunate, Miss Hackworth. No machine has yet learned how to make fine furniture by itself. Though the time may come, and soon."

"These chairs, over against the wall, they are your work?"

Fisk watched the slim, dark woman appraisingly. He liked her black hair and unusually large, sea green eyes. He didn't mind that she was no longer in the first blush of youth, nor that time and work had left their marks on her. He thought her sharpened features gave her a look of refinement.

"Yes," he answered.

"Very beautiful. You do fine work. The kind of work I did in clothe, once. Now there is never any time to do really good work," she said as she ran her hands across the carved central piece of a chair back. The wood was smooth as satin, yellow as honey with a pattern made up of small markings like a thousand birds' eyes.

"Thank you, Miss Hackworth."

"What does an angel look like?" she asked suddenly as she turned back to face him.

"They are all beautiful but all different. As are we."

"But they are winged?"

"Yes. Their wings have a peculiar beauty, at once very light, yet very heavy and strong. Why do you ask me these things. Do you think me mad or foolish?"

"Oh, no, sir." she answered looking at him earnestly. "I-I would just like to see one."

"Why?" he asked, gently.

"I just think it would help to, to bear things. That is, actually to see the Lord's favourites and know absolutely that they are here with us would help us bear any of our trials. Is it not so for you?"

"Yes, though I had not thought of it that way before. I believe anyone who loves the Lord and who really wants to see our celestial brethren can see them. The Lord does not have favourites. We do not have to do anything to please Him. Mostly it's a matter of undoing."

"I don't understand."

"Here, sit down," Fisk said pulling one of the chairs she had admired over to her.

"Oh, I have never sat on such a beautiful chair," she said as she sat down. "Thank you."

"We need to undo all our false ideas about what we should be, should do and realize that Christ loves us all just as we are. That is the chief message of the Lord. That is what the angels tell me."

"And what of this iron beast you speak of?"

"That is a creature of man's own distorted thoughts and antithetical to our natural state, which is pure and loving. The grip of this beast and its oppression, the oppression of the masters and the churchmen, comes from the blindness of their greed. They in turn seek to govern us by laws that say one person has the right to set and limit the value of another. If they can keep us convinced that this is so, they can keep us in subjection forever. Really, we are free. We need only to know that the Lord loves us as we are, and we are free. Our own soul's uniqueness will guide us once we are free of the laws, shoulds and musts that the churches and the wealthy would impose on us. Each human is a magazine of power and creativity if only each of us will claim it for himself or herself. The more we rely on God, the more will He be with us."

"Tell me more about angels," she said.

"What do you want to know?"

"The one you said you saw in the park today? What did it look like? What was it doing there? I know these sound like a child's questions but I feel a hunger for a glimpse of the New Jerusalem you speak of. I want to believe it, but I feel I shall not until I see it with my own eyes." A few dry coughs followed her question, so he paused before answering.

"I am all right," Cynthia said as her coughing subsided into hoarseness.

"I shall tell you then, Miss Hackworth, the angel I saw this afternoon had hair like spun gold and long silver wings. His eyes were as brilliant as stars. He flew over your head and pointed you out to me. He showed me that you would be my helper, would help me manifest the New Jerusalem for all."

"I wish I could do such a worthy thing. But I am nothing..."

"No! You shall. I don't believe that angels can be mistaken."

"It will all seem like a mere fancy tomorrow when I am back with the others in the thick air with the clatter of the presses below us."

"That need not be. It is your choice. You can change everything if you trust the Lord's love."

"These beautiful things you speak of, how can I believe them when the machines are pounding and the air is close and choking?"

"Do not go back to them."

"What shall I do? How shall I live."

"Live here," Fisk said in a suddenly changed voice.

She met his steady gaze with her own and said,

"I am married. To a man I have not seen for two years."

"I don't care," Fisk said, looking into her face intently. "I do not need anyone's permission to love you. I think the angel meant this to be. It is better to be together in our hearts than by law."

Cynthia stood up suddenly. "This cannot be. I cannot do this."

"Why?"

"I hardly know you...it is a sin."

"But you are fond of me already, I can see. There is no sin except the sin against your own true nature, your own heart. Blake says, 'One law for the Ox and Lion is Oppression.'"

She blushed.

"You speak so, so, wildly. More likely you are just seducing me with tales," she replied"

"Do you truly believe that?"

She looked down at her hands which were gripping each other, tightly.

"No. I do not, really. But how can it be? It is all wishes and fancies. I must leave, now."

With those words, she abruptly stood up and walked to the door. She coughed dryly a few more times.

"Goodbye then, Cynthia Hackworth, for now."

She paused at the threshold for a moment without turning around or speaking and then passed out of the building.

Fisk felt a great calmness after she left. It had started. The ones who attended him today would be his brothers and sisters and more. Cynthia would come back to him. She would be his helper and support. It was only that her heart was so unused to happiness.

Chapter 9

Richard entered Manchester under a cold rain that made the soot darkened streets and buildings look as if they were paved with black iron. Yet, after he crossed the Medlock River and passed beneath the hovering canopy of smoke, Piccadilly, one of Manchester's most important streets, astonished him. The elegance and opulence of the shop windows and the beauty of the buildings was remarkable. The finest goods of every type were displayed with such magnificence, on both sides of the broad street, that the town might have been expecting a visit from the Sovereign.

In the same profusion that he had seen the cheapest goods displayed in the poor markets in London, so were rich fabrics, jewels, precious metals, works of art and all things of quality, laid out in shop windows here. The glitter of wealth seemed to surround him on every side, but beneath the din of the fashionable crowds clogging the street, he could hear and feel a deeper note, the rhythmic clanking and shuddering of the mills.

As Carlyle wrote of the city, "The rushing of its thousand mills like the boom of an Atlantic tide. Sooty Manchester was constructed upon the infinite abysses." Their smell and dark discharge were everywhere. Richard could feel the particulate matter in his nostrils and lungs as he walked along. High above the tallest and most magnificent warehouses and stores in the centre of the city, rose the mightiest structures of the place: huge brick smokestacks, looking down on mankind like the gods of Olympus, deities visible from every part of the city, omnipotent and omnipresent creators of the wealth displayed on Piccadilly and Market Streets.

Richard walked back and forth, across the centre of the city, on these broad, magnificent streets, eventually finding his way to the square towers of the beautiful, ancient cathedral and the other medieval buildings of Chetham's at the center of the city. He had read that among this venerable cluster of buildings, was the oldest public library in the English speaking world. How he would like to stop there, once he found Fanny. He paused to admire the same ornamental pond and fountains off of Market Street that had delighted Victoria and Albert when the royal couple visited the city five years earlier. Then, growing hungry and fatigued, he began to think about food and lodging and knew he must find a less fashionable part of the city. With this purpose in mind, he turned down another great thoroughfare, Oldham Road, and walked toward the poorer looking buildings which he now saw abounded behind the magnificence of the broad avenues. It was as if the city's ugliness had been deliberately hidden behind the beautiful shops, handsome ware-houses and public buildings.

He walked in the direction of the poor district on the other side of Great Ancoats Street and soon became lost among the rotting three story houses, packed together in the most prolix alleys and courts he had ever seen. Even the rookeries of Rosemary Lane and Bethnal Green were nothing to these. The condition of many of the houses was ruinous. Foul odours assailed him at each doorway. Attempting to find his way out of the warren, he ended in a lane so narrow that the walls rubbed his shoulders on each side while a low roof held in an odour of disgusting foulness. The passage abruptly let him out into a court with a large mound of human dung in the centre. Holding his breathe so as not to gag, he turned quickly back the way he had come and walked along the street from which the lane had led him. He walked past poor shops, houses and markets as the heavy, ominous beat which seemed to underpin all other sounds in the city grew louder and louder. Suddenly, directly ahead, Richard came upon the largest building he had ever seen.

Redhill Street Mill was a monstrous rectangular box made of black-ened red brick. A single, huge smokestack pierced the middle of its roof. The enormous building loomed some six storeys above the street, like the palace of some giant demon. Its great smokestack rose upwards many storeys more before finally vanishing into its own black billows of smoke. The pounding and shuddering that issued from the building were unlike anything Richard had ever heard. He could feel the unrelenting beat of the machines in the pit of his stomach and in the paving stones under his feet. He stood dumbly, staring at the monstrosity for a few moments until the urgent clanging of an ear-splitting bell made him jump. Another moment, and the abrupt silence seemed as loud as the noise of the manufactory had been. Then, a sound like the wind rushing through a great forest swept toward him as literally thousands of factory operatives left the building to eat. Their voices were not loud, but rather sibilant, wheezing out their words with a breathy, asthmatic sound. Their eyes were lowered, their step halting and their skins white as the bellies of fish. As he watched them pass, Richard began to notice the deformities: one boy had a shoulder six inches higher than the other, a young woman could not seem to stand up properly and as she drew closer, he could see there was a huge hump on her back. Another man walked with a curi-ous rolling gate as though his hip were in some way afflicted; another walked sideways because he could not turn his head forward and so could not see where he was going if he tried to walk without twisting his body. These were the factory cripples that Fisk had spoken of so often. Richard had never seen such a legion of deformities. This was the price for the luxuries lining the great avenues of Manchester, a price, that astonished and horrified the young, healthy school master.

He started to approach the humpbacked woman, but before he could speak she fixed him with bitter glance and said, "No work, here. All full up."

"Could you tell me of a decent lodging house where I might get a meal and a room?"

"If you want decent food, and working man's lodgings better than most, try the Mitre Inn on Hunt's Bank," a nearby man called to him.

"Thank you, sir," Richard called back. "But I am strange here. Can you tell me how to go?"

The man stopped for a moment and came over to Richard.

"You give me less time for my meal," he said grumpily.

"I'm sorry. Would a shilling compensate you for your time?"

"Aye, lad. I'll be glad to have that," and he held out his hand.

After receiving and following the expensive directions, Richard finally came upon the Mitre at the edge of the commercial centre of the city. Even though the street was poor, it was paved and was not filthy, unlike many which lay hidden behind the brilliant storefronts of the great avenues. He followed it until he saw a sign shaped like a Bishop's mitre. Almost as soon as he walked through the doors, the warm steamy atmosphere and the odors of good food turned his thoughts to rest and ease.

"You've been on the tramp for some time," a big man behind the bar said to Richard. He had curly black hair tied back in the style of the last century, what in our century we would call a pony tail. His arms were thick and strong; his eyes blue and piercing. He looked nothing like any of the factory workers.

"Yes, sir. I have. All the way from London."

"And what would be your destination?"

"Here. To find my sister."

Richard had already decided that he would make his purpose known to any who would listen. There was no telling where he would find a clue to Fanny's whereabouts. She could be living in the next lane.

"And she's been lost long?"

"Taken. Not lost."

The big man looked up at Richard with genuine sympathy. "That's a bad business."

"The worst."

"I'm sorry for you, lad. What can my house do for you?"

"I thought you the landlord. I need a room and to find work. I have money but not much. What are your charges for room and board?"

"Two shillings a night and that includes one mug of bitter and a hearty dinner."

"Then I'll take a room for three nights. He put the amount specified on the counter."

"There's a slate over there on the wall for those who can read. People who come and go put notices up for work wanted and workers needed."

"And where in town will I find a respected solicitor's chambers?"

"Do you want to make your trouble worse? That's all a solicitor will do for you. Respected or no."

"Perhaps. But I need to find one."

"Well, if you're set on it, take the street outside toward Salford. The courthouse is on the other side of the River Irwell. Take the New Bailey Bridge across. I'm certain you'll find plenty of what you seek. The foxes all have their dens around the hen house, a big building with columns in front. The streets all around there are piled high with solicitors."

"Is there no name in the legal profession that is often repeated here?"

"I've no direct knowledge solicitors, lad, thank the Lord. I've a man who helps with accounts but that's all."

"Do you think he might know the name of a professional man?"

"He's in tomorrow to work on my accounts in the morning. I can ask him then."

"Thank you, sir."

"My name's Tom Weedon. And I am glad to be of service to you. I will shake hands with you on the success of your quest."

After what seemed the most delicious meal of his life, Richard looked at the slate the landlord pointed out and was surprised to find the notices not altogether illiterate. However, they asked for men of trades like mining, steel-making and factory machine operation, of which Richard knew nothing. He ordered a drink of mulled cider to take the chill out of himself which had stayed with him in spite of the hot meal. He sat in a corner near the fire and savored his drink, looking at the half-empty tavern as dusk allowed the log bright light of the fireplace to become the primary illumination. As the cider penetrated him, his arms and legs began to feel leaden. He felt sorrow once again for Fanny's loss, but it set his thoughts going in a practical vein: The lack of employment for his skills posed a real barrier to his search for her. Teaching was out of the question because it would require references he did not have. There would be too many questions about why he'd left London and come to Manchester. He thought of the landlord's instructions for finding the law courts and suddenly thought of the elderly law writer with whom he had studied to improve his hand. If the demand were great enough and law writers few, his hand might be just good enough to get him some work. He needed ready money soon and so resolved to try his luck first thing the following morning, after a good night's sleep. With that thought, he stood up and went to find his room.

The next day was bright, cold and sharp as a new knife when Richard started off in the direction of the ancient city of Salford, just on the other side of the Irwell, one of two horribly polluted rivers that ran through

Manchester. Salford was originally the great seat of the area, now overtaken by the mighty wealth of Manchester.

Just seeing the sun lifted Richard's spirits a little and he hoped it a good omen. He was soon back again in the neighbourhood of the Cathedral. Nearby were several bridges which led across to Salford, just a stone's throw away beyond the narrow river. He crossed over on the New Baily Bridge and saw the courthouse close to the river. As the inn keeper had said, all around it, like fawning dogs, were lesser buildings of gray stone striving to look as large and important as the court itself. Brass plates announced that these held the chambers of many legal professionals. Somewhere among the tangle of streets around the commons there must be a law stationers that would do job work copying legal documents.

After walking down innumerable echoing corridors and asking a small army of dusty clerks hunched over their tall desks, Richard finally found what he sought. Ardmore's Legal Stationers was a large glass fronted shop that stood out among the soot covered stone of the professional inns. With the carefully lettered gold script on its sign and the substantial mahogany cases behind which four bustling shop assistants were hurrying to fill customers' orders, it exuded an air of prosperous busyness.

Richard patted his pocket which held the handwriting sample he had prepared in the day's earliest light and stepped into the shop. He left a quarter of an hour later with the job of writing a one page letter for Barnes and Cameron, attorneys at law.

"It's a small assignment, worth only a shilling," the kindly, middle-aged clerk had said, "but as you know, it's for one of the most important firms in the city. If they like your hand, there may be more work for you. But you must have it back to us by opening time tomorrow. Seven sharp."

It was with a feeling of great excitement and hope for the future that Richard returned to his room. He sat at the bare wooden table cutting several pens as he prepared to execute what he believed would be the first of many jobs for Ardmores. He ran his eye over the page of the loosely written draft from which he was supposed to work. When he got to the second paragraph, there was a Latin quotation, which Richard knew was incorrect. What should he do? Perhaps it was a test. If not, would it seem impertinent if he corrected it? A moment later, he could hear Charles Wilney's voice telling him, "In matters of knowledge, always do your best. Do not guess at something of which you are uncertain, but never hide what you really do know."

With that happy memory of his mentor in his mind and heart, he began to write in a fair facsimile of the round, clear script known as "law hand."

Several hours later, he looked at his finished work and told himself that he had made a real step toward finding Fanny. The thought made him feel expansive. He pushed his chair back and looked once more at the clothes he had carefully sponged for his early appointment at Ardmores. Then he went downstairs to have some coffee and gossip with the friendly landlord.

Richard's glow of pleasure over his work made the young man rather more talkative than he'd intended. He told Tom more about himself and Fanny than was prudent. But Tom showed no signs of slyness as he listened to Richard's story about old Maudie and the great London house to which she'd led him. The innkeeper's few comments were remarks critical of the wealthy. They reminded Richard of his friend, Fisk. Both men had a forthright quality that Richard liked and trusted. But on his way up to bed he cautioned himself: "Just because Tom is like Fisk in his manner and appearance, it does not mean they are similar in all ways. I must guard my tongue with greater care."

The following morning, it was with optimism and a surge of youthful strength that Richard pushed open the heavy glass and oak doors of Ardmores. The early hour had slowed the activity in the big store and Richard quickly found the clerk who had given him his work. He was disappointed that the gray-haired man hardly glanced at his letter and handed it back to him as he leaned confidentially across the counter.

"Be so good as to take this over to Barnes and Cameron for me. I will count it as a special favour. Get a receipt from Wilson, the head clerk, come back and I shall pay you."

Not wanting to seem a stranger to Manchester, Richard did not ask where the solicitors' chambers were located since, apparently, this firm was a household name among the city's legal trade. The narrow lanes around the courthouses were already filling with people, horses and wheeled conveyances of all kinds. Richard looked around him and saw a young man, about his own age who had a rather dusty, withered air in spite of his youth. He was reading from a sheaf of papers he held in his hand while he waited for the crossing sweeper to clear the way through an already thick layer of muck.

"Excuse me, sir" Richard said. "Do you know the whereabouts of the chambers of Barnes and Cameron?"

The dusty looking young man shifted his extremely tall, hat back on his head and looked up owlishly at Richard. A lock of dry, yellow hair, stiff as straw, fell out from under the brim.
"Oh, ah, my, Barnes, Oh, my, yes, of course. Highly placed members of the profession. My, yes. None higher. Their chambers are on my way. If you care to walk with me."

"With pleasure, sir."

As the two young men stepped quickly along the crowded pavement Richard spoke, "If it is not an impertinence perhaps you could tell me whose acquaintance I have the pleasure of making?"

"Well, if chaps our age can't be informal, who can? I'm Quidley, John Quidley. Articled at Swopes and Swiveling."

"Richard Darrow, law writer, employed only for next few minutes in delivering a small document to Barnes and Cameron."

"Modestly said, Darrow. Perhaps I shall see you again. Now, I have some tenants to squeeze for my principal and here's your place. Chambers are third on the left, quite far back in building. Bit of a warren. Don't get lost."

95

With that, the oldish young man bobbed away into the passing crowd, his tall hat visible far down the street until he turned at the next corner.

Immediately upon crossing the threshold of the building indicated he heard his own footsteps echoing hollowly along the marble paved halls. The smell of old aging paper and binder's glue mixed with stale cigar smoke and permeated the air. It was actually a pleasant change from the omnipresent smell of the mills. Almost immediately the hall split into two staircases and Richard had no idea which to take. The footman's chair was empty so there was no one to direct him. When he got to the upper floor, the corridors were even more confusing and half an hour later he was still no closer to his destination.

As he hurriedly turned a corner, now anxious about delivering his job on time, he almost tripped over an elegantly dressed, beautiful little girl.

"Oh, pardon me, Miss," Richard said, stopping to look at the little beauty. "Are you lost?"

"No sir. Are you?" she answered with a self-possessed upward look.

"Actually, Miss, I am." Part of Richard's success as a teacher was that he always spoke to children without any assumption of superiority.

"And where are you going?"

"I am looking for Barnes and Cameron."

"Oh, that is easy. Come with me." And she reached out her hand for Richard to take as though he were the child and she the adult.

"What a lovely and remarkable child," Richard thought, taking her hand.

With an air of complete certainty, the little lady took him through the windings of the corridors without a single hesitation until they stood in front of a door which bore the name of the firm Richard sought.

"What an excellent guide you are, Miss. You must come here often?"

"Oh, no sir. But it's easy to see where to go in the light."

Richard did not entirely understand her comment about the light but he let it pass without comment. "Are you coming in?" he asked as he opened the door.

"Oh, no sir. Those rooms are for big people only. I must wait in the hall for my guardian."

"Well, I must go in to complete my business. Pray excuse me. And thank you."

"You are welcome," Emily said as she turned away and skipped down the hall in the direction from which they'd come.

The offices into which Richard stepped were unlike anything he'd ever seen. He was staggered by the richness of the turkey carpets and the handsome leather furniture, the tall windows that rose almost to the ceiling and the silken curtains. Seated at a tall desk, wearing a handsome black suit and perfectly white shirt was a silver-haired man, whose skin was so pale it could have been powdered. There was nothing rusty or redolent of dusty papers about these chambers. Richard approached him.

"I am looking for Mr. Wilson. With a letter from Ardmores."

"I am Mr. Wilson." the man said reaching down to Richard from his high seat.

"Then sir, I must tell you something. I did the copying and there was an incorrect Latin quotation which I changed."

Before the man could answer, the door to one of the inner chambers opened and out came a very supercilious young woman, a ruggedly handsome middle-aged man and a tall, distinguished looking man.

"You changed my text?' Wilson said.

"Yes, sir. I'm sorry, sir. But I know that quotation from Virgil, well, and it was incorrect."

"Really?' The clerk said frostily.

For a moment Richard thought he would be dismissed in a blast of chilling politeness. His heart sank. He desperately needed the work from Ardmores. But before Mr. Wilson could answer, the tall elderly, distinguished looking gentlemen detached himself from the young woman and middle-aged man and stepped to the head clerk's desk.

"What's this Wilson. We have now a copyist who knows Virgil by heart?"

"So he says, Mr. Barnes."

"Tell me how the passage should read. If you can do it from memory, young man."

"Yes, sir. 'At regina gravi iamdudum saucia cura
volnus alit venis, et caeco carpitur igni Multa viri virtus animo, multusque recursat gentis honos: haerent infixi pectore voltus verbaque, nec placidam membris dat cura quietem'"

"Wilson, go and get my Virgil from my office. Pardon me for a moment, Mr. Blackwood. My memory of the classics has been challenged and I must defend myself."

The rugged middle-aged man bowed to Mr. Barnes with a slightly amused expression on his face. He waved his hand, granting his leave. Richard immediately knew that the man was an important client and realized the text he had questioned was not the clerk's but the master's. It had been written by the highly regarded attorney, himself.

A red calfskin volume of Virgil was produced and Barnes turned the pages, peering into the book like a great bird wading on a river bank, looking for its dinner.

Finally, he spoke, "By gad. You are entirely correct, young sir. To the letter. It is time for me to go back to my classical authors. I thank you for your service. I have always taken great pride in my knowledge of the classics and it would have hurt my vanity if my fellow practitioners had learned of this. What is your name?"

"Richard Darrow, sir."

"Well Richard Darrow, in future when we have text with classical quotes, we shall tell Ardmores that no other writer shall do for us. Are you as familiar with the ancient Greeks?"

Richard nodded. "Homer is my favourite classical poet, sir."
As he turned away, the distinguished looking solicitor slipped several coins into the younger man's hand.

"Thank you, sir." Richard said, bowing low. "When I am ready, he thought, this is the man I shall consult about Fanny."

"Come Barnes, let us lunch. You can ride your favourite hobby horse on someone else's time," the middle-aged client said. "I find that my daughter has allowed a child to run around the hallways of this building by herself. I must gather her up. You must talk to the child at lunch, Barnes. Emily will amaze you."

The pretty, haughty young woman looked at the man with asperity, her eyes flashing her irritation. Richard thought he could see the whole story at a glance: one spoiled daughter jealous of the family's brilliant late arrival, the tale of a too talented younger sister.

Richard retraced his steps out of the building, was lost once more, but now did not care. He was bursting with pleasure. How well guided he had been by Charles Wilney's clear, honest precepts. He would write and tell his friend about the value of his words. "God bless you, Charles. Once more, you have been the good angel of our lives," he muttered under his breath, as he finally stepped out from the chilly stone halls into the rare morning sunlight and the now familiar smell of the mills.

The coach Emily rode in passed Richard just as he was getting his bearings in front of the law offices. Emily leaned out of the window to wave to him.

"Sit up straight, Emily," Pamela said sharply. The older girl was annoyed, jealous of her father's having taken any notice of the "little stray." In addition to the boredom of taking care of Emily that had set in so quickly was now added a real jealousy as her father had begun to take note of Emily's rapid learning and her intelligent, self-possessed remarks. He sometimes called her his "little minister" and even petted her as he had Pamela when she had been little. Instead of becoming a source of prestige for Pamela, Emily had become a wedge between her and her father.

"So, Barnes, you were bested back there by that young man," Blackwood said abruptly as he saw Richard on the street.

"Not bested, Mr. Blackwood. I have loved the classics since I was a boy. I am always glad to be corrected and to meet someone who knows great literature better than I. The boy's learning is, I think, prodigious. Of course, I would not want my professional opponents to know he corrected me. But that is merely business and appearances. Real learning is the greatest of prizes."

"And are there no other qualities that deserve recognition," Pamela asked, once again feeling left out.

"Will you answer, Barnes?" Blackwood asked.

"If you wish it, sir."

"I do."

"Well, there are few things in life as valuable as learning, Miss Blackwood. Especially today. Learning is the great bridge to a higher station."

"But is there nothing else in life, sir?"

"Well, for a woman, I should say that you have the greatest prize of all, Miss Blackwood: great beauty and the power to attract. All male endeavours are made extraneous in the presence of great feminine charm."

For a moment Pamela felt pleased with this courtly speech. Then it seemed to her that the solicitor's words also meant that women could do nothing except be attractive to men, that by themselves they were mere passive ornaments. All afternoon, she meditated on this thought, saying little to her father, Barnes or Emily during lunch.

Later that night at the Blackwood's home, Pamela approached her father in his library where he was reviewing the documents Barnes had given him.

"Papa, I must talk to you about something important. May I have some time now?"

Blackwood put down the papers he was holding and looked at his daughter.

"Of course, dear. These can wait."

"Papa, I want to study music seriously." She told him.

"Well I'm sure Mrs. Peevey can help you find a better teacher, my dear."

"No, papa. I don't want to play just in our own salon. I want to become known as an artist. I want to be a great musician. Like Lizst or Chopin. It is the one thing I have real talent for and I am still young enough. I believe I can do it."

Blackwood looked up at his daughter appraisingly.

"How could I possibly countenance a stage career for my own daughter? It is unthinkable.."

"No papa, it is not."

He held up his hand to forestall her,

"I shall make this contract with you. If you find the best teacher possible who will come to us for the next year, and if you will work extremely hard during that time, practicing long hours, I shall abide by that teacher's decision as to your talent and fitness to be a professional musician."

"Oh papa. I know you think I shall just let this fade away. But you're wrong. I don't want to be merely someone's wife. I don't want to take orders from a husband. I want to be someone with important accomplishments of my own."

After Pamela went to bed, Blackwood sat up and wondered, in the face of his daughter's request, how to tell her about the house guests they would soon have. How could he make her understand the power and value she would have if she encouraged the alliance that these visitors might present? Had she not also read of the great women of society who directed the course of culture through their salons? Such a marriage as the one he now envisioned for her would give her that kind of power and prestige. She could pursue her musical education, too, even if she were married. It was perfectly acceptable for a wife to be accomplished to the level of professional performer, as long as she did not appear in public for pay, but only to enhance her husband's house. He could see nothing but benefits arising from the possible marriage he now hoped for.

With the presence of his "little minister" in the family circle, Blackwood no longer feared being alone. In the six months Emily had been in the house, the financier had realized what a remarkably intelligent and charming child she was. It was amazing to find such gifts wrapped in coal dust and dirt.

He had already been thinking about educating Emily at home with a first-class tutor. The scene with the young man in Barne's office that afternoon once again brought up the idea of Emily as a highly educated person, who could be of material assistance to him. She was not his real daughter, so it would not seem odd if he did not settle any money on her, but instead gave her good employment. Her chances of a good marriage as a dependent of the Blackwood family were insignificant, so she could be with the firm for years. Pamela had never had talent for learning anything other than music, nothing that might have been useful to Blackwood, but Mrs. Peevey said that Emily soaked up knowledge like a clothe, and remarkably, her manners were much better than might have been expected. The governess had been completely against Emily's presence until she began teaching her. Now, she could not praise her enough. It would be good to get Pamela married so that she would not feel so jealous of Emily. She would then have a separate life of her own and not be so dependent on her father's affection. Emily would be free to grow and develop without Pamela's animosity. He lit a cigar and leaned back from his beautiful desk. They would both be young women of whom he could be proud. But he had to make sure that Pamela was at her best when she met their house guests. Her outbursts of temper toward Emily must not be allowed while there were guests in the house. It might be a good idea to send Emily away for a term at school, just until Pamela was married. He stood up and looked out at the dark line of the Winter Hill in the distance. The possibilities that this marriage could open for his own fortune and future position were beyond calculation. A term with highly qualified tutors would be a solid foundation for Emily's education as well. As he watched the moon rise above the dingle below his house, Blackwood congratulated himself on his own acumen.

Chapter 10

U nder the tutelage of Samuelson and Booth, Bradley was fast becoming one of the few MPs in Parliament who really understood the technology, managerial and financial issues of railway building. In less than a year, he found himself on three different committees that assessed applications for new lines. Even though it was known and accepted that other MPs had specific railway interests, Samuelson insisted that Bradley's connection with his interests remain absolutely obscure. All of Samuelson's payments to Bradley were made through other clients who patronized his practice. Bradley's knowledge coupled with the Members' belief in his financial neutrality made his support on private member's bills very sought after. These bills allowed new railway companies to offer stock issues to raise money and to force the sale of land that lay on their railway's designated route. The majority of bills that had Bradley's blessing passed both houses and went on to receive Royal Assent. This had made Bradley a very powerful man both in Parliament and on the Stock Exchange, or 'Change as it was commonly known. The bills that Bradley helped to pass in his first year as an MP enabled Samuelson to force four powerful landholders to sell land to four different railway companies which, through a deliberately labyrinthine network of companies, were apparently controlled by different interests but secretly controlled by one man, Samuelson. By the time Bradley realized how illegal these activities were, he was too involved, too much enriched and too swollen with his own importance to undo anything he had done. Also, he watched many of his parliamentary colleagues line their pockets by using inside information they had acquired in the House to speculate on new railway stocks. It seemed to him that many Members of Parliament were taking money from railway interests, or getting stock for their votes, or simply using privileged information to speculate.

Eventually, over eighty directors of railway companies sat in Parliament at one time. During the mid-nineteenth century, the railways made more money for more people than any other industry in history. So given the tenor of the 1840s, it seemed to Bradley that his activities were comparatively blameless. The close liaison between politics and railway interests on this vast scale is why the spy at Fisk's Chartist meeting had said that, "money sat on the throne of England." It was the first time in history that the corporate money of a specific industry so strongly influenced political activities. With the building of the British railways, modern political corruption was born in the form we recognize in our own time. But the early Victorian age was also a time before the idea of individual rights had taken root in society. In other words, modern corruption began while the idea of class privilege still held many aloof from closer scrutiny by society at large. Many of the great reforms of the age came decades later. On the other hand, it would be difficult to find single instances of railway building that cost the public as dearly as such things as the Enron scandal in our own time.

Booth and Samuelson were well pleased with their protegee. Bradley's name had begun to be mentioned in some of the papers. He was becoming, as Elspeth put it, "a public character." As his public reputation grew, he felt more and more need to be away from his too-clever wife. He preferred spheres where he was always treated with deference. The higher he rose, the more he needed to feel protected from falling. The world in which he now moved seemed to be a bauble that existed for his own delight, a priceless gem he must clutch tightly in his fat, red hands. As he rose in public estimation, the private man had begun a strange descent. Bradley was regularly visiting London's most exclusive brothels. In early Victorian times, pleasures for sale were limited only by the wealth of the purchaser. It was relatively easy for these houses to find girls who were alone and unprotected by family or law, and in a society where young children were routinely sent into coal pits to work for hours in dark airless chambers, perverse pleasures of all kinds were for sale in brothels protected by wealth and privilege. Mrs. Gaskell's novel, "The Rag Nymph" details the abduction and attempted violation of a girl from the lower orders, and shows with chilling clarity how dangerous life was for attractive, unprotected young women. The brothels were often operated by dangerous, unprincipled, well-connected men. It was in one such pleasure house that Bradley's true nature began to emerge.

One cold January evening, after listening to Elspeth hold forth about railway stock for several hours to guests, Bradley slipped out the servants entrance of his house and took his carriage to the door of one of his favourite establishments.

"How does my wife get all the intelligence she seems to have about the railways," he wondered as he was ushered up the white marble steps.

He stepped through the richly carved oak and brass doors. As usual, the attractive, elegant middle-aged french woman bowed to him with great deference. She took his greatcoat and hat and he wandered into the lounge where the girls sat, displaying themselves in various states of undress. The lounge was a huge room with thick, soft carpets on the floor and tiled pools holding brightly coloured fish. The walls were covered with flocked wallpaper in the latest fashion. Large plants in Chinese porcelain pots stood under the dome of glass that roofed the room. At night, the effect was of sitting outside without the pernicious effects of the London night air, by day, when the sun was visible, the luxuriant foliage, pools and the girls gave it the feeling of a seraglio out of The Arabian Nights. Burton's classic translation was not yet available, it would only be published at the end of the 1880s, but there were lesser, bowdlerized versions available in the forties.

"Gad," Bradley thought, "how I would like to wipe that perpetual smirk from Elspeth's face."

His eyes traveled around the room. He saw some former partners who tried to catch his eye. But he ignored them. In one dim, distant corner of the room a thin young girl with red hair and very white skin knelt on the floor. She was tiny and wore a plain nightgown of poor white muslin. She paid no attention to anyone but seemed lost in her own thoughts as she gazed into one of the pools set into the floor. Occasionally, she played with the fish by stirring the water gently. There was a frailty about her that appealed to Bradley. She was also the youngest looking girl in the room.

"She can't be more than eleven or twelve," he thought.

He sauntered through the chairs and divans that stood scattered around the richly appointed room, making his way toward the girl.

"Good evening, my dear."

A pair of frightened blue eyes looked up at him, almost pleadingly. Her submissiveness immediately aroused his interest.

She said nothing, but looked down nervously at her hands. She was truly afraid of him, he realized. It made her somehow more exciting.

"Are you engaged this evening?"

The girl didn't speak or look up but shook her head negatively.

"Then, shall we go upstairs?" he held out his hand. Her tiny palm was cold and moist.

"Don't be frightened, dear," he said as he led her away. But he found her fear an exciting tonic that leapt through his body. Though he had earned the respect of his fellow MPs and been praised by Samuelson and Booth, no one had ever been afraid of him before. Elspeth had never feared him, even when she was at her most obedient. He found there was something exhilarating about the young girl's fear. It made him feel a sense of strength that was new to him. He was becoming aroused before they even reached the door of the room he had reserved for the evening.

He unlocked the door and entered without letting go of her hand. He felt her almost resist his pull. How different she was from the others, he thought, as he watched her sit down limply on the edge of the bed. Then he thought, "I wonder if she is just acting or really fearful?"

"What's your name," he said in his gruffest tone.

"Anne, sir."

"Well, come over here, Anne."

She rose obediently and faced him at arm's length.

"Kneel in front of me, Anne."

Just as obediently she got down on her knees.

"Take off your shift."

Anne's thin arms began pulling the white muslin over her head. Bradley looked at what was revealed with the air of a connoisseur. The shift lay in a heap next to her. She knelt, looking down at the floor. She wore only garters and white stockings. There was hardly any hair between her legs. Her breasts were almost non-existent. Her whole posture was one of submission and fear.

"Undo my flies." Bradley could feel himself getting harder by the moment. The girl was affecting him like a drug. Anne fumbled with the buttons until Bradley proudly felt his erection exposed.

"You know what to do?" he said.

She nodded and moved her head close to his penis. She took him in her mouth.

"Look up at me while you do that," he said hoarsely.

Her frightened blue eyes looked up into his face and in spite of his desire to prolong the pleasure, he felt himself erupt into her mouth. He grabbed her red hair and pulled her face hard against him while he had his orgasm. She coughed as he ejaculated and forced himself deeply into her mouth. She sputtered and gasped, as though drowning on his sperm, but he kept her pressed hard against him until he had finished. Then he used her hair to jerk her away from himself. She fell limply onto her back at his feet where she lay unmoving, her knees resting against each other protectively. She looked absolutely helpless, her thin arms bent at the elbows at right angles to her body. Her eyes still looked frightened. Without knowing why, he momentarily put his booted foot on her thin, white belly, but applied no pressure. Then he pushed her thighs apart with his heel and she let her legs fall open. The sole of his boot now rested on her genitals with his heel on the floor. He pushed down on her a little experimentally. She twitched slightly. Her frightened eyes held his own.

"Why are you so afraid of me? Surely you've done this often?"

"No, sir. I think, sir, your-your thing is too big for me. I'm afraid it would hurt me." She spoke to him like a young servant girl. Not like the shameless women he'd had here before.

Her fear of his genitals was very exciting to him. "I'll show you there's nothing to fear," he said getting down on the floor and mounting her as aggressively as he could manage. He held her small thin legs apart and battered against her as hard as he could.

Finally, her tension and fear turned to what appeared to be lust, and she moved against him until they were both spent.

Later that night, riding home in his carriage, Bradley wondered why Anne had been so arousing. It was the most exciting evening he'd ever had. He had already arranged to have her the following night. Next morning, sitting in his library, trying to read surveyors' reports on a new bill, his mind kept wandering to the submissive young girl. He wanted more of her, much more. He wanted to really frighten her, though, to see her terror of him. That evening, he had his first orgasm when he hit her thin buttocks with his belt and she cried out. The third night he entered the house where Anne resided, the hostess approached him and drew him to a private alcove in the hall.

"Mr. Bradley, you know what a valued client you are here. But I must tell you that there are kinds of entertainment that will entail extra charges to you. After all, if a girl is damaged and cannot work..." she let her voice trail off.

"Yes, of course. All right. I accept the extra charges." he answered impatiently. He couldn't wait to get upstairs. He had been fantasizing about seeing Anne all day, about what he would do to her.

When he opened the door, she was sitting quietly on the side of the bed, looking down at the floor. She only glanced at him as he entered, then she looked back at the floor in front of her. He walked over to her and gently forced her to look up at him by lifting her head up by her long red hair. Then he kissed her on the mouth. He bit her lower lip and she let out a whimper at the unexpected pain.

"What do you think of me?" he asked her suddenly.

The girl looked down again, away from his gaze. "I don't know, sir. You are my master. I'm supposed to give you pleasure." Her voice was low and toneless.

"What would happen to you if I was displeased with you--what if you refused to do what I asked?"

"I-I'm not certain, sir. But I have known girls here who disappeared."

"Disappeared?"

"Yes, sir. I don't know where they went."

He suddenly smacked her across the face. "Do you like that?"

"No, sir," she said touching her bright red cheek. "Please don't hurt me, sir."

"But what if I like hurting you, Anne. Suppose that is how you can give me pleasure?"

"You liked fornicating with me, sir. I can kiss your..."

He smacked her again, harder than the first time. "You filthy whore. I don't want to hear your dirty talk. Get down on the floor and lick the mud off my boots. They're cleaner than your dirty mouth."

"I don't want to, sir.." she said as she cringed and held up her hands to protect her face.

"What do I care what you want." He grabbed her arm and dragged her off the bed onto the floor. He kicked her in the buttocks. "Now clean my boots with your tongue or I'll really hurt you."

Several hours later, after they were finished, Bradley went downstairs to find the Madame.

"Is there a private place where we can speak, confidentially?" he asked her.

The handsome matron led him down a secondary hall running off the main foyer where he usually entered the house. The corridor turned sharply a few times until the Madame stopped at the open door of a handsomely appointed room. A big, moustached man sat inside reading. He was a broad shouldered man with a fleshy face and a tight suit, a typical swell who wore too much gold jewelry.

"This conversation has to be private," Bradley insisted.

"This gentleman is my associate," the Madame explained. "It is a sign of our trust for you even to see him."

"I don't care. I must talk to you alone," Bradley insisted.

The man got up and left the room. The Madame closed the door.

"Now, sir. How can I serve you?"

Bradley paced back and forth as he spoke. He avoided the Madame's eyes.

"That girl..."

"Anne?"

"Yes, you know. Is there any way I can make an exclusive arrangement regarding her?"

"We have done that on rare occasions, Mr. Bradley. But it is very expensive. You have to pay for all of her time..."

"But suppose I want this to be permanent..."

"You want to take her away from this house?"

"Yes, perhaps. I don't know—I'm not sure, yet."

"I have to warn you there are difficulties involved in maintaining the kind of girls we have here. Most gentlemen prefer to come here. It could involve you with the Metropolitan Force. Here you are safe from prying."

"Yes, privacy is essential," he said. "In my position I cannot risk exposure." Bradley paced faster and lit a cigar. "I feel I must have her to myself. I want to own her. Use her as I like. Without any limits placed on our activities."

"Oh. I comprehend you now, Mr. Bradley. Why didn't you say so. You want to buy her? Yes?"

"Buy her? Can I buy her?"

"Mr. Bradley, in this house we do not place limits on our clients' pleasure. But this kind of arrangement is very expensive. If anything were to happen to her...we would have to furnish a certificate of death that could not be questioned. There are great costs involved."

Bradley was shocked at the words "certificate of death." He stopped pacing and stared at the Madame.

The woman replied coolly to his look "You know, Mr. Bradley sometimes in our passions things happen that we do not intend and then..." she let the sentence hang in the air.

"How much?" he asked.

"That little girl? She has a limited clientele but those who patronize her are very generous. If I restrict her to you, the house will lose a large sum."

"How much do you want?" he asked again.

"I could not take less than £5,000."

The sum staggered Bradley. There were thousands of inexpensive child whores on the London streets. Why did this one have to cost so much? But he didn't really care about being cheated. He wanted Anne. He only wondered if he could hide such a large expenditure from Elspeth?

"I need to consider your terms, Madame. At least overnight. Perhaps longer."

"Of course, Mr. Bradley. You will want Anne tomorrow at the same time?"

He nodded abruptly, went to the door, opened it, looked back and was gone.

The Madame sat down at her Louis Quatorze desk and wrote a quick note, folded it, placed it in an envelope and handed it to her "associate" who waited just outside the door to her office.

"Take this to Mr. Booth," she said.

Two hours later, Booth let himself into Samuelson's estate with his key to the private gate.

"I don't like this, Booth," Samuelson told his agent after listening to his report on Bradley. "He could end by involving himself in serious crimes. He's been doing good work for us, but if his connection to my interests were ever discovered, we would be seriously injured. Especially in our ability to float new stock issues. You know what sheep investors are. A breath of scandal and they will all melt away like snow on a summer day. Especially this kind of scandal."

"But there is another way of looking at this," the Booth said.

"Yes, yes, I know. It gives us absolute control over him. Like my control over, Collins."

"Yes, sir."

"I dislike the idea of ending our association with Bradley. He has been working well for us. He has turned out to be more talented than we first thought. Prestige and money easily keep him up to the mark, and he has actually earned the respect of many MPs."

"Then, let us use this situation to our advantage," Booth urged.

Samuelson picked up his brandy, sipped it and rolled the liquor around in his mouth. "You know that in a navvy camp, the price of a woman is a bucket of beer."

"And did anyone go to prison because women were bought and sold.?" Booth asked.

"Life is different in a navvy camp, Booth."

"No. It isn't," said the scotsman. Look at the lives that are bought in London society everyday. Captialists make fortunes by shutting up small children in mines and working them until they die. Women expire from carrying loads ten times their own weight. Young women marry rich old men and trade their virtue for a title and a carriage. As long as those with money do not have to look directly at anyone's misery and suffering, it easily slips by any cries for reform. No one cares. As long as investors get their percents.

No one cares about a girl who has lost her virtue. She has put herself beyond the remotest interest of respectable people. Believe me, there is no one to care about this girl unless we decided to make a cause célèbre out of Bradley's use of her and put it into the newspapers. If people saw this girl's story in the papers on their breakfast tables, then they would cry out. Otherwise, the women who occupy houses like Madame's are creatures who don't exist for society. They are merely shameful pets who are kept until they are sick, old or have lost their attractions. Then they are discarded."

"Bradley will have to pay a great deal more than a bucket of beer for this girl," Samuelson said, more to himself than to Booth. "Sometimes, the cost of our pleasures often can't be calculated with accuracy until it is too late."

"That's true," Booth said.

There was a long silence. The only sound was the wind in the chimney, and then the railway king turned back to Booth. "But essentially, I think you are right. The girl is owned already by the house. There is no one looking after her. The money I give Bradley is invisible and he is valuable to us. If we ever need to separate ourselves from him, this transaction with the girl would see him end on a gibbet. Just be certain that none of this ever reaches Collins' ears. That could precipitate a true disaster. Now, what about the matter of the armed group in Manchester?"

"Collins says that whoever they are," Booth answered,"they have covered their tracks well. I think we can assume they are educated men, a different group altogether from those who merely write letters, attend meetings and give fiery speeches. These are men with brains, money and determination. I have traced one of their sources to an arms dealer in Germany where they have bought weapons. I know only that over one hundred carbines have been purchased and were probably shipped to England. But that is all I have been able to find out. This firm is well protected by the Hapsburgs, which is why they are so daring in their international trade. So the trail simply ends there."

"None of the men who are building the future of England want to see these arms reach the hands of those able to use them in an organized way. If we can trap them, I will have a stock of goodwill that will enable me to plan a coordinated railway system the length and breadth of England. The Prime Minister himself told me as much. And you, Booth, I will make rich and independent of me, forever. Like all dangerous situations, these insurrectionists are an opportunity as well as a hazard. You must make some progress with this. Do not waste our resources on small problems like Bradley. He is under our complete control. You will take care of any little problems with Bradley and this girl."

After the secretary left, Samuelson sat, looking into the flames of the fireplace. Shaping the railways of England into a unified system was worth Bradley's life and all those of the insurrectionists if it came to that. Navvies' lives were lost every day in accidents and brawls. Look at what he'd already paid, himself, and what he still risked. And his task was nowhere near completion. The people who swarmed around him trying to enrich themselves would run from the cold, dark way he had to take to build England's iron roads and make it the greatest nation on earth. He'd been given the chance and the strength to rise from the muck of a navvy's life and become a major power in his own right. He had not shrunk from doing what was necessary to attain his great aims.

"If there is a God," Samuelson thought, "certainly He has meant me to succeed, regardless of the costs.

The progress and betterment that a national railway system would bring every Englishman would be his legacy. Let his sins be measured against that. He would be remembered for what he had built, not for his misdemeanors along the way.

"It is late," he said aloud to the dark room as he stood up. Tomorrow he was traveling with Paul to Manchester. He had explained to the boy how much stronger his railway interests would be if he could combine with Blackwood's mining interests. He only hoped the two youngsters liked each other. It would make the alliance that much stronger. If not, he might have to force Paul into the marriage and everything would be more difficult, especially during the initial stages. It was crucial that during the courtship of Blackwood's daughter, Paul should offer no insult to the girl. Later, once the alliance was made Paul would be free to do what he liked so long as he managed it well in public. Recently the boy had been so little at home, it was almost as if he were living somewhere else. He looked pale and dissolute.

"Unfortunately," he thought, "Paul's weak character will never permit him to run my business. He will never be able to take over from me, and that, too, must be hidden from the Blackwoods. Perhaps it was..."and a thought formed in his mind that he forcibly turned away from before it could take shape. Instead, he locked the French doors Collins had used and left the room.

Chapter 11

Pamela sat in front of her dressing table mirror as she brushed her hair. Her life had not been smooth in the three months since her ward, Emily, had been living with the Blackwoods. Once the child had been bathed adequately, it had been fun to do her hair, dress her and be seen with her. But then, Mrs. Peevey and her father had begun to take an excessive interest in the little girl. Emily had been her idea but then everyone else had taken her up and ended by ignoring Pamela. It was especially vexing of her father to talk about Emily as though she were a family member, and to constantly praise her progress with reading, writing and arithmetic. She hated it when he asked the little girl questions and called her his "little minister."

Since Mrs. Blackwood had died, Pamela had never had to share her father's affection with anyone. Now, when it was too late, she would have liked to send the miner's child back to where she had come from, but knew her father wouldn't countenance such an act. He had warned her that taking Emily home was not to be done lightly. Now, Pamela knew, the little girl was a permanent fact of life in the Blackwood house. The only good thing about her father's decision to educate Emily was that Pamela didn't have to spend much time with her anymore. Now, she could use all her time for music.

Though not shaken out of her childish self-absorption by Emily, Pamela's discomfort had at least forced her to think about a life outside of her father's home. In her own mind and in the social context of the time, there were really only two choices open to her: she could marry or, and many would say this was no choice at all, she could go on the stage as a concert musician. Going on the stage was something that would be severely censured by all of her friends and acquaintances. It would put her beyond association with any of the minor nobility she had danced with on visits to London. A female entertainer, even a concert pianist, was only one or two steps removed from a prostitute. But Pamela viewed marriage as a prison where she would have less freedom, more responsibilities and be at the beck and call of a husband. She could never love any man enough to allow him the liberties that a wife was supposed to allow. She liked being admired, but anything beyond that was repulsive to her. When she talked to her friend Alicia in York, who was now engaged to be married, Pamela could never understand why a woman who was petted and spoiled at home would ever want to risk the chance of matrimony. It seemed a dangerous and unpleasant gamble to her.

Pamela's true love was music. Throughout her adolescence and young adulthood, it was the only affection she felt that went beyond a desire to make an impression on others. Most young ladies of her class played M. Chopin or M. Lizst's music to the point where it could be said that they, "played all the notes." But Pamela had an innate feeling for the inner harmonies of a phrase, for a tempo that was correct without being mechanical. Her large strong hands were capable of testing the limits of a pianoforte and though she played far beyond the level of most young ladies of good family, she had always known she could do much more if she worked harder. The pressure of Emily's presence had made her resolve to develop and polish the one gift in which she had absolute confidence. She would become a concert artist and astonish her father and everyone who thought they knew her. She particularly wanted her father to see her merit. Ever since Emily had come into the house, Pamela felt her father saw his own daughter as little more than a handsome doll.

As usual, she dressed herself. She did not like being undressed in front of anyone, even servants. Then she went downstairs to the grand salon where the rosewood pianoforte dominated the room. She sat quietly at the keyboard for a few minutes with her eyes closed. She wanted to cross that threshold within herself to find the place from which she could listen with perfect detachment to her own playing. If she was out of practice, it was always hard to find at first. Once she felt settled in herself, she opened her eyes, set her metronome ticking and began to drill herself on scales, arpeggios and the exercises of M. Czerny. For the next two hours she played the dry notes with rigid precision, striving for articulation and velocity. Then, for two hours more she took several of M. Chopin's etudes, playing them first very slowly but in scrupulously exact rhythm and then playing them faster and faster until she was racing through them at a breathless speed. Dimly, she heard the door open behind her and close again. She knew it was her father. Even so, she would not let her concentration falter. For another hour, she played for her own pleasure, starting with Chopin's brilliant and famous Polonaise in A major and ending with some of her favourite selections from Herr Beethovan's Piano Sonatas. When she stopped, she had the familiar sensation of waking from a brief daydream, as if all her hours of practice had passed in an instant. She noticed that her shoulders and arms were mildly sore. It was always hard to begin practicing again but once she did, she always wondered why she had stopped.

"What a foolish thing I am," she said to herself. "Ever to be led away from music by lesser pleasures, or ever to be bored when there is music in the world."

Then the thought crossed her mind that if she hadn't left off practicing and become so bored, Emily wouldn't be living with them. No matter. With her musical talent and handsome appearance, Pamela believed she could become a concert artist, successful enough to earn her own way in the world. She knew the idea would be hateful to her father, but she also believed that he would never force her to marry. Still, it was better to rely on her own ability to earn money. The more she saw of life, the more personal independence seemed the only way for a woman to live without feeling degraded by having a master. She would keep to a rigid schedule of practice, earn her father's respect for her effort and then insist on getting an outstanding teacher, such as the one Alicia had just written to her about.

Alicia wrote that a very fine German pianist named Bruckner would be staying as a guest of the Thornsbys who lived only a few miles from Blackdale at Rivington Hall, one of the grandest estates in Lancashire, boasting extensive formal gardens as well as a large park. Rivington Pike, a beautiful tower built on the top of Rivington Moor dominated the area and was a destination of choice for the more athletic walkers of the county.

Alicia said the German musician would accept only a few pupils during his stay, which was rumoured to last through the summer. His greatest attraction as a teacher was that he was a pupil of the greatest musician of the century, Franz Lizst.

Pamela had attended one of Lizst's concerts in Paris. Sitting only three rows from the legendary maestro, she had seen that the reports of his remarkable personal beauty were not exaggerated. In addition to his elegantly chiseled features, shoulder-length blonde hair and slender figure, he had a very masculine air of reflection and sensitivity. He looked to Pamela like a young god, which in fact he was.

Franz Lizst was the world's first larger-than-life performer, a direct precursor of the rock stars of the twentieth century. He was a celebrity who was lionized by royalty from Paris to Petersburg, and pursued by beautiful women wherever he went. His love affairs with great ladies were the talk of Europe, his enormous gifts as a pianist, composer and teacher were irrefutable facts. Only Thalberg ever posed even the remotest challenge to Lizst's position as the greatest virtuoso pianist of the age, and he was easily defeated when the two gave concerts in the Paris at the same time. In addition to prodigious musical talents, Lizst was also a born showman, leaving his gloves on his piano so that women in the audience would run to the stage to pick up a personal momento. Few women ever got a whole glove. The delicate kidskin was usually torn into pieces by ladies vying for a souvenir. But Lizst was much more than a showman and virtuoso, he was a musical innovator and a great champion of other musicians. He was quick to praise the talent of others and help build their careers, as he did, most notably, with Chopin. He very actively promoted the music of Ricard Wagner and many other composers, conductors and performers. One of Lizst's illegitimate children, Cosima, daughter of Countess Marie d'Agoult, eventually became Wagner's wife. Liszt scandalized Paris by eloping with the beautiful married countess and living in seclusion with her at Lake Geneva. By 1845, Lizst had already spoken of giving up performing for a more meaningful life of composing and teaching in Weimer. He withdrew there in 1848.

Pamela had no illusions that she would be another Lizst, but she believed that as a remarkably handsome woman, with a genuine talent, if she worked hard enough, she would be free to live as she liked. The world would be at her feet, and no one would be able to tell her what to do. She would live and breathe music for the rest of her life. She would win back her father's respect and he would realize that she, as well as little Emily, was exceptional.

Later that evening, after Emily was in bed, Pamela brought her father some cocoa in the library. It was a custom that went back to Pamela's childhood years, when she thought it great fun to wait on her father. She had not done it recently and he was pleased when he saw her in the doorway with a tray. She was already in her bed jacket and her hair flowed down her back unimpeded in a cascade of ruddy gold. She had always worn it so when she was little. As he watched his grown-up daughter act out the childhood ritual, it struck Blackwood as an excellent time to talk to her about the coming visit of Samuelson and his son. He had not yet decided how clearly he would state that matrimony was one of the definite objects of the visit. Probably, he thought, it would be best to infer the possibility and see how things developed on their own.

"How good of you, Pamela," he said as she put the tray down on a corner of his desk. "Cocoa is exactly what I wanted after this long day of papers and dry figures."

With a cup of cocoa in her hand and her nightgown tucked under her feet, she snuggled into a large green velvet wing chair that faced the desk.

"We haven't sat like this in a long time, my love," the father said.

"Oh, I know, papa. I feel as if I have been living in a ugly dream recently and have just awakened to myself."

"Playing music always seems to help you feel at your best," he remarked.

"Yes. It's true. That's why I wanted to tell you about a teacher I have heard of."

"Well, that's very fine my dear. I have something to tell you as well."

"Oh, but do let me tell you about this teacher first. His name is Herr Bruckner. He will be all summer staying at Rivington Hall with Lord and Lady Thornsby. He'll probably take one or two students while he is here. It would be a wonderful chance for me. And I would even stop asking you to go to London. The lessons would be given right at the Hall, I'm sure. Almost certainly with Lady Thornsby in attendance."

Her voice rose as she contemplated studying with a great musician in the fine ancient manor house of the Thornsbys.

"Thornsby is rather an old stick, you know," Blackwood said. He has no great love for me after I won my lawsuit for the right to run my coal cars across the northwest corner of his land."

"Oh, but that won't matter to Lady Thornsby, Papa. She is herself a fair musician and devoted to the art."

"Well, I suppose I must say, yes."

"Oh, you are such a good papa to me," she said putting her cocoa down and throwing herself into his lap.

"My dear, you are rather big for my lap, or rather my lap feels small," he said smiling.

She nestled her head into his neck. "You are so good, Papa. I promise you, England shall ring with the concerts I shall give."

"Oh, wait, missy," he said pushing her away to look at her face. "I have not given you permission to perform in public."

"What else can I do, Papa? You are my father and there is no other man I would marry. I must look after myself somehow," she said archly.

"Hmm." Blackwood scowled. "You know we agreed on a year of hard work before anything was decided."

"That's why I want to go and play for Herr Bruckner and see if he will take me as a pupil."

"All right. Well, go and play for this German in that heap of old stones the Thornsbys live in. But now I have something to tell you."

"Yes?" she responded still tugging on his neck.

"We have guests coming from London."

"And who will be in the party? Any young people?"

"Yes. A young man will be coming with his father, the famous John Samuelson."

"Really? Mr. Railway Samuelson?"

"Now, that is disrespectful," Blackwood said, pushing her off his lap.

"I just meant, is it that particular Samuelson?"

"Yes. And his son, Paul."

"And you want me to wind them both around my little fingers," she said smiling as she half stood and half leaned on her father's chair, twisting her long locks through her long fingers.

"Well, I would like you to act as my hostess for their stay. Especially for young Paul when his father and I have business to discuss."

"Oh, is the younger Mr. Samuelson not a businessperson, too?"

"Samuelson's interests are so vast that he does not easily trust anyone who is not directly a party to a particular discussion. I think you may find him a little forbidding. But his son seems a pleasant fellow."

After hearing his daughter's latest thoughts on marriage and future occupation, Blackwood had already decided that he would present Paul's presence as incidental to that of his father.

On the day following her discussion with Blackwood, Pamela sent a note to Lady Thornsby, saying that she understood Herr Bruckner was visiting for the summer and perhaps accepting a few students. Could she, Pamela, make an appointment to audition for the maestro? Her note was answered promptly by Lady Thornsby on a crisp piece of her private stationary saying that Pamela's musical accomplishments were well known to her from various houses where she had heard the young woman play. The maestro had condescended to give her an audition next Wednesday at two o'clock.

Pamela was glad to find that the day offered was nearly one week hence. That would give her sufficient time to practice and show herself to best advantage. She wrote to her friend Alicia immediately and asked for any particulars on Herr Bruckner himself. This was so she could choose the music that would be most likely to please him and demonstrate her abilities at the same time. By return post, she learned that Bruckner had some Preludes published, which were difficult to get in England. Alicia had tried to get them in York, and even from London without success. So, Pamela decided she would play The Paganini Études by Lizst. Fortunately, she had an account with a music dealer in London who kept her abreast of all new piano music as it was published. She already had a copy of the brilliantly difficult études, which Lizst had written as an homage to the greatest virtuoso of all, the demonic Genoese violinist, Niccolo Paganini.

Day after day, Pamela remained at the pianoforte for hours on end, working to make the most of her chance. Her father was proud and at the same time a little worried by her passionate desire to be accepted by Herr Bruckner. It seemed unfortunate to him that just at the time he would like her to be thinking about their visitors and Paul's suitability as a husband, she should have set herself so forcefully at this other object. He was much more used to his daughter in the role of spoiled child. Of course, she had always been more passionate about music than anything else. But the hours of toil that he now saw her apply to something that, for the most part, had come easily to her was new. The strength of her desire to win over this new teacher surprised him. Of course the life of a public performer was out of the question for Pamela, but he would deal with that if her ambition was sustained, which he doubted.

When the day of the audition finally arrived, it was sunny and surprisingly cold for the time of year. Pamela climbed into the brougham and bundled herself up in traveling furs. Her music lay beside her on the seat in an oilskin envelope. Her father was from home on business and could not see her off, but it had been arranged for her to be delivered to Rivington Hall and later to stop the night near Manchester to visit Alicia.

Pamela felt elated, her mood as bright as the day itself. She wondered what Herr Bruckner would be like. Probably old with a guttural accent and a great bushy head of white hair like the legendary Herr Beethoven. Such was her confidence after a week of practicing that not for a moment did she mistrust her abilities or fear her examination by the music master. She looked forward to seeing the Hall again, one of the most beautiful old homes in the county, redolent with history and built of light-coloured stone. The wide, level lawn on which the Hall's ten front windows looked out was bounded by water and woods, all part of the very extensive grounds of Lever Park.

Lady Hornsby graciously met Pamela at the door her home. Her deferential treatment of Pamela was not because of Blackwood's wealth, but because of the daughter's musical ability. Though she had not heard the girl play in some years, Lady Thornsby remembered her undoubted talent from musical parties she used to give for talented children in the area. The thin, elderly lady was a true votary of music and had for years upheld a tradition in her house of having the best musicians in the world come and stay for extended periods of rest, composition and music making. She was a patron in the fullest and deepest sense of the word. In her house a great artist was treated as a member of the nobility. She, too, would have picked up Titian's brush.

"So nice to possess you at the Abbey," her Ladyship said as Pamela stepped out of the carriage. "You must be quite chilled with a ride in this wind across the moors."

Pamela curtseyed. "I am quite all right, Lady Hornsby. I am so excited, I felt no cold at all."

"Even so, come in near the fire, my dear. It is so cold for the time of year that I had one built."

She led the way through the high arched doorway into the huge hall, which soared some forty feet high, then through a series of modern partitions that had been used to create smaller more comfortable rooms. Finally, they entered the salon where the family spent most of its time. Below the high ceiling a fire burned in the cavernous fireplace that was half again Pamela's height. In one corner of the room was a massive black Erard concert grand pianoforte. Behind the instrument was a fine example of a Flemish tapestry dating from the 1600s. It depicted a scene from one of Eleanor of Aquitaine's courts of love. The knight on trial knelt in his armor to his lady, who stood in front of him. They were surrounded by a group of seated women, the judges who would pass sentence on him. In the foreground sat one of the greatest of the Provençal troubadours, Bernard De Ventadorn. He was poised to strike the strings of his lute.

Pamela had visited the Hall before, but never as a private guest and so, she had never seen this room before. She was particularly struck by the tableau formed by the magnificent pianoforte and tapestry. It seemed wrong to the young girl to connect romantic love and music. Music carried Pamela far above the sordidness of love, with its sufferings, misunderstandings and enforced behavior.

"I am sorry, Miss Blackwood, I had forgotten you have not visited us since you were a child. The tapestry behind the pianoforte depicts a court of love, a favourite preoccupation of ladies and knights of the time of Eleanor of Aquitaine."

Pamela looked at the tapestry for some moments and then said, "I wonder, Lady Thornsby, how grown men and women of that age could have been so absorbed by romantic love. It seems so much less important than other things."

"I am surprised to hear a young woman say so. I don't know if you are very mature or too worldly wise. What do you rank as more important?"

"Music," Pamela answered, looking at the piano.

"Would you like to try it?" Lady Thornsby asked.

Pamela looked up, all her eagerness lighting her eyes, "Oh, yes. If you please, your Ladyship. That way I can be ready for Herr Bruckner."

"Then play something for me, if you would. Nothing brilliant. Play one of Herr Mozart's divine adagios. I haven't heard you play in some years."

Pamela sat down in front of the vast keyboard and softly touched the keys. So perfect was the mechanism of the pianoforte that the sound seemed to float out of the instrument without any pressure on the keys at all. The tone was round and bell-like, even pianissimo. She sat quietly for a moment and then, very softly began the orchestral part to the Adagio movement of Mozart's piano concerto number twenty-one.

When she reached the singing, opening, notes of the solo part, the voice of the great pianoforte utterly bewitched her and Pamela felt transported beyond awareness of anything but the music.

She woke from the tones of the last chord to the sound of applause echoing through the hall. Near the fireplace stood a well-dressed young man only slightly older than herself. His dark curly hair was worn long and thick and rested on his shoulders. His full, wide mouth smiled at her. His startlingly dark eyes were bright with pleasure.

He bowed to her.

"Bravo, mademoiselle. In Mozart's slow movements there is no place to hide. But you do not need to hide, I think."

"Herr Bruckner?" she ventured.

He bowed again, more stiffly, in the German style. "At your service, Mademoiselle. What music did you bring to play for me?" he asked as he walked to the oilskin case lying on the piano.

"Ah, the Maestro's Études. You are a very courageous young lady. There are few musicians who do not quail before these difficulties. Most young ladies prefer M. Chopin."

She looked into the dark eyes that surveyed her so appraisingly and they seemed almost as deep as the music she had just been playing.

"Can you play these well?" he asked her in a forthright way. The spell was broken and her eyes turned away from him and she looked down at the floor in front of her. She spoke quietly and sincerely.

"I ask nothing more, Herr Bruckner, than for you to listen and judge and tell me yourself if I do or do not play them well. I have not had the advantage of playing for a great musician like yourself before. What has sounded excellent to others, may have many defects to you."

"Please begin, then, Mademoiselle."

The ringing tones of the Thornsbys superb instrument quickly enraptured her once more. It was particularly well suited to the bell-like effects in Lizst's interpretation of Paganini's "La Campanella". For Pamela the sublime, dancing arpeggios did not rise like impenetrable barriers. They carried her up and ever higher and higher, returning her to earth only after the final silvery cadence.

This time there were no applause as the final notes faded into the air. Pamela looked up at Herr Bruckner and found that she was being stared at with an expression she could not comprehend.

As the moments of silence passed she thought "I wish he would say something, anything," Finally, she stood up and began putting her music back into the oilskin envelope.

Then the young musician moved around the piano so that he was standing directly in front of Pamela. She felt his eyes touching her, looking into her thoughts while he held her still with the power of his gaze.

"Mademoiselle, you are a musician." and he took her hand in his and kissed it.

She looked at him standing before the great tapestry and what only a short time ago had seemed so ridiculous and unimportant, suddenly was not. She felt her cheeks grow hot.

Abruptly he turned away from her.. "But I think you could even be better. If you will let me help you."

"Oh, yes, Herr Bruckner, I should be honoured if you would instruct me. My teachers have only been local musicians."

"But they have taught you the correct things. The right basis for your technique. It is only your intellectual knowledge of the music that could be improved. Your feeling is superb, mademoiselle. Quite remarkable. Here, I will show you."

He sat down at the pianoforte. "At this point where the theme returns..." and he demonstrated his words. Pamela sat down next to him and for an hour he guided her through the most difficult transitions and alterations of tempo and key in the piece she had just played. She watched his fingers dance over the keys while his voice rode on the music itself as he explained his own brilliant playing. It was the most exciting hour of Pamela's life.

"It was like fireworks inside of me, papa," she told her father the next night when he returned home. "I felt my entire life had been a dream, but for that one hour, I was awake. Oh, he is such a great musician. I told him of my aspirations and he thinks I can have a concert career."

She went on to describe the great musician and without realizing it, every time Pamela referred to Herr Bruckner there was a special emphasis in her voice that was not lost on her father. Blackwood said nothing, he was too experienced a negotiator and knew his daughter too well to attack her fondest wishes in the heat of her ardor. The next day, a letter from Lady Thornsby reached him and he realized that the case was even more serious than he'd supposed. It seemed that combined with the musical experience there had been a personal experience with this young musician which had been noted by Lady Thornsby.

"The intensity of both young people as they examined the music together could ignite into a truly dangerous situation for Pamela," Lady Thornsby wrote to Blackwood, "Though it is my belief that Herr Bruckner is too honourable and has too great a career before him for anything overt to happen in my home. Also, I can promise that I shall not leave them alone for an instant when she takes her lessons here."

Blackwood put down the letter and silently thanked Lady Thornsby for her sharp observation. He had only two weeks before Samuelson and his son arrived.

Pamela's thoughts were in the worst possible state for such a visit. It might even be preferable to send her to London and make an excuse for her absence. Such a trip would also get her out from under the apparently "mesmeric"(Lady Thornsby's word) influence of this German music master.

Chapter 12

In the weeks since his first law writing assignment for Ardmores, Richard's knowledge of Latin and Greek literature had continued to provide a firm foundation for his relationship with the principal of the chambers, Mr. Barnes. Mr. Barnes was such an avid student of the classics that he often asked Richard into his private office to examine a point of classical language which he found obscure. As a result, the elderly Wilson, the chief clerk, gave more and more work to Richard through Ardmores. Richard was busy for the firm nearly every day, constantly running back and forth to Mr. Barnes' chambers. During one of his visits, Mr. Barnes had even condescended to introduce Richard to Mr. Blackwood, the important client who had been present during Richard's first visit. For a man whose name was so often in the papers, Blackwood seemed a man of natural ease and friendliness with few affectations.

As the weeks passed, Richard felt proud of his new connexions and the importance of the people with whom he was now associating. He had not yet broached the subject of Fanny with Mr. Barnes. He wanted to wait until he had saved more money before confiding his reason for being in Manchester to the solicitor, in case his patronage was withdrawn when he heard the truth about Richard's sister.

One morning, some two months after his arrival in Manchester, Richard entered the law chambers to find a handsome young lady in the outer office. He recognized her as the supercilious young woman he had seen on his first visit to the chambers. She was accompanied by the beautiful little girl who had guided him through the hallways on his first visit. What was clearest in his mind about Pamela from their first meeting was her haughtiness.

"Well," the little girl said glancing up at him, "I see you have learned the way by yourself."

Richard smiled.

"Yes, miss. Your instructions have been most effectual."

"Good. I am glad you are such a good learner," the child replied. Pamela looked briefly at the young man who spoke so familiarly with her ward.

"Emily. Don't be impudent to your elders," Pamela said.

"Oh, she is not being impudent, Miss, begging your pardon," Richard said. "The young lady did guide me here one day when I was lost in the hallways."

Richard stood near Wilson's empty desk, looking over at Emily. She was holding a copy of "Robinson Crusoe."

"Are you reading that, Miss?" he asked the child. "That is quite advanced for your age."

Without looking up from the text in question, Emily answered, "Miss Peevey says I am quite advanced for my age."

The two adults looked at each other and Pamela couldn't help but smile as the young man grinned in appreciation of Emily's precocious answer.

"You know," Richard continued to the child, "many people think that "Robinson Crusoe" has a great deal of wisdom in it."

"Why else would one read it?" the child answered as she shrugged without taking her eyes away from the page.

Richard chuckled audibly.

At just that point in the interchange, Mr. Barnes' door opened and Wilson came out. When the clerk saw Richard, he smiled, an expression Richard had never seen on the clerk's haughty, narrow face.

"Ah, Mr. Darrow. Mr. Barnes would particularly like to see you before you take away these documents. You may go right in. He is expecting you."

"Thank you, sir," Richard answered, stepping toward the heavy mahogany door of the solicitor's office.

"Come in," a muffled voice answered in reply to Richard's knock. "Ah, close the door, Richard and sit down," Mr. Barnes said gesturing to one of the leather chairs where clients usually sat when consulting him. Richard was surprised by the invitation. In all the times he had discussed classical language with Mr. Barnes, he had always remained standing. Once Richard was seated, Barnes looked at him thoughtfully.

"You have been doing good work for us, Richard. And you have considerably improved my classical reading. I don't know you well, but I see that you work hard, are punctual and appear trustworthy."

"Thank you, sir. From a man of your reputation and position, I am sensible that what you have said is high praise."

"As I say, however, I do not really know you. In spite of that, I propose to offer you a position here as a clerk in training. The addition of my son to these chambers will create a heavier work schedule for Wilson. I want him to have help. What you lack in specific legal knowledge, I am convinced you can acquire. You are a remarkably well-read young man and your tastes and views are unusually sound for your age. In the practice of law, however, reputation is everything. So I must ask you if there is anything in your past or antecedents which would not bear full disclosure and scrutiny—should you become articled here?"

Richard stood and bowed to Barnes. "Allow me to say, sir, how deeply honoured I am by your good opinion. I must say, however, that there is no way I could pay the premium for my articles here. And, I must now disclose something to you that I have for some time been meaning to discuss with you as a client."

"As a client?" Barne's thick, slanting eyebrows twitched upward in surprise.

"Yes, sir. When I came to Manchester I had a settle purpose which I knew would require the assistance of someone as respected and knowledgeable in the law as yourself. I have waited this time, sir, because, while I needed your advice, badly, I did not want to lose your respect and I needed the money from Ardmores so I could offer you payment."

"Sit down, Richard," the solicitor said blandly. "I freely give you the next hour of my time to explain yourself fully, in return for all your generous classical coaching. Besides, if what you have to say touches on your suitability for working in these chambers then I must hear it in any case."

In as few words as possible, Richard outlined what had happened in London, regarding Fanny. The solicitor than asked some pointed questions about the past of both brother and sister. His interest in Richard, he explained, necessitated probing farther back in time than Fanny's disappearance. Quickly, Richard described his early childhood in a navvy camp and his good fortune in meeting Charles Wilney. He quickly passed over the tramp to London that he and Fanny had made together and his subsequent years of study and teaching. When he had finished, the solicitor looked more thoughtful than ever.

"I must tell you, Richard. Your narrative is extraordinary, and as a solicitor I have heard many remarkable tales."

"It is entirely true, sir," Richard began defensively.

Barnes raised his long arm and waved his hand to quiet Richard.

'I did not say I did not believe you. But it is remarkable in any case," Barnes said sitting up in his chair, "And you are a most remarkable and fortunate young man. This Mr. Wilney has placed you forever in his debt."

"Well I know it, sir. He has been the good angel of our lives. I doubt Fanny and I would be alive were it not for him."

"Well, your own fortitude is most impressive as well, Richard."

"Again sir, I must say, I am honoured by your good opinion. But I must say that as honoured as I am by your offer, I simply do not have the resources to take advantage of it. And there is the matter of my sister."

The tall solicitor rose from his chair and reached for a humidor behind him. "Do you smoke, Richard?"

"No, sir. I could never afford it. And when I could, it still seemed too costly a pleasure."

"Well," said the solicitor, running his hands through his thick woolly white hair, "it helps me think. Touching on the matter of your sister's whereabouts, I shall do the following: I shall set some enquiries in motion. The results of those enquiries shall determine how far I act in this matter. Is that understood? I reserve the right to drop the matter entirely, if I so choose."

"I am deeply grateful, sir." Richard asked. "I could not have hoped for so much, sir. Oh, your fees. I have saved money for just that purpose..."

Barnes took the young man's hand and held it while he asked, "And will you take the position offered? I will forego the premium until you are more settled."

"I hardly know what to say, sir."

"Say, 'yes.'"

"Then, yes, indeed sir, and thank you."

"And we'll deduct the fees for the enquiry gradually from your salary. How does that sound?"

"Extremely good of you, Mr. Barnes."

The two men sat down again and the solicitor spoke, "This man who attacked you with a sword stick sounds a particularly notable villain. He will, I believe, be easier to trace than your vague description of your sister's abductor. I shall most certainly be able to find out who lives in the grand villa you describe through a private enquiry agent I have in London. With those two threads in our hands, we shall be able to make a beginning at locating your sister. I hope you will not be too dismayed by what we may learn."

"No sir. I assume that the worst has already taken place," Richard said quietly.

"I think that is probably wise," the solicitor concurred.

By the time the consultation with Barnes had ended and Richard re-entered the outer office, the little girl and the young woman were gone. Richard felt mild disappointment. He was charmed by the child and the young woman was very handsome and beautifully dressed. A glance at Wilson's concentrated face in the outer office brought Richard back to the present and his own changed connection with the chambers.

The clerk adjusted his metal spectacles and glanced down at Richard and then looked back to his documents.

"Tomorrow morning, Mr. Darrow," he said in his driest voice as Richard opened the outer door. "Seven-thirty, sharp, mind you."

"Yes, sir. Thank you, sir."

Outside, Richard's step was buoyant. In a few short weeks he had made greater progress toward helping Fanny than he could have imagined possible. It seemed years since he had crept into the iron-coloured city, friendless, tired and hungry. Not only did he now have the very best professional counsel, he, himself, had a career that formerly he could have only dreamed about after many years of study and saving. Charles would be proud that his teaching had borne such fruit.

"But I wonder," he muttered under his breath. "Is being a solicitor's clerk is as high a calling as teaching?" Certainly, the chances of enrichment were greater, but what would Charles say if he abandoned his plans to go to Cambridge. Now, Richard thought, I shall write to him about Fanny. Clearly, my duty is to help her first. Staying with Mr. Barnes is the best way to do that at present. Charles would understand.

In spite of the fact that Richard had not seen his mentor face to face for more than ten years, Charles Wilney remained a very tangible presence for the young man. His first reading lessons and the world they opened for him, a ragged and dirty boy, were events that remained as vivid as anything in his life. Walking down the streets of Manchester on that unusually clear afternoon, he could still hear Wilney's deep, mellow voice, reading The Fairie Queen and making acrostics out of the letters of the first word of each new line to keep his young student interested. A small brook had splashed around their dangling feet. A row of low pale coloured hills had risen above the distant green plain. This tableau of memory lay across the present moment like a piece of painted glass, past and present superimposed and intermixed for some minutes. Then, Richard saw the back and shoulders of a man on the street in front of him that reminded him of the man who had threatened him and sent him to Manchester. It was too fleeting a glimpse to be certain, but Richard walked the few blocks to Ardmore's with all his speculations about Fanny reawakened. Pushing open the heavy glass doors, he could see Ruskin, the store manager, the man who gave him his first chance at the law stationers standing just inside.

* * *

As Richard was reflecting on his new calling, Pamela, too, was thinking about her future. She and Emily were in Blackwood's carriage returning home from the shops where the older girl had picked up a gown ordered weeks ago, ordered especially for the dinner her father was giving that night. Pamela sensed that there was some special parental object connected with these important guests. Ordinarily, she would have been happy and pleased to play the great lady for her father's male associates. Now the prospect just bored her. She had even begrudged the time she had taken to come to Manchester and have the gown fitted. Any time away from the pianoforte seemed wasted time to her, now. She also sensed there was something special about these guests, something connected with herself. She amazed herself by the coolness with which she thought,

"Perhaps he wants to get me married. Now that he has his 'little minister'." She glanced over at the self-possessed Emily, who was looking out at the town. Strangely, the thought did not fester as it had done just a few weeks before, before she had met Herr Bruckner and had the validity of her plans for the future confirmed. Not for an instant did she fear that her father would force her to marry, or give up music.

The two young ladies watched the city's parade pass the carriage window until, near the edge of town, on a quiet, empty street that straggled out into the country, they saw a well-dressed young man and a beautiful young woman kissing each other hungrily on a street corner. It wasn't a usual sight to see so handsome and well-dressed a couple indulging their instincts in public. Pamela was repelled but could not take her eyes off the pair until the young man put his hand under the woman's skirts. Then she spoke sharply,

"Emily, look away!"

"From what, Miss?" the little girl asked.

Pamela realized the young girl's indifference and the heat that was spreading upwards from her own abdomen in the same moment. She blushed, looked down into her own lap and said nothing to the little girl for the rest of the ride home.

The Blackwood estate was too far out in the country to be connected to the city gas mains that lit the great thoroughfares of Manchester. The Blackwood household had to burn old-fashioned oil lamps and candles, in spite of their wealth. This lack was something Pamela had always felt keenly whenever she returned from London. Now, however, as she and Emily arrived at the candle lit house, in the fugitive sunlight of the late, overcast afternoon, she admitted that the flickering candelabras set in the windows in anticipation of visitors were ornamental. She slipped out of the carriage without a glance at Emily and went straight to the parlour where her pianoforte stood. She closed the doors behind her, sealing off the rest of the house. As soon as she entered the room, she was in another world. Here was the world Herr Bruckner occupied, the world of Herr Lizst and the other great artistic geniuses who were guests on an equal footing in the aristocratic houses of Europe. When her teacher spoke of these world-famous artists, his humble reverence for his art and for its great practitioners shone like a pure flame, a flame that had ignited all the ardor of the young girl and was transforming everything in her life.

She worked on Chopin's Études now with a new understanding given her by Bruckner. In his words, she had come to understand the harmonic greatness of the music that underlay the brilliant surface. The articulation she strove for had musical purpose and was no longer merely to dazzle the listener. Without knowing it, without knowing all the reasons why, Pamela was learning to serve something greater than herself.

It was not until she heard her father's insistent knock that the spell was broken, but she knew that even then, it was only for a little while. She opened the door, pecked her father's cheek and ran toward her room.

"I shall be ready on time, father. I shall be very quick."

Blackwood watched his daughter dart from him with the lightness of a small bird. The change in her amazed him and he hardly knew what it meant for her future or for his. At that moment, the footman called him to the door to greet his guests.

Blackwood had met Samuelson several times, so he was not surprised, as he had been on their first meeting, by the man's aura of sheer physical power. The great man's son, by comparison, seemed weak, though he was handsome enough in a way that would please a women, Blackwood thought.

The men settled into the thick, heavy chairs in the smoking room and talked about business, local politics and railways, all in a general bland tone. Paul said little, Samuelson and Blackwood carried the conversation.

After an interval which Blackwood judged long enough for Pamela to dress, he said, "Gentlemen, allow me to offer you some refreshment in the salon."

The three men left their cigars and filed out of the womb-like smoking room that was hung with heavy maroon curtains. Blackwood led the way for his guests into the large bright room where the servants were waiting with a light wine, a prelude to the heavier wines that would be served with dinner. Through the arch of the room's entrance that gave onto the main reception area, Blackwood saw Pamela cross the hall toward the men. He was proud of her beauty as she seemed to float toward them in a magnificent gown of blue velvet that perfectly set off her hair and eyes. She drew near and Blackwood said, "Gentlemen, my daughter, Pamela."

As the men turned to face the young women, Pamela's graceful step was frozen in mid stride. Her cry shattered everyone's demeanor.

"Not you," The obvious scorn in her words burst from her as she looked straight at Paul. Without another word she turned and ran from the room. All the men looked baffled.

"Have you met Miss Blackwood, before, Paul?" Samuelson asked in a quiet but accusatory voice.

"No, of course not. How could I?" Paul answered defensively.

"Well, she certainly appeared to recognize you."

Like a night landscape revealed by a lightning flash, Blackwood saw in a single instant the personal distrust that lay between father and son.

Putting down his drink, Blackwood spoke, "If you will excuse me, gentlemen, I shall take a moment to find out what is troubling my daughter. I apologize to you both for her outburst. She has been working too hard lately. The footman will take you to the table and I will join you shortly."

As he climbed the marble staircase to the upper storey, Blackwood's thoughts echoed his words. Pamela had never been so wanting in decorum. The only possible reason must be illness due to overwork. He would lock up the piano and see that the German music teacher left the county. He would send Pamela to London for a round of social pleasure to help restore her balance. He should have granted her request before her nerves had become so affected. At the same time, he wondered how to repair the damage to the young man's vanity. Pamela's marriage to Paul would propel Blackwood Holdings into the forefront of British industry, and eventually could create a company that would lead the world's industrialization. It was too good a chance to be destroyed by Pamela's two words of scorn. In the end, Blackwood felt certain that Samuelson would see it in the same light. He knocked on his daughter's door, confident that eventually all would be well. He was totally unprepared for the next half hour he spent with his daughter. On leaving her room, his face wore a frown of perplexity. It was bad enough that a young woman should actually see a prospective husband take his pleasure with a low rival, and so lose her respect for him, but what most worried Blackwood was the attitude Pamela expressed toward her musical plans. She was adamant that nothing would interrupt her lessons. She refused to go to London and said she would follow the music teacher if he were banished. She did not say she loved the musician, but the man had somehow fanned the flames of her passion for music to a fire that had turned to icy determination. Pamela almost seemed a stranger to her father. Nothing Blackwood had said, moved her in the slightest. She feared neither disapproval nor any financial sanctions he might place on her. She was ready to sell her clothes, jewels, all of her personal property to continue her lessons. He felt, with an inevitable shock, that pang all fathers must feel when they are no longer the adored god of the young woman they have raised. Nor could he, after years of treating Pamela almost as a partner, invoke his legal authority in the face of her powerful desires. He sensed that her outrage at such an attempt, borne of her independent upbringing, could precipitate almost anything.

"No," he thought as he started down the stairs, "Paul must win her himself. That is the only practical solution. He must somehow gain Pamela's respect and confidence."

Chapter 13

When Richard saw the initial agreements that were being drafted between Samuelson and Blackwood, regarding the railway that was being sponsored in Parliament by John Bradley, MP, he felt he was truly participating in events that would shape his own epoch. He did feel a conflict between some of the affairs Mr. Barnes handled and the more idealistic teachings of Charles Wilney. It was true that Blackwood and Samuelson were enriching themselves, but they also provided work for others and were contributing to the many new benefits industrialized society was offering to working people. The condition of the mill operatives here in Manchester was horrifying. But neither Blackwood nor Samuelson were involved in the cotton or woolen trades. Richard told himself that even Charles would have found Barnes a good man. Blackwood, too. Richard believed Blackwood a kind and thoughtful man, talked of throughout the city as an enlightened master who provided good working conditions for his people. Emily had told Richard proudly,

"There are no little girls like me in Mr. Blackwood's mines."

Richard still had not written to his old mentor about all that had taken place. As when Fanny ran away, he felt Wilney would not entirely approve of his present situation. His position with the solicitor was not quite what Charles would have hoped for from him. For Wilney, learning and giving the gift of learning was the greatest of all vocations. And though the law was a respectable profession, using it in the service of men who sought to enrich themselves way above their fellows, would not have met with his entire approval. Richard was also uncertain how Sally and her Chartist family would feel about his new profession. For her safety and his own, Mr. Barnes had advised him not to write to her until they knew more about the man with the sword cane. Richard's old life in London seemed far away, indeed. His new clothes, occupation and substantial salary, made him feel, at times, like someone else. So far, Fanny's whereabouts remained a mystery.

The days and weeks passed quickly in the bustle of the law chambers. He had little time to himself except the early morning when he rose and breakfasted at Tom Weedon's inn where he still maintained his room. It was during one of these quiet times in his day when his old life came back to him in a dramatic and unexpected form.

Richard was perusing "The Union Pilot" the newspaper his landlord took, one popular with Manchester's working people, when the name, "Charles Fisk" leapt suddenly out of the thickly inked type of the crudely printed page.

"Charles Fisk, carpenter, gives fiery speech on the rights of working people," a bold heading ran. The article was short and said only that Charles Fisk, carpenter, had spoken to a small crowd of people on a rainy afternoon in Hyde Park. "His remarks were well received by those gathered to listen," the story concluded.

Richard put down the paper and was thinking about his friend's idealism when Tom Weedon put down the tin plates that held Richard's breakfast.

"You look like you have seen a ghost, Darrow," the landlord remarked.

"I just had the remarkable experience of reading about an old friend in the newspaper. Someone I haven't seen for some time."

Even though the landlord thought little of solicitors and the law, the two men had struck a casual friendship and were on easy terms now.

"Surely not some famous London solicitor," Tom said, smiling at his own jest.

"No, look. Right here," Richard answered pointing to the article. Tom looked suddenly serious as he read the words Richard pointed at.

"You are acquainted with Mr. Fisk?" the older man asked, looking at Richard narrowly.

"Yes. He has been my good friend. Without him, I might not be here."

"But Charles Fisk is a downright Chartist. Some would even say, revolutionary," Tom answered.

"How do you know that?" Richard asked.

"Wait here. You should know who your friend is. A good man and none better."

The big landlord went behind the private bar and came back a moment later to Richard's table. He dropped a well-thumbed pamphlet next to the younger man's plates. The title on the cover read, "A New vision of the New Jerusalem and why the Monied Classes Wish to hide it from The Working People of London by Charles Fisk." A very poor black and white engraving of William Blake's "Nebuchadnezzar" was printed under the title.

"The face of my enemy," Richard muttered under his breath."May I borrow and read this, Tom?"

"Keep it hidden. The mayor and his friends have named it seditious. It's prison or a fine to be caught with it. There will be a meeting very soon, on

Kersal Moor, not far away. Would you come? Many of the words spoken will be similar to those of your friend."

"I shall think of it, Weedon. I shall think of it, maturely."

***

As he walked to work, thinking about Charles Fisk, Richard pulled his coat close around his shoulders. An oily rain was pelting down on the shop windows and settling in viscous pools in the streets. The morning was blurred and dirty and added to Richard's feeling that his own life lacked clarity and direction. He wished that he had Fisk's certainty of conviction about the course he was following. Taking care of Fanny had been a clear duty and often, a labour of love born out of their shared hardships. His short time in Mr. Barnes' chambers had already shown him that simple, black and white ideas about society didn't encompass the more complex, gray realities of the century in which he lived. Now that Mr. Barnes had introduced him to two of the great industrialists of the age, he could see that one was a truly good man, while the other, Samuelson, was——what——he wasn't sure. Richard's own relatively comfortable present life pricked his conscience when he thought of the chances Charles Fisk was taking to express his ideals, or the lives of the people he'd seen who lived in Ancoats and worked in the Manchester mills. Manchester itself was a greater argument in favor of Chartist ideas than anything Fisk had ever said. Perhaps the carpenter was a little mad on the subject of William Blake's ideas of a spiritual revolution. Still, one could not but admire his courage and conviction. Yet, Richard's first duty was still to Fanny. Only when she was found and her abductor punished, would he be free to take up these larger questions, questions that would also touch Sally, and all English people. He knew instinctively that Sally would have her own well-formed opinions about the present changes in society, though he was not clear what they would be.

As he walked through the city, proud of his new suit, Richard could not see the assumptions through which he was viewing the world. The imperatives he applied to himself and those near him were based on beliefs about morality and duty hidden from him by the nearly universal acceptance of these values by people in all levels of society. To put it succinctly, in Richard's age, most people still believed themselves children of God, and sincerely wanted to live under His laws. When survival and religious idealism were in conflict, many people of the Victorian era would become morally blind, but not by consciously and deliberately eschewing their faith. In spite of all the abuses, it was a time of hope and idealism, faith in man living under God's laws. It produced men like General Gordon, a public celebrity who taught in the ragged schools without pay and who rescued many young boys off the streets of London. Society had not yet seen clearly the human capacity for evil, a deliberate, horrific evil, much worse than the lashes of a fallen angel. The assumption of an absolute good and an absolute evil, each governing with specific laws, was implicit in everything Richard thought and did.

When Richard opened the door of Mr. Barnes' chambers, he saw

Emily sitting in one of the big leather armchairs reading a periodical. Wilson was, of course, at his post looking as neat and polished as ever. Richard sometimes wondered if the Head Clerk ever went home or even if he had a home other than his high chair in the chambers.

"Good day, sir," he said to Wilson.

"Good day to you, Mr. Darrow."

Emily looked up at him with a bright, purposive expression on her face. Her personal beauty had now been enhanced by a neat yellow print dress that set off her blonde hair and dark brown eyes. Pamela had chosen it for her.

"Mr. Richard," she said in a piping eager voice. "I've been waiting for you. Could you help me with something?"

She held out a twelve-year-old copy of *Bentley's Miscellany* which advertised on the cover that it was carrying the most recent chapters of Mr. Dickens' "Oliver Twist".

Richard had already been told by Wilson that anything a client asked of him which didn't overstep his knowledge of the law was to be carried out with alacrity, so he had no doubt about acceding to Emily's request. "Of course, Miss. Show me the place where you are having difficulties."

"Well, I think there is something very odd about Bill Sykes and Nancy," she said as Richard sat down next to her.

"Where did you get this old publication?" Richard asked.

"The complete set of Oliver Twist was in the hall below stairs at Blackdale. Mr. Blackwood borrowed them for me from Mr. Gates, the butler."

The door to Mr. Barnes' office was opened just as Emily made her comment. The solicitor was speaking in low tones to Mr. Blackwood.

"So what is it you find odd about Nancy and Bill Sykes?" Richard asked.

"I can't understand why Bill Sykes would beat Nancy to death when she had a good reason for going to see Mr. Brownlow. And Bill could even have run away with Nancy to France. Why do you suppose he kills her instead? He's far worse off afterward than before. It seems very horrible and wrong and it has been bothering me ever since I read it."

"Well, Miss, I think Mr. Dickens meant it to be very horrible."

Neither Richard or Emily noticed that Blackwood and Barnes had ceased talking and were now listening to the dialogue of teacher and pupil.

"But why?"

"I think Mr. Dickens wanted to show people how horrible someone who steals and drinks and is mean to others can become. He wanted to show that crime always leads to worse and worse crime. Bill Sykes' character is also contrasted with that of Oliver who would not be mean or vicious no matter what Fagin did to him."

"But don't you think in real life, Bill Sykes would have run away to France instead of killing Nancy?"

Richard was silent for a moment, then he said, "Weren't you a little afraid when you first went to Mr. Blackwood's house, even though it was a wonderful home?"

The little girl was absolutely still while she thought. Richard could feel the play of her powerful young mind reaching beyond itself.

"Yes. Oh, I see. You mean he didn't go to France because it was too different. He was afraid because it was strange, even though it was better."

"That would be my idea, Miss. But you'd have to take it up with Mr. Dickens to be certain."

"Oh, no. I shall not bother writing to him now. I think you are right. Thank you, Mr. Richard."

"My pleasure, Miss."

The discussion at an end, the two became aware that they had been observed. Barnes looked at Blackwood and said, "You see what I mean, Sir." It was obvious to Richard that the remark referred somehow to himself and Emily.

"Yes, I do," answered Blackwood looking straight at Richard.

"Do you like to teach, Mr. Darrow?" the financier asked.

"Well, yes sir, I do."

"You did quite a bit of teaching, I understand, before you came here."

"Yes, sir. In London at Miss Reade's Academy. Quite a good school, sir."

"If she agrees, would you teach Emily, history and mathematics? Can you teach those subjects as well as you teach literature?"

"Geometry, trigonometry and a smattering of algebra is all I have learned of mathematics, sir."

"Ah, yes, just about what is needed to build railways. Is that not so, Mr. Darrow?"

Here Barnes broke in, "I hope you won't mind, Richard that I told Mr. Blackwood your history."

"Not at all, sir. I am entirely in your hands."

"Do you know anything about the mechanics of digging a cut or building an embankment?"

"I have, of course, watched these things done many times as a boy, sir. Mr. Wilney, my tutor, was a self-taught but able surveyor. He worked as such on the Stockton Darlington line and several others. It was he who taught me the little mathematics I know."

"Better and better, Mr. Darrow. If I searched the world I do not think I could find a better tutor for Emily."

Then the great financier turned his attention to Emily who was smiling and nodding her head up and down with an exaggerated movement. The "lion of the North" walked to the armchair and knelt down so that he and the little girl were on the same level.

"Does my little minister approve, then?" he asked.

"Oh, yes sir, if you please sir. Oh, thank you, Mr. Blackwood," she cried, clapping her hands.

"What do you say, Mr. Darrow?"

"Well, I am very sensible of the high trust of your offer, sir. But I have a previous commitment to Mr. Barnes, as I'm sure you must know." The solicitor spoke up, "Our agreements would still stand, Mr. Darrow. Miss Emily has a governess and you would only be needed to supplement the gaps in her knowledge. Two or three afternoons a week at most. You'd stay to dine with Emily since it's a long ride."

"But I have so much to learn about the law, sir."

"You could make it up in the early evenings. Mr. Wilson could probably give some time around dinner hour. Eh, Wilson."

"And I keep a few horses here in town," Blackwood added.

Wilson looked up from his papers as though he had not been present for the last few minutes, but he spoke with perfect clarity on what he had been asked. "As you know Mr. Barnes, I dine at a chop house very near here, sir. If Mr. Darrow would meet me there and we could work as we ate and then return to chambers for an hour, I think I might manage to cram enough law into him given that time."

"Are you willing to work that hard, Mr. Darrow?" the solicitor asked.

"Of course, sir. It is a great chance for me to study and to teach at the same time."

"I will compensate you well for teaching Emily," Blackwood said. "I know you have expenses here...shall we say £100 a year?"

"My goodness," Richard exclaimed, blushing. "For two afternoons a week? Very handsome, sir, I am sure," His head was spinning with his sudden rise in fortune.

"You'll also need the use of a horse to come and go from my house. I have several stables here in the city. Arrange it, Barnes."

The solicitor gave a slight bow of acknowledgement.

"Then we shall expect you, Mr. Darrow, say, tomorrow week at one o'clock in the afternoon?"

"I am at your disposal, sir. May I shake your hand?"

"Keep on as you have started here, Mr. Darrow and I predict great success for you," Blackwood said as he gripped the younger man's hand. The financier then slipped his large gold watch out of his pocket and consulted it for several seconds.

"Come, Emily, we still have time for our business at the mine." When the two had left the office Barnes looked over at Richard.

"A remarkable opportunity, Mr. Darrow."

"Indeed, sir. It shows the greatness of our age that such things can happen."

"When one has a friend like Mr. Blackwood, almost anything is possible. He is a man who makes things happen. No doubt of it," the solicitor finished as he turned back into his office.

* * *

Richard's day was a long one. After attending to the firm's business until six o'clock, he adjourned with Wilson to the chop house. In contrast to Tom Weedon's Inn, this was a fashionable establishment with large plate windows and waiters who wore smart uniforms and moved noiselessly through the handsomely appointed dining room. Many brass gas jets illumined the walls, which were covered in a dark green patterned material, one of the new amenities made possible by the recent production techniques for printing patterns on large pieces of paper or fabric.

Wilson ordered for both of them, and when the waiter had left them asked Richard almost immediately, "What is a contract Mr. Darrow?"

This was the beginning of a long and detailed explanation of how contract law had developed and what, fundamentally, its present condition was and its importance in law.

Richard had the foresight to bring several quires of paper with him, several pens and ink. He wrote furiously while trying to eat and answer the questions Mr. Wilson fired at him. By the time the two men finished eating, Richard was exhausted.

After dinner, as they stood out in front of the chop house on the pavement Wilson said, "I think we shall omit returning to chambers tonight, Mr. Darrow. I have given you enough to consider, I am sure." Then with a curt nod, "Good evening to you, Mr. Darrow."

"Good evening, sir," Richard said wearily.

The ugly rain had stopped and the violence and duration of the storm had, for a short time, made the air and city seem almost clean. This was the first moment since Mr. Blackwood's offer that Richard had time to consider his new position. His first thought was of Sally. Once he made sure of his situation with both Mr. Barnes and Mr. Blackwood, he was resolved to ask for her hand. With his increased income, his prospects and the protection of his powerful connections, he felt sure, based on their last visit together, she would say, "yes," to his offer. If Fanny could be found and convinced to accept the shelter of Richard's new home, there would be nothing lacking to his happiness. Was it really only six weeks since he had entered the city, poor and friendless? It seemed hard to believe. Now he was actually able to consider marrying Sally within the year. But it was a sign of the great age in which he lived that one could rise so rapidly and gain such great improvements in situation in so short a time.

When Richard reached The Mitre, the common room was crowded and noisy. Its steamy air held the odors of men, wet wool, cooked cabbage and tobacco. Richard passed through it quickly and went up the stairs to his own little attic room. He sat on the wooden chair with his long legs stuck out in front of him, imagining his future life with Sally. His fatigue had dropped away and one happy picture after another passed through his mind. It was probably the first time in his life he had felt such unalloyed pleasure in the anticipation of the future. It was only later, when he turned down the counterpane before sleep, that he saw Charles Fisk's pamphlet lying on his pillow like a reproach for his happy visions.

Surely, he thought, as he lay down and waited for sleep, it is because we live in a fallen, imperfect world that such terrible contradictions existed between the good and bad in society. People were abused but also raised up by men like Samuelson and Blackwood. The new machines were terrible in what they exacted from workers but great in what they gave back. What could he do, other than obey the laws of man and God and do the duty he saw immediately before him? It was not for him to pass judgment on the great people and events of his time. He would leave that to men like Charles Fisk, men who were certain of their own way. He was, by then, too tired to read the pamphlet his friend had authored. He saw Sally's face rise before him as he found his way into the other world of night where wishes and fears are all given form.

* * *

Richard looked forward to his visit to Mr. Blackwood's house. He was curious beyond measure to see the home of the great man. He had never seen the inside of such a house and had only the vaguest idea of what it would be like. The closest he had ever been to such a place was when he had hunted for Fanny, following the mad old lady past the great villas of west-end London.

On the day of his visit, Mr. Barnes gave him directions to the stable where he would find a horse and a note identifying Richard to the chief groom. The bright sunshine of the countryside as he rode out of town added even greater brilliance to the extraordinary occasion of his visit: to be riding to Mr. Blackwood's manor on horseback as an invited guest almost seemed a dream to the young man. As a teacher, Richard also looked forward to teaching Emily, undoubtedly the most intelligent child he had ever met. All that was really necessary with her, he felt, was to introduce a subject and then stand by to answer questions while the little girl eagerly drank up new knowledge. Of course, there would be things that would not be easy or pleasant for her but he sensed that self-discipline would never be a problem with the extraordinary child. Her hardships, tempered with the kindness and affection of Mr. Blackwood, had added to the gifts of her native character. Mrs. Peevey loved learning and had passed that affection on to the little girl, providing the best of all foundations to an education. Nor had Richard's thoughts about teaching ever been corrupted by the use of mechanical repetitions and dull formulae. His ideas about teaching had been formed by Wilney's enthusiasm and natural ability, and the great good fortune of having had mostly good learning experiences himself.

Richard rode north out of Manchester and then skirted the mill town of Bolton, which stood at the edge of the Manchester coal fields. He had no desire to see the town or the "black country" farther to the west. If anything, he thought, the misery of the mill operatives and miners would be more concentrated in a smaller town than in the city. The farther north he went, the fresher the air and once away from the scars of industry, the green, rolling landscape delighted him with its beauty. As he continued northward, the mountains of Yorkshire rose in the distance. Finally, after a ride of more than fifteen miles, the sandstone and iron gates of Blackwood's home marked the entrance to the estate.

"Blackdale," as Mr. Blackwood styled the manor he had built was a handsome building of classical lines constructed in the light reddish-brown stone of the region, the same that had been used in Manchester for the Chetham Library, hundreds of years before. The distance from the gates of the property to the house was a feature all guests noted, and Blackwood had wisely preserved enough of the old timber to have some truly majestic trees in the park around his house. The great trees stretched high above the sloping ground and had been thinned to provide enough light for the lawn and seemingly random patches of wildflowers. The effect was a handsome informal combination of garden and park, ideal for walking, riding or any form of outdoor entertainment.

To the rear of the house, the ground was open to permit views of the long slowly curving hills of the moors whose colours changed so beautifully with the seasons. To a city-dwelling young man as inexperienced as Richard, Blackdale and its park seemed like a paradise.

Only moments after his arrival in front of the great building, Emily came out to him. The perfectly trained servants asked him no questions but simply took the horse and led it away.

"Mr. Richard, I was afraid you might be late. I finished reading "Oliver Twist" and I have so many questions."

Richard smiled and took the child's hand which she offered so artlessly as she led him off to a large outdoor table not far from the house. Richard was a little sorry not to see the beautiful Pamela, but he had no time for such regret since Emily was, even as they walked, asking one question after another. And finally, the uncanny child put her finger directly on the weakness of Dickens' early book.

"All of the reasons for things happening come right at the end of the story. I think they should come mixed into the story," she said.

"Well, you have many good ideas, miss. I think you should write them down and send them to Mr. Dickens."

"You do?"

"I should like to see how well you can express yourself in writing."

"Oh, you mean we shall not really put it in the post bag?" said Emily, sounding disappointed.

"If the letter is clear and expresses your thoughts clearly, I promise that I shall get the address of Mr. Dickens' publishers and we shall post it." Emily was up and running toward the house almost before Richard had finished speaking.

"Don't leave, please, Mr. Richard. I shall just get some paper and a pen."

In the first few moments while he was free to contemplate again the beautiful park, Richard heard the soft singing notes of a pianoforte, seemingly carried by the wind.

Though the young man didn't know it, he listened to the opening theme of Bach's Goldberg Variations played by Pamela. The beautiful fall sunshine, the magnificent park and house and the music that floated toward him all combined to form a memory that the young man would treasure. Then, the faces of Charles Fisk and Charles Wilney appeared in his thoughts.

"Surely," he said to the images of his friends. "Such great beauty could not exist without goodness residing in this house. I must believe that it is so. I cannot believe that the Lord would permit his Enemy to have any hold in a place such as this."

Chapter 14

Simon Oakley, the young man who had joined Fisk's followers, chose the factory where the accident would take place with great care. When the steam boiler exploded the workers would be at lunch. No one would be hurt but the machines would be destroyed, with luck, the factory itself would catch fire. Simon did not tell Fisk of his plans. He wanted to keep his inspiration hidden and then produce evidence that the "accident" had been of his making. He particularly wanted Fisk to acknowledge and praise his achievement. In a few short weeks, Simon had come to admire the visionary carpenter more than anyone he had ever known. Fisk's fire, his vision and the purpose he had given to Simon's life, made the young man ready to die for his chosen leader and his cause. He often appeared at Fisk's workshop early in the morning with a freshly baked loaf and would then spend the entire day watching Fisk work, helping him in small ways around the shop. He spoke little, for in proportion as he felt Fisk great, he felt himself small.

Fisk could see that the young man was burning to act and prayed to find a task for him, One evening after the young man had left the shop, Fisk saw a daemon sitting in the shadows in one corner of the room. By this time, Fisk had seen many creatures of the upper and lower air, angels and devils. His experiences were similar to Emmanuel Swedenborg's reported conversations with devils and angels. So Fisk had no fear of the fierce looking creature he saw floating in a corner of his studio. It somewhat resembled Blake's etching, "The Soul of a Flea." It was a creature whose unquenchable thirst for strong emotions of human suffering had been attracted by Simon's longing and emptiness.

"What do you want here?" Fisk asked.

"I enjoy your friend. He feeds on himself."

"I fear that is not good for him," Fisk answered. "I fear he will one day burn up in his own fire."

"You feed his fire," the devil said in a genial tone.

"I?"

"He loves you and burns to win your praise."

"I would prefer he did not."

"But he gives off such a heat with his yearnings. His desire is very pure. It could be harnessed to almost any object."

"Begone, spirit. I like you not at all. You are a parasite, like the flea you resemble. I banish you now."

Fisk was displeased with what the devil had said about Simon because he knew it was true. The young man's desire to act was a palpable pressure on Fisk to plan something specific that would satisfy his followers and strike at the forces he had seen coalesce as the iron beast. He had believed when he saw the New Jerusalem that his next acts would be inspired, that a vision would always show him the way, but as yet, none had spoken of how to begin destroying the monster of the age. He had the weapons from Newcastle hidden now, in the east end of the city on the Surrey side of the Thames. He knelt down on some folded canvas and began to pray to quell the vague feeling of uneasiness that he felt growing within himself, but rather than waning, the feeling grew stronger. His inner vision saw nothing. All was dark and empty. Gabriel seemed to have deserted him. He waited for some time while the shadows grew longer and twilight darkened the corners of his shop, but no one spoke to him.

He was relieved and puzzled the next day when Simon did not come. Fisk worked steadily on the table he was making, part of the same dining set as the chairs he had shown Cynthia. The wood felt good in his hands. He felt grateful for the certainty and solidity of his craft when all else seemed uncertain and evanescent. He kept thinking of Gabriel, the angel who had shown him the New Jerusalem.

"I beg you, speak to me again," he said to the image of his vision that he carried in his mind, but all was silent but for the sound of his tools as they shaped the wood.

As night drew on, he tried once more to pray but his unease was even greater than the day before.

"What have I done?" he asked out loud. "Why have you deprived me of your guidance? Why am I separated from my own inspiration?"

Just as his own voice died away, there was a knock at his door. When he opened it, he saw Cynthia standing on his threshold with a bundle slung over her back. She looked more worn than when he had seen her last. She obviously needed rest and to leave the thick air of the place she worked.

"I hope you were sincere in what you said to me, for I cannot go back," she said. Her voice was hoarse.

"I am glad, indeed, to see you Cynthia. Walk in."

"Am I disturbing you? You look distracted."

"I am. I am feeling a little lost."

"You? Lost? Surely, not you."

"Oh, yes. I am only a man, Cynthia."

"A man who talks to angels."

"That is part of what is troubling me. They are silent."

"Why should that be? Where shall I put my things?"

"Here, I shall take them for you."

He took the bundle from her and carried it to the corner away from his tools, where he had his bed. He spoke to her as he crossed the big room. I don't know why they are silent. I did not call them in the first place. Perhaps they have deserted me."

"No," she said. "You were chosen by them to do their work. I feel sure of it."

He came back to her and took her hand in his. "May I borrow some of your certainty tonight?"

"Yes," she said, allowing herself to be drawn close to him.

Before the sun had risen again, Fisk had told Cynthia all he could about his inner life. He was particularly anxious that she should not think him a prophet or wise beyond other men.

She was kind and generous and spoke her understanding in soft tones, but her dry coughs often punctuated her speech.

"I like you for yourself and what I know you can teach me," she told him. "I do not expect more. If your vision is dark for a time, perhaps you will need me all the more. I should like that."

Days passed and turned into weeks but Simon did not reappear. Fisk knew that the relief the young man's absence gave him was without value, for it begged the question of what he should do next with the people who had decided to follow him. There were eight of them, now. Joseph Becker was an apothecary who had a vast collection of spiritually oriented books. He was particularly enamoured of Jane Lead's Philadelphians, a very secretive mystical group which had thrived some forty years earlier. Becker had been drawn to Fisk because of the carpenter's first-hand visions and revolutionary sentiments. He was more interested in visions and metaphysics than social change, so he was the least discontent with Fisk's inaction. But the other six men, all of whom had worked in the factories of the northern cities, were impatient to express their anger and dissatisfaction with the incarnation of the iron beast they had encountered in the factory system.

Had it not been for Cynthia's support and confidence in him, the carpenter would have felt alone and empty without his celestial visitors. He consoled himself in the steady glow of Cynthia's affection and faith. He worried about the cough that never completely left her. He tried to stop her from doing any work in the house, but she would not listen. Each day after his work, as Cynthia cleaned his shop and made food for them, he strove to understand his blankness. Before his vision of the New Jerusalem, he had presentiments of the world of light when he read Blake's words or those of other great teachers, such as Boheme and Swedenborg. After his vision, the tangible reality of the spiritual world was the most powerful fact of his existence. Now, that world had been withdrawn from him. The world of man seemed much darker and more dense to the carpenter than ever before.

Had it not been for Cynthia, he would have felt the loss of his spiritual companions as despair. He spoke less often in public and met with his followers only once a week to read the Bible, Blake and other inspired teachers. When the others asked him for guidance in understanding the texts, he tried to respond, but given his own inner darkness, he felt like a mountebank. Some of those who had been drawn to him drifted away because there was no active programme, but he couldn't go forward without a feeling of connection to the world of spirit. His own inspiration, of which he'd felt so certain, was gone. The last vision he'd had was of the daemon who had been attracted by Simon's hunger.

One morning, after Cynthia had gone to market, there was a light tap at his door and Fisk opened it to see Simon standing before him. He had on new clothes and wore a strange self-satisfied smile.

"Simon, how are you? I have been concerned about you."

"Well, enough. And you? What steps have you been taking against the Iron beast?"

"None."

"Well, I have brought you a programme for terrorizing the high and mighty that will make the nation ring. Here," he said, handing Fisk a folded newspaper.

Fisk opened the journal. The headline read: Twelve Killed in County's Worst
Factory Accident.

"What is this?" Fisk asked the younger man.

"This was no accident, Fisk. I did it."

"What do you mean?"

"I caused it. I exploded the boilers that drove the machines and the factory burned. If the men hadn't rushed in to save the building where they sweated their lives away, no one would have died. But the great thing is, no one has the least idea it was anything more than an accident. Don't you see, this is how we can pursue our goals. We can cause as many accidents as we like and no one will know. We can wreak our destruction one factory at a time. This is the result of my own technical training. We can train some of the others how to strike the machines as well. Then we will tell the world how and why it happened. They will never know where we will strike next. They will never know who we are. Is it not fine? Are you not pleased? I did it for you, Fisk."

Fisk began to notice a strange sound as Simon was speaking. It began like a hissing from a boiling kettle and gradually became deeper and louder until it grew into a gale. He could hear nothing else and could see only a gray light around himself which grew darker and darker. Then, Gabriel came to him. Tears were running down his face.

Fisk suddenly understood the months of silence.

"Angels cannot be connected with any taking of human life," he told Cynthia later. "They were afraid that I was going to act with Simon. They told me that we must not take life under any circumstances, no matter how justified it may seem. The Great Laws are such that it is simply impossible to achieve our goal if we harm others."

"What will you do, then?" Cynthia asked him.

"Pray, wait for guidance, listen to my celestial friends."

"What about Simon?"

"I will go and talk to him. All he could see was that I fell down in what looked like a faint. He tried to revive me and when he could not, went outside and waited for you to return. I fear he will be disappointed and angry when I tell him we must give up any violence. These people he killed and the factory that was destroyed was done largely, I believe, to please me. A devil warned me of it."

"A devil? You are listening to devils now? I am frightened for you, Fisk."

"You know by now that they are more to be pitied than feared. You have read the conversations of the great Swedish master I gave you. They are little more than nuisances unless you put yourself into their power through your own thoughts and acts."

"This other world you live in is difficult for me to comprehend," Cynthia said, "but how I should like to see as you do," she said.

"If you are in earnest, my dear, I believe you shall. But it is not to be comprehended. We are not great enough for that. When an angel speaks to me, I know he cannot tell me the full truth he knows because I could not grasp it. So he tells me what little I can understand. But do not be frightened. We are safe from daemons. It is men who worry me."

"If you tell me that," she said, holding herself tightly against his side, "I shall not be afraid." He put his arms around her and later they had a quiet dinner together and then sat in bed, listening to the rain drumming on the workshop.

The following day came gray, quiet and weeping softly, like an exhausted child. Banks of fog were deep and impenetrable. The moisture in the air had been bad for Cynthia. She had coughed much in the night and she was still sleeping restlessly. The sun was a vague orange blot when Fisk got dressed and left the shop to set off for Simon's lodging house. It was a day when the world of vision peculiarly overlapped the world of men. Several times, reflected in the fog, Fisk saw insubstantial faces of daemons, creatures whom he knew were connected with Simon. It made him worry about the younger man. It was not good that creatures of the lower air were so attracted to him. It meant there was some strong correspondence between Simon's thoughts and those of the daemons. He would warn his friend when he saw him.

As he approached Simon's rooming house there was a foul odour in the air. It was sweet with corruption and rot. It was the smell of hell's own wickedness. It increased his anxiety about Simon. Standing on the threshold of the building was a large, menacing devil.

"You are not wanted here," it said and moved toward him threateningly.

"You cannot frighten me, spirit. You have no hold on me. Why do you stand between me and my friend?"

The daemon made a menacing sound like the growl of a large dog, but Fisk ignored this and passed right through the insubstantial body. The creature became a wisp of smoke and trailed him up the stairs to Simon's room, wrapping them both in the stink of hell. The smell dissipated as Fisk knocked on the door.

In the bright lamp light of the room, the vapours of the other world seemed to clear, but Fisk realized that this was only a semblance to make him think the evil creatures were gone. He felt there was danger but stepped into the room anyway. The daemons could not hurt him, but Simon might.

"Hello, Simon."

"Fisk, I am glad to see you well. You gave me quite a turn yesterday."

"I am sure I did. I apologize."

"Are you all right now?"

"You know, Simon, there are many foul spirits about you in this room. Come out with me for a walk."

"A walk? In this weather? Come over by the fire and have something to take the damp out of you."

Fisk did not argue. He took off his coat and sat down. Simon's eyes were preternaturally bright.

"Well, now that I know you are well, what do you think of my programme?"

"We cannot use violence, Simon. I have been wrong. For almost the entire time you were away, I had no visions. Then, when you showed me the paper, reporting on the accident, I saw Gabriel weeping. He told me that we cannot kill others no matter what our goal."

A strange unnatural smile twisted itself across Simon's thin face. His sharply cut features cast a strangely distorted shadow upon the white mantle.

"You mean, you did not invent it, so it cannot be used."

"No, Simon. I tell you, Gabriel told me, ordered me, not to."

"Well, I have presentiments of my own, Fisk. And they tell me that you don't want me or anyone else to have anything to say about accomplishing our ends. It is very convenient to have one's own guardian angel to tell one what to do and give one authority. Up until now, I have believed you and done everything to please you. Look," he said, holding up a pamphlet. "I even paid to have some of your ideas printed for others to read. You can take them with you when you go. Now, I shall follow my own inner voices and so will some of the others. John Cary among them. I have already told him about my programme and he is ready to back it, financially. So, what do you think of that, Mr. Fisk?"

Fisk shrugged. "I only came here today, Simon, because I was concerned about you. I sensed that some spirits of a lower order were drawing close to you."

"My ideas and my plans are inspired by spirits of a lower order. But yours come from the angels," he said in a sneering voice as he turned and put his back to the fire. You know what I think, Fisk? I think you are the falsest of prophets."

"I never claimed to be a prophet, Simon."

"Oh, you let us all follow you as if you were one while you were being so modest and self-effacing. I think in future, I shall follow my own plans with my friends. You may join us or not, as you choose."

Fisk stood up, went to the coat tree and took his pea jacket. "I am sorry, Simon, that you choose this. Truly, I am. Please be watchful. You have enemies all around, even if you don't see them."

"Oh, yes, you would like me to believe that and lose my resolution. Well, I'm not going to."

"Very, well, Simon. God bless you."

"Don't forget your pamphlets, Fisk. I don't need them any longer."

Fisk caught the small bundle that Simon threw at him.

As soon as he stepped out into the hallway and closed the door, the smell of corruption finally ceased altogether.

Chapter 15

After the disastrous dinner with Pamela, Paul and Samuelson, Blackwood had insisted on another visit. The opportunity for the expansion of his business was too great a chance to be passed up easily. After much negotiation with Pamela, she had finally agreed to be present at table with Paul and Samuelson, but adamantly refused to speak one word to the young man or to sit next to him. She seemed to feel that the merest suggestion that she might marry someone who kept a prostitute touched her sense of feminine dignity at its deepest and most tender place. Music had entirely supplanted her interest in meeting handsome young men, even meeting them at fashionable balls in London. Two events had become defining experiences for her, the lesson with Bruckner and seeing Paul with Fanny. They had combined to set her character into a firm mould that Blackwood would never have anticipated.

He hoped that if they kept bringing the young people together, eventually, Pamela could be shown the advantages of being married to Paul. Samuelson, for his part, could not understand why Blackwood didn't exert more parental pressure on Pamela.

"If your hand were really firm, Blackwood, she would do as you told her," the railway giant had said.

Blackwood found the suggestion of coercion crude. He attributed it to Samuelson's navvy background. He also knew that pressure would not work with Pamela, not now. She had already sold her jewels and deposited the money in her own bank account. She was of age and she was in deadly earnest about making herself independent.

"She has lived without a mother for many years and has had her way in most things," Blackwood replied. "I cannot simply tell her what to do. She will not do it. She would leave home and go on the stage before she would comply with an order to marry."

"Well, is the future of the northern railways to be balked by a girl, then?" Samuelson had asked.

"I think we must be patient and Paul must exert himself to create a better impression."

This conversation had resulted in a bellicose encounter between Paul and his father in Samuelson's hotel suite.

"No, I will not get rid of my ' whore,' as you put it," the young man said angrily. "I will not live for your business interests. I..."

Paul's sentence was cut off by Samuelson's huge hand striking his cheek, knocking him against the wall. The big man closed with the younger and grasped him by the throat, pining him against the hotel room door as easily as if he were holding a puppy.

"These are not merely my interests," Samuelson said through his clenched teeth. "We are talking about the history, the future of a nation, an empire, you idiot boy. I do not act for my interests but for Britain's. I would have hoped, by now, that you would understand as much. Do you think I could have climbed this far only to enrich and enlarge myself? Ahhh," he finished in a tone of disgust as he released his son. "I offer you a place in history and you quibble over the price of a whore."

Samuelson walked to the decanter, took two glasses, filled them and handed one to Paul.

"You have no idea of what I have done to achieve what I have. No idea of what I have sacrificed. Perhaps one day I shall tell you. I wonder how you will like it?"

"All I desire is to live a life of my own choosing," Paul replied as he tossed back a large portion of his drink.

"A life of poverty and disgrace?" Samuelson shot back.

"Fanny cannot do that to you, to us. What are you threatening me with?"

Samuelson was quiet for a moment as he looked into his glass.

"It is not I who threatens, Paul." he said in a tone become suddenly quiet and reflective. "You have no idea how easy it is for any man to slip down the steep slope of society's approval and slide to the bottom."

"Well, certainly," Paul said, finishing his drink, "it won't be Fanny who brings us to that precipice. No one cares enough about her even to notice her presence at the hotel."

"No," Samuelson agreed. "It would not be Fanny who would bring us low. But she can block a very advantageous marriage that could make you powerful and wealthy for the rest of your life. Blackwood's settlement alone would make you independent of me forever."

"And you would let me have it in my own name? You would not try to keep it from me?"

"If you marry Blackwood's daughter, you shall have the settlement for yourself. Here is my hand on it," he said reaching out his huge hand.

As much as he distrusted his father, Paul knew that this phrase was a guarantee that the famous railwayman had never broken. It was known throughout the length and breadth of England how Samuelson would make a binding contract with a simple handshake.

Paul took his hand and at the same time wondered where he could hide Fanny, now.

Paul would have cut off his right arm rather than give up Fanny. The totally uninhibited pleasures she offered him as a fond partner were not to be found easily in the England of Victoria's reign. Apart from her exotic appearance, she would do things with him that would make a whore blush, and he was convinced that she was sincerely fond of him. Everything about her body fascinated Paul. The way her skin felt. The way she touched him and made love with him, not with the jaded movements of a whore but with all the enthusiasm of a young girl's first love, an enthusiasm that was rarely experienced in the marriage beds of the time. Fanny let him explore every inch of her body with his fingers, his tongue, anything. The sexual fascination that she had for Paul had mesmerized him from their first encounter on the night they'd left her market stall. He had thought he was merely picking up another tramp from the street, albeit a very handsome one. But once alone, Fanny had leapt on him like some great jungle cat, tearing at his clothes and riding him hard until he lay exhausted under her gently swaying body that sought more pleasure even after he was spent.

Paul had no conscience about lying to his father. He would do anything to free himself from Samuelson. Once he married Pamela and got the settlement, he and Fanny could do what they liked. More than anything else, Paul wanted to be free of his father's suffocating presence.

Paul's mother had simply faded away in the small Scottish cottage where Samuelson had marooned her and the boy, completely isolating them in the lonely wilderness of the highlands. Among the heather and stony hills, shut in by thick forests of pine, Paul grew up in the circle of seclusion Samuelson drew around his family. Samuelson visited only often enough to prevent gossip, three or four times a year for perhaps a week at a time. Samuelson's "vacations with his family," as they were referred to in the press usually consisted of a week of salmon fishing by himself amid the lonely, icy cold streams fed by highland snows. As Paul grew up, Samuelson had arranged for a tutor, a young Cambridge graduate named, Phillips. He gave the man a cottage within walking distance of Paul and his mother and paid him so well that no one had ever heard a breath of gossip from him. In fact, after Paul left the seclusion of Scotland, his tutor disappeared into the wild country of Northern India where he was said to have built a tea plantation on a grand scale. Paul never liked the man, whom he knew was entirely his father's creature. It was the sadness of his mother, a tall, pale ghost-like woman who might have been a little pretty once, that had first set Paul against his father. Sometimes as she and her son sat in front of the peat fire in the main hall of the lonely, silent cottage, tears would run down her face, for no reason that her son could see. Sometimes after hugging Paul to her, she suddenly sprang away from him as though he were made of hot iron. Somehow, Paul always believed that this bottomless well of sorrow had to do, not with himself, but with his father.

She spent all day turning the pages of a large, illustrated bible for children. She could not read, nor was Phillips, the tutor, instructed to correct her deficiency.

As Paul grew older, his father paid more attention to him, mostly cross questioning him on his studies, gauging his accomplishments. It was in these sessions that Paul first knew his father's adamantine will and relentless pursuit of the goals he'd set for his son. Paul grew to dread Samuelson's visits. In the later years of her seclusion, Annabelle Samuelson's sadness lapsed into a vague illness that kept her in bed more and more of the time. She slept long hours day and night. Then, one day she sat up suddenly, clapped her hand to her forehead and cried out, "God forgive me," and died. Neither Paul nor any of the servants could imagine what the poor, unhappy woman needed God to forgive her. Paul was seventeen.

After his mother's death, Paul moved to his father's house in London where he realized for the first time just how rich and what a public figure his father was. Here, another Scotsman began to train him in business matters, Samuelson's confidential secretary, John Booth. For two years, Booth cleaned up after Paul's mistakes in arithmetic and bookkeeping. Then, in disgust, Samuelson gave his son an allowance and told him not to get into trouble, by which he meant public scandal. This was two years before the proposed marriage to Pamela. Father and son had seen little of each other before the trip to Manchester.

The sudden shift from the isolation of the Highlands to Britain's greatest town, from close scrutiny to complete freedom resulted in Paul's living the dissolute life of a wealthy man's idle son. His isolation hadn't made him thoughtful, only resentful of any authority and arrogant with those he considered beneath him. His favourite sport was picking up working girls willing to give up their virtue for a price, girls who had not yet become regular prostitutes. He thought himself a connoisseur at distinguishing girls of the demimonde from established professionals. This had been his daily round up to the time he met Fanny. His desire to keep her to himself and her desire to be kept had resulted in a large, nicely appointed apartment over an upholsterer's shop in the neighbourhood of Vauxhall Walk, not far from the bridge of the same name on the Surrey side and near the site of the once famous Vauxhall Gardens. Here the two set up housekeeping while Richard had searched for his sister with poor old Maudie far to the north in Kensington, on the other side of the Thames.

Paul also had a room in his father's house where he put in the occasional appearance to ask Booth for money or to be present for a particularly important dinner or triumph of his father's. This helped keep his relationship with Fanny from becoming a commonplace domestic arrangement, though the girl's own moodiness and the days on end when she withdrew into total silence helped to keep Paul's undeveloped emotional nature off-balance. For, under his resentment and arrogance was the heart of an abandoned child that longed for affection and approval. Fanny's laughter or long silences that alternated with her fits of heat kept Paul completely fascinated and always hungry for her, always trying to draw her out and elicit expressions of affection. Though he had begun as the seducer, in the months that followed their meeting, Fanny's stronger character had made her the one who controlled the ebb and flow of their physical and emotional relationship. She was with Paul mostly as an alternative to costering. She liked him, but did not love him. It would have been Paul who suffered if they were separated. He could not bear the thought of being without her, while she grew more and more self-reliant. So for Paul, the financial freedom that marriage to Pamela offered was irresistible. Fanny was indifferent to the other woman, confident of her own power and glad for Paul to have a seemingly inexhaustible source of money that could not be withdrawn. She was fond enough of Paul so that she hated to see him brow beaten by his father. In this, she was genuinely sympathetic. These were the reasons the pair had not separated even when Paul went to Manchester to court Pamela. Now that they had been seen, Paul would have to find some secluded country cottage for Fanny while he tried to convince Pamela to marry.

* * *

The weeks that followed Richard's first lesson with Emily were the happiest of his life. If Sally and Fanny had been with him, all his hopes would have been fulfilled. Three days a week, he enjoyed the long, slow rides out to Blackdale where he was engaged with the brilliant child, often teaching her as they sat out in the beautiful park during the unusually warm fall afternoons. Every so often, Mr. Blackwood would appear, placing himself just within hearing distance of teacher and pupil. He never stayed long or spoke, but it seemed to Richard that he was well pleased with what he heard. The dire predictions of Fisk's pamphlet, which Richard had finally read, about a future filled with world cataclysm because of man's machines and the greed that powered them sounded especially absurd when he sat on the lawn with Emily at Blackdale. Each time he arrived beneath the mighty trees of the great park in the dappled sunlight of late afternoon, he saw a true picture of what man could achieve and the greatness of Britain's industry. At times he was so content and happy that he felt guilty for not yet finding Fanny, even though all his hard work at Mr. Barnes' chambers was done with her as well as Sally in his thoughts. He, was still equivocal about the profession of law. However, his grasp of the fundamentals of the common law was progressing, and even Wilson occasionally said a word of praise about his choice of case law citations. His knowledge of classical languages had continued to prove useful. Mr. Barnes took great delight in baffling many of his adversaries by adding long quotations and comments written in Latin or even Greek, comments which Richard reviewed and corrected in his own room away from chambers.

By late fall there began to be snow on the distant Yorkshire hills, visible across the green plain where Manchester stood. Richard had become so accustomed to the smooth course of his life in Manchester, he was almost resigned to Fanny's disappearance. None of Mr. Barnes' enquiries had borne fruit. The villain with the sword cane had vanished like a ghost, though it was suspected that he had been one of three different spies used by the British in the last war with the "little corporal". Where he had come from or why, no one knew or could guess.

Pamela continued her lessons with Bruckner and steadfastly refused to consider marriage with Paul. Richard heard that the great railwayman and his son were planning to spend part of the winter in Manchester, at least through the Christmas season.

Things continued in this easy, uneventful way until a damp, chilly morning late in November. Ice had started forming in some of the streets. Rooks called down hungrily to the people below. A cold, whistling wind cut intermittently through the town, rattling loose panes of glass, warning of harsh months ahead. As he trudged along, braced against the damp chill wind, Richard looked forward to the coal fire which he knew would be burning in Mr. Barnes' chambers. When he arrived and opened the familiar door, he was momentarily shocked into immobility by seeing the man who had abducted his sister sitting in the outer office. Paul saw Richard moments sooner and rushed past him out of chambers into the corridor. By the time Richard had recovered himself, Paul was out of sight. The schoolmaster ran down the hall in the direction of the outer doors. He jumped down the steps at so break-neck a pace that he nearly fell. Regardless of his efforts, Richard finally found himself looking out of the building with no sign of the other man anywhere on the street. Realizing that the chances of finding the man on the crowded streets were poor, Richard turned and raced back into the building to the law offices. He burst into the outer office.

"Mr. Wilson, who was that man?"

Wilson, too surprised at what he had just witnessed to do anything other than answer said, "That was Mr. Samuelson, the younger, Mr. Darrow. And I am most surprised that I must remind you of the dignity of these chambers."

At that moment the great solicitor himself entered the chambers. Richard's appearance and Wilson's scowl alerted him immediately.

"Sir," Richard said. "I have just seen the man who abducted my sister. Mr. Wilson says he is Mr. Samuelson, the younger. I demand to know where this villain is, sir. I cannot believe you have him as a client, sir. I chased him but.."

"Richard, you will stop and listen to me quietly," Barnes said, holding up his hand. "I am conducting some business for Mr. Samuelson at Mr. Blackwood's request. His son was supposed to meet me this morning..."

"Sir, this is the man..."

"Richard. You must calm yourself, now. Are you ready to listen?"

"Yes, sir. Pardon me, sir."

"That's better. The truth is never got in anger or haste. First point, since I was not here. I cannot be certain that this was Mr. Samuelson the younger. Was that the name given, Wilson?"

"Yes, sir."

"Point two, how long did you look carefully at this man's face before you chased him?"

"Long enough to know him. And he ran when he saw me. Before I knew him."

"Now think carefully, Richard. You chased him, so of course he would run. You also told me that you only saw this man once with your sister and that it was under gaslight, out of doors, on a rainy night."

"I am not mistaken, sir."

"Many, many times, Richard, I have heard witnesses speak, under oath, with absolute certainty only to be proved wrong."

"Sir, I am not mistaken. That was the man. Whose house was the address you had investigated by the private inquiry agent in London? The address I gave you. You told me that the lead had failed. Whose house was it?"

"Richard, I think you should go home until you can speak more rationally. You sound as though you are accusing me."

"I am not accusing you, sir. I only ask that you review the private enquiry agent's report. I only ask that you believe my identification of the man."

"Richard, I must insist you go home for the rest of the day and reflect on two things. First, many certain witnesses are proved wrong every day in courts of law. Two, what is the likelihood that the son of one of the richest and most respected men in the country would abduct a poor costermonger, no matter how beautiful?"

Before Richard could respond, Barnes once again held up his hand.

"Do not answer me now, Richard. I want you to think about these things and give me your thoughts tomorrow. Understood?"

"Yes, sir."

That afternoon, while riding against the sharp wind on the way to his lesson with Emily, Richard resolved to speak to Mr. Blackwood. His reading of law in recent months gave Richard an understanding of the solicitor's reluctance to believe him, but that did not change the fact that he was correct about identifying Samuelson's son as Fanny's abductor. Of course, he knew what Fisk and Tom Weedon would both say: he was being hoodwinked by the rich and powerful, including the solicitor, Barnes. You could not trust any of these men, they were all in league. Richard promised himself that he would not be turned aside by anyone until he found Samuelson's son and Fanny. He could only hope Mr. Blackwood would come to listen to the lesson today. Richard was confident of his kindness and good opinion and was resolved to ask him for advice.

Now that the weather had turned, Richard usually taught Emily in a pleasant small room that had been fitted out with a child's desk and bookshelves next to Blackwood's own library. The industrialist nearly always looked in when he was at home.

Emily was, as usual, waiting eagerly for her tutor. She always met Richard in the large front entranceway when the weather dictated that they were to work inside. The pair then walked through the house's east wing with it's long, sunny picture gallery and prospect of the moors. At the end of the gallery, Blackwood had his library and Emily her little school room.

Each time Richard came, Emily had new questions that the teacher tried to use as the starting point for their lesson.

On that gray afternoon, her question ran: "Mr. Richard, how can I measure the height of the biggest oak on the front lawn without actually holding a ruler to it? I can't think of any way to do it. I am too little to climb such a big tree," she added. "Anyway, Mr. Blackwood says there is a way to do it without a ruler and he said you would teach it to me."

"Well, that would take us into the realm of mathematics, Miss. Many pupils find that subject quite difficult. Are you sure you want to neglect our maps of America we were going to look at in favour of the rudiments of trigonometry?"

"Trigomonetry?"

"No," Richard said, "Trigo-nom-etry."

"Trigonometry," Emily repeated, as they entered her room.

"That's correct."

"Will it give me the head ache?"

"Why should any subject do that?"

"That's what Pamela always says when she does not want to listen to me or Mr. Blackwood. She says it will give her the head ache."

"Trigonometry will not make your head ache, miss. But it is a difficult subject."

Emily thumped down into her wooden seat and cupped her hands under her chin.

"Is it not better to do the difficult thing first? That way I shall not be too tired to do it later. I'll only have the easy thing to do."

"I think that is a very good plan, miss" Richard agreed.

He could hear someone moving about in the next room and then heard voices raised in argument, one of which he knew was Blackwood's. The other, he quickly identified as Pamela. The voices were muffled but very close, just on the other side of the door between the two rooms where Mr. Blackwood had his desk.

"Father, even if I wished to marry, which I do not, I would not marry a man who keeps a prostitute, even if he is Mr. Samuelson's son. You amaze me. It is unthinkable."

"Pamela, it is not fair to condemn the man without speaking with him. I've tried to explain what this alliance could mean for me and for our part of the county."

"I saw what I saw. He touched that beautiful, dark gypsy girl where no man will ever touch me. And she was laughing as he did it, in public. The child saw it too. I do not want to talk about this anymore, Papa. Please consider the subject absolutely concluded."

Richard felt rather than heard her rapid, heavy footsteps retreating from the side of the room near the door where he stood.

"Mr. Richard, do not be worried," Emily said, tapping Richard on the hip. "Pamela is always saying she don't like something when she is not playing the pianoforte. What about trigonometry?"

It took all of Richard's self control not to rush into the next room and question Pamela Blackwood about what she had seen. But her description of a "dark gypsy girl" fitted Fanny well. And Emily had seen it all, too. She would answer his questions artlessly, but his natural respect for the position of trust he had established with the little girl made him shrink from abusing it.

"All right, Emily," he finally answered. "We shall begin trigonometry by discussing triangles."

Through the lesson, Richard kept thinking about the opportunity that had been cast in his way. He now knew that Samuelson's son and Fanny were in Manchester together. If he did try to find out what the little girl knew, he might be able to trace them. As the lesson proceeded, he fought back and forth with himself about questioning the child. It was apparent that Samuelson and Blackwood did have strong reasons to unite their business interests through marriage. The conversation he had overheard seemed to raise a chorus of voices in support of Fisk's views about wealth and the wealthy. Any claim Fanny might have on Samuelson's son would be completely ignored. She would certainly be thrown into the gutter once Pamela gave way.

While the little girl was working on some simple problems, he thought bitterly of the happy preceding months. Indirectly, he had allowed himself to be bought, too, made comfortable enough to let Fanny disappear without a struggle. Blackwood's pressure on his daughter showed how right Fisk was. The rich cared for nothing but wealth and power. The only reason Blackwood was good to his workers was that he was wise enough to know that he would get more work from them that way. Blackwood maintained that he was building the empire's future. Perhaps he was. That did not permit the use of Pamela or any person as a paving stone, something thrown down to make the way to empire smoother. For whom, then, would the empire exist? The suffering he had witnessed among the labouring poor made him suddenly want to pull down the beautiful house and cry out against the easy arguments of improving society and creating employment for the poor. Who made them poor? he suddenly wondered. For a while, he had allowed himself to accept the arguments of his wealthy patrons. But what he had heard that afternoon made him realize that these fine words only masked a more subtle lust for wealth and power. Even a thoughtful man like Blackwood would sell his daughter for a great enough profit. That was the bald fact of the matter. Not one of the respectable working men he had known in London would have dreamt of such a thing. He recalled one of Charles Wilney's favourite sayings: "Either God is there or He is not".

153

By the time Richard rode out of the handsome gates of Blackdale's beautiful park, he felt completely disillusioned. The woman whose child Richard had buried was part of human society. Maudie and the mudlarks of the London waterfront were society. The street arabs and the poor pedlars like Fanny, these were society. The society that Blackwood, Samuelson, Barnes and all their kind claimed to work for would be a society ruled by themselves, new kings, madly chasing wealth. But, in fact, they were not all or even most of society. Yet, it was their interests which were consulted first.
As he rode away from Blackdale, Richard was wrapped in a dark cloud of frustration, sadness and anger. All seemed false and uncertain, but he still had not questioned Emily. There was such complete trust in the child's eyes when he spoke to her, he simply could not trespass against it, even if his questions brought no harm to her. He had thought of many excuses why it would be permissible to gain what he wanted from the child, but he knew they were excuses. He would find Fanny, himself, somehow. Then, perhaps, he would go back to London and join Fisk, return to his old life and ask Sally to marry him. So much had happened and nothing had happened, though he now knew that he would shun the wealthy and their servants as if they were a plague.

He welcomed the sting of the wind and the bite of its chill, a large white moon was rising as he rode back to town in the deepening darkness. The sudden change that day from unseasonably warm weather to the present blast of cold wind, rushing down from the high ground of Yorkshire, matched his mood and made him feel less the pain of his own disappointment in Blackwood and his former grand vision of empire.

That night in his room at the inn, Richard reviewed his resignation from Mr. Barnes' practice. Legally, he had accepted the terms of his articles, but he had little doubt that if he pressed the matter, he would be released, especially once he presented his grievance against Barnes for shielding the son of Blackwood's partner. For in his anger and sorrow, Richard was convinced that all of the wealthy men of his recent acquaintance had betrayed him. He had decided that he would be like Fisk and draw a sharp line between himself and anyone who had the motives and privileges of wealth. He sat in his dark room for hours on the wooden chair , reviewing his life and all the people and places he had known. It seemed that everything had been divided into high and low. The beauty of the wildflowers at Blackdale and the smell of bad privies at the navvy camp; poor Fanny selling her virtue for a gown and the haughty Pamela who would not take an empire for her freedom; burying a child by the roadside and riding along on Mr. Blackwood's handsome horse. The brilliant little Emily taken out of the darkness and mud of a mine by a rich girl's whim and now being trained to serve the purposes of her new guardian. The empire was divided into two parts, the high and the low. The high cared not at all for the lives of the low. Pictures of this deep contrast passed through his mind one after another. He had not read any of Disraeli's novels which spoke of "the two nations," but Fisk's idea of a need for a spiritual revolution seemed less foolish to Richard as he sat through the night in his drafty room. What seemed foolish was the idea that such a war could be won. He felt he would have much to say to Fisk when he got back to London with Fanny, for he was determined to take his sister from her seducer by force, if need be. He would not leave her to be thrown away when Pamela's refusal to marry was finally overcome by her father's will and money.

Chapter 16

Richard left for the law chambers very early the following morning. The light in the sky was only the faintest gray tinged with orange. Frost coated the paving stones of the streets with silver while curtains of mist hung in the autumn air. He wanted to write his resignation at his desk and hand it to Wilson as early as possible. Then, he would be free to search for Fanny. Some of his anger from the previous day had subsided. He was now simply determined to find his sister and sad at the falseness of much of what he had thought worthwhile in his new acquaintances.

Richard had learned that the law building where Mr. Barnes had his chambers retained an old soldier who acted as a footman through the night, allowing access to messengers in case one of the solicitors had urgent letters to send or receive. The door to this man's rooms was just after the entrance to the building. Richard was certain he would have to wake the man up to get into the chambers, so he was very surprised to find carriages standing near the building and servants milling about. He recognized two of the carriages as belonging to Mr. Barnes and Mr. Blackwood. A huge barouche with six horses also waited near the curb.

"What has happened?" Richard asked a haughty looking man in livery who sat atop the barouche.

"A death," the man drawled sleepily.

Without waiting to ask more, Richard leapt up the steps into the building and ran down the hall. The door to Mr. Barnes chambers was wide open. The rooms were brightly lit against the darkness outside. The young man rushed inside.

"Good lord, what has happened?"

The first people he saw were Emily and Pamela. Emily was weeping against Pamela's shoulder. The older girl was white faced and seemed not to notice anything.

"Mr. Richard," Emily said in the watery tones of a child's tearful voice, as she turned and reached up her arms to him.

Richard responded without thinking and took the little girl from Pamela.

"Miss Blackwood," Richard said looking over at Pamela's frozen countenance. "What has happened?" he repeated. But already he felt the chill of a terrible presentiment pass through his body.

"Oh, it is Mr. Darrow," Pamela said, in the manner of one waking from a dream. "My father is dead."

Her voice was flat and lacked any accents of emotion. But as Pamela spoke the words out loud, Emily began a long keening cry, unmuffled by anyone's arm or shoulder. For long moments, Emily's voice was all that Richard heard or knew. Then, suddenly the door to Mr. Barne's office broke open and the solicitor came out.

"Ah, Richard. How fortunate you are here so early. Would you take the young ladies home to Blackdale? We have finished the necessary formalities for now."

In what way this formal statement touched Pamela, Richard never learned but she, now, began to sob. It was unthinkable to Richard to ask for particulars of the death and so he simply reached out his arm that did not hold the child and offered it to Pamela.

"If you'll allow me, Miss Blackwood," he said.

"Thank you," said Pamela with tears trembling in her voice now. She rose, leaning on his arm. The three moved toward the door but before they could pass into the hallway, another voice was heard from Mr. Barnes' office.

"Have your man stop at my son's hotel, Mr. Barnes, and give him this note. I've written the address on the outside."

The tall form of John Samuelson loomed in the doorway. No one thought or said anything, the only sounds in the room were the crying of the two girls: Emily's having grown quieter as her head nodded on Richard's shoulder and Pamela's which grew louder as some of the shock began to fade. Richard thoughts were frozen nothing as he simply took the envelope in hand and all three left the chambers. The strange emptiness that death in the midst of life leaves seemed to envelope the three travelers as they set out in the carriage for Blackdale. It was as if, for a time, the life that had been left a palpable emptiness in the carriage, a space which none of the living could occupy. Each of them was pressed back against the sides of the vehicle. None spoke and it was only when the two girls fell asleep from exhaustion that Richard felt able to reflect on the tragedy that had overtaken his little pupil and her sister. In spite of his bitterness the day before, Richard deeply regretted the death of Blackwood, remembering now only his ready wit and laugh and his handsome, smiling face. His death, Richard knew, would affect many, in addition to the two quiet forms that slept through the jostling of the badly paved road. It could even affect Fanny since, there would no longer be anyone to pressure Pamela into marriage with Paul. Mr. Barnes would lose a large source of income, as well as a friend. Samuelson would not have the Blackwood interests with which to align himself in the north. And given the unrest of the working people in Manchester, the death of a respected and valued employer could erupt into illegal combinations of companies. Only time would tell what the effects of Blackwood's unlooked for passing would be.

During his melancholy journey along the now familiar road to Blackdale, Richard felt for the first time, the personal nature of death. He felt it eclipse all other questions--even of society and morality. It was the first time that death had taken someone the young man had known and liked.

The ride into the gray dawn seemed to last for hours. Then, as the carriage passed in at the gates of Blackdale, Richard suddenly recalled the letter in his pocket, bearing the address of Fanny's seducer. He had ridden out from the valley of shadows back into life. In just minutes after handing Pamela out of the carriage and saying goodbye to Emily, he departed Blackdale on a swift horse borrowed from the stables and was racing back to Manchester with the cold air on his face, bracing him for the confrontation with Paul Samuelson. The familiar road now seemed to fly past the galloping horse. In something just over an hour, he reached his destination: Paul's suburban hotel, away from the center of the city. This was where Paul had taken Fanny after the confrontation with his father.

The new, straggling edges of the town where the hotel was located made Richard think of an uglier version of the north London suburbs where he had taught at Miss Reade's. Here, however, the countryside obstinately obtruded itself into the newly constructed streets. Spindly forests grew between the buildings. The edges of the roads were paved only with grass and weeds. Richard heard an owl hoot to the fading darkness as he tied his horse near the ugly square building whose address matched the railway king's sharply pointed handwriting on the envelope. Damp patches of mold were already appearing on the sides of the new hotel. In the gray light of a wet morning, the place had a dank, unwholesome appearance. A thickset rough-looking man in ill-fitting livery dozed on a barrel as he leaned against the building near its front door.

Since Richard had a real commission to perform, he did not fear identifying himself if the man woke. However, he preferred to find the room himself and surprise the occupants. The man stirred but did not wake as Richard stepped into the lobby. The cheap, bright colours and thin carpet made Richard think of the painted women he'd seen walking the London streets at dawn. The light from the fixtures lighting the staircase were turned down very low, so as Richard started up the wide uneven staircase, his form threw distorted, wavering shadows onto the lobby floor below. The room number on the envelope was two-twelve, and Richard was relieved to see that each accomodation was clearly identified with black numbers on an oval plate of white enamel, quite easy to see in the dim light. A long corridor of several turnings brought him to what he believed would be the crisis in his search for Fanny. He stood in the gray light of the corridor for a moment and paused to pull out the letter and reread the number on the envelope.

Confirming that the number was repeated on the plate in front of him, he softly tried the door. It was unlocked, but within all was silent.

The interior of the apartment was even darker than the hall. Heavy curtains fell across the window. A settee was placed against one wall. Clothes were strewn about. Unwashed plates, some with empty oyster shells and other detritus were piled on tables and chairs. Several empty wine bottles on the floor added to the disorder. The door to the bedroom was ajar. Richard approached it cautiously and looked into the room. The darkness of the room and the odd tangle of bedclothes at first made it difficult for him to resolve the shapes on the bed into something recognizable. Then, slowly, his eyes unwound the sheets from a naked arm, leg and finally male genitals. The pair was fast asleep. The completely uncovered and unclothed Fanny had wrapped herself around the naked male body. One of her delicately formed hands, an aspect of her Richard had always admired, rested in the man's crotch.

"Good God," Richard's voice exploded into the gray padded stillness of the room.

In a reflex of surprise, Paul leapt off the bed and was struck by Richard who thought he was being attacked. Paul fell back against the bottom edge of the bed, the bed struck the night table and a porcelain ewer was smashed against a mirror. A sleepy looking Fanny sat up.

"Richard," she said.

Rushing feet were heard on the stairs and the dozing man in the ill-fitting livery burst into the room a few moments later.

"Oh, I see what sort of a party this is," he exclaimed, at the same time devouring Fanny with his eyes.

Fanny, completely unconcerned at her nakedness got up on her knees to see better who was in the room. For a moment, none of the men could take their eyes from her sinuous body. Then, Richard threw a sheet at her. "For heaven's sake, Fan. Cover yourself."

The center of interest in the room having gone, the big hotel guard rushed at Richard saying, "Now this is a matter for the constables. I arrest you all in the name of the law. I am an official deputy." He finished by holding out a tattered and dirty piece of paper.

Paul huddled on his pants. "You shall pay for this, you lunatic," he shouted at Richard.

"You shall all pay for any damage," the hotel guard bawled.

Once all were fully dressed, they re-convened in the poorly decorated lobby.

Richard had his arm around Fanny's shoulder.

"Poor, dear Fan." He said as he kissed her cheek. "Are you all right? Everything will be all right now, dear. We shall clear this up and you will come away with me."

Fanny pushed him away and detached herself from his arm.

"I don't want to come away with you." She moved to Paul's side.

"Paul is my home, now, Richard."

"Fanny, you don't understand. He's going to cast you off. He is here in Manchester to marry another woman."

"I know. A rich little thing with no feeling for anyone. We plan to live well from her money."

"Fanny!" her brother exclaimed. He turned back to Paul, his fists clenched.

"This is your fault, you monster."

"I told you I was not a good girl, Richard," Fanny said. "Just leave me your kind wishes. I thank you for all the care you've given me, brother. But it will be better for all if you just leave us."

"Don't do this, Fan."

"Please, Richard. I shall be all right."

He looked sadly at her for a few moments and then answered, "Very well, Fanny. If that's what you truly want. I see I failed with you, utterly." "You were a good brother. But I need a man of my own now. Don't you understand?"

"But someone who will marry you."

"There are some things between a man and a woman more important than words in a church."

"Oh, Fanny!"

She touched his cheek in the old gentle coaxing way. "Let us part friends. The good, dear friends we have always been. I am sorry to displease you so."

He turned away from her abruptly and before any member of the now fully awake hotel staff could stop him, he handed his card to the hotel guard and said, "This is my place of business. I am a solicitor's man and can be found at this address during business hours. I will defend any legal action to the utmost and, I am sure, to the disadvantage of your hotel. Good day." He started to the door and then turned back to Paul.
"This is yours," he said reaching into his pocket. He handed him his father's letter.

As Richard rode Blackwood's horse back to the stable in Manchester, the cool air made him suddenly feel his own fatigue. The events of the last twenty-four hours seemed to weigh on him all at once. He left the horse at the stables and stumbled, exhausted, through the streets. When he reached the inn, all was strangely quiet, but Richard hardly noticed. He was too tired to do anything but go to his room and sleep.

He would see Mr. Barnes later in the day, tell him what had happened with Fanny and give him his resignation. He was too tired even to console himself by thinking of seeing Sally again. He saw no one downstairs but went to his tiny attic room, lay down on his bed and immediately dropped into a deep sleep.

* * *

Richard woke in darkness. Rough hands were shaking him.

"Richard, Richard," someone was whispering in his ear.
He sat up suddenly. Tom Weedon was standing near him, a candle in one hand.

"Tom," Richard said hoarsely.

"Shh," the big man replied, putting his finger to his lips. "There may still be some constables or soldiers downstairs."

"Soldiers? Constables?"

"I warned you about that pamphlet, Richard. There is a warrant now for Charles Fisk on the charge of sedition. They want to hang him in London, but they are afraid to arrest him. They are afraid of his preaching liberty for all in God's name. His words and visions unite the pious and the working men. Here in the north, matters are even more dangerous for the gentry and the factory owners. They are uneasy here even with the infantry and cavalry barracks they've got here and in Salford. They all fear strikes or worse. Now that you're a wanted man, I can tell you that we are making weapons at Newcastle and shipping them to London to some friends of your friend, Fisk. We will have the Charter, one way or another. We must. All Europe is rising. The gentry is terrified that what happened in France will happen here and they know that the men of Manchester and Birmingham are the staunchest Chartists. That's why they've begun making Manchester an armed camp. I told you not to let anyone see that pamphlet. It was found at your office and the soldiers were fetched."

"Not by Mr. Barnes?"

"Oh, someone much more dangerous. The king of railways, himself, ordered the soldiers to look for you."

"How do you know all this, Tom?"

"Stubbs, the old porter at your law chamber, is one of us. He came round as soon as it happened. Samuelson was there, giving orders to the soldiers as if he were their general. And some of our people have told me that you had a fight with his son in a hotel, early this morning. A young lady was involved. A good day's work for one man, Darrow."

"My sister, Tom. The one I was looking for."

"It was Samuelson's son who took her? God's blood, man, you've made yourself a deadly enemy. Any road, with things as they are right now, they'll hang you for nothing. All the rich here shake with terror in their beds, except Blackwood, the squire who just died. You cannot stay here. I waited until it was dark before waking you. It is just luck that they have not yet searched up here in the attics. But they will come back if they don't find you elsewhere. Some soldiers were seen riding out of town towards the great manor house of Blackdale."

"Yes, they might look there," Richard nodded."Tell, me, Tom. I am in your hands. What shall I do. I have no experience with this sort of thing."

"Aye. But we need learned men like you, Darrow."

"Tom, in the last twenty-four hours, I've realized that there can be no trust between the rich and poor without the legal equality of the Charter."

"Those are true words, Darrow."

A noise from the bottom of the attic ladder made both men start.

"Get your things and come with me," Tom said. "There must not be any sign of you here."

"Where shall we go, Tom?"

"You're fortunate that we are sending a shipment of arms to London in several days time from Liverpool. You shall travel with them by barge. You'll leave here in my kitchen wagon, stuffed between sacks of potatoes, which I can say I am selling to another inn, if asked. The soldiers who watch the roads won't lift two hundred pounds of spuds from your back to look underneath. It won't be a pleasant ride, but it will be better than being caught. Once we are away from the city, I'll lift the sacks and you can sit up. Now, let's depart. No more talking. Step as quietly as possible. The horses are already hitched."

So Richard left Manchester on a clear night, beneath a moon he could not observe, buried under many sacks of potatoes, a hunted man with enemies at every turn. He lay down in the wagon and was soon insensible of everything except the weight of the potatoes that were piled on him. When the movement of the wagon over the ground began, it hammered him against the rough wooden floor. The bruising ride seemed to last forever, but it was actually only a few minutes later when the wagon stopped for some moments. Faintly, he could hear Tom speaking to someone and then the jolting, crushing ride began again. From the harder jostling of the wheels on the poor paving, Richard knew they were now setting out on the roads outside the town and away from the watchful eyes of the soldiers. It seemed an eternity before the wagon stopped again. Moments later, Richard felt the crushing weight lifted from him.

"Now sit up against the sacks, Darrow, and I'll arrange them round you so that from a distance you will still be hidden. If there are patrols on the roads, we shall be seen and stopped in this brilliant moonlight. But I am going to travel by way of Blackdale where we know the soldiers have already searched. I think they'll be loath to disturb the family again in their grief. Especially with Mr. Blackwood having been so thick with the railway king."

"Why are we riding north, Tom?"

"Because it is less likely the soldiers will look that way."

The big man went around to the front of the wagon and resumed his seat.

"Don't talk. Voices carry strangely through the hills."

"I understand," Richard answered.

The moonlight gave the long hills and patches of fog a strange glamour. Richard could almost feel that he had left the world he'd known altogether and entered the world inhabited by the faerie, which the farmers and people of the countryside still talked of and feared. Here and there he could see the scraps of uncultivated ground that had been left for the fair Folk, left so the supernatural denizens would not hold their revels and ceremonies in proximity to humans.

The slowly curving hills bent down and up in the ghostly light. From high ground all that could be seen were more hills with more shadowy declivities between. Occasionally, small silvery patches of fog would cling to the lowest point between two hills. On the steepest inclines, Richard jumped out of the wagon to make the task easier for the two great white cart horses who, lit by the moon, their breath steaming in the chill air, also looked like spirits from another world.

The moon had begun to set and Richard was walking alongside the wagon as they were approaching one of the deepest points in a dingle that lay not far from Blackdale. A thick patch of fog hovered across the road. Suddenly the wagon stopped and Richard felt his blood drain out of his head and upper body. Coming straight toward them, seeming to float out of the silvery fog was a tiny robed figure.

"Heaven protect us," Weedon exclaimed.

At his exclamation the small figure began to run off the road and into the darkness.

The stride of the small figure identified it to Richard as a child rather than any supernatural apparition. He ran after it into the heather. The vegetation caught and pulled at both Richard and the small figure he pursued, but the man's longer legs gave him the advantage and he quickly had his arms around the child.

"Emily!" Richard exclaimed as the moon caught the child's face. "What are you doing here?"

"Oh, Mr. Richard, Mr.Richard. Help me. I am going home."

"Home? But what are you doing out here? You are walking toward the town, not toward Blackdale."

"I am going home to the mine, Mr. Richard."

"The mine?"

Tom Weedon had steadied the horses and gotten them to the bottom of the incline. He left them standing and came to where Richard and the little girl were talking.

"What's this, then? Is this a child you know, Darrow?"

"Yes, Tom. This is Emily, the adopted daughter of Mr. Blackwood. I was her tutor."

"Please help me, Mr.Richard. I must get to the mine before they all go down for the day's work."

"But you must go back to Blackdale."

"Please, sir. Miss Pamela doesn't want me there. Only Mr. Blackwood was my friend, and you, Mr. Richard. Now all the servants have been pinching me and calling me names. Please, Mr. Richard. I want to go back to the mine."

"Darrow, we've got to get off this part of the road as quickly as we may," Tom Weedon interrupted. "If you mix in this, you will surely be caught. You can't go to Blackdale, they may have left soldiers there, and we cannot turn back to Blackwood's mine. The barge will go without you."

The face of his own dear Sally flashed through Richard's thoughts.

"Well, I can't leave her here, either. She will have to take her chances with me."

"You're mad, Darrow. You'll be hung for her abduction."

"I shall be hung anyway, if we are caught."

Richard knelt down so he could look into the little girl's face."What do you say, Emily. Do you want to come with me to London? You might be hungry and cold. There are men with guns chasing me. You may be left alone in the great city of London. But I think I know someone who would prize you as much as I do, and would make a home for you. You see, my dear, I cannot go back with you. It is my life to do so and the life of this good man who has helped me.You either come with me into the unknown or stay here and find your way. Which do you choose?"

Richard knew it was an impossible choice for the little girl, but his own fondness for her made parting with her in the darkness impossible, too. He could not send her back to the mines to live in isolation, dust, heat and darkness and the likelihood of premature death.

The little girl quickly took his hand. "Oh, I shall come with you, Mr. Richard. Please, sir, just keep me as long as you are able."

"That I shall, Emily," Richard answered, lifting up the child. "Nothing will part us, if I can help it, I promise."

"I don't know that the men we are meeting will take her on the barge, Darrow. It's death to any man caught with those weapons," Weedon put in. "If she cries or whimpers at the wrong moment, it could be the end of everything."

"Then I shall walk to London with Emily in my arms. I did something similar once before. I am afraid there is no choice for any of us but faith in God's goodness." Richard walked toward the wagon with Emily in his arms. "If our cause is as just as it seems to me to be, I cannot believe in a world made by a deity who would forsake this child and the cause of justice for the poor. I shall talk to the men in Liverpool. And Emily can speak for herself. My friend Fisk, I know, would do as I am doing. If I have to speak in his name, I shall. You, Tom, can leave us anywhere. You have had far more than your share of danger, already, because of me. Only tell me the name of the barge and its captain."

"I am not a coward, Darrow, as you ought to know. I would not desert you or the little one here, on the high road. Besides, you will never find these men unless they see me with you. So, if you say the little one has to go with you, then the three of us go together until you are safely on board or the men refuse to carry you."

They trudged on through the darkest hours and took lonely country lanes and winding dirt tracks once the sun came up over the hills. Traveling this way and sparing the great horses as much as possible, it took nearly two days to reach Liverpool, close as it was, only a few hours by train, but they dared use only back roads. By the time they entered the port city, they were eating raw potatoes. By then, Tom's feelings for Emily had grown into a genuine affection and respect. As they entered the city, the little girl was sleeping under Richard's coat in the drizzle that had been falling all day, Tom glanced back at her.

"A mighty soul, that little one is," the big man said. "Not a whimper, a cry or complaint. I have known many men who do not travel with as much fortitude as this child.

"Yes," Richard answered. "She is what we all are supposed to be: brave, wise, fearless and gentle. To know and teach her is a privilege."

"I can believe that, Darrow. I can believe that. I will tell the barge men that she is no ordinary child. I only hope it will help. They are mostly a sober, god-fearing lot, these lightermen. No one would trust a drunken man with a barge, especially in the locks of the canals that you shall travel."

Chapter 17

The world was empty, a blasted sorrowful desert for Pamela Blackwood in the weeks following her father's death. Anything that had been his, even his ugly mine, was now dear to her. His most personal possessions, such as his pipe, hat, gloves and cane had become sacred relics for her. She had gathered them together, blinded by her own tears as she collected them from his study, and placed them in a trunk in her room. For, she could not look at or touch them without bursting into tears, nor could she bear to be parted from them and so kept the trunk locked but near her. She gave orders through the housemaid that nothing of Blackwood's was to be removed or touched, changed in any way. She kept trying to think that there was some meaning in the fact he had died in one of his own mines. There had to be some meaning, she kept thinking. Surely the Lord of Hosts would not desert her just as she had found her own way in life. But perhaps that was the meaning: that she had found her vocation which was to provide the strength to go alone into the world, without the being who had been little short of a god to her for most of her young life. At the same time, she could not bear the thought that in some strange, mystical way, perhaps her own independence might have robbed her of her most beloved friend. She even tried to read the Book of Common Prayer, but found nothing in it but meaningless black marks on the white pages. No matter where her thoughts began, they always led her back to the terrible blank wall of death which she could not pass, which shut her out from the kind, loving presence that had always been near. All she could do was stare out of the window in her room at the moors, the landscape her father had loved. She did not even know that Emily was missing until Miss Peevey insisted on bringing it to her attention.

"I cannot think of her now," Pamela said through her closed door. "Do whatever you think right." Then she sank back into her despair, refusing to talk to Barnes or anyone else.

She sat at her window for days, sometimes seeing the landscape, sometimes seeing only memories of the times when they had been together.

The aching weeks closed over her, a tomb of death in life. She did not want to leave her room for fear of seeing or touching something that would surprise her thoughts and suddenly bring her, unwarned, to some unbearably poignant memory of the time he was alive. It was easier to pretend he had been a dream, her perfect, dear friend. At other moments during those early days, she even thought she was suffering from brain fever and had only imagined his death. For three weeks she ate almost nothing that was left at her door. She could not attend her father's funeral.

One night she woke from a blank sleep to find that the terrible ache which had greeted her at the very threshold of every waking was dulled and softened. An enchanted light of a full moon was spilling into her room. The silvery chiaroscuro made everything familiar appear strange and different. The house was silent. For the first time in days, she slipped from her room and looked down the marble staircase to the floor below. The white stone of the staircase glowed in the moon's brightness and felt deliciously cool under her feet. Downstairs, she stood silently in the brilliant shafts admitted into the many-windowed entranceway of the house. Then she turned and went down the hall to the parlour where her pianoforte had remained untouched for weeks. She entered and saw the massive form outlined against the moon-bright hills which looked in from beyond the large french doors. She lifted the cover, caressed the shining keys and at the sound of the sonorous notes, her sorrow was elevated to a higher, more spiritual plane. The harmonies of Herr Bach's fine old church music gave her the holy comfort she had sought for in vain, in words of prayer. She spoke to the Lord through the keys, and felt His response in the blessed, joyous voices of the music. She released her pain into the harmonies and her heart was renewed by them. In a few moments she knew that music would make it possible for her to live. Her love for it was stronger than her sorrow.

To everyone's surprise, including her own, Pamela was awake and out of her room early the next morning. She felt there was much to do. She began by sending for Mr. Barnes. She must find out what her father had wanted her to do with his business interests. She knew that his businesses had been his greatest personal delight, as music was hers. It now seemed sacrilegious to have abandoned his interests for the past weeks. She was also ashamed of abandoning Emily. She knew only that the little girl had not yet been found, nor had she reached her former home. Knowing her father's great regard and fondness for the child, Pamela berated herself for her inexcusable neglect of Emily. This, she felt, must be looked into quickly and thoroughly. This, too, she would take up with Barnes. The disappearance of a pretty young girl on the road could be the result of the greatest possible infamy. She knew her father had wanted the child to be protected and educated at the very least. Pamela acknowledged to herself that her behaviour had been opposed in all ways to her father's desires. Over and over again she thought, "through my own wickedness, Emily may be lost, forever."

The solicitor would be the one best qualified to sift this matter to the bottom. She wondered how long it would take for Mr. Barnes to come. She did not know that on his side, the solicitor was waiting to act on her behalf. He knew much better than she that there were affairs which brooked no delay. He had tried to call several times at Blackdale and was on his way to Pamela within minutes of receiving her note. The solicitor called for his carriage and picked up the briefcase next to his desk which he had prepared days ago. It contained Blackwood's last will, as well as notes on other pending affairs that the heiress should know about. He did not look forward to discussing any of these matters with Pamela. Mr. Barnes stretched his legs comfortably in his coach and tried to prepare himself for what he expected would be a difficult interview. Pamela had not one shred of her father's businesslike way of ordering his ideas and getting things done. He had always found her rather sulky and wilful. He looked out the window and tried to enjoy the sunshine as he rode out to Blackdale.

* * *

Pamela received the solicitor in her father's study where Blackwood had done all his accounts, written letters and generally conducted his business. Books lined the walls along with large flat chests of drawers that held technical drawings related to different mining and railway projects. The only personal adornment in the room was a fine painting of Pamela which hung behind the desk. It was not a sentimentalized portrait and, along with its subject's beauty, it also captured her spoiled, petulant nature. For the first time in Pamela's life, the original of the picture sat in front of it, in her father's large, carved Chinese chair.

As Barnes entered the room, he found the mirror-like effect of the girl and picture disconcerting, but he also noticed that the likeness was no longer as true as it had once been. Pamela had changed markedly since he had last seen her. He felt she watched him with a new interest.She came around from behind the desk and offered him her hand as a man would. Her large hand was strong and firm.

"Thank you for coming so promptly, Mr. Barnes. Do sit down." The voice was steady, he noted. There was no hint of dullness, nor of tears. He saw a new gravity and poise in her. It boded well for business.

"I know," the young woman continued, "there is no one my father trusted more than yourself, Sir. Therefore I have asked you to come here and guide me. To speak, with my father's voice."

"Thank you for your good opinion, Miss Blackwood. I shall certainly do my best, for you must know that your father was not only a friend and client. He was also a major force in the growth of our county and of the north. The way his interests are carried forward will affect many."

"Wait, Mr. Barnes. I know these are weighty matters and we shall speak of them, directly. But first, I have two more personal interests of which I wish to speak."

The solicitor nodded his acquiescence.

"The little girl, Emily, had become very near my father's heart toward the end of his life. I want to know if there is any report of her. If not, I wish to offer a reward for information regarding her whereabouts--with--what is the phrase, no questions to be asked if she is produced unharmed."

The solicitor's face tightened into a grim mask.

"There has been no definite word about the child," he said. "But you must know that, God forgive me, the former tutor, Richard Darrow left my service at the same time under a very dark cloud. There is some suspicion that the two left the region together."

"What is this very dark cloud of which you speak , Mr. Barnes? I liked Mr. Darrow and I believe he was genuinely fond of the child. My father was favorably impressed with the progress she made with him. I would actually worry less if I thought the two were together."

"But he had no business taking her away, if he has. Especially with what has been revealed about his activities," the solicitor remonstrated.

For the first time since the interview began, Pamela looked uncertain and vulnerable. "I do not think he would take her, sir. But she may have left on her own."

"What do you mean?'

"I mean, sir, that I was not the best or kindest friend to Emily. She may well have felt that with my father's death she would not be welcome and certainly not loved as she had been at Blackdale."

"Nonsense, Miss Blackwood. Richard Darrow has been shown to be a revolutionary of the most incendiary kind. A dangerous man who gained our confidence while he was secretly plotting armed insurrection."

"Sir, I cannot believe that. On whose authority do you speak?"

"No one less than John Samuelson, Miss. And my own eyes. A dangerous pamphlet written by a rabble rouser in London was found in his desk in my chambers. Soldiers actually searched the premises for Darrow. Samuelson says that Darrow physically attacked his own son to get money from him. The woman you saw Paul with was Darrow's degenerate sister, a vile, plotting woman of the worst sort who has sold herself since childhood. She seduced young Samuelson and has been ruining him for several months. The boy grew up very quietly in Scotland and had no idea of the kind of creature the girl was when she attached herself to him. Darrow and sister appear to be equally desperate and lawless people. They were apparently born and grew up in the utter lawlessness of various navvy camps. Samuelson himself saw them as children in the camps. Two more vicious children were never met with according to his personal report.The Darrow woman was another factor in Mr.Samuelson's hoping for your marriage to Paul. In addition to uniting your fortunes and industries, he felt that an engagement with a decent woman would remove this creature from Paul."

Pamela was quiet for a moment then said," This is all horribly shocking, Mr. Barnes."

"It is indeed."

"We all felt a great liking and respect for Mr. Darrow, here. Everyone from the governess to my father and myself. I cannot hide that the portrait you paint seems hardly to be credited."

"Yet, it is so. I have the word of John Samuelson, who has no reason to say otherwise than the truth and, there is also this." The solicitor opened his briefcase and drew out Fisk's pamphlet.

"This was found in Darrow's desk. I have also learned that Darrow and the author of this madness were neighbours in one of the most dangerous parts of London."

Pamela put out her hand for the pamphlet. "May I have that for a while, Mr. Barnes?"

"To what end, Miss Blackwood?"

"I wish to read it. The Blackwood interests have many people in our employ who have probably read it. I wish to know what they read and think."

"But it is arrent nonsense, Miss Blackwood."

"Nonetheless. I would know the nature of the arrent nonsense to which our people give credit."

"But these are not things for you to worry about, Miss Blackwood."

"If Emily is with this man, whom you claim is a thorough blackguard, it is my business. Nor am I ready to disbelieve so easily my own opinion of Mr. Darrow. I would find it much easier to dislike and disbelieve Mr. Samuelson."

"Excuse me, Miss Blackwood. That is a woman's logic. Mr. Samuelson is a hard man who has rough manners. He drives like one of his own locomotives toward his goals. He has none of the charm and obvious kindness of your father, but he is helping to build the empire for all of us. It is hard work and not always polite in character. That does not make him wicked."

"Pardon me Mr. Barnes," the young woman said, mimicking the solicitor's condescension,

" But I must say that I feel many of the great capitalists of our age are wicked. or at least self interested to the exclusion of anyone else. My father thought so and always tried to do more for his people than others of his acquaintance. There are other men like him, I know, good men who have built great fortunes. But my feelings tell me that Mr. Samuelson is not one of them."

"Miss Blackwood, I am afraid we have reached that impassable gulf that lies between the sexes. You talk of feelings and I of facts. And after all, your father was willing that you should marry Mr. Samuelson's son."

"And I believe he was wrong in this. I think his own desire to build the Blackwood interests into a great northern empire of railways and mines may have blinded him to what was good for me. Fortunately, the choice was left to me to do as I wish. I shall not marry Samuelson's son under any conditions. And what you have told me this morning about his weakness for Mr. Darrow's vicious sister does not make him more attractive to me. Now, I should like to know the exact terms of my father's will. Though, I believe I know most of it in outline."

Barnes found Pamela both easier and more difficult than he'd expected. She was far firmer and more decisive than he'd anticipated, but she stubbornly refused the logic of some of the actions he urged upon her during the interview.

Blackwood's will left Pamela unusually independent as to the disposal of a large portion of the income generated by his businesses, though she was was not allowed to touch the firm's existing capital or money invested in land that, in Blackwood's judgment, would sustain the future of Blackwood Holdings. Barnes had argued with Blackwood that Pamela's access to the income should be more limited since, the income might be needed to see the companies through difficult times, should they come. The holdings in land were a matter of very long term capitalization, not liquid enough in the case of unforeseen reverses. Blackdale was also hers, unconditionally, to dispose of as she pleased. Again, the solicitor had argued with his old friend, but Blackwood told the solicitor, "I have loved twice in my life, Barnes. My wife and my daughter. All I have was built on the foundation of that love. It is what has always sustained me in all my efforts. I know that I have built something that transcends personal interests, but I believe Pamela will understand this. Until recently, I was not sure that she would be capable of that understanding. Now, I am quite certain of her. I shall trust her wisdom and not place strictures on her. I do it out of respect for the openness and strength of the relationship we have always had and as an acknowledgment of her recent personal development.. The actual ownership of the companies' shares shall remain in trust and only be released if and when Pamela marries a man who is capable of running the businesses. Judging that capability of a future husband I shall leave to you, Barnes."

In vain had Barnes tried to change Blackwood's outlook, but to no avail. At a certain point when the great financier was being brooked by someone or something he just began making a joke out of it. This is what he had done with Barnes.

"I think, Barnes, that you are afraid my daughter will not retain you. That she will prefer some younger more handsome man to handle her business. Perhaps your son."

It was patently impossible for the solicitor even to respond to this so he had no choice but to let the matter drop.

When these points had been covered with Pamela he asked her, "Do you feel able to begin managing the day to day affairs of Blackdale?"

"I don't think my father did very much of that. He trusted our steward, Harrison, in nearly all things. If there are issues about tenants or land which I do not understand, I know I can call on you. We have good friends and servants, and I shall endeavor to treat them all better than I have."

The young woman's next pronouncement took Barnes utterly by surprise. "Since I am obviously unqualified to make business decisions, I should like to give you power of attorney regarding the operations of the companies."

"But Miss Blackwood," solicitor burst out, "how can I accept such a thing?" The young girl smiled, knowing she had shaken the solicitor's professional aplomb and poise, on which he prided himself, to its foundations.

"I have thought about this well, Mr. Barnes. I could never trust another capitalist like Mr. Samuelson with the companies for he would always be trying to gain the upper hand and acquire more and more control. You, however, are the perfect executive. You shall always act for someone else. It is your training and your nature. Naturally, these increased responsibilities shall call for greater remuneration for you. I wish you to consider that figure and tell me what it shall be. I shall pay it out of company income."

In all his years, the seasoned legal warrior had never been so totally caught off guard.

"But Miss Blackwood, I must protest. This should be discussed with corporate officers."

"No. I give you my first order, Mr. Barnes, as owner in trust of Blackwood Holdings Limited. You may not protest. This is the only way that I can expect to do reasonable justice to my father's legacy. I think it is what he actually intended, in fact. But was kind enough to leave it to me to delegate this authority. These subjects are now closed," she went on. "Now I wish to return to the finding of both Emily and Richard Darrow, regardless of whether or not they are together. I want to know what has happened to both of them. I shall read this pamphlet and make my own judgment about Mr. Darrow's culpability. If we ever find her, Emily, herself, shall tell me what took place. I wish to offer a reward of ten thousand pounds for the safe return of Emily to this house."

"That is a huge sum, Miss Blackwood."

"I know it is what my father would do. If anyone is holding her, I want to make it more worth while to bring her home than to carry out any plan that may injure her. I believe it is my fault that she is gone. I brought her here as though I were buying a pony. When she turned out to be not only beautiful but to possess a brilliant mind, I was stupidly jealous of her and of my father's affection for her. His plan was to educate her and give her good employment in his businesses. I daresay that he hoped she would become his private secretary in time. I shall do everything possible to carry out my father's plan and atone for my own thoughtless behavior."

Once again, the solicitor tried to remonstrate with the young woman.

"But a sum like that will attract the notice of every mountebank and swindler in the country."

"Then you, sir, shall meet every swindler and mountebank in the country and sift their stories to the bottom and decide what is true and what is false. I would rather have too many applicants with information about Emily than too few."

"Then I think we should also set enquiries afoot in London, for that would bethe easiest place for Darrow to hide with the little girl," the solicitor ventured.

"I am not ready to assume Mr. Darrow's culpability in Emily's disappearance. "I reserve for myself that blame. I believe she left this house on her own."

"But surely under the influence of an adult?"

"I am not certain of that. All of us in this house know that she is a fearless and extraordinarily self-possessed child. At any rate, I do not want Mr. Darrow made the object of a police search."

"But he already is, Miss Blackwood. I am sure that Mr. Samuelson will urge the authorities in London to find him, or perhaps even hire his own agents for the purpose. Highly placed men in Her Majesty's Government whom Mr. Samuelson knows are deeply interested in finding the men with whom we believe Darrow to have been in contact. There is a ring of weapon makers in Liverpool which has been tied to this man, Fisk, Samuelson tells me. Based on Mr. Samuelson's assertions, it is believed that Darrow is one of his lieutenants. Mr. Darrow's chances of slipping through the snares that have been laid are small, indeed. Especially if he stays with the little girl. They make too striking a pair."

"Oh, Emily, Emily" Pamela said out loud, "I am so sorry. So sorry. I shall be the best sister in the world to you if only you will come home."

* * *

At the very moment of Pamela's repentant words, Emily was splashing in warm soapy water in a large copper tub.

"Miss Sally," she called out. "I am getting out now. I shall dry myself."

A moment later the door opened and Sally Howard entered the room holding a thick, freshly washed cloth.

"No you don't, little imp. You'll get water all over the floor. First, I'll wrap you up," Sally said as she accompanied her words with the promised action, "And then," she continued putting her hands around the little girl's waist, "I shall take you out."

With her last statement, she lifted the little girl and swung her so her feet cleared the edge of the tub in a long arc. The child giggled with delight at being handled like a sack of produce.

Sally Howard was the first person who had ever treated Emily as an ordinary child. Growing up with three younger brothers had given the young woman much practice with children. Two weeks earlier when Richard had arrived on her father's doorstep in the middle of the night with the child, Sally had immediately taken her over in a motherly, businesslike way. Being an unconventional family of engravers who frequently worked at night, the family was not too upset by the midnight callers. Once Sally had bundled the child off to her own bed and the other family members had gone back to their bedrooms or the studio on the first floor, Sally sat down at the kitchen

173

table and faced Richard.

They looked at one another for a moment and then Sally reached out her hand to the young man.

"It is good to see you, Richard. Though the child is quite a surprise. Is she a relation?"

"No. I know it is a great presumption to bring her here, but I had nowhere else. And as long as she is with me, she is in danger."

"In danger? Are you in danger, Richard?"

"Yes. And if you want me to, I shall leave when I've told you..." Sally got up, walked around the table and put her fingers on Richard's lips to silence him.

"Do you not think I have been waiting for months to hear from you--as I told you I would? I have kept my promise. I have waited. But perhaps you feel differently. You look as if much has happened to you," as she spoke she searched his face intently.

"It has. But I must tell you, so you know what you will be facing if you help me and Emily."

With that introduction, Richard began a full account of his movements since leaving London. When he got to his flight with Emily across the moors, Sally interrupted him.

"What a tale, Richard. It is as thrilling as any of Walter Scotts' romances," the young woman said, her eyes shining as she admired the man sitting across from her.

"I had not thought of it in that light, Sally. We were simply scared and wet. But taking Emily commits me to her for life. She absolutely wants nothing to do with Blackdale or Pamela Blackwood. I am now a wanted man, thanks to John Samuelson and his son. So, I am now a poor protector for the child. I am also no one to look after you. I know we are not formally engaged but I feel I should release you from any..."

"Oh, you can be such a pompous ass, Richard," Sally said in a sharp derisive tone.

"Sally, this is dangerous. I am a hunted man. The child needs a place to stay and though I tried very hard to make sure I wasn't followed here, I can't be certain."

"I understand all this. But I won't have you making decisions or assumptions about our friendship as if you were the only one who is involved in it. The risk is mine to accept or reject. And I accept it. I know you will win back your place. You are a strong man."

Sally bent over him and he felt her lips on his. Her body melted into his lap. She kissed him for a long time.

Afterwards he said, "All right, Sally. I know I'm not to make decisions for us by myself. But what about your family? Will they want this threat hanging over them?"

"Everyone in this house is an ardent Chartist, Richard. We all believe in Tom Paine's ideas and admire many of the words of Charles Fisk, even if he is a little mad. Everyone here will gladly run a risk for the child and for our future together." Her head was rested on his shoulder. Her lips very near his ear. "My family loves me, Richard. And they all know that I love you."

"I may end on the gallows, you know," he said softly.

In answer she turned and stopped his mouth with another kiss, then she said,

"Somehow, I am certain you will not. They have not even dared to arrest Fisk, yet. And there is more proof of his sedition than of yours."

"Yes, but through Fanny, Samuelson and his son are now my sworn enemies. They have the power to hound me to my death."

"You must beat them, Richard. For yourself, for me and for Emily."

"How to do that, then, my brave girl?"

"I don't know, yet. But we shall. For now, you and Emily must stay hidden."

"I cannot stay here, my dear. I have told Fisk I would meet him at dawn."

"Fisk? You've seen him? Associating with him will be an extra risk."

"We were old friends from the time when Fanny was living with me. He helped me get away from the man who threatened me here, the man with the sword cane. That man is one of my greatest concerns. He is somehow connected with Samuelson. I saw him at his house that night I was out with old mudlark, though I didn't know him then. He is the one most likely to find Emily here, I fear. Fisk met the barge Emily and I came to London on earlier this evening. I believe that joining his cause is my best hope of winning against Samuelson and his minions and clearing my name."

"My brothers are good and brave men, Richard. They will protect Emily even from this scoundrel."

Richard shook his head. "The only protection from this man and those he serves is to remain hidden and to win the Charter."

Richard made a move to stand up. Reluctantly, Sally got off his lap.

"I must go to Fisk, my dear, before the sun is up. I will endeavor to find a way to get messages passed safely between us. Give Emily my love and tell her I shall see her soon."

"And me?"

"What do you mean?"

"You do not give me any such assurances."

Richard put his arms around her waist, which was slim, he noted, and without laces or stays.

"If there is a way to win, my dear, I will take it. But it is not up to me. I believe that we are acting in God's name and purpose and that if He sustains us, as I believe He will, we shall win against Samuelson and we shall win the Charter. Fisk says that if we do not win, the world will end in less than two-hudred years. In his visions he has seen great engines of industry, powered by greed, destroying the world. He says that if we do not stop our greed there will be a kind of Armageddon of machines."

"Oh, Richard," Sally said, tears catching in her throat as she threw

her arms
around him once more. "I am made so proud by everything you have told
me, tonight. But do you really think that Fisk can see into the future, like one
of the Old Testament prophets?"

"I don't know. They are his visions. He must believe in them. For my
part, I shall believe in you, in Emily and in the Charter." Then, he hugged her
to him and was gone.

Chapter 18

Richard splashed through the city toward the river, and the workshop of his friend, in a hard rain that forestalled the coming of dawn. Fisk had told Richard when they met on the quay that he would be watched by those who believed in the carpenter's visions. If anyone tried to arrest or assault Richard, they would be stopped. However, the agents of the law were very different in 1845 than in our day.

The purpose of the Metropolitan Force was to prevent crime by being a visible presence, not to detect crime and arrest the guilty. In fact, most people were deeply concerned about the idea of "police spies." There was a fear that if the police were given this right and power, England would become a nation filled with spies. During the eighteenth century, if someone was robbed, they would have to hire a Thief Taker to recover their goods. These private agents were like bounty hunters who worked entirely for profit. One of them, Jonathan Wild, became the criminal mastermind of London for nearly fifteen years, before he was finally hanged.

In 1842, the plain clothes detective force was formed with nine men who worked out of Old Scotland Yard, but it took decades before the detectives were given the powers and training to be effective. Many of the men hired for the Metropolitan Force were formerly agricultural workers. They were chosen more for good character than shrewdness. In fact, there was constant fear on the part of the police commissioners that the men would be corrupted through contact with criminals. Separate police forces did not work well together and were often in conflict with each other. Even today, the city of London has a separate police force. In 1845, it might take weeks for a warrant to travel from one end of the country to the other.

In short, Richard was in no immediate danger of being arrested, though he and his friends were too inexperienced to know this and tended to magnify the powers of the authorities. It was primarily in the north, with a long history of labour unrest that soldiers acted quickly and forcefully on any seditious whisper. In London, Fisk had been left alone. It was only Samuelson and those in his pay who knew of Fisk's connection with the weapons maker's in the north. And for the time being, it was a card the railway king held back. So Richard was quite safe as he approached Fisk's shop. The sentry's who watched the quiet waterfront streets all around were superfluous. Fisk did not now lead any who wanted a violent overthrow of the government. Fewer would follow him on the spiritual path he had chosen, but followers, the visionary carpenter still had. His writing had made him known and respected by many Chartists throughout the country, especially those with strong, unconventional spiritual beliefs.

As Richard made his way down the familiar streets, only the earliest birds were at large. Nut sellers, who would cry their wares on the muddy streets, with shouts such as "Hot warrnuts," were getting their cheap stock for the day from the strangely empty and dilapidated storefronts of the Jewish market at Duke's Court. Poor fish mongers were on their way to Billingsgate to get the leavings of the wealthy shop owners, while the fruit and vegetable costers pushed their carts or drove their donkeys toward Covent Garden to get the bruised produce they would sell to the poor at inflated prices. At a cab rank in Cheapside, only two cabs were left when Richard passed. The horses were dozing with their heads down to their knees, and the windows of the cabs were both covered with the warm breath of the drivers sleeping inside. As Richard neared the City, being that it was Monday, a market day, he encountered a mass of sheep and bullocks, tramping with eerie silence to Smithfield, their breath a portable cover of fog that parted to reveal the drover and his eager black and white dog following the drove. At some of the poorer markets, there were customers wrapped in every kind of rag, shuffling up and down as they waited for the vendors to open. A pair of pathetic, barefooted children, a boy and girl holding hands, who later that day would sell little bunches of watercress, trudged to get their day's stock, their legs and feet so cold, Richard could see that they were blue when they passed under the gas lights. In the quiet of the early streets could be heard, far in the distance, the occasional scrape of milk cans being moved, and here and there other sounds were added as London woke. Those who traded in some sort of vice, the outright prostitutes, the flower girls who often sold themselves along with a bouquet, the poor pickpockets whose trade was in cheap, silk handkerchiefs found the hour too early and the weather too wet, as did most of London's better society. These familiar sounds and smells, along with the rhythm of the early morning street, gave Richard the feeling of being at home. He wished that Fanny were with him, on her way to a day of honest work, though he had made his peace in his heart with her. He had done his best and she had rejected him utterly in the end. He wanted to talk about his sister with Charles Wilney, whose last images of Fanny would be of a silent, pretty child, not of a lewd woman in bed with a lover. It was an impulse that arose from wanting to return Fanny to a past that rose before his eyes as he walked the streets where he had raised and protected her. He wanted that younger Fanny to blot out the Fanny he had seen in the suburban hotel in Manchester. It was of the child-Fanny that he was thinking as he rapped on the door of Fisk's workshop.

A dull, red blade of the light from an oil lamp slipped from the door as it was opened. Richard stepped quickly inside.

On the other side of the door, there was a woman standing next to Fisk, looking at Richard shyly.

"Richard, it is good to see you safely here. This is Cynthia Hackworth. She lives here, now."

"How do you do, Miss Hackworth."

"How do you do, Mr. Darrow. I am pleased to make your acquaintance. Fisk has told me so much about you."

Richard smiled broadly, "And he's told me absolutely nothing at all about you, Miss Hackworth."

"We only became acquainted some weeks ago," Fisk said gruffly.

"Well, this is great news, Fisk. And thank you for all your help on our journey. I got the impression from the men on the barge that you no longer work with them to arm London's labourers?"

"No. The Lord has shown me that violence of any kind is an error. We are all one people," Fisk replied, "Or, we should be. And we shall, once the Iron Beast is defeated forever."

Richard nodded his agreement and water splashed off of his broad-brimmed hat.

"Let me take those wet things. I'll put them over by the kiln." "Please," Cynthia interjected, "Allow me."

Richard unwrapped himself and handed his wet things to Cynthia. He looked around at the rough studio of the carpenter. The unfinished wood walls and floors hadn't changed, but here and there, Richard noted small improvements that were the sure signs of a woman's hand. The two men looked at one another carefully.

"You've changed, Richard. Grown into a man with a decisive brow. I've seen that you'll serve our cause powerfully, though the manner of your service is dark to me."

"Can you really see the future, Fisk?"

"Yes, he can," called Cynthia from the other side of the shop.

"I see pictures in my mind's eye. I look at the pictures and sometimes I know what they mean."

"People talk of you as they would a prophet, even the arms-makers on the barge," Richard said.

"People always make the unknown into the form of their own wishes or fears."

"He is a very wise man, " Cynthia said as she came to the carpenter's side and took his arm.

"You are different, Fisk. Your eyes are different."

"For a brief time, I did actually see the New Jerusalem, Richard. It would change any man's eyes."

"I read your account of your vision in your pamphlet. It was for that evidence of sedition that Samuelson ordered the soldiers to arrest me."

"Well, if it brought you to our cause, by whatever circuitous path, I am glad I wrote it. And where is Fanny? Did you find her?"

"She plays wife to Samuelson's son, Paul."

"Good heavens."

"It is of her own choosing, Fisk. She chose to stay with him instead of coming with me. I even told her that I knew Samuelson's son was going to marry another woman. I had blows with him over her. And now I am persecuted by the father. It was he who called for my arrest in Manchester."

"You choose great adversaries, Richard."

"I chose him not. I wanted only to bring Fanny home. It was he who decided to revenge himself on me. I was surprised that such a great force would bother to strike out at someone as insignificant as myself."

"Do not underestimate the vanity of these self-made heroes. They think all who obstruct them should be swept aside as the Lord did Pharaoh's men in the Red Sea. They think themselves the true prophets of the age. They think they see far, but they see too little and not far enough."

"Fisk," Cynthia broke in, "Perhaps your guest would like some hot tea on a morning such as this??"

"He is your guest, as well, Cynthia. Ask him yourself."

"Would you care for some tea, Mr. Darrow?"

"Thank you, Miss Hackworth. I should very much enjoy a hot drink."

"It will take a few minutes, Mr. Darrow. Pardon me," and with that Cynthia crossed the room to the far end where Fisk's make-shift kitchen was set up.

"You surprise me, Fisk. I had never thought you the marrying kind of man. Except once or twice when I caught you looking at Fanny in a certain way."

"Miss Darrow was very young, Richard," the carpenter said, colouring slightly. "Perhaps I had just not met the right woman of my own age. Anyway," he said dropping his voice, "Cynthia is still married to someone who disappeared two years ago. She cannot legally remarry. I only tell you so you will not say something that might embarrass her."

Richard nodded.

The carpenter paused and was silent for a moment. Then he said, "But on another subject, Darrow, have you seen a newspaper recently?" Fisk asked suddenly.

"Not at any time in the last two weeks. Why?"

For an answer, the burly carpenter turned away into the shadows of the shop and came back holding a newspaper in his hand. He dropped it on the bench in front of Richard.

"Murder and sacrilege in country village!" the bold headline read. In smaller type another headline read: "Bloody deed done for no reason—Bible desecrated." What followed was a detailed account of Charles Wilney's murder.

"No, no, no," Richard cried out punctuating each negative with a blow on the bench with his fist.

Finally, Richard finished reading. His cheeks were wet.

"We always said we should meet again and smoke a pipe before his own hearth. Oh, Lord, what new calamities shall befall?"

Fisk clapped his arm on the younger man's shoulders.

"I knew he was much to you. That's why I saved it."

"Thank you, Fisk, but I see this is from almost two weeks ago. All this time and Charles dead and I did not know it. All these months I have been meaning to write to him, and now the chance is lost forever. I have even missed his funeral by some weeks. though, according to the paper, his neighbours in the hamlet gave him a fond ceremony. He was known as a good man by all who met him, Fisk. Vicar Franklyn delivered a eulogy. Franklyn was his great friend there."

"Well, now we must look to the future. I saw the child you brought from Manchester. She is very lovely."

"Yes, an extraordinary child who had been working in a mine and then was adopted by the mine owner."

"These capitalists know their own sins and try sporadically to wipe them out. But they cannot. The world itself will be consumed by their greed if they are not stopped. I have seen it, Richard. Poison air, and water that kills, food that does not nourish, winds and tides that destroy nations, the natural order, itself, perverted."

But it was obvious that the younger man was not listening. He was re-reading the article on Charles Wilney's murder. Fisk stopped speaking and waited. After some moments, Richard looked up at him.

"I must know more about this, Fisk. I must know who wanted to kill such a man."

"It would seem likely that it was some tramp who looked for valuables, was surprised by your friend and then struck him down in his fear of being caught."

"Then why desecrate the bible? Why take the time to tear it? Charles used that very bible to teach me to read. I wonder if any part of it has survived the attack? No, Fisk, I must know more about all this. I must go there."

"Where?"

"To the rustic, little Dorsetshire village where Charles was living. I must pay my respects at his grave and see if I can find his killer. This man was more than father to me. He gave me a vision that enabled me to see the world beyond the mud of the railway camps."

Cynthia returned to the men with two steaming beakers.

"Thank you, Cynthia," Fisk said.

"Thank you, Miss Hackworth," Richard said, taking the second cup.

"You are both welcome," she said. "I do not wish to interrupt you, Fisk. If you wish to speak, privately."

"Richard?" Fisk asked.

"No, I do not mind if Miss Hackworth hears us."

"Than I was about to remind you that you are now hunted. You will be caught more easily on the road to Dorsetshire, especially if this railway king decides to send men after you. Out in the country, a stranger shall not pass unnoticed. Here we can offer you some protection. How would you start your search for your friend's killer? What would you do in a place where you are not known and have no one to help you?"

"I would begin with Reverend Franklyn. I am certain Charles has mentioned me to him. I would start by getting all the particulars from him. As to my own risk, I should be a poor friend, indeed, if I let that stop me."

"And what of the child?"

"She is safe for now. She is staying with a fine family, the father and brothers of my be-be-betrothed," he stumbled over the word. It was the first time he had described Sally as his future wife, even to himself.

"This is glad news, Darrow. You have been busy, indeed. Who is she?"

"No busier than you, Fisk," he said, smiling at Cynthia. "Sally is a fine young woman whose father and brothers are engravers. They are all for the Charter. I am surprised you don't know them. I understood they had done considerable printing for Chartist authors."

"Well, what is the name? I cannot know them without a name," Fisk said, grinning."Do you think all the world knows your betrothed? Does she always addle your mind so?"

The younger man flushed. "Her name is Sally Howard."

"Is she of the Howards who operate Howard Engravers in Cheapside?

Richard nodded.

"Of course, I know them. I have only glimpsed the young woman, but the men of the family I know well. Michael, Henry and Richard and the father, Roderick, an old lion of a man. They are all men who know how to work with their hands and think with their heads and hearts. You have not met them yet, Cynthia."

"Well, I'm glad you approve of them so highly. I scarcely know the rest of the family."

"Their home is a good place for the child," Fisk said thoughtfully. "It will be easy for me to have it watched. If there is trouble we might be able to get them away by way of the Custom House Stairs and the river."

"I am most worried about the man with the sword cane who drove me to Manchester. I fear him. He is a killer, I think, and would stick at nothing. And I do know that he serves someone I have now made an enemy, the railway king, Samuelson."

"So, that is where he came from. A man who murders for pay, perhaps an old soldier."

"Oh, he is more than just a soldier. But what, I cannot say. But he makes me fear for Sally and Emily."

"We shall watch them. And surely, no matter how deadly he is, he is only one man."

"With Samuelson's wealth and power at his back."

"True. But we could defend your friends against anything short of the army or the Metropolitan Force. I have good men with me, Richard."

"I have met some of them and they are good, indeed. It will be a great comfort to me to know that Sally and Emily are being watched over. It makes it much easier to leave London."

"Mr. Darrow," Cynthia said, "I should be very glad to go and call on Miss Howard and the little girl. I could not protect anyone, but I might be able to watch the child if your betrothed needs help."

"That is very good of you, Miss Hackworth. I shall tell Sally. Thank you."

"I certainly understand your need to go," Fisk said. " Get this business done and come back as quickly as you can. Within the coming year I think we'll try once more to present the Charter to Parliament. I think you go to Dorset on a hopeless errand, but I understand the need. It could have been any passing tramp who killed your friend. I do not know when the storm will break here, exactly, but I think, soon."

"But do you not decide when the storm breaks?"

"To a very limited extent. Movements like ours have their own life. Part of the problem is that there is no central leadership. And the ones who would lead are the least to be trusted."

"You mean O'Connor?"

"Among others. But there will come a moment when something must be done or the whole thing may collapse. Nor am I the only leader, or even the one with the largest following, or even among the best known. But I have seen what lies ahead and know that we must stop this unwholesome progress or future generations will see God's hand strike the world as it did in Noah's time."

"I hear your conviction in your voice, Fisk. But I hope you are wrong."

"I do not want to be wrong, Richard."

"Nor do I want him to be," put in Cynthia.

"We say that, Darrow, because I have also seen the chance of great beauty and joy," Fisk said. "And if the one were false, then so would the other be. I have seen the flames if we are not wise, but I have also seen and heard angels singing above the roofs of the New Jerusalem."

The sound of the heavy rain that had punctuated their conversation stopped. Day was gradually forcing itself through the damp soot and coal smoke of the city air. They all stood quietly for a moment, then Richard spoke.

"I must have a holiday with Sally and Emily before I go. It may be the only time we have. I know it isn't prudent. But my heart forbids me to leave the city without a day together as a family. I missed my chance with Charles, I would not miss it with them."

So as the sooty morning dried out into a brighter, more promising afternoon, Richard, Sally and Emily took a cab to the Greenwich ferry. On the other side of the river they could walk on the open lawns, meander along the river, watch the great ships and eat plates of oysters at waterside stalls with tables out under the trees. Richard watched approvingly as he saw how Emily already looked to Sally to tell her how to behave in this new place with brightly dressed crowds, promenading beneath the trees.

Greenwich was like no place the little girl had ever seen. There had been few people at Blackdale and the paths had not been wide and paved. Nor had there been great ships close at hand bound for India and all the points of the globe. Emily looked out over the water with rapt attention whenever a ship came near.

"That's an east indiaman," the child said pointing to a ship. "It can go to Bombay in just forty-five days. And that is one of the new steam packets they are trying out on the river, I think. And there's a..."
"How did you learn so much about ships, Emily?" Sally asked.

"Mr. Blackwood told me about them. He says, said, that soon there will be steam ships that travel on the ocean. They will make England's sea power and wealth even greater. He said Mr. Brunel will build them."
"And who is Mr. Brunel?" Sally asked.

"Oh he's a friend of Mr. Blackwood's. He builds things. He makes railways with a wider gauge track than the ones Mr. Stephenson is using. They will be more re-reliable."

"You certainly know a lot about mechanical things," Sally said.

"Oh, no, Miss Sally. I know very little. Mr. Blackwood knew all about them. He showed me drawings of, of, new ventions.., that's not right," she muttered to herself,

"New in-ventions, things that aren't made yet. He said looking at the drawings was like seeing into the future. I wish he was here now. He could tell us everything about every ship on the river. He told me many things. I miss him, Mr. Richard," she said, reaching for his hand.
"I know, Emily. I miss him, too."

They walked in silence for a while and then Emily spoke, "I think, I would like to have my own steamship and sail all over the world when I am older."

Richard looked down at the little girl staring raptly out at the ships. "Sea captains are men, Emily,..ouch" he said suddenly looking over at Sally, rubbing the arm she had just pinched.

"There are no reasons why a woman couldn't command a ship," Sally said.

"Perhaps you could be the first one, Emily."
As a peace offering she reached over and rubbed Richard's arm and kissed him quickly on the cheek.

"Is your arm all right now, Richard?" she asked.

"It's much better, thank you," he replied tucking one of her arms under his.

They continued walking, resting, eating and drinking late into the afternoon.

The sun finally broke through and gave the moist air a rare golden colour. After Manchester's clogged sky, it seemed like brilliant sunshine to Richard. Here and there on the lawns were a few standing patterers doing their pitches for the crowd. One mountebank offered a pill that was guaranteed to right any ailment of the major internal organs, stomach, liver and heart. Another was selling "a true account of Rush, the greatest murderer and villain of all time". The patterer said he was offering the killer's last true statement, made on the scaffold, which heretofore had never been repeated accurately. There was a ragged brother and sister on stilts and their two little dogs. The children danced together on the long poles, the dogs danced below on the ground while a gray-haired gypsy played the fiddle for the them. Emily got peculiar pleasure from watching the dogs and applauding their antics.

The day was exactly what Richard had wanted for them, a time to be a family, a day to forget about politics and enemies. Sally squeezed his hand as they walked along. Emily skipped in the grass or ran from one speaker or musician to another. All three were at the pinnacle of happiness. Only once or twice more did Emily murmur within Richard's hearing, "I wish Mr. Blackwood was here."

By the time the cab brought them back from the ferry and stopped in front of Sally's house, Emily was fast asleep in Richard's lap. He lifted her out and followed Sally inside. Roderick, Sally's father, who did in fact resemble a grey lion with his thick beard spilling onto his chest and shoulder-length hair greeted them silently when he saw the sleeping child.

Richard found it odd to be completely accepted by the family without closer scrutiny. He and Sally might have been already married. How different from all his vain fears when they had first met. Sally led the way up a long flight of stairs and Richard followed with the little girl in his arms. At the top, Richard found a large airy apartment with a sitting room and a separate bedroom. These were Sally's rooms. He put the little girl on Sally's bed. He had held off telling Sally that he would be leaving the city again. He had put it off all day. Now it was time.

"Dearest," he said, tenderly as he took her hand in both of his. "I do not want to spoil our beautiful day but I must show you something." From his pocket he drew out the article Fisk had given him about Charles Wilney and silently handed it to Sally. She read it without speaking. She knew of Wilney's importance to Richard since the day they'd met at the lecture. He had rushed to tell her of his humble origins and how Wilney's gift of teaching had raised him up. He had blurted it all out almost as soon as the lecture was over. If she was going to reject him for his low station, he had wanted to know right away.

"Oh, Richard, this is terrible," she said putting down the paper. "It seems so senseless."

"That is what I have to find out, Sally. Why? Why was he killed? Why was his bible torn apart? Who committed the horrible crime? I must know all I can, my dear. Do you understand."

"Are you telling me that you are going away from us? Now? Immediately?"

"I have a better protector for you both than I could be. Even now, Fisk's men are watching this house to keep you both from harm."

"But I don't want Fisk's men. I want you."

"I'm sorry, Sally, I must go. And I must go right away. Every day I wait, traces of Charles' killer will become harder to find. Every day diminishes my chances of catching him. You may be sure the local constables will not find the killer. I leave for the southwest tomorrow."

"Why do you think that you shall catch the criminal if he has not been caught yet by the constables?"

"I don't know that I shall, Sally. I only know I must try."

The young woman took hold of his shirt front and pulled him down to the settee in the sitting room.

"There's something else you must do first, then" she said kissing him deeply, more passionately than on the previous night. Then she began unbuttoning his shirt.

"Sally, what are you doing?"

"I love you and I want to be yours and I don't know that I shall have another chance."

"But we're not married and Emily..."

"I don't care. I shall have you now if you can't promise you will come back safely."

"But Sally, this isn't..."

"Right? We are betrothed, and a women's passions are just as deep as those of men. I find that with you mine are peculiarly strong." She bit him on the neck.

She had unfastened his shirt and she now slipped her hands across his naked chest.

"I want you to stay with me tonight," she said breathlessly. Her cheek burned against his as she continued undressing him.

He was too dumbfounded to move. He had little experience with women and certainly nothing like what Sally was proposing. He felt himself slide down into a well of passion. His body caught fire and Sally made herself irresistible. He became vaguely aware that she stood naked in front of him. Then she made him touch her in all of her secret places. She showed him explicitly what she wanted. She put his mouth on her nipples and then bit his lips. A thousand times during their torrid night together, memories of women in the navvy camps haunted him with their lewdness but each time his love for Sally and the young woman's deep affection drew him back to the present. Finally, a timeless warmth seemed to spread out over everything, engulfing them both.

Later, as they lay together in the darkness, Sally asked, "Richard, did you like me, did I please you?"

"What do you imagine? My dear, girl. Why do you have to ask after the way..."

"I like your voice. I would like to hear you say what you feel. I need your words as well as action. Do you understand?"

"Dear, Sally. Of course, I love you."

"So it wasn't me that made you hold back at first? It wasn't the fact that I was forward or that you didn't like me as much as you thought you would?"

"No, my own. It was me. It was all the years I spent trying to look away from the loose women in the camps. All the years in the navvy camps watching people rut like animals in the mud. And, poor Fanny."

"I believe that the taking of sexual pleasure with one's spouse is part of the divine plan," Sally said. "Without it, we would not procreate."

"But there must be marriage."

"Then," she said turning her face to his, and looking at him very searchingly "are we not now married in the sight of God? Oh, dear Richard, please say that you do not censure me for not waiting. I knew I would feel like your wife if we did this. That was what I really wanted. All the time you were in Manchester, I felt how tenuous was our connection. I had to feel more strongly bound to you when you went away this time."

"You surprise me, Sally. You have always been so strong and independent. I used to think you were just laughing at me when I came to call."

"Oh, no, Richard. I wanted you to know that I wasn't going to be a pet or an appliance, something to pick up and put down. I wanted you to know you would have to win my respect, by respecting me as a person with ideas and feelings that might be different from yours. Also, you were a boy when I met you. You have become a man while you were away. Now you are someone I can look up to as a protector. You even have a child now."

"Yes, she is a wonderful child, isn't she? I've not seen her like anywhere, not even the most intelligent children I've taught. Can you accept her as your own, do you think?"

"No matter what other children we have, she will be our first. I do love her already, Richard." Sally said as she pressed herself close to him and softly ran her hands across his stomach.

"And how many children shall we have?" he asked, turning toward her.

"As many as God brings us," she answered putting his hand on her breast.

Chapter 19

The following day, in spite of the cost and the possible risk of being watched by police, Richard took the coach to Dorchester, a place later made famous in Thomas Hardy's "The Mayor of Casterbridge." Like Casterbridge, Dorchester was the county centre of the corn trade, which was the main business in the area. It was the closest large town to the hamlet which had been Charles Wilney's home.

Richard felt there was not a moment to be lost if he were to find traces of Charles Wilney's killer. According to the newspaper, the constables had no idea of the murderer's identity. The coroner's verdict had been simply: "murder by person or persons unknown." Once the coach crossed the river and got out of the tangle of wagons, carriages, pedestrians and animals leaving London, it passed through the Surrey hills at nearly ten miles an hour, rolling easily on the smooth, paved road. They arrived at the coach house in Dorchester just after midnight. Not wishing to spend more of his money than necessary, Richard waited for sunrise on a bench near the great fire that burned in the fireplace of the large hall. At first light, he slipped out the door and continued to Higher Woodsford without speaking to anyone and, as far as he knew, without being observed.

In the rosy morning, he was once again by himself on a strange road. His heart lifted. The sun at his back threw his own shadow far ahead of him, pointing the way, and he thought, "I shall get to like being a tramp if I am not careful. My wife wouldn't like that."

He walked for several hours, sharing the road only occasionally with carts and wagons but more often with pedestrians whose dress and manner marked them as agricultural workers. Most people wore pattins, thick leather leggings almost knee high. Even the women wore them as protection against brambles and other low growing plants. Most of the carts lumbered along at a leisurely pace, occasionally overtaken by a smaller and speedier carriage: a physician's dog cart, a country lawyer's phaeton.

The further he went from Dorchester the more empty the road became until, perhaps an hour after noon, he turned into the ancient Roman thoroughfare which would take him, eventually, to the hillier and more heavily wooded country where his friend's village lay. At this turning he stopped and took out the bread and cheese Sally had wrapped for him on the morning of his departure. Nearby were some branches that had been lopped from an oak that had stood where now only the stump remained. When he finished eating, he picked up one of the smaller pieces, weighed it in his hand and decided to take it with him. The country was starting to feel lonelier and the afternoon shadows deeper. There were often tales of country tinkers and other itinerant merchants being assaulted and robbed, sometimes even killed in isolated places. Like the labouring poor, criminals too had their regular routes and houses of call. Richard had deliberately worn his London coat and hat to make a favourable impression on Vicar Franklyn. A hungry tramp might think him worthwhile prey. He tucked the cut wood under his arm and set off once more.

After following the old road for several more hours, Richard began the ascent of the hill that wore the village of Higher Woodsford on its crown. The shadows had filled in with advancing dusk. Nothing untoward had happened on the road and
Richard knew from Wilney's letters that the village was now just ahead. This was the same place where a hypothetical observer might have watched Wilney's murderer as he came along the road at almost exactly the same time of day. Now as then, the wooded edges of the thoroughfare were dark but the white dust of the ancient roman track was luminous with the ruddy rays of the nearly departed sun.

Richard knew from letters that Charles' most intimate friend in Higher Woodsford was the Vicar Franklyn, who lived in an ancient stone house next to the old Saxon church at the end of the high street. After Richard climbed the hill and entered the village, he could easily see the thick, square tower reaching up into the great oaks. The other stone buildings also spoke of antiquity and some even wore the same kind of heavy buttresses seen on the church. The additions since the time of the Norman Conqueror had been few. Here and there were a few low walls, visible relics of an even earlier time when Roman lords had made a local market of the town. Richard felt there must be a spell on the ancient place that had kept it hidden in the distant past. If the inhabitants had never heard of Bonaparte, he would not have been surprised. If Chaucer's pilgrims had passed this way, it might have been only yesterday. He thought of Charles' many references to local antiquities and the hours he had spent digging for small archaeological treasures: a bronze spear head, an ancient spade green with age, and his greatest find, a thick glass bottle brought all the way from Rome by a homesick settler who had come to this distant edge of the Empire.

Richard lifted the iron ring on the thick, wormy door of Reverend Franklyn's cottage and let it fall. The old wood and metal gave a dull boom. After a few minutes the door swung open and Richard saw a tiny, white haired woman with cheeks that looked like apples.

"Mrs. Franklyn?" Richard asked.

"No. Lad. I am Grace Damson, vicar's housekeeper. If you're looking for vicar, he's in garden."

Richard looked at her blankly.

"In back of house," she said closing the door.

Passing between the house and an ancient low wall thick with moss, lichen and vines, Richard soon saw a man, tall and thin as a stork, wearing a clerical collar with a rough canvas jacket. He was wrestling with a thick root that he was trying to pull out of his garden. If he had hold of the Leviathan, he could not have struggled any more vigorously.

"Sir," Richard called out, "Let me help." The vicar didn't even seem to hear him, so engaged was his attention.

Richard removed his town coat and laid hold of the root, adding his strength to the vicar's. In a moment the fibrous coil released its hold on Tartarus and both men nearly fell.

"Ah, finally." the vicar panted, "Thank you, young man. That monster has been in my way all through the summer. Ever since I added this patch to my garden. I doubt I could have pulled it without you. I have tried before."

"Vicar Franklyn?" Richard asked.

"Yes, sir. And whom do I have the pleasure of addressing?"

"I was a good friend of Charles Wilney, sir. My name is Richard Darrow."

"Oh, my. Richard," the older man said taking Richard's hand in a frank, friendly manner. " Of course, of course. Charles spoke of you many, many times. This is a great pleasure. You were his adopted son. I know I never wrote to you as Charles might have wished. I had no address for you. His death was so sudden."

Richard flushed with pride and sorrow when he heard himself described as Wilney's adopted son.

"I quite understand, sir."

The thin old man pulled out a venerable briar pipe from his pocket. On one side, the bowl had been badly scorched and blackened.

"Please come in to my house and refresh yourself. Have you come all the way from London?"

"Yes, sir. I left yesterday."

"Goodness, imagine. So far in such a short time. I was in London once. But it took nearly a week to get there. We had to walk most of the time because the roads were so bad. Come, come," he said taking Richard's arm and leading him in through the garden door.

"Mrs. Damson, we have a visitor. All the way from London. Poor Charles' adopted son."

The little lady reappeared and began her preparations for tea."Go to parlour, vicar," she ordered in her telegraphic north county speech.

The rooms of the house were half the size Richard would have expected from the exterior, because the stone walls were at least two feet thick. The fireplace in the parlour looked like a pile of loose stones with a fire burning in it. The wooden floor was rough and uneven, made of massively thick boards. The vicar reached into the flames that burned on his tumble down hearth and pulled out a burning brand, dexterously managing to light his pipe with it. Only the ancient brier the old man puffed on appeared to suffer any injury.

"Do you smoke, Richard?"

"No, sir. Thank you, sir."

Somehow the pipe made the sharp featured old man look even more like a stork. It seemed to complete the likeness. His gestures too, Richard decided, had the deliberation of one of the great birds wading in a marsh. There was a faint resemblence to Mr. Barnes.

"I suppose you have come to pay your respects and collect Charles' personal effects?"

"Yes sir and..."

"Wait," the vicar said suddenly holding up his pipe at arm's length,

"There is something...I have forgotten something in connection with Charles. It will come back as we speak."

"Yes, sir. I would very much like to visit Charles' grave and to see his home and all things that were his."

Richard was relieved to find himself so readily known and accepted. It would make it easy to go to the place of the crime and to ask as many questions as he would like.

"And you shall, young man. But first you'll dine with us and have a good night's rest. I am too old to pick my way through the woods in the dark, and you don't know the way. Charles lived quite a distance from the village, you know. And there is no road. But I do have some of Charles' archaeological treasures here. I am sure you will like to see those, and hear about how and where we found each one."

In the course of the evening, it developed that Charles and the vicar had done a great deal of digging together, both being avid antiquarians. Richard knew that Charles had first developed his interest in antiquities at railway excavations when strange looking creatures embedded in stone had been unearthed. Richard remembered Charles showing him odd-looking shells and telling him they were from a very early time, shortly after the world had been created. As a boy, Richard had thought the creatures very strange to be permitted in Eden, which he had pictured as a garden of unsurpassed beauty where all plants and animals were handsome.

The old man was a good story-teller and Richard enjoyed hearing about his teacher and friend. Charles came alive in an entirely new way as Richard shared the experiences of a man who had spent years as a neighbour and friend of the dead man. It almost made Charles more alive than reading his letters. Richard's relationship with Wilney had been one of student and teacher. The vicar spoke as a friend and equal which gave the younger man a different perspective of his departed friend.

When finally the old man lit the way up to the tiny room under the eaves, he said, "Now if you hear any noises in the night. Do not be alarmed. It is only the mice in the thatch and they shan't bother you."

Richard had thought he would lie awake, plot and plan, think about finding the murderer, how he could look for traces and, in general, how he should get on the following day. But after asking God to guard Sally and Emily, he quickly fell asleep, listening to the mice digging in the thatch and the voices of owls outside in the darkness.

* * *

After Richard had his tea and biscuits the following morning under the watchful eye of Mrs. Damson. She was pouring a second cup from the young man when the vicar appeared wearing heavy canvas gaiters and working man's clothes. Together, the two men walked through the ancient town in the fresh, dappled sunshine. The vicar pointed out a fragment of an old roman wall and a very ancient well that was believed to be of pre-roman, Celtic, origin. Then he led Richard off the road very near the crown of the hill. Down and off to one side was The Pilgrim, Cantle's inn. In that direction the country was an open network of hedgerows and fields, but in the direction the vicar took lay a thickly grown mixed plantation of trees. The path was well-worn and obviously used often, even though the area was heavily wooded. Richard mentioned his observation.

"Yes, this is a very old track," the vicar replied. " A right-of-way that dates back to the eleventh century. Everyone in the area uses it, though it crosses no less than seven holdings between here and Foyle's farm."

The notion that Charles had lived far from the village rested upon the way country people measured distance. For in slightly less than a quarter of an hour, Richard stood at the edge of the clearing where Wilney's cottage was situated. It was a very simple building, but in good repair, Richard thought. There was a pen for chickens which was empty. As they pushed open the rough door of the house, Richard saw a dark stain on the boards of the threshold.

"Is this where Charles was found?"

"Yes. The poor man's head was horribly broken. The monster must have been a giant to knock down Charles that way. He was himself a very strong man and still able bodied."

"Do you not keep his things locked up?"

"No. There is nothing here to steal. Charles never kept anything of value for himself, as I'm sure you know."

"But the papers...perhaps there is some trace of his killer."

"That's a romantic notion, young man. But here is something I know he especially wanted you to have."

"His bible," Richard said touching the thick leather covers reverently.

"He taught me to read using this book. I wondered how much of it had survived the outrage. He used to scramble verses and I had to unscramble them. He would make up doggerel to give me clues. It was a game to keep a restless child interested in reading."

Richard lifted the heavy book, nearly dropped it and an envelope fell out from the pages.

"That's it," the vicar cried out.

"What?" Richard asked looking at the envelope. His name was inscribed on it in Wilney's handwriting.

"This was the thing I had forgotten. Charles especially wanted you to have this bible and to read his letter carefully. This letter I really should have taken home. He was so adamant that you should read it carefully if any mishap overtook him. It was odd to see him so concerned about something so improbable, something that has now come true. Charles mentioned the letter and the Bible often. He knew how bad my memory could be."

"But I thought there were pages torn from the bible. I can see them myself. How could the letter be left inside the book without being soiled or damaged when the pages were torn?"

"Oh, the letter was not kept in the book. It was always on the mantle shelf. I put it in the book myself to keep the constables from taking it. I also reglued the covers back onto the book. You know that the killer was interrupted in his gruesome work?"

"No."

"Oh, yes, or he probably would have found the letter. All the drawers of the desk with papers in them had been turned over. It appeared that the killer had been looking for money among the papers. Mrs. Damson's niece, Suk, who used to do needlework for Charles, nearly saw him. She heard someone running into the trees when she approached that night. She is the one who found poor Charles."

"Well," Richard exclaimed excitedly. "If the killer was searching Charles' papers, then there is a good chance that the killer was someone Charles knew and not just some passing tramp."

"He may have just been looking for money and not the least bit interested in the papers. The constables are sure he was looking for money."

"Perhaps," Richard agreed reluctantly."Could we take the papers that are here along with the bible and letter and bring them back to your house, sir. I should very much like to have an opportunity to look through everything."

"Of course, of course, we may take them back. You know that this house is now yours?"

"No. I had no idea."

"Oh, yes. I was a witness when he made his will not six or seven months ago. There is only one acre with it so it is not very valuable and the surroundings are rather wild."

With this last comment they began collecting the few bits and pieces of Charles Wilney's life that lay scattered about the room. They left the dead man's house carrying the bible, the letter and other papers that the vicar had gathered from the desk, along with trinkets that Charles had unearthed on his archeological explorations with his old friend.

"Good heavens," Richard said suddenly after they were outside. He stopped walking. "Perhaps he made his will because he was uncertain of his life. This letter, too, and his instructions to you could indicate some foreboding. Perhaps in some way he foresaw this."

"Perhaps," the vicar was now the one who agreed reluctantly.

"You said he was able-bodied. No signs of weakness or illness in his last months?"

"No, he seemed in his usual strength."

"Then why else? Tell me, vicar. Did he seem at all apprehensive in recent months? Did he mind going out at night or anything of that kind?"

"Well, we were all apprehensive when the navvies began working in the neighbourhood. I would say Charles less than others. Though as it turned out, they were just surveying and have departed without any incident. Everyone wonders what will come of their work here. Perhaps we will have a railway even in our little out of the way corner."

"There were navvies here at the time of his death? And you tell me that it would take an unusually strong man to knock Charles down? Could it not have been a navvy?"

"I suppose, perhaps," the vicar said, shocked at the idea. "I think we were all much more comfortable believing that it was a chance tramp. No one at all connected with our village. Not even the navvies, who were well-behaved here"

"Well, the navvies would have been strangers."

"Yes. That's true. I just thought of them as belonging to the railways."

"But this kind of thing has been known to happen around navvy camps before, sir. That I know for a certainty."

"Oh, dear. I wonder if we should do anything about your observations. Perhaps send for the constables in Woodsford."

Richard thought of his own questionable status in the eyes of the law. Trying to explain it all to the old man seemed beyond his ability.

"Well, sir. It cannot do poor Charles any good. I think on the way back I should like to stop at his grave. Is he in the village churchyard?"

"Of course. This was his home and parish for many years. I shall leave you at the church gate. You'll find his marker just out in the far right hand corner of the yard. I am sure you would like to go alone."

"Thank you, sir."

The churchyard was old and crowded with crumbling stones. At the edge of the yard where it tapered off into the woods there were even a few stones with lengthy Latin inscriptions. Some were so weathered as to be almost illegible. Charles' modest white stone stood out in the brightness of the stone and the clarity of the inscription :

Charles Wilney, born 1785, died 1845. "A friend and teacher to all who wished to learn." The epitaph touched Richard to the quick and called forth memories of his own early years. It evoked the smoky smell of the stone and peat shanties and the odor of stale beer; the noise of many people talking, fighting even fornicating in one room. He had always felt better outside the shanties. The only company he sought was Fanny's and later Charles'. He saw himself guiding the little girl through the camp, around the most dangerous men, keeping her out of the way of their fights, rages and blows. He saw again Charles standing out in a field on a raw morning in early spring, the wind blowing his thick dark hair, preaching a sermon on temperance to a small group of Irish navvies. Richard could hear his clear tenor voice saying, "To be drunk is to become a weakling and join the lower orders. Sobriety is for the strong and total abstinence is for the strongest." There was a memory of his first copybook, given him by Charles. The boy had to fill page after page with the words, " The lord is my shepherd, I shall not want." The vividness of the past surprised him. Without knowing it, he had buried these experiences for many years. But to recall them and watch their passage through his mind at Charles' grave side seemed appropriate, even necessary. He suddenly put his hand on the gravestone and said aloud, "I swear, Charles, that if heaven allows, I shall find your killer and bring him to justice." As he said the words, he felt a strange kind of shudder pass through him, he described it later to Sally as a sort of magnetic current, hardening and strengthening him. It was as if his oath had unlocked new magazines of strength. A few moments later, he felt a drop of rain on the hand that was resting on Charles' stone and realized that the sky had grown dark with clouds during the time he'd been standing at the grave side. Then, the storm broke over the churchyard in earnest. It was time to go back to the vicarage and read Charles' letter.

The vicar was out "comforting the sick," Mrs. Damson informed him. "He put things in study. Up stairs, turn right," the old woman told him.

Richard found a snug room that had a prospect out over the garden and the wild, forested edge of the village. The number and quality of books on the shelves lining the stone walls surprised Richard. An old leather arm chair with holes in the upholstery had a colourful crocheted blanket thrown over it, and since it was the only chair in the room, Richard settled into it, sharing it with a large, smoky gray cat who accommodated him with sleepy good grace. Overhead, the undressed logs supporting the roof were clearly visible, giving the high-ceilinged room the character of a primitive cathedral. He looked briefly at the sheets of rain cascading down the window, and wondered at the vicar being out in such heavy weather. Then he picked up Charles' letter and bible and put them on his lap. He unsealed the letter addressed to himself and began to read.

"Dear Richard, If you are reading this, the worst has happened." As the young man's eye fell on this line, his heart beat fast. He had been right: Charles had known he was under threat of death.

"Do not grieve. I have lived a rich life. I am strong in faith and am going to meet my Maker, with whom, for many years, I have endeavoured to be on good terms. I exhort you to be certain you are of the same condition when your time comes. I am at peace, but my chief concern, now, is for you and little Fanny. I have thought long about what to do to protect you..."

Richard broke off reading for a moment. How right he had been to come here as quickly as possible. How else would he have ever learned about this message from beyond the grave. It could have lain forgotten forever by the vicar and may have ended in dust. He picked up the letter once again, breathless with excitement.

"...and could think of no better way to proceed than to write you this letter of warning, exhort you to read with extraordinary care the Bible I have left you, and recall the word game we used to play called 'doggie in the well.' I hope you remember it clearly. I am counting on it. I cannot say more here. I only hope the good vicar's memory doesn't betray me and that he passes this and the Bible on to you.

I want you to know that I have always thought of you as my own son. Your intelligence, learning and probity have made me feel that my life as a teacher has been a great success. May God bless you and Fanny always. I am sorry that I could not have seen you in later years and done more to advance you in life. It is the only thing I have ever regretted about being poor. This once I allow myself to close by signing,

Your Loving Father who knows you stand in the Light of Christ, Charles Wilney."

By the time he reached the end, Richard's tears were falling as thick and fast as the rain on the window. He sat for some time in the darkening afternoon, lost in his melancholy. His sadness over losing Charles was intermixed with his sadness about Fanny. He was glad he had not told Charles about her fall. Losing them both was a heavy blow. But finally, he roused himself by thinking about Sally and Emily. "The lord giveth and the lord taketh away," he murmured. Thinking of the present, and the crime he had come to solve, he was able to shake off his sorrowful mood.

He began to think about how to solve the problem of the letter. He bent his memory back in time to try to remember the game, "doggie in the well" that Charles mentioned. Charles had always loved word games and had used them as effective teaching tools with Richard. The younger man had used some of the same techniques in his own classroom. But the obscure reference to "doggie in the well." eluded him. He could not remember such a game. Charles had made many acrostics out of biblical passages. They had always used his family Bible. He picked up the big book, opened it and in shifting its weight disturbed the cat, who found the seat too unsettled to remain. The animal jumped down on the floor and looked back at the young man with an expression of disgust. Richard, however, paid little attention to the feline's displeasure and opened the bible.

The vandalized pages had born the names of Charles' family for three gen-

erations and had been savagely ripped out of the binding. Had there been some indication of identity that the killer had wanted to destroy? Richard wondered. The rest of the book was perfectly intact. The covers were of thick leather stretched over carved wooden forms so that each cover was itself was nearly an inch thick. The vellum pages gave
the old book tremendous weight and size. Tearing out the thick pages from such a strong, heavy binding would require a very deliberate effort and a powerful hand. Why the names? Richard wondered. What was there about Charles' family that the killer wanted to hide? Could it be a family member who had committed the brutal crime? The only relative that Richard had ever heard the dead man mention was the cousin who had once disputed his claim to the little cottage. Charles had told Richard that when the man had lost the cottage to Charles, he and his family had emigrated to the Americas.

He re-read Charles letter, then dropped it into his lap.

"He exhorts me to read very carefully the bible and to remember an obscure word game we once played," the young man said out loud. "He says he is counting on my recollection of the game. Why?"
Then, suddenly, five words seemed to leap off the page at him: "I cannot say more here." Surely, this implied that more could or would be said elsewhere. He began slowly turning the pages of the bible and noticed a series of very small dots alongside different passages. The dots were present in the margins all the way through the huge volume. They had been neatly and deliberately marked. They were not accidental. He suddenly realized that they must be part of one of Charles' acrostics.

Charles had never marked the Bible when teaching Richard, he had always copied out verses that were part of an acrostic. Perhaps what he had wanted to say was too long to write out all the verses needed. If that were so, it would make sense simply to mark the verses in the book. The game mentioned in the letter might give him the key to the scrambled meaning of the verses with dots next to them! If the game ran true to form, it would have a verse component and a numerical component. The verse component was given with the marks. The numerical component would unlock the meaning of the marked passages. But he had forgotten the game, utterly, lost the numerical component, the pattern for unlocking the word order to be used in reading the marked lines. He could not even remember
having heard the name, "Doggie in the well." In his frustration, Richard sprang out of the chair and paced back and forth like a caged beast. He grabbed his hair and tugged at it.

"Doggie in the well, doggie in the well, doggie in the well, I cannot even remember hearing the name before."
The rules themselves, he knew, based on other games Charles had invented could be complex.

"Oh, lord," he muttered. "That is the key to unlocking the secret meaning of the verses Charles has marked and I have lost it. Probably lost it forever, along with Charles' complete message which very likely included the identity of his killer! I am given all this help only to fail him in the end. No, no, it must not be. I must remember."

"Wouldn't you like a lamp in here, Richard?" the vicar's voice seemed to cut through his thoughts. His briar glowed in the near darkness of room.

"Oh, vicar, pardon me. I have made such extraordinary discoveries but I have lost the key itself."

"This sounds exciting, indeed, Richard," he said reaching over to light a second oil lamp on the desk.

"It is exciting, sir. I believe I am on the edge of knowing everything about Charles' killer. But I have lost the key."

For the next quarter hour, Richard acquainted the vicar with his discoveries and what they might mean.

"Oh dear me," the vicar said. "Charles and his word games. He was always inventing them. But he rarely gave them names. Hmmm. Doggie in the well? You know it actually does sound familiar. I think I have actually heard of it. But goodness, that is all I can remember."

"Well, it is more than what I can offer, vicar."

"Perhaps if we let it go for a while and try to enjoy the mutton that Mrs. Damson is baking, it will come to us. Come, my young friend," he said taking Richard's arm. "Let us go down to the table and refresh ourselves."

With a sinking heart, Richard let himself be led to the stairs.

***

The plain but excellent meal seemed to Richard to last forever. Conversation was taken up with the vicar's day of rounds and the younger man heard the names of many people he would never know. Finally, the older man rose, signalling that the meal was over.

"Let us stimulate ourselves with some fortified wine," he suggested, "and retire to the study. You go up. I shall bring another chair."

Richard carried the two glasses upstairs and left the vicar mumbling about furniture in the dining room. The bible and letter were both where he had left them. The mere sight of them made him feel irritable and frustrated. After some minutes he said aloud, "I am letting him down. If his killer is not brought to justice, it will be my fault."

"Now, now, Richard. That kind of self-punishment will produce nothing," the vicar said as he was preceded into the doorway by his glowing pipe and the chair he carried.

"But what else can I think, vicar? If I cannot remember this game, if I do not remember it, I have let Charles' killer escape."

"Well, Charles had faith that you could remember it. So why don't we just talk about Charles and the times we spent with him. Let us give the Lord time to help us. That's what works best for prodding my own memory."

"Very well, sir. You, at least, remember the name of the game."

But the evening of reminiscences dragged on until after eleven. The lamp burned low and the vicar began to yawn. Richard, too, felt worn out.

It was twelve when he took the watch out to wind and crawled into bed, exhausted more by frustration than by exertion. He resolved that on the following morning, if there were not new developments, he must return to Sally and Emily in London.

When he told the vicar of his intentions on the following morning at breakfast, the older man disagreed.

"There are still other papers to look at. There may be other indications of what we seek. The cottage itself has only had the most perfunctory examination. You see, Richard you have shown me that solving crime is very much like archaeology. The criminal agent and the archaeologist are both trying to unlock the past from small crumbs of evidence. I know from experience that one has to be very methodical and look at every tiny grain of information, if one wants to unlock the past. I honestly believe that leaving is not a good idea. I believe it is only your own restlessness speaking. You have made a big discovery, that is true. But very often something very small will provide the key to unlocking the larger meaning of a site. I urge you to stay a while longer, at least. I, too, am anxious to see if we can learn anything more."

"Then I must send a letter to London, advising people how I am to be found if needed."

"I can have a rider take it to Woodsford. If it gets there before four o'clock, it should reach the London mail coach in Dorchester in time."

"Then, if you'll excuse me, sir. I'll write my letter immediately. And, sir, thank you for your help and hospitality."

"Charles was my dearest friend, Richard. I, too, want to catch his killer, not for revenge. But because I believe that apprehending the culprit will help relieve everyone in the village."

***

Busy days flowed by Pamela in the weeks after she began recovering from her father's death. Instructing the servants and having final authority on all things relating to Blackdale took up more time than she had anticipated, even with the very excellent help of Harrison, the steward. She met with Barnes whenever he had a letter from someone who sounded as if he or she might know anything that could help find Emily. In the end, though, out of hundreds of letters received, there was only one letter whose writer was invited to Manchester for closer questioning. With all of this, however, Pamela never failed to practice a regular six hours a day and to have her lessons with Herr Bruckner well-prepared. At her most recent lesson at Rivington Hall, he had said to her, "You have attack, you have velocity and articulation. Now, Miss Blackwood, we will concentrate on tonal shading and rhythmic subtlety. For me these are the things that separate good pianists from great ones. When Herr Lizst plays old Master Bach's simplest music, he could make angels weep with his tonal shading. You must learn to do the same."

"But Herr Bruckner, how can you mention me in the same breath with Herr Lizst. I am just a votary of music. He is a god."

"Do not think that way, Miss Blackdale. Herr Lizst has his weaknesses and you have your strengths. We will build on those. We must all strive to do our best. Not for ourselves but for our art. Also, we need to spend more time on your knowledge of harmonic structure. You must be a skilled improvisor to be a great performer."

To achieve his ends, the handsome young music master insisted that she now play the music of Bach and Mozart, exclusively.

"These are the two greatest geniuses of music in all of history, though they are out of favour right now. When you have learned to understand and express all the harmonic and tonal qualities of these masters, you will be a great musician, indeed. With these masters everything is pure music. There is no passage which is merely brilliant. Study them well and listen with close attention even to the simplest phrases.

Listen," he said sitting at the keyboard. "Mozart at first seems simple." The fingers of Bruckner's right hand danced over the keys, playing the opening solo of Mozart's D Major violin concerto. The attack was sharp, percussive. "But then," and he continued the lilting answer to the opening phrase. "You see? A different face. A different character entirely. Yet these two faces must be one. His harmonic ideas must be stitched together perfectly. He changes musical character often. It is like changing his face. He wears so many different faces in one piece of music, your rhythm must be absolutely perfect to make all of his faces a single one—without sounding like a ticking clock. You must reveal the genius that lies beneath the apparent simplicity of Mozart, while retaining his purity and simplicity. It is one of the greatest musical challenges you will ever have. You did this well but unknowingly when you first played Mozart for me. That is why I was so impressed with you."

A few months earlier, Pamela would have argued and been bored with composers she had played well long ago. But she had already learned the difference between being playing notes and playing music. When Bruckner played she could hear that difference immediately. She had submitted herself entirely to Bruckner's judgment, bending herself to his will more readily than she had ever done with anyone else in her entire life. She saw her own father, now, in these terms, as well. He had been a master of the world he occupied, not a mere fortunate speculator. His results in business had been as certain as Bruckner's were at the keyboard. When he gambled with some of his holdings, he made certain that his other enterprises were secure. He provided workers with good conditions and paid them well so that he could choose the best ones. As she had already learned from her music teacher, great achievements and brilliance were not enough to be a master. Mastership required also, evenness , consistency and wisdom. Mastery was now her goal, even more than a successful career. If she never played anywhere but in an empty room, it would not matter, providing she had mastered her art. Developing this attitude, to serve the art and not oneself, was Pamela's most important attainment. It is the most important attainment for any artist, for it is precisely at this point that the practice of art transcends technique and becomes a spiritual process. When Bruckner saw this attitude grow in Pamela, he knew she had acquired the key to becoming an artist. She was no longer a talented little girl trying to gain applause, nor a seductive young woman at the keyboard. She was allowing the music to have more importance than herself.

Lady Thornsby was also gratified by the progress of the lessons, which she still attended. She felt it a duty to keep a watchful eye on the young people. Also, Pamela's playing had become a joy to hear. Never had the old lady had such wonderful music in her house for so long a time. In order to continue the lessons, Bruckner had been invited to stay until the spring when, he would go on tour again. He, too, practiced most of the day, sitting beneath the tapestry depicting the court of love. Occasionally, Lady Thornsby would enter the room without shoes on her feet, so as not to disturb the maestro. Then, she would slip out again after an hour or so.

Pamela had been playing Bach and Mozart for several weeks when Mr. Barnes received a letter from a man with the obviously invented name of Mr. Darkwinter, "creator," his letter said "of a unique and valuable stenographic system." The letter explained that Darkwinter sold his system on printed cards, and had often stood near Fanny's stall. He and Richard used to exchange greetings in Greek and Latin. For he, too, the letter claimed, was a classical scholar. And several lines of good, literate Greek followed the assertion. Barnes translated it as "He can only offer what he truly possesses." The letter went on to say that the writer believed he might be able to offer information useful to those seeking Richard. He had spoken with brother and sister often. He was much more vague in his assertions about the little girl. The letter was written in long, flowing sentences that were certainly the work of an educated man, even if he was a London street merchant. He would not be the first scholar to take to the streets through misfortune or out of a gypsy-like temperament that could not bear a fixed address or mode of work.

Barnes summoned Darkwinter, offering to pay for his return transport. His reply to Darkwinter made it very clear that the reward was not yet his and would have to be earned. Barnes reminded him that the reward would only be paid to someone who offered information that led directly to the return of Emily to her home at Blackdale. With this stipulation, Mr. Darkwinter was invited to come to Mr. Barnes' office at such a time and date.

Since Darkwinter was the only person they had culled out of hundreds, Pamela awaited the appearance of Darkwinter with some anxiety. She had never regretted any- thing in her life as much as the way she had treated Emily. Contrary to her father's own wishes, she had ignored and neglected the child. Everything she was learning about music from Herr Bruckner made her behaviour with Emily seem even more reprehensible.

The day that Darkwinter was due to arrive at Mr. Barnes' chambers, Pamela preceded him by half an hour, so anxious was she to hear what he had to say. She was also in some measure curious about the species of man she was about to meet since the idea of a highly literate man who made his living selling cards on the London streets seemed an extraordinary contradiction to her.

She sat alone in the outer office, except for the ever-present Wilson, whose pen scratched monotonously over the foolscap. His lines were written so regularly that Pamela compared the commencement and cessation of each line to the ticking of a metronome. Finally, on the stroke of the great courthouse clock, the door to the chambers opened and there stood Mr. Darkdwinter. He was a slender, wiry man of middle height, his face shaven so closely that his chin had a blue tinge. His nose was roman and rather short for his face and on either side of it each eye was of a different colour, one green and the other blue. His hat had been brushed so often that it was bald in spots. His linen was dingy but starched to perfection. The points of his collar looked as though they would cut his neck if he turned his head too quickly. He met the world with a smiling, confident countenance, in spite of the fact that his umbrella, clothes and gloves all showed signs of having been patched and darned many times. Even so, he was spotlessly clean and his clothes carefully pressed. He gave his name and card to Wilson with an air that said, "You, a head clerk in a prosperous law office may think me poor, but I am here to do Business and require the deference that you must pay to Business." In short, if Mr. Darkwinter had been the proprietor of the law offices, he could not have looked more in possession of himself or his circumstances.

"Mr. Darkwinter?" Pamela said.

"Do I have the honour of addressing Miss Blackwood?" he asked, and as he asked, he stepped backward with a slight bow and looked at Pamela directly in the eyes.

His expression was at once so bold and so obsequious that for a moment she hardly knew how to respond. Her impression was of a highly intelligent and rather charming knave. He was quite good-looking in a very shopworn way. It was hard to think of him as a man of scholarly attainments.

"You do, sir," she said finally. "And are you the Mr. Darkwinter who is a classical scholar?"

"Ah, the lady is herself a scholar? Especially admirable attainment for a woman.""I am not a scholar but my attorney, Mr. Barnes is, sir." She already doubted his honesty but had to admit to herself that she liked him for his smiling roguishness. Would he really know anything about Richard or Emily?

Mr. Barnes entered the chambers and the introductions were repeated. The solicitor, who from years of being exposed to knaves of all sorts, was proof against their charm in any form, was colder than Pamela. He began by speaking classical Greek to Darkwinter. To Pamela's surprise, Darkwinter smiled even more broadly and began smoothly to run off a long speech in the same language, delivered in a courteous tone to Mr. Barnes. He appeared more at home in the strange tongue than did the solicitor.

"Let us go into my office," Mr. Barnes said, finally interrupting what might have been an endless demonstration. "Miss Blackwood is the client for whom I act in this matter. She will be the final judge of the value of the information you provide."

Darkwinter bowed deeply. "My condolences, Miss, on the loss of your child. There are terrible rogues on every corner who will do anything to those weaker than themselves. It is positively shocking, Miss Blackwood, that in our own great metropolis children are not safe." As they all sat down in Barne's office,he continued smoothly, "But in my own uninformed opinion, Richard Darrow seems an unlikely person to have taken your little girl."

"Oh, do you think so, too?" Pamela asked.

The girl looked too obviously pleased with what Darkwinter had said about Darrow, Barnes thought. I must take control of the interview, but before the solicitor could speak, Pamela asked,"Do you know Mr. Darrow well?"

"No, miss. But customers who have need of my unique system of stenography are accustomed to find me and my system, neatly printed on fifty cards complete, Miss, next to the stall where Mr. Darrow's sister customarily sold her excellent vegetables. When he visited her, which was twice a day, when coming and going from the school where he taught, he would stop and we would exchange a few words. Sometimes classical words, sometimes English words. Mr. Darrow is a fine scholar and a man of many excellent acquirements as to knowledge."

"And have you seen him recently, Mr. Midwinter," Mr. Barnes asked.

"No, I have not."

"Tell us of this sister," Barnes said. "Does she sell herself to men?"

"Gracious, no sir. She is certainly very handsome but I have never heard her solicit any gentleman for other than vegetables. Though many gentlemen do stop at her stall. I always thought brother and sister quite respectable, sir. And I, sir, in addition to my stenographic and classical achievements have also taken orders as a deacon."

"Really," Barnes said dryly. "Very respectable, indeed."

"Yes, sir."

"You see Mr. Barnes," Pamela said. "I told you Mr. Darrow would not take Emily. And certainly not against her will."

"So far," the solicitor said, "this man's statement is entirely inconclusive, Miss Blackwood."

"I don't know," Pamela said archly, "I think this man would know a rascal if he saw one."

In spite of the clear implication of Pamela's remark, Darkwinter rose and bowed to her, meeting her with the blandest of bold faces. "You do me no more than justice, Miss. Years of working the London streets has, I believe, given me a penetrating insight into human character."

It almost seemed to Pamela that his green eye winked at her. Pamela was smiling broadly when she said to Barnes, "How much do you think we should pay Mr. Darkwinter for coming all the way from London,

Mr. Barnes?"

"Pay him? He has not told us anything. Why should we pay him anything."

"I will definitely undertake, Miss Blackwood," Darkwinter said, "that if I receive any intelligence of your child, I shall forward it immediately to you or your solicitor. I want to be of service in any way I can."

"Give him fifty pounds, Mr. Barnes."

"What! That's a very large sum, Miss Blackwood," the solicitor remonstrated. Darkwinter began pulling on his darned gloves with great deliberation. He could not have looked any more pleased with himself if he had been a cat who had just stolen the cream.

"Please see that he gets that amount, Mr. Barnes," Pamela repeated. "But first, I should like to ask some additional questions."

"I am at your service, Miss Blackwood," Darkwinter said bowing slightly before sitting down again.

Both Pamela and the solicitor tried for the better part of an hour to get more information from Darkwinter, but he really had nothing more to offer, other than his own life story of academic successes and pecuniary failures, punctuated with quotes from classical authors and Dr. Johnson, whom he called "the leviathan of literature," and William Shakespeare.

Barnes finally rose with a look of irritation plainly written on his face. He went to the door and held it open for Darkwinter.

"If I can be of some future service to you, Miss," Darkwinter said, "do not hesitate to contact me. Allow me to offer you my card." Then with a slight bow, he turned gracefully on his heel and was gone with the solicitor into the outer room to collect his fifty pounds.

Pamela glanced at the card. It read: The Darkwinter Method of Modern Stenography, developed by O. Darkwinter, M.A. classics and divinity, Cambridge.

The London address given was in a part of the metropolis unknown to her. Though she was disappointed in his information, Darkwinter had amused her. She had never met anyone so honestly a rogue in all her life. It made it a little easier to bear that she had gotten no closer to finding Emily. She also had faith in Darkwinter's assessment of Richard and Fanny. She now believed that it was Samuelson's son who had ruined the girl and not the other way around.

"The rogue I have just met," she thought, "is harmless. But Samuelson is a rogue who is truly dangerous. He would like to take and control my father's companies if he could. I must talk to Barnes and make certain he is never given the opportunity."

She broached the subject when the solicitor returned. His response alarmed her.

"I don't think you realize, Miss Blackwood, the extent to which your father wanted Samuelson's money to help him complete several large projects he had in mind. Without Samuelson's money, Blackwood Holdings would have to reduce its projected undertakings or you might have to sell Blackdale to cover business expenses."

"But I thought we were very solvent. I thought there was a surplus of money."

"Well, you are, Miss Blackwood. But you can't cover the cost of the investments your father wanted to make out of your own pocket. You must use other people's money as well, and Mr. Samuelson was a natural investor. He grasped the ideas and he had the money, and they dovetailed with his existing business."

"I do not want that man involved in our business," Pamela said sharply."I do not trust him."

"I shall have to speak with him then, Miss. Certain agreements have already been signed."

"Do they bind us to using his money?"

"Not really. They are just letters of intent that lay the basis for a possible future relationship."

"Tear them up."

"I cannot do that, Miss Blackwood without consulting the directors of the company. And it is my own judgement, that this would be a mistake."

"We must not sign anything that would bind us to that man in any way, Mr. Barnes. I insist upon it."

"If you insist, I shall talk to Samuelson and to the directors of the company. That is all I can promise. While you do hold the majority of shares, you do have four partners. They act as directors. You don't want to do anything to make them want to sell out and reinvest."

"To whom could they sell? Doesn't it have to be to one of the other partners?"

"Other partners get right of first refusal, but after that, they could sell to anyone."

"Even to Samuelson?"

"Even to Samuelson."

"So unless I buy all the shares, I may be forced to do business with Mr. Samuelson."

"You do not have sufficient capital to buy all the shares. And the company should have money to expand. A business must grow, or it will die."

"Can we not sell stock in a company to increase capital?" she asked.

Barnes frowned. "I do not like joint stock companies with publicly traded stock. I know they are the rage now among middle-class investors who are putting their money into things they know nothing about, but I highly disapprove. The investors end up with something they don't understand and the company ends up with investors who don't know the business of the company. It puts the company at the mercy of strangers. No, Miss Blackwood. I highly dislike that method of raising money."

"But it could be done, if need be?"

"It could be done with your portion of the assets," Barnes

said reluctantly.

"Well, sir, I will do anything rather than have Mr. Samuelson as a partner in my father's businesses."

"As your business advisor, Miss Blackwood, I must tell you that your prejudice does neither your judgment or your father's judgement in trusting you with his holdings, credit. Mr. Samuelson's holdings and your own make an alliance highly desirable."

"Explain exactly why that is, Mr. Barnes," Pamela said sitting down again.

"He builds railways that run on coal. He is considering retaining partial ownership of some of the lines he is going to build. That would be an expansion of business for him. Until now, he has only built for other owners. This would invest some of his money in the actual railways themselves. Some of his lines run close to your father's collieries. You have coal. If you sold him coal at a lower price than you might currently, and in return got some of the profits of his railway building activity, you would both be more diversified and would probably make more money into the bargain."

"Probably but not certainly," Pamela said.

Pamela stood up. I shall think about all this, Mr. Barnes. I shall think very carefully about it, but I must tell you that I distrust, Mr. Samuelson in my bones. The thought of having him as a partner makes me very uneasy."

Pamela rode home in her carriage with a feeling of foreboding. She knew she did not know enough about business to command Barnes. The only thing she did know was that she distrusted Samuelson more than ever after hearing Darkwinter's account of Richard and his sister. It had agreed with her own opinion of Richard. And what was Barnes talking of when he spoke of speculations her father wanted to undertake? Perhaps there would be something among her father's papers at home that would help guide her. There was no one else to help her except the solicitor and she could see he was reluctant to do as she wished. She resolved to search her father's papers immediately on arriving at Blackdale. All of this made her suddenly feel less in control of her life than she had. It seemed there were forces that could make changes in Blackwood Holdings without her consent. She wanted to protect her father's legacy and to remain free to pursue her own vision of the future. So strong had this instinct for freedom become that she was morbidly sensitive to any possible reduction of her self-governance. For the first time, at the solicitor's office, she sensed vaguely that it might be next to impossible to avoid a business relationship with Samuelson. It made her so uneasy that she shut herself in the library as soon as she got home, ordered the servants not to disturb her on any account and worked right through the diner hour, reading over her father's papers. She finally fell asleep in her father's chair.

When Pamela woke, it was dark and the house was quiet. Once more, she began poring over her father's correspondence, looking for something, she knew not what, that might clarify her situation. What she finally found, shocked her deeply. It was a draft of a letter sent to Samuelson and copied to Mr. Barnes. It discussed Pamela's future marriage to Paul as a thing already done. "As long as she is permitted to study music with this German and Paul is not too foolish about this harlot, I see no reason why we shall not have them married by the spring. Then our interests will be truly united and we'll control a vast network of railways and coal from Manchester southward. We'll be able to deliver more coal to London, at better prices than any other single competitor."

The spoiled and loving daughter could hardly believe that her father would speak of her almost like another possession, part of a business plan. The letter went on to detail how Samuelson's investment money would be used and how many shares of each company he would get for his funds. After the initial shock had passed Pamela realized that her father had behaved as she would, herself: he used every available resource to realize his vision of the future, just as she would stop at nothing to master her art. Both attitudes were ruthless. However, her resolve affected no one other than herself. Her father's ruthlessness would have changed her life, changed it in a way that he knew she had not wanted.

"Apparently," she thought, "he did not take my ideas of remaining unmarried very seriously." Nor had he understood my relationship to music and what it meant to me.

It was a difficult moment for Pamela to discover her father's less than perfect understanding of his daughter. She had always felt such a fondness and respect for him that at no time had he ever seemed less than perfect in his love and understanding of her. It would be years before she could integrate her idealized love of him with the contents of the letter she had found. She could little understand the grip of the empire-building fever which had spread across Britain and her colonies, nor why machines and money should become more important to her father than the feelings of his daughter's own heart. For the moment, the young girl simply felt betrayed and beset by powerful enemies who were united in their goal to make her marry, or do business with someone she neither liked nor trusted. Far from finding a solution to her predicament, the letter had made it seem worse. She felt she had only one real ally left. She must speak with Herr Bruckner about her future very soon. She resolved to find a way to speak privately with the music master.

The following morning she wrote to him:

"Dear Herr Bruckner, My pianoforte is not behaving properly and I would consider it a great personal favor if you would come to Blackdale with my friend Alicia when she comes from Manchester in our carriage on Thursday next. I know you could explain what is wrong with it and tell me in a way I can write down for the mechanic. Your grateful student, Pamela Blackwood."

Then she penned a short note to Alicia telling her of the ruse she was using to get out from under Lady Thornsby's watchful eye. Alicia would never be picked up by the Blackwood barouche. Pamela wanted to talk to Bruckner alone. These two letters dispatched, Pamela tried to quell her restlessness until the appointed time and continue to practice and carry out her duties as mistress of Blackdale.

Pamela's general uneasiness since the meeting at Barne's office was magnified when, two days after posting her letters to Bruckner and Alicia, two dozen fresh-cut roses arrived from Mr. Samuelson senior with a card requesting a personal interview.

"He wants my father's holdings and has decided to approach me directly," Pamela thought to herself. "What should I do?" Samuelson's sudden direct appeal made her interview with Herr Bruckner seem more important than ever. She looked at the card once more and noted the bold flourishes of the signature, John R. Samuelson.

He will be able to see me if he likes with Barne's connivance at the solicitor's chambers, she thought. Here I shall be on my own ground, and there will only be one person I have to fend off. I might as well see what his next stratagem will be. I can't protect myself if I cut myself off from information.

She quickly strode to her desk and dashed off a reply, "Come today or tomorrow. Pamela Blackwood." That would give her several days before seeing Herr Bruckner. If seeing him failed to help her see her way, she was lost.

* * *

Samuelson's response was prompt. A note arrived later in the day naming four o'clock as the time for their interview, which just gave Pamela time to finish her practice. She knew from experience that the calming focus of practicing would strengthen her mind and feelings for dealing with Samuelson. She deliberately played right up to the moment that a servant knocked on the door and announced that the railway king had arrived.

Pamela met him in the entrance hall. The servant explained that the visitor had declined to be seated. He had ridden his own horse and was dressed simply in a long, bottle green shooting coat. He extended his hand to Pamela as though she were a man. In his other hand he carried a briefcase bulging with papers. On meeting him in the front entrance way what struck Pamela most was the strength of his jaw and intelligence of his brow. The long shooting coat made him look even taller than his already great height. His address to her was so direct and forthright that she was thrown off her guard almost immediately.

"I have come to discuss business with you, Miss Blackwood."

"You mean the marriage of your son, sir?"

"No. That is between you and Paul. My honest opinion is that he has acted the fool."

"Then to what business do you refer, Mr. Samuelson?"

"I wanted to brief you about several projects that your father and I were hoping to undertake together."

"Why brief me about them, sir?"

"Because you would be my new partner, if I can convince you of the value of these projects. Can we sit down somewhere so that I can go into the details with you?"

Pamela was surprised and she had to admit, pleased, by the direct, respectful tone of the railway king. The fact that he did not want to talk of marriage to his son was a great relief to her. Now, she felt, any other question would be comparatively easy to handle. It never occurred to her that complete openness could be a powerful tactic, especially when an adversary is expecting deceit.

She led the way to her father's library, sat down beneath her own portrait and gestured to a chair facing her seat.

"Do sit down Mr. Samuelson."

"Thank you, Miss Blackwood."

"Would you care for any refreshment after your ride?"

"No thank you, Miss Blackwood. I would rather go right to the point."

"Very well," Pamela said sitting back in her chair.
Samuelson drew out a large map of England.

"If you'll excuse me, Miss Blackwood. I think I can make things clearer if we look at this map together." He got up, came around the desk and spread the map in front of her. "The railways I am already planning to build are marked in red. Unlike other lines I have built, I am planning to retain partial ownership of these lines.

"Mr. Barnes told me of your plans, sir."

"Blackwood Holdings' mines and rail links in the midlands are marked in blue. The essential idea of joining these enterprises was that your father's interests which are local would connect with mine which are on the verge of being truly international in scope. One of the great advantages of an alliance is that we would have our own source of coal near to our lines. Do you see?" he asked as they looked at the map together.

"Then tell me, sir, what do your larger operations acquire from Blackwood Holdings?"

"Your father's mines are the best run pits in this part of the country. I wonder if you know what a wise and clever man your father was? I mean as regards his businesses?"

"I know only what principles guided him. They seemed wise to me. I do not know the particulars."

"Well, then, Miss Blackwood, allow me tell you that the way he has bought land and built his local railways to deliver coal to the most likely routes to important markets was brilliantly conceived. For example, for years Worsley coal has reached Manchester by water or land in a route that has gave the Bridgewater Canal run by Bradshaw a monopoly and the ability to fix prices. In essence, Bradshaw controlled the flow of coal to Liverpool and kept prices artificially high."

"And that is no longer so?"

"The Manchester & Liverpool Railway broke the Bridgewater monopoly very quickly. The union of your father's mines, coordinated with the routes I've planned, will enable us to carry far more coal, much faster to destinations other than Liverpool. Prices will come down. We will beat the competition on price and take their markets. That is the strategy in brief"

Without realizing it, Pamela was flattered by this explanation. Not even her father had ever talked to her of things like this. He had told Emily more about his businesses in a few short months than he had ever discussed with her. It did not occur to her that prior to the events of the last few months, she had had no interest in these things. But since her father's death, she had grown up quickly. Now, she found these explanations interesting, not only because the railway king was treating her as an equal, but also because the issues themselves began to seem important.

"And what will the result of that be, Mr. Samuelson?"

"Profits for our companies and growth and strength for England and the world. Has your father told you of the amazing ship that Mr. Brunel has built?"

"No."

"An ocean going steam ship that is driven without a paddle wheel, Miss Blackwood. I think I can show you. I'm certain your father had copies of Mr. Brunel's plans."

The big man stepped lightly over to the case of large, flat drawers where her father's plans and blueprints were kept. Each drawer was labeled alphabetically. He pulled several open and closed them again. While he was doing this, Pamela marveled at the way Samuelson had taken command of their meeting. Not against her will, but because he had interested her in what he had to say. He pulled two large sheets of vellum out of a drawer and brought them to her desk.

"Here it is, The Great Britain, an all metal ship with a unique method of locomotion. Look at this propeller in this detail down near the corner."

"It looks like a common carpenter's screw," Pamela said.

"Not quite. But that is the idea. It allows ships to push through the tremendous ocean currents and waves without being swamped by them. Ships like this one will dominate the seas and need coal to run them, a great deal of coal. If we can deliver more coal, more cheaply to more ports, we will make a great deal of money. Ships like The Great Britain will make England the world's greatest power for decades, perhaps centuries to come. They will move English goods all over the world, faster than ever before. We could be a highly profitable part of that great future, Miss Blackwood."

The young woman looked up at the big man who towered over her. His excitement and energy were palpable. He believed in his ideas with a strength that was nearly irresistible. She felt this force tugging at her. Part of her wanted to be drawn to the source of it, Samuelson himself. She understood now this man's enormous success and power, the force that had lifted him from the mud of navvy camps to the pinnacle of society. The expression "force of character" came to her mind. For the first time in her life, she knew what it really meant. If it had not been for the spiritual joy and exultation she experienced daily at the pianoforte, she might have succumbed to the plans of the railway king then and there. But her profound experience of the immortality of art and her own pledge of service to music gave her another perspective from which to see this future of profits, national growth and mercantile greatness, which, in the past, might have tempted her personal vanity. Now, however, music had become a sacred thing, something more valuable than any earthly treasure or gratification. Until that moment she had not known how holy a thing her art had become, nor how much strength her vow of service to it had given her. But she did know that she dared not make any business judgement while in Samuelson's presence. He was far more dangerous than she had known, and in a much more personal way than she had imagined.

After Samuelson had finished speaking, she sat quietly, focusing her mind as though she were about to start practicing. When she felt very calm and clear she said,

"What you say is very interesting to me, Mr. Samuelson. I should like to reflect on it and discuss it with my own advisor, Mr. Barnes. I should like you to write down your precise proposal as regards money, shares and ownership of any companies we might own, together. Only then will I be in a position to decide what I wish to do."

Samuelson reached into his briefcase and pulled out a thick sheaf of papers.

"Barnes already has most of this. But I have added more accurate figures. You can discuss it with him. This copy is for you."

Once again, Pamela was taken off guard at the way Samuelson managed to retain command and initiative with her.

"Thank you, sir. I shall certainly look at these proposals soon." But even as she rose to end the interview, she felt he was already taking charge of her business, and perhaps of herself as well.

* * *

Pamela's last thoughts as she closed her eyes that night were of Herr Bruckner and the cool, pure, eternal beauty of the world he inhabited. He would never take control of her. Samuelson, on the other hand, naturally commanded and ran any situation. If she was not very careful, he would command everything that belonged to her. More than ever, she needed the strength of Bruckner's spirituality and his help starting a new life as a professional musician.

Chapter 21

Richard was in the garden with vicar Franklyn when the special post from London arrived. The cost of these special messengers made them rare and neither Richard nor his host had ever received one before. Richard was apprehensive before he opened the envelope, which had been addressed to him in Sally's hand.

"Dearest Richard, Do not fear, we are well," the first lines read, "but something has happened that makes me concerned and I have taken certain actions as a result.

Emily and I went marketing yesterday. As we came out of a shop, we were accosted by a well-dressed, respectable looking older man. He was of medium height and was clean shaven. His hair was dark, though streaked with gray.

"Pardon me, miss," he said very politely. "You don't know me, but I know some of your friends."

Of course, after the things you have told me, Richard, I was quite frightened. Especially with Emily present. I didn't know who this man could be. I was afraid he was from the police or perhaps from this railwayman whose son is now with Fanny.

"Don't be frightened, miss," he continued. "I mean only to warn. Not to harm. You and the baby should change your place of residence."

At this point in the conversation Emily spoke up, "I don't know you sir, but I hope I know that I am not a baby. My name is Emily."

The man actually knelt down then, right on the sidewalk, so that he could look very closely at Emily. 'You are a beautiful child, Emily. Perhaps even as lovely as my own little one. Ah, I have not seen her in such a long time. Looking at you gives makes my heart hurt. I hope your friends will take excellent care of you, Emily, and guard you well.'

As you may imagine, Richard, this speech terrified me. But then the man stood up and patted Emily's head with what seemed genuine tenderness.

"Tell your friend he is well hidden. You and the child should also be hidden. The carpenter, too, is in danger."

With that, Richard, he patted Emily once more and said, "Ah, ma petite, I will do the best I can for you, for her sake, wherever she may be."
Then he turned and seemed to disappear in a moment.

Do you know who this man was? There was something very unusual about him which I find hard to put into words. He was elegantly dressed in black. His age I would put at about fifty. He had a quality that made him— transparent—as if he could be standing in front of you in broad daylight and not be visible. I am convinced that whoever he is, his warning was sincerely given. He looked at Emily with such tenderness. I believe he wants her to be safe. So I decided to take his warning seriously and have moved us far from my family's home. My father gave me some money and Michael helped us move our things. Out of my whole family, only Michael knows where we have gone. We are much farther east now, and though the streets around us teem with the working poor, we are much better hidden here, I believe. I have taken rooms over a poor draper's shop. Here is the
address: 27a Penny Fields, Poplar.

I do not let Emily leave our rooms alone, though she certainly chafes under the constraint. Fortunately, her wonderful intelligence understands the need for caution. You'll never imagine how she amuses herself. She spends hours drawing pictures of the new machinery Mr. Blackwood showed her. Her drawings are very carefully done and remarkably detailed. She has an astonishing grasp of machinery. She also made a drawing for me of the metal shutters which she used to open and close in the mine. I was having difficulty understanding her description, so she drew them for me. So we are safe and comfortable, though we both miss you, my own, dearest love.

I have taken a post box address and include it here. I thought that would make it harder to trace us if anyone is trying to find or watch us. Write to us immediately so that I, I should say, we, know you've received this and know where we are. I leave it to you to contact your friend the carpenter. Emily has asked me several times when you are coming home.

All our love, Your Sally and Emily."

The letter had been signed by them both. Richard folded it carefully, kissed it and placed it into his pocket book. Then he went to his room to write to Fisk. There was no time to be lost. Fisk's danger was probably greater than his own. The only person he could imagine who could have given the warning to Sally was Samuelson's spy. But why had this man twice offered warnings and information that would help Richard or his friends? Twice he had been a friend, but he had also told Richard that he would kill him if their paths crossed again. It was alarming that this man had found Sally and Emily so easily. He must have followed them home. Would he be able to find them again? Why was this warning being given now? What had happened to once again interest this man in Richard and his wife and child?

Richard's note to the carpenter was short and to the point: "I have been told by the stranger with the swordstick that you are being watched, and that there may be some sort of move against you.

P.S. You can direct letters to me at General Delivery, Dorchester, Dorsetshire."

That way, if the letter were intercepted by enemies, it still would be difficult to find him. He would only have to be careful when he went to get mail in Dorchester. He had adopted the same plan with Sally. Only the express messenger had been given the actual direction to the vicar's house.

After sending off his letter to Fisk, Richard decided that he had no right to stay at the vicar's house and not let him know he was a fugitive. But even if he told the older man exactly how things stood, his presence at the vicarage might still endanger Mr. Franklyn and his housekeeper. The solution to this problem lay right at hand, he realized. He could move into his own house, the cottage left to him by Charles. It was a perfect place to hide, being quite out of the village which was itself an isolated place.

Of course, Richard thought, if the man with the swordstick finds me in that house out in the woods, he could dispatch me and no one would even know. Richard hated to make any plans that supposed a long separation from Sally and Emily, but for the time being, his presence would probably increase rather than reduce their danger. How he would ever become respectable again in the eyes of the law after Samuelson's denouncement was something he could not even be concerned with until he had found Charles' killer. With the new facts he had discovered and the vicar's views in mind, he knew he must persist in Dorset for some time, at least. He was as well hidden as possible in Charles' cottage, and he could talk with the vicar and continue his search for the key to Charles' acrostic, which he hoped would reveal the identity of the killer.

In preparing for his move to the cottage, Richard borrowed some blankets, tea and sugar, He also borrowed a tin bread box from Mrs. Damson. He would have to hide the bible whenever he left the cottage. If the killer had tried to destroy the book it confirmed the idea that the book could reveal his identity., or provide important information. The killer knew where the cottage was, so it was of the last importance to keep the Book safe. If the killer returned when Richard was there, the young man would have to trust to his own strength and to God.

The vicar had also penetrated to the possibility of danger lurking near the cottage and would not hear of Richard taking his belongings there alone. The older man insisted on carrying the household items in a large portmanteau. In vain, Richard protested, but the hale old man was stubborn and seemed to feel it was his special duty to establish Richard safely in his old friend's house.

They arrived at the edge of the wooded clearing around Charles' cottage at dusk. The dark trees, which had started to lose their leaves, gave the place a mournful, desolate look. The stain on the threshold was something that Richard could not look away from when they swung the door open. Almost the first thing the vicar did was to throw a small drugget over the ugly blot on the floor.

"I wonder if Mrs. Damson would know how to get that mark out of the wood?" the vicar mused.

"No, vicar, I do not want to forget what has happened here. We will erase that mark once his killer is caught, even if we put new floor boards down."

The vicar, much more accustomed to using hardwood as fuel than Richard, soon had a fire blazing on the hearth which gave light and cheered the room considerably. He also lit two of the tallow candles he had brought from the vicarage.

"Come," the older man said. "I shall show you the well." They went outside and drew water, filled an earthen pitcher and an iron kettle and brought them back inside. As he placed the kettle on the fire, Richard thought that Charles must have used this same kettle many times during his years in the cottage. Most of Charles' life had been spent here, except for his railroading and his time studying Latin with a priest in Bath.

As Richard and the vicar sat in front of the fire, they both felt the place imbued with their friend's spirit. The very rudeness of the building and furniture spoke of Charles' desire to own nothing but essentials. Outside, the wind moaned softly in the twilight, mingling with the many songs of birds preparing to sleep.

"I have not sat here since the tragedy," the vicar said, almost to himself. "It is cheering to sit here now and remember him with you. It helps to exorcise the horror of his death."

Then, the two men sat quietly, each remembering their absent host in different ways. For the older man, the passing of Charles Wilney was recalled in all the convivial hours they had spent smoking in front of the fire, or digging for the treasures of the past. It also reminded him that he must soon follow his friend into God's mercy. The younger man simply felt that he was still under Charles' protection, hidden in his cottage, surrounded by his homely things.

Even in death, Richard thought, he is still the good angel of my life. I will find the key to the riddle he has set me and catch his killer, and someday, if God wills it, Sally, Emily and I shall live here with the same purity and simplicity as Charles.

While walking the vicar back through the woods to the village lane, Richard finally told the older man of his true situation with regard to the law. Even after hearing of Samuelson's denouncement and Richard's friendship with Fisk, the vicar expressed his trust in the young man by asking him to come back to the vicarage.

"It seems to me that this man, Samuelson, harbours very bitter feelings about you."

"As I have told another friend, it seems strange that one so mighty should even have me in this thoughts."

"Some men who rise in the world have a very great idea of their own importance and take any real or imagined, slight very easily."

"That's what my friend, Charles Fisk, said, too."

"All the more reason for you to come back to the vicarage with me." In spite of this heartfelt invitation, Richard went back to the cottage alone. He felt he would commune better with Charles' spirit by staying in his woodland home. However, upon returning, the silence of the country at night and the lonely situation of the house began to unnerve the city dweller. He was restless and wandered aimlessly about the two rooms until he remembered the one task he must perform before retiring.

He took the tin bread pan he had borrowed and the Bible and Charles' old spade outside and buried the book in the garden. He would take this precaution every night so the book could not be taken while he slept. The night was so dark, Richard doubted if anyone could have seen him in the thick darkness that surrounded the cottage, even if it was being watched at that very moment. When he was through digging, he entered the cottage once more, sat down, and finally fell asleep in Charles' chair in front of the fire.

Being of a practical turn of mind, Richard rarely dreamed but this night the influence of his surroundings worked on the young man to produce a strange sequence of events: The cottage door opened suddenly and Charles entered the room. He came over and shook hands with Richard. Then he said, "Look what I have brought you." He handed Richard a small brown puppy. Then he said, "I did not escape." As soon as he spoke, the shadows cast by the fire around them became shadowy navvies covered in dirt. They were digging, hauling and blasting and looked like grinning devils that had risen out of the ground. Their bodies were writhing. Some flew up in the air as a blast went off, but they were laughing and unhurt. They terrified Richard. Behind all this activity however, a huge shadow loomed. Richard could not see what it was, at first, but gradually the shadow got smaller and denser until its outline was clearly that of a daemon bigger than any of the others. Charles pointed at the dark figure and said, "This is one devil I can cast out. But do not let the doggie fall in the well." Then the devil-navvies began digging, blasting, and grinning in Richard's face. There was an enormous iron kettle in which the devils were lowered into the tunnel where they were digging. The shaft where the kettle descended appeared to be a bottomless well of darkness. Suddenly, Richard became terrified that the devils would lower him into the darkness in the iron kettle and that he would be blown up when the next blast went off. A devil reached for him and...he woke muttering, "doggie in the well, please guard him well, don't let him fall, don't pull his tail and all shall be well: one, two, three, four, five, five, six. The dear little dog will get better quick."

Richard stumbled out of his chair and as he searched frantically for ink and pen, he continued reciting the rhyming sequences. Images from his own memory flooded into his mind as he searched. He saw the sun burning brightly in a blue August sky. He and Fanny were sitting in a field of tall grass; Off in the distance he could hear the cries of the men as they worked. Occasionally there was a blast from the tunnel where the crew was digging. Then, he and Fanny heard the grass swishing as someone walked toward them quickly. There was something frightening about the sound, but then Richard looked up and saw his friend, Charles. He was holding a little brown puppy in his arms.

"Look, Richard and Fanny, what I have brought for you."

"A puppy!" Richard yelled. "A puppy for me?"

"For you and Fanny."

"Look, Fan." Richard said, taking the puppy from Charles and holding it in front of her. But the little girl turned away. She just shook her head.

"I think he needs a drink, Richard." Charles said. "He has had a long hot ride from town."

Richard got up, holding the puppy. Fanny followed her brother as he walked toward the water wagon. Charles walked in another direction to confer with the head ganger. It was late in the afternoon and the men were coming off the tunnel as Richard began to give the little dog sips of water from a big, tin ladle. While holding it steady for the little creature, he suddenly felt a hard, powerful hand pinch his own neck and shoulder in a painfully tight grip. A huge drunken Irish navvy grabbed the ladle in one hand and the little dog's tail in the other. He used the tail to throw the puppy over his shoulder, high into the air. The poor creature flew up into the sky and was thrown so far that he fell many yards away down into the shaft the men had been working on for many days. It was a vertical drop of sixty or seventy feet.

Later, when the man was sober, Charles made him apologize and offer to get Richard another puppy, but the boy shook his head. The memory of the poor thing flying through the air was too terrible. He didn't want another creature that could be hurt by the men. Protecting Fanny was already a heavy burden. A few days after this shocking event, Charles had been giving a lesson to Richard and tried to make light of what had happened by basing an acrostic on the tragedy. This may seem heartless to a modern reader, but prior to the late Victorian era, children were not regarded as having particularly tender sensibilities. From the middle ages up to Victoria's later reign, children were simply small adults. There was no special literature written for them. Public executions and gory accounts of murders and other terrible crimes were very popular forms of entertainment for all ages. So Richard's mentor shouldn't be judged from a modern point of view. He hoped that by making the puppy's death a game the boy would be able to get over his horror of what had happened. Richard learned the rhyme quickly but Wilney could see the boy was sad whenever he repeated it. The teacher left off using the game in a few days, but at night, he could hear the boy muttering it in his sleep for weeks afterwards.

217

As these memories flooded his mind, Richard scratched out the sequence of numbers on a piece of paper. He stood up when he was done. The fire in the grate had burned out but there was already enough light in the sky to see clearly what he had written. Yes, he had it. There, on Charles' own table was the key to his killer's identity. Richard felt sure of it. All he had to do now was take the lines marked in the bible and substitute the word order in each marked line with the number sequence given in the rhyme. This was the way Charles had set up his acrostics for Richard long ago.

The adult Richard seized the bible and the piece of paper with the key on it and ran out the door to tell the vicar what had happened.

Mrs. Damson was pouring tea in the kitchen when Richard unceremoniously burst into the house. The vicar was just sitting down to his breakfast.

"Vicar, I have got the key. It's all here," he said, holding up the sheet of paper on which he had written Charles' word game. He dropped the Bible on the table with a thump. Mrs. Damson glared at him disapprovingly and lifted the book up almost the moment he put it down.

"Table is no place for scripture, young man," the old lady said. The tiny woman lifted the big volume easily and carried it out of the room. "I will put it in study, vicar," she called as she left the room.

Richard sat down and breathlessly told his story to the vicar.

After listening closely to the dream and Richard's recollection, the old man suddenly broke into Richard's narrative, "I knew I had heard that phrase, 'doggie in the well', before. I remember the incident clearly, now that you have jogged my memory. Not long after Charles returned from railroading, he received a letter from you. I believe you told him you were safely arrived in London with your sister. Charles talked at some length about you and Fanny, saying he was glad you were now both safe in London. He began telling me about occasions in the camp when one or both of you had been threatened, and, among other anecdotes, told me what happened that day your puppy was killed. In retrospect, he felt it was very wrong of him to make a game out of an event that would be so terrible for a young boy."

"But you can see why he would have chosen this game,' Richard said. Only I would know it. And after listening to me say it over and over in my sleep, I'm sure he thought I'd never forget it during the whole course of my life."

"Yes, Richard, I'm certain your assumptions are correct." the vicar said, as he looked ruminatively at the ceiling. "He told me how horrifying the death of the little dog was for both of you. I'm certain he never forgot it. In fact, before he went to work building railways, he had never had a dog living with him. But after he came back, he always had one in the cottage. I believe he felt in some way responsible for what happened to your little puppy. Always having a dog to care for in later years was his way of atoning for what had happened. He always had one, always a stray that no one else wanted, until just six months before he was killed. That's when old Roamer died."

"If he had had a dog with him when this villain attacked, he might still be alive," Richard said.

"Well, that sort of speculation leads to melancholy, my young friend," the vicar said, patting Richard's arm. "After dinner we shall go up and look at the Bible and try applying this, "key" as you call it."

The effort of just a half hour was sufficient to show the two men that the task was going to be much more formidable than Richard had at first thought.

"And just imagine the time it would have taken to pick out the right sentences to use with the key," Richard said. "It's nearly a superhuman task. Some pages have as many as sixty or seventy lines marked."

"Ah, but for Charles this kind of game gave him great pleasure," the vicar replied. "He could peg away at this sort of thing for hours and come away fresh and smiling. I would only find it a source of frustration. I think Charles always regretted my lack of aptitude for this sort of thing."

"Yes, he was much more skilled than I ever was," Richard agreed.

"What have we got so far?" the vicar asked drawing his chair closer to the desk so he could see what Richard had written.

"It isn't much vicar. But it is certainly provoking. I'll read it out loud. I'm sure you'd have trouble reading my scrawl."

"But I thought you'd done legal copying work?"

"I have, but copying and doing acrostics are two different things. My own hand when I am composing is as ragged and blotchy as anything you'd care to see. Here are Charles words to us thus far:"

"I shall attempt to tell my story as a connected narrative related by one omnipresent person, though, in fact, many of these facts were gleaned from different people ...in different times and places whom I questioned. Rather than force you, Richard, to put all these small pieces together, I shall connect them into a coherent whole. I know the patience it must have taken to get this far with my acrostic. "

"That is all?" the vicar asked.

"I am afraid so, vicar."

"Good heavens. This will take weeks."

"It could, indeed. But I am very gratified to see that all my surmises about the meaning of my dream have resulted in a coherent text."

"That is certainly true, Richard. Now, however, I must go. I must not neglect my other duties. It is time I started my rounds."

"I understand, sir. I suppose I shall just work at this as long as I can stand it."

"Good fellow," the vicar said as he rose and patted Richard on the shoulder. "Plan to dine with us again and I will see you here at dinner."

"I shall do my best to move this forward."

"I'm certain you will, Richard."

Left to himself, Richard made better progress, though he still felt the work painfully slow. The hours dragged on and he realized he had to guard carefully against small mistakes that would substantively change the meaning of a phrase. The task began to seem endless. The afternoon wore on, shadows lengthened and the light began to fade. After many hours, the young man finally got up to stretch and stand at the window. Beyond the garden, the tops of the trees were losing their foliage. Their sharp upraised branches pointed to the coming winter, and Richard wondered how long it would be before he would see Sally and Emily again. He had only been from home a few days, but there was no telling how long his task would take. When he had left London, he had not thought about a long absence. He missed his dear ones very much, though he knew they were safer without him. How, he wondered, would he ever get clear of Samuelson's charges and his? Perhaps he would have to emigrate with Sally and Emily once Charles' killer was caught and punished. Possession of Fisk's pamphlet would not, in most cases, have been enough to make him a sought after fugitive but the fact that there was so much fear of insurrection in Manchester and that he had had a row with Samuelson's son had sealed his fate. It was probably Samuelson's ill-will that was most to blame for his predicament.

If Samuelson wanted, Richard thought, the great man could hound us for the rest of our lives. He struck his fist against his palm.
"It is unjust that wealth should have so much power," he said out loud. The Charter was fair and equitable. Yet, the wealth created by the railroads and other industries was a juggernaut that overturned everything in its path. It could destroy this fine old village. It could give a child like Emily a short life in a dark mine. It could crush the Charter and ruin his own and Sally's life. Perhaps, as Fisk foretold, man's greed could provoke the Lord to destroy the world once more. He turned away from the window and his own dour thoughts and went back to the work at hand.

When the vicar returned several hours later, he found that Richard had the lamp burning and had added the following lines to the ones they had read earlier in the day:

"...in different times and places whom I questioned. Rather than force you, Richard, to put all these small pieces together, I shall connect them into a coherent whole. I know the patience it must have taken to get this far with my acrostic. But I know you would do it if the worst happens.

My story began on a particularly rainy Saturday when I was on the tramp from my little Dorsetshire cottage to the new construction being started for the ambitious Liverpool & Manchester railway, where they were planning to build one of the longest tunnels in the world, to run 1 1/4 miles under the city of Liverpool itself, all the way to the docks.

I had heard that on this new line they had need of a surveyor and someone with some engineering experience. Since my former place had been that of a navvy, I was anxious to advance myself and use the little learning..."

"I'm sorry I am so slow, vicar," Richard said as the older man read the text that the younger man had carefully written out from his notes.
"No, Richard. You mustn't berate yourself. Let us trust that we are on the

Lord's side and doing his work in what we are attempting and not complain of the tasks he has set us. Who knows when or how he will stretch out his all-powerful hand to help us?"

Richard's long afternoon of dull work left him feeling the need of an outing in the fresh air. Immediately after Mrs. Damson served supper and they had eaten, the young man set out to stroll through the village lanes and see some of the surrounding countryside before nightfall. Having no fixed purpose in his walk other than exercise, Richard re-traced the road he had taken when he came to Higher Woodsford. He passed the old inn and began his descent into the deep dingle that would lead him to high ground again and eventually into the more level country beyond. At almost any time during late fall or winter, at an hour in late afternoon, the woods on either side of the road at this low point were extremely dark. This was due to the depth of the dingle and the density of the fir and cedar trees that grew almost like a high hedge near the road. Richard noted this gloom as he descended. With each step, the road plunged deeper into twilight, until, at the bottom, it seemed nearly night. He began climbing the road on the far side of the small valley when, suddenly, he felt himself seized from behind. A heavy blow fell on his shoulder, numbing his whole arm. He broke free and raced upward, away from his assailant. In a backward glance he saw two large, ill-dressed tramps who must have been hiding in the woods to wait for whomever might pass through the deep notch in the road's course. One of them carried a stout cudgel.

Richard wished with all his heart he had the oak bough he had carried on his journey to Higher Woodsford. He was a good runner, but hunger and desperation seemed to drive the two tramps on to astonishing bursts of speed and they steadily gained on him. As all three men neared the top of the long hill, the tramps closed on him. At almost the same moment, Richard heard rapid hoof beats approaching, but the desperation of the tramps was such that they did not fall back when the mounted man came into view. The attackers now turned away from Richard and attempted to block the rider.

One man lunged for the horse's reins while the other tried to hit the rider with his club. A sound of ringing metal was heard, as of a sword being drawn. The horse and rider wheeled about in a tight circle, giving a fine demonstration of a difficult manoeuvre. A cry of pain was heard, and the tramp who had tried to seize the reins clutched his right shoulder with his left hand. He turned and ran for the wooded edge of the road to evade his mounted foe. The man with the cudgel continued running on the road until the rider drew close and then he, too, ran off the road and into the brush.

The rider turned and cantered back toward Richard.

"Mr. Darrow," the rider called out, "we meet again."

In a few moments more the mounted man drew close enough for Richard to make out his face in the gathering dusk. He was shocked to see Samuelson's spy, the man with the swordstick, looking down at him from a huge red horse. After just witnessing the martial skill of horse and rider, Richard could do nothing but stand and await his fate. The rider drew near and then, to Richard's surprise, dismounted.

"Are you hurt?" the man asked.

"No, sir. Not really," for the moment he was too surprised to say anything else.

"Good. Are you going back to the village?" the spy asked.

"Yes, I suppose."

"Then I shall walk with you, though I think it unlikely those men will return."

"I think not," Richard agreed.

Slowly, they walked up the hill. Richard began to feel the pain in his arm more. He wondered what would happen next. He noticed that the swordsman's well-trained horse followed behind his master like a dog, without being led.

"How came you here, sir?" Richard asked.

"I might ask you the same question," the man replied.

"I am visiting friends here."

"And have you deserted your friends back in London?"

Richard stopped walking and turned to face his questioner.

"I do not see how my actions can be a source of interest to you, sir. Nor do I choose to answer any more of your questions."

Completely ignoring Richard's last statement the man asked, "Have you made much progress at finding out who killed your friend?"

"Yes, I mean, no. I do not wish to discuss my unfortunate friend with you."

"That may be, but when you do find your friend's killer and can prove your assertions, I shall wish to know of it. And I think you know I make no idle boast if I say that I hold all you love most dearly in the palm of my hand. I expect a report if you succeed in tracing the killer. Letters addressed to the Hotel de Louvre in London shall find me. If you do not contact me, you'll regret it deeply," the man concluded as he mounted his horse. Then, he turned the animal.

"Good fortune, Mr. Darrow," he called as he rode back the way he had come.

Richard stood in the middle of the road listening to the hoof beats long after darkness had hidden horse and rider from sight. In moments, man and horse seemed more like twilight spirits than flesh and blood.

* * *

Gregory Barnes, esq. prided himself on being a well-moderated man. He prided himself on being classical in his thought and opinions, cleaving to the clear rules of living laid down by the Roman and Greek thinkers. Marcus Aurelius was his favourite. He did not care for the thought of Plato or Heraclitus because he did not like anything unclear or mystical, even in a classical author. When confronted with legal difficulties he liked to say to his clients, "Common sense is the best way through life and litigation. Common sense will see us through this." Fundamentally, he was a simple, uncomplicated man, and had the good sense to make virtues out of the qualities he knew were his. He did not doubt himself, and that lack of doubt had made him successful in his profession. His client of twenty years, Edward Blackwood, had liked him and worked with him because he had what the entrepreneur described as a "healthy optimism" about people and any new undertaking. At the same time, the solicitor was prudent and careful when he was uncertain of his ground. By the time of Blackwood's death, Barnes felt he knew himself quite well. He prided himself on being able to regain his equilibrium in almost any situation with a brisk walk and a cigar. His disposition was studious and fairly placid. He had never faced any profound personal crises. He had been born into a prosperous family of solicitors who rose with the mercantile opportunities of the times. He had read law at Oxford and been a modest student. He had never been in love and was not sorry for it when he saw how it unbalanced many people. His marriage had been financially prudent and companionable, but not terribly emotional. His son had lived up to Barnes' expectations, but they were not particularly close. When his wife died of cholera, Barnes decided to move out of his house and into rooms above his chambers. He had never needed to be ambitious to be successful. People trusted him. He never felt lonely, liked people and tried to do others a good turn when the chance arose. The greatest passion he had ever known was for the history and languages of the classical world.

John Samuelson, Barnes sensed, was his opposite. There was an energy and power in the man that was wild, raw, enthusiastic, magnetic and definitely, not moderate. He knew that Samuelson wanted Edward Blackwood's holdings. His plan for marriage had failed and now Barnes was all that stood between the railway giant and Pamela Blackwood's financial interests. Barnes felt a great loyalty to the memory of Pamela's father, but one had to be realistic. A woman could not run such a business, and Blackwood Holdings touched many lives and affected the whole north western county. Pamela was not even interested in business matters, nor did she seem to care much for money. He could not go on acting as a proxy for a dead man. These thoughts were uppermost in the solicitor's mind as he dressed carefully in his elegantly appointed apartment above his chambers. Like its owner, the rooms were muted in colour but were furnished with solid, valuable things, kept very neat and clean by his Swiss housekeeper, Madame Egremont, with whom Barnes liked to speak French.

"The question is," Barnes said to himself, "how can I make the most advantageous arrangements for Blackwood's daughter?" Unquestionably what Pamela needed most was a substantial income that required very little management to keep it secure. He knew that Samuelson's request for an interview this morning had to be for the purposes of making some kind of business proposal. Barnes knew the railway king had already met with Pamela, but what that conversation had been, he knew only in very general terms.

He had the papers Samuelson had left with Pamela. This morning, he felt, Samuelson would get down to fundamentals. And if he did not provide adequate information, then Barnes would force the issue. The Blackwood interests had remained too long in suspension. He had tried to explain all this to Pamela, but the girl simply wasn't interested and wanted to leave everything to him. So be it, he would plan the future for his friend's daughter, and make her as secure as he could.

He gave his collar a final pat and turned to go down the stairs that led to his chambers below. Samuelson was already sitting in the outer office. Wilson, as usual, was at his post.

He greeted Wilson and then "Good day, sir," Barnes said heartily to Samuelson.

"And a good day to you, Mr. Barnes."

The solicitor led the way into his inner sanctum.

"Pray be seated, Mr. Samuelson," the solicitor said, eyeing with satisfaction the briefcase that the other man carried .

"I have come this morning," Samuelson began, "to make an offer to Miss Blackwood."

"To her directly? What about the other partners of the companies?"

"My offer is to Miss Blackwood," Samuelson said. "It is an offer of marriage." Barnes was thunderstruck. It was the last thing in the world he had expected from the railway king.

He sat speechless for some moments. Samuelson was the first to speak.

"I see I surprise, you, sir."

"Well, I, ah, yes you do, Mr. Samuelson. I thought the idea of marriage between your son and Miss Blackwood had already been categorically refused by Miss Blackwood."

"It has. I, myself, who is making her the offer of marriage."

For an instant, Barnes let his professional mask slip. He was profoundly startled by the railwayman's words.

Samuelson hurried forward, "Understand, sir. It is a business arrangement that only may become something more. It keeps the company in the hands of the present owners. In essence, I will run Blackwood holdings for the rest of my life, utilize it to help build my plans for a national railway within strictly defined limits. The company profits from the joint activities of Blackwood Holdings and my business interests. Then, the whole of Blackwood Holdings will revert to my wife or any heirs."

"You stagger me, sir." Barnes finally said pausing briefly to recover himself. "You stagger me, only because of your son's original offer. I can see that this might make perfect sense.." As he spoke, the solicitor was thinking of Pamela's words regarding Samuelson when he last met with her. Then he answered his own thoughts by saying to himself, "But who knows when or how a woman's moods might change? Perhaps her rejection was a sign of a secret attraction. It was impossible to know with such mercurial creatures. He reached for his snuff. "It makes perfect sense. I understand now, sir, better than ever, your business success. It is like cutting the Gordion Knot. But I don't know if young Miss Blackwood will see it in that light. Young ladies tend to view such topics emotionally."

"I think you mistake her, Barnes. I think she will see this as a way of permanently having her freedom without losing control of her father's legacy for future generations." Without waiting for the lawyer's reply, he hurried on, "You will see that the terms of the marriage as specified in the agreement I have had drafted call for separate residences for as much of the year as the law allows. She shall remain at Blackdale, or wherever she chooses and I in London. If we grow closer at a later date that will be our own affair."

Barnes thought of Pamela's likely response and decided it was best to provide some gentle warning for Samuelson. "But your son, sir...Do you not think she may see this as rather cynical?"
"I believe when you talk to her and examine the details with her, Mr. Barnes, both of you will see the benefit to the Blackwood family. All the details are here."

Samuelson reached into his briefcase, pulled out a large folio and handed it to Barnes.

"I see you have been thinking about this for some time, Mr. Samuelson."

"Time is not the issue. But I do believe it is well-considered. My offer remains good indefinitely, sir. She is not a woman to be rushed or bullied, but only to be won. That is where my son made a foolish mistake."

"I thank you for my client, sir," Barnes said, reaching out his hand.

"Good day to you sir," Samuelson said. "Oh, I shall be returning to London on Tuesday week. I may be reached at my house there."

"Thank you, sir. Good day."

"Good day. No, don't bother. I'll show myself out."

Chapter 22

In the months after his separation from Simon, Fisk had ceased giving
public talks Ironically, more and more people called at his humble shop
to ask to speak with him. Some friend or relative had heard him speak,
or read of his vision, and the visitor was interested in his message. Fisk gladly
talked with all, setting out his beliefs. The small store of pamphlets that Simon had printed was quickly handed out to visitors and more were requested. Fisk began to charge for the pamphlets since his carpentry work was so
often interrupted by visitors that it was becoming difficult to earn a
living. The shop became a meeting place for Swedenborgians, a small group
of admirers of William Blake, latter-day Philadelphians and others of a mystical and political turn of mind. More and more, Fisk believed that spiritual
principles must underlie social action. This was some six months before the
warning that he received from Richard in Dorset.

For a time it had seemed that even Cynthia's cough was getting
better, thanks to the bustle of new, friendly faces that came and went all the
time. Fisk was often asked to speak privately about his visions and conversations with daemons and angels to different private groups of people interested
in original religious thought. Many Americans visiting London came to the
carpenter, since the Swedenborgian church had taken firm root in the soil of
the new world, alongside the transcendentalism of Ralph Waldo Emerson.
Fisk tried always to stress his political beliefs: that the poor were blessed in
the eyes of heaven and that the rapacity of the Iron Beast should be defeated
by any peaceful means. He warned listeners repeatedly of a future time when
the Beast would lay waste to the world— if mill owners, speculators and the
established churches did not cease in their greed and in their support of the
factory system and the brutal treatment of the poor.

"The Beast shall rise up and create a vast desert," he told people.
"Like Babylon, our entire world shall become a dwelling place fit only for
'snakes and dragons'."

Few paid attention to Fisk's words about a distant future, but one
afternoon, just a few days after he received Richard's letter of warning, an In-

spector from the new detective division of the Metropolitan Police called on Cynthia and told her that he had been instructed to warn Fisk about stirring up the poor. He was a tall, heavy man, blond and stolid, a portrait of middle-class respectability.

"It is sometimes a fine line between sedition and expressing political opinions, Miss," the detective told Cynthia. "In times like these, statements about factories and the poor must be guarded carefully, otherwise the Commissioner will send us again. The next time, to arrest Mr. Fisk, since there is already a warrant that has been issued for him. The government is not anxious to arrest its good citizens, Miss, but Mr. Fisk should take no more chances. We are glad to see that he has stopped speaking in public. You understand, Miss? You also better tell him to stop printing these pamphlets, Miss. They could be made out as written proof against himself."

Cynthia, who had grown much bolder through Fisk's teaching answered,

"Where in his writing does he say anything illegal? Does not an Englishman still have the right of free speech?"

"A word to the wise is sufficient," the Inspector said, tipping his hat to her. "People will read what they want to read, Miss. Good day."

***

An hour after the policman had left, Fisk returned from delivering a small marquetry table he had made . Cynthia was fearful and told him so. He noticed that she was coughing again as she spoke.

When she finished recounting her contact with the police inspector, Fisk was silent for a long time. Finally he looked over at her and said, "Would you mind very much if we found new quarters, Cynthia?"

"No. I should be happy to do whatever you think best to protect ourselves."

"We may have to move more than once. I shall not be muzzled by these government roughs. Nor do I want to spend time in jail, if I can help it. We might be able to beat them in a court of law. But I do not like to take that risk. Perhaps a change of air, away from London, will get rid of that cough once and for all."

"I do not want you to take any risk, either. Your work is too important." Cynthia added, putting her arm around Fisk. "A change from the London air might be good for me."

"Do not worry," he said patting her hand. "I knew this persecution was bound to come. Until we have the Charter, we shall not be really free to speak our minds."

"How soon shall we leave?"

"Within the week."

"Would it not be prudent to leave sooner?"

"A messenger has told me we have that long before any evil befalls us. I knew of this before this policeman came today.

"A messenger? You mean Richard's letter?"

"No dearest. One of Gabriel's kind. So don't worry. I want to make some arrangements for us and say goodbye to our friends here."

"You know where we are going to go?"

"Yes. We shall go to Birmingham. Rather, outside Birmingham. I would not subject you to the soot and cinders of another city for anything. We shall find a little cottage near the town. But I have friends in Birmingham. They are among the most determined Chartists I know. Don't scowl so, my dear girl," he said catching sight of Cynthia's worried face. He put his arms around her.

"All shall be well, my dear. I promise."

"And did a favourite angel tell you that?"

He kissed her. "You are my favourite angel, dearest woman."

"Don't talk so, Fisk," Cynthia said. "I'm certain that none of the Lord's host would want to be compared to a creature of clay. You might make them angry."

"Remember what I told you, what Swedenborg says, 'The Lord is never angry, never takes revenge, hates, condemns, punishes, throws anyone into hell, or tempts anyone; thus never does evil to anyone.' Do not fear, dearest woman. The angels of the Lord never abandon us. It is we who abandon them, as I was just recently taught. Now, let us start packing," he ended as he released her from his embrace.

***

On the eve of their departure, the empty workshop filled up with friends who had come to say goodbye. It was given out to all that Fisk and Cynthia were going to live quietly in the country in Essex. Only a handful of people knew their real destination.

A huge bowl of punch was made, some of the seamstresses who had worked next to Cynthia baked a brown cake laced with sugar and rum. A very old man who had been a fiddler of reels in the farming towns of Dorsetshire during the Napoleonic wars kept hearts gay and people stepping lively until well past midnight when the party broke up. As the last stragglers were leaving, a street arab in torn trousers and a man's jacket buttoned across his bare chest entered the shop. He seemed to recognize Fisk and went right up to him .

"This is for you, sir. I am to deliver it and get a penny for my trouble."

"Who sent you, lad?" Fisk asked.

"Dunno a name. Said you should give me a penny, if you please," and he held out one hand with a bold, insistent gesture while he held back the envelope in the other.

Fisk dug deeply into his pocket, found the required article and deposited it into the soot-blackened palm whose owner disappeared the next moment, leaving Fisk holding an envelope, which was large and yellow and of a type generally used by solicitors. Inside was a folded sheet of paper pasted on one side with a dozen cut out newspaper articles, each describing more factory accidents, in which workers as well as machines were affected. Two men had died in one incident. Cynthia looked over Fisk's shoulder as he read the accounts.

"Simon?" she asked.

"I am afraid it must be, Cynthia. Eight more people killed altogether. In each case there was no mention of sabotage. He glories in fooling the authorities. He sends this to me as a boast. Ah, Simon, Simon. It's a black star you've chosen to light your way."

After receiving the paper all gaiety left Fisk for the rest of the evening. He said goodbye to the last of his friends with a serious mien.

Fisk's purpose in going to Birmingham was that he had decided to write more about his experiences and what he believed about the future of mankind. He knew that he must be hidden, otherwise the authorities would try to silence him, but he had many friends who were printers capable of producing cheap pamphlets that could be distributed surreptitiously. Fisk would have the finished publications shipped to different small merchants of second hand books throughout London at general delivery, "to be held until called for." Some of the places that would offer his work would be the same ones who, years earlier, had sold cheap editions of Tom Paine's essays, usually slipped between the covers of old books on innocuous subjects. With the little money he and Cynthia had saved, and the skills they each possessed, they would manage to live obscurely and cheaply and he would have time to write.

They left London and traveled by coach to Brimingham. Three or four coaches a day went back and forth between London and the city made renowned for mechanical and metal manufacture. Mathew Boulton's great enterprise, the Soho Works on the Hockley Brook, helped make the town famous for quality metal work. This great building near Birmingham was filled with craftsmen and was nothing like the mills of Manchester. But Mathew Boulton was the man who first saw the potential of Watts' Rotary Steam Engine and suggested the cotton mills as a ready market for it. The industry of Birmingham tended to be made up of better educated, well-trained artisans who understood the value of the Charter and what it could mean for themselves and their children. Hence, the working men of Birmingham were known as England's most ardent Chartists.

Fisk and Cynthia found a cottage well outside the city, away from the madding crowd of the burgeoning town. There were grassy fields around their house and the change in air seemed to improve Cynthia's cough, though Fisk was concerned that she looked so thin. He tried to feed her delicate foods, but she would not have fine food unless they shared it equally. So Fisk grew fatter while Cynthia became even sharper in outline.

Fisk's first work was called, "The Apocalypse will be Man-Made : The

Iron Beast and the World's End." It was attacked from a handful of Church of England and Dissenting pulpits on the basis that it was a distortion of the meaning of Revelations.

"The anonymous author," wrote one clergyman, "has abused the true meaning of scripture and twisted it into a revolutionary and dangerous philosophy whose only result can be social upheaval and the destruction of property."

His second pamphlet, "The End of Time," was widely read by Chartists throughout the Midland factory towns. It argued that mechanical time kept by watches and clocks created an unreal view of the world. It created the false impression that one moment followed the next in sequence. In heaven, Fisk claimed, all times were understood as existing simultaneously. There was no past or future, all was the eternal moment, "eternity's sunrise" as Blake had called it. Further, mechanical time was the basis of slavery, the basis of forcing men to behave like machines, the basis of the factory system and a weapon used to beat down the poor, forcing them into a single mould of behaviour, making them an actual part of the factory, thus destroying their uniqueness and their Imagination.

"Nowhere is the factory system's blasphemy against the intention of the Creator more hideous," he wrote, "than in the Methodist Schools set up by factory owners which aim to destroy the Imagination and individual character of every child before the age of speech. Reading matter such as Foxe's Book of Martyrs aims at attacking the child's will with images of terror. Whatever the avowed goal, all this is done to make the children of the poor pliable and willing tools for the factories and their owners. Angels in heaven regard this as a terrible blasphemy because they know it is only through the power of our Imagination that mankind can realize our unlimited grace and the enormous creative power that the Saviour has purchased for us. It is only the power of the Imagination that will kill the Iron Beast. And it is essential that we utilize this power. For, from that Beast born of the perversion of man's greatest faculties, will come droughts, deserts, raging storms, poisoned water and air, wars and death for all. It is the poor who will save us from this eventuality. It is the poor who must rise up and smite the Beast in his dwelling places, The Factory and the Railway." he wrote. "Avoid factories as if they contained all the Plagues of Egypt. Purchase only things made by hand from those who shun factory machines and their shoddy work. Starve the Railways of all profit by not using them. Remember that the Factory Clock is the mechanical tool of the beast's blasphemy against spirit Do not allow it to diminish you."

***

The early months in Birmingham was a fruitful period for Fisk, though he missed the many friends and conversations of his days in London. He had often wondered about Richard and how he had fared in his quest for Fanny and, whenever he heard of a factory accident, he feared it might have been caused by Simon. With every month, it seemed that the grip of the Railways spread across the land like the coils of the Leviathan.

In spite of these large thoughts and concerns, the hours and minutes he and Cynthia shared were filled with happiness. Fisk had admired young Fanny Darrow for some years before meeting Cynthia and there had been someone else long ago, but Cynthia had become his heart's true delight, a companion and equal in all things. He worried about her coughing and thinness constantly, but she would not see a doctor.

"They will always find disease when they are asked to," she said. "We cannot afford their fancies."

For Cynthia's part, she believed implicitly in what Fisk wrote, and regarded him as a truly great man who had lifted her up and placed her on a level with himself. Some of Fisk's essays had been requested by a Swedenborgian printer in the United States, who found Fisk through a Chartist bookseller in London. Fisk began to correspond frequently with the New Jerusalem church that had been founded in the New England states. All might have continued in this comfortable way but for a letter that was forwarded to Fisk through another of his London printers.

"The Beast grows," the letter began without greeting, "Soon, however there shall be a conflagration that will terrify all. Then the money that grows the Beast shall be cut off by this fear. I shall make your essays prophecy, Fisk. We shall win."

The letter had been made by cutting out type from different printed publications and pasting them on a sheet of paper. It was unsigned, but Fisk knew who the author was. The letter cast him into black despair for the rest of the afternoon noon.

Cynthia tried to comfort him, "It is not your fault that Simon uses the wrong means for the right ends, Fisk."

"But people are going to die and I know about it," he replied. I know, too, that Simon is in a hell of his own making. I saw all this coming the day I went to visit him. Daemons and low spirits had flocked to him like bats to a tumble-down barn. His own thoughts had attracted them. I have to do something."

"What can you do, Fisk? You tell me all the time that each one of us is responsible for our own thoughts and actions."

"But we are also our brother's keeper, Cynthia. I must try to find him and stop him from pursuing this reckless course. It sounds as if he has some great mechanical disaster planned. Who knows how many lives it may cost?"

"Why is he so bent on destruction?" Cynthia asked.

"I preached it to him when we first met."

"But Fisk, your few words to him months ago cannot be the force behind all his crimes. Otherwise, I should be destroying manufactories as well."

"No. I know that I am not the cause. Only the excuse. It is the fear he was taught as a child that is the cause."

"I do not understand," she replied.

"Fear often turns into hate and hate will find any excuse for its own existence. When a child is taught to distrust its own inner experience and is threatened with a wrathful, scolding God, the child cannot hear the voice of his own genius and learn God's plan for him. He lives his life in fear, and that fear separates him farther from God. Without knowing his own unique soul, he feels lost and often comes to hate himself because it seems he has nothing solid and clear that he can hold onto."

"Can you change that for Simon? Can anyone change it for another person?"

"I do not know. But Simon came to my nets. He heard my words and came."

"But perhaps it was the violent deeds you preached that lured him to you."

"Perhaps. But I think Simon also loves me, truly loves me and wanted me to love him in return and introduce him to the kindness and mercy of Our Saviour. Perhaps it can still be done."

"Could you not ask Gabriel to do this for you?" she asked. "Surely one of the Lord's host..."

"No. Simon could not hear the voice of any angel right now. He is too lost, too far away from the light. I must help him, if I can."

"And what am I to do?" she asked with a touch of asperity in her voice.

"You are comfortable, here, are you not? You shall have enough money while I am away. My writing brings in a steady trickle. It would not be good for your health to go back to London. There are our new friends, here."

"No. That is not the point, Fisk. I am your wife in my heart, if not in law, and I will not have us parted this way."

"If I stay, I shall be worried about Simon and the deaths he might cause."

"So, I shall have to go with you, then."

"But your cough, dearest."

"No, you must take me. That is an end of it."

"Well, wife, I shall fear for you." he answered, hugging her.

"Then you will have to fear. I shall not be put aside. When I am away from you I feel farther from the Lord's great ones, like Gabriel. More than anything else in life, I should like to see him and talk to him as you do."

"That's settled, then," Fisk said. Who can we lodge with in London? We cannot afford an inn or hotel."

"I think I could ask the Howards," Fisk said. "My friend Richard Darrow is betrothed to the daughter of the family, Sally. You remember, they are engaged to be married. And the Howards own a large building where they live and work. I feel sure we shall be able to stay at the Howard's."

"I shall need a day to prepare for the journey," Cynthia said. "It will be a long ride in our wagon."

"No, I would not have you ride in an open wagon all the way to London. Either we must take the coach, or I'll not go."

"But the expense," Cynthia protested.

"I don't care. I would not risk your health in an open wagon all the way to London." Fisk put his arm around her. "You must take care, dearest. What should I do if anything happened to you?"

"But I was all right coming here."

"It was warmer and we were not as close to winter. And, when we get there, you shall be breathing London air once again. We must take the coach."

Chapter 23

The testament of Charles Wilney

Richard saw and heard nothing more of Samuelson's spy in the weeks following the attack on the road. Letters from Sally and Emily assured him that the two were doing well in their new quarters. There was no sign of any kind that they were being watched by the spy or anyone else. The special bond of daughter with mother, which Emily had never experienced before, was daily growing stronger between her and Sally. Sally wrote that the little girl asked every night for a kiss and for the two to say their prayers together. Emily continued her drawings of machines, and continued to amaze Sally with her intelligence. One day, after a long walk with Sally, Emily came home and drew a very strange looking series of machines. When asked what they were she answered: "They make the gas for the lamps, I think. At least, that's the way I think they would look. I cannot see them because they are behind a brick wall." The little girl spoke to Sally often of the day they had spent watching the great ships at Greenwich, and she dreamed of future voyages on "Mr. Brunel's great steamships."

Chartism seemed quiescent at the moment, or at least, it had no public face. The soldiers were still quartered in Manchester and the leaders of the movement were quiet, which was probably why the press began again to focus on Fisk's publications,

John Bradley, MP said on the floor of the house that "A warrant should be issued for all incendiary writers and speakers. The country cannot afford their dangerous agitations."

The weather was beginning to grow colder. The year progressed inexorably toward winter. The vicar told Richard there had already been a hard frost in the higher meadows surrounding the village. Apples had been harvested in large numbers and cider was being made by presses that came through the area at this time of year. Mrs. Damson was making apple butter in the kitchen and her niece, Suk, brought the vicar a jug of cider spiced with cloves, cinnamon and dried currants. If it had not been for his many pressing concerns, Richard would have enjoyed the brittle sunlight and deep shadows of the chilly country afternoons. He would have enjoyed rambling through the meadows to watch the farm workers change their occupations with the season. As it was, he was a prisoner in the vicar's study where he worked long hours each day to unlock the mystery of Charles Wilney's murder. The vicar had pressed the younger man into staying under his roof, where there would be less danger to Richard and to the Bible, which had already been attacked when Charles was killed.

The disclosures thus far had been startling, indeed, and had altered Richard's mind about his own future course of action. He was racing to finish the narrative so he could lay it complete before the vicar and get the older man's opinion of it.

"It is a terrible knot of dreadful crimes that Charles relates, vicar," Richard had said to his friend. "It touches on many lives. I would even say it touches on the future of many lives. It tells of acts almost too awful to think of. It places a burden on...But wait, and very soon I am going to ask your help in examining some of the conclusions I have drawn from it. Soon you will hear it complete, and examine it with a fresh and impartial eye. And help me decide what to do. It explains much about my own life, as well."

"It is your legacy, Richard," the old man had said, lighting his briar in front of his tumble down hearth. "I am content to play whatever role you and Charles assign to me."

"You understand, sir, that it is precisely because your judgment is so important to me that I ask for this delay. One of us must have an absolutely clear head about Charles' tale."

The old man reached out a long, thin arm and with the iron poker pulled a clay jar out of the ashes of the hearth. A generous measure of Suk Damson's spiced cider gave its fragrance to the room as the vicar lifted the blackened lid.

"I assure you Richard, I feel privileged to be given your confidence at all. I want nothing better than to help in any way I can. If you feel it will help if I read Charles disclosures all at once and not before, that is what I shall do." Weeks after that conversation, Richard sat in the study racing to unravel the final pages of Charles' strange testament. So many issues had been raised by this document, Richard felt that finishing its transcription was of the last importance. He was hoping to have the manuscript complete before the vicar came home after his rounds. Once they both knew about the terrible events that had led up to Charles' murder, perhaps they could forge a plan of attack together that would result in justice being done. Richard hoped it could be so.

That evening, in the flickering light of the fireplace and a constantly guttering oil lamp, the vicar heard his dead friend's story. It had taken Richard more than three weeks to get a cohesive version of the coded Bible. It began:"I shall attempt to tell my story as a connected narrative related by one omnipresent person, though, in fact, many of these facts were gleaned from different people, in different times and places, whom I questioned. Rather than force you, Richard, to put all these small pieces together, I shall connect them into a coherent whole. I know the patience it must have taken to get this far with my acrostic. You will see why I had to resort to this manner of secret writing to tell you what I know. I could not take the chance that it might become known that you knew the truth. Then your life might have been forfeit as well as my own.

"You see, vicar," Richard broke in, "it was no casual tramp. Charles knew he was in danger."

"Yes, Richard. You were right. Please go on."

"I hope that this document will give you a weapon with which to defend yourself if the need should ever arise. I pray to God that you will simply be passed over unnoticed.

My story begins on a particularly wet Saturday in May of 1826 . I was on the tramp from my family's little cottage in Dorsetshire to the diggings of the Liverpool & Manchester Railway where the world's most ambitious railway tunnel was to be built. When finished, it would be one and one quarter miles long, and run beneath the city of Liverpool right to the docks! It was a fine opportunity for a young lad to get hired as a junior surveyor. I knew that the great George Stephenson was the Chief Engineer. Someone with a little engineering experience might get to assist the engineer on the site, John Dixon, a protege of Mr. Stephenson's. Or at least, so I hoped. Since my former place had been that of a navvy, I was anxious to advance myself and use the little mathematical learning I had gained from Dr. Winslow, the elderly priest who was my mentor in all I had thus far studied. Of course, this was the site where you and I met, Richard. When we first met, Richard, I had a piece of the secret I will relate in these pages, but it is my conviction that I now possess all its parts. I am sorry that I have to burden you with it. I hope it is for good and not for ill.

To continue my narrative, I was walking alongside of the highway that was the first leg of my journey to Liverpool. I planned to walk near the sea all the way to Weymouth and then strike out north to Bristol and up to Manchester. The rain was pelting down, beating steadily on me and the macadam. The sky was almost black with storm clouds and it appeared to be dusk, though in fact it was only past mid day. The storm had blown up in just moments and I could only imagine what the nearby sea was doing on the other side of the near hills. I seemed to be completely alone on the wide road, with the high wind and stinging rain. I remember admiring the work of the road builders, how they had banked the road's turnings and blasted to keep it level and less tiring to the horses. The water rolled off neatly into culverts on either side of the paving. The storm was so sudden that I could still smell the sweet clover of early spring in the air. The rolling hills, dotted with black-faced Dorset sheep, stood naked under the Lord's fierce heavens with not a tree or shelter of any kind in sight, otherwise I should have stopped rather than walked in the inundation. Since I was alone with my Creator in the midst of his creation, I took the opportunity to call on our Lord in my heart and thoughts and ask if there was anything I could do to please Him at that moment. Almost immediately, I heard footsteps begin to echo my own. I turned around and some hundred feet behind me saw a huge man striding toward me. He seemed to have sprung up out of the hard surface of the road. I was certain he had been nowhere in sight just a few minutes before. As I said, he was a huge man with a strong, angular face, a broad intelligent brow and two burning dark eyes that told of a troubled soul within. His clothes were foul rags that hung from his brawny arms and shoulders in wet tatters. I wondered why a man on the high road should be as ragged as an Irish beggar in the worst London slum.

I held my strong briar staff close to me, ready to defend the life my Lord had given me or ready to befriend another of his creatures and share what I had with him. I stood and looked back at the man. He quickened his step when he saw me standing still, watching him. His long legs ate up the distance between us in seconds.

"Good sir," he called out. "Can you answer me a question?"

"I shall try," I replied.

"Can you tell me what county this is?"

"Surely, sir, you must know this is Dorsetshire."

"No, sir. I know it not. My ship was wrecked some hours ago and I am the only swimmer who has arrived at shore."

"You think all hands lost?" I shouted into the wind.

"Yes, I believe so."

"Let us go to the water and see," I shouted back.

He seemed reluctant to follow my steps in the direction of the hills that hid the beach from us.

"Come," I urged him. "There may be others we can help to land. I have twenty yards of stout rope in this bag." With his mighty arms to anchor me and my rope, I could wade into the surf and see if there were others close to land. Visibility at the water's edge might only be a few yards out, but I knew the Lord had heard my question and had answered clearly. Even now, after all that has happened as a result of this meeting, I do not question that the man's appearance was the Lord's doing. It is not for us to question why He does certain things. It is only our simple duty to obey without question when we know He has spoken to us. I had a clear task before me and the means of performing it. I left the road and began to jog in the direction of the sea. The big man followed more slowly, reluctantly, I would have said.

There were three rows of hills with deep gullies between them, hiding the beach and water. The storm-tossed sea was only visible when we ascended to the top of each row. As we drew closer to the sea on the unsheltered hill tops, the howling rage of the storm grew in intensity, until on the last hill above the beach, we looked out at a horizon of boiling white foam and black clouds. The beach below was intermittently masked by the breakers by the towering breakers and the curtains of gray air heavy with water droplets, which rose from the crashing surf. I insisted that we climb down the cliffs to the water's edge, though the beach was empty of any human form, as far as I could tell from the height where we stood. The closer we got to the water, the more reluctant seemed my companion to go forward. Finally, on the third and last height, I took his arm and motioned to the way down. When he hesitated, I shouted into the wind and rain that was screaming at us from the sea to make myself heard,

"I cannot go out alone. I need you to hold the rope. There may be helpless souls out there. You must help. The Lord commands it."

As I said these last words a huge bolt of lighting was seen very close by, almost instantly followed by a deafening explosion of thunder. The big man turned white as a sheet, and I thought he might faint, but when I tugged his arm again he followed.

The way down was treacherous. We clung to the cliff and inched our way along a narrow, twisting path of wet, sandy ground. Between the wind and the stinging, blinding whips of rain, I sometimes thought I had been called to die on that beach, and that I had taken another innocent man to his doom with me. When we finally stood at the bottom on the wet beach, I immediately realized that we could do nothing against the ferocious elements. Advancing into the sea was an impossibility. I could see little or nothing farther than three or four feet in front of me. There was nothing but a shifting gray wall of water and wind through which I could see glimpses of the boiling surf. The wind blasted at us, heavily laden with water, whipping us back from the water's edge. If there were people in the white, churning water, they would be hidden by the pall of churning water. I had already endangered our lives by climbing down. I knew we must stop where we were or commit the sin of self-destruction. Almost as soon as I had this thought, the storm began to abate and in a very short time we could look out over the whitecaps and see far out into the water. There was no sign of any human creature in the subsiding troughs of the sea. I could see no piece of wreckage or sign of a foundering ship anywhere. If the man who stood next to me on the beach were not a giant of strength, he would never have reached the shore.

I looked over at my companion and saw that he was still white as a sheet.

"What is it, my man?" I asked. "Are you all right?"

"I saw the lightning strike you and illuminate your flesh, yet you live." His teeth were nearly chattering, no doubt from fatigue and cold as well as fear.

"What are you saying?"

"When you said, 'the Lord commands it' the lightning struck you and you looked like one of the mighty Archangels who will defeat Satan on the day of judgement with their holy fire."

"A trick of the air and your own eyes, no doubt," I replied and slapped him on the shoulder. "I think you have need of food and drink after your ordeal, my friend. I thank you for coming down here with me."

"Yes," he said looking out at the dark green troughs still heavily crowned with white foam, "I'll never go near the sea again."

I shared my food with him there on the beach, gave him a drop of my brandy and we both tucked up behind some rocks above the surf line.

Before falling asleep, he asked me, "What is your name? I want to know your name."

"Charles Wilney. And yours?"

He hesitated for a moment and finally said, "John Samuelson. I was a warder on a prison hulk bound out for Australia." He looked out toward the water. "Poor devils," he added.

"And now," I asked, "what will you do?"

His eyes grew dark and furious for a moment and then the inner storm passed.

"Find my si..find someone. And find some work. My old position is no longer open," he chuckled and I could hear the dangerous imbalance in the laughter. "And you?" he asked me.

I told him where I was going, and he said,

"Railroading, now that sounds a good trade."

"Other than the trade we all have," I answered.

"What's that," he asked as he stretched out to sleep.

"Obeying the Lord."

When I woke the next morning, the sea was as comfortable and peaceful as a sleeping cat. But my uneasy companion was gone. He left no word, no sign, just slipped away. I wondered if his story were a true one. His rags did not seem like something a warder would wear. And it seemed next to impossible that anyone could swim through the surf I had seen. He was a giant of a man, but the sea had been furious. I let my speculations slip from my mind and thought no more of the whole incident. I retraced my steps across the hills and returned to the road.

A week later, without further incident on the road, I found the railway crew out past the edge of the city. Men, horses, wagons and supplies were all huddled together around the track that had already been laid. Everything was covered in mud. Near the actual works were the navvy shanties, and as soon as I saw them, I promised myself I would find quarters with a nearby farmer even if I had to rise two hours early every morning to walk to the works. The best of the buildings were white-washed stone, thrown together with tar paper for the roof. Some of the worst were simply cuts made into the side of a hill with a roof of rafters and tar paper. You, Richard, were living in one of these with little Fanny when I met you. I do not know if you remember, Richard, that inside, all the shanties were verminous. They stank of cooking, spilled beer and unwashed human beings. When I saw you and Fanny later on, I could not bear the thought that you were growing up in such a verminous hole. I can never forget the fate of Mrs. J, the filthy crone, or so I thought her when I first saw her, who was supposed to look after you and keep the house clean. She beat her own children with an iron bar and behaved so viciously, the navvies killed her by throwing her into the cooking fire. It was when she died after being put in the fire that I resolved to somehow find other quarters for you and Fanny. For, in that shanty, especially, all was disorder with the strong taking what they wanted from the weak. The big shanties had as many as three rooms, which mattered not at all, since men, women and children slept in the same beds. The small sites I had seen in the past left me completely unprepared for the slovenliness, sin and utter chaos of this big navvy camp on this major line that was to be thirty-three miles long. When I saw what disorderly, hopeless lives the men lived, I felt that part of what I must do in the camp was to help spread the Gospel to the navvy heathens who were as ignorant of the Lord's word as savages from the south sea islands.

I remind you of all this horror so that you will understand from an adult perspective the conditions which fostered the secret I am writing to divulge. Even so, crime need not beget crime. Anyone can all choose to follow the Lord. It was from this sink of crime and misery that you grew up to be the fine, intelligent man you are, an achievement that would only have been possible with your own strength and fortitude and the Lord's love and special blessing.

I went to the Ganger right away and told him I wanted a position with the crew. He asked me about my last railway employment and was satisfied with what I said, but almost immediately we had a falling out over accommodations. He wanted me to live on the site. He said there were too many long shifts and emergencies. If I wanted employment, I would have to live in the camp. I said I would live in a tent but not in any of the shanties and he agreed.

"As long as I can lay my hand on you day or night," he said. He was a rough Irishman who wore purple suspenders and a rainbow waistcoat. He was known as Punching Jack because he was well-known as a prize fighter among the navvy camps. His fists had made him Ganger because he was good at keeping order in the crew. When he wasn't drunk, he was an easy-going man except for his violent hatred of Yorkshiremen. He liked to hire his own countrymen, who were the worst paid and most ignorant men in the crew. I believe he had ways of keeping back some of their wages for himself. "You look black Irish to me," he told me when he hired me. I didn't bother to correct him. "Give me an Irish back any time. They may bend but they never break," and he chuckled and slapped me hard between the shoulder blades. When Punching Jack was in his cups, however, he was a dangerous man. Many was the time, Richard, that I had to steer you or Fanny away from him. A single blow from his bony fist would have killed either one of you. He always repented of his drunken rages when sober, which made him better than many of the others. He was one of the first men to attend the sermons I began giving in the field alongside the track. He came very regularly, and he beat up the other Irish who had been baptized to force them to attend and listen to the Lord's word. There were about twenty out of the seven or eight hundred men who came regularly to hear the Lord's word on Sunday when I began. Punching Jack made a wonderful usher and I believe he was a good man at heart. He had been brought up in a Catholic home and it was he who started the custom of confessing to me after the sermon every Sunday. He knew I was not a priest, but my sermons and my quiet ways made him think of me as a clergyman, I guess. When some of the other men saw Punching Jack kneeling in the field, telling me his sins, others wanted to confess, too. I believe they liked the sacrament of confession because, in their minds, being forgiven meant they could go out and sin again the following week with a clean slate. I tried to explain otherwise, but it was no good. And I felt that any small glimmering I could give them of any church and of our Lord and Saviour was worthwhile.

In a couple of months, I had earned the nickname Father Wilney. They all loved to give themselves names and this was the one they chose for me. It was very strange to me that after failing to become a priest, I should be ministering to this tribe of savage men. Many of the others modeled themselves after Punching Jack and gave me the same respect a good Catholic gives their priest. After I broke the skull of a big Yorkshireman with a shovel, I never had another fight in the camp. Some of the men even gave me a portion of their money to hold when they didn't want to waste it all on drink. I felt honoured that these wild, brutal men gave me their trust and respect. For I knew it was not I to whom they bent their knee, but the Lord. And that was a good thing in their rough, short lives. Every day we worked on that line, we were facing death, and we all knew it. As long as I live, I shall never forget the noise, smoke and heat of the shafts that were sunk for the tunnel. When the man who was handling the blasting caps was drunk, which was often, any of us could end up buried under tons of rock and muck. At first, at first I was horrified by the pain and suffering of the navvies' lives, but their own code of stoic behaviour did not ask for my sympathy. When a man was mortally injured in a blasting accident, or had his legs crushed under a barrow he was handling, he might call for me and ask for "the holy words," as he lay dying or waited for the surgeon to come and cut off his legs. Anything in the Latin tongue would satisfy them, though generally, I read passages from the new testament and not from the texts reserved for priests. I also started to give reading lessons to the men and children who were interested. In all the time I did this work, Richard, no other man or lad took my lessons as much to heart as you did. To this day, I feel that you were a special blessing the Lord sent me as confirmation that I had done the work He wanted me to do.

I found my work very interesting and absorbing, not the labouring so much, but the strange ministry I had been given. Even the management of the site recognized the value of what I was doing. One day, Punching Jack brought me over to Mr. Dixon, Mr. Stephenson's man in charge on the site. He was very young. His eyes always seemed to be looking far away, past the person to whom he was talking .

"This is the man?" he asked Punching Jack.

"This is the man, yes sir," the sober Jack answered.

"I understand that for the last few months you have been giving sermons and helping the injured men. You are teaching some of them to read."

"Yes, sir. I have tried, inadequately, to share the Lord's word with them."

"I shouldn't say inadequately, Mr. Wilney. It's very hard for educated divines to come down to the level of the navvies. The last parson we had ran away from camp in the middle of the night when one of the men pissed in his face while he was sleeping. The men like and respect you. And we've had fewer fights since you've been here. I would like to install you as our pastor, Mr. Wilney. I shall increase your pay by seven shillings a day."

"But, sir, I am not ordained. And I am a Catholic."

"Ordained or not, you know how to get the men to listen the words of Jesus Christ. To me, that is ordination enough. And I don't care if you are a red Indian, if you reduce the brawling. Will you do it?"

"It would be my duty in any case, sir."

"You won't have to go down into the tunnel anymore, either. It must be hard for a man like yourself."

"Being a navvy is hard work for any man, sir. I am proud that I can work with them. And, if you'll pardon me, sir, I think the reason the men trust me is that I share their hardships, and except for my clean tent, I live as they do."

"Well, the tent won't do for the winter," he replied. "I've told Jack I want a new house built for you from stone, with a wooden roof."

"I would prefer to clean one of the existing buildings, sir."

"As you like, Wilney. You are an unusual man."

"We are all the same, sir, in the Lord's eyes. He loves us all if only we would know it."

"Yes, yes. Well, if you need anything come to me or talk to Jack."

"Thank you, sir. There is one more thing."

"Yes?"

"There is a young boy and his little sister here in camp. They have been living in a particularly foul shanty and I would like to have the children come and live in the one I will clean. He is an excellent student, sir. One of my best."

"Oh, was that Mrs. J's house?"

"Yes, sir."

"I suppose their parents will have no objection?"

"I'm sorry to say that their mother is rarely sober, sir. No one knows who the father is."

"Do as you like."

He turned away and that was the first and last conversation we had.

I was glad to have the extra money, though, it meant I could buy some additional books for the men and children. So now you know, Richard, how you came to live with me and I found my true vocation. I thought I wanted to be an engineer, but ministering to the men and children was much more important."

Chapter 24

The testament of Charles Wilney continued

About three months after I began working on the Liverpool & Manchester line, I approached the Tommy shop wagon one late afternoon. I was looking for a birthday gift for little Fanny. Among the exorbitantly priced goods that the wagon carried, I was sure I would find a small hand mirror for the little Miss. I knew she liked looking at herself in the nearby river. I suppose I should not have encouraged her vanity, which is the bane of her sex, but I knew she would like to have a mirror and there were few pleasures for her in the camp. The rains had been heavy and the mud was worse than usual for this time of year. The sky was just beginning to clear as I approached the wagon. We all hoped it would dry out for a time before everything froze again. There was a huge man in line ahead of me. My head only came to the middle of his upper back. I didn't think I'd seen him before, but men came and went so often from the camp that I thought no more of it until he finished his business and turned around. It was my shipwrecked acquaintance from the road.

"You," I said. "So you came here."

"Yes, I came. Though I must say it does not look much better than a shipwreck."

I looked around at the men, animals, lumber and wagons wallowing in the mud and replied, "No, I suppose it does not."

I turned back to look at him. I remember thinking there was something strange about this man. He looked very rough, though his clothes were better than when I'd last seen him, but he was well-spoken. When we had first met the contrast between his speech and appearance had not struck me as it did now. Perhaps because of my concern over the other victims of the shipwreck. Now, it seemed very marked.

"Did you find that person you were looking for?"

"What person?"

I felt he was almost angry at seeing me.

"You mentioned there was someone you had to find."

Just at this point in the conversation a tall, clean, plain-looking woman came over to the man and stood next to him in the proprietary way women have with men.

"Jack, I have found a place for us."

"Annabelle, this is Charles Wilney. The man I told you about."

"Mr. Wilney, this is my wife, Annabelle."

"Ah," I replied, "She must have been the person you were looking for. Pleased to meet you Mrs...I'm sorry, sir, I've forgotten your family name."

"Christian names are fine for us, Mr. Wilney. Annabelle and Jack."

"Very well. Pleased to meet you Miss Annabelle."

"Thank you, sir." She made an awkward curtsy. She was nearly as tall as her husband. Too large for any normal sized man to find pretty, but she and Jack seemed well suited.

"What work have you been given?" I asked Jack.

"They want me for the embankment. To handle a barrow."

"Ah, that's because of your strength. At least, you shall not have to go down into the tunnel."

"I've heard from some others that tunneling is the most hazardous of all jobs," he answered.

"Yes, but all work here is hazardous if men are drunk, and many are. Watch closely who works next to you."

"I'll do that, thank you. And where do you work?"

"In the tunnel. I try to make certain that the men handling the blasting caps are sober."

One of the men I knew, nick named, Cocker Jones, came up as I was talking with the husband and wife.

"Father Wilney, could I have your word on something?"

"Father?" Jack said. "Are you a priest?"

"I'm not ordained, but I've been doing some preaching here and there around camp and the men gave me that name. I try to help the men when I can."

For a moment, the big man looked at me and I saw the ghost of the fear I had seen when he said the lightning had struck me.

"Aye," he said, "you'd make a priest, all right. Especially for this band of devils. I mean, sir, they would respect you."

And at that moment, I knew he was seeing me lit up by the lightning again.

"Father, can you come?" Cocker said pulling my sleeve.

"Excuse me," I said to husband and wife. "I am certain I will see you both again soon."

"Yes, of course," he answered.

But I wasn't at all sure he wanted to see me again. Something had happened down on the shipwreck beach that made the big man uneasy around me.

The next incident I remember, regarding Jack, took place when I wasn't present, so what I relate is hearsay. Jack was making the running, which is the hardest and most spectacular of all navvy work. Only the strongest men are chosen for this. It's done when dirt from a cutting cannot be used somewhere close by and must be removed by barrow. Jack was going up the steep slope of the cutting on boards laid down on the ground to keep the wheels of his barrow from sinking into the ground. A rope attached to the barrow and also to Jack's belt, ran up the side of the cutting, and then around a pulley at the top, where it was attached to a horse. If, on the upward climb, the horse above slipped or faltered, or if a man lost his balance on the muddy plank he had to throw the half ton of muck in the barrow away from himself or risk being crushed by it.

The man working on the boards next to Jack was Happy Dave. He was about forty feet away to the left of Jack. He suddenly slipped when he was close to the top of the hill. He got tangled in the ropes and suddenly half a ton of muck was flying down the hill toward Jack with Dave knotted up in the ropes. Apparently, Jack whipped out a knife, cut his own ropes, dropped his barrow and jumped in the way of Dave and the tumbling barrow of muck to which he was tied. As the barrow and man careened toward him, Jack grabbed Dave and the barrow in both arms. His size and immense strength enabled him to slow the barrow enough so he could cut the ropes that would certainly have hauled Dave to his death at the bottom of the cutting. Once Dave was free, Jack jumped to one side and the barrow still had enough momentum to go tumbling down the slope to the bottom. It was over in seconds but many men had seen Jack choose to jump toward rather than away from the tumbling barrow, in order to free Dave. The incident combined the three things navvies prize above all else: strength, courage and loyalty. After this, all the men clapped the big man with the name, Mighty Jack, and he became an instant hero in the camp. With every telling, his feat, already amazing, became downright fabulous. The incident made it easier for me to believe that he had survived a shipwreck and swum through the boiling sea, though I still didn't believe he was a warder, and I think Mighty Jack caught me looking at him several times, with an appraising glance. He said nothing, but I could see that he didn't like being noticed by me, though he was always very polite and soft-spoken when we met.

The incident with the barrow was the first thing that set Mighty Jack apart from other men in the camp. Navvies are always glad to follow a man stronger than themselves and Jack was undoubtedly the most powerful man among the nearly one-thousand navvies we had on the site. It took an ordinary labourer a year at a railway camp before he was really strong enough to do the work of a navvy. Mighty Jack had started out with the most physically demanding work and made it seem easy. Navvies admire physical strength above all else. All the men deferred to him and soon Dixon, Mr. Stephenson's man, was asking Mighty Jack to do especially difficult jobs, sometimes by himself, sometimes by getting the other men to work with him. This notice from the Engineer brought out the fact that Mighty Jack was not only strong, he had an uncanny instinct for railway building. After only three months on the site, he could look at a task and tell exactly what resources would be needed and how long it would take. This ability to estimate time and materials is the key to profitable railway contracting. A contractor must be able to know how to bid on building a particular line. How many men, what materials and most important of all, how long it will take. Most railway companies fail because the estimate of time, money and men has been inaccurate, or because some obstruction arises which requires more resources. Mighty Jack had a sixth sense for this essential work. Once this was noted by the Dixon, he began offering Mighty Jack one subcontracted task after another. This was possible on the Liverpool & Manchester because George Stephenson was acting as his own contractor on the line, something for which he was criticized when the Exchequer Loan Commissioners sent Thomas Telford out to look at the works. If there had been another big contractor involved, I doubt that Jack would have had a chance to do as much of the work. Dixon knew Jack and his men would always finish on time and within the budget he estimated for the work they did. This was exactly what George Stephenson needed. He had become famous mostly for building locomotives and constructing the Stockton Darlington Line. But with the technical demands of the L & M, the tunneling under the streets of Liverpool, the cutting and work at Mount Olive and crossing Chat Moss, he needed his group of bright young engineers: Dixon, Locke and Allcard. They in turn, needed all the help they could find on site to get the line actually built within the terms of the bill under which the railway was authorized. This is how Jack Samuelson got his chance to become one of the greatest railway builders of all time. He earned it with sweat, skill and the Lord's help. Many times I saw his giant form, naked from the waist up, literally covered in mud, moving gigantic amounts of muck for hours at a time, while the other men struggled to keep up with their leader. Any man Jack chose for a crew was proud of the fact, for it meant the man was one of the best and strongest navvies in the camp. It also meant he was a sober man. Jack would not work with anyone who was drunk, and once he was a ganger and choosing his own crews, he could make the rules. I appreciated the sobriety of his crews and the seriousness with which he worked on any job he was given. Mighty Jack also took care of his men. I was present one day when a lift was being made, that is, a cut into a vertical face. Deciding how much of the face could be removed from below before men got up on the top to blast, was a piece of critical judgment. If they dug too far in on the bottom, the whole rock face could come down on the men. If the digging was too shallow, more blasting and time were needed at the top. There was a great tendency to make the digging on the bottom deep, because it meant the work went faster. The men were in the process of making a lift when Jack came back to the site after a talk with Dixon. He immediately started calling the men names.

"You jackasses," he said, can't you see that this stone is going to split off any second and crush you all? Get out from under there."

Jack grabbed the arm of the man working closest to him, known as Gipsy Joe, and pulled him out from under the rock, and just as he did, the rock face began to slide down. The other men, already on the alert, got out, too. At least three men would have been crushed to death if Jack hadn't issued his warning.

I was standing right there and I didn't know the rock face was about to drop, but Jack did. It is fair to say that by himself, Jack raised the standards of the navvies on our diggings. Yet, in spite of the fact that everyone looked up to him, I never saw him really laugh, or keep company with the other men when he wasn't working. He spent all his free time with his wife shut up in their shanty. I felt he brooded deeply on something in his past and I was convinced it had to do with the day we had gone down to the sea together. Finally, I decided to walk to his shanty and talk to him about my intuitions.

At this time, I was still living in my tent out in the fields. The shanties were built without regard to order of any kind. One faced east, its neighbour faced north, another lay directly in front of the doors of the other two. Like everything on the site, the shanty settlement had the appearance of complete disorder, as though the Father of Lies himself had touched each stone with his hand. As I approached across the clean grass of the rolling meadows, the shanties of whitewashed stone looked like a misshapen mouth of broken teeth set in mud. Surely there are no dwellings in the foulest rookeries of London as bad as the homes of navvies, the men who carry the future of Britain on their backs. I have always believed that the navvies must be especially beloved by the Lord to be given such short, difficult lives. They are maimed, broken and live in poverty in the service of their country and countrymen. They are given little honour in this world. Surely, they will be honoured in Heaven. Those, however, who make their excessive and sinful profits by the sweat of these poor broken heroes will end in the lowest circle of Hell. I have often asked the Lord to make it so.

I could smell the shanties from at least two hundred yards away. Mighty Jack's habitation was on the outer edge of the settlement. A few untrammeled patches of meadow formed his back yard; all else was mud. Occasionally, I could hear the boom of explosions as the crews worked twenty-four hours a day to sink four, hundred foot vertical shafts for the great tunnel. I knocked on the ancient boards that had been tied together with baling wire. In a few moments, Miss Annabelle peered out from a crack just wide enough to see who it was.

"Oh, Father Wilney," she said in her very soft, almost inaudible voice.

Though an exceptionally tall woman with large hands, she always impressed me as unusually gentle and mild, not just among navvy women but among any of her sex.

A moment later the door was pulled out of her hand and jerked wide open. There stood Mighty Jack, glaring out the door. When he saw who it was, he moderated the grimace that had been on his face and softened it to a frown.

"Father Wilney, I've just finished a day of lighting blasting powder under that wall of stone they hit. I am tired. What do you want?"

"Sorry, Jack. May I come in?"

"I don't like people in my house," he growled.

But Annabelle tugged on his sleeve and looked up at him in a mute appeal for sociability.

He looked down at her mild face and then back at me. He stood aside and said,

"Very well, Father Wilney, Come in."

"Thank you, Jack."

I could see immediately that the interior was unusual in that it was extraordinarily clean. Sand had been used to polish the wood floor into a shining state. There was still some small deposits of it in the corners of the room Every article was hung neatly on a hook. Scrubbed pots dangled from a rope above the stove and the copper kettle was polished to a bright shine. There was no disorder here,

"Miss Annabelle," I remarked, "what a fine housekeeper you are. I am certain this is the cleanest house in the settlement."

"Thank you, Father Wilney. Would you like tea?" she asked looking over at her husband.

"No, thank you, Annabelle."

"Well, then I had better go out. That is, I have to get something at the shop." She tied on her bonnet and fled out the door while the two of us sat in silence.

When she was gone, her husband visibly relaxed.

"Now, what can I do for you, Father Wilney?" he asked.

"Well, Jack, I just wanted to be sure there was no ill will between us. I've had the feeling that there is something about me that bothers you. I thought perhaps I could change it to suit you better."

The big man stood up again and walked around the room rubbing the back of his neck.

"No, no, nothing, Father Wilney. I, well, I just can't forget the way you looked the day I met you."

"You mean when it looked like the lightning struck me?"

"Yes."

"And?"

"I told you. You appeared like a ghost or some creature from, from somewhere else."

"Like heaven or hell?"

"Yes."

"Well, the Lord made us all in His image. So if I looked that way to you for a moment, maybe you were just seeing more clearly, then."

"Yes." The big man sat in a tense silence and I felt there was more he would say.

"I did not believe, did not believe in God until that day," he said slowly. "It was easier when I did not. Ever since that day I feel that I'm being watched, day and night."

"You are, Jack. The Lord knows us all, because He made us all. He knows your every thought."

"I don't like it."

"Don't like his knowing?"

"Yes."

"Well, there's not much can be done about that, Jack There is no escape from His all-seeing eyes."

For the first time since we started talking, the big man raised his face to mine. In his eyes, I saw a look of terror that I shall never forget. Involuntarily, I burst out, "For heaven's sake what is it, Jack?"

"No, no," he said getting up out of his chair as if he'd been stung. "You get out of here, now. You can't use your priest's tricks on me."

"I don't want to, Jack. I just want to help, if I can."
"Well, you cannot. Get out."

He moved to the door and pulled it open so forcefully one of the boards slipped down and its end hit the floor.

"Get out and don't come back."

I rose immediately and I blessed him silently in his terror and confusion in the Lord's name. I felt his eyes on my back as I walked away from the house.

My next incident with Mighty Jack was much more public.

There were over one thousand men working on the L & M and the feeling of competition between the men working on different sections was often heated. Later on, when there were more railways being built, the contractors themselves encouraged a sense of competition between their men and those of other contractors. From time to time, they would send their navvies against each other in pitched battles when a site was being contested or a contract not yet awarded. Most often, these are relatively minor bloodlettings where no one is killed and perhaps fewer than twenty seriously injured. Sometimes, however, there are deaths and the dead are toasted as heroes with buckets of beer. A less demanding sport which the men liked nearly as much as outright warfare was prizefighting. The prizefighters could be from the same camp. Sometimes it was just two men settling a grievance with each other, but the fights that the men really looked forward to were those between the men who were recognized as champions. There was a prizefighting champion working on the L & M whom I had never seen. He was known as Hammer Fisted Mick. It was said he had won all of the several dozen fights he had. The men on his part of the diggings boasted that Mick was going to quit being a navvy to become a professional prizefighter. In the end, his followers said, Mick decided that he'd better stay a navvy because nothing else could keep him in such good form.

One day, some six months after I began my ministry on the Liverpool & Manchester Line, two wagons, one with Hammer Fisted Mick aboard, with a crew who was working primarily in the tunnels in Liverpool and one that I rode in, passed each other on the road from Liverpool. The road was narrow and the two wagons could not pass at the same time. The men in the other wagon, had clearly been doing a lot of drinking. They began calling to our men to pull aside and let their wagon pass. Naturally, hoots and jeers followed and Hammer Fisted Mick rose off of their wagon and hit one of our cart horses in the jaw. The horse was staggered by the blow and lost the advantage. The other wagon pulled ahead. One of the men on our wagon called out to Mick, "You wouldn't get away with that, Mick. if Mighty Jack was here. He'd make sausages out of you."

Mick, not wanting his prestige as a fighter to become tarnished, called back, "I'll meet your Mighty Jack any time and any place and I'll smash him. Then I'll grind him under my boots til you dain't see anything but mud."

Of course, the men in our wagon came racing back to our site with this insolent challenge, and a deputation immediately went looking for Mighty Jack. They all converged on him at the tommy wagon where he and I were both buying some necessaries.

To the men's surprise, Jack was reluctant to fight. He said fighting was a waste of strength and time. But then Crazy Mike spoke up, "Yer can make lots of money, Jack. We'll all bet you up. We'll back you."
When it was observed that this argument seemed to carry weight with their champion, the men called out loudly, "Aye, aye, we'll back you, Jack."

"Ah, ah, ahn and you know what,what he said he, he do to you, Jack?" Crazy Mike stuttered. "He sa, sa, said he, he could grind you into mud under hi,hi,his boots."

"You hear that Jack?" some of the men shouted. "You can't let him say that."

At just this point Dixon, the engineer, walked into the group and took up a place near Jack.

"Jack," he said, "the honour of our part of the line is in your hands. If you don't pound this man down, The other men will say we're all daisies. And your men couldn't live with that, could you?" he asked turning suddenly to the several hundred men who by this time were crowding around.

"No," they roared with one voice.

"Aye," Jack finally said, after a long silence. "I'll beat this man for you. But I want ten percent of all bets placed. Mr. Dixon has to hold all bets. Their money and yours."

"Done," said the Engineer. "Who will carry the challenge into Liverpool?" he asked.

Someone shouted my name, "Wilney," and immediately it was taken up by the whole crowd. "Father Wilney, he'll know how to tell 'em the rules. Yes, send FatherWilney, he'll talk to them proper. No fools on this part of the line. Father Wilney will tell them."

While this was being said I was being pushed to the side of Jack and the Engineer. When we all stood next to each other, the men cheered.

In all my years of railroading, I never saw a prizefight so anticipated by the men in a camp. For the three weeks before the fight, it was all the men or women could talk about. It was Mighty Jack who insisted we wait three weeks so that the bets could pile up. He wanted to get as much money as possible out of the fight. He planned to use it to buy equipment so he could expand his independent contracting. When the day of the fight arrived and the betting was closed, there was over one thousand pounds at stake. Samuelson stood to make one hundred pounds. That is the often-repeated true story how the famous John Samuelson started his career as one of the kings of railway building. But what I will tell here is not so well reported.

The day of the fight was cold and dry. The ring had been built out in the field away from the works. If there was rioting afterwards, the company did not want its property damaged. Four saplings had been cut and driven into the ground to form the four corners of the fighting arena. Then we tied the ropes to these posts. Almost from sunrise, men began arriving from both camps. The Engineer had pressed for constables from Manchester to keep the peace. Ten of them in blue jackets were stationed in highly visible locations. Soon the big field was choked with men, horses and wagons. If the ground hadn't been frozen hard as iron, it would have been trampled to mud. The sky was cloudless, a brilliant blue, when at noon, Hammer Fisted Mick stepped into the ring bare-chested but wearing his moleskin trousers and bright red suspenders. His favourite dotted red kerchief was tied around his neck. He was greeted by cheers and hisses. He was a huge man, bigger than Samuelson, though not as well muscled. His technique was to literally pound his opponent down from above, using his great height as an advantage. After Mick appeared, we waited and waited for Samuelson to arrive. After a time, angry comments began to be heard from the men of the other camp. Mick, himself, just stood quietly in the ring looking absolutely certain of victory. Finally, almost a quarter hour later by my pocket watch, Samuelson pushed his way through the crowd. The cheers of our men drowned out the hisses from the others.

Mighty Jack was also bare chested but he wore no suspenders, only black canvas pants and boots. The crowd began murmuring when he stepped into the ring. The men from the Liverpool gang were probably seeing Jack for the first time, some probably began to think that there was going to be a real job for their undefeated champion. I had been elected referee by unanimous acclaim on both sides. Our side felt it gave them an advantage and the other men felt they would take their revenge on me if I made a call with which they disagreed. I did not mind the fact that I could be mobbed if I made an unpopular call on a fighter. I would only feel the burden of deciding the fight if both men were still standing, which was unlikely. This was a bare-knuckle prizefight with few rules: no hitting below the belt. Hands, head and elbows only to strike blows. The fight was over when a man went down and could not get up. Each round was to last five minutes with a one minute rest in between.

Finally, the stating bell borrowed from a locomotive was wrung. Neither man rushed at the other. Mick just let his long arms dangle at his side. Samuelson had his fists up like a man who had fought before and knew his business. Mick landed the first blow but it seemed not to affect Jack at all, glancing off his powerful shoulder, which he used to good advantage to protect his chin. Then, Mick moved in closer and began to try to rain blows down on Jack, but they all fell harmlessly on Jack's mighty back. Up to this point, it looked like Mick was going to win the fight, since he was out-punching Jack nine times over. Suddenly, however, when Mick came in close again, Jack closed with him in a corner and began to hit him. The first blow landed on Mick's ribs. I could hear a crack and see a spasm of pain on Mick's face. Jack was smiling like a man who enjoyed his work. He pushed Mick up against the post and began to batter him. In a few moments, Mick could not even hold up his hands. Only the post of the ring kept him standing, and Jack pressed him against it with his own body, refusing to let the other man fall. Our men were cheering as Jack began drawing blood from Mick's face. Jack refused to let his opponent fall and escape him, but kept pressing him against the post. I went to Jack and tried to pull him off, but his face was the face of a fiend. He was a man possessed as he pounded Mick's face into a bloodier and bloodier pulp. I could see the daemonic rage in his eyes as he crushed the weaker man. Mick's eyes rolled up in his head. He was unconscious but still, Jack held him up with his own body and battered him for a fearful interval of time. Through all this bloodshed, Jack was smiling. I felt the evil in him and all I could think to do was to pray to the Lord to bring this terrible mayhem to an end. By this time, I could no longer see Mick's face. His features were a smear of blood and broken bone. Both eyes were swollen shut.

"Dear Lord," I said out loud, "End this wicked assault on one of your children."

Jack seemed to hear me, or at least, he turned his head and took a step back from Mick, letting him drop to the ground. I think even our men who could see how badly Mick was injured were shocked. I have never before or since seen a beating like the one Hammer Fisted Mick was given that day. Once Mick hit the ground, I could see he was no longer breathing. Mighty Jack had beaten him to death, as cold-bloodedly as if he had been pounding rock with a twenty pound hammer. When he turned his back to walk away from Mick, Jack's face changed. He lost his daemonic look. He glanced over at me and smiled a cruel smirk. Watching him that day makes me believe that one of the lesser daemons of hell possesses Jack Samuelson's body, or, at least, possessed it the day he killed Hammer Fisted Mick.

Jack walked right from the ring and over to Mr. Dixon. The crowd was quiet, uncertain of what to do now, with the winner, hardly out of breath, collecting his money and his opponent lying stone dead on the ground. Finally, some of Mick's friends went over to the body, tried to wake him, realized he was dead and finally carried him to one of their wagons. After the fight, with the money he'd won, Mighty Jack was able to take on more work. He took on larger pieces of the line, and even began to work directly with Mr. George Stephenson, himself, now often called, "the father of British railways." Mr. Stephenson was glad to use him because he ruled his men with a strong hand and his work was always finished on time and finished up to the highest standards.

So, I watched Jack Samuelson rise from the sea with rags on his back to become a ganger, a contractor and finally a friend of the highest in the land, with his own empire of iron roads. In spite of the heights he has reached, he could lose everything and end on the gallows if the truth about the man were known, Richard. My narrative will demonstrate that Samuelson's empire is founded on the deepest deceit a man can practice. You will learn that everything about the railway king is based on a fundamental lie and the darkest of crimes. If you are reading these lines, you must know that my knowledge of these secrets is the reason I have been killed. You must use the secrets I impart here however you think best to protect yourself and Fanny. Do not use the secret for revenge. Vengeance belongs to the Lord, alone.

Chapter 25

The testament of Charles Wilney continued

By and large, navvies are illiterate labourers who travel from one site to another seeking work. They have no power as individuals, but when a contractor gathers them together, sometimes by the thousands, they can become the most formidable army on earth. It has been estimated that in the year of our Lord 1845, there are over 100,000 navvies at work in Britain, nearly as much as the combined land and sea forces of Great Britain itself. Samuelson learned about this power very quickly, for power was always his goal, the power to shape the iron roads of Britain and thereby shape the future. I believe that profit has always been secondary to him. Money was simply a way of keeping score of his achievements, a way of counting the iron roads he built.

Some months after the fight, a company director visited our site. He was an elegantly dressed man who, it was said in camp, had come all the way from London. We all knew that the titled owner of a key parcel of land was now holding up our progress. Each day's delay cost the company a great deal of money. Of course, a private member's bill introduced in Parliament could have been used to compel a sale of the land in question, but it could take months and would mean ruin for the company and its shareholders. It was because of an unexpectedly deep vein of stone in the original route that this parcel was needed so suddenly. To put it more succinctly, the route had to be changed at the last minute. So this one land owner could hold us to ransom.

Jack Samuelson was called in to speak to the man from London. A few hours later the word went around camp that there was going to be some "fun" out at the home of the man who owned the property we needed. The men who worked regularly with Samuelson marched out of camp. There were about one hundred of them, I would say, armed with picks, shovels and blasting caps. A holiday feeling prevailed in the camp. Work was suspended for the day and quite a few of us followed Samuelson's men out to the home of the land owner. I forget his name now, but he was a Baronet or had some such title and he had a grand house and grounds. You could see it from miles away: surrounded by a clump of forest on a high hill. A paved road ran into the wood and eventually to the gates of the house itself. We marched into the woods and in a short time, Samuelson's one hundred men were setting fires in the Baronet's park. In less than a half hour, most of us were coughing and blinded from the smoke. The grand house had burning trees on every side. The only thing between the fire and the Baronet was the wall and gates that encircled his house and park.

Jack Samuelson went up to the gates and told the gatekeeper that he must see the Baronet. There was a terrible fire raging around the property, he said, but if his Lordship would give us leave to come on to his land, he believed we could put the fire out and save the house. In just a few minutes the steward was fetched to the gates. Samuelson talked to him briefly and handed him a paper, which I understand, gave the company's men a permanent right of way across the land in exchange for putting out the fire. The paper came back very quickly, signed by the Baronet. Then, Mighty Jack used the water wagons he had brought with us to put out the fire in the Park. Every man who participated in setting the fires and putting them out was given three days extra pay. It was rumoured that Jack himself received some shares in the L & M. This was only eleven months after Jack had arrived in the camp. It was from watching this man, Richard, that I developed my understanding of what is generally called "business" or "capitalism". Samuelson's highly successful tactics enriched his masters and himself at anyone else's expense, yet it could also be said that they enriched England and helped make us a greater nation. I never raised a hand against my employers, but neither would I break the law for them if so commanded. I have kept the Lord's commandments and rendered unto Caesar what is Caesar's. You know my views. Watching Samuelson helped form them.

Mighty Jack also played an important part in what is still considered George Stephenson's most famous engineering feat: laying track across the Chat Moss. It was Samuelson's men who were hand-picked for working on this particular segment of track, which took a full year to build. It was Samuelson himself who actually led the way across the four miles of soggy moss. It was Mighty Jack's will that kept his men throwing endless bundles of brushwood and heather into the morass after the parallel drains were cut so that a stable embankment could be formed. Ton after ton of these materials were tossed into the morass, and promptly disappeared. Many believed the morass was bottomless and that the undertaking was doomed to failure. From what I saw of this famous bit of railroading, I believe that Stephenson, himself, would have given up on his legendary achievement if it had not been for Mighty Jack's will and his men working day and night to forestall the criticism that was being leveled at the Engineer for his handling of the Chat Moss problem. It took a full year before a solid embankment appeared above the swamp. It took year and a half before the track was laid across Chat Moss. Part of my aim in telling you all this, Richard, is to make you realize the sort of man against whom you may have to struggle. He is an implacable foe. This is one of the reasons I urge you to dismiss all thoughts of revenge and to stay away from him.

On another occasion, we were building an embankment that the tracks would ride on across a deep ravine. The embankment was nearly built when Jack and his men got to that part of the track. Jack wouldn't start working right away but spent a full day walking around the works, looking carefully at different soils that had been thrown up while the bank was being built by the men who had preceded his own. For that whole day he refused to let his men work. They were idle but he paid them and lost a lot of money because of the delay, but he came back to camp and told Dixon that the soil underlaying the embankment was no good. It should have been removed and filled with a better base. He said if it was not done, the embankment would be unstable and could collapse at any time. He would not allow his men to risk their lives on the existing embankment. They would only work if another embankment was built with a stable foundation. He nearly lost his place over this delay, but finally, Stephenson agreed. One week to the day after the new embankment was started and the men shifted over to it, the earlier one, now abandoned, collapsed after a heavy rainfall. Men on the site told me that as many as fifty of them could have been buried alive.

As I have already said, Mighty Jack had a sixth sense for railroad building. When Jack looked at a handful of dirt it was as if he was reading printed words in a book. It was uncanny the way he could sense trouble before it happened. Of course, this made the men respect him even more. His crew did the toughest jobs but without unnecessary risks. He wouldn't let them work on the tunnel. I, for my part, was fascinated by the tunneling. Every aspect of the work interested me. The big gins drilled into the surface so the explosives could be planted to sink the vertical shafts. Then the blast. Even the heat, even working in the dim candlelight below ground did not bother me much. Perhaps, like many of the other navvies, the risks of tunneling gave it a certain savage excitement for me. Once the vertical shafts were dug, we worked with hand tools to cut away at the walls until we had a horizontal shaft that connected the vertical ones we had already sunk. Working at the bottom of the shafts, there was terrible and unpredictable danger. The Liverpool tunnel kept filling up with water. Standing in the half light at the wet bottom of a shaft, or worse, midway between two shafts under tons of soil and stone, there was no way to get out if we hit something soft and the earth above us started to give way.

The Lord took care of me. I was never injured or buried but many men lost hands, legs, eyes or died to build that tunnel. The Lord put me elsewhere when the accidents occurred. I suppose He had other work for me to do. Part of what I tried to do was to comfort those who were injured. After we came out of the tunnel I would go and find out the men who had been hurt that day. Sometimes I would write a letter to a mother and explain as gently as I could that she would never see her son's earthly form again. Sometimes I would read the scripture over a dying man. But the most heartening work I had in those years, Richard, was teaching you and the other men and boys. Those were the best hours of the day for me. The ability to learn has always seemed to me to be the Lord's greatest gift to His children. If we could not learn and reason, we could not repent and become better. Learning is the golden key to salvation that the Lord's grace has given us. It is not to inflate the vanity of learned men. Always remember this, and always use learning to draw near the Lord, Richard. Your life can never go wrong if you do this.

Jack and I spoke little to each other. After watching him beat Hammer Fisted Mick to death, I was troubled by the daemonic, murderous spirit that I had seen in him. I think he knew it and, for some strange reason, I think he always wanted my good opinion. It made him uneasy around me. I was the only man in the camp who had met Jack before he joined the crew. I was sure there was something in his past that pricked his conscience. I could not forget the rags he had been wearing on the afternoon of the shipwreck, nor his reluctance to go down to the beach and rescue his shipmates. Finally, there was his strange vision of me being illuminated by lightning so that I appeared as a fiery angel to him. His superhuman feats of strength, the way he drove himself and his men, spoke to me of a desperate soul within. I felt he was being consumed by a terrible inner struggle. I felt he wanted the Lord's word but was afraid of it. He made me think of Saint Augustine who once said, "Make me good, Lord, but not yet."

Sooner or later, I believed, something would have to happen in Jack Samuelson's life to end his wrestling match with the Lord. He was a man who wanted to believe, but was afraid to believe. I did not know then if it was because he felt his sins were too great, or if he was afraid that if he did believe in the Lord, Our Saviour, would disappoint him by proving false and unreal, simply a tale for children. At any rate, I saw Jack Samuelson as a man locked in a great spiritual struggle. In those days, I believed I could have helped him win that struggle. But I could also see the Enemy was tempting him with gifts of power and greatness among men. If you are reading this, Richard, then I know he has finally given in, and gone over to the side of the Wicked One. God save his eternal soul!

The crisis of Mighty Jack came about one night when even his sixth sense about railway building failed him. I believe that this failure was actually the Lord's way of offering him a last chance. He was working at night with his men and they were trying to blast a small ridge of stone out of the way of their cutting. As usual he was driving himself and his men to their utmost limits. In a split second, in a blast and blinding flash of black powder, the world tumbled down on him. The ridge of stone, much smaller than the crew thought broke free from the ground and tumbled down the hillside where Jack and the men were working. He was caught in the tons of soil that the tumbling rock pulled into its wake, burying the mouth of the cut where Jack had been working. Moments later, when the dust cleared, Mighty Jack had disappeared. His men began digging like furies to find him. Any man who was awake and sober came to help. Many times that night, his life was despaired of and had it not been for the great loyalty and determination of his men, Jack would have remained buried forever.

I shall never forget the scene when he was finally found. As I write these words in front of my own hearth a vision of the event rises up before me, as clear as that terrible morning: It was a little after dawn. There was a hard frost on the ground. The rising sun was throwing long black shadows from each clod of earth and rock that had been turned up during the long night, magnifying the size and shape of every particle. In that eerie light, a pebble looked like a boulder, and the boulder that had broken free and caused the catastrophe loomed over the pit like a mountain. The men were working so hard, I could see their breath rising from the pit where they dug, thick as steam from a boiling kettle. Dixon, himself, stood by, watching, clenching and unclenching his fists. and next to him, a leading doctor from Liverpool who had partaken of our vigil most of the night, a lean prematurely bald man with thin tightly compressed lips. I remember watching as the sun rose and a golden sliver of light glinted off the polished iron rim of the doctor's spectacles. At that moment, I saw there was no spark of hope in his eyes. The muddy sweating bodies of the men worked on with the relentless power of a steam pump, their shadows large as Titans risen from the Underworld. All were tense with expectation, though the chance of anyone surviving these long minutes with tons of soil and rock lying on him appeared an impossibility.

I had been praying silently most of the time I watched, hoping that Mighty Jack with all his gifts and powers would survive to become a good man and welcome the Lord into his heart. Suddenly, without being able to see clearly, the sounds told me there was a break in the nearly mechanical regularity of the men's digging. Then one man shouted. "Got him." Another voice echoed into the absolute stillness that had suddenly prevailed, "He's breathing."

The doctor began to climb down to see his patient. The men made way for him without making a sound. Then I heard a third voice.

"I cannot examine him here. We must get him to shelter and light," the doctor's voice was a thin, tinny rattle, muffled against the tons of earth that surrounded him.

"Thank you, my Lord," I whispered under my breath, as the men shifted Jack upward. They carried him as tenderly as a newborn babe. As they passed him near me, I got a glimpse of blood and bones breaking through the skin. He looked so crushed to me that I could not imagine his survival. Then I rallied myself in the Lord's name, and began praying again as I walked back to the shanty I had cleaned and fitted out for you and Fanny and myself. I had been away all night, but both of you were fast asleep. I lay down on my bunk and the tension of the long night of suspense came crashing down on me all at once. I fell into an exhausted stupor immediately. The camp was quiet when I woke, yet the light told me it was past noon. You and Fanny had gone out. I got up to hear the latest report was on Mighty Jack. I left our shanty and walked over to the Engineer's house where I knew Jack had been taken. I was amazed to see all of Jack's men standing quietly, their heads bowed while one of their number tried to read from scripture. Most of these men couldn't read at all, yet here they were trying to get help for Jack by reading the Lord's word. I was deeply touched, but I was afraid the worst had happened. As I approached, the man who had been reading haltingly, immediately handed the book to me with the words, "We're trying to call on the Almighty to help out Mighty Jack, Father Wilney."

"Is he living or dead?" I asked as quietly as I could. I felt that somehow I had been put in charge of the soul of this gifted man and that the Lord had brought us together for a purpose. In some way I didn't understand, his fate was bound up with my own.

"Hardly living, Father Wilney," someone answered.

I took the Bible and immediately turned to Mark's reference to Lazarus' return to life. I read the passage and handed the book back to the man.

"Please Father," one of the Irish navvies asked, "Would you tell our Holy Saviour how much better we can do if Jack's here instead of up there," he pointed to the sky.

I think that the man believed the Lord would simply carry out any request I made. He was a man who had come to most of the open air sermons I had preached.

"I'll tell him, but I'm sure He's heard all of you," I said. I knelt down on the ground and all the men knelt down, too, an unusual demonstration for a gang of navvies. It is not that I think they believed fully in the Lord, but they wanted Jack to live so badly that they would take any measure that might help him. I was just about to enter into prayer when the door of the Engineer's house was opened and the doctor stepped out. Even now his voice had a thin, tinny quality,

"I know you are all anxious about your injured comrade inside. The best thing you can do is pray for him very quietly. I must tell you that he is very badly injured. I think you should prepare for the worst. I will return this evening at six to look in on him." With that announcement he put on his very new hat, walked to his handsome gig, got in and drove away. We finished our prayer and then rose.

How long we all stood around the Engineer's house, I don't know, but the weary day dragged on and Jack's wife came out to talk to us from time to time. Her report was always the same: He was resting easily and was still unconscious. It struck me that with her calm, quiet way, she would be a good nurse. Finally, late in the afternoon the men began to trickle away from the house and I was left alone, sitting on the only front porch in the camp. Once the men were gone, there was nothing for me to do. I thought of you and little Fanny, whom I had not seen all day. I got up and walked home. Do you remember, Richard, telling me that the men were betting for and against Mighty Jack's survival? The poor heathens! They didn't mean it disrespectfully. It was their way of being with Jack when they could not see him or talk to him. You and Fan did your lessons with me, and by that time it was getting near the hour when the doctor said he would come. I went back to the Engineer's house to wait. About half Samuelson's men were there. I saw that the doctor was already in attendance. His handsome horse and gig waited in front of the rough cottage.

"Any news?" I asked the men.

They shook their heads.

After what seemed a very long time, the doctor came out. I stepped forward and asked him, "How is he, sir?"

"Still alive, I am surprised to say. And where's there's life, there's always hope," the tinny voice answered.

I could hear the copybook phrase drop mechanically from him. He was surprised Jack had lasted this long. He didn't expect him to last much longer.

As the doctor rode off the men began to leave. Once again, I was the last one, standing in front of the house. Just as I was about to leave, the door opened and Miss Annabelle came out. I remember she was neatly dressed in brown. As usual, her cleanliness was striking as she stood on the rough mud spattered boards of the porch.

"Father Wilney," she said.

I could see she was discomposed. It was the first time I had seen the big woman so. She was twisting her long hands together in a gesture similar to that of woodlanders when using a wimble, an odd sort of twisting movement.

"Yes, Miss Annabelle? Is there anything..." I let my question trail off.

"Well, yes, sir, there is. I," she stopped and her face coloured up in a flash of scarlet. "That is, sir, I'd like to..." She paused for a long time and looked down at the ground. Her colour was still high.

"I'd like to talk to you, sir, privately. It, it's a matter of conscience, you see."

"Well, of course, Miss Annabelle. I am at your disposal."

"Not now, sir. Not with Jack lying just in there." She glanced back toward the house behind her with a startled look in her eyes, almost as if she expected the sick man to walk out the door. "But soon, sir."

I understood there was something she wanted to tell me but only after Jack had died. Then she turned abruptly and slipped back inside.

How many days Jack lingered between life and death, I can no longer remember, exactly. The doctor, I could see, was puzzled by Jack's unwillingness to die, and resented it. Coming out to the camp all the way from Liverpool, riding through the mud in his fine equipage was a nuisance for him, I'm sure. Navvies' were not in his line. I, frankly, did not like the man. He didn't have a healing manner about him. I do know it was weeks later when, one day, I called to see how Jack was and Miss Annabelle answered my knock. She had said no more about the "matter of conscience." Her bright look told me that something had happened for the better.

261

"He's been awake, sir," she said. "Twice since this morning. He hopes he shall feel a little better tomorrow." From the light in her voice and face, I can tell you that in those days, at least, she loved him well.

He was a little better the next day, and the next. His men now came each day to pay their respects to Miss Annabelle and ask about Jack. I have never before or since seen anyone command this kind of respectful interest from a gang of navvies for such a long time.

The weather was getting milder, the heather was putting on fresh colour and one could smell the waking earth in the air. It was a state of nature I always associate with the Blessed Virgin, Her gentleness and mercy after the winter. Jack was better than he had been, but the doctor warned us all that he was still very damaged inside and that it would be many months before we would know for certain if Jack would go on living. None of us had yet seen him. Only the doctor and Miss Annabelle were allowed into the house, so I was very surprised one evening after an especially grim day underground, with several serious injuries in our crew, to be summoned from our dinner table by Miss Annabelle, herself.

"If you please, sir," she said dropping one of her clumsy curtsies. "Jack would like you to come and see him right after your dinner."

"I shall come immediately, Miss Annabelle."

"No. Please, sir. Jack said very particularly that your dinner was not to be disturbed."

Then, she began wringing her hands in the same way she had when she had told me she wanted to talk to me. She looked away from me and down at the floor.

Suddenly she said, "He has much to say to you, sir." The words seemed to break from her almost against her will and she bolted out the door.

Do you remember all this, Richard? The very tall woman standing in the doorway as we ate dinner? Well, no matter. We finished our meal and I left you reading at the table by the stove, while Fanny played with a dolly I had bought for her.

I had no idea what to expect as I approached the house where the injured man had lain for so many weeks. I wondered, if at last, Jack would loosen his iron grip on himself and share the burden of his trials with me.

I was shown into the sickroom by Annabelle. She spoke not a word. Jack's face was mercifully unscarred but the rest of him was wrapped in clean bandages. All over the white cotton strips, I could see spots of blood that slowly blossomed here and there, pushing up like curious red flowers in a field of snow. Annabelle had kept his hair neatly cut and his face clean shaven. Jack said nothing until Annabelle left the room.

"Sit down, Father Wilney. There is a chair, I believe."

I did as he directed.

"How are you feeling, Jack?"

"About like a piece of uncooked steak."

"You wanted to see me?" I asked.

"You, know, father, I was raised a Catholic."

"No, I didn't know, Jack, but I suspected it."

"I thought you might have. Uhh," He cried out suddenly.

"Is there much pain? Can I do anything?"

"Only our Lord can do anything, now, Father Wilney."

"I am gratified to hear you talk like that, Jack. We are all in His hands at all times. But mostly we are lost in sin and forget the fact."

"Yes, Father. Oh," he writhed in pain again. Then he went on, "I have lived the last few years as law unto myself. When I feel death's hand on me as I did a moment ago, I wonder what awaits me."

"Repentance and forgiveness are always there for you, Jack. You know that if you were raised as a Catholic."

"But I have to confess to be absolved of my sins, don't I, Father."

"Yes, you do, Jack."

"Then I should like you to hear my confession, Father Wilney."

"You know I cannot, Jack. You know I am not ordained. I am not a priest."

"I saw the Lord touch you with my own eyes." The big man writhed in pain again. "I have seen you here. You are more a priest than some the Church takes as its own."

"But I am not allowed to absolve you from sin. It is a sacrament only a priest can perform."

Suddenly, I saw the sick man's eyes blaze with an inner fire that had seemed all but extinguished. He grabbed my arm in a convulsive grip that still had the crushing power of a pair of iron pincers. The strength the Lord had given the man seemed almost supernatural.

"I must confess to you. In the sight of God, if you are not a priest, there are no priests."

His hold on me did not lessen. My arm began to grow numb from his grip. Then he used his hold to jerk himself more upright and closer to me. He held himself upright by pulling on me.

"Damn you," he said with repressed rage. "I'm a dying man. Do you think I cannot tell?"

I began to fear that if I did not give him what he wanted, he might injure himself.

"Easy, Jack. Of course, I shall listen to anything you want to tell me. I cannot absolve you as a priest, but I do know that he who truly repents of his sins shall be received in heaven by our Saviour. I can listen to your repentance, and the Lord shall hear. He shall absolve you."

"Very well."

He let go of me and fell like a stone back onto the bed. In a few moments, he was asleep. I waited for him to come back to himself. I felt certain that such a strong willed man would not allow himself to die without having a chance to ask the Lord's forgiveness.

I had been tired from a long day before I got to Jack's bedside, but there is always something about Jack Samuelson that can call forth greater than normal efforts from the people around him—for good or ill. He can make them better or worse than themselves. I felt fresh and able to sit at his bedside all night, if need be. The lamp burned low and guttered. I waited in the darkness praying for the soul of Mighty Jack.

To this day, I am uncertain whether my prayers were answered. I suspect, however, that soon I shall know. Through the small deep window in the sickroom, I watched the moon rise and set. Slowly the camp grew more quiet, until, finally all was silent except for the occasional drunken shouts of the very few men who were still awake. Several times I heard the cries of nightjars and other nocturnal birds. A strange peace settled over me as I sat by Jack's bedside. For the first and only time in my life, the gifts of vision and prophecy were given to me. This is what I saw:

Jack and I were standing in a very high place. It reminded me of the hill overlooking the sea where we had stood looking for the shipwrecked men, except that the distances we looked out over were infinitely greater. There was a strange glow in the sky, a kind of light I have sometimes seen after very violent storms have passed, a particular very bright yellow light that changes the colour of anything on which it rests. Within it, shadows always seem darker than normal.

I felt there was a great choice to be made. It was to be made by all humanity in a general way but it was to be made by Jack, specifically in his own life. If he chose to walk with the Lord, he and I would be like brothers. If not, he would cast me down off the high cliff where we stood and dash my life to pieces on the rocks below. I was not frightened, but I hoped that Jack would choose the way of the Lord.

When I became aware of myself again, sitting on the chair in the sickroom, I heard the sounds of the camp waking up for a day of work. The sky that was visible through the window showed me the rosy streaks of dawn beloved by classical poets. Jack was speaking to me.

"Wilney, I am in a lot of pain. listen to me. Wake up. I know not how much longer I shall last. You must hear my confession, now."

Here I set down this confession in as close to his own words as I can recall. Even though it was spoken in repentance felt in the shadow of death, the horror of his words still burns in my memory, Richard.

***

"I shall say things quickly and simply for I know not how much longer I can draw breath. I was born in Ireland in 1792. My father was a large landowner who was loyal to Erin. He was betrayed to the English king for a bag of silver plus the lands that belonged to us, and was shot. His betrayers were good church-going Irish Catholics.

From this, I first realized the power of money. I came to England to make my way in the world and found I had a talent for handling animals. I became a very successful farrier and blacksmith. Soon I had a small forge and began manufacturing farm tools. Small improvements I made in their design were much appreciated by my customers. I was already making a fair sum when a robbery took place in our neighbourhood. Plate was stolen from an English churchman's palace. The criminal was described as very large and strong. There were only two such men near the palace who fitted that description: myself and the man who committed the crime. But, he had the money from the crime to buy his way out of his troubles—and he was an Anglican, a member of the English church. All of my property was seized by the crown when I was accused and I was tried and summarily sentenced to transportation. Once again, I saw the power of wealth to shape events. When I stood in the dock for this crime I had not committed, I was more determined than ever that somehow I would manage to become rich and call the tune that other's would dance to, instead of being the one who danced. I did not know how this would happen, but when the hulk I was on was broken up by the sea, I was given my chance and took it.

When we met, Father Wilney, I told you I was shipwrecked. But there was more to it than that. There was a warder on the boat whose name was Samuelson. He was a decent man, God forgive me. His face sometimes gets between me and sleep. But I had to choose between his life and my own and I had already been cheated twice by what wealth could do with the laws of England—especially if it was against someone who was Irish.

As the ship foundered and began to go down, this warder, Samuelson, was the only one who came below decks to loose us from our leg-irons. He could have let us just drown. But he did not. He kept his gun trained on us. The hull was filling up fast. The water was rising right behind us as we walked upward to the deck. Men were running and screaming, soldiers were jumping overboard to swim for it. Some were fighting among themselves to get into the few available boats. But Samuelson was determined to do his duty and kept his gun on us. Suddenly, the ship lurched. I saw my chance and took it. I seized Samuelson by the throat and while I looked straight into his eyes, I choked the life out of him, stole the papers and money he had on his person in an oiled leather bag and jumped into the sea. A short time after that, I met you.

Later, when I came here, to the camp, I discovered I could do something that others would call good and that would bring me wealth at the same time. I found that men would follow me. I started to believe I had finally found my way to a place in the world none could take from me."

"But why did you kill Hammer Fisted Mick, in that fight," I asked. "It was so unnecessary."

T'was a fair fight. He would have killed me if he could. He told me so in the clinches. He said, "You better kill me you Irish bastard, or I will get you, sooner or later. I'll flay your thin Irish hide off of you. Things like that, he kept cursing me any whenever I was close enough to hear."

A spasm of pain shot through the injured man, and he cried out.

"Father, absolve me of killing that innocent warder on the ship and stealing his name. And there is another crime, but it is not...Ahh," the injured man cried out again, he shuddered and I thought his life was passing from him.

"If you truly repent of this crime, tell the Lord that it is so and he will receive you. This I believe with my whole body and soul. God bless you, Mighty Jack."

The big man reached out his hand to me and swooned. In that moment I did not know if it was sleep or death that overtaken him.

Chapter 26

Charles Wilney's testament concluded

In a few minutes, the crisis passed and I could see that Jack Samuelson, for to this day, I know no other name for him, was breathing easily and very much alive. Having done what he had wanted of me, I got up and went out to Annabelle in the large outer room. As soon as she saw me, her face again coloured up and her eyes avoided mine.

"Did Jack speak to you?" she asked, studying the old, broken floorboards with great care.

"Yes, he did."

"And you do not revile me?" Her tone was so soft it was almost a whisper.

"You? You are not guilty, good woman. Why should I revile you? I am not here to judge anyone. Neither you nor Jack."

"Oh, thank you, sir" she said, suddenly seizing my hands in a strong passionate grip and pressing her lips to them. "You are so good."

The extreme gratitude that she showed me was unwarranted. To this day, I do not understand her burning kiss on my hand. But her manner made me pull away and go to the door.

"You will come back to see Jack again?"

"Whenever he asks for me. Day or night. Goodbye, Miss Annabelle."

But Jack did not ask to see me again for a long time. From the day of his confession, his health rapidly improved. I think he truly felt that a great sin had been lifted from him by the Lord. Weeks passed. I heard that his men had been allowed into the house to see him and were so quiet and respectful, you would not have known them for navvies. The proud doctor disappeared, having proved himself entirely superfluous. When I saw her around camp, Annabelle looked almost gay and lighthearted. By fall, Jack was up and around, talking to his men, overseeing their work sites. It was truly a miraculous healing the Lord had provided for Jack.

I did not have a conversation with Jack again until a dark night in nine months after I had listened to his confession. Strong winds were battering a lone maple near our shanty, rattling the half dried leaves. You and Fanny were asleep and I was reading. Between the howling wind and the branches hitting the timbers of the roof, I did not at first hear the soft knock on our door. Then a blow fell that made the whole wall shiver. I
opened it and there stood Jack.

"May I see you, Father Wilney."

"Of course, Jack. We are friends. Let me shake your hand. It is good to see you up and about."

His grip had lost none of its power.

"Sit down and have some tea," I said.

He sat down and I realized something in him was different. I could feel his driving, burning spirit had been softened. As he sat at the table and I made tea, I thought that it was the first time I had ever seen Mighty Jack simply wait for anything or anyone without pressing it forward with his own relentless force.

"How do you feel, Jack."

"Well enough. A few aches and pains. Nothing serious."

"I am very happy to hear it. And Annabelle?"

"Always strong and willing," he replied. "She's with child."

"Praise the Lord!" I exclaimed. Then I noticed that Jack didn't seem to share my enthusiasm.

"Are you not overjoyed, Jack?" I asked.

"Oh, aye," he said blandly, then added. "But I've heard it said that sometimes a woman's first child can hurt her."

"You must not harbour thoughts like that, Jack. The Lord has been very good to you already. He elevates you with strength and the power for great acts. He has saved you to do his work. There is no reason to expect anything but His blessing on this child."

Jack was silent for a moment. "Father, I feel indebted to you. It seems to me that you are the one who is singled out for supernatural gifts. Because from the day I confessed to you, I began to feel stronger."

"The weight of sin was lifted from you by the Lord, Jack. Not by me."

He leaned forward across the table and looked at me very intently. "I don't see it that way. There is something about you. I knew it when I met you. I feel it more strongly now than ever. You have a strange kind of power that I don't understand."

"I have no power, Jack. The Lord is the only power. All things come to us from Him."

"But it seems that some men are better able than others to wield that power. He listens more to those men. It is so even in the Bible."

"But I am no saint or prophet, Jack."

Jack banged the table with his fist. "You are something more than common," he insisted. "I know."

"You sound almost angry about it, Jack."

He let himself fall back in his chair. "You make me feel that way. You are my friend and my enemy. And you know something I've done that's a hanging offense."

I thought of my vision in the still hours of the night when I kept watch over him.

"But Jack, you must know that anything you told me that night, I listened to under the most solemn seal of secrecy. Nothing could persuade me to tell it any where, or at any time."

"Yes. But still it is a strange thing that lies between us. I have to say that though you have done things for me without reward, you make me uneasy. I feel strange when I am about you."

We both sat silently for a few long minutes. Finally, I spoke. Jack sat passively, looking down at the table.

"I think you are still wrestling with the Lord, Jack. You want to command His power rather than follow His commandments. The way to His strength lies in obedience not in the violent force of your own will. That will, that strength you regard as your own, is a daemonic thing, Jack. I have seen it. No matter what you tell me about killing Hammer Fisted Mick, I know that a daemon possessed you when you struck him down. It is the desire to sweep all before you into your own way that is your greatest enemy. I would even say it is the Great Enemy talking to your heart. Do the work Our Saviour has given you, do it in His name and you shall have His strength and power, infinite and good in all its effects. The other way lies darkness and your eventual undoing."

Jack looked up at me, meeting my gaze.

"I do know now that I have a special task to perform with my life. I know what it is and I shall do it even if all the fiends of hell were ranged against me. I found it here in this camp. Men will see and use my work for generations. It will help change the entire world. I am certain of it. I shall help build a new kind of empire, an empire of iron roads for Britain, roads that will bind us together and make us stronger than anyone in the world. It will bring me wealth, and the power to shape events for the good."

He suddenly reached across the table and gripped my arm in his iron grasp. "I am only beginning now. Great things will be done in the coming years. By me and others. We shall be known and remembered."

He released my arm and the fire died out of his eyes.

"That is why I'll soon be leaving here with my men," he went on.

"You cannot run away from the Lord, Jack. He is everywhere."

He suddenly hit the table so that it danced on the old wooden floor. "I can get away from you, Wilney. I show you an empire and you make it sound like a crime. Why? What is the matter with you? Can you not see the greatness of shaping history itself?"

"I can only ask in whose name you work?" I answered. "If you labour for the Lord and for his creatures and creation then what you build will be a great good. If you labour for yourself only, it will be daemonic. Remember Our Saviour's words: 'I give you life or death. Choose life'."

Jack stood up suddenly and looked down on me.

"I choose to make the world better here and now. If the priests and men of God fear this new world then I say it is they and not I who will be done away with." Then he paused and looked at me with a quieter, more thoughtful eye. "I wonder if we'll meet again. You have been strangely bound up with my life here. I came to thank you and ended by becoming angry. I am sorry."

He held out his hand to me and I took it once again.

"When do you leave, Jack?"

"Tomorrow, early."

"So this is good bye?"

"Aye. It is."

"God bless you and Annabelle in every way."

He turned and left.

After he was gone I thought of our words together and my vision. Even then, I could not tell what choice he had made. My heart told me, we would meet again.

You, Fanny and I moved on to other camps together, Richard. From time to time, I heard of Jack Samuelson. Everyone did who had anything to do with railway building. You both grew until you and I felt it would be dangerous for Fanny to continue to live in railway camps. I returned to Dorset, thanks to my tiny inheritance, and you and Fanny tramped to London to make your way. Fortunately, your academic achievements far outstripped my ability to teach you by this time and I felt quite confident that with the Lord's help, you would be successful in London.

It would seem that this should be the end of my history of Mighty Jack. I gave up railway building and settled into a retired life. Jack continued building iron roads and became rich and famous but, as I had suspected, the Lord was not finished with me and Jack. This last time we met my prophetic vision almost came to pass, and I wonder if it yet may yet be fulfilled.

You know, Richard, something of my quiet life and pursuits here. I interest myself much in the history that lies buried in our venerable soil. In pursuit of these ancient secrets, I often ramble the countryside hereabouts, trying to read the hidden signs that would tell me something of interest is present beneath my feet. It was during such a ramble just a few weeks ago that I again met Jack Samuelson.

As the hill of Higher Woodsford dips to lower ground on the southeastern side, its slope is moderated and becomes fine agricultural land with a thick covering of good black topsoil. The day of which I speak was in midsummer so that the corn was already well grown, making it hard to discern the details of the men and wagons I could see from my lookout on the high ground. I had planned to carry my antiquarian researches in that direction in any case, so I set out to descend the hill on a line that would intersect with the activities of the strangers. As I drew closer, I had actually less view because my prospect dropped lower and lower until I was on the same level as those I wanted to observe. Between us lay several fields, thick with corn. So it was not until I was within several hundred feet that I recognized the men as a railway survey crew.

There were two wagons, about twenty men on foot and two on horseback. The high stalks of corn prevented my seeing the faces of the men until I was quite close to them. Suddenly, I saw Jack Samuelson sitting astride a huge chestnut horse, looming over me, his restless glance following every move of the men. He did not see me until we were within an arm's length of each other. It must have seemed to him that I had sprung up out of the vegetation.

"You," was all he said when he saw me.

"Hello, Jack, are you going to build a railway here, in our quiet little corner?"

He jumped down from his horse. I could see from his easy movements that he had lost little of the strength and elasticity of youth.

"Wilney. You here?" He did not put out his hand to me.

"I live nearby. I am a woodlander now and have not seen a railroad camp for more than a decade. But I take several London papers, so even here, I know you have gained the renown you wanted. Are you happy now, Jack? Is Miss Annabelle well?"

"Well enough. As to happiness, I am doing my work, and I have the privilege of building the new Queen's nation. Life offers no more than that, I think."

"Not more?"

"What do you mean?"

"I mean are you at peace in your heart with the past?"

He stopped walking and looked at me. The fire that suddenly flared in his eyes told me that the daemon still lived in him.

"You had better not threaten me, Wilney. The word of a false priest won't mean much, now. I shall crush you if you threaten the work I am doing."

"I'm sorry, Jack. I did not mean to threaten. I asked out of concern for you."

He turned his back to me and got on his horse, then he looked down and said, "I gave you my confidence once. Now, you see me in a high place. I think it is a little more than you can bear. So hear me, Wilney. Go quietly home and leave me to do my work or you shall regret it." He paused and looked hard at me again and then said, "It were better for you if we had not met today."

He pulled on the reins of his horse and rode away.

Since this meeting I could not help but think about my own prophecy regarding our future and Jack's choice. In the field of ripening corn this afternoon, under the noonday sun, I have learned what Jack's choice will be. It tells me that in all probability my time in this world is drawing to a close, for I believe that the man who has called himself, Jack Samuelson, will find some way to strike me down. As long as I live, he will feel I am a reproach to him and the work he has done. He wants to erase all traces of his past, even in his own mind, and I am the only link between who he is now, and who he was the day of the shipwreck when he started a new and successful life, albeit on a false foundation. He would like to be certain that he never looks on my face again.

I was chosen to play the role of the Lord's messenger to his soul. Now, I believe he has chosen to disregard the message I was given to carry. I do not think he will wait long to do away with the messenger. Richard, I do not know how you can use my narrative to defend yourself if the man called Samuelson should notice you and suspect you know his true story. You were a boy then, and you may have passed entirely unnoticed by him, or have been completely forgotten. I do not know. I hope the two of you never meet, on the other hand, the Lord may ask you to carry to the end this strange story I have begun in these pages. Perhaps He means you to be the instrument of Mighty Jack's downfall. But leave all to the Lord. Do not try to take revenge on Jack. Do not seek him out. Use what I have said only if you are pursued and persecuted by Jack's power. Remember that in spite of man's laws, God has told us that vengeance is His alone.

I feel better now that you are in full possession of the history of the man calling himself Jack Samuelson. My advice is this: Put all the seas of the earth between you. Avoid him at all costs. This is your best protection. If you dig under the elm stump at the edge of my property, you will find 25 gold sovereigns. It is everything I have saved for you and Fanny. God bless you and Fanny,"

Vicar Franklyn looked up from the manuscript Richard had given him. The fire had burned low in the grate and the room was nearly dark.

"Good heavens, Richard." he said after a long silence. "What an astonishing document."

"It is extraordinary," replied the younger man who had been staring into the fire, remembering the goodness of his dead friend. "The question now is, what do we do about it?"

"Do about it?" the Vicar asked.

"How do we bring this villain to book for his crimes?"

"I do not know. Charles did say that you shouldn't use this information for revenge, Richard. He felt you should have nothing to do with this man."

"Not revenge, but justice. Surely we can't be passive when we know that this man's high place in society is built on a stolen identity and at least two murders. How can we let that pass, even if we can forgive him for destroying our friend whose work lay in tireless goodness. Is it not our duty to act?"

The older man shook his head. He stood up stiffly. "Richard, I am too tired to talk rationally about this tonight. I feel unbalanced by these amazing revelations. I need some time. My mind is too full of sinister thoughts to see you return to that lonely cottage in the darkness—even if you left the Bible here. Stay here tonight, please, and we shall talk in the morning.

"Very well, Vicar."

As the older man rose to go to bed, Richard sat and stared into the fire, as if somehow he could divine the future in the glowing coals. It was extraordinary that this testament of Charles' should come to light just at the time when Samuelson had chased him from Manchester back to London. Was it because Mighty Jack knew who Richard was, and feared he had knowledge of the confession made to Charles? Or was it simply because of Richard's quarrel with Paul over Fanny? Would this situation qualify for Charles' idea of "persecution?" It should be the railway king who was fleeing from the law. Instead, it was Richard. Whatever the cause and however unjust, Mighty Jack cast a long shadow over his life and the lives of those he loved. How he was to extricate himself and live peacefully with Sally and Emily was more than he could imagine. It seemed impossible without a new beginning in another country, especially if Mighty Jack knew the nature of Richard's connection with Charles Wilney. Samuelson's spy already knew of it, so probably Samuelson did himself. If they did have to leave the country, what would Fanny do? Would she stay behind or could he convince her to come, once he acquainted her with Charles Wilney's statement about Paul's father. With these fears and suppositions buzzing in his mind, he finally fell asleep in the chair in front of the fire.

* * *

The following morning Richard woke with an absolutely clear understanding of what he must do. He needed an excellent legal opinion about the value of Charles' written testimony. Would it or would it not put Jack Samuelson within the power of the law? He needed to know what other evidence he would need if the testimony were not enough. He needed to know how another solicitor would argue against Charles' disclosures. In short, he needed to prepare his case against the man who called himself John Samuelson. So, in spite of Charles' advice, he must go back to Manchester, where Samuelson might still be, and consult his former employer, Mr. Barnes. He felt there was no one else he could trust with the revelations about the man the world knew as one of the great railway kings. If it were possible to prosecute the imposter, it would remove the dark shadow from the lives of those Richard loved, and bring Charles' killer to justice.

"I entirely disagree," Vicar Franklyn told him when he heard his new resolve. "It flies in the face of everything Charles has said. How will you even get this solicitor to listen to you? By your own statement to me, he thinks you a dangerous revolutionary."

"That is the one obstruction I must overcome. But if there is any chance, however slight, that I can rid Sally, Emily and myself of this nemesis, it is worth any risk."

"Of course, the decision is yours, Richard. But I am certain it is not what Charles hoped and intended for you."

"That may be true, but Charles did not know how I was situated in regard to this imposter. I'm certain he would want me to free myself of him. It may even be that the imposter hounds us because he remembers me from the early days and fears I know his secret. If that is true, he will not stop until I, too, and perhaps even Fanny, have followed Charles into the next world."

"I had not thought of that," the Vicar said.

"Like it or not, I have been given the task of striking down this villain, before he strikes me down...or Sally...or even Emily."

Richard's face was flushed, and his eyes bright with anger and determination when he finished speaking.

"I understand, Richard. Either choice seems poor under the circumstances.

Action or inaction could be equally, ah..fatal."

"Exactly."

"Will you first write to this solicitor?"

"No. I think that would only give him the opportunity to have me arrested. He is too respectable a man to take a chance on someone he sees as a lawless Chartist. I must appeal to him in a more personal way. More directly."

"How shall you do that?"

"I do not know as yet."

"Then will you set off on this journey without a clear plan? I think that is a dangerous way to achieve your end. I think you should remain here, in comparative safety, until you know how you will get Mr. Barnes to listen to you."

"I do not know, Vicar. I think sometimes it is necessary to begin before the right means can be found. But one thing I must do before I leave: I must write to Sally and Emily. And I must wait for their reply. They must be made aware of what I am going to attempt and have an opportunity to give me their thoughts on how best to do it. Their interests and mine are no longer separate. We must think and act together as much as possible. I know this is what Sally would want."

In less than a week, Richard received Sally's answer to the letter he wrote to her. She said there were still no signs of anyone following either herself or the child. It appeared that their whereabouts were unknown to anyone who might be seeking Richard. In short, Sally felt there was no apparent reason why she and Richard could not now meet in London with some safety. For his part, Richard was anxious to see Sally so he could communicate the full significance of Charles Wilney's statement. She did not know that it dealt with capital crimes committed by Samuelson. He would not trust his copy of

Wilney's story to the post or even let it out of his sight. The bible and the key to the acrostic would stay with the Vicar in Higher Woodsford.

Once the decision to go to London was taken, Richard told Vicar Franklyn. In spite of the cleric's unease about the young man's plans, Franklyn could see that no argument about Richard's safety would keep him from those he loved, nor from attempting to prosecute Charles' murderer.

The two men were closeted in the study when they discussed the immediate future.

"One thing you must give me time to do, Richard, is to write a corroborating statement as to Charles' letter and how you used it and the bible to make his revelations intelligible. My statement can be witnessed by people who know me here. They do not have to know what is in my statement, only attest that I have made it freely, and that my signature is a true one."

"That is well thought of, Vicar. At least, I shall not be a single voice telling Charles' story. But I wonder if you might not involve yourself in a great deal of unpleasantness if we ever have to use your statement in a court of law."

"Perhaps, you can use it to show Mr. Barnes. I should hope that the word of a clergyman, supported by three or four highly respectable people here in Dorsetshire, will help to get you a hearing with him. Then, you could ask Mr. Barnes what his opinion was about using it in actual legal proceedings."

"Thank you, vicar. I will gladly accept your help under those conditions. Sir, please let me shake your hand. You have been, throughout this whole affair, steadfast and helpful in the extreme."

The vicar moved to Richard's side in front of the window that overlooked the yard. A thin mantle of snow lay on the ground, but inside the two men shook hands with great warmth.

"Charles was my friend, too, Richard," the vicar said, "and I have never known a better Christian."

When the documents were ready and the requisite signatures obtained, Richard and Vicar Franklyn went to retrieve the money that Charles had buried at his cottage for his foster son. The covering of snow made the afternoon bright, although the early winter sunset would come soon and both men were anxious to get their task done. As they approached the clearing where the cottage stood, a vixen and her cubs, red coats ablaze against the snow, watched the men warily and then silently vanished into the trees. Much to the relief of Richard and his friend, the only tracks on the ground were those of the foxes. Both men had acquired a deep feeling of unease about the isolated cottage, especially since they now were aware that it was a place known to the imposter. If Samuelson had connected Charles Wilney and Richard, the cottage was indeed a dangerous place, but with his usual selflessness, the Vicar had insisted on accompanying the younger man.

The ground was hard, but Charles had left a rusty pickaxe near the chicken coop, and they soon found the old iron box Charles had buried beneath the elm stump. Inside were twenty five gold sovereigns, a tidy little fortune for the schoolmaster. As Richard looked at the gleaming coins, he promised himself and Charles that he would use it to bring the murderer to justice.

Later that night, Richard and Vicar Franklyn sat before the tumble down fireplace once more, each aware that it might be for the last time. It was Richard's hope that he and his family would return to live in the cottage that Charles had left him, but so much remained to be done and so little was known about the difficult task ahead that nothing could be regarded as settled. Sadness lay on both of them as they looked into the coals together. The vicar smoked his half burnt pipe in silence, while Richard wondered how he could ever repay the help and kindness that the clergyman had given so generously. They also both thought of their absent friend whose death had brought them together. They felt him presiding over this last evening of conviviality. As with all farewells, anticipation of the future was mixed with a reluctance to depart. Richard was eager to see Sally and Emily, to find them safe and well and see the light in their eyes when they beheld him once more. But as the evening drew to a close, he was peculiarly sensible of the vicar's kindness and concern. Once more, the vicar lit his way to bed in the attic room under the eaves. Once more, Richard heard the mice in the rafters, Once more he fell asleep listening to the cry of owls in the darkness.

Chapter 27

The journey to London which had seemed so swift to Richard when he came to Dorsetshire, seemed excruciatingly slow as he returned to those he had missed so much. When the coach finally stopped in the yard of the White Horse Cellars inn on Piccadilly, it was past midnight. Even so, Richard did not pause but set off immediately, on foot, to the address Sally had sent him. His eagerness was such that he did not even notice the slush and manure of the streets or the heavy, sulphurous fog which was so thick, it was impossible to use a cab.

Ironically, Richard's way to the poor neighbourhood of Sally's new home lay through some of London's more respectable quarters. As he thought of this contrast, he was walking through an area that had been new in the time of George III and rather far north of the river. The houses were handsome without being elegant. There were bow windows and brass door knockers, but the buildings were shabby, not really grand in the manner of those farther south. Richard made his way along the silent, gaslit streets where he felt the respectable facades seemed to try to stare him out of countenance with their tall windows and prim doorways, as if to say, "it is too late to be walking on our street." As he passed out of this quarter, the fog became suddenly thicker, blurring the gas lamps so that anything within their glowing yellow light had a dim bleary look. Shapes seemed to loom suddenly out of the night and then disappear again like flotsam on a strange sea. As he turned into a street on the west side of Warwick Square, Richard nearly tripped on something large and heavy, lying across the sidewalk, cloaked by the fog and shadows,. When he stopped, bent over and looked down at his feet, he saw the form of a well-dressed young girl lying in the slush. There was blood on her face.

"Good heavens," Richard exclaimed. "You are injured."
He knelt down and propped the young girl against his knee in time to see her eyelids flutter toward consciousness.

"Oh, I did not realize I had wandered outside," the young girl said.
"Let me help you, miss. Where do you live? How came you here?"

"I shouldn't wonder if I ran away this time."

"Ran away from where miss?"

"From my lover. ...when he was beating me."

"Good Lord," Richard again exclaimed. The tone in which the girl uttered her shocking revelation was so bland and lacking in violent feeling that it staggered the young man.

"How can you speak, thus, miss? Can I help you stand? Yes? Are you sure you're quite strong enough?"

In the dimness of the street, Richard thought the girl looked years younger than Fanny, too young to have a lover, certainly, if she were respectable. But then, her whole manner of expressing herself did not seem at all respectable, though she herself was well dressed in a genteel way. His overmastering impressing was of her weakness and fragility.

"You must tell me where you live and I shall take you there," he said looking down into her face. Even in the gaslight, her skin was extremely pale, contrasting strongly with her hair which was an extraordinary shade of deep red. Her eyes were very blue, like cornflowers, and looked up at Richard with perfect docility.

"You are too good, sir. Don't bother about me. I'll be all right."

"No. You must tell me where you live and, of course, I shall take you home," Richard answered. "I refuse to leave you here in the street. Shall you be safe at home?" He asked.

"Oh, lord, yes, sir. He will not damage me too badly. That would stop his fun."

"How you speak, miss. Where are you from that you should talk of things that no young girl should even know of? You must tell me where you live."

"Just over there, sir," the girl said pointing to one of the lesser houses on the Square.

The girl suddenly staggered and Richard put his arm around her waist and walked her across the street.

"Are you quite certain you'll be safe at home?" he asked again.

"Oh, yes, sir. I'm all right. He won't come back tonight."

"But if he does this to you, why have him back at all?"

"Well, if I did not have him, it would just be someone else, a stranger, who I wouldn't know at all. Perhaps someone who'd give me no little presents."

Against the evidence of his own senses, Richard finally realized that the frail looking little child-woman was a prostitute, but it did not make him draw away from her. He held her closer to him as they climbed the stairs.

"Miss, you must not let this man harm you this way. He has no right."

"Oh, yes he does, sir. He tells me so all the time. He bought me."

"He bought you?" Richard's mind recoiled at what the girl was telling him. In spite of all his years of looking after Fanny, he had never met so young and frail a woman in such depraved circumstances. A navvy woman in a muddy camp was one thing, but to see this very young, rather genteel girl on the streets of the metropolis seemed an outrage. His heart was moved to pity and anger at the hound who had hurt her.

"Have you no friends? No protector?" He asked, knowing full well that scores of girls in the great city were absolutely alone. It was her frailty, youth and calm acceptance of her horrible fate that made it seem doubly terrible to him.

"I have my nice stories and my chocolates, and I have him in the evenings. I do not want more. Think nothing of me, sir. But you are very kind." She looked up at him, her eyes were shining with unshed tears of gratitude. "Take this," she said suddenly pressing something cold into his hand, and then in complete contradiction to her own words, she said, "When you look at it, remember the lonely girl you met late one night. And I shall be able to think that somewhere in the world there is a kind young man who knows of me."

Before Richard could reply, the girl slipped her latchkey into the door and disappeared inside.

The lateness of the hour, the respectability of the neighbourhood and the girl's profession all prevented Richard from knocking on the door. He turned away, feeling pain for the wounded creature he had found lying on the sidewalk. Her situation he immediately connected with Fanny and wondered if Paul were still good to her. Did he ever beat her as this girl had been beaten? This girl wanted nothing more than to get back to her master to lick his hand. Would Fanny be so spiritless? He could not believe she would be so negligent of herself. During the rest of his trek across the metropolis, Richard could not shake off the horror of the young girl's life, or of the thought that one day Fanny might share something like her fate. He resolved that he would talk to Sally about trying to bring Fanny to live with them once they were married. But when would that be? Could he marry Sally while the giant shadow of John Samuelson loomed over them? Did he really have any right even to court her? But then he thought of the night they had spent together at her father's house. She had already given herself to him. He could never abandon her for any reason, even her own safety. There was no going back. And for the first time, Richard realized why Sally had acted as she had. She had wanted to make their separation impossible. She had been afraid that Richard's scruples about exposing her to danger might drive him away. Now, however, in the sight of God she was his forever, a fact which should be solemnized soon with a marriage ceremony. The thought cheered him as he trudged on through the cold, damp night.

The sky was gray with coming day when he finally approached the quarter where Sally had taken lodgings. It was fortunate, he thought, that the streets were still deserted. He swept his glance up and down the narrow lanes before approaching the address Sally had sent him. The empty streets reassured him that no one could be following or spying on him.

He heard the faint tinkle of a bell as he pulled the wire. In just moments this was followed by the sound of feet running upon the stairs. The door flew open, the yellow light of a candle shone on him briefly and Sally was in his arms.

"My dear, dear, girl," he murmured as he held her close.

The joy of their embrace kept them standing in the doorway for some moments before Sally separated herself and held up the candle to look at Richard.

"Oh, you are covered with mud, Richard. You've walked a long way. Come in right away. I shall fix us some tea."

It was not long before the sound of voices had their effect on the other member of the household, and Emily staggered sleepily into the kitchen where Richard and Sally sat with the manuscript of Charles Wilney's statement open in front of them.

"Mr. Richard," Emily mumbled, holding out her arms for someone to pick her up.

Sally rose and took the child in her arms. "Come little captain. It is too early for you to be out of bed."

Richard watched with satisfaction as Emily snuggled against Sally's shoulder. This, he thought, is why I must prove Samuelson's guilt. Then the three of us can live without fear. He settled back in his chair and put his hands in his waistcoat pockets, awaiting Sally's return. Unexpectedly, he felt something hard and cold, an remembered the young girl and her wish that he would think of her. He drew out what she had given him and was surprised to see a beautifully carved image of the Emperor Napoleon. Even though he was not a connoisseur, Richard could see how finely the cameo portrait had been cut and mounted on the flawless green stone. On the other side was a second portrait of a man Richard had never seen.

Richard was still looking at the jewel when Sally returned.

"What is that, Richard? More of Charles' legacy?"

"No, my dear. Part of a very strange and sad tale that occurred on my way home tonight."

He quickly told Sally of the young girl's plight.

"Then what is the keepsake she gave you?" Sally asked, looking closely at the stone.

"I do not know. It looks valuable to my untutored eye," he answered passing the jewel to Sally.

"Oh, it is very fine," she said at once. "It is a work of art. I will show it to my father. He may be able to tell us who the engraver is, if not the artist. But the girl's story is very, very sad. It is odd that she gave you something so valuable."

She handed the carved stone back to Richard and he slipped it in his pocket, little thinking how the tiny jewel would affect them all.

They both bent over the manuscript again and read in silence as daylight stole into their humble lodging.

Finally, Sally spoke, "Are there really such people as navvies, Richard? I mean, I know there are. But do they actually live like this and take such odd names? Surely your friend was exaggerating."

"No, my life. I am afraid it is all quite true."

"And this is how you grew up? In such a place?"

"Yes, my dear."

Suddenly Sally clasped him tightly around the neck.

"You are a hero, Richard, dearest. You are truly a hero."

"I am not, Sally. Why say you so?"

"Just to survive it and become the fine person you are."

"If anyone other than the Lord is responsible for that goodness, Sally, it is Charles. You must now realize how great is my debt to him."

"He was very fine, and very good" she said. "Not least because he taught you his goodness." She nestled her head on his shoulder and yawned.

"Let us finish this," Richard said pointing to the manuscript.

"Yes, Emily will be awake again soon. I do not want her reading this document. And she will read everything that falls into her hands."

Richard chuckled. "Yes, I remember once at Mr. Barnes' chambers, I caught her reading a legal citation on incest. She found the word in a newspaper article and thought the casebook was a dictionary. She is an absolutely omnivorous reader."

The reunited couple finished reading Charles' statement about Mighty Jack just as Emily came running out of her bedroom, asking for breakfast. With the three of them in the small apartment, it was impossible to advert to the contents of the manuscript without involving the child in the discussion. Only after she was put to bed at the end of the day following Richard's arrival could the adults talk amongst themselves with some sense of privacy.

"I understand your reasoning, Richard," Sally said as she put the tea down on the old table that had been hired with the lodging. "But I can't say that what you propose does not make me shudder with fear for you. For all of us."

"I know, my love," he said slipping his arm around her waist. "But until this villain is brought down, we may never be free of his persecutions."

"You don't know that he will persist against you," she said.

"He certainly will if he thinks Charles has disclosed anything to me. But even if he does not, what about his responsibility for Charles' murder? Do I not have an obligation to Charles?"

"Only if it can do some good and little or no harm, I think," Sally answered.

"And that is why I must see Barnes."

"But how? How will you get him to see you without having you arrested?"

"I know how," a bright young voice chirped from the other room. Emily came into the kitchen wearing her sleeping gown. Her beautiful golden hair had been carefully brushed out by Sally before bedtime and hung down to her shoulders.

"What do you know, imp?" Richard said, taking her on his knee. "You are supposed to be asleep. I shall take back my good night kiss and be cross."

"No you will not be cross when you hear what I shall say," said the child definitively. "I know how you can talk to Mr. Barnes. It is easy."

"How can you know all these things, little captain. Especially, when you belong in bed," Sally said as she pulled Emily off Richard's knee.

"No. You must wait. I must be heard," Emily insisted, pulling away from her foster mother.

The child stood in the middle of the kitchen, her little arms crossed defiantly across her chest. Her manner was so assured and contrasted so comically with her childish appearance that both adults were forced to smile.

"No. No. You must listen, Mr. Richard. I know how to do this thing you want to do."

"What do you know, little captain?" Sally broke in.

"I know all about it," the little girl said. "I know about Mighty Jack, about the murder of Charles Wilney, about the navvy camp. I know what it means, and I know that Mr. Richard wants to find a way to get Mr. Barnes to listen without calling the constables."

Both adults were staggered at the child's statement.

Finally Richard said, "How did you learn all this?"

"I read the pages you brought home while the two of you were having a rest this afternoon."

Richard and Sally exchanged glances.

"Well, no one said I was not allowed to read it," the child said.

Richard put his hands around the child's waist and pulled her gently to him.

"That is true, Emily. So now tell me how I can get Mr. Barnes to listen without having me taken away by the constables."

"Richard," Sally remonstrated.

"Wait, Sally. I know this child's capacities, well. Let us listen to her."

"Yes," Emily agreed somewhat put out. "I really do know what to do."

"Then tell us," Richard said.

"It is very easy. Write to Pamela Blackwood and tell her you have me with you. Enclose this note that I have written to her and ask for a private interview at Blackdale."

So saying, the child produced a sheet of paper from the pocket of the little wrapper she wore over her nightgown. She handed it to Richard.

"Dear Miss Pamela," he read out loud, "I want you to know that I am good and happy. When Mr. Richard found me I was running away from you because I knew you did not want me. We were both very sad about Mr. Blackwood. Mr. Richard took me with him because it was night when he found me on the high road.

He has taken very good care of me. I do not want to come back to Blackdale. I want to stay in London with Mr. Richard and his wife, Sally." "I had to write 'wife', you know," the child broke in, otherwise they would not let me stay."

Again, Richard and Sally exchanged meaningful looks.

"I shall come back," Richard went on reading from Emily's letter, "if you help Mr. Richard. Please help him and do not tell anyone. If you do this, I shall do what you want. I will open and close the shutters in Mr. Blackdale's mine once more.

Your ward,
Emily

Richard clasped the little girl in his arms.

"You astonishing and wonderful child," he said hugging her to him. "You shall never go to any mine. You shall stay with us and be our daughter if I have to fight every policeman in England."

Then he detached one of his hands from the little girl and reached out for Sally.

"You and I, Miss Howard are overdue for a wedding."

"Are you sure that now..."

"We will be better able to protect Emily and if anything should happen to me, you will have the legal rights of a wife."

"If that is all you can say, Richard," Sally said frostily. "I decline." Richard then knelt down in front of Sally and said, "Please, my dearest girl, to whom I can offer little except my whole heart, will you have me?"

"And absolutely no one else," she replied, smiling.

"Can we have breakfast now?" Emily asked. Everyone laughed.

"Will you solve all our problems every morning before breakfast, little captain?" Sally asked.

"Well," the child said slowly, "I shall try."

***

Sally and Richard were married quietly within the week. Sally's father and brothers were present along with Emily. Otherwise the little east-end church, was empty and cold. The parson kept sneezing into his handkerchief. It was so drafty that the candles would not stay lit. No one minded the cold but the clergyman. Two days after the ceremony, Pamela's answer to the letter Richard sent with Emily's enclosure was received by the new family.

"She has agreed to a private interview at Blackdale. And has promised not to divulge my presence to anyone, including Mr. Barnes," Richard told his new wife and daughter.

There was just before he left, they all agreed, for one more outing to Greenwich. They went on a chill damp day, the sun was a faint outline in a bright but heavily overcast winter sky. They all put on their warmest coats and planned to spend the day.

The scene was very different from their last promenade along the river. There were few pedestrians now. The wind from the river was sharp. The only merchant was a man selling hot chestnuts from a cart. Once again, Emily was mesmerized by the ships and their cargo as they passed. She seemed not to notice the cold at all, keeping up her own patter of information about the ships. Richard and Sally were in their own world of newly married joy, drinking in each other's looks and words. Sally's heart-shaped face was alight with her happiness and that same light was reflected in her husband's countenance, as well. There could have been icebergs in the Thames and none of the three would have been bothered in the least.

The happiness of being together in a holiday spirit kept them out late and, instead of returning home for their evening meal, they had dinner at one of the smart Greenwich restaurants, through whose windows Emily could continue to watch the ships as they passed. If any one of them could have chosen a time in their lives to be remembered perfectly, forever, it would have been this winter evening: watching the sun go down over the water, the great ships floating by beneath a whitened sky fading into delicate shades of lavender, and the delicious food before them. God's bounty seemed great, indeed, for the new family. Richard even managed not to think about the dangers ahead. For the first time since reading Charles' statement, the shadow of Mighty Jack was extinguished completely, for a short time.

Chapter 28

It was decided that the trip to Manchester to see Mr. Barnes should not be made by public conveyance. The continuing agitation by certain elements among the poor in the factory towns, had made the authorities too alert to anyone who might be connected in any way with the troubles. Samuelson could try once more to set the authorities on Richard. His spies or the police could be watching out for Richard, either in London or in Manchester. The couple's only hope was that the location of Sally's new lodgings had remained unknown. Fortunately, Sally's father owned a wagon that was used for deliveries. It was rough, but sturdy. A frame had been built over the back to keep the weather off of art works and finished printing when being delivered. A team of two old cart horses went with it. Roderick had named them Titian and Raphael.

"You must not drive them too hard, Richard," Sally's father told him when he brought him to the stable. "They are old friends of mine and must not work more than six hours a day. But feed them well and care for them and you'll find no finer creatures on God's earth, man or beast. Your progress shall be slow but certain."

"Thank you, sir," I am very sensible of their value and importance to you." I thank you," Richard said, patting Titian's neck.

"I don't mind, Richard. At least my daughter married a man who understands Tom Paine, not some Jack 'O Napes solicitor or money mad man from the City."

Richard thought of his time spent at Barnes' chambers. It was as well that he had not studied the law.

"Go on. Get along with you now. When you are ready to depart, you know where to find them and they know you." Roderick said. " Just remember the beasts have the same rights we do."

***

Sally spent several days shopping for food and preparing it for the trip. To Richard's great surprise and delight, she was an excellent cook. When he said as much, she replied: "

"In a family of nothing but men, I had to learn to cook. Otherwise we should all have been poisoned. My father used to let the meat hang until it was green and maggoty. Then, he would cook it and try to serve it. He simply never noticed."

Emily very much wanted to accompany Richard. "It was my thought," she said. "Miss Pamela will listen to me. I know she will. The note to me she put in with her answer said how sorry she was three times. I know she will help us if I ask her. Even though she did not say it, I am certain she expects to see me."

"That may be, Emily," Richard had answered. "But the trip could be a dangerous one and you are too precious to us to risk in any way. I shall take your letter to Miss Blackwood."

"We made a dangerous trip before," the child persisted.

"Only because we had to. Finding you on the road in the middle of the night left me no choice. You know that. Now, I will not permit it. Do not ask again."

And there, the matter was left.

"This time," Sally said to Richard, "I want you to be well provisioned. My father even wanted to give you his old musket. But I thought it would be quite useless against a regiment of regulars."

"You were right. Our only hope is in stealth and in winning Mr. Barnes' goodwill."

The day of departure finally arrived. As luck would have it, rain fell and the city lay under the blanket of what Miss Flyte in Bleak House styled a "london particular," a thick, brownish-yellow fog with high amounts of sulphur dioxide gas in it, a fog which could be fatal for the elderly or infirm. Richard had to lead Titian and Raphael through the barely visible streets, but as long as they were in the east end, the wise old horses knew their way and could be relied upon not to startle or miss their footing. It was five in the morning and very dark as Richard led them out of their stable to begin the journey.

Leaving London in the fog was difficult but at the far edge of the city, the dreary pall began to thin. By noon, Richard was able to ride in the wagon. Next to him, under the seat, he had a strong blackthorn cudgel in case he should be bothered by any roughs on the road.

"Once again, he thought," sitting behind Raphael and Titian, "I am off on a journey. But this time I am a married man. I have some means, and I shall rid us of this villain who has broken so many laws of God and man."

He chose to avoid the post houses where he and the horses could have found accommodation. In the hubbub of these places it would be easy for someone to pick up his trail and follow him, if they so desired. He would trust his chances to the open air and the goodwill of the highly intelligent animals Sally's father had lent him. In the wagon, he had oats and hay for the beasts. Water was provided by a small stream where he removed the traces and stopped for the night. It was a lonely country, just outside the city, an area likely to harbour tramps finding their way into or out of the metropolis. Since the rain had stopped, he resolved not to sleep beneath the canvas covered frame in the wagon, but in the open air. That way, he could hear more clearly if anyone approached. Since he was going to call on Miss Blackdale, he had brought respectable clothes with him. Sally had even done her best to finish a new shirt for him. Now that no longer looked like a tramp himself, he would have to be especially careful on the road.

Once he'd made sure the horses were cared for, he went to get his own food from under the canvas at the rear of the wagon. He lit his lantern and held it underneath the canvas and there, on the floor of the wagon, Emily lay fast asleep.

"You wicked imp," he exclaimed.

The little girl woke sleepily.

"We have not arrived already?" the little girl said.

"Of course not. How could you disobey like this, Emily. Now you force me to return and lose an entire day."

"Oh, please, Mr. Richard. What I am doing is for the best. Please, oh, please, please trust me. Your chances are better with me than without. Miss Pamela will do for me what she might not do for you."

Richard turned his back and slumped against the wagon. The thought of going back into London was more than odious to him. Then, too, the child might be right. She had lived with Pamela Blackwood and knew her well. The note she had written Emily had begged her to come home and was filled with expressions of contrition. In addition, leaving Sally again was more than he could bear.

He turned back to the child, "All right, imp. You are a very, very, very bad imp, you know. Deceit is very bad. You do know that don't you, Emily?"

"Yes, sir. I am sorry. But I knew this was right."

"Do you solemnly promise me never to do such a thing again? Never to lie to me or Sally, no matter what the circumstances."

"Yes, sir, I promise."

"If you feel so strongly about something, Emily. I shall listen to you, I promise. I know you are wise and clever way beyond your years, but Sally and I are still your guardians and you must be honest with us and trust us. And we shall do the same. And when we get to Blackdale, you must write to Sally and beg her pardon for tricking her. I am sure she will worry about her little captain when she finds you have gone missing."

The child stood up and came to the opening in the canvas. She gently put her arms around Richard's neck with a great expression tenderness. "I know that I am yours and you are mine, Mr...father." the little girl said."Please kiss me good night and say prayers with me."

Richard clasped the child to him and pressed his lips to her forehead. There were tears in his eyes. Together, Richard and Emily repeated the 23rd

Psalm. Sally had told Richard that Emily had been very struck by the Psalm because of the phrase, "the valley of the shadow of death." It made her think of the mine where she had worked. She liked the idea that God could be present even in the darkness, and that He could make green pastures in such a place. So they both slept peacefully through the night, trusting that God would take care of them.

Their journey was slow and uneventful. Once or twice Richard had to flourish his cudgel at a tramp, but he suspected that the sight of the beautiful little girl with her long golden hair and dark eyes turned away other itinerants who never even made themselves known. It was a time for Richard and Emily to grow even closer.

Once they got north of Manchester and the surrounding industrial towns, the country began to look familiar to them both. When Emily saw the moors, she became excited and began talking about Blackdale.

"I wonder if Hilf is still there?" she said.

"Who is that, Emily?" Richard asked.

"He's a wolfhound who guards the stables. He's this big," and stretched her arms out as far as she could.

Richard smiled.

"Really, he is," the child repeated.

"I believe you. He is a special friend?"

"Mr. Gibbs says that Hilf listens to no one as well as me."

Emily's conversation was now peppered with allusions to her previous life at Blackdale, and Richard began to be troubled by them. He wondered if the little girl might not have a better life with the advantages of growing up on the estate at Blackdale, instead of living in a small cramped lodging in London. Oh, he was confident that he and Sally could give her a good education, as far as it went, but they could not provide money for travel and elegant clothes, which would become important as the girl got older. The new clothes Emily had already required was a strain on their limited means. If not for Sally's father, and Richard's inheritance from Charles, it would have been difficult to make ends meet. They would have to provide Emily with more opportunity than he had been able to give poor Fanny. How would he do it? At the same time, they all loved each other dearly. Pamela Blackwood, on the other hand sounded like an inconstant and fairly indifferent guardian. He wondered which was best for Emily. When he heard her talk enthusiastically about something on the estate, he felt it might be wrong to take her back to London with him. He even wondered if the child felt this way herself and had stowed away because of her eagerness to see Blackdale again. As they entered the rolling hills, drawing closer to Blackdale with each step, these nagging thoughts troubled Richard more and more. Finally, he decided to broach the subject with Emily.

"Do you think you might like to live at Blackdale again?" he asked her.

"Oh, wouldn't it be jolly if we could all live there and play with Hilf and eat Cook's wonderful cakes? And Sally would have maids to wash and clean?" the little girl cried merrily.

"Well, you know that can't be, my little dear. Blackdale is Miss Blackwood's house."

"I don't want to live there with just her," the child said decidedly. "The only one I see when she plays the pianoforte is Hilf, and I think sometimes he is bored with me. I cannot run fast enough for him," she said, shrugging her shoulders resignedly, in a very adult way.

When they were perhaps a day from Blackdale, at the very slow rate of the two old cart horses, Richard began to worry about how they looked. There was straw in Emily's hair. He had a change of coat and some clean linen but nothing for Emily.

"Perhaps we should get you a new dress before we see Miss Blackwood," Richard said.

"Why? I brought my red one, the new one that you Sally bought me Friday week."

"Truly. You have that, here?"

"I put it in one of the old potato sacks that looked clean."

Richard put his arm around the little girl who sat next to him.

"How did you become so neat handed, Emily?"

"Oh, women just know about these things. That's what Sally says."

"And what shall we do about the straw in your hair?"

Emily hopped off of her seat and jumped into the back of the wagon.

"Look. My hair brush. Sally bought it for me."

"Then we shall dazzle Miss Blackwood with our handsome appearance."

"I must look well cared for, otherwise Miss Pamela will not like you and she will not help you."

"You are too clever, even for an imp," Richard said tousling the child's hair.

"That is not a very nice thing to say, father. I looked up "imp" in your dictionary. It is a kind of small devil."

"Sometimes you are a small devil, child."

"Like hiding on the wagon."

"Precisely."

Richard resolved that rather than present themselves at the estate looking travel stained and weary, they would stop the night nearby, be assiduous in their toilet in the morning and only then proceed to Blackdale. Emily was disappointed.

"I thought we should get there today."

"But you agree that our appearance is important. We don't want to look like tramps."

"No. You are right."

But the child had trouble sleeping that night as they camped not more than a mile from the great gates of the estate. The thought of being reunited with Hilf and other people at Blackdale kept her unsettled until there was light in the sky. Throughout the restless night, Richard worried about the effects of their arrival on Emily. He also wondered if Pamela Blackwood could be trusted to keep her word about not telling anyone of his presence in the neighbourhood. There was little he could do if soldiers or constables were waiting at the estate to arrest him. Yet, they had to go on. He must see Barnes. That was the clear path of his duty. He could not ask Emily and Sally to live under Samuelson's shadow.

Contrary to Richard's expectations, Emily was quiet and subdued the next morning when they arrived at the gates of the estate. It was fortunate that Gibbs, Emily's friend from the stables was on duty. The house servants were the ones who had been jealous of the child, but Gibbs was not a member of the house staff.

"Hello, Mr. Gibbs," Emily called out with a wave.

"Bless me, it's the little Miss," the stable hand replied. So the rough wagon rolled unimpeded through the gates, into the park and up to the grand front doors of the manor house.

Pamela met them in the large front hall. She held out both hands to the little girl.

"It is so good to see you well, Emily."

"Thank you, Miss Pamela. I am glad to see you and everyone at Blackdale." The little girl curtseyed daintily, just as Pamela herself had taught her.

"Mr. Darrow," Pamela held out her hand. "I am so relieved that you placed yourself in communication with me. Shall we go to the library?"

Emily ran toward the front door. "I am going to see Hilf," she called over her shoulder. Then, she stopped and ran back to Richard. He bent down and she put her little arms around his neck.

"It is all right," the child whispered reassuringly. "She's does not have the headache. I can tell."

"I shall see you later, little captain."

Then the child ran down the hall and out the doors into the beautiful park.

"She seems very fond of you," Pamela said when Emily was gone.

"My wife and I love her dearly, Miss Blackwood."

"Your wife? You were not married when you were last here. Come." She began leading the way down the gallery.

"No," Richard answered. "We were married only recently."

"And does your wife care for Emily as you do?"

"As if she were her own, Miss Blackwood."

"I am glad to know it, sir. Nothing is more important to me than getting Emily settled in life. I postponed a very important appointment of my own so I could meet with you both."

When they entered the library, the first thing Richard saw was the portrait of Pamela hanging above her father's desk and chair.

Pamela sat down behind the desk and motioned to a chair.

"Do please sit down, Mr. Darrow. Would you care for tea or some other refreshment?"

"I will join you, Miss, if you are having some, thank you."

A few moments later a pretty young maid not much older than Pamela entered.

"Yes, Miss?"

"Tea, please, Effie."

"Very good, Miss," the girl closed the door softly.

Richard took in the richness of the room, the beautiful patterned paper, the heavy green velvet curtains and thick carpet, the magnificent empire desk which sat in front of him. Was it right to take Emily from all this, he wondered?

"Mr. Darrow, Emily's note told me in the clearest possible terms that she does not want to come back to Blackdale. She wants to stay with you and your wife. After seeing you with her, I am sure that her letter was written without prompting."

"I honestly did not know she had written, Miss Blackdale, until she showed me the letter and asked me to enclose it with my own. My coming here was her idea. She thought you would help me see Mr. Barnes."

"Well, it seems we have two pieces of business to transact, sir. First, some decision about Emily needs to be taken. Second, I must learn more about your reasons for wanting a meeting with Mr. Barnes. He is extremely busy now. He has taken over the day to day operation of all my father's business interests."

Richard sat quietly, saying nothing. For some moments, the two studied each other. Pamela thought the tutor very much improved, almost handsome, though his clothes were obviously poorly made. Richard thought Pamela less sulky and more gentle in her demeanor. It gave him hope. On both sides, first impressions were positive.

"What is your opinion about Emily?" Pamela suddenly asked. "I mean where ought she to live, in your opinion?"

"I have been wondering about that all the way here from London, Miss Blackwood. Emily is very fond of Blackdale but..." he hesitated.

"But not of me?" Pamela finished for him.

"I would say, rather, that she is not sure of you Miss Blackwood." exhaling the breath he had been holding.

"She has good cause to complain of me, Mr. Darrow. I was a jealous sister and an indifferent guardian. I assume you have continued giving her the benefit of your teaching abilities?"

"Of course, Miss Blackwood. Teaching Emily is not work, it is a pleasure. She learns so quickly."

For the first time in the interview, Pamela smiled at Richard. He was surprised at how kind and sweet she looked. For, Pamela Blackwood had one of those faces that seemed distant, cold and beautiful in repose, but could light up with tender expression and look even more handsome when animated.

"I was so jealous of the way she learned," Pamela replied, obviously smiling at the memory. "My father taught her things he never even mentioned to me."

"She talks often of those subjects a great deal, Miss Blackwood. The ships, railways and the technical details touching on them. Mr. Blackwood's teaching made a great impression on her."

"My father never discussed such things with me," Pamela said, her voice momentarily husky. She sat quietly for a moment.

"But this does not answer the purpose at hand," she said suddenly. "It does not help us, does it, Mr. Darrow? For I, too, have been wondering what is best for the child, especially since I have seen the two of you together. Unquestionably, you and your wife are fine guardians for her. Much better than myself."

"Oh, Miss Blackwood..." Richard began to remonstrate.

"No. Let us be truthful, sir. Emily loves you and probably Mrs. Darrow. She does not love me. At the same time, Blackdale is an ideal place for a child."

"You put the conundrum with great clarity, I think, Miss Blackwood."

"So in one place she has the best parents. In the other, the best home. What shall we do?"

"I.."Richard began.

"I think I know what to do, Mr. Darrow, if you will allow me to answer my own question. I think Emily should live with you and your wife. I plan that in future I shall often be away from Blackdale. Emily will always have free access to the house and the park. Her room and her things will always be here for her when she wants them. During the nice weather , when I am at home, perhaps you and your wife will come with her and be my guests for several weeks at a time. Most important, when Emily's future education and personal refinement are concerned, I must be allowed to bear any cost you deem necessary."

"You are too good, Miss Blackwood. I am overwhelmed by your generosity."

"It was what my father wished. His desires are sacred to me, now, sir."

"I have only one other thing to ask, regarding Emily," Richard said.

"What, after being overwhelmed by my generosity," Pamela said ironically. "No, please," the young woman continued, "that was arch but meant as a jest, sir."

"I understand you have a wolfhound on the estate. His name is Hilf."

"Yes, Gibbs cares for him."

"Do you think, Miss, that the dog could live with Emily? She is passionately fond of him. And I must tell you, Miss Blackwood, touching on other business we have yet to discuss, I should like her to have a protector who can always be near her."

"Is there some particular danger to which you allude, Mr. Darrow?"

"There is a danger of a kind, Miss Blackwood. It requires rather a long explanation and is part of why it is of the last importance that I see Mr. Barnes. You are aware that I was denounced to the authorities by Mr. Samuelson?"

"Ah, yes. That business. I remember. I must tell you, Mr. Darrow, I have little liking for Mr. Samuelson."

"Miss Blackwood, I am going to ask you to read a rather lengthy document regarding that person. It was written by a very good man whom I knew since childhood. You will find it rather shocking."

"You interest me enormously, Mr. Darrow. The more I can learn about Mr. Samuelson, the better. He has made several important proposals to me and I want to reject them. Mr. Barnes feels that my reasons are simple prejudice and nothing more."

"You have good cause for rejecting anything that belongs to Samuelson, Miss Blackwood," Richard said drawing Charles Wilney's testament out of his pocket and placing it before Pamela.

"I shall call for more refreshment before I start," Pamela said. "What can I have brought for you, sir? Lunch hour is long past. Emily, I know, can find her way to the kitchen."

"Whatever you have, Miss Blackwood, shall certainly do for me."

Pamela once again rang for the maid, ordered a fresh pot of tea and cucumber sandwiches. When the refreshment arrived she directed Richard to the technical drawings that had served as the models for Emily's pictures.

"That whole chest of shallow drawers contains plans and drawings of machinery. These are the things that made such a strong impression on Emily. Feel free to look through them while I read. Of course, you may go where you wish while I am occupied, but I should prefer to have you here, in case I have any questions regarding this document."

Richard tried with little success to put his mind on the drawings he'd been invited to peruse. All his attention was really directed toward Pamela and her reaction to Charles' statement. She said nothing but from time to time, her exclamations told Richard that the document was having an effect. Many times his eyes roved away from the elegantly drawn plans of fabulous machines and over to the desk where the beautiful young woman read, completely immersed in the story of Mighty Jack and Charles Wilney. Next to the desk was the beautiful antique globe made in Venice, showing the many misconceptions about the world that existed in previous centuries. Emily had told Richard that Mr. Blackwood had taught her geography by showing her the globe and pointing out all of its beautifully painted errors. From there, Richard's gaze went to the portrait of Pamela and to the young woman it mirrored. The portrait looked haughty and distant. The original was thinner and kinder looking, Richard thought. Her generosity to Emily relieved him of the chief concern he had had about keeping the child.

Then the rattling of the papers in Pamela's hands tugged him back to Samuelson and the help he needed from Mr. Barnes. The fact that Pamela had her own reasons for distrusting the railway king, made Richard hopeful that she would want to sift the matter to the bottom and get him an interview with the solicitor.

Finally, after nearly an hour of reading, Pamela put down the manuscript and looked up at Richard.

"Mr. Darrow, you have done me two very great services this afternoon. First, you have relieved me inexpressibly about Emily's future and, second, you have given me something with which to fight the villain described in these pages. Until now, I have had nothing substantial to offer Mr. Barnes as a reason for my desire not to have Samuelson concerned in our business interests."

She rose from behind the desk and walked over to Richard, who had also risen from his chair.

"Thank you, sir," she said holding out her hand. "I will insist that Mr. Barnes read this manuscript. Then, I shall instruct him to help you with any advice he can offer. Your behaviour with Emily and this document remove any slur that may have been cast on your reputation. At least as far as I am concerned."

"Thank you so much for your many kindnesses, Miss Blackwood."

"I shall send to Barnes and tell him to come to Blackdale. He shall not know of your presence until he arrives. I will attempt to have him here when we dine this evening. Now, we have yet to discuss the danger you spoke of earlier. I must be sure that Emily is not in danger."

"Of course," Richard agreed. "I think, however, that is a subject which would be well to discuss with Mr. Barnes present."

"Then," Pamela said, standing, "Let us go and find Emily, now. Let us tell her of the plans we have made for her so that she can be glad and cease thinking that her terrible step-sister will send her back to the coal mine."

After a brief search, child and wolfhound were found lying together on the thick carpet of the elegantly appointed front parlour. Hilf was an enormous gray haired animal whose back, when he stood at their approach, was nearly as tall as Emily's shoulder. His tail began sweeping back and forth when he recognized his mistress. Then he lay down again and rested his head once more in the little girl's lap. Pamela and Richard sat down on the soft carpet and the four made an odd looking party: Richard poorly but formally dressed, Pamela in a ravishing and frightfully expensive gown of green silk, Emily in her jumper and the huge grey beast with his head in the child's lap.

Emily was stroking her friend's fur when she said, "Do I have to work in the mine again, Miss Pamela?"

"Of course not. I regret you should think me so mean."

"Not mean, but..."

"You are going to go home to live with Mr. and Mrs. Darrow. But you can come to Blackdale whenever you like. Your room and your things will always be here. And...Hilf, (the great beast lifted his head when he heard his name), is going to live with you in London."

The little girl hugged the shaggy head against her body so tightly that a lesser creature might have fought to get free, but Hilf's tail only thumped the ground with delight.

The three sat together talking quietly as the short hours of daylight faded. Finally, Emily fell asleep next to Hilf, listening to the murmur of Richard's and Pamela's voices.

* * *

"Now what do you think, sir?" Pamela demanded of Mr. Barnes as her solicitor put down the manuscript she herself had read earlier that afternoon. It was late in the evening. Dinner, as usual at Blackdale, had been excellent and Barnes, Richard and Pamela were seated in her library. Emily was long since in bed. The solicitor had been very surprised by Richard's presence at table. At first, he had been hostile but once Richard explained where he had gotten the pamphlet and how Paul Samuelson had taken Fanny from her stall on the Ratcliffe Highway, he was somewhat mollified.

"I'm not in the habit of dining with revolutionaries, sir," the solicitor had said somewhat stiffly. "The rule of law is paramount. I want no mobs in the streets, no matter how poor are the poor."

"Nor do I, sir," Richard assured him.

Pamela had done her best to prepare the solicitor for what he would find in Wilney's document. But once he had finished reading, he quietly put it down, took off his spectacles and said, "It is definitely a remarkable tale. But I must ask, Miss Blackwood, who wrote it? How did you get it? It all comes back to this one young man, who is a fugitive from the law. He put the words on paper. He doesn't deny it. The dead man, if there was such a man, was his friend. The presence of the railway survey crew near the village could be verified. But there is absolutely nothing to say that this is not a work of fiction, Miss Blackwood. A complete fabrication libelling an eminent man."

"Pardon me, Sir, but there is something else," Richard said, producing Vicar Franklyn's statement with the four signatures on it. He handed it to the solicitor.

"Hmm, yes, well, this is a little better. Your statement at least is verified by a respectable clergyman who provides his own testimonials. This was well thought of, Mr. Darrow."

"It was Vicar Franklyn's suggestion, sir. He thought his voice might give weight to mine in your estimation."

"Hmm, Well, yes it does. But it by no means proves that this tale is anything more than a tale. It is hearsay from an individual now deceased with few facts that can be independently verified. I feel certain that Mr. Samuelson could explain away all of these charges if given the chance."

"You may not discuss this with him, Mr. Barnes," Pamela put in. "You must respect my confidence, by law."

"Quite so, quite so, Miss Blackwood," the solicitor agreed blandly. "If that is the course you wish to take. I advise against it, but if that is the course you wish to take... I just wish I could give him a clear cut reason for your refusal of his offer."

The solicitor ceremoniously produced a snuff box and took a pinch as if to emphasize his opinion.

"I want you to tell me," Pamela went on, "How you would go about proving this statement from a legal point of view?"

"First, I should look for verifiable facts. Was there a prison ship that went down near the southern coast at the time of which Mr. Wilney writes? Second, was there a warder aboard that ship by the name of Samuelson? Understand that even if the answer is, "yes," it does not prove the statement, it only helps lend it weight. Do the records of the Liverpool & Manchester Railway support any of these claims? If no such records exist, are there individuals that could be found to support them? The problem, Miss Blackdale is that there is no way of proving or disproving any of this in an incontrovertible way. And when going against a man like John Samuelson, you had better be able to prove your assertions. Otherwise you could be sued for slander."

Richard's heart sank.

"I see," said Pamela.

"Now if it were a matter of marriage where there are definite records, or a question of inheritance, these are things relatively easy to prove in a legal sense. Questions of identity are generally extremely difficult to prove. Especially when the question goes back so many years."

"So you regard this document as worthless from a legal point of view?" Richard asked.

"Yes sir, I do," Barnes said. In fact I do not even like to use it as a reason for rejecting Mr. Samuelson's offer to Miss Blackwood. I wish there was something truly incontrovertible and final. I should feel more satisfied."

"Is it not enough that I don't want the man?" Pamela said sharply. "Is marriage nothing more than a business arrangement?"

"I'm sorry to say, Miss Blackwood," the solicitor replied "that in your case, marriage is very much a business arrangement. Your father's legacy and your marriage are bound together. The two things cannot be separated. It would be better for you and your business not to unnecessarily annoy Mr. Samuelson. "

All were silent for some long moments.

Then Richard spoke excitedly, "Wait. There may be something else. Remember when Mighty Jack confessed, Charles mentioned something about another secret. And remember, too, Annabelle's odd behaviour with Charles, her seeming embarrassment. Perhaps there is something related to the wife, something hidden behind the plain statement."

"I must tell you, Mr. Darrow," the solicitor said, "that when an English judge or an English jury are confronted with plain facts and hidden meanings behind the plain facts, the hidden meanings will not even be noticed."

"So it is hopeless?" Richard asked somewhat bitterly.

"Well, if the wife were alive and you could find out about her, I don't say that there is nothing there to be discovered. Perhaps there is, perhaps not. I doubt very much that it will prove much against John Samuelson."

"And what about this man whom Samuelson employs. Collins. The man with the sword cane?"

"I could find no history of him, Mr. Darrow. And when I can't find a man's history, or any traces of his past, he probably never existed, is dead, or is a practitioner of the black arts."

"You give me very little hope, sir," Richard said.

"In my view, the shortest way is the kindest way. In my view, there is absolutely no hope of bringing John Samuelson to justice for the murder of your friend unless physical evidence can be added to this statement."

"Or any other crime?" Richard pressed.

"I can't say," the solicitor replied. "It certainly seems unlikely."

"And what are the chances that the authorities will seek to arrest Mr. Darrow?" Pamela Blackwood asked.

"If he is quiet, lives obscurely and does not run afoul of the law, especially in London, there is probably little risk."

"Unless they are inflamed against me by Samuelson," Richard added.

The solicitor said nothing, but merely nodded.

"Mr. Darrow, what of the danger you mentioned in connection with Emily?"

"Well, Miss Blackwood, I was thinking of this spy who Mr. Barnes could not find. He has twice presented himself to me or to those I am concerned with. Not long ago he saved my life."

"Really, sir," the solicitor exclaimed. "You interest me enormously. This man made a complete fool of my own agent in London. He simply walked into an alley and turned into anyone of three different men, none of whom could be found."

Richard recounted Sally's meeting with the spy and his own narrow escape on the road. When he had done, Pamela was the first to speak.

"The man sounds not so much like a danger, Mr. Darrow. Almost more like a guardian."

"But he has threatened me and I have seen him entering the grounds of Mr. Samuelson's house with a latchkey."

"Yet, he saves you from a vicious attack," the solicitor commented. "Very curious,
Mr. Darrow. Very curious."

"Do you have any thoughts about him, Mr. Barnes?"

"No. It would be mere guesswork and supposition. But from what he said to your wife, it sounds as though he has lost a child. Apart from that and the fact that he felt protective toward Emily, I can see nothing else."

"But his swordsmanship and the way his horse was trained. He easily drove off the tramps," Richard said.

"Yes, Mr. Darrow. That does suggest something to me," the solicitor said thoughtfully, getting up suddenly and looking out the window next to Pamela's portrait. "But, mind you, it is only a suggestion and pure guesswork."

"What is it, sir?"

"It suggests cavalry training. A professional soldier turned spy. The army is the only place that a man is likely to learn to use a sword and horse so expertly."

Barnes suddenly turned back to face Richard who sat opposite Pamela. "How old did you say this man was, Mr. Darrow?"

"Somewhere between fifty and sixty," Richard replied.

"Hmm. Yes. It is just possible," Mr. Barnes said more to himself than to the others.

"What is it, sir?" Richard asked.

"I have the histories of the three identities my agent came up with in London. Perhaps in those stories I will find something to confirm or eliminate my theories."

"Can you tell us, sir, what those theories are," Pamela asked. "The welfare of a child may be involved here."

The solicitor moved toward the door of the room and just before he reached it, turned back, took out his snuff box and again used a pinch as emphasis for what he said,

"I prefer to reserve my comments, Miss Blackwood. But I doubt very much if Miss Emily has anything to fear from this spy. I shall let you both know what I learn. You will be here for some days, Mr. Darrow?"

"Yes, sir."

The solicitor held out his hand to the younger man. "I am glad to have heard your side of things, Darrow. I am glad to know that I had not misjudged you."

"I am a Chartist, sir," Richard said stiffly. "But I shall never hold with mob rule in any form."

"Let us hope that those who share your views do not become a mob, sir."

"Thank you, sir," Pamela said to the solicitor.

The solicitor bowed curtly to Pamela and Richard and left the room.

"Well," Richard remarked. "He thought rather more than he said."

"Yes, well, Mr. Barnes is a solicitor," said the young woman. "It is his nature and
training to suppress his thoughts and words most carefully."

"I fear I would not have made a good legal practitioner," Richard remarked.

"Do you find that a shortcoming in yourself, sir," Pamela asked.

"No," he replied.

"Nor do I," the young woman said, smiling.

Chapter 29

The following morning, Richard insisted that Emily write to Sally by the first post. "But Hilf needs to go outside," the little girl protested, looking over at her shaggy companion who watched her anxiously. "I am glad to see you are aware of his needs, Emily. But your first duty this morning is to write to Sally and apologize for your deception. I shall go outside with your friend," Richard finished. "Come, Hilf,"

With a quizzical backward glance at Emily, the wolfhound led the way to the front door and outside.

It was a gray, wintry day in the moors. The clouded sky hung low over the horizon, patches of wet snow lay on the ground, but after the muck and bad air of London, Blackdale Park looked beautiful in the sun and shadow that rolled over the folded hills beyond the trees.

Hilf knew his own ground so Richard felt free to ramble under the trees. Things had gone very well so far, except for Barnes' opinion on proving Samuelson's guilt. If only the solicitor had suggested another way to approach the problem. But then, Richard admitted to himself, Barnes had been extremely cool toward him until near the end of his visit.

"Mr. Darrow," a voice called, breaking in on his thoughts.
He looked up and saw Jason, the big footman coming toward him, holding a letter in his hand.

"Sir, this came for you by first mail. Miss Blackwood felt it should be placed in your hands immediately."

"Thank you, Jason," Richard answered, taking the letter.

The missive was from Mr. Barnes. Richard knew that the informality of the salutation was a sign that the solicitor was ready to deal with Richard on their old footing of familiarity.

"Darrow," the note ran. "After a good night's sleep, I think if I were you I should try the chance of the marriage records turning up something regarding the wife. Remember, the only certain thing is that if someone is legally married, they must be married in a Church of England ceremony and the church would probably (though not necessarily) have the record of the marriage. That is the only certain thing about the recording of marriages before 1837. Unfortunately, records relating to births and marriages prior to 1837, when such recording became law, are notoriously inaccurate. I know this is not much help, but it is all I can offer. Otherwise, I believe you really are at a dead end. I shall advise you if I learn anything of value regarding the old cavalryman, for so I think him to be. Lie low and good luck. Sincerely, Barnes."

The solicitor's words seemed to hold out a very slender hope. If he and Sally and Emily could live quietly, perhaps it was better to let Mighty Jack go his own way in the world, but even as the thought came to him, the calm, patient face of Charles Wilney rose in his mind.

"No, there has to be some way. I cannot believe that God will allow Charles' murder to go unpunished."

But he had to admit he was not looking forward to the trip back to London, nor to yet another journey back to Manchester. According to Charles, Manchester was where Mighty Jack had said he was going with Annabelle when he left the Liverpool & Manchester railway. The pair may have already been married at the time Charles met them in camp, then again, if there were secrets to uncover that might be proved with marriage records, Manchester was probably the logical place to start. It seemed such a remote chance that the thought depressed Richard's spirits. He had done so much traveling of late. Yet, in spite of the fact that Manchester was close to Blackdale, he was not comfortable with the thought of leaving Emily at the estate while he looked in the industrial city for records that might unlock the secrets of Mighty Jack and his wife. Samuelson was still having business dealings with Pamela Blackwood. He might still come to the estate, and Richard did not want the little girl within Samuelson's grasp, nor did he want to take her to the industrial city. He had no idea what kind of danger there might be if he got close to the secrets of the railway king's past. The man had killed twice to preserve those secrets. Far better to take the child back to London and Sally, and then return to Manchester alone. So far, at least, no one had bothered Sally and Emily in their new lodgings in the metropolis. Having made this resolve as he walked under the trees at Blackdale with the great wolfhound, he allowed another two days of rest at the estate before starting back. Emily was having such a good time, romping in the woods with Hilf, in the clear air and sunshine.

Pamela was absent from breakfast and lunch, spending her days at the pianoforte. But it was nice for her to have the visitors in the evening. All day she had the solitary pleasure of music and at dinner and afterward, she could have the conversation and companionship of Emily and Richard. Having the opportunity to treat Emily fondly, was especially important to her. During the same interval, her good opinion of Richard was strengthened. She felt he was highly intelligent, balanced and had a deep, affectionate regard for Emily. It made their short time together very pleasant for her and she felt she would be sorry to see them go. Richard had the joy of rambles, where he could take in the scenery of the moors. He climbed the Rivington Moor with Hilf and visited the eighteenth century Rivington Pike, which dominates the landscape for many miles around is part of the lands of Rivington Hall.

In spite of injunctions to the contrary by Richard and Pamela, Emily established her own bed as Hilf's regular sleeping place. As with all pleasant times, the hours and days passed rapidly and soon Richard and Emily started back to London.

* * *

Sally was inexpressibly relieved to get Emily's letter of apology, definitely informing her of the little girl's whereabouts. With that worry alleviated and Richard and Emily away from home, she now had time entirely for herself. When Sally had lived with her family, she had naturally helped her father and brothers as much as possible, but unlike young ladies from more conventional homes, she had not been expected to do more than her equal share of housework. Her brothers swept, cleaned, cooked and sewed as much as she did, but with indifferent results. Where any of the children had learned these domestic arts was something of a mystery since their father was entirely ignorant of the skills of housewifery. Perhaps the children had learned in simple self preservation.

Sally's mother had died in giving birth to her youngest brother, so there had never been any woman to oversee or train her. Thanks to her father's skill and prudence, there had always been enough money for a maid of all work. With three younger brothers and a radical father who believed in the equality of all living things, Sally had been encouraged to develop her mind to a remarkable degree. She cooked well and was good at needle work, but she particularly liked going to scientific lectures and keeping a journal where she could fearlessly record her own opinions and ideas. One day a week, Sundays, she gave her time to the poor by mending cast off clothes at her non-conformist church. She had a great interest in the poor, especially in the women among London's poor, for she felt that women in poverty and working children were the most oppressed people of her time. She believed fervently in the suffragette movement but was too independent to join any specific group. In short, Sally would have been judged "advanced" even by the standards of the "new women" of the 1880s.

As she poured out her tea after reading Emily's letter, Sally's thoughts turned to the young girl, whom Richard had described as living in such degrading circumstances. She determined to find and visit the young woman and try to become her friend. Sally thought the girl's loneliness must be excruciating if she gave a stranger such a beautiful keepsake just so that he would think of her. The jewel the girl had given Richard still lay on a shelf in the kitchen. Sally got up from pouring her tea and reached over to examine it. Coming from a tribe of engravers and being exposed to some of the best artists in London, who came to have their work prepared for printing, Sally had a fine judgement and a keen appreciation for the visual arts. She thought the engraving in the stone very well drawn and exquisitely executed. In fact, it was one of the finest pieces she had ever seen. She promised herself to show it to her father before going to see the young girl. She might learn something that would help her draw the girl out. With that resolve, she rose from the table, put on her bonnet and heavy wool shawl and left the house. The Howard's establishment in Cheapside was not a long journey from the apartment Sally had taken. In less than an hour, she was entering the shop. In the big, open room that smelled of lithographic ink, two of her brothers were explaining, each to their own customer, how they would execute the commissions the customers were presenting. Her father, standing at the counter, his arms resting on the polished wood regarded her with twinkling eyes. He was a tall broadly built man with a handsome full beard of gray that blended with his hair, which was worn long in the style of the last century. There was an expression of friendly frankness that was permanently settled on his wide but well-defined features. His full mouth was smiling at his daughter, as it usually was. He was liked by everyone. His bluff honesty and great competence at his trade made him respected by all, and a leader among the neighbourhood tradespeople.

"What are you doing, here, Missy? I told you it wouldn't last. He's a nice enough chap, but why marry the lad and go away from us? I knew you'd be back."

"Father, don't make jokes at my husband's expense," Sally said with the same twinkle in her eyes that one could see in her father's.

"If I can't make jokes about my family," the old man roared over the din of the shop, "who can I make them about, I should like to know?"
He came out from behind the counter and embraced Sally.

"I came here for an expert opinion, sir," Sally said archly. "Not vulgar, ill advised humour."

"Humour is the food and drink of the gods, Missy. Sometimes I believe you are too serious by half. I can't understand how that happened to my daughter."

"Here, father," Sally said reaching into her purse. "Look at this."

"Oh, my," he said as he took the jewel. "That is a rare thing. Where did you get it?"

Sally quickly described Richard's meeting with the young girl. As she did, her father was holding the jewel up to the light and turning it around.

"It is very, fine, Sally. Eh? You want to know something more about it? Well, it wasn't cut in England. There was a man in France who did extremely fine miniature portraits like these. I'd heard he'd been given some sort of a small kingdom by the Little Corporal, in the Emperor's heyday. His name was Lauzon. And anyone who has his work must have been well-off at one time. Either that, or someone very rich must have bought this for her. The backing for the two cameos is a very large beautiful emerald, my dear. Very rare. Very expensive. Not usually used in this way."

"And you're sure it's French?"

"As sure as one ever can be about the provenance of anything."

"Is it old?" Sally asked.

"If it is the work of Lauzon, which I believe it is, it is at least fifteen years old. He has been dead that long. More likely something like twenty-five or thirty years. You see the border? It is in the style of the First Empire. Even then, there were few who could pay a man like Lauzon for this sort of objet d'art: a fine quality emerald with two superb cameos on it. One portrait of the Emperor, a very fine one, as well drawn as David's, I think, and a portrait of some unknown man. Ask your young lady friend where she got it. I should be interested."

"I shall, father," Sally said reclaiming the stone. "But I thought I might learn something that would help me draw her out."

"Well, that is the best I can do."

"Thank you. You are all well? Where is Donald?"

"Out delivering some folios in a rented wagon, thanks to your peripatetic husband. If Raphael and Titian complain when they get back, I shall scourge that man of yours."

Sally grinned at her father's scowl.

"He is the kindest man in the world, father, after yourself. He will not neglect our friends. In fact, Emily tells me she is coming home with a wolfhound from the estate."

"Someone to keep the wolves away, that is good, my dear, after what I've heard about some of your husband's acquaintances."

"Yes. I shall be glad of the dog. If he listens well."

"Any of god's better creatures will listen to you, daughter, except me. Now get out of here and stop engaging me in idle gossip. It may not look like it, but I have work to do."

Sally smiled, waved and went out the door. She said nothing to her two brothers who were still with customers. She went from the shop directly to Warwick Square, where the young girl lived. Richard had given her a description of the house but no address. He had not noted it after the girl left him. He only knew that it was on the northeast side of the square, that the porch needed paint and that the door had a knocker in the shape of the famous fixture at Durham cathedral, a rayed sun with a face on it. She had to approach eleven or twelve houses before she found a house with the distinctive door knocker. It was about one in the afternoon. The brass knocker was grown green with tarnish and was stiff with desuetude, but Sally wrenched it hard and forced it to make a satisfactory sound.

An odd startled cry came from behind the door. After a few moments, a small crack appeared and through it, Sally could see a long strand of red hair and a pair of frightened looking cornflower blue eyes.

"Yes?"

"Hello," Sally said trying to make her voice low and soothing. She held out the token the girl had given Richard.

"Oh. Did he give it to you? I don't want it back. I want him to have it."

"I only brought it so you would know I was a friend," Sally said quietly. "May I come in and talk to you?"

"You want to talk to me?" But the door was opened enough for Sally to enter. The tone of the question was one of genuine surprise.

"Why ever should I not?" Sally said stepping inside.

"No lady ever wanted to talk to me. Not in all my life."

The interior of the house was dark and stuffy, as if the windows had not been opened for years. There were no lights or candles burning. The curtains were drawn.

Still, Sally could see the girl clearly. Not more than twelve, Sally thought as she looked at the smooth, pasty skin and undeveloped body. The girl wore a kind of white negligee over stockings and a garter belt. When the negligee fell open, the girl's half developed pubic area had no covering, no drawers of any kind. There was a roll of blankets on the floor. The girl seemed sleepy.

"Oh," the girl bent over and picked up the blankets hurriedly and threw them into the hall closet. Then she pulled her clothes tightly around herself. "I'm ashamed, Miss, to meet you like this. You won't tell him, will you?"

"Tell whom?" Sally asked.

"Oh, that very kind young man who had the jewel. I did so want him to like me and think well of me, even if I never saw him again." Sally knew immediately that she would not tell the girl she was Richard's wife. "Did he send you?" the girl's eyes grew large at the idea.

"Well, yes, in a way. He told me about you and asked me to come and see you."

"My goodness. It's quite like a novel, ain't it."

"What is, dear?" Sally asked.

"Him. You. It is like a story in a book."

"Do you have a maid, my dear? Someone to make us tea?" Sally asked, taking her gloves off.

"Oh, Mrs. Griffiths is only here, when, that is, in the evenings."

"Otherwise, you live here all alone. All day?"

"Yes. Sometimes I feel so lonely." The girl's head drooped. Then she looked up. "But I read novels then."

"What is your name, my dear?" Sally asked, gently lifting the girl's chin so their eyes could meet.

"Anne, miss,"

"Well, my name is Sally. I should like very much to be your friend."

"Really? I mean, are you sure?" She let her head droop again and looked down at the floor for a few moments. Without lifting her head, she said, "You are almost as kind as he was. And you are a lady."

Sally did not have to ask who 'he' was. Richard's native gentleness had made an enormous impression on the poor girl.

"Remember what a great author has written, Anne," Sally said, 'a lady is nothing more than a woman in a silk dress and her night's food and lodging in her pocket.' Nothing more. No one is any better than you are." The innocent blue eyes looked dazed. She obviously couldn't grasp the idea.

"Shall we go out, my dear, to have our tea?" Sally asked. She found the house and it's atmosphere suddenly horribly oppressive. She wanted to remove its gloom from their meeting.

"I can't go out like this," the girl said looking down at herself. "You should have to wait while I dress." The blue eyes looked at Sally tremulously, fearing the gentle lady would not wait.

"Of course. I can even help you dress, if you like."

"I do have some nice things," the girl said, enthusiasm taking hold of her.

"Come upstairs to my room and I'll show you."

The poor child's desire to please and fear of rejection touched Sally deeply. She promised herself that the child should not remain in this terrible life much longer. From the girl's complete lack of feminine modesty, it was obvious that she had been accustomed to a dissolute life for a long time, from an early age. Sally was almost ready to take her home, immediately, but she would have to write to Richard about it first. Then, too, the girl's own fear might prevent her from coming. It would take time for Anne to really trust anyone, even a "lady".

After the boredom and isolation in which Anne had lived, her afternoon outing with Sally seemed, indeed, like a novel. They went to a tea shop on the Strand where they could watch all the elegant passersby from their table. Anne was very well up on all the latest fashions explaining all the nuances of men and women's dress to Sally. As the fashionable world passed, the girl became animated.

"You see that man's hat. Too tall. They haven't been worn like that all year. And that one, he's trying hard to put on a brave front, but look at his shoes. Oh, just look at that beautiful cape that woman is wearing. Wouldn't you just die for it? And that dress. I'm certain that fabric cost a fortune."

"You certainly notice a great number of details, Anne," Sally said, interested only because the girl was.

"Well, clothes make the person, don't you think? Anne said. "At least that's what Anna Ripley said in, "The Kings Men." I just finished reading it." She took another quick sip of tea, "This is such fun. I've never had a conversation like this before. I mean, with a woman, about these sorts of things. You are so nice to me," she blurted out.

"And why ever not, dear," Sally said, reaching over and patting the girl's hand.

Sally also noticed that Anne was very well-spoken for a common prostitute.

"It is such a beautiful day, Anne, why don't we go for a ride in the park?"

"Oh, I should love to. But I don't have any money for a carriage, miss."

"Sally, dear, call me Sally."

"I don't have any money, miss, I mean, Sally."

"Does not your friend give you any pocket money?"

"Oh, yes. But I spent it all on jewelry. Now I'll not get any more until next month."

"Well, I can afford a ride in the Park. So let us go."

"Oh, that is my favourite thing, miss, Sally. Riding in the park. I asked him to get me a little gig and pony, but he says it is too expensive to keep horses."

They rented a cab at a rank not far from the restaurant and ordered the driver to go back and forth along Rotten Row. Then they drove all over the west end. They both enjoyed looking at the beautiful water birds who made the area around Green Park their refuge even in early Spring. It was one of the few places in the metropolis where such birds could be seen. The poor air and lack of sunshine favoured pigeons and wrens and little else in most parts of the city. Sally was relieved that the birds gave them something of mutual interest. Now, it was her turn to tell Anne all about the birds, where they came from, their habitats, what they were called, and so on. She pointed out the male and female colours of their plumage. To her surprise, Anne was truly attentive.

It was an unforgettable afternoon for the girl. She had never been so happy in her entire short life as when she and Sally rode down the beautiful avenues with all the handsome ladies and gentleman, walking and riding around them. Sally's interest in her amazed the girl, but after a time she simply accepted it.

"Tell me, Anne, where did you get the jewel you gave Richard?"

"Richard? Is that his name? Oh, thank you, for telling me his name. It's very good of you to tell me."

"Where did you get this, Anne," Sally said holding up the stone.

"Someone gave it to me a very long time ago." The girl turned away and looked out the window.

"Who was it, my dear?" Sally asked gently.

"I do not know. I cannot remember. Oh, look at the swans! They are so pure and white, are they not?"

Sally admired the swans as directed but thought, there was something about the jewel and its source that was extremely important to the girl. So important that she had given it to Richard and had trouble even talking about it. Sally's deep feminine sensitivity told her that there were many closed doors in Anne's soul. They would have to be opened one at a time, very slowly and very gently. It might take many visits before there would be any point in returning to the subject of the jewel. Sally's forthright nature chafed under the constraint when she thought of the degradation that Anne would be subjected to as long as she stayed where she was. The jewel might be a clue to her past, even a connection to someone who might help the girl and care for her. Sally's father had often told her that no living thing was willingly a slave except those who had been trained to be. If that were so, Anne had certainly been trained in a hard school. It broke Sally's heart to think of what the poor child's history must have been to have produced someone utterly unfamiliar with simple acts of kindness.

Rather than press the girl anymore, Sally set herself the task of giving Anne a wonderful, happy afternoon. She dismissed the cloud of any other thoughts regarding the child's situation. As they walked, rode and looked about in the rare sunshine of a London afternoon, they peered into shop windows together and stopped to refresh themselves in yet another tea shop. Sally couldn't help but compare Anne to her own, dear Emily. She felt no one could ever have broken Emily's spirit. Thank God, the hours in the darkness of the mines seemed to have done nothing more to Emily than make her character strong. The mystery of why people think and behave so variously was one that interested Sally deeply, and by thinking about Anne and Emily, she could compare two remarkable examples of human beings. Did God make them as they were? Or were there other, more commonplace things that formed people as well? She mused upon the question throughout the afternoon. She realized that it would take some time to build a friendship with Anne and get her to talk about the past. The past was where all her unhappiness and disappointments were rooted. It would be painful to remember and talk about. But Sally felt sure, without knowing why, that the key lay in the jewel. It was much more precious than anything else the girl had, and it showed a cultivated sensibility as well. It meant something special to the girl, something that was painful to remember. Sally promised herself that she would find out what it was and use it to help Anne.

As the shadows lengthened and the air began to grow cooler, the holiday feeling began to fade and suddenly Anne said, "It is getting late. I must go back."

"Must you really, Anne?" Sally couldn't help asking. "What would he do if you weren't there when he came?"

"Oh, he should be very angry and call me names and accuse me of being with other men."

"And what if you told him you'd been with me?"

"I do not want to bring trouble on you, miss, I mean, Sally. He is a very important person." There was a touch of pride in the girl's voice.

"Oh, really?" said Sally, feeling more truculent with every moment, as she thought of Anne returning to the dark, stuffy house and the foul man who provided it.

"Oh, yes. He's an MP. He makes laws that we all have to obey."

"What is this MP's name?" Sally asked.

"His name is Bradley, Sally. He makes laws about railways.

It did not seem remarkable to Sally that the girl knew these things about her lover, but she would have been surprised to learn that these were the only scraps the girl did know, had been pieced together out of boasts that Bradley had made. Where he lived, how he lived, what being an MP was, exactly, were all dark mysteries to Anne. She knew only that it made her lover an important person. Given Richard's situation with the authorities, Sally could not press Anne to leave the important person until she had somewhere safe to go. Unfortunately, if the man really was an MP, he could cause trouble for Richard. She felt frustrated and irritable at the thought. She wanted to act and she felt herself prevented by circumstance. She was determined, now more than ever, to win Anne away from the disgusting man who was keeping her. Somehow she would find a way, once Richard had resolved their troubles with the railway king.

They ended their day together by walking a long distance to the house where Anne was living. There was frost in the air as they stood on the peeling porch holding hands. Sally looked at Anne tenderly. A few tears trickled down the girl's pasty cheeks.

"Do not be sad, Anne," Sally said wiping away the girls tears. "I shall see you soon. We shall be great friends."
"Really? You're not just saying that? And you will tell him that I am not so bad as he might think?" the girl asked.

"I am quite certain that Richard thinks no ill of you, Anne."
Sally could feel that the girl wanted to pull away and go inside to her other life, but at the same time could not bear to part from her new friend.

"I shall come again, soon," Sally said. "Here, let us make an appointment and we shall each write it in our pocketbooks. That way, we shall each know when we'll next meet."

"Could he come, too?," the girl asked shyly.

"Richard is not in London right now," Sally replied.

"Oh. You sound as if you know so much about him. I wish I could know him as you do."
"Perhaps you shall, one day, Anne." Sally bent down and kissed the girl on her cheek. "Now which day would you like me to come next week? What day is best for you?"

The girl took out her latchkey.

"Oh, if it is in the day time, it does not matter," she said in a listless tone. "Goodbye." Then she stopped and turned to face Sally. "You really will come again? You won't forget?"

Sally put her arms around Anne and hugged her tenderly.
"I promise, I shall come again, soon, dear."

Chapter 30

J ust two weeks after Richard and Emily left Blackdale, Pamela received the following letter with several enclosures:

"Dear Miss Blackwood,
Here is a letter which I found among the papers of Charles Wilney after my return to London. It describes the very underhand tactics that Samuelson used once to obtain a right of way across a Baronet's land. These papers document the entire affair. Perhaps, Mr. Barnes could put these to good use in refusing Mr. Samuelson's addresses to you. As you will note, the letter is from an MP sent to the engineer on the site where John Samuelson was working. With it, I have also included the Baronet's original letter to the MP which was sent to the engineer as well. All are signed and dated.
Thank you again for all your kindness during our recent visit.
With Sincerest Regards,
Richard Darrow."

Now, Pamela thought, as she read over the enclosures, Barnes has every reason to break off all contact with Samuelson. She put the letters down on the desk in front of her with a sense of satisfaction. He could show these documents to the other partners and make them understand what sort of man Samuelson really was. Then she rose, went to her own room to prepare for her interview with Herr Bruckner. When she had written to the maestro asking for a meeting, she had vague forebodings of Samuelson convincing Barnes to permit some combination of their business interests. She had written to her music teacher with the feeling that, perhaps in founding her own career as a musician, she could simply walk away from Barnes, Samuelson and all the complications of her father's legacy. Now, that seemed unnecessary. Barnes and the other partners could not refuse now to break with Samuelson. A number of her father's partners, she knew, were Quakers, like

Edward Pease. They were hard, but very moral men who would have nothing to do with anyone who broke the law as Samuelson had.

Still, she felt, as she selected one of her most flattering gowns, if she could be truly independent and earn her bread in the service of music, it would be the most complete life she could have. Now that Emily's future was settled in a way that would have pleased her father, she felt entirely free to once more put music at the centre of her life.

She waited for Bruckner in the parlour where she practised each day. It was the first time she had seen the music master away from Rivington Hall. She felt older and more mature somehow, meeting him in her own home. Then, too, she had now studied enough to have some idea of her own powers. She was no longer the uncertain girl she had been when her lessons first began. With the elimination of Samuelson, Pamela felt more in charge of her life than she had since her father died.

She opened the pianoforte and began playing the very lovely theme of the second movement of Mozart's concerto number twenty-one, a great favourite of hers and the first music Bruckner had ever heard her play. As the gentle final cadence died away there was a soft knock at the door. Effie, her personal maid, opened the door.

"If you please, Miss, Herr Bruckner."

"Thank you, Effie. Please show him in." she answered rising from the pianoforte.

When he entered the room, Bruckner saw her, facing him, standing next to the massive Érard wearing one of her loveliest gowns, cut out of a fabric the colour of twilight, a colour, he had noticed, that she often wore. He bowed formally and then cocked his head to one side, his admiration of her obvious in his glance. It was the first time they had met without Lady Thornsby. It surprised Pamela how different everything felt without the presence of a chaperone.

Pamela felt all the blood rush to her face as she said, "Do please have a seat, Herr Bruckner."

"Thank you, Miss Blackwood." But he walked over to the pianoforte where she was standing, instead, and said, "Is this the instrument that is not functioning correctly?"

Suddenly, Pamela felt very embarrassed at the subterfuge she had used to see the musician alone. "Oh, no. I had the mechanic. It was only something minor, which has now been fixed."

"You are certain?" His dark eyes were serious and showed no sign that he suspected her deception.

"Yes, Herr Bruckner. Quite certain."

"May I try the instrument, Miss Blackwood? To make certain the mechanic overlooked nothing?"

"Herr Bruckner, I had another reason for wanting to see you today — without, without Lady Thornsby present."

"Ah," the slender young man said sitting down on the piano bench.

He looked up at Pamela, studying her face.

His scrutiny was too much for her and she turned away from him and walked over to a small petit-point chair from the reign of Queen Anne. She slipped behind the chair, placing it between herself and the musician, and said, "I-I-wanted to know your honest opinion on my progress, sir."

"You do not feel your lessons have progressed well?" he asked.

She could see he was genuinely puzzled.

"I feel they have been very satisfactory. But my opinion on this topic is not important. Yours is. What do you think, Herr Bruckner? Please be direct with me."

"Of course, Miss Blackwood. I hold your playing in high regard, you know that."

"But..."

"Yes?" he said, trying to understand what she wanted.

"Am I yet accomplished enough to make my way as a professional musician?" Pamela finally blurted out.

The young man's handsome smooth forehead crinkled into a frown for a moment.

"Do not spare me, sir," Pamela said. "Please give me your honest assessment."

"As a concert artist, performing in respectable homes?," he asked.

"No. I want to perform in public. As you do. As Maestro Lizst."

"Performances entirely open to the public?" He frowned as he asked the question.

"I do not want to have to rely on the invitations and good offices of others to earn my living," Pamela replied.

The young man nodded. "But you must know, Miss Blackwood, that any performer must court society's good opinion. No one is entirely able to do his or her own will without experiencing consequences."

"Does not talent and art purchase some true independence?"

"Yes. But no one is ever completely free, except perhaps for a handful of divine geniuses like Liszt. And even he was without friends when he eloped with Countess D'Agoult. I'm sure it effected his income."

"I understand."

"When?" he asked.

"When?" she repeated, uncertain of his meaning.

"Yes. When do you want to begin giving public concerts?"

Pamela began to walk nervously back and forth, her long fingers sneaking up to the locks of hair that fell to her shoulder. To her horror, she realized a few moments later that she was twisting her hair around her fingers as she had when she was little girl, or when she was alone. The dark eyes of the musician followed her with interest.

She could almost feel his quiet, tender glance on her burning cheek. She pulled her hand away from her hair.

"I should like to begin as soon...as soon as you think me ready."

He frowned again, whether in disapproval or in thought, she could not tell.

"Many of your friends will not approve, Miss Blackwood."

"I know that," Pamela said, blushing unaccountably. "I care not for my friend's opinions. I want to be independent, as independent as anyone can be of society. I want to be independent of my father's money and of anyone's good opinions. No, that isn't correct. I do care about the opinions of other musicians. I will court their good opinion, assiduously. I want to earn my place among them." She paused for several moments and looked away from him. Then she went on in a much more tender accent then she had meant to utter, "But I care especially about your opinion." Then, hearing the tone of her own voice, she said quickly, "What I mean, sir, is that you know my playing better than anyone."

He was silent for what seemed a long time to Pamela. His lips were pursed as he looked down, away from her. Finally, he spoke.

"If you are certain about risking the dangers of this step, I should be proud to offer you a place on my programme when I perform at Manchester next month."

"You are giving a concert? Here? In our hall. The one on lower Mosley Street, near St. Peter's Square?"

"I do not know the streets. It is a very plain building from the outside with six columns in front and a pediment above. But the inside of the hall is very grand. It's fitted out much more handsomely than most public halls."

"That's because it is not a public hall. Concerts are by subscription only, and subscribers must be invited to join and attend."

"I see," he said.

"I wonder why I haven't been told?" she mused out loud.

"Perhaps Lady Thornsby was afraid of somehow disrupting your lessons by telling you. But I know that I must stay before the public so I am not forgotten. It is one of the hard facts of earning one's bread from the stage, Miss Blackwood."

"And you invite me to play at the concert?"

"I should be proud to introduce you as my pupil, Miss Blackwood. If you permit, I shall put your name on the bills and give you a portion of the total subscription. After all, you want to support yourself entirely with music, yes?"

"Oh, but it is you people will come to hear. I could not take anything for being given such an opportunity. I should be taking advantage of your kindness."

"Nonsense. I am being a selfish beast by making the offer, Miss Blackwood. Many more people will come to hear you, who are known as a young lady of fortune in the region, than me."

"Surely not."

"This is lesson number two of earning money on the stage. Novelty improves earnings. Many people who do not know you well will come expecting that the wealthy, handsome Miss Blackwood will play badly. They will be shocked and amazed when they realize you are no dilettante. My prestige as a teacher will certainly wax in the county. It is I who am taking advantage of you, Miss Blackwood. I am certain that is how your friends also will see it. Lady Thornsby, especially, will not be pleased"

"Oh, I shall write to her and explain that this was entirely my design. That I lured you here with a falsehood. Her disapproval will not be directed at you if I can turn it away."

"I advise you to think very carefully, Miss Blackwood, before you step out onto a stage. The people you have known will see you differently afterwards."

"But you do not believe there is anything immoral about playing music in public? You would not think less of me for it?"

"Of course not. People who are as gifted as you are and who share that gift with others should be praised and celebrated. But often, when the applause die away, performers meet with opprobrium. Herr Lizst was regarded as a criminal when he eloped with the Countess d'Agoult. And it was less because she was married, I believe, than because he was a performer. I want to make certain you understand that you will be separating yourself from many of the people you know in Manchester and elsewhere. You will never again be quite respectable in the eyes of society. This is true of all artists. Especially performers. Especially women performers."

"But I shall be an artist," she said with a thrill in her voice. " I shall pass my entire life in the company of the immortal masters, striving always to be worthy of them. With that as my reward, what do I care for opinions that will die like mayflies in an hour. Was it not Goethe who said, 'All else dies but art'."

"Truly," he said looking up at her with shining eyes, "you have the sublime soul of a true artist. Only a great and sensitive soul would be capable of such lofty sentiments. All the more reason why I must make you realize that not many people are capable of such refined perception. I am concerned that your own sensitivity may make the slights you will feel as a public performer that much more bitter when they come—as they are bound to do."

While they had been engaged in this impassioned conversation about art, Pamela had slipped from behind the chair and had slowly made her way back to the piano. She now stood very close to Bruckner.

"If people do not feel the greatness of music and what it can bestow," she said "then I do not care what they think about me. Through your lessons, music has become more to me than food or air."

"Dear lady," Bruckner said, impulsively reaching toward her, his mask of decorum slipping, his pleasure showing in his soft, limpid eyes. He took her hands in his and then, as if suddenly remembering his role, dropped them, but not before Pamela felt a gentle pressure from his long, supple fingers. For the brief moments that the elevation of their art mixed with more personal feelings, they were enraptured with the most profound emotions of the human heart. It was a slight span of time that touched eternity. It would always be one of the greatest treasures of Hans Bruckner's life. Had Mephistopheles stood at his elbow, this was the moment when he would have said, "Let this moment never pass."

Pamela blushed down to her shoulders. "And when are we to perform?" she asked, avoiding the tender, dark eyes that she could feel resting on her.

"The twenty-seventh."

"You will choose something for me to perform?" she asked, rearranging the music that lay piled on the piano in front of her.

"No. I should rather you chose for yourself," he said.

Something in his tone made her look up. His eyes were wide and seemed to look into her soul.

Suddenly, she felt a pang of emotion pierce her, so sharp and unexpected she had to turn away.

"Please go now." she said without turning around. "And thank you." She suppressed her tears until she heard the door close softly, then she wept from the fullness of her heart.

She remained alone near the pianoforte for what seemed like hours. She could not understand what she was feeling. Was it joy, gratitude? Then, for the first time, the question came to her, was this love? Was this the master passion racing through her mind and body, turning her into another person, someone she didn't know? Her memory tossed up strange bits and pieces of conversations with Alicia when they had each fantasized about falling in love. They had pictured it as something delightful and fun, like a role in a theatrical that one could put on or take off. But this was terrifying, to be so governed by unpredictable sensation. She remembered the way she had felt almost physically pulled toward Samuelson the day he had come to the house and shared his ideas with her. And now, good God, she was being attracted by another man. Was there something wrong with her? Perhaps she had always wanted to avoid marriage because she feared her own ardor? Perhaps she feared the power it would give to the man she allowed herself to love. The more she tried to penetrate the mystery of her feelings, the more confused she felt. Finally, she just wanted to escape, so she opened the pianoforte and began to play Mozart's pure, serene theme she had been playing before Herr Bruckner came. The music spread around her like a perfectly clear pool with expanding silvery rings on its surface. She plunged gratefully into the cool beauty of its embrace.

During the next few weeks of preparation for the concert, Pamela often found herself strange and unaccountable. Her emotions tossed and rolled like the moors. She took to long walks on gray, rainy days, seeking to feel the drops and wind on her face, wanting their touch to pull her attention outward, away from the maelstrom of her feelings. Incomprehensibly, it was both Herr Bruckner and Samuelson who came into her thoughts unbidden, as if they were in some way connected. Yet, in her quieter deliberations she could not see what the two shared. Samuelson was a dangerous, powerful man with whom she wanted no contact at all. She feared him. Herr Bruckner was like music itself, cool, perfect and tender. It had been his generous words and the touch of his hands clasping hers that had released the storm in her. She had not allowed the feelings she'd had with Samuelson to become nearly as strong. She seemed to live in two worlds: one waking and ordinary in which she did the things necessary to the running of the house, practicing, reading a letter from Emily, writing letters, sending the evidence against Samuelson to Barnes. But she also inhabited a world painted with her own sudden strong emotions. She imagined being in conversation with Samuelson or sometimes Bruckner. She felt Bruckner's eyes rest on her gently when she played the selection she had chosen for the concert. One night she woke from sleep, upset by a dream about Samuelson putting his hands on her. She got out of bed, pushed open the window in her room and let the rain cool her face. If she loved Bruckner, why dream of Samuelson this way? Why should her skin grow so hot while dreaming of the railway king? She could not explain any of it. She grew more and more uncertain of herself as a woman as she grew more and more confident as a musician. For the concert she had chosen the music she played at her first interview with Bruckner: the terribly difficult Paganini Études by Bruckner's teacher, Franz Liszt. When she wrote to Bruckner and told him of her choice, he highly approved, remarking that no woman had yet played the études publicly. If she conquered its extraordinary difficulties from the stage as well as she did in a private salon, her performance would astonish Manchester and lay the foundation for her future with a single stroke.

As predicted, Lady Thornsby replied to Pamela's letter about the public performance with a letter of strong disapproval, verging on condemnation.

"You must realize, my dear, a woman's reputation is very fragile," the letter began. "Especially the reputation of a young woman so handsome, wealthy and gifted as yourself. Jealousy adds to the likelihood of malicious gossip. You have no guardian, no husband, no male authority in your life and these facts will magnify any imagined misconduct that can be connected with a public performance. I must strongly urge you against the public concert, but I open my doors to you, at any time, for a private presentation of your acquirements. It is imperative that you start to present yourself at balls and places where society can know you in an appropriate way. Becoming known first as a public performer will place you under a very dark cloud, socially. Your wealth and beauty will only add fuel to the fire. If your father were still alive, I should appeal to him, as it is, you must be the guardian of your own reputation. Remember, that no one can afford to set society's rules at defiance. With your fortune and your beauty, there will always be young men who will aspire to your hand, but if your reputation is tarnished, there will be fewer of the better sort and more of the fortune hunters. I write candidly, my dear because I have a high regard for you and want to protect you from being damaged by the opinion of society when you are just starting out in life."

She does not understand, Pamela thought, that I want to be able to earn my own bread. No one can imagine me independent of my father's money or a husband. She contrasted Lady Thornsby's attitude with those of Bruckner and Samuelson. The railway king would snap his fingers at anyone else's opinion about his actions. His powerful egoism would simply sweep all before him. Bruckner, on the other hand, believed that the artist was the true leader of society, that he showed the way where later fashion would follow. Still, he maintained appearances for the sake of earning a living. For entirely different reasons, both men were inwardly independent of society and its opinions. Was this why they had both been so much in her thoughts? In spite of, or perhaps because of, her emotional confusion, she worked harder than ever each day at the piano. She ate and slept little, feeling herself transported into a pure realm of music, yet when she did sleep, she felt more and more often the touch of a man's hands on her body. She could not always tell if she dreamt of Bruckner or Samuelson.

Bruckner sent her a copy of the handbill that was being posted throughout the city of Manchester it read: Anton Bruckner, pupil of Franz Lizst, presents a concert of modern music: Chopin, Lizst and Beethoven and is pleased to introduce Miss Pamela Blackwood in her début concert, where she will play Franz Lizst's Paganinni Études...the first public performance anywhere by a woman.

Both young musicians had acceded to Lady Thornsby's request and had changed the venue to Thornsby Hall. In recognition of Pamela's aims, the noble woman had offered to pay both musicians out of her own pocket. The young woman was deeply touched by the value her friend placed on her standing in society.

Pamela read the handbill with a racing pulse and a great sense of pride, even exultation. This was something she had won for herself. None could take it from her.

"I would not trade this for all the rich, handsome husbands in England," she muttered smiling to herself.

Her former life of longing for London and the amusements of balls seemed like the life of another person. Only the ache of her father's absence connected her with that former time. She missed him and the love and protection he had given her. How true had her conception of that life been, she wondered, now? Her father had been a wonderful man, beloved by many, but he had also been ready to marry her to an unworthy boy. She had sensed that Paul Samuelson was weak as well as grossly carnal. What would have happened in that former time, if it had been the father and not the son who had been presented to her as a future husband? She pushed the thought away. The strange attraction and repulsion she felt for John Samuelson was an unnecessary complication when she had music and the admiration of Anton

Bruckner. She had to make her performance worthy of him and of his legendary teacher. These men would be remembered down through the ages. Here was greatness in a form one could not doubt.

After Lady Thornsby's first letter and Pamela's reiteration of her intention to perform, the noble woman had written again. This time, she offered Pamela the opportunity to give a private preview of her public concert at Rivington Hall. This way, society would know that the young musician was under the patronesses' protection.

"I believe people will be less ready to say malicious things, my dear, if you appear here a few days before the public concert. Since you are decided on this course, I should be honoured to have your great talent known first in my home."

Pamela was deeply touched by the noblewoman's offer. She had expected a curt dismissal. But she now realized that Lady Thornsby was a true friend, whose interest in her and in music went beyond social forms. Herr Bruckner would not appear with her at Lady Thornsby's as an artist, though he would be an invited guest.

As the night of the private début drew close, Pamela felt no nerves, no concern about her performance. She felt carried forward on the certainty of her own ability. In spite of her personal confusions, she felt she was embarking on her life's work and was doubly pleased to have that beginning sanctioned by Manchester's leading musical authority, Lady Thornsby.

The day of her debut, Pamela left Blackdale in her carriage in the cool twilight of an evening that promised to be really cold once darkness fell. The prospect of her own park enchanted her with its beauty in the gathering night. Beneath the foliage on the ancient trees, she saw a doe grazing. A glimpse of its quiet liquid eyes, when it turned to look at the carriage, seemed to mirror the serenity and certainty that music had brought her. For that one moment, that brief time, Pamela knew absolutely that nothing could ever hurt or diminish the essential goodness of life. The memory of this one casual glance, this ordinary but unique moment, was a glimpse of perfection that would never, in Pamela's entire adventurous life, be surpassed for its beauty and completeness.

She arrived in good time at Rivington Hall. Numerous carriages were drawn up in the drive, and it looked as though the high and the mighty of Lancashire and York had once again honoured the summons to one of Lady Thornsby's musical evenings, regardless of what they thought of the announcement of Pamela's public concert. What Pamela did not know was that ever since the public handbills had appeared, she had been the town talk, discussed high and low, by all who interested themselves in the doings of society. The most notable among those attracted more by her personal history than by musical attainments was George Hudson, from York, greatest of the railway stock promoters.

Pamela let herself into the Hall by a private entrance to which Lady Thornsby had sent her the key. It led her down a narrow stone stair hidden behind a curtained archway which led into the main salon. Near the curtained arch sat a neatly dressed maid, looking crisp and fresh in her black dress and white apron and cap. On the other side of those curtains, Pamela knew, waited her audience. She handed her wrap to the maid and waited while the servant helped perfect her hair and gown. She regarded herself in the long mirror placed in the hall. Then, she confidently strode through the heavy brocade into a new life.

Pamela had no interest in who sat in her audience. The music was everything to her, and by the time she reached the magnificent instrument she knew so well, she had already entered the deep, inner quiet music always gave her. As if from a great distance, she saw Anton Bruckner and not far from him, she was aware that John Samuelson watched her with interest. She did not know that the corpulent man who sat next to Samuelson was George Hudson, nor would she have cared.

Even before she sat down at the pianoforte, the silence she commanded was sudden and complete. Her red gold hair, fair skin and beautiful gown of twilight coloured velvet took the breath away of all who saw her. Since she had not been much in public, none but Lady Thornsby had observed the recent changes in Pamela, the greater definition of her features and figure. Her face was more perfectly delineated. Her handsome chiseled features, exquisite nose and large oval eyes above a superbly carved mouth had a firmness that had not been present before. The mouth, which some might have thought a little too wide, now combined with her other features in a rare balance of line and form that rivaled the ethereal, yet profoundly sensual beauty of Botticelli's *Venus*. Everyone, but especially the men, felt the spell of her striking appearance. Concert goers of the next four decades would always comment first on her extraordinary personal beauty. Throughout the début, no one spoke or coughed except between études.

Attention was riveted on the exquisite figure who hammered and coaxed the keys of the huge keyboard with the power of a man and the delicacy of a woman. All were astonished, even Lady Thornsby, who knew Pamela's playing so well. The piquancy of performing before an audience had added an even greater brilliancy and power to her already considerable gifts.

As the last notes died away, the applause thundered in the high, stone-roofed hall. The din was so sudden and loud that for a moment, Pamela almost lost her balance as she rose to acknowledge the praise, but she regained her poise without anyone noticing. She stood next to the pianoforte and made a deep curtsey to the audience.

She rose and turned quickly away. The epoch-making concert was over and she disappeared behind the curtains. The maid waited for her with a beautiful silk robe that Lady Thornsby had provided. Pamela wrapped it around herself and felt suddenly, her utter exhaustion. A moment later, her patroness appeared.

"My dear young woman," Lady Thornsby said, clasping the girl to her. "I had no idea that I had invited a goddess here tonight. You are truly a great musician, my dear. Even Lizst, himself, could not have found fault with you, tonight."

Pamela started to sob against the motherly shoulder of her patroness.

"Oh, thank you, Lady Thornsby. You are so kind. I feel quite over-come by your goodness."

"Nonsense, my dear. You are overcome by your huge effort and suc-cess," the old lady said as she hugged the girl proudly.

"No." Pamela said drawing back and looking into Lady Thornsby's eyes.

"I am overcome by gratitude to have been given the gift of music. It is such a holy and wonderful thing. Where is my teacher, I must thank him."

"He has gone back to his chambers at my suggestion. I thought it better if society did not see the two of you together at what was bound to be an emotional moment for you and him. Now, go off with my maid and change your dress to meet your other admirers."

Without thinking, Pamela allowed herself to be led away, full of gratitude to the man who had given her so much.

A half hour later, Pamela emerged, refreshed, dressed in a gown of autumnal brown-gold silk. She followed the maid to the Hall's ballroom.. Stone walls and the uncarpeted wooden floor echoed the sounds of talk, laughter and movement. But as soon as Pamela appeared, applause burst spontaneously from the gathering. A moment later she found herself looking up at John Samuelson. As soon as their eyes met, Pamela felt the heat in her face, as images from some of her dreams flitted through her thoughts.

Both of his enormous, calloused hands enclosed one of hers.

"You are a very remarkable woman, Miss Blackwood. It makes me doubly sorry that you have had Barnes turn me down in such a cold, legalis-tic way. I can only say in my own defense that I have been ruthless in doing what I thought best for the people and nation of England. If I have at times overstepped the bounds of society's idea of propriety, it was because I served something more than personal interest. I believe, after tonight, that you are the same sort of person. Will you not allow me to come and call? Without any kind of business dealing entering into it? You have compelled the most profound admiration I have ever felt for a woman."

Pamela withdrew her hand.

"You overpower me, sir, with your statement."

"Give me the chance to make my true self known to you. That is all I ask. Let me come and take a walk with you in your own park. Please."

During this speech, Pamela alternately felt hot and cold. They were feelings she did not understand and she was startled to hear the railway king speak to her in such a warm, direct manner. For a moment, it seemed like the memory of one of her dreams. For a moment, she felt the strange sensation of something new that is also familiar.

"It is not my intention to be rude or cold, sir. You and my father were good friends, I know. Of course, you are welcome at Blackdale," she heard herself say.

Chapter 31

On returning to London, Richard told Sally of Barne's discouraging comments about catching the killer of Charles Wilney.

"Perhaps, Richard," she said, "you should take Charles' good advice one more time and let the matter drop."

"I should like to, dearest, but I cannot. Even if I could accept Charles' word not to see justice done for him, Samuelson could seek us out to do us harm at any time. If he had any idea that I knew the full story of Mighty Jack and how he got off the prison ship, he would hunt us to the ends of the earth. I cannot simply sit here and wait for that to happen."

"But you do not know that it will happen, Richard. Could we not just wait and see?"

"Perhaps some could, but I cannot. My whole being rebels at the thought. I must go to Manchester and follow Barnes' slender thread about Annabelle. The more I read over Charles' testament, the more it seems that there was something Annabelle had a bad conscience about. I want to know what it was."

"But it may not involve her husband at all."

"No. I feel certain it did. After Charles had heard Samuelson's confession, Annabelle asked specifically if Jack had told Charles about 'us'. Then, when he said 'yes', she asked if he did not revile her and when he said, 'no', she was grateful to a degree that made Charles uncomfortable."

"But she must be dead if Jack Samuelson is now courting Pamela Blackwood. I do not see how it is possible to find something in all this that could possibly touch him. All this pursuit does is to put you at risk." She turned to her husband and put her arms around him, "I do not want to lose you, dearest. It frightens me to see you stalking such a dangerous man."

"I tell you, Sally, we shall never be safe as long as he is at liberty and remains unpunished for Charles' murder. I also feel that a trip to Manchester is very unlikely to uncover anything of real value. I am not anxious to go north again, but I truly believe there is no choice. I should also like to hear from Miss Blackwood before I leave, to see if the papers I have sent her are of use."

"I do not like what Emily has told me of Miss Blackwood. She sounds a spoiled, willful creature with no thought of anyone but herself."

"I do not find her so. At least not since her father died. And the provisions she has made for Emily are extraordinarily generous. A mother could not do more for her own child. Even Emily found Miss Blackwood very changed. It is probably because of the loss of her father. They were very close."

"And I have heard," Sally said as she dusted the counter with particular energy, "that Miss Blackwood is very beautiful and is quite fond of you."

"Sally, dearest," Richard said, coming up behind his wife and putting his arms around her waist. "You could not think there is any feeling between Miss Blackwood and myself except concern for Emily?"

Sally continued cleaning, pulling Richard behind her as she moved around the kitchen.

"I think the fair sex is often taken with you, Mr. Darrow. You should hear poor little Anne talk of you."

Richard took his wife's shoulders and turned her toward him.

"The only member of the fair sex whose good opinion I court is yours." Then, he very wisely stopped her reply with a long kiss.

After a long embrace, Sally finally said, "How soon shall you leave for Manchester?"

"The journey soonest begun is soonest ended."

"I believe you have a classroom homily for every occasion, Mr. Darrow."

"And you are a saucy, wife, Mrs. Darrow. "Everyone else respects my learning."

"Those phrases are not learning. They are turned out by hacks to keep working children in submission. I am sometimes surprised that someone as literate and intelligent as I know you are can use such copybook phrases."

"Good heavens, ladies and gentlemen," Richard declaimed smiting his breast with a theatrical gesture, "I have married a shrew."

Sally shook her fists over her head, adopting the melodramatic stance of a defiant shrew and said shrilly, "You were warned, sir."

The two smiled at each other, laughed and embraced again.

"In seriousness, dear, when will you go?"

"As soon as I can. By now, Miss Blackwood must have received the documents I sent. I had wanted to get a letter from her acknowledging receipt of the evidence against Samuelson. But I shall not wait much longer."

"For all his crimes, Samuelson must be an exceptional man," Sally remarked.

"From the little I know of him, I believe he is. But he is hard, Sally, like stone or iron that will crush the life out of anyone without notice. Hard like the age we live in, a totally self-centered man, immensely strong, physically, financially, and in his character.

One can feel it when one is in his presence."

"Do not make me more afraid of him just when you are going off to do battle with him," Sally said, putting her hand to Richard's lips.

"If I did not believe in a God who loves justice, I should think I could never beat him, and we should be on a ship to America" Richard said quietly.

"I think that is why I love you, Richard. You believe in the power of goodness with a certainty which I do not possess."

"That is because you are a part of that goodness, dearest," Richard said, kissing his wife on her forehead. "Tell me more about your visit to the injured girl I found lying in the street."

Sally looked through the door toward the bedchambers. "Wait, I just want to be certain Emily is still asleep." She listened for a moment.

"It is all right. She sleeps deeply."

"You can hear her breath from here?"

"It is an ability that many mothers have. Any way, Anne."

"Yes, tell me more of her."

Sally reached into her apron, took out the jewel the child hand given Richard and put it on the table.

A sharp, brittle tapping on the upper door of their apartment interrupted their dialogue.

Richard opened the door.

"You!" his wife heard him exclaim. The door was pushed open to reveal the middle aged man in fine clothes who had met her and Emily on the street. It was Samuelson's spy.

"What do you want here?" Richard asked with some truculence.

"I told you I should want to know the results of your investigation. What did you learn about John Samuelson?"

"You are his spy. Why do you ask me?"

The man did not even flinch at the insulting word Richard had used.

"Because I believe you may be privy to some information that I have not been able to obtain."

"I do not see that it is your business, sir."

"You must admit, Darrow, I have twice saved your life. Could you not offer me a little more civility? I have watched over those you care for and protected them from harassment. Will you not tell me willingly what you have learned? I have my own cause to debate with John Samuelson."

"Richard," Sally said, "Why not tell him?"

The jewel which had been left on the table was suddenly seized by the spy. He sprang on it, grasping it and then holding it up to the light for a better look

"Where did you get this?" he demanded in a suddenly shrill tone. "Tell me this instant." His hand played with the silver grip of his swordstick.

"I met a young, injured girl lying in the street late one night on my return from Dorset. She gave me that jewel."

At that moment, there was a loud thumping on the lower door.

"Police," a voice called. "Open in the name of the law, Richard Darrow."

"Quickly," the spy said. "Go out your bedroom window and jump to the parapet below. From there you should be able to reach the ground without being seen."

"How do you know this?" Richard asked.

"It is my trade," answered the spy. "I shall slow them. But you must give your word to meet me in two hours time, here. And he quickly scribbled an address on a scrap of paper.

More thumping and shouts issued from below.
"Police. Open or we shall use force."

"But they might hurt Sally or Emily," Richard said. "I cannot leave. It is better if they take me."

"Or if they take all of you?' the spy said.

"At least we should be together."

"I give you my word they shall not be taken."

Richard lunged out of the window without hesitation, fell to a parapet a short distance below and was able to get to the lane behind the building without being seen. He stopped to catch his breath, his heart beat rapidly in his chest.

"Mighty Jack," he said between his clenched teeth. He read the address the spy had written and stuffed the paper back into his pocket. He would go to the place named. If the spy spoke the truth, he might be a powerful ally in the fight against John Samuelson, but fear plagued Richard as he forced himself to walk away from home. Would the police do anything to Sally or Emily? The spy said he would slow them. Did he really have the power to protect Richard's wife and child from the authorities?

The address was distant, a place on the south east edge of London. All the way there, Richard worried about his family. He felt alternately frightened for them and furious at Jack Samuelson for harassing them. Could someone so rich and powerful, he wondered, actually want to put Sally and Emily in prison? He knew what Fisk would have said. But did Fisk really know? The spy said he would protect them. Richard's only hope now was to meet him as promised and to tell him what he wished to know.

Thinking that he knew the worst streets and rookeries London had to offer, Richard was appalled as he followed his way down to the address the spy had written. He had seen the Irish rookeries off of Rosemary lane, where the courts had other courts branching off of them, making the whole area a perfect labyrinth of blind alleys so that, once the heart of the maze was reached, it was difficult to find the way back to the main road. He had looked through the narrow openings between the houses, so close together that neighbours conversed across the passages, while children lay in the dirt next to piles of refuse even the dustmen didn't want. But, here buildings were just as close together but even more decayed. They were deserted and on the verge of falling down. They reminded him of Manchester. Foul smells and pools of water with putrefying vermin in them assailed his senses. Once or twice he saw filthy human beings lying in the streets, whether dead or drugged or ill, he did not know. All was decay, and loneliness, as though the buildings themselves moaned against their utter abandonment, like a child left at night in the gutter. Richard wondered if perhaps the spy had brought him here to kill him and leave his body in one of the dank, oily pools that oozed across the mud and cobblestones. When Richard had seen the man mounted, brandishing his sword on the country road, he had no doubt about his expert ability to deprive his fellows of life. The address to which he had directed Richard exuded the same misery as Dickens' imagined slum, Tom All Alone's. In addition, the atmosphere of the place was enlarged by Richard's fear: for himself, for his wife and child. Fear walked arm and arm with him as he crossed the ghastly courts and twisting alleys, following the blurred numbers ever deeper into the narrow ways that afforded no more view of what lay ahead than a darkened peep show. Eventually, hours after leaving the spy at Sally's lodgings, he found himself in a hideously ruined courtyard, surrounded on all sides by buildings whose very bricks were crumbling and turning to dust. Here and there, wooden beams poked through the dissolving facades like broken bones protruding through ruptured skin. The only way into the court was the one Richard had just taken, otherwise he was confronted on all sides by the empty, wasted fronts of the ruined structures. The only noise was the slow drip of water in some place he could not see.

Then, from a dark hole that may once have been a door, the spy stepped out to meet him.

"Now, tell me what you have learned about John Samuelson," he said without preamble.

"I have learned to call him by the name of Mighty Jack, which was the name my dead friend knew."

There, in the pit of all that is most hopeless and forlorn in London, the story of Mighty Jack was told once more. For a long while the only sound other than Richard's voice was the seemingly eternal drip of the foul water. The spy spoke not at all but stood like a statue as the tale was unfolded before him. At last, when Richard reached the end and described the most recent meeting between Charles Wilney and Mighty Jack, the spy finally spoke.

"You have stood by your word to me. Now, in return I shall tell you this. You have made Samuelson angry because of your interference with Pamela Blackwood. The documents you sent her have infuriated him. His offer of marriage to her was not altogether a matter of business. He would have you destroyed the way one would swat a fly. He knows nothing of your knowledge of Mighty Jack, or your well-founded suspicions about Charles Wilney's death. But I shall tell him."

"What?" Richard cried. Why? You tell me to my face that you will betray me?" Richard said.

"It is not a betrayal. You are already pursued. But by making him more anxious to find you and by letting him know how close we both are to the hidden facts of his early life, I hope to provoke him to imprudence. I am now in your debt, Darrow. This," he reached into his pocket and took out the jewel he had taken from Richard's table, "has placed me in your debt, forever. It is the first and only trace I have had in years of someone I have long sought. I shall keep it for a while, yet. Tell me, please, where you found this girl. I promise you, I mean her no harm."

In as few words as possible, Richard told of his meeting with the girl. He said nothing about her profession or the fact that she had been attacked. He said only that she had stumbled and fallen. He felt that the matter of her mode of life was not his to tell to a stranger.

"This was on Warwick Square?" The spy asked in a voice strained by some emotion Richard could not recognize.

"Yes, not far from the Old Bailey."

"I am doubly in your debt, Darrow. Now, I shall tell you this: your wife and child are not in harm's way. They stop at home. Your sister, once again, resides in London with her rich boy at the Albany. I shall make certain that none of your family is harmed or harassed. Their safety shall be my sacred trust. You, on the other hand, once I tell John Samuelson about what you know, shall become my cat's paw. He will seek you out to crush you and silence the long-buried story of Mighty Jack. I give you my word that he shall not succeed."

"But why..." Richard began.

"Because I want to provoke him. I want to provoke him into revealing any evidence of his crimes that may yet exist. Behave like a good soldier and do your part. Go to Manchester and seek this other secret you believe exists. There will be more eyes on you than you shall see. And take the safety of your family as a done thing. Now, it is time for you to leave."

The spy walked across the yard to another hole that yawned in the face of a ruined building. From this he led a magnificent chestnut horse, the same that Richard had seen him ride when the tramps were driven off.

"This is Samson, Darrow. I lend him to you for your journey. He is trained as few horses ever are in these days of peace. If you are ever in danger, let him think for you."

"You forget, sir, I have seen his prowess. It is a great gift."

"Not as great as the gift you have given me this night," the spy answered, still clutching the jewel. "Now away with you to Manchester to shine a light in all the dark corners of John Samuelson's soul. Let us hope he will soon be in pursuit of you and lead you to evidence of his crimes. Do you have money?"

"Not much," Richard admitted. "What I had was left with my wife."

"Here," the spy said throwing Richard a small, heavy leather pouch.

"This is the first portion of what I owe you. Now get on Samson and ride north."

Richard weighed the pouch in his hand for a moment.

"Wait, will you take a note to my wife since I probably dare not approach her for some time. Even my letters may be read."

"You may survive this, Darrow, after all. Perhaps you are more of a soldier than I thought. Yes, I will carry your letter. I was planning to visit your wife, in any case. And I repeat that her safety and the child's is now my sacred trust. You have nothing to fear on their account. But guard well your own life for their sakes."

Richard quickly scribbled these words in the moonlight made ghastly by the surrounding yard:

"Dearest, the man who bears this note is a friend, strange as it may seem. Help him if you can. He has helped me on my way and he has sworn to guard you and Emily. I have seen him fight and there is no one who could guard you better. So, fear not.

I may not write again for some time. Our letters may be stopped and opened, so I do not know when I shall be able to contact you again. You have money and you are protected.

Perhaps you could see Fanny for me, and make yourself known to her, for I have learned tonight that she is now living again in London at the Albany. But, be careful. Remember that she is living with Samuelson's son. I am of two minds about this. On the one hand, I would like her to know what sort of man the father is. Perhaps that knowledge will make her think again about changing her situation. On the other, I do not like you to have anything to do with the subject of Samuelson. I leave it to you to decide, but be careful. Believe me, dearest, with God's help we shall prevail and be reunited soon. I love you both, Richard."

He folded the note and handed it to the spy who placed it in his pocket.

"Now, take Samson. Whenever you break your journey, board him outside of town on some farm or country stable. Anyone who knows animals will see at a glance what he is and perhaps become curious about you. Now, you must let him lead you through here." He pointed at the large ruined opening of the building. There seemed only darkness inside. "Put your hand on the saddle and let Samson guide you. He knows the way."

The tall horse looked down at Richard, flexed his neck eagerly, as though looking forward to the night's journey and began to walk fearlessly into the blank darkness ahead of him.

"I do not know your name," Richard said.

"Nor does any living man. But you may call me Collins, Darrow."

Then Richard found himself walking into the ruined building. In a moment all was dark. He felt only the warmth and easy moments of the great creature who walked next to him.

Collins watched while man and horse disappeared, and then slipped into one of the other dark openings in the courtyard. Utter silence fell on the terrible place, except for the unvarying drip of the pestilent water.

* * *

Sally could not have been more surprised when, the morning follow-ing the attempted arrest of her husband, Collins returned. She opened to his tapping to find him standing and holding out a folded sheet of paper in his hand.

Sally read quickly and said, "Oh, thank the Lord. He is safe. And you have been his friend. Come in, sir. Thank you for your help. We are persecuted by a monster. Will you have tea? We are just finishing breakfast, as you see."

Emily was seated at the table and looked at the guest with interest.

"Did you find the little girl who was taken from you, yet?" the child asked.

The spy, for once, was caught utterly off his guard.

"What do you know about my child?" he asked sharply.

"Only what you told me the last time we saw you."

"I did not tell you I was looking for my lost daughter."

"No. You said I reminded you of someone you had looked for a long time. You said to guard me well, so I thought she must have been taken from you. The things you said made me think that I must remind you of your lost daughter."

"Mon dieu," the spy said. "She is a sybil. She understands more than the wise."

"Yes, she does," Sally agreed pouring tea."I am sorry, sir. I do not know your name, even though you have befriended my husband in a dark moment."

"The name I give friends is, Collins," the spy said picking up his tea. With his other hand, he reached into his waistcoat pocket and took out the jewel which interested him so much and placed it on the table.

"I must apologize, Mrs. Darrow, for borrowing this when I was here last. I needed to study it."

Sally looked at the man with a new interest in her eyes. "Why?" Sally asked.

"Because..." and here he paused. "Because, Mrs. Darrow, a long time ago I knew the person for whom this jewel was made."

"Mr. Collins, you interest me inexpressibly. I was trying to learn about the history of this jewel only yesterday from my father."
"And who is your father that he should know such things?" the spy asked suspiciously.

"He knows a great deal about art, Mr. Collins. It is his business. He is an engraver."

"Ah. Tell me what he said." But even as Collins spoke with Sally, his eyes were on Emily. The two watched each other.

"He said that it was made in France during the reign of Napoleon the First."

"True."

"He said it was the work of a great french engraver named, Lauzon."

"True again."

"And that the stone itself was very valuable. That is all."

"All true, as far as it goes. Now, I will tell you its complete history, Mrs. Darrow. It is sad and I don't know..."

"I shall leave," Emily said getting up from the table. "I do not like sad stories. Only merry ones. Goodbye Mr. Collins."

Collins watched the little girl leave the room.

"She is a most extraordinary child, Mrs. Darrow.'

"Yes, Emily amazes us everyday with her intelligence and penetration. She is like someone who was born as a grown person. But now tell me sir, this sad history. I have my own reasons for wishing to know it. It is not mere curiosity."

"Your concern for the girl you visited?" he asked.

"Oh, my husband told you?"

"Yes."

"Yes, well I have felt all along that this jewel was somehow the key to her. Perhaps, the key to helping her. May I ask if she is the daughter you search for, Mr. Collins."

"I cannot answer, Mrs. Darrow, for I have not seen the girl, yet. I have not seen my own child in a decade. I have searched for her all these years without success. This jewel is the first hope I have had."

"I knew it!" Sally exclaimed, picking up the stone. "I knew this held the key to her identity and perhaps to helping her."

"I am almost afraid to ask if she is badly off? Your husband did not tell me anything about her condition except that she had fallen in the street. I sensed he was holding back information."

"Did he know you were her father?" Sally asked.

"I did not say so."

Sally thought for a moment, weighing things in her own mind, finally she said, "Mr. Collins, I will tell you about her only on one condition. You must promise that if you are to see her, or try to know her again, you must proceed in only the most gentle way. You must not judge her harshly."

"Look," said Collins fumbling at his collar and opening his cravat. From his shirt front he drew a small linen bag, from which he drew a lock of bright red hair. It was tied with a cornflower blue ribbon."I have carried this next to my heart for ten years. Never would I be cruel to her, madame."

Sally started at the personal mementos Collins showed her.

"How old was she when she was taken from you?" Sally asked.

"Only two, madame. A tiny, helpless thing. Only this big," he held his hand a short distance above the table top.

"And you have been searching for ten years?"

"Yes."

"That is a most unusual hair colour, sir," Sally said. And that ribbon matches the colour of her eyes. The age would be right. I believe, sir, that you may have found your daughter,"

"The Saviour is good to me," the spy said. There were tears in the old soldier's eyes. "I thought she might be dead. But I could not give up," he said wiping the tears away.

Sally took the soldier's hand in hers and held it as he wept. They were both quiet for some time.

Then Sally spoke, "I must tell you, Mr. Collins, that if she is your daughter, she has had a very, very hard, a very cruel life. She has been badly used, sir. I fear that if you were to make yourself known to her, it could un-balance her reason, so strangely is she situated right now. She is very delicate, sir. I warn you. Not ill, but delicate."

"Will you help me, Madame?" Collins suddenly asked. "Will you introduce us in a way that seems fitting to you when you have prepared her? You have an understanding heart. You are her true friend. I can see that. Will you help us to know each other again without our connection harming her?"

Sally's inward glance showed her to be considering his words.

"It will take some time, Mr. Collins. But, yes, of course, I shall do everything I can. But I do not know what sort of a cloud my husband and I will be under. As long as I am able, I'll help you and her."

"And I have already told your husband that I answer for the safety of you and your child."

"God bless you, sir, if you can protect us from the evil man who persecutes us."

Chapter 32

"Yes, of course I was very worried about Richard when he left," Sally said to Fisk and Cynthia, who had just arrived in London. "But Mr. Collins got him away and says that unless he is careless or has very bad luck, he does not think the constables in Manchester will search for him. He is going to tell Mr. Samuelson something which he thinks will make him reluctant to call on the constables again. I can't say I understand it all, but I do trust Mr. Collins."

Fisk had been anxious to meet Richard's new wife and so had suggested that he and Cynthia immediately go from the Howard's family home to the lodging Sally had taken in the far east end. A week had passed since Richard had left for Manchester with Collins' help.

"Your brother gave me the address, knowing what good friends Richard and I are," Fisk explained. "I hope you do not mind our visit. Richard and I were always thus with each other."

"No, of course, you and Miss Hackworth are welcome, Mr. Fisk. Richard has spoken of you often. I am pleased to know you better."

"It is remarkable to me that this fellow has ended up helping you and Richard," Fisk said. "We thought him a particularly dangerous enemy in the past, an assassin bought and paid for by Samuelson."

"Yes," Sally replied, "I know Richard had misgivings about following his instructions, but there really was no choice. The police were at the door. Now I believe he has good reason for helping us."

"But they were at the door because they had been set on Richard by this same man's employer," Fisk said. "There is some other meaning here of which we are ignorant.

But I am certain Richard will be well on his guard."

"Well, I like Mr. Collins," Emily said, wandering in from the other room, holding a doll. "He is trustworthy, I am sure."

"And, who is this, then?" Fisk asked.

"I am Emily, sir. I came with Mr. Richard—who is now my father—

from Manchester. I live here now, and Sally is my mother and looks after me. I know who you are. You're the man who sees things other people cannot see. I read your little book."

"She reads everything," Sally explained. "We tried for a time to regulate her reading, but it could not be done. She used to read even the law books in Richard's office in Manchester."

"And tell me, Emily, why do you think Mr. Collins trustworthy?" Fisk asked.

"I do not think someone who loves his daughter so much and wants to find her so badly could be wicked. That is all," the child told the carpenter with a shrug. Then she wandered away, carrying on a private conversation with her doll.

"She has met this fellow?" Fisk asked Sally.

"Oh, yes. He made a point of talking to her," Sally answered. "That was when he warned us to move here because we might be watched at my father's."

"Oh, I wonder if Fisk will be in danger, then, at Mr. Howard's house," said Cynthia.

"My friends are on the look out for us, dear," Fisk said. "Do not worry. Sally did not know that some very good men were watching over her father's house."

"No, I did not, Mr. Fisk," Sally said. "Thank you, sir."

"I suppose things moved too quickly for Richard to tell you, or perhaps he just forgot."

Sally nodded and then said, "Before he left, Richard did ask me to call on his sister, Fanny. I know he has been very worried about her. Do you know her at all well, Mr. Fisk? I know you were once neighbours."

"Yes, Mrs. Darrow. Richard and Miss Darrow used to be my neighbours."

"What were they like, in those days?" Sally asked.

Well, I can't say I knew them well. I was often away from home. But I do know those young people had a hard time of it after they tramped up here from the railway camp near Manchester. They'd never lived anywhere but in one of those hellish camps. I helped them make their lodging more like a home with some shelves and cabinets. Richard was always studying and working hard at his books.

"And his sister?"

"Oh, she was a very pretty little thing. Full of mischief and laughter."

"But she grew up to be very beautiful, did she not?"

"Ah, yes. Fanny grew up to be very handsome, I should say."

"Oh, Mrs. Darrow," Cynthia said,"This hot tea is so warming and refreshing. Thank you."

"I am pleased you find it so, Miss Hackworth."

"My father says you have become a great writer, sir," Sally continued.

"Just some little pamphlets."

"My father says that your views on religion are most original. I must say that after reading some of your work, I must agree with him. I should like to write one day."

"About what, Mrs. Darrow?" Cynthia asked.

"About the plight of working women," Sally said. "I believe that we and our children are worse off than our men."

"You are right, Mrs. Darrow," Cynthia replied with feeling. "What do the angels say about that, Fisk?"

"Now, please, Cynthia..." Fisk began.

"And why ever not?" Cynthia said. "They already know, if they have read your work."

"Your mystical writing reminds me much of Boehme or Swedenborg," Sally said. "The gift of spiritual vision must be a great gift, indeed. I have myself never touched on such things. The ordinary world of nature is more than I shall ever manage. It already seems miraculous to me. I should have to learn much more about that before I could converse with angels."

"I should have thought that, too," Fisk said. "But they came to me and told me I was to write what they said. It is they, not I, who have something to impart. I am merely the hand that holds the pen."

"Howard," Fisk said standing up as Roderick Howard entered the apartment from the hall.

Roderick Howard filled the small room with his presence. He stood a head taller than Fisk. His long gray hair and beard did, indeed, make him look like an aging lion.

"Yes," the big man said, "I thought since everyone had deserted me, I would also join the party now that work is done. Fisk, I meant to tell you when you first arrived that I thought 'The End of Time' was a fascinating essay. Very provoking thoughts and very true," Howard's deep voice rumbled. "But I just wondered..."

"Father," said Sally getting up with the dishes she had just collected off the table, "Perhaps you and Mr. Fisk could go back to your studio so that Cynthia and I can speak together as well."

"Are we preventing you, my dear?"

"You are in my way, father. I have to make dinner and you fill up the room."

"You see Fisk, we men need a Charter of Rights in the home, too."

"Oh, father, you can hardly say that I persecute you."

"Not persecute, dear, just push me from place to place," he winked at Fisk.

"Go on with you now," Sally said smiling as she pushed her towering father toward the door.

"You see, Fisk?" Howard said as the carpenter got up to follow.

"I sometimes think," Sally said when the men were gone, "that my father never grew up."

"Mr. Fisk has a high regard for him, Mrs. Darrow. He told me that

333

your father was one of the most intelligent men he knew."

Sally flushed with pride. "Oh, he is very clever and even wise, but he often acts like a great boy."

"Do not all men?" asked Cynthia. "Is that not part of their charm."

"Richard is not like that," Sally said. "Sometimes, I should even say he is too serious."

"Do please tell me about him. I have only met Mr. Darrow, once, very briefly. Though, Fisk has talked of him often."

"Right now, he is away from London, trying to apprehend the murderer of his dearest friend."

"Fisk has told me. What a terrible thing— to have someone you love, murdered. How dreadful for Mr. Darrow."

"He would not rest even a day when he heard of it from Mr. Fisk. I believe it was the day he met you."

"Yes, it was," Cynthia affirmed. "I remember that right after he heard the news, he wanted to leave us almost immediately."

"Yes," Sally agreed. "Nothing would satisfy him but to go and visit his friend's grave and see what he could do to apprehend the villain responsible. Miss Hackworth, pardon me for changing the subject, but do you know Fanny Darrow?"

"No, I'm sorry. I have not met her."

"Well, I have not met her either, so I only know her by Richard's report. I have seen a portrait of her that Richard had made for a locket. He says it is a good likeness."

"Does she have a remarkable face?" Cynthia asked.

She is very, very handsome," Sally answered. "Richard says that when she was a costermonger, men swarmed about her wagon more thickly than the flies."

"You are very handsome also, Miss Howard," Cynthia said.

For a brief moment, a rose blossomed on each of Sally's cheeks.

"That is very kind of you to say, Miss Hackworth. But Fanny is really extremely handsome. Richard was afraid she might go on the stage."

"Oh, no. Now that I think of it, I do believe Fisk rather admired Miss Darrow at one time," Cynthia said.

"I should not be surprised," Sally said, as she kneaded dough for dinner buns.

"From what Richard has said there are few men who meet her who do not admire her."

Cynthia was quiet for some time and when Sally looked over at her, she could see she was thinking deeply about something.

"Are you all right, Miss Hackworth? Have I said something to distress you?"

"Oh, no. I was just thinking that I am fortunate Fisk was still free when I met him."

"You mean because of Miss Darrow?"

"Yes."

"From what Richard has said, it is hard to see such a deep thinker as Mr. Fisk with a woman whose greatest pleasure is laughter. Even Richard says she has a light character. Mr. Fisk seems opposite."

"That does not always act as an impediment," Cynthia said. "Especially when a woman is very fair..."

"Yes. Sometimes I think that a woman's face and figure are all men can see. I sometimes think that if I had not had a good figure and long golden hair, Richard would not have asked me to marry him."

"Mrs. Darrow! What a thing to say."

"Oh, it is different now. But in the beginning when Richard would talk about my excellent mind, I could see his eyes running over my hair and wandering all over my figure. I told him I didn't think it was my mind that interested him."

Cynthia tittered for a moment and then lapsed into coughing. With the return to London, the dry rasping edge had returned to her cough.

"Oh, dear," Sally said wiping the flour off her hands and pouring a glass of water for Cynthia.

When the spell passed, Cynthia had tears in her eyes, so hard had she struggled for breath.

"My dear good woman," Sally said. "You must rest. London is not a good place for someone with a weak chest."

"I did not want to be separated from Fisk. He does not know how long his business in London will take."

"There, there," Sally said, "Let us not talk anymore. I shall put a shawl on you and make some more hot tea. I have a lemon here as well. I shall put some in."

So saying, Sally took the shawl she had been wearing before she started kneading dough and placed it on Cynthia's shoulders. As she wrapped the warm garment around Cynthia, Sally felt the other woman's extreme thinness. "Heavens," she thought, "I hope she does not have consumption." She resolved to talk to Fisk about it.

Later that evening after dinner, when Cynthia was resting in Emily's room, Sally pulled Fisk away from her father.

"Mr. Fisk, are you aware that Miss Hackworth is ill? She is far too thin and her cough sounds dangerous, sir. In my work with the poor at our church, I have heard coughs like the one she has. I hope we can give her some extra nourishment and try to build her up while you are here."

"I thank you for your concern, Miss Howard. I have tried to get her to rest more and take delicate food, but she will not let me do anything to save her labour. She insists that it is her part."

"Well, she shall not resist me in my own house," Sally said. "I think I shall keep her here with me and make certain she rests and is well nourished. You can stay with my father and see to your business."

"You are very good, Mrs. Darrow. Thank you."

"Sir, might I ask what your business is that brings you back to London? I fear that the London air is not good for Miss Hackworth. I know she would not stop at home without you. She told me."

"My business is of a most pressing nature, Miss Howard."

"Well, if anything less than life and death turns upon your stay here, I am of the opinion that you should leave very soon."

"Unfortunately, Mrs. Darrow, it is life and death and a duty which no one else can perform. When Cynthia insisted on coming, I thought long and hard about what to do. But I was told to come by those much wiser than I."

"Do those holy beings who visit you then oversee your actions, Mr. Fisk?

"Never oversee, Miss Howard. Only suggest."

"But Miss Hackworth's health. I am sorry, sir, if I am being disrespectful of your privacy, but I am deeply concerned about Miss Hackworth. I have known people who have died of consumption. I fear that Miss Hackworth might be afflicted with it."

Fisk took one of Sally's hands between his. "I could never be offended by an act of kindness, Mrs. Darrow."

"I will go further, then, sir, and say that even when it is great authority that counsels something, if the counsel is not consistent with common sense, I should protest against it."

"You are quite right to do so, Mrs. Darrow. However, this is not a matter in which I have any choice but to do what I know is my duty."

"I hope, sir, I might come to know you well enough that I should be convinced that what you say is true. But I certainly shall find fault with you if Miss Hackworth sinks any lower than she already is, even if all the angels of heaven stood behind you."

Her cheeks were flushed and her eyes bright with the strength of her feelings. She glared at Fisk for a long minute.

"Three angels press around you this very moment to catch sight of such passionate goodness, Miss Howard," Fisk said in a very serious tone.

Sally was struck dumb by his rejoinder and before she could recover herself, he had released her hand and left the room.

The following morning, Fisk rose early. His mind was somewhat easier about Cynthia, because of Sally's offer to watch over and nurse her. He set out for Simon's lodgings.

As he approached the old Georgian house that had been cut up into apartments, he had no sense of any palpable wickedness in the air as he had on his last visit. When he stood close to the door of Simon's apartment, there was a perfumed odour which spoke of a female occupant. He knocked and in a few moments the door was opened by a woman of faded attractions, who stood before him in a revealing wrapper of silk or some shiny material.

"Hello, love. I haven't seen you before. Which one of my gentlemen friends sent you over?"

"No, miss. I am looking for the man who used to live here."

"Oh. Don't know nothing about him," she said as she closed the door.

Fisk was not surprised that Simon had moved. Since he had started his programme of destruction, it made sense that he would want his whereabouts to be unknown. The activities he was engaged in were clearly hanging offenses. The letter he had mailed to Fisk had been postmarked from an altogether different part of London.

Fisk now had no choice but to try some of the radical public houses and booksellers. If he made it known in these places that he was looking for Simon, he might hear something. After visiting two booksellers, his third stop was The Lamb and Flag, a public house which had a long history of radical political gatherings reaching back to the early-eighteenth century.

"Charles Fisk," the tall, thin landlord hailed him, reaching out his hand over the bar. "I have not seen you in my house for some time. I heard you had gone from town because of the stir your writing had caused in certain circles."

"Hello, Joshua. Yes, it's true. I now live elsewhere than London."

"Can I get you something?"

"I'd like a half of that ale of yours. It is one thing about London I deeply regret."

Joshua's flabby cheeks and high, broad forehead crinkled into a smile, making his round face look like a withered apple.

Fisk drank deeply from the earthenware cup put before him.

"Some good things do not change, thank the Lord," he said.

Joshua's smile broadened.

"Joshua, I am looking for a friend of mine. He came in here a few times with me. A young man named Simon, Simon Oakley. Do you remember him?"

"Oh, aye," the landlord said wiping the wooden surface of the bar with great care.

"Do you know where he is, now?"

Joshua leaned forward and dropped his voice to a whisper. "I have heard some strange things of him. He doesn't come here anymore. You would have to try way out east and down near the docks. Do you know *The Darkling Thrush* in an alley called Lancashire Mews, between Narrow Street and the river?"

"A place of evil report, if it's the one I'm thinking of," Fisk replied. "The reach of the Police doesn't yet even touch that district. A bad and lawless place."

"That's the one. Between St Katharine's Dock and Limehouse, nearer the Ratcliff Stairs. I can offer no more than to say go there and ask around for him. But mind yourself, the place is filled with cutthroats. If I had a penny for every pound they have stolen off the river, I should be a rich man. The flotsam of the seven seas drifts through that house of call. Heathens of every colour, too."

On his way to the *Darkling Thrush*, Fisk debated whether to ask Roderick Howard to come with him. The big man would be a valuable ally in such a place, for he feared nothing and was a giant of strength. On the other hand, if he found Simon, it would be difficult to talk with him if someone else were present. In the end, rather than stopping for Howard, Fisk went on his way alone to the lawless slum which boasted the notorious pub.

Lancashire Mews was not on any map. It consisted of a narrow opening between two buildings and continued for only one block, ending in the mud of the river bank. *The Darkling Thrush* stood by itself at the very edge of that mud. The tides came and went beneath its side door. The area was not quite as foul a slum as the courtyard Collins used as a place of business, but it was considerably more dangerous. The dead end lane that ran off of Narrow Street to the water gradually shrank to little more than a footpath before it expired into the muddy ground of the river's edge. The few buildings that stood on either side of the Mews were low dark piles of lumber and brick that appeared to be tumble down improvisations, but were rumoured to have been warehouses at some time beyond the memory of the living. Those who lodged in these venerable estates during the eighteen-thirties and forties were some of the most desperate and dangerous thieves in London. If it became known that a particularly valuable cargo was on the river, Lancashire Mews and the surrounding streets would empty out to attack and board the vessel, providing it was not too heavily guarded. These good citizens had not far to go then to earn their living, for they usually brought their swag to one of area's several rag and bone shops, establishments with illegible signs and large windows filled with a miscellany of ill-gotten goods. A little further west, between Fleet Street and the river lived a large tribe of those who, rather than exerting themselves to steal, simply coined their own money. After a night of enterprise, many of these riverside capitalists, whatever their business, could be found enjoying their new wealth and leisure at the *Darkling Thrush*.

How long the *Thrush*, as it was known by regulars, had stood in its dark, damp corner, at the very end of Lancashire Mews, none knew. If one were to judge by the crooked clay bricks of its face, its age might seem to approximate that of the river mud, out of which it appeared to have grown by some malignant organic process. When Fisk reached the building through the lane after a long, muddy tramp, a party was in progress. A rousing, bumptious melody played by a tin whistle and an out-of-tune pianoforte rang out from the *Thrush* into the dark, empty streets that straggled away down to the water. Fisk looked into the brightly lit interior and could see men and women dancing on a floor strewn with sand and sawdust. The cracked walls had, in another age, been painted with a woodland scene that was now faded and discoloured. Near the bar, in colours more vibrant than the rest, was painted and repainted, larger than life, the thrush that gave the place its name. It glared down at the room with an eye and beak more like that of a bird of prey. Beneath that avian insignia, it seemed that all the nations of the world took their pleasure, for Fisk saw faces of every colour gathered round, from coal black to a fairness so light, the skin looked bleached. One swarthy, thickly muscled man with bushy black hair and beard wore the feathers of a red indian. His left earlobe was pierced by a large golden ring. Next to him, within easy reach of his powerful arm, was the long iron shaft of a whaler's harpoon. This sentinenal, for so he seemed to Fisk, turned his head constantly, watching every corner of the room. If any man were foolish enough to disrupt the proceedings of the regulars, he would probably find himself pinned to the wall like a butterfly and then thrown out into the river to be disposed of by the convenient tide.

Fisk stepped over the threshold and was almost immediately dragged into the hurly burly. He was swept up by a buxom, heavily painted woman whose smile of greeting would have been more attractive if she had had more than two or three teeth. Mixed with the odours of overheated bodies, stale drink and the dry rot of the building, was a sweeter aroma that told Fisk opium was being smoked somewhere nearby. He whirled around with his grinning partner for some minutes but when the music stopped, he quickly stepped away from her and moved over to the barmaid. The holy of holies was presided over by an incongruously sour-faced middle-aged matron who would have done for the wife of a Methodist minister. Fisk leaned over to her so he could be heard over the din.

"I am looking for Simon Oakley. Do you know him? I am a friend."

The woman shook her head in the negative.

Fisk put a pound note on the bar.

"I tell you, I am a friend. I am trying to help him."

"Write your name on this," the woman said, slipping the bill into her pocket and pulling up a scrap of soiled paper, a cracked pen, and a bottle of nearly dry ink from underneath the counter. Fisk scratched out his name and handed the paper back to her.

She kicked at something on the floor and bent over to mutter a few words. A ragged, tipsy child of about ten rose unsteadily upward from his gin-soaked dreams. She handed him the paper and he wobbled his way through the dancing couples and out the door.

Fisk waited at the bar among the noise, heat and smells for what seemed a long time. Finally, the boy reappeared in the doorway. Without entering, he nodded his head that Fisk was to come outside with him. The carpenter felt some apprehension as he stepped out into the dark street. He followed the boy east through a labyrinth of the small twisting alleys and lanes that slipped in and out of boat yards, warehouses and sheds lying between Queen Street and the river. Finally, in a small dark yard that smelled of creosote, the boy stopped and nodded toward a lit window on the second floor of an ancient, tilting shed. Two narrow, crooked flights of stairs led up to a doorway near the light. Fisk turned back to the boy to ask him if this was the place where Simon lived, but the boy was gone. The air in the yard was strangely close, as if no wind had ever touched the place. Beneath the smell of creosote was an odour of decay. He felt none of the evil sprites who had guarded Simon's other lodging on their last meeting, but there was a chill dampness from the river, and he had an overwhelming presentiment of death. The spidery steps swayed under his weight but held him.

Two storeys up in the air, he stopped on a small shelf of wood and knocked on the door. At first, he could see nothing other than a silhouette of a figure holding open the door. But the figure's extreme thinness and the high, tight set of its shoulders told him it was Simon.

"It's good to see you, Simon." Almost as he said the words, he stepped inside and the light fell on Simon's face. The younger man's eyes were wild and staring and yet, were in strange contrast to the rigid immobility of the rest of his face. All of the young man's movements were poised and slow, but his eyes were frozen wide open, as if with horror.

"Are you all right, Simon?" Fisk asked.

Simon's mouth curved into an expression that was more of a rictus than a smile.

"I am well, Fisk."

"You look, different."

Simon's pupils dilated even more. "Of course, Fisk. I have found out who I truly am."

"And who are you?"

"I am the one sent to slay the Beast. Oh, you were my John the Baptist, Fisk. But I am the Appointed One."

A cold shiver went up the carpenter's back as he realized that Simon was mad.

"Ah, you see it, don't you Fisk? You see what I have become."

"Yes," Fisk said reluctantly, uncertain of Simon's meaning.

"I knew you would see it and understand, if we met again. You would realize I had surpassed your understanding. I am completely in charge now of the Lord's work, Fisk."

"Could you explain these changes to me, Simon. I sense them, but I do not see as you do."

"No, you do not. My vision has been purified in the blood of the Beast. You can't kill the Beast, Fisk, with words, as you tried to do. I have spilled his blood. I have watched the colour bloom from his wounds when I have struck him." Then in a more strident, fearful tone that ended in a shriek,

"He can be killed, Fisk."

"When did all this happen, Simon?"

"As soon as I left you and realized my own power. Ah, I have been hoping you would come, Fisk. So I could tell you these things. I may yet find a use for you."

"I should like to help in any way I can, Simon. Where is John Cary, by the way?"

Simon's eyes drooped. Instead of being held wide in an expression of horror, they were suddenly suspicious and cunning as they regarded Fisk.

"I do not know if I should tell you about him," he said as he began pacing back and forth. "You were quite wrong about him, you know. He wanted to give way to the Beast, Fisk. And my army needed his money. He would not spend it. He was always worrying about what things cost. I soon realized that the Beast had left its mark on him, already. I think, actually, that he wanted to die and help us in that way. Yes, I really do."

"So he is dead?"

"Oh, yes," Simon said very calmly. "I gave him a quick, easy death right in this room. Look," he said suddenly rushing across the room. "Come and see this, Fisk. The mark is still here."

Fisk rose slowly from the barrel he had perched upon and crossed the room. What, he wondered could he say to Simon? He had no idea. He could not betray him to the police, nor could he let him kill more.

"Look, Fisk," Simon said pointing to a large brownish stain on the floor. Then he turned away and began pacing quickly back and forth. Finally he said to himself, "We have not told him everything yet. No, we have not. Shall we tell him?" He walked faster and faster, back and forth across the large attic room.

Fisk stood quietly and waited.

Suddenly, Simon stopped and stood still. "We shall tell him, yes, we shall. He, of all my followers will understand. We, I, have also had a vision. A great vision. A greater vision than yours, a glorious vision of the Beast's end and the coming of the New Jerusalem. I know how it is to be accomplished. We, I have been chosen...Come with me," he said suddenly hooking his finger through the buttonhole of Fisk's coat lapel and pulling him over to the door. He opened the door and released Fisk. Then he ran down the rickety stairs to the ground and waited for the carpenter. He was obviously bursting with excitement.

Simon led the way on a long forced march up Narrow Street to Queen to Cock Hill and Shadwell. Then, they walked rapidly past the London Dock, past St Katharine's Dock, Tower Hill and Billingsgate. They passed four bridges: London Bridge, New London Bridge, Southwark Bridge and finally Blackfriars. Just past Blackfriars bridge, Simon stopped and stood, staring with shining eyes outside the iron gates of a brick fence that completely enclosed a group of squat brick buildings. A peculiarly acrid smell emanated from the complex. These fumes contained high concentrations of ammonia, and were, in fact, the caustic result of distilling the coal gas used in London's street lights, first introduced in the eighteen-thirties. There were several sets of pipes protruding from some of the buildings. Mounted on the fence, a sign whose paint looked leprous, announced that the buildings and fenced yard belonged to: The London Gas Company.

Simon had forbidden conversation during the march. He had moved with a strange, stiff gait that was extremely fast. He was waiting for Fisk at the Gas Works gate when Fisk arrived.

341

"This is how the Beast shall end, Fisk. We, I,I, shall explode the works of the London Gas Company, and the old London shall ride into the New Jerusalem on a ball of flame. I have seen it, I have seen it clearly in a vision, a vision of flames, burning lakes of acid...running men covered in flames,...A fire many times greater than the Great Fire shall consume the Beast and those who worship him. The City itself, where all the temples of greed are built shall burn first. Then, the rest. That is the vision given me. This is the destiny appointed for me. Is it not great? Is it not greater than any of your visions?"

Simon turned back to Fisk, his face alternately twitching, grinning and scowling. His arms were wrapped tightly around himself. He seemed frantic with delight.

"And now you," Simon said, "you have been sent to help me. I have done all the thinking and planning. I even have a confederate who works nights here who will let us into the yard. All we have to do is turn down the outlet valves from the purifier boxes. Then we'll push a couple of wagon loads of drip barrels near the boxes. The drip is like naptha and while it has a low flammability" it will burn intensely once lit. No one shall be able to put it out. We'll position the wagons between the purifier boxes and as soon as the pressure builds up in the boxes, we'll ride into the New Jerusalem on a wave of cleansing flame. If it turns out as I hope, this whole part of London will disappear in a burst of flame. Then the holy city will descend. I shall have done my part and be honoured by the hosts in paradise. Just think of it, Fisk. Just think of it."

His voice rang out with a terrible ecstasy on the edge of tears. "You shall be my anointed helper. I shall show you what to do when the time comes."

"And how will you avoid the flames yourself?"

"Why should we avoid them, Fisk? We shall be in heaven with the Lord and his hosts. Now, enough for tonight. Come tomorrow night. We may be watched."

Then, the younger man scuttled off into the darkness, going back in the direction of the lair where Fisk had found him.

After parting with Simon, Fisk walked north, away from the docks and alleys of the river toward the Howard's home. He knew it was his task to stop Simon. He did not doubt that the younger man had the technical knowledge to explode the gas works and create a terrible catastrophe. There were minor explosions all the time in gas works. He supposed that the key to Simon's huge explosion were the naphtha barrels which would make a fire so hot it would explode the accessory gas pipe and ignite the gas storage tanks. Fisk only hoped he could stop Simon without hurting him. He would pretend to help him right up until the last minute so that he could keep a close watch on the progress of the scheme. Then, he would have to hope that he would find some way to prevent the final conflagration.

Chapter 33

S ally had more than a little curiosity about the beautiful sister of her husband, the companion who had shared his early years in the navvy camps. She also knew that Richard was anxious to have them become friends. There could be no harm in approaching Fanny that Sally could see. Collins said that there was presently no question of anyone proceeding against her or Emily. It was the trumped up charge of sedition that hung over Richard that made him susceptible to Samuelson's persecution. Collins had spoken with the police downstairs and they had left. Sally had never even seen them. Under the circumstances, she felt quite safe approaching Fanny. She could not believe that Richard's sister would connive in any way to harm her brother or his family. She resolved to take Emily to her father's shop, where the child was always welcome, and then proceed to the Albany. Of course, everyone knew the Albany, the odd collection of small houses let out as chambers where many wealthy men had *pied a terres* in London, especially during the early years of Victoria's reign. The Albany's houses ran from Burlington Gardens to Piccadilly, in one of the best quarters of the city. Many famous literary men had lived there: Byron, Macaulay, Bulwer, "Monk" Lewis and others. In fiction, it was the home of one of Dickens' worst scoundrels, a money lender called "Little Eyes" by the dolls' dressmaker in "Our Mutual Friend." Raffels, the Robin Hood of London cracksmen, lodged there, and many others of more respectable stripe. In 1845, the young society gentleman who lodged at the Albany was a recognized phenomenon and was described as such by Dickens in his "Dictionary of London, An Unconventional Handbook."

Though Fanny's presence would have been frowned upon by the management, The Albany provided more privacy for Fanny and Paul than an hotel. A few well-placed five pound notes from Paul had settled the staff. For her part, Fanny was delighted to live in such an elegant part of town. Green Park, St. James and the shops on Regent Street were just steps from her door.

Sally left Emily and her father deep in conversation about the mysteries of lithography, got a cab on the street and gave the address to the driver.

With the special attention to detail that women pay to personal appearance, Sally had worn one of her best dresses. Fanny, having had no communication of Richard's wedding was puzzled when the porter came to the chambers she shared with Paul, when he was not at his father's. Who was this Mrs. Darrow? Could it be that she and Richard had some unknown relative? Her curiosity was piqued as she looked at the card that had been sent in to her. After searching her wardrobe carefully for her most demure costume, she chose a simple brown cashmere dress and stepped lightly into the sitting room where she had told the maid to seat the caller.

Fanny could not imagine who the quietly handsome woman was. Fanny had had very little to do with other women. Most of her acquaintances had been men, usually men who admired her. She was not a woman who attracted other women, especially women who looked as modest and respectable as the handsome, blonde Mrs. Darrow.

"What would such a woman want with me," she asked herself?

When Fanny crossed to the seated stranger, she was surprised by the sudden, warm smile the woman directed at her.

"Hello, Fanny," Sally said, smiling and rising to greet her hostess.

"Hello, Mrs. Darrow. But I am sure I don't know you," Fanny replied awkwardly.

"I am Richard's wife, Fanny. Now that we are sisters, I have come to make your acquaintance."

"Richard's married?"

"Yes, as I said."

"This is news. When?"

"A few months, Fanny."

"Where is Richard, then?" Fanny asked, once again showing her uncertainty in a social conversation that did not involve some form of banter.

"Can we not go somewhere to get some refreshment and talk?" Sally replied. "I noticed a very nice looking tea shop nearby."

"I could give you something here, Mrs. Darrow."

"But it's a lovely day. Why not go out?"

Fanny stood stiffly, not knowing how to escape from the very respectable looking stranger who smiled at her and claimed such a close relationship.

Sally stood up and took Fanny's arm easily. "Come, Fanny. Don't disappoint me. I have so looked forward to meeting Richard's sister."

"He was none too pleased with me the last time I saw him, I can tell you, Miss, Mrs. Darrow."

"I know," Sally said. "He was just surprised to see you with--with your friend. I know how much he loves you. He was peculiarly anxious that I visit you. I do so want us to be friends, and so does he."

"Well, lord bless me, Miss, Mrs., I believe you. Just looking at yourself somehow makes me feel comfortable, though I can't think why. Perhaps it is because other women don't commonly take to me."

"I am sure that is because you are so handsome. They are probably jealous."

Fanny had never had compliments or interest from anyone but men who wanted something from her. Sally's honest interest in her was an entirely new experience.

Slowly, as the two walked to the tea shop, Fanny began to feel less guarded with Richard's smiling, friendly wife. She looked so respectable, but she talked so easily and kindly, Fanny thought.

"You are not as stiff as he is, Miss, Mrs. Darrow."

"I should like it so much better if you would call me Sally."

"All right then, Sally. My brother has got himself a wife with a better temper than his own."

"But you know, Fanny, all those years that he took care of you made him feel more like a father than a brother to you. It is natural, I think, that he is a little gruff and grim with you."

Fanny laughed loudly. Heads turned toward the handsome pair as they walked along Regent Street.

Fanny put her hand up to her mouth. "Gruff and grim. I like that. That's good, Sally. Suits your husband, my brother. Excuse me. I like to have a good laugh, even if it ain't genteel. Where is he, anyhow, my brother?"

"He had business in the north."

"Not teaching school anymore?"

"Not right now."

"I'm surprised she didn't get him, Sally. Though, you're much nicer looking and younger."

A man in livery opened the brass trimmed door of the tea shop for the women as they passed inside.

"Who?" Sally asked.

"The lady who owned the school where he taught. I see he didn't tell you about her."

"You mean Miss Reade?" Sally asked.

"That's the one. You didn't know she was sweet on him, though, did you? Now, tell me the truth."

Sally blushed and answered quietly, "No I did not know she particularly liked him."

"Oh, she particularly did, Sally. Very particularly. She wasn't too bad looking, but she was older, you know, a lot older. But she had money and t he school."

"And Richard?" Sally asked.

"Oh, I'd say a look at the shop window was as close as he got to buying."

"You mean he didn't return her feelings?"

"No. He would only have taken her for her money and the position at the school. We were very poor, Sally. Yes," Fanny said almost to herself,

"He might have done it for me. My brother took good care of me. But I think he met you at some place where people were making speeches and it was all decided for him."

"Did he talk about me when we met?" Sally asked.

"Lord, for a while I couldn't get him to talk about anything else. He was afraid you wouldn't have him. He said your father was in a very good way of business and had high friends."

Sally's eyes glowed with pleasure as she heard these confidences from her husband's sister. She so respected Richard's character, now, that she could hardly think that there had been a time when she found him boyish and lacking firmness. She could also see that the topic put Fanny at ease.

"I think quite a lot of women like Richard," Sally said, thinking of Anne.

"Oh, yes," Fanny said without special enthusiasm. "I think they do."

"Were there any other particular woman who liked Richard?"

"No. Not really. He worked all the time. When he wasn't teaching, he was studying. Lord, he had a head for it. Not me. I like to laugh and dance."

"Yes, I can see you are a carefree person. It is a nice quality, Fanny." Fanny looked away and Sally realized that the compliment had made her uneasy.

"Her character is an odd combination of boldness and self-deprecation," Sally thought to herself. The quality of innocence that her uncertainty lent Fanny was striking to Sally and made her think of Anne, once again. Without considering all of her reasons for speaking Sally said, "You know, I have a young woman friend who would benefit from knowing you, Fanny."

"Lord, Sally. No one has ever said that to me before."

"What, Fanny?"

"That knowing me could be a benefit."

"I think this young girl would be better for knowing you. May I introduce you to her?"

Fanny blushed. "Well, Miss, Sally. Of course... I mean, if you truly want to."

"I just have a feeling she could be comfortable with you. I think you could be her friend and be a good influence, too."

Fanny dropped her eyes to the table. "A good influence," she murmured to herself. "Surely, Sally, Richard has told you I am not a good girl." Then she looked up defiantly. "But I'm not altogether bad, either."

Sally took Fanny's hand. "Do you love this man you are living with?"

"I don't know, honestly. I went with him at first because Richard and I never had enough money. He was nice looking. Now, I don't know."

"Will he marry you?"

"It's his father, Miss..."

"He's a terrible man," Sally plunged in suddenly.

"He's very hard on Paul, that's certain," Fanny said. "He is always making him feel that he is not fine enough for him. As if he was not good enough to be his son."

"So they do not get on well?" Sally asked.

"Not at all. He wanted Paul to marry some woman who is in a big way of business in the north. It was all for his father's business interests. You will think me terrible when I say I did not mind much. You see, I know I have Paul. He will never want anyone else as much as he wants me. And I thought if he had the money from marrying her, we would both be better off. The money would make him free of his father. He wouldn't be able to twist and bend Paul and nag him to leave me."

Fanny was silent for a moment and then added, "You're right, Sally. Paul's father is a terrible man, hard as iron."

While Fanny's adulterous speech about Paul's intention to marry a wealthy woman did shock Sally, she had long believed that poor women were subjected to almost constant harassment, injustice and degradation. The terrible circumstances of Fanny's birth and early childhood made Sally ready to forgive almost any impropriety from her. Even though Richard had protected his sister, he could not blind her to the terrible examples she saw daily in the navvy camps. Richard's immunity to the moral environment of the camps was due in large measure, Sally believed, to the fact that much of his attention and energy had been absorbed in trying to protect Fanny. Sally knew before she married Richard that the more difficult circumstances became, the more protective and helpful Richard would be. He had learned this behaviour taking care of Fanny and it had made him proof against the degenerate life of the camps.

Anne and Fanny shared a strangely innocent familiarity with vice, and it was this quality that connected the two women in Sally's mind. It was also the quality which made her feel that Fanny could help Anne. Fanny was older and better off in all ways than Anne. Yet, she would understand Anne's life much better than Sally could, herself. They would both like topics and amusements that she would find dull. On the other side, Fanny might learn to see herself as someone strong and useful to others. Sally felt, rather than thought, these things about Fanny and Anne. She often found herself understanding people without knowing how she had gained the understanding. Her intuitions were rarely wrong.

"Will you come and meet my friend?" Sally asked again.

"I really believe you could help her."

"That's a foolish idea, Sally. But I shall try. For the sake of your friendship and your kind thoughts about me."

"Then, let us go," Sally said taking Fanny's hand and standing up.

Unfortunately, a light fog had settled on the city and it had started raining while they had been inside, so they took a cab to Anne's house at Warwick Square. On the way, Sally explained to Fanny what Anne's situation was.

"The bloody brute," Fanny exclaimed with spirit when she had heard the story of Sally's last visit. "Just let him be there and I shall teach him a lesson he won't soon forget."

In the gray afternoon light, the house appeared even more run down and inhospitable, but, arm and arm with Fanny, Sally marshalled her cheerful nature, climbed the steps to the porch and tugged at the sticky door knocker.

"It is Sally, Anne. I have come to see you."

After a long pause, she heard Anne's muffled voice answer without opening the door.

"I don't think I can today, Sally."

"Are you alone?"

"Yes."

"Then open the door and we'll have a pleasant afternoon together. I have a surprise for you."

"A surprise? Sally...I,"

"Please, Anne, please don't send me away. I hoped we were better friends than that. Open this door so that I may see that you are all right. I can tell something is wrong. What is it?"

The two women on the porch heard the bolt snap. The door opened slightly and stopped. A few soft sobs could be heard through the gap in the doorway. Sally pushed open the door further. Anne, dressed in undergarments, much as she had been on Sally's last arrival, was attempting to stifle her sobs in her hands.

"My poor, darling," Sally said putting her arms around the young girl. "What has happened?"

"I feel ashamed to have you see me," Anne said between sobs without showing her face.

"What is it, my dear?" Sally asked tenderly as she lifted the girl's fingers away from her face. A large welt ran down one of the girl's cheeks. One of her eyes was black and blue and puffed shut.

"He doesn't usually hit me in the face," Anne said as if in apology.

"He doesn't does he?" Fanny said. "Ain't that bloody nice of him."

"Oh, Anne," said Sally with her arm still around the girl's shoulder, this is my sister, Fanny Darrow. I thought the two of you would like to know each other so I brought her along."

"Oh, I'm so ashamed, Sally, before you and your sister."

"There, there, dear," Fanny said, taking Anne's free hand and pressing it to her lips. "You're not the one who should be ashamed. Just let me get my hands on this brute. I should make short work of him, I promise you." Fanny reached out and lifted Anne's face into the light, "Lord, she's just a child. Who is this great bully?"

"Oh, he's very important in the City, Miss..."

"Fanny," Fanny said briskly as she and Sally piloted the girl to the parlour.

"Very important? Really? If he has a position to lose, I know we could scare the life out of him, Anne. Important gentlemen are always afraid of losing their reputation. And if that don't do it, I still have a few navvy friends who would dress him up proper, so he'd never lay a hand on you or any other woman again."

"You are so brave, Miss Fanny," Anne whimpered as the three sat down on the sofa.

Fanny jumped up from her seat. Probably no iodine in the house?"

"No. I don't think so," Anne answered.

"I'll send to the apothecary for some things," Fanny said. "We don't want any permanent marks on that fair skin of yours, Annie, do we? I'll just go out and give this order to a passing cab."

"A cab?" Sally said. "How can you trust a London cab driver with money for the apothecary?"

"I just let them think that there may be something extra in it for them when they come back, if they do as I want. Nothing improper, mind you. I just give them a little encouragement to think what they are already thinking, that's all." And she sprang away to the front door.

Sally was amazed and pleased at the way Fanny took charge of the crisis, even if her way of doing it was unconventional. The quality of independence was so unlike what she would have expected, but perhaps Fanny, like Emily had developed a high degree of self-reliance from her difficult early life.

***

By the time the cab returned with the medicines, the three women were the best of friends, sitting in the parlour drinking the tea Sally had made. Sally paid the driver and once again, Fanny showed her true colours. She picked up the various bottles that had been brought, took them to the kitchen and began mixing them together in a bowl she found. The other women and girl followed her.

"What are you doing, Fanny?" Sally asked.

"Well, if there is one thing we women know about in a navvy camp it is black eyes, cuts and bruises. This mixture, which we called, "Black Dog" will take the sting out of the cuts, bring down the swelling and keep that beautiful skin from being scarred," she said, touching Anne's cheek softly.

"Heavens, Fanny," Sally exclaimed. "How useful you are. Richard never told me any of this."

"Well, he wouldn't would he, being a man. I patched him up many times when the other boys beat him because he liked books. Even though I was very little. I dare say, he's forgotten all about it. He like's to think he's the only one who knows anything. And all he knows, comes from books. If it is not in some book somewhere, it doesn't even exist, even if you are describing his own nose."

Sally chuckled at Fanny's humorous portrayal of her husband's character, but Anne reacted very differently.

"Oh, you must not talk that way about him, Fanny," Anne said in a very serious tone. "He is so good. You can't know how good he is. But how did you know him as a boy? Will you tell me about him?"

Now, Sally realized, the truth about her relationship to Richard would come out. She had neglected to tell Fanny that she had kept her true connection with Richard secret from the girl, nor had she told her why.

"Why, I am his sister, Annie. I have known him all my life."

"But I thought Sally was your sister? Is she his sister as well?"

"Sally is his wife."

"His wife?" the girl gasped turning bright red and clapping her hands to her injured face. "Oh, dear. I am such a fool."

"No, Anne," Sally said putting her arm around the girl again. "I could see how much you liked him and I did not want that to keep us from being friends. So I was not honest with you. I am sorry. But he did ask me to come here and see you."

Anne stood with her head hanging down, her face hidden once more by her long red tresses. She was sobbing quietly. In between her sobs she said:

"I never thought...Sally...that is...I never really, truly hoped that...but just to have it to think about..."

Sally hugged the girl to her bosom.

"I am truly sorry, Anne. I do want us so to be friends."

"But you're not mad at me for..wishing, that is..you know..."

"Of course not, dear. Only, do not let the truth make you unfriendly. It was wrong of me not to tell you right away. Please accept my apology?" she finished still hugging the girl.

"You are both so good...so good to me. I can hardly believe that I have such friends," Anne said clutching Sally ever more tightly.

"Come, now, Annie," Fanny broke in. " Let me finish fixing your face. There are plenty of men in the world as good as my brother. A great deal better, too. You'll get one of your own."

"Do you think so?"

"Of course. You just need to get rid of this cad. And choose more carefully next time," Fanny said.

"But I didn't choose Bradley. He bought me."

"Worse and worse" Fanny exclaimed.

"From the house where I was.. working, you know. I'm a whore, Fanny. You should know the truth right away."

"Lots of so called respectable married ladies are also paid to sleep in their husband's beds," Fanny replied. "They're paid with position, with money, even respectability. But they're not honest about it. My man's father has called me a whore every time I've seen him. According to men, immorality is always the woman's fault—they're such helpless things. How could they fight against their natural passions?"

Here Fanny held up her hands in a gesture of puzzlement.

"Most men know nothing about real goodness," Fanny continued, "They only know they should get what they want from us for nothing," and she chuckled.

"Oh, Fanny," Sally said, "Richard said you liked to laugh, but I had no idea..."

Anne finally managed to suppress her giggling and went over to Fanny and kissed her on the cheek. "You are wonderful, Miss...Fanny."

Fanny blushed with pleasure and then said self-deprecatingly, "Yes, when the Lord made me, he threw away the moulds as soon as he saw how I came out of his kiln. Heavens I'm hungry. Let us get some food."

"Does the range work?" someone asked.

"A little," Anne replied. "About enough to boil water," and they all laughed again.

"Then, I shall go out and get us something," Sally said.

"There's a nice oyster stand not far from here. Just down on the next street. The man's son is a fisherman and brings his dad fresh oysters when it's still dark, before he goes to Billingsgate. He keeps his stall very clean," Anne said.

"Fanny, you stay with Anne. I'm certain you don't want to go out until your face is better, do you, dear?" Sally asked.

"No."

"I like lots of vinegar on my oysters, and pepper. I'll make some more tea," Fanny volunteered, and so the afternoon was arranged.

In a short time, Sally returned with oysters, hot eel soup and a beautiful red apple for each.

"Lord," Fanny said, "Here's a feast. That is lovely fruit. You didn't get that from a coster."

"Yes," Sally said. "There's a woman selling apples within sight of the oyster stand. They looked so lovely, I could not resist."

"Yes," Fanny said, examining the apples, "these are no coster's apples, I can tell you. She must get them from someone in the country."

"This is like a party," Anne said. "I have read of them, but I never was at one before. Oh, thank you both for being my friends."

After the feast was over, they all settled back comfortably on the sofa, half leaning on one and other. Then Fanny spoke up:

"Now the next order of business is to squash the insect who keeps you in this house, Annie."

"Oh, he is not so bad," the girl answered.

"Not so bad," Fanny replied, taking the girl's chin in her hand and turning her injured face to look at it. "Next time, he might kill you. I've seen women beaten to death, Annie. It ain't fun for the woman, and it makes for an ugly corpse."

"Fanny!" Sally remonstrated.

"Truth's truth, ladies. You need to get rid of this man before he hurts you even worse, Annie."

Anne looked down at her lap. Sally reached over and took her hand. "She is right, Anne. When I see what he's done, I believe now that this man could kill you. We must do something to protect you. For reasons I have no control over, I cannot bring you to my home just at this time."

"And why should she leave here, when he is the one at fault? It would be a fine place to live if he never came here." Fanny said. "Where did you say this fellow worked, Annie?"

"He is an MP. Do you know what that is? I did not."

"Better and better," Fanny said popping another oyster into her mouth. "He will be easy to tame."

"What ever do you mean, Fanny?" Sally asked.

"That lot are more worried about their reputations than a flock of nuns. If you will write a note, Sally, with a much nicer hand than I have, I'm sure, I'll show you how we'll undo this bully so that he leaves Anne alone and keeps paying her at the same time."

"You mean that I will be able to stay here without Bradley?" Anne asked.

"Yes, dear," Fanny said. "That's what I mean."

"You know, I have been so lonely here," the girl said, "that I actually used to look forward to having him come. But now that I have two such friends as the two of you, I do not care if I never see him again. Especially after this last time."

"That's right, my dear," Fanny said gaily. "Let us get rid of him for good and all and just keep his money."

"How can you do that?" Sally asked, feeling truly mystified.

"Just write down what I say, Sally. I saw pens and ink in the kitchen. I'll get them for you."

Once Sally was ready to write, Fanny began, "Dear Sir, your immoral behaviour with a certain young lady at a certain house in Warwick Square has not gone unremarked.

If the lady is not allowed to keep the house and her income for at least two years without any further harm by you, your activities shall become known to the Morning Chronicle. Personal statements by reliable people shall be offered as evidence of your immorality. The young lady, herself, has no control over these actions, so it is pointless to try to bully her. Your reappearance at the above house for any reason will immediately bring about the publication of the complete facts of your disgusting behaviour.
The house is being WATCHED." Signed, Paul Samuelson.

"Gracious," Sally said when the signatory was named. "Will he permit this?"

"He will not like it, I am sure. But it will be sent by then and I'll make certain he won't withdraw the threat."

"How?" Both women asked, echoing each other.

"If he withdraws his name, I shall withdraw from his bed." Fanny said.

"You are shocking, Fanny," Sally said, hiding her smile behind her hand.

"Yes, ain't I?" Fanny agreed. "But just watch what's going to happen. It's going to be fun to put an end to this rat and the nasty way he's treated Annie."

Chapter 34

Ardsley was a country house whose fortunate situation on lovely, rolling land and well designed interior made it far more pleasant than many more venerable and larger Somerset homes. Though small, the preserves had been lovingly looked after, and since the county was famous for its fox hunts, the superb horses of the Ardsley stables had been seen and remarked upon throughout Somersetshire.

Elspeth's father had acquired the house in early life when he first received his patrimony, which had consisted of money but no property. At Ardsley, Elspeth had grown up with rather countrified manners, having been permitted to rove the fields and orchards on horseback. Her governess had been French and so tended to stress the subjects that country was famous for: art and languages, which was congenial to Elspeth's native tastes.
She had a somewhat solitary though particularly happy girlhood. Her father was an easy-going man, who lived well, but within the income generated by his capital.

Elspeth's mother was a great sportswoman who liked nothing better than riding to hounds and enjoying a genteel sporting country life. As a young woman, Elspeth lived in her mother's shadow, having neither her trim athletic figure, nor her ease among other people, usually shrinking off by herself during social gatherings to read quietly under a tree in good weather or in the attics in bad. Consequently, in spite of her father's ability to offer a generous settlement, Elspeth was passed over by all of the most eligible men of the county. This suited Elspeth very well, and she would have been happy to live out her life among the fields, hedges and streams of her father's property. But, her mother had insisted that marriage was the only suitable state for a woman and had found Bradley when all other, more elegant young men had failed to make offers. Elspeth did not particularly like Bradley, but she did not think him any worse than the other men she had met. His greatest virtue, in her eyes, was that he was so involved with himself that, as long as she flattered him occasionally, he would leave her alone to think, dream and read. At least, this was her perception of him before her marriage. After the ceremony, however, when they began having an intimate life, her feelings changed. From their wedding night, Bradley treated her roughly, sometimes really hurting her. Fortunately, Elspeth had little physical fear and simply hit back. This cooled her husband toward her and his advances became short spasms of lust that were soon over. From then to the time that Bradley became connected with Samuelson, her life had been one of enduring and ignoring Bradley's petty hurts while giving him enough compliments to keep him from bothering her too often. His business absorbed most of his time and attention, and the pair lived well in town on what he made, and what her settlement had provided. But once Bradley became an MP and the servant of Booth and Samuelson, everything changed for her. Life was no longer a matter of endurance, but of active thought and even greater personal distance from Bradley. Then, Rowells had come along, presumably as nothing more than a way to provide an escort for her so she wouldn't complain of being neglected by her husband. The men he worked for saw Rowells as a vacuous, well-connected doll. But his extreme good looks and gentleness had worked on Elspeth until she had become truly attached to him. She had maneuvered through considerable obstacles to take Rowells to her father's pretty, quiet house in the country. The excuse had been that they were working on some parliamentary presentation for the railway king together. That eliminated her mother and anyone else from bothering them. In fact, they roved the fields of her girlhood, holding hands, kissing and making love in the tall grass and wildflowers. How often the lonely girl had walked here, dreaming of a beautiful man who would love her. The completeness with which the interlude with Rowells fulfilled those early dreams, dramatically strengthened their bond and Elspeth's determination to somehow change her life and get away from Bradley. Six months after the romantic interlude, Elspeth's mother broke her neck while hunting and Elspeth and Rowells had another opportunity to go to Ardsley together—for the funeral. They jumped at the chance. Bradley was, of course, too busy to come.

"Pressing parliamentary business, my dear," Bradley had said. But Elspeth knew there was another reason he did not want to leave the city, though she did not know the girl's name. All she cared was that Bradley's attachment made her affair with Rowells easier to have and enjoy. Both had been living parallel lives, especially separate in any of the ways that married couples were usually intimate. They went to dinner parties together when necessary. She applauded his speeches when he made them, but their late evenings were spent away from each other. Rowells' presence in Elspeth's boudoir was invisible to all the servants and to Bradley, who was pursuing his own interests with Anne and so was glad to have Elspeth's attention fully engaged.

The idyllic interval at Ardsley with Rowells was a turning point for Elspeth. It made her utterly discontented with the life she and Bradley had been living. The only thing Elspeth enjoyed about living with Bradley was the pleasure she got from helping to shape railway development through him, and here, Bradley had, at first, seemed to be a necessity. Or was he? Rowells was looked down upon by Samuelson and Booth, she knew. Changing their minds about him would be difficult, especially since her ideas and contributions to Bradley's speeches had been so effective in enhancing their opinions of him. The question was, how could she diminish Bradley and improve Rowells' standing without substantially hurting Samuelson's interests? She was musing over this very question late one evening when her husband himself provided the answer.

"Come in," she replied to the knock on her door. "I wonder what he wants at this hour?" Elspeth wondered, feeling fairly certain that only Bradley would dare disturb her so late. Bradley opened the door only enough to thrust his head and shoulders into her room.

"Am I intruding, Elspeth?"

She immediately knew that there was something troubling him. This tone of consideration was only used when he felt in great need of her help.

"Not at all, Bradley. Do come in. Would you care for anything?"

"Perhaps a brandy."

Elspeth turned to her cabinet and poured a brandy for her husband, who sat down opposite her in front of the fire. Now that he was closer to her and lit more fully by the fire, she could see real fear in his eyes. Only once had she seen him thus: when he'd made a speech on his own initiative which had turned out to be antithetical to the stand that Samuelson had been planning for him to take. Now, he sat in silence peering into his glass. Her interest was piqued by his slowness in coming to the point. He downed his drink and wiped his sweating forehead.

"Elspeth, I believe we have both been happy with our, ah, domestic arrangements?" he began. "I mean, you have what you want, do you not?"

"By and large, Bradley. Why?"

"I need to ask your ad..opinion on something rather delicate that may touch your feelings as well as our position in society and mine in Parliament."

"Really?" Elspeth managed to say blandly, though she was now alert to the fact that some truly extraordinary revelation was about to be made. For him to mention her feelings was something entirely without precedent in her experience of him.

"Yes, Elspeth." He stood up and began to pace the room. "May I smoke?"

"Of course."

He lit his cigar. "I got a letter this morning and I am entirely at a loss to know what to do about it."

"Goodness Bradley, I have never perceived you to be so inadequate a correspondent."

She could see that he was wrestling with how to say as little as possible about his letter and still get her advice.

"You have been happy with Rowells, have you not?" he asked

suddenly, breaking their unspoken pact that neither should refer directly to the other's amorous life.

"It is a little late to be jealous, Bradley," Elspeth replied, deliberately misunderstanding him. She knew that he had only brought up Rowells because whatever he had to say referred to his lover.

"No, no, Elspeth. I shouldn't presume to be jealous. We have each pursued our interests while preserving appearances. No room there for jealousy. That would rock our snug little boat. But this letter may have the same effect on us and bring us unpleasant public notice."

"Oh?"

"Yes, well, I hardly know where to begin."

"Just give me the letter, Bradley," she said, knowing full well that this was exactly what he had wanted to avoid.

"Oh, I could not, Elspeth," he sputtered. "Parliamentary business, you know. Came to me at the House, at the House. Just imagine if it had gotten into the wrong hands."

"I cannot imagine, Bradley because I do not know what is in this scandalous letter."

"Yes, yes, of course," he answered, puffing hard on his cigar as he paced more quickly.

Elspeth held out her hand. "Just give me the letter Bradley, and I promise I shall do my best to help you, no matter what is in it."

He suddenly stopped pacing in mid stride turned back to his seat at the fire and sat down heavily. He looked at her intently for a moment and then roughly pulled an envelope out of his inner coat pocket.

"I have been fortunate in my wife. You are a good friend, Elspeth," he said, "an understanding one," he finished by handing her the envelope. It contained the letter Fanny had dictated to Sally.

"Well, this seems simple enough, Bradley. Pay and keep away." Bradley got up and started pacing again. After a time he muttered, "But the expense."

"The price of a whore and the rent on the house she is living in?" Elspeth said.

"Well, yes," he said.

"How much can that be?" Elspeth asked sharply.

"I rented a house in a respectable neighbourhood. Thought it best."

"Where?"

"Warwick Square."

"So you are paying some hundreds a year in rent? For a trollop?" Elspeth said, feeling somewhat annoyed. "And this allowance that is mentioned, what does that come to?"

"Ten pounds a week." he said, his breath growing ragged.

"Good heavens, Bradley. What sort of pleasure does this woman give you for over a thousand a year? Let her go to blazes for that kind of money."

Even in the firelight, she could see that his face was a dusky red.

"And Samuelson's son, should he go to blazes, too?"

"I wager he did not even write this, Bradley. Looks like a woman's hand to me. Turn your back on her and her friends and she will do nothing. Go to Samuelson's son and ask him if he wrote it. Be incensed."

"But if certain facts came out..." he trailed off.

"What facts? Facts from a whore's imagination? Samuelson does not think much of his son. We both know that."

"But there may be other..."

"What are you not telling me, Bradley? What do you do with this girl?" She watched her husband intently while he squirmed under her questioning. "Go ahead. Tell, me. I think I can almost guess. Would you like me to make it easy for you and tell you. Yes? Very well. You beat her and then fornicate with her, don't you? Yes. I thought as much. It doesn't matter. I still think you should face this down."

"There's one other thing..."

"Yes? What else, Bradley."

"She's rather young. About twelve."

"Good lord, Bradley. If you had set out to ruin us with your tastes, you could hardly have done a better job, could you, or behaved more foolishly? Especially after the way you were helped to defeat Atherton." Elspeth finished, unable to hide the disgust in her voice.

"Yes, I have been foolish, Elspeth. But it could affect both of us, now. Possibly even Samuelson. I must decide what to do."

Elspeth let him remain in suspense for a long period of silence, before speaking. "If you want me to help you in this matter, I must have some time to think about it," Elspeth said, finally. "Let us make our plans regarding this tomorrow evening. Agreed?

He nodded.

"Then good night, husband."

Bradley nodded again and left the room.

Inwardly, Elspeth was trembling with excitement. This was the very chance she had been looking for: a way to finish Bradley without materially affecting Samuelson. First thing tomorrow she would talk to Rowells. Then she would see the great man himself.

She rose early and wrote a note to Rowells. She would meet him for lunch. Then she considered the second appointment she needed to make. She had never been to Samuelson's house. She knew it only by Bradley's description. She did not like to send a note because that was something that could be shown to Bradley. Finally, she decided to wait before contacting Samuelson. She needed more information, first. So, the next thing she did was to write to a private enquiry agent used by some of the railway speculators she knew. She made arrangements to have Warwick Square watched for signs of Bradley's lover. She wanted to know the address and the girl's name. The agent could then get proof of her age and other lurid particulars Elspeth might want.

She met Rowells at Goldini's restaurant, a small garishly decorated place with surprisingly good food. It was enough off the beaten track of MPs and City men to give them some privacy. When he entered the restaurant, Rowells looked especially handsome to her.

"Soon, my love," she thought as she watched him, "we really shall be together." As he made his way to her table, his tall commanding figure made her proud to be his lover. She held out her hand to him affectionately as he approached.

"Hello, dearest," she said in a voice too low to be heard by anyone else in the restaurant.

"What is this all about, Elspeth? I had to make all manner of excuses to get away from the chaps I usually lunch with."

"Are you complaining, my dear?"

"Of course not."

"I have some great news, Arthur," and proceeded to tell him about the conversation she had the night before with Bradley.

"After what happened to Atherton, the man who should have had his seat, you would think Bradley would be more careful with that sort of thing," he remarked after he heard her gossip. "I can certainly understand that Samuelson would not want it known that Bradley was involved in this kind of scandal. As you know, Elspeth, a lot of other directors of railway companies are MPs, but Bradley and Samuelson have convinced everyone that he is above private interests. If that came out along with this story...well, Samuelson certainly wouldn't want this kind of liability. You know how investors are, especially small ones. They won't put a penny into anything that has anything where there is a breath of scandal." He paused. "But how are you going to use all this to benefit us?"

"I have been thinking of nothing else all day," Elspeth replied. "First, I think I need some more facts." She told him about the private enquiry agent she had retained that morning. "Once we have his report," Elspeth went on, "I shall simply write to Booth and tell him I should like a confidential interview with his master. I shall not allude to the subject I wish to discuss. I shall only say that it would be in his master's best interests to see me."

"And when you do see him?" Rowells asked.

"I shall name my price——Bradley's dismissal."

"You are going to blackmail John Samuelson?" Rowells said, sounding alarmed.

"Why not? Bradley is really nothing to him. It will be a minor inconvenience to find a replacement for him. I am not asking for money or a favor. I can even play the incensed wife and take the moral high ground with him."

"Yes," Rowells said, thinking it all through. "If you put it in the form of being outraged at Bradley's immoral behaviour, but you were letting him know before you went to the press..."

"He might actually think I am doing him a favour," Elspeth said, finishing his thought. "And, I shall be certain to let him know how much I have had to do with preparing Bradley for Parliamentary battles. He will certainly not be surprised by the girl."

"I am certain Booth knows every move Bradley makes. He must know about this girl," Rowells said.

"I would have one of the very few grounds for leaving Bradley that the public would sanction. Once Bradley was detached from Samuelson, our separation would not materially affect our future." Elspeth said. "We would be free, darling. I could go to my father's and you could join me there while it all quieted down."

"What about Samuelson? Don't forget that I am still working for him."

"Why not continue? He may know about us, but he has no reason to want to destroy you in parliament. How many men will he find to work for him who come from a family as old as yours with such prestigious connections? If there is not a pressing reason to eliminate you, why should they? In fact, I believe that I'll be able to write you some speeches that will change his opinion regarding your value. I do not believe either he or Booth know how much I have had to do with shaping Bradley's public pronouncements."

"I am not good on my feet, Elspeth."

"We shall just have to anticipate the questions and rehearse your answers until you are comfortable. I know you can do it, Arthur."

"Well, I shall certainly try," he answered. "I must confess, I wouldn't mind being rid of Bradley. He is so awfully unpleasant when we are with Booth and Samuelson."

"The girl shall be cut off, of course. Bradley shall have nothing to lose once Samuelson casts him off."

"Oh, I do not think Bradley will want the details known publicly. He might be able to salvage a small income and live quietly on the Continent. If his ugly behaviour were to be fully known, he would never enter a decent home again," Rowells said.

"You're right," Elspeth said. It will that much nicer if Bradley is forced to meet the terms the girl has made. I think she is really quite reasonable," Elspeth said smiling.

"You heartily dislike him, don't you Elspeth?"

"Yes, dear, I do."

"It is odd but I cannot help feeling sorry for him," Rowells said. "He is such an obvious climber. He has no breeding or land or anything of real consequence. I suppose he hoped to get Ardsley. Or is it entailed away from you?"

"No. It will be mine one day. I shall make sure he does not get it. My father doesn't like him either."

"It is not part of the settlement?"

"No."

"It is a lovely place, Elspeth. We could be happy there. I like it much better than my old seat at Broadsmore."

"Broadsmore just needs some modern conveniences. It could be charming too and it is steeped in your family's long history."

"Well there is more work to do now before we can arrange such a pleasant future for ourselves," Rowells said.

"You're right, Arhur. As soon as I have the private enquiry agent's report, we'll be able to begin. The scandal from a press story alone should be all we would need, but the girl might be willing to help us. First, I have to learn more about her."

***

That evening, Bradley came to her room as arranged.

"Well, Elspeth?"

She could see that the problem had been plaguing him all day.

"Pay her," Bradley. "I think it is the most prudent way."

"Such a lot of money, Elspeth. It makes my blood boil to think of giving her so much. After all, she is beneath the notice of anyone who counts in society."

"Yes, but if you pay her, she will be quiet. Of that you may be sure. She has a nice house to live in for a while and a good income without any labour. What girl of her kind could say as much?"

"It just makes me angry to keep on paying..."

"Without getting what you are paying for?" Elspeth finished archly. "We must all take the sour with the sweet, Bradley. A thousand a year won't ruin us."

"So you think we shall be safe if I pay her?" He asked.

"Yes, husband. I told you. But if I were you, I should write and tell her you intend to pay. Tell her right away. Let her be certain so she will remain quiet."

"Yes, yes. I suppose you are right. If the thing is to be done, it should be done quickly. I shall go and write to her now. Good night, Elspeth."

"Good night, Bradley," she said.

Now, Elspeth thought to herself, all she would have to do would be to get the note Bradley was writing by approaching the girl and offering to pay for it. It should give them all they would need with Samuelson or anyone else. She only hoped that Bradley's temper would get the better of him when he wrote. Perhaps she could insure that the letter suited her purposes.

She rang for her maid and when she answered said, "Go to my husband and tell him I want to see him again."

A short time later," she heard Bradley's knock.

"I just wanted to suggest, Bradley, that you show me the letter you write the girl before you send it."

"I had planned to do so, but I am not finished composing it yet."

"Then perhaps we could write it together?"

"That would be most kind, Elspeth. You are a much better writer than I."

"Sit down, then, and let's get the thing done," she said. "Would you like another brandy?"

"Yes, thank you, Elspeth. That is most considerate." For his part, Bradley was delighted that his wife was taking Anne in her stride.

"You write, Bradley. I shall speak," she said.

After various drafts and emendations, the note to Anne read as follows:

"Madame, while I do not think that I owe anything to a woman who sells herself to men for a living, I shall, out of kindness, agree to pay for the house at number 12 Warwick Square for two years. The allowance, as you call it, was meant to be paid for services rendered and as I shall not be receiving those services, Anyone would conclude that I should not pay.

However, knowing that you are quite young and would otherwise be destitute, I agree to give you the amount you ask. As you grow to maturity and see more of the world, you will realize how generous I have been. Signed John Bradley.

"That should certainly make her feel the sting, Bradley," Elspeth said.

"Yes, I think it is nicely put, Elspeth."

"Now," said Elspeth to herself, "I have him." All that remained was to contact the girl and offer to buy the letter from her after she received it.

Chapter 35

Fanny's letter seemed to have the miraculous effect of making Bradley disappear from the house on Warwick Square. Once they felt sure he wasn't coming back, Fanny, Sally, Anne and Emily cleaned the house as it hadn't been cleaned in years. The place was more dirty than worn, Sally had decided. What it really needed was a good scrubbing which, during the time Anne had been living in the house, it had never had, and probably not for some years before.

For Sally, the cleaning was also a distraction from caring for Cynthia, who daily seemed to sink lower. Fisk insisted that he could not leave London and Cynthia would not leave without him. So even after Sally's original suspicions about the illness had been confirmed by a Harley Street specialist, there was little more to do but keep Cynthia resting, well-fed and quiet. The bustling tempo of house cleaning on Warwick Square gave Sally and Emily, a welcome respite from the sick room at home.

Anne knew nothing of housekeeping and it was a good opportunity for her to learn from the other women, though Fanny was not very adept either. They were all willing workers, Emily included, but it was actually Sally who took the lead and directed the work. Neither of the other women had ever even washed a sheet. First, Sally called in a workman to clean the stove and get it to draw properly. Once that was done they had hot water and it was possible to cook and clean. The stove and plumbing were actually quite modern and efficient, but tenants had neglected to clean the stove to a point where it filled the house with smoke when it was fired. It would be some years yet before the range made its appearance in ordinary kitchens. Having to heat water on coal burning stoves made the simplest household tasks onerous. The women also cleaned the water closet and got it sparkling. The whole house took four days to get up to Sally's standards of cleanliness. Only after all the really hard work was done did Sally suggest that Anne get a real maid of all work to help her keep the place in its present condition. Sally, herself, fired the old woman Bradley had hired to wait on him in the evenings.

The hard work also helped distract Sally from worrying about Richard. Spending time at Warwick Square gave Emily a chance to visit St. James park with Anne. She played once or twice in the park with other children there while the cleaning was being done. Anne reported that while Emily liked watching the boats the other children were sailing on the little lagoon, she didn't care much for the company of the youthful yachtsmen. At first she was quite enthusiastic about meeting the other children. She would ask them questions about the kind of boat they had, how much water it drew, its tonnage and so on. But none of the other children had ever even considered these details and their lack of response soon made Emily dull with them.

Sally also insisted that Anne get fully dressed every day. She began sending her on small errands around the neighbourhood. The girl needed to start living a normal life and give up the habits she had acquired living in brothels. On her side, Anne was so grateful for the time the women spent with her that she never complained of the hard work or the demands that Sally made on her.

Fanny was the first one to get bored with scrubbing and cleaning. She began to get sulky and Sally knew she would have to give her workers a holiday.

"Why don't we go over to Regents Park and see if we can get glimpses of the animals that have been brought in for the zoological garden," Sally suggested. "My father has a friend who is a keeper there. He sometimes lets us in, though the zoological garden is supposed to be reserved for famous animal specialists. Let us hope there is no eminent expert there today."

"Really," Emily said, her eyes getting big as saucers.

"I should love to see some of the animals," Anne said.

"It would be better than just doing more cleaning," Fanny responded. "It is a fine day outside."

They all agreed that the weather demanded an outing. So they got into two cabs and instructed the drivers to take them to the north edge of Regents Park where building was still being done for the zoological gardens. Unfortunately, they were told by Mr. Brock, the friend of Roderick Howard who worked at the animal hostelry, they would only be able to see a few of the inmates that day. But everyone in the party was excited to be allowed in at all. Emily walked like one in a dream. When she saw the giraffe house she let out a little scream of delight.

The huge scale of the building and its gigantic roman columns thrilled her. She looked awestruck as they all walked through the sixteen foot doors and saw the looming animals housed within.

"Sally," Emily whispered, "They must be the tallest animals in the whole world." The little girl had a special thrill when one of the huge creatures lowered its neck and head to get a better look at the human child. Then, they were escorted to the Clock Tower where the llamas lived. To Emily the Tudor style building looked rather like a castle.

"What's a llama, Sally?" the little girl asked before they got to the Tower.

"In two more minutes you shall see, little captain," Sally answered.

Anne was only slightly less awestruck by the structures and animals than Emily.

Fanny was most blasé, though she did particularly like the ravens who looked at her so wisely from their cage with their bright black eyes.

"I don't know," Fanny said as she and the ravens regarded each other. "There is something uncanny about those birds. I almost feel as if they could see into my thoughts."

"They are extremely clever beasts," Mr. Brock informed her. Fanny smiled her nicest smile at him. She could tell that the animal expert found her very fetching.

Everyone agreed it was a marvelous afternoon. Roaming in the thirty-six acres of woods that would one day constitute the London Zoo made all of them feel they were spending a day in the country. All were sorry when Mr. Brock had to escort them off the grounds, even Fanny. Emily could not stop talking about the animals.

"Giraffes' favourite leaves are the ones near the tops of the trees," the child said. "That is why they grow so tall, so they can reach them. Just think of getting all your meals from the tops of trees."

"If I were a giraffe," Anne said, "I should get dizzy and fall down. Heights make me dizzy."

Even Fanny spoke up, "Well, I liked those ravens. They know what you're thinking, I am certain. But they don't judge anyone. They just watch and know all."

"And in future they will have a whole house full of snakes," Emily said, her voice ringing with excitement.

"But not for a long while, yet," Sally added.

"But when they do, can we go to see them?" Emily asked. "Please, Sally?"

"Uggh," Fanny said, "Nasty slithery things. I don't like snakes. We dug up many of them around the camps."

"You did?" Emily said. "I wish I could dig up snakes."
And so the conversation went all the way back to the house on Warwick Square.

As they opened the front door Anne saw an envelope that the postman had slipped through the slot. She bent down to pick it up. The other women gathered around her.

"This is the first letter I have ever had," Anne said.

"Who is it from, Annie?" Fanny wanted to know. "Open it. It can't bite you."

"Yes, Anne," Sally added, "Open the letter."
Anne read Bradley's letter of capitulation with her friends reading over each of her shoulders.

"Well that settles him," Fanny said with an air of triumph.

"What does it say?" Emily wanted to know. "Who is it from?"

"It is from a very unpleasant man, Emily," Sally answered. "That is all you need to know."

"Why?"

"Because it is private."

"But you read it."

"There are some things even you do not need to know about, yet, little captain," Sally said gently but firmly. "Someday when you are bigger, and if Anne chooses, she may tell you. But not now."

"Very well," the child said, knowing she would get no more out of anyone at present. "Perhaps I could go to the park with a big pot and a spoon and dig for snakes along the side of the lagoon."

"I don't want you that near the water by yourself," Sally said.

"I shall take her," Anne said to Sally.

The girl usually acted so helpless that the idea of her caring for someone more helpless was odd. However, if Emily did fall into the water, Anne could help her. It was a good sign to Sally that Anne was ready to be responsible for Emily.

"Thank you Anne," Sally said.

When Emily had gotten her pot and spoon, Fanny and Sally were left alone.

Sally started sweeping the parlour hearth, but Fanny turned away and said, yawning. "I am going to take a nap. Paul was over last night. We had a row about the letter I signed his name to, but he'll say nothing."

"So you did get your way," Sally said, obviously curious.

"Of course."

"Do you have some kind of enchantment I could use with Richard. I am not good at debating with him."

"Of course, not, dearie. He's a man. There's only one place to settle arguments with him."

"Where? What do you mean?"

"In bed, Sally. That's how to settle a man."

Sally blushed deeply.

"There's nothing to be ashamed of," Fanny said. "It's true. If you..." Fanny's sentence was interrupted by the thump of the doorknocker. She stopped speaking and walked toward the door. "I shall see who it is."

When Fanny opened the door she was very surprised to see a very smartly dressed woman in her thirties, who regarded her with a look of surprise.

"Oh," the woman said. "You are not what I expected."

"And who were you expecting?"

"I believe her name is Anne. Quite a young person, I understand."

"And who are you, miss?" Fanny asked.

"May I come in?"

"I suppose," Fanny replied unenthusiastically.

"Who is it, Fanny?" Sally called from the other room.

"I think I can guess," Fanny said, her eyes held appraisingly on the woman, "but I am not certain, Sally."

Sally stepped into the hallway from the parlour.

"You are definitely not what I expected," the stranger commented when she saw Sally.

"Please be so good as to state your business, madame," Sally said.

"I am looking for a very young person named, Anne," the woman said. "My business with her is confidential. Can you direct me to her?"

"You are correct, madame, in stating that Anne is very young. We are her confidential friends, however, and you shall tell us what business you want to transact with her or you shall not see her."

"I see. Are you in this with her?"

"What do you mean, miss?" Fanny said with an edge in her voice. "We are respectable women who are looking after a very sad young girl. Now, who are you and what is your business?"

"My name does not matter. But I believe that one of you, or this Anne, recently sent a letter to Mr. Bradley and received one back from him. Is this not so?"

"I don't know your game, dearie," Fanny said, pulling the door open, "but we don't talk to people who don't give their names."

"I heartily agree," said Sally.

The woman fidgeted with her purse and looked put out but finally said, "Very well. My name is Elspeth Bradley."

"Ha," Fanny exclaimed. "The wife. You have quite a husband, Mrs. The terms offered were generous. Just what is it you want?"

"Oh, I quite agree that the terms were generous," the woman said. "When I dug all the facts out of Bradley, I told him that very thing."

"Then why are you here?" Sally asked

"I--ah--want to buy something from Anne."

"And what is that?" Fanny asked. "What could our friend have that you want to pay for?"

This difficult cross-questioning was not what Elspeth had expected when she set out to get what she wanted from Anne. She felt in a very false position with the other women who knew her only as Bradley's wife. Her vanity was pricked and she wanted to correct what she felt was a misapprehension. That was what prompted her next remark.

"You see," she said, "I want to be rid of him, too."

"The letter," Fanny cried. "You want the letter he wrote. It will prove his scandalous behaviour."

Elspeth found it a great trial to be inspected by the two women, but she had no choice. She wanted Bradley's letter desperately.

"Yes," she said softly. "I want the letter."

"What exactly are you going to do with it?" Sally asked. "I would ask

Anne not to give it to you without knowing that."

"I agree to that," Elspeth said shrugging.

"And," said Fanny "How much are you willing to pay for this valuable document?"

"Fanny!" Sally exclaimed, sounding shocked.

"Our young friend needs a start in life," Fanny said. "Money can make all the difference. Believe me, I know." She turned back to Elspeth.

"So how much will you pay?"

Sally could see the woman was feeling pressed by Fanny.

"Would you care for some tea?" Sally asked suddenly. "I think we could all do better over a cup of tea."

"Yes, thank you," Elspeth answered, glad to have even a brief respite.

"Do come into the parlour, in that case," Fanny said leading the way while Sally went through to the kitchen.

When they had sat down, Fanny and Elspeth regarded each other warily.

"Who exactly are you, Miss?" Elspeth asked. "And how do you and your friend come to be the protectors of my husband's former mistress?"

"I do not know if that creature, your husband, treats you in any of the ways he has treated poor Anne. If so, you have our sympathy. But he has left this girl cut, bruised and broken. I treated the wounds myself. They are some of the worst injuries I have seen inflicted by a man on a woman. When I think of it, I feel that hanging is too good for him."

"I think I can understand your feelings," Elspeth said quietly. "He can be quite cruel. But he has never treated me as you describe. I have only really known--known about this kind of behaviour when he came to me with Anne's letter and asked me what he should do."

"He came to you and asked for your help? Good lord, nothing is too low for him. How can you live under the same roof with him?"

"I wish to leave his roof," Elspeth answered. "I want to be rid of him for good and all."

"Well," said Fanny, "at least we are all agreed on his character, or lack of it."

As Sally entered the room with the tea tray, Elspeth said, "Then you will help me get the letter?"

"She is trying to get away from the monster," Fanny said to Sally. "That's why she wants the letter he wrote to Anne."

"Does it prove anything, legally?" Sally asked.

"I do not know," Elspeth replied. "But it would certainly give me a very strong hand to leave his house under conditions advantageous to me. If I threatened to make it public..."

"But that would also call public attention to Anne in the worst possible way," Sally said.

"Let us deal with that after the question of money," Fanny said, firmly. "How much money Anne has will have a good deal to do with repairing any public scandal, should it arise. So I want to know what you will offer for the letter."

"Fifty pounds."

Fanny shook her head. "Not nearly enough after what the girl has suffered."

"And are you going to answer for her?" Elspeth asked.

"Yes," Sally said. "I really think we must."

"And get part of it for yourselves?"

Fanny stood up and glared at Elspeth. There was murder in her eyes. She was furious.

"We want this poor girl," Fanny said, "to have a chance in life. The clothes on your back are worth five times the price you name. Her future is everything. If it weren't, I'd pull that monster into the gutter for the amusement alone." Fanny's rage was far too palpable for the other woman to doubt it. She knew she would have to make terms with her, and that she knew that she faced a shrewd, worldly woman instead of the young girl she had thought she would find.

"Five hundred," Elspeth said, with a slight breathiness in her voice as she named the amount. She and Rowells together could get the money.

"Not a penny less than two-thousands," Fanny snapped.

"But I do not have that kind of sum available," Elspeth protested.

"You can get it," Fanny said, "I am certain. I know the signs of a woman who spends a fortune on herself and her household. You will just have to tell cook she'll have to stop shopping at Fortnum's for a year or two. That is all the harm you'll come to."

Elspeth stood up suddenly as though about to leave. "I shall have to think about it."

"If you leave here without writing a cheque, the letter will go to the Morning Chronicle," Fanny said in a voice hard as flint.

"Fanny!" Sally gasped. "Don't be so unyielding."

"You think because she is smooth and soft that I am being hard, Sally. But I can see that this woman will not suffer long for two thousands. For Anne, it could change everything in her life. Poor child."

Elspeth was breathing quickly. Her bosom heaving under her dress.

"So you are not going to give me any quarter?"

"No, I shall not," Fanny answered. "You only came here to get something you wanted. You thought nothing of the girl, your husband was ruining. You are a woman who pretends to be a gentlewoman. If you truly were that, you would have started by asking us what the girl needed to recover from your husband's monstrous behaviour."

While Fanny spoke, the colour rose in Elspeth's cheeks. She had to admit to herself that the handsome, fiery girl was right. She had not thought of her husband's child-mistress at all, only of her own freedom.

"Well?" Fanny said sharply.

"Very well. What you say is true. I do feel ashamed of not being concerned for the girl. How old is she, really?"

"About twelve, we believe. She is not certain, herself," Sally replied.

"I must get away from him, quickly," Elspeth said to herself as she drew out her cheque book.

"I shall give you as much as I can out of my private funds and the balance I shall post to you tomorrow? Is that all right?"

"This draft shall not be cashed," Fanny said, "until the rest arrives. When it does I shall send you the letter. If it does not..."

"No. You were right. I can get it. You shall have it tomorrow. You have reminded me of the decency which I owe myself. Goodbye. Sally escorted the guest to the door. When she returned to the parlour, Fanny was holding the draft in her hands.

"It is good, I am certain," she said.

The two women hugged each other.

"At least now," Sally said, "poor little Anne will have some sort of start in life."

"Yes. It is a tidy little fortune," Fanny agreed. "And money is the one thing that can repair a woman's reputation."

Chapter 36

During the weeks whilst Fisk watched Simon and listened to him lay his plans for destroying the London Gas Company and a large part of the City, Cynthia grew worse. In spite of Sally's best efforts to feed her well and amuse her, she became weaker and weaker. As Fisk watched her face become thinner and thinner, he, too, began to fear that the worst might not be far off.

"I only ever wanted to help you, Fisk," Cynthia said, her large eyes looking larger than ever in her wasted face. "And to see an angel. Not to burden you."

"It is no burden, dear woman. I will see you get the best care, or I shall be constantly worried and affrighted."

"All right, then," she said in a soft, sighing voice. "I shall do whatever you want. Now, I should like to sleep some more." With that, she turned over on the day bed that Sally had made up for her in the sitting room. The room had been made as pleasant as possible for her with large bouquets of fresh flowers that Fisk brought every morning from Covent Garden.

"Fisk," Cynthia said one morning as she looked around her colourful, sweet smelling room, "these blooms are too expensive. You are spending too much money."

"They are not just for you, my dear, They are also for Sally who has been so kind to us."

"Yes, she is very kind. What a lovely woman. I am so sorry I shall not see her husband again."

"Why shall you not?" Fisk asked.

Cynthia just sighed and turned to the wall.

Fisk leaned over her and stroked her hot forehead.

"Is there anything you would like, dearest?" he asked.

Cynthia turned back to him and with the ghost of a smile on her lips said, "I told you before, Fisk, I should like to see an angel. Perhaps if you prayed very hard to Gabriel, he or one of his brethren would come to me."

"Let us do so together, dearest," he said sitting down next to her and taking her hand.

He bent his head and Cynthia closed her eyes. Silently, they each prayed that an angel of the Lord would visit Cynthia.

Later that evening, when Fisk had gone out to watch over Simon's mad venture, and Sally was sewing at church, Fanny came to sit at the sick bed. Emily was asleep in her room so the two women were alone. "Why do you long so to see an angel, Cynthia?" Fanny asked.

"Because, I have been present when Fisk is talking with them. During a few of those times, I felt I could sense their presence, too. So I have some direct experience of
them, even if my faith is weak in other ways."

"What an extraordinary thing," Fanny said, "To think of angels visiting that way with Fisk, someone I have known since I was quite small."

"Did he admire you very much, Fanny?" Cynthia asked suddenly. The beautiful girl blushed all the way down her arms.

"Did he?" Cynthia persisted.

"We never spoke of it," Fanny finally said. "He was my brother's friend. My brother was like a father to me then. So I didn't think of it."

"And he never said anything? He never made any kind of declaration?"

"No. Probably for the same reason. To him, I was just a little girl."

"But still, you knew, did you not?" Cynthia pressed.

Fanny looked at her hands lying passively in her lap for a long time and then reached over and took one of Cynthia's hands in hers.

"I suppose I had some idea. But I paid no real attention to it. It seemed a commonplace."

"You mean because of all the other men who admired you?"

This time Fanny's face turned crimson. She bit her lip for a moment before answering. "I suppose I have been used to men admiring me, yes. That is probably a great sin. Isn't it?"

"No. I don't think so. You do not seek admiration. It comes of itself."

"And what about Fisk, now? Do you like him, now?"

"Good Lord, Cynthia. How can you ask me that? I like him very well as, as a friend."

"And nothing more?"

"Cynthia! What are you trying to get me to confess?"

"Whatever is in your heart, dear Fanny."

Fanny gripped Cynthia's hand more tightly and the sick woman squeezed back.

Fanny looked down at her lap when she replied, "I always thought Fisk a very kindly, warmhearted man whom I could trust entirely, which is something I can say about no other man I know, except my brother. And I have always thought him very nice and manly looking. There, have I said enough?" she asked looking over at Cynthia.

"Fanny, when I am gone..."

"No, do not talk so," Fanny protested. "I shall not permit it."

"Yes, I shall speak. When I am gone, do you think you could love him?"

"I have never thought it. I have been living with Paul, who is very different. He looks like more and more of a boy to me, now. As you know, I've seen little of him in recent weeks."

"I only ask you to consider it, Fanny—when I am gone. I feel certain Fisk would marry you."

"Do not speak so. It is wrong."

"No. It is not wrong. If Gabriel comes to me, I shall be satisfied."

"Gabriel the Archangel?" Fanny said, sounding rather shocked.

"Yes. He talks with Fisk often."

"Goodness. I do not know if I could get used to such miracles going on in my parlour. It is rather a droll thought in some ways," she said with a chuckle. "I mean, I am such a lover of laughter and lightheartedness. For someone like that to have an Archangel in her parlour..." and she laughed.

"Fisk says that the angels love to laugh. He says that laughter is holier than solemn prayer."

"Really?"

"Yes. I am certain that your smiling goodness and mirth would be much appreciated by the heavenly hosts."

"Oh, but I am not a good girl," Fanny said, looking downcast. "You know that. Why would someone like Fisk or such beings as angels want to know me at all?"

"In heaven, Fanny, it is the heart that counts. Fisk has often said so. You are naturally good and honest without premeditation. Goodness flows from you without thought or calculation."

"I am certain you credit me with too much, Cynthia. No one has ever talked of me this way."

"That is why I am doing so, now. I want you to know that you are worthy of every good thing. Including, Fisk."

"I promise you, Cynthia, from the bottom of my heart, if you are not here, I shall look after him. He shall not be alone. More than that I cannot say."

"What if Paul should come back?" Cynthia asked.

"I do not think it will have much effect on me now, at all," Fanny said. "I know he lusts after me, but I do not think he loves me. The more I am around good friends, like you and Sally and," she hesitated for a moment, "Fisk, the less I am interested in him. I suppose, I shall have to find a new place to live."

The sick woman pushed herself up from the pillows so that she could plant a tender kiss on Fanny's glowing cheek."

"God bless, you, Fanny. I am so glad we have been able to talk like this. Don't forget your promise."

"Well I certainly hope and believe you shall be here, because now we are friends and I should miss you terribly. Before I met Sally, I had never had any women friends. It is so wonderful to have such dear ones as you and her, and poor little Anne."

"How is Anne, now?" Cynthia asked."Sally was telling me her terrible story last night. Is she growing used to company and a more regular life?" Cynthia asked. Then the talk flowed away into the present and away from the darker current of the future. Presently, both women fell asleep, hand in hand, Fanny's head resting on the side of the divan where Cynthia lay.

* * *

In spite of Cynthia's worsening condition, Fisk felt he had to spend more and more time with Simon. The younger man's increasing agitation convinced the carpenter that the time when Simon would attempt to detonate the gas works was not far off. This enforced separation from Cynthia at a time when he would have liked to be even closer to her, he accepted as part of his atonement for having preached violence as a way to gain freedom. At the very moments when Cynthia and Fanny were plotting his matrimonial future, Fisk was striding, as rapidly as possible, through a dense fog which hung over the city and imparted a blurry, dream-like appearance to the most ordinary objects and streets.

"Tonight," he thought, "would be a good time for the realization of Simon's plans." The streets were obscure, and the yard at the works would be even darker. It would be less likely that any of the men who were not in Simon's pay would see what Simon and Fisk would need to do to cause a large explosion.

For three weeks, Fisk had watched the plant where coal gas was manufactured with Simon, learning the movements of the men inside and the schedule of the constable on the beat. He knew that Simon's plan required that they would first shut off the outlet valves from the purifier boxes, which were filled with crushed limestone. As the impure gas passed through them, the limestone took out the impurities and made the gas safer. But if the outlet valves were closed the pressure of the gas would build up inside the purifiers and cause an explosion. Before the explosion was triggered, Simon wanted at least two carts packed with drip barrels of naphtha pushed between the purifiers and the tanks which held the purified gas. Naphtha had a low flammability but would burn very hot and cause a fire difficult to extinguish. Simon would add to the explosion with black powder to make certain that the accessory gas pipe and the storage tanks would be punctured, so that the naphtha fire would ignite the gas lines all around the plant.

Simon believed that a large part of the City would go up in the ensuing conflagration. He had estimated that it would take two hours and twenty-eight minutes for the pressure to cause an explosion. The black powder would be detonated by the explosion. The experience of the last three weeks had shown that the men who came on at midnight, were quite punctual in their movements and usually worked twelve-hour shifts. The three men Simon had bribed were only too glad to take his money. They were dissatisfied with their working conditions and wages and felt that the gas company management had no regard for them. One of the men in Simon's pay, a very bad man, would look for any excuse to do away with anyone who might interrupt them. Fisk was supposed to bring the carts in between the tanks while Simon closed the outlet valves and began monitoring them. There should be plenty of time for the five of them to get away before the pressure built up and the works exploded. Of course, all the other men in the works would die in the explosion and fire. Fisk had at least convinced Simon that immolating themselves in the fire was sinful and wrong, and served no purpose, so the younger man had agreed that they would all flee together. Fisk also pointed out that if any of the men in their pay got wind of Simon's suicidal intention, they would rebel. After several lengthy disputes, Simon had finally agreed not to die in the gas works.

"Now all I have to do," Fisk thought as he walked toward the river in the heavy fog, "is understand how I shall stop four determined men from carrying out their horrible intention. Gabriel will have to help. There is no other way."

During the weeks he watched Simon's preparations, Fisk had thought of going to the police but felt that stopping Simon was his responsibility. He also doubted if the police would listen to someone with his reputation as an incendiary. He couldn't take that chance. Fisk knew it was Simon's belief that as soon as the explosion took place, the one-thousand year epoch of the New Jerusalem would begin. Where he had gotten this idea, or why he believed the New Jerusalem would last one-thousand years, Fisk knew not. To have asked, would have been to court danger. It was the type of question that Simon seemed to feel was disloyal. He seemed to need to feel that he and he alone knew how things were to be done. His state of mind seemed extremely unstable to the carpenter. Like the gas works, Simon could blow up without a moment's notice.

When Fisk turned into grimy Dorset Street, which ran from Salisbury Square all the way to the river, and lay within a stone's throw of Blackfriars Bridge, he knew his goal was near. The fenced grounds of the London Gas Works was bordered by the ugly street on one side and solid gray stone warehouses on the other, but the night was so thick that he could not even see the brick fence which ran around the entire perimeter of the huddle of brick buildings which composed the gas works. The closer he got to the river, the heavier the fog became until he was groping his way through the air, waving his hands in the air in front of him like a blind man. Finally, he banged his palms on the iron bars of the single gate which pierced the fence surrounding the gas works. He stood for a few moments and waited. Everything was shrouded in the thick fog. The effect was one of standing in the middle of a smoky nothingness. He felt so separated from the tangible world that he wondered if what he saw was entirely physical or whether Simon's own troubled mind was adding to the obscurity that curtained him on all sides.

"Fisk," he heard Simon's sibilant rendering of his name come at him from the impossible direction of the fence directly ahead of him, as though Simon were standing inside the perimeter.

"Simon?" he whispered. "Where are you?"

"Inside, Fisk. Tonight is the night. The guard is dead and our men are watching the yard. We have two carts of naphtha ready to push into place. I was waiting for your strong back. The shift lasts twelve hours so we have hours to work without interruption. Walk to your right along the fence and you'll find the open gate."

Fisk felt a stab of regret when he heard about the guard. He had arrived too late to save the man. He felt his way along the fence and in through the open gate. Then he felt Simon's arm across his shoulder.

"Well done, Fisk. Is this not perfect?"

"I can barely even see the buildings let alone tell which building the storage tanks are in, the fog is so thick," Fisk answered.

"The big mass over there are the storage tanks. The big building on our left that we're passing now houses the retorts where the gas is distilled. Those are the purifying tanks of lime and water that remove the sulphur. That's where you and I shall begin working. The space between the tanks is where you will have to place naphtha carts. You see, the dark alley over there. You know where everything is. We've been over it often enough. You are just disoriented by the fog. Follow me."

The difference in their ability to see their way through the fog told Fisk that at least part of the thick atmosphere was produced by Simon's own mind. Fisk perceived a physical result of Simon's psychic condition. The younger man's darkened thoughts and distorted ideas lay on Fisk like a suffocating curtain. Simon had only the fog that blocked his physical sight. It gave the younger man a great advantage in moving through the gas works' yard.

The odour of ammonia was very strong as they passed the building which held the retorts. In spite of the clay seals, some of the fierce odour seeped out from the big chambers where the coal was distilled and the ammonia and coke were deposited by the distillation process. The fumes burned Fisk's nostrils, searing them as if someone held an open flame under his nose. The chemicals given off from the process of coal distillation released some of the worst, the most caustic and dangerous pollution to be found anywhere in London. The grip of the deadly toxins seized Fisk by the throat. How, he wondered, would he stop Simon without hurting him. This was the moment he had put off for weeks. It had already cost the life of the guard. He felt responsible for the deadly avocation of the younger man and so was anxious for him not to come to harm, but now, he really had to be stopped. What would happen if a huge explosion spread this poison over the city? His own seared nose and throat showed him how deadly Simon's plan was. He could not let his concern for Simon stay his hand any longer. Simon led the way into the black notch between the purifiers. Fisk followed him and was surprised to find that he could actually see better in the narrow space. Perhaps the fog was shut out by the tanks. He saw Simon stop beside two large valves, the outlet valves. He picked up a twenty pound hammer from the shadows. Fisk realized that he was not simply going to close the valves, he was going to damaged them so they could not be opened. If Fisk allowed this to happen, the very least damage would be an explosion from the tanks when the pressure became too great. This was the point where Simon had to be stopped. As the saboteur lifted the hammer, Fisk leapt on his back. Even though the carpenter was the larger man, Simon threw him off. The young man was in some sort of trance. His excitement was at fever pitch.

"I thought you might lose heart at the end, Fisk. That's why I decided to break the valves."

"Simon, I do not want to hurt you, but I shall if you try to damage the valves."

"Nonsense, Fisk. This is just a momentary fear. All men are afraid of death. Even you. Even I feel some fear. But perhaps it is not fear. I am the chosen one. Perhaps it is just anticipation."

"Simon, I will warn you no more. Put down the hammer, or I shall take it from you."

An eerie, ringing laugh issued from the young man. "You cannot, Fisk. No one can challenge while I fulfill my appointed task." And the mad laughter echoed off of the huge tanks.

When Fisk got close to Simon, he reached suddenly for the hammer and almost tore it from the young man's grasp."

"No," Simon shrieked. "You can't do this."

Simon turned away and ran farther into the dark narrow slit between the tanks. Fisk looked at the valves closely, they were jammed shut and looked bent. If they remained that way, the explosion would be inevitable. But if there was no black powder to augment the blast, the danger of blowing the huge storage tanks of purified gas would be diminished.

A sound from the other side of the tanks alerted him to someone else's presence. A moment later he saw a wagon loaded with barrels of naphtha being pulled next to the purifiers. Fisk jumped on the man who was pulling it and found that it was not Simon but one of his paid helpers. The man wheeled around and was holding something shiny in his hand. Though he couldn't see it, Fisk assumed it was a knife. The man lunged, Fisk dodged and hit him hard with the twenty pound hammer he had wrenched from Simon's grasp. The man cried out but did not get up again. Fisk ran to the largest building and opened the door. He had to warn the other men in the works. Standing in the doorway he yelled, "The outlet valves on the purifiers have been hammered shut. Everyone must leave the works." Before anyone could question him, Fisk ran into the yard to get rid of the black powder which was supposed to amplify the explosion and ignite the underground mains. That would be the night's most spectacular damage. The gas mains ran like knotted roots for many blocks around the gas works. If they were ignited by the naphtha, there was no telling how much of the City and how many lives would be lost. It would make the Great Fire look like a candle. He turned back to the dark notch between the purifiers. Someone had already pulled a wagon-load of naphtha into position. A dark figure stood between Fisk and the black powder. It had a long length of pipe in its hands.

"You, there," Fisk saluted the man, "If you don't let me pass you'll have the blood of countless people on your head. Stand aside." The figure made no move.

"If you don't stand aside, I shall use deadly force," Fisk said. "Do you really want so many people to die?"

"City swells, that's all who's dying. Why should I care? I got paid to torch 'em. Can't think of a job more to my liking. And I'll be happy to break your head, too, you narc."

Just as Fisk was about to rush the man, he felt someone slam into him from behind. In a matter of seconds he knew it was Simon.

"Fisk," Simon hissed in his ear. "I knew you were a yellow dog. You aren't suited for this great task, so I'm going to kill you. You will not see the New Jerusalem." and he drew a revolver from his hip pocket.

Fisk could hear men emptying out of the main building into the yard. But would they run for the gate and ignore the alley between the purifiers? He could just make out Simon, arm extended, pointing the gun at him. A split second later there was a loud report and a cry. For a moment, Fisk did not know what had happened. He only knew he did not seem wounded. The air around him cleared slightly and he was able to see Simon lying on the ground. He reached him in three running steps and knelt down beside him. His hand and face was shattered. The gun was nothing more than a lump of exploded metal. It had misfired, killing Simon.

"Dear Lord," Fisk said out loud, "release him from all fear and pain, now. Take him into the Heavenly City. Free him from his own darkness. Have mercy on me that I should have had any part in bringing him to this. Love him in paradise and quiet all his terrible fears." He prayed for some moments, kneeling in silence near the purifiers.

Then, remembering the black powder, he ducked around the tanks and began searching for the keg and long fuse. It had been moved! He turned his head back and forth, peering into the darkness and finally glimpsed a flicker of light in the darkest corner at the far end of the gas storage tanks. The fuse must have been lit before Simon came to attack him. He raced around the tanks. It could blow at any second. Every moment, as he was running toward the tanks, he dreaded the explosion that he was certain would come. He reached the tanks, threw himself on the sparks and saw no other light. He lay panting on the ground as men shouted nearby in the yard. Then, a strange glow like moonlight seemed to wash the alley where the purifiers stood. A tall figure in white stood in front of him. Gabriel had descended once more.

"His soul shall be cared for. Now you must leave this place. I am well pleased with you," was all the luminous figure said before fading away.

Fisk crossed the gas works yard where many men were still running around in confusion. He slipped out of the gates before anyone was aware that an outsider had been in the yard.

Exhausted, walking with a dragging step, the carpenter returned to Sally's lodgings to see how Cynthia was. Now, he would be able to spend more time with her. They could leave London. He thought about nothing but Cynthia all the way to Sally's. His friends met him at the door with solemn faces.

When he saw the two women Fisk said, "She is worse?"
Sally answered in the plainest terms, "She is dying."

Fisk quickly entered the flower strewn sick room. Cynthia, barely conscious, looked up at him, her eyes rolling in her head. Her brow was wet with perspiration.

"Fisk," she said in a reedy, gasping whisper, "He hasn't come, yet. Please, please beg him to come. I should not be frightened, then."

Fisk knelt down next to the bed. "Dearest," he murmured.

"Please ask him, now. I feel he'll come if you only ask him, now. Hurry, all is growing dark," she finished breathlessly.

"Very well, dearest. I have just seen him, myself. He is near. I know." Sally and Fanny watched from the door of the room. Both women's cheeks were wet with tears.

"Dearest Lord," Fisk prayed out loud, "whose angels have visited me unbidden, I beg that you send the great Gabriel now to this deserving woman who craves the comfort of his presence. Please, Gabriel, come now and comfort her."

A sob made the last word catch in his throat and he said no more. He remained, head bent, hands clasped on the pillow of the dying woman for what seemed an eternal, silent moment. Then, to Fisk's eyes, the gas lamp seemed to flare into a greater brightness, but instead of dying down again as a lamp would, the brightness grew and grew. There was light everywhere. The walls of the room disappeared and Fisk could see Cynthia in the arms of the great winged figure of Gabriel as he lifted her up into an even more brilliant light.

"I see him. I see him, Fisk," she murmured. "Thank you." Then the brightness ceased, as did Cynthia's breath.

Chapter 37

"With one phrase," Pamela said to her solicitor, "you tell me we need more money if we are to go forward with my father's plans, but with the next, you tell me we have not enough money. Your solution is to use John Samuelson's money. Mine is to issue stock and sell it on the 'Change. My father was known and I'm certain the stock will do well."

"I have no doubt, the stock will sell," Barnes said. "But I must advise against that alternative. With Samuelson we have a wealthy rascal who understands our business and has sufficient funds for our purposes. With a joint stock company, we don't know who or what we shall have as partners, nor do we know how deep their pockets will be if we have future needs. What good will it do for the company to make calls on men who may have no cash? We have no way of knowing what our real resources will be. Let me write to Samuelson. I shall make it clear that marriage is not part of the transaction."

"No. I feel sure we shall do well with a joint stock company," Pamela said. She had not told Barnes that Samuelson would soon be visiting Blackdale. "Form the company and have the stock issued. At one point you were willing to allow Mr. Samuelson a large proportion of the partnership," Pamela pointed out.

"Yes. But that was because it was a partnership. Both sides had specific expectations and commitments. But this wholesale cutting up of Blackwood Holdings and selling the bits to unknown people is something quite different. "

"Those are my desires, Mr. Barnes."

Mr. Barnes gave her his stiffest bow.

"I have done my best. Good day, Miss Blackwood."

He turned and left the library at Blackdale where the two had been meeting over the future of Blackwood Holdings.

Pamela remained in the library, looked out over the moors and dreamed away the long, gray afternoon as she used to do before she had committed herself to music. The rain kept up all day and it was not until early evening that the dark sky broke open into a beautiful orange sunset.

In just three days, she and Hans Bruckner would play in Manchester. They had been writing to each other two and three times a day with thoughts about the concert. They had decided jointly that if an encore was called for, they would play a Schubert duet.

Ever since her appearance at Rivington Hall, Pamela had felt a strange kind of excitement. She described it to herself by saying that she wanted to begin her new life. The old things, even the dear ones, no longer held her. She was eager to hear the applause in Manchester, a tribute which she knew was bound to be offered. But that was just the starting point. She wanted to be on the road, going from town to town with Hans Bruckner, daring the weather, the roads and whatever adventures might befall. She thought about Barnes. What if he were right and Blackwood Holdings dissolved? Would she be miserable if the worst happened and they lost the companies and her money? Or at least a large part of it? No, she realized. Once, these things had meant everything. Now, the luxuries were pleasant but not at all important. She had made peace with her father's memory by setting aside money for Emily's education and even a marriage settlement for the little girl. So, everything now was connected with music and the life she imagined for herself. The only exception to this sense of wholeness were the persistent dreams about Samuelson. Why, she wondered? She had a very passionate regard for Hans, though nothing improper had happened between them. In a real sense, Hans had given her everything she wanted. So why have such strange, stirring dreams about another man, a dangerous man, a man who was to dine at Blackdale tomorrow evening?

It had not taken the railway king long to act on Pamela's remark that she would be glad to welcome Samuelson at Blackdale as a friend of her father's. Why had she said it? she wondered as she watched the sky break open into brilliant orange rays. She certainly did not want to encourage him. Especially now, with Barnes talking of raising money from him again. There was something about his presence that affected her strongly. It was almost as if she had asked him in order to find out what lay at the bottom of his power to affect her. Well, in any case, the die was cast and he was coming. She would just have to see what she thought of her own behaviour when he came. The rain continued all day and all day following. So, Samuelson arrived in the midst of an autumnal gale, his waterproof streaming as he stood in the front hall until the footman took it from him. He had just gotten off his wet things when Pamela appeared in the hall, wearing the same gown she'd worn on the night of the concert.

"Well I can see we won't go for a walk in your park on a day like this," Samuelson remarked.

Without knowing why Pamela said, " One can always dress for the weather, as you did when you rode here."

"And you would enjoy such a wet turn in your own woods?"

he asked.

She had been inside for two days. Why not go out and meet the weather as she had often done before?

"Yes, I believe I would. I'll go and change my dress. Can I have something brought while you wait?" she asked.

"No. I shall just wait."

She turned, went back to her room and took out an old riding jacket. She had a pair of men's breeches that she liked to wear when there was no one around to see. Somehow, she didn't mind how Samuelson saw her. Perhaps it was because she felt his own indifference to appearances. She emerged from her room dressed like a country game keeper, her hair tucked into a snug fitting riding hat. Jason was standing in the hall near Samuelson with his waterproof and hers.

"I am prepared for anything, now," she said.

"I would not have taken you for someone so rough and ready," he said. "Especially after having just seen you in that beautiful gown."

"I think I actually like these clothes best," she said as they passed out into the wet blustery weather.

The groom was waiting with their horses as they stepped from under the protection of the porches. As they rode down the driveway, little water fell on them because of the tenacity of the leathery oak leaves which still clung to the branches of the venerable trees that had been saved when the house was built.

"Now, you shall really see Blackdale," she called over her shoulder. She was surprised at how easy she felt with him, in spite of her odd feelings and dreams. Being with Hans felt more strained, as if his sensitivity made it necessary for each thing she said and did to be perfect, like her playing. She urged her horse into a gallop and turned off the main drive onto one of the trails that criss- crossed Blackdale's considerable acreage. She gave herself up to the wind and droplets of water hitting her face, the motion of the horse and her own feeling of youth and strength. She was not surprised that Samuelson easily kept pace with her on his huge red stallion. He, too, seemed to like the wildness of the blustery weather. As long as he did not get to close to her, she felt surprisingly easy in his company.

After a long gallop, they came out to a high ridge overlooking the moors. Here she reined in her horse. Samuelson drew alongside of her.

"Everything you see down into the valley," she said, moving her arm across the horizon is part of Blackdale."

"Do you love it much?" he asked.

"Well, yes, of course. I grew up here. My father built it. But even so, if I were a stranger," she said, "I should love the moors. Only in my worst, most childish moments did I crave a more superficial entertainment away from here."

Her eyes were shining with pleasure as she spoke. Her cheeks were flushed with exercise and a few locks of her red-gold hair had slipped from under her hat.

The big man leaned across the horses and suddenly kissed her on the cheek.

"I can't say I am sorry for that," he said. "because I am not. You looked so fresh and beautiful in that moment that I am not responsible for my lack of restraint." He was smiling at her.

Pamela met his eyes with a glance and then looked down. She did not feel embarrassed or angry. She felt drawn to the man instead, the same pull she had felt that day in the library, as if there were a maelstrom of energy around him that drew in people when he was near. Almost before she finished her thought, he reached over again and now kissed her on the lips until she pulled away breathlessly and urged her horse to a sudden gallop. She felt stunned by her own, not his behaviour. She felt her own desire, her own animal nature racing in her pulse. She rode as fast as she could away from him and he let her get away, cantering after her easily, not forcing the big red horse's pace at all. As she rode, she resolved that this would go no further and that there would be no more social visits with Mr. Samuelson. Her life was planned and was on the verge of beginning anew. She would not allow it to be thrown into turmoil. Her sense of her own destiny was more powerful than the fascination that Samuelson exerted. She could not, would not, allow anything more to happen. She thought, too, of Darrow's sister whom she had seen with Samuelson's son. She remembered the flash of heat she had felt then. She would not be ruled by such things and urged her horse to an even faster gallop.

In spite of her pace, Samuelson was waiting on the steps of Blackdale when she got back. His horse had already been led away. He looked much at home and in fact, he looked as though he were the proprietor. An impression that she felt contrary to all she had just resolved. She would not show any signs of disturbance whatsoever with him.

"You ride quickly, sir," she said.

"Mouse has long legs."

"Mouse? You call that great beast, Mouse?" she said smiling, in spite of herself, as she slipped off her horse and handed the reins to the groom.

"I found him out in a field. His mother was dead and the poor colt was wandering around in a daze. To this day I don't know how he got there. There was a cut on his leg and I resolved to carry him back to our camp. I did not want him to be permanently injured by walking a long way when his leg was injured. So I carried him on my back and kept telling myself that he was just a little mouse to help me bear the weight."

Pamela could not help glancing after the great red horse as he was led away.

"Oh, he was smaller, then," Samuelson said. "But he was still very heavy. And he did not like being carried."

As they stepped inside she said, "That sounds like a tale from the nursery," Pamela said. "But I recall that you were a navvy in your early life."

383

"Yes, I was, Miss Blackwood. I believe it has given me great advantages in my business life."

Pamela led the way into the front parlour where she knew the maid would be on duty.

"What sorts of advantages, sir?"

"Hardness in the face of adversity. A first-hand understanding of what it means to take the short way whenever possible."

"You have obviously thought about your advantages much, sir."

"Knowing one's strengths and weaknesses is part of accomplishing one's ends, Miss Blackwood. Your father knew that. He was one of the two strongest, yet most gentlemanly men I have ever known."

"And who was the other, sir?"

A sudden scowl broke across the big man's face, making him look almost frightening for a moment.

"It was a very long time ago, Miss Blackwood," he said, his face clearing. "That gallop stirred my appetite."

"We shall eat soon, sir. In moments, perhaps." She wasn't entirely sure of his meaning but she certainly wasn't going to provide an opportunity to allude to a subject which she had decided was closed.

The rest of the evening passed surprisingly easily. Pamela would not have thought it could be so comfortable to make table conversation with a man who had kissed her passionately just a short time ago. Yet, it was so. He did not ask for another appointment, nor did he say anything about the kisses he had stolen when they were out riding.

He stayed far enough away from her so that she felt no uncomfortable pull toward him. She walked to the front door, said good night and he was gone. She slept restlessly and woke feeling cross and tired. It was the day of her concert when she most needed to be at her best. Without having any clear memories, she attributed her bad sleep to Samuelson, and promised herself that she would simply avoid him altogether in future.

From her father's study, she spent the day lazily watching storm clouds gather and break up over and over again. She would practice only two hours that day, enough to stretch her hands and keep them flexible, but no more. Later, as she rode to Manchester in the barouche, her excitement rose. Her confidence was absolute and she felt like a new queen going to her coronation. She kept seeing the smiling face of her father in her thoughts. She felt he was watching over her.

The smells and sights of the great hall's backstage pleased her. The exposed mechanisms of the curtains, the unlit footlights, even the smooth well-varnished wooden surface of the stage itself gave her a feeling of being at home, even though she had never been backstage, not even in Manchester. The closer she got to her public performance, the better she felt about the life she had chosen.

An old porter, hunched and wrinkled, his skin the colour of dirty mahogany, led her to her dressing room: a tidy little room that had been filled with baskets of flowers.

Undoubtedly, she thought, the blooms were the work of Hans. But when she read the card on a tremendous bunch of roses in a silver ewer, it was signed, John Samuelson. Hans had signed the cards on many of the other bouquets. There was a knock on the door as she was reading them.

"Yes," she called. "You may enter."

The door opened and she saw Hans, resplendent in a black frock coat and creme coloured pants. His welcoming smile made her glow with pleasure.

"How are you?" he asked. "No nerves?"

"I am fine, Hans. Please walk in. As he entered the room she took his hand.

"I owe all this to you, Hans. You have given me the life I wanted most."

He looked around the room. "You have many well wishers."

"Mostly you. One of these blooms are from an associate of my father's, John Samuelson. He is in pursuit of my father's companies. But you have given me what I most prize."

"Perhaps he is also in pursuit of something else," the musician said smiling at her.

She took his other hand and stood looking up at him. "I would not trade this little room for all the palaces of the earth. Your skill and patience has given me the right to be here, about to take my place on stage. That is what I owe you, Hans. I want nothing else."

They had begun calling one another by their given names in their letters. It now seemed perfectly natural to continue the habit.

Pamela couldn't help but compare her feelings with Bruckner to those she had felt with Samuelson on the previous day.

The one had tremendous power, a kind of frightening energy that was barely under control. The other had a delicacy of perception and fineness of sentiment that would one day, she was sure, be remembered as an essential part of his art. She could not have imagined then that Bruckner would be remembered primarily for having been her teacher.

She stood on her toes to kiss him gently on the cheek. His fine eyes looked at her lovingly and she felt his lips brush hers.

"Bon chance," he said.

"Thank you, Hans," she answered. "For all you have given me. I am so grateful."

"You have won your own place and shall win it tonight and every night you perform. I have done little enough. In any case, it is not your gratitude I want." His slim, high boned face looked to her like a beautiful carving in ivory, so well-formed and refined.

"I shall see you on the stage," he said and left the room.

* * *

The concert was a stunning success. Bruckner had been correct about the Blackwood heiress drawing a large audience merely because Pamela was her father's daughter. One critic even came from London, though he was rather inarticulate in his praise because he ordinarily reported on business matters. The fact that Pamela was a superb musician seemed secondary to the facts of her beauty and fortune.

"I told you," Hans said, as they read the notices together in the study at Blackdale.

Pamela was angry. "You are scarcely mentioned. And they speak more of my gown than the music," she said with asperity. "It is absurd."

"No," he said smiling. "It is the press. And, you played like an angel last night, better than I have ever heard you play before. You surpassed yourself and deserve all the notice you have gotten. Do not be discontented if the notice is not as refined as you would like. Remember, there will be many sharper thorns along the way." He raised her hand to his lips but she pulled away and held up the Manchester paper. "They certainly liked our encore," she said.

"A murder or a love intrigue sells more journals than anything else," he said smiling.

"But we were very, very good together, were we not? I felt that the duet was my best playing of the evening."

"Yes. But with the press that is secondary. As you can see. Now, we have to talk some business. Good notices, bad notices, they all come and go. Do not think of it too much. What I need to know is whether or not you are ready to commit yourself to a tour in the spring?"

Pamela looked up from the paper. "But of course, Hans. What else has all this been for, if not that?"

"This is really what you want?" he asked. "Perhaps you want to talk to some of your friends first."

"I do not care about the town talk. I am a musician. I want to get my own living doing what I love. That is all."

"Touring is very exhausting, bumping along on muddy roads, break downs, bad food..."

"Hans, why are you talking this way, now? Have I done something to make you think me unworthy to come with you?"

"Not at all. It would break my heart if you did not come. How would I leave you, then. No. But we must not make a commitment to the impresario if we are not certain to fulfill it."

"You think I haven't the strength for the life?" she asked.

"I do not know," he answered. "It is a hard life."

"But it is the life I know I want. I look forward to traveling. Even to the hardships. It excites me."

"From the comfort of Blackdale," he said, "But once we are stuck in the mud and find the inn closed and miss an engagement and still have to pay for the hall, how will that be?"

"A wonderful adventure. The only thing I shall miss is not practicing every day."

"Very well," he said, "I shall commit us to Herr Schlibein."

***

Several days after this conversation, Pamela received a note from Barnes asking to come to Blackdale that afternoon. He wrote that he had urgent business to discuss.

When she saw Barnes, Pamela was alarmed. He looked ten years older than the last time she had seen him, only a week earlier. His cheeks had fallen in. His eyes were red and his tall figure was more stooped.

"Mr. Barnes, what has befallen you?" she asked as soon as he stepped into the library. "Are you unwell?"

"It is Blackwood Holdings that is unwell, Miss Blackwood."

"But you, sir, tell me of yourself."

"I am merely tired after an exhausting week of trying to stem the flow of our shares into the hands of the bandit who is taking possession of your father's companies."

"And have you learned who that is, Mr. Barnes?"

"John Samuelson."

Now it was the solicitor's turn to be alarmed for, at the mention of the name, Pamela had turned white as chalk. She fell rather sat down into her chair.

"John Samuelson," she repeated. "He is more of a knave than even I suspected."

"And you do not know all, yet," the solicitor said.

"He was here last week trying to court me."

"And he does still," said the solicitor holding out a piece of paper.

"Dear Sir," the note began. "I know you have been trying to trace my activities on the 'Change since you set up the joint stock company with the assets of the Blackwood Holdings. I shall leave you in suspense no longer. I now have enough shares to control the voting of the other partners of the late Mr. Blackwood. Please tell Miss Blackwood that if she will reconsider my offer of marriage, she shall have the shares as a wedding present and they shall be put legally beyond anyone else's reach, including my own. I also undertake that no matter what she does now or in future, she shall have Blackdale for the rest of her life.

I know she is a girl of spirit and I do not expect her to say, "yes," now. My offer remains good indefinitely. Please tell her, contrary to all my expectations, how passionately I love and admire her."
John Samuelson.

"The scoundrel," Pamela said after finishing the note. "In one breath, he would blackmail me with my father's own property into marrying him; in the next tell me he loves me. I have never heard of anything so scandalous. Is this really legal, Mr. Barnes? Can he do as he says? Can he fulfill the promises he makes?"

"He has no power whatever over Blackdale, Miss Blackwood. But as far as the shares go, I am afraid so, Miss Blackwood. When I tried to get you not to offer shares on 'Change, I did not consider this possibility. But you can see how a public market makes it very difficult to control a business."

Suddenly, much to the anxiety of the solicitor, Pamela burst into peals of laughter.

Barnes seized the decanter and rushed to her side with a glass of brandy.

"Drink this, Miss Blackwood, it will help you over the shock. You are unwell. You are not yourself, now."

"I am very much myself, sir. I was laughing because that is precisely what this villain has failed to recognize. He thinks that my father's wealth is still important to me. He would buy me with something that has already lost its value to me. Though, I am glad to know he can do nothing with Blackdale. Not for myself as much as for Emily."

"I don't understand your attitude, Miss Blackwood," the solicitor said. "You can't be indifferent to poverty."

"You have not heard of the concert I have recently given in Manchester?" she asked.

"I have been engaged in nothing but trying to stop this attempt to steal your companies, Miss Blackwood."

"Then I shall tell you, Mr. Barnes. Sit down again and don't trouble yourself about me. Yes, I do insist. Yes. Before I go on. You look very fatigued, sir. That's better. I am now a public performer, sir, a concert artist. I have appeared in front of a paying audience in Manchester and intend to go on doing so. I shall soon be booked for a tour of European cities starting in the spring. It is music I love, and getting my own bread without reference to anyone else. Samuelson has missed his mark by about a year. I find it comic that he should rob me of something that I now think of little value. So, all his money and power is spent for nothing. I snap my fingers at his offer and his threat. What a villain he is, though," she ended, glancing at the letter.

"He is a villain, indeed, Miss Blackwood. In all my years of practice I have never seen such scurrilous behaviour. Both on a business and personal level."

"I shall write to him myself, Mr. Barnes. You may be sure that I shall deal with him summarily. But I am afraid, sir, that you will now have to serve him if you continue to work for Blackwood Holdings."

"That I shall not do, Miss Blackwood. There is enough left of my other clients that I'll be able to reduce my work day and still have an income. I have not lived in a profligate way. There is no circumstance that would compel me to work for such a blackguard."

"I am glad to hear it, sir. I would hate to think of him controlling my father's old associate as he will control my father's companies. And he has the nerve to give me Blackdale for life, when it is not his to bestow," she added picking up the letter again for a moment and glancing at it.

"He is an unmitigated blackguard," the solicitor agreed vehemently. "It galls me bitterly to think that there is nothing I can do. It is the fault of today's way of doing business, of raising capital from the public. I warned your father against it and I tried to warn you against it. It makes such disasters as this plausible. If there is any way, any way at all that I can serve you, Miss Blackwood, please call on me."

"I should like you to come and dine with me here at Blackdale, sir, a few times before I leave in the spring. I grew up seeing your face at our table. I would deem it a very great favour if, for a short while, we could reinstate the custom of that happier time when my father was alive."

Barnes bowed stiffly. Pamela could see he was strongly affected by her words.

"Miss Blackwood, it will be a great pleasure to await your invitation."

"Poor man," Pamela thought to herself after the solicitor had left the room. "He has spent his life building and defending my father's companies and he lives to see them taken away by Samuelson and rejected by me in his old age. Poor man. I am sure it is far worse for him than for me."

Now she would deal with that consummate scoundrel, she decided, picking up her pen.

"Dear sir," she wrote, "Mr. Barnes has just left me with your absurd offer of marriage. You little know or understand me, if you try to win me this way. I reject you, not because I am "a girl of spirit," but because you have no understanding of what I hold truly dear. You have no idea of my essential self.

What better reason could there be for rejecting utterly and forever an offer of marriage? Pamela Blackwood."

As for her own peculiar feelings about Samuelson, she would regard them as nothing more than strong animal sensation. She had to admit to herself that the animal part of herself was very strong, indeed. She had not known that women could have such feelings. She thought again of the day she and Emily had seen Paul Samuelson and Fanny together. She remembered the heat that had risen through her body. She would guard these impulses carefully in future, not just with Samuelson but with any man.

In spite of this resolve, during the ensuing decades, the amours of Pamela Blackwood would be almost as notorious as those of Franz Lizst.

Chapter 38

At times during the journey back to Manchester on Collins' warhorse, Samson, Richard felt certain that the Lord would deliver Samuelson to him through the discovery of some secret crime. Manchester was a city where the contrast between rich and poor, high and low were more extreme than anywhere else in Britain. It had also been the birthplace of the British railway industry. While these things indicated nothing about Samuelson, it felt to Richard that they did have meaning. At other times, these intuitions seemed like a will of the wisp, and his venture like a hope of the hopeless. He had built all his suppositions on the fact that Annabelle had been afraid Charles would blame her for some terrible misdeed after Mighty Jack's confession. Why had she thought so? Why had Charles not pursued the "matter of conscience" with her?

Now, according to Barnes, only marriage records might provide legal proof of crime connected with Mighty Jack's wife. Richard surmised that a crime provable by marriage records would be, like Jack Samuelson's original crime, one that falsified identity, and that would be a serious crime, indeed. Richard would follow the courses indicated by what Barnes had told him: Anglican churches were the only places to look for legal marriages. Marriage in any other church was not considered legal. If contracted before 1839, the year when the registration of births and marriages became law , it was less likely there would be any record at all. Before that date, Barnes said, people often just stated they were married and didn't bother with the ceremony. But even after recording became law, many vestry clerks were careless about records. Was Mighty Jack's claim to have been married in Manchester even true? Finding records that would turn up a weapon that could be used against Mighty Jack was a slim hope, Richard admitted in his less sanguine moments. At such times of doubt, he would say to himself, "I must believe it is possible to win, otherwise I shan't try. I must do it for Sally and Emily."

If Samuelson had been married in what was now the city of Manchester, records were most likely to be found in the hands of the vestry clerk of the fifteenth century Cathedral which stands next to Chetham College, facing Victoria Street. It had been the original parish church of the suburb of Manchester before Victoria granted the city its patent of incorporation in 1838. Of course, the Samuelsons could have been married outside of Manchester proper, in any one of the many nearby towns that had made up the old Salford One Hundred. No matter what the chances, he told himself, he must try every single one.

As Collins had instructed him, Richard stabled Samson outside the city at a small but clean blacksmithing establishment that had two or three stalls for boarding. During one of his stops en route to Manchester, Richard had been told of the place by a coachman who knew horses and the road well. The blacksmith whom he'd recommended, one Silas Anderson, was a small, squat, gray-haired man who held long, one-sided conversations with the animals he boarded.

"To Silas," the coachman said, "only a horse is worthy of notice, never the rider."

When Richard had first arrived at the stable, he'd heard a lengthy discourse coming from the barn. He had expected to find a whole crowd inside. He'd found only the proprietor talking at length to each of the horses in turn as he fed them.

When the farrier came out and saw Samson, he gave Richard a hard suspicious look, and said, "Surely this great war horse is not yours. You hardly look a soldier."

"He was lent to me by a friend and he needs a place to stay for a short time. Can you take him or no?" Richard answered curtly, disliking the man's curiosity.

"Aye, we shall be honoured to have such a guest," the blacksmith said reaching up to stroke Samson's nose. "I have not see his like since the Duke and I fought Boney together, more'n twenty years ago. Is he trained? He wears a warrior's leather."

"I am told he is."

Anderson slipped some pieces of freshly cut apple from his pocket to Samson's inquiring nose.

"How are you called?" he asked the horse as he stroked the great head.

"Samson," Richard said, smiling, in spite of himself at the farrier's obvious passion for horses.

"Aye, well, Samson, you would have ridden with the Duke himself or some great man who carried a sabre. I saw none better than you in the Duke's own stable." Then he turned back to Richard. "You have a great hearted friend to let you ride a grand animal like this. You'll want him to have only the best oats?"

Richard nodded.

"He shall have the care here, sir, as befits his rank."

As he led Samson away, Richard heard the man say to Samson, "You are a very general's horse, and in my barn. Think of it, sir. A general's horse, looked after by Silas Anderson, once more. We shall keep you glad and glossy, ready for inspection at any time. You may depend on it, sir."

Richard, himself, did not fare so well. He took a room in the centre of town at the ancient Seven Stars Inn, whose labyrinthine cellars were reputed to have once sheltered Guy Fawkes. The ancient wood frame building might have been redolent with history but it had few amenities. As he stood in the dark, low-ceilinged lobby, Richard had to admit to himself that he was seeking a needle not just in a stack of hay, but in a field of it. But there was simply no other course to take. There were fourteen parish churches in Manchester. He might have to look at the vestry books for them all. All other avenues had been closed, and he could not accept the idea of allowing his benefactor's death to go unpunished. He had to be able to free himself and his family from Samuelson's persecutions and bring the villain to book. What would happen if Collin's protection was withdrawn from Sally and Emily? He had no idea. They could not go on living under Samuelson's long shadow. Either he must succeed in Manchester, or he and his family would go to the Americas, he told himself. He went to sleep in the drafty, antique room, grateful that he could escape from his own dark thoughts.

He woke from a dream about Sally and Emily at Greenwich to smell the sulphurous air of Manchester, exuded by the mills. The air was thick with the fumes, even in his room. He knew that outside the sulphurous pall was even worse. No wonder all but the newest stone and brick in the town was painted black with soot. He left his lodgings and trudged through the busy streets toward the Cathedral.

Anyone who has ever been to Manchester knows the venerable Cathedral, the widest medieval cathedral in England. It's delicate, square tower is beautifully ornamented in each corner with three finely-cut stone spires that dominate the cluster of medieval buildings in the centre of the city. Inside, are many treasures of ecclesiastical art. Richard had not seen the elegant, antique interior on his last trip to Manchester. Here, the wealth of the city was even more apparent.

An officious looking man dressed in black told Richard that the vestry clerk, the person responsible for the marriage register, was a solicitor who had offices nearby on St. Ann's Square, one Mr. Pagget. When Richard found the clerk, sitting at an old-fashioned desk, he proved to be a legal practitioner of the hearty, confiding school. His well-fed face and figure were reminiscent of Mr. Pickwick but with the added characteristic of slyness around the eyes and mouth. A man who invited superficial trust but who seemed, on second look, entirely bent on serving himself. This was the character Richard found when he presented himself at the handsomely appointed law offices, not far from the Exchange building.

"A marriage as far back as 1829? Then, you will be wanting to consult the old registry book. The one retired about ten years ago," the solicitor said. "I do not have it here. It is kept in one of the cellars of the cathedral itself."

"Is that safe, sir?" Richard asked.

"Absolutely. The cellars of the church are dry and guarded by stout oak and are locked and chained. When my work here is done, I shall meet you in front of the church. You know," he said, dropping his voice as if imparting a secret, "the cathedral has been the parish church time out of mind. Ever since the fifteenth century. A very venerable house of worship, sir. Say, at about six?"

"Thank you, sir. Six o'clock." Richard said, realizing that this sort of delay was likely to be the rule rather than the exception in trying to obtain the information he wanted. He left the solicitor's office determined to continue his rounds of other churches in the area. What he found was that three had no appointed vestry clerk at all. The responsibility was shared among members of the congregation and he had trouble even finding out who presently had the responsibility. It could take him some days to track down all these people. The remaining five churches had professional, salaried appointees like Pagget. Three of these had the registry book at hand and found nothing. These, at least, Richard could strike off his list. So the day went, walking the chilly, busy streets of Manchester, once more growing used to the soot and the booming of the mills. He stopped for a bun and coffee at one eating house just before meeting Mr. Pagget back at the Cathedral.

The attorney looked just as cheerful, fat and pleased with himself as when he met Richard earlier in the day. Richard, on the other hand, was spotted with mud and exhausted after a discouraging and fruitless day. He knew he might have many more similar days and the weight of that knowledge told on his face.

"Searching for family, sir?" the attorney asked cheerfully as he showed the way to the cellars.

"In a way," Richard replied.

"Often a difficult undertaking. Especially when the search begins so long ago as yours. But very rewarding to find lost relations. Yes."

Richard found the man's confidential manner very irritating after the day he had had. Yet, he said nothing to the man, who had probably been chosen as Vestry Clerk for the very traits of superficial jollity which Richard found so unpleasant.

They passed through several heavy oak doors which the solicitor opened with keys from a large iron ring which he had picked out of a locked cabinet near the inside of the main church entrance. The solicitor then led Richard down several flights of stone stairs. Finally, they reached a small room that seemed deep underground. It smelled of dust and paper but was dry, and clean, and when they entered with the lamp that the solicitor carried, Richard could see that all was in order. There was no trouble at all about pulling out the three or four heavy, leather bound volumes that covered the years from 1800 to 1840, the years when Richard supposed the marriage would have taken place.

"I have some business upstairs with one of the churchwardens," the solicitor announced. "Here is another lamp. I shall leave you to your work. I shall come back in half an hour."

"Thank you, sir," Richard said.

In the dim, stuffy atmosphere of the room, with only a candle to light his way, Richard thought the thick vellum pages of the huge books seemed endless as he ran his finger down column after column of names. Something about the act of poring over the books brought the difficulty of his task home to Richard in a way that nothing had yet done.

"Still at it, I see," the solicitor's cheery voice hailed him from what seemed somewhere far away. "I shall come back, never fear. Take your time."

Richard did not even look up but mechanically kept running his finger down the names of a multitude so great that it could have been a list of all those who had been lost by Pharaoh under the red sea. He grew dull and sleepy in the dusty quiet of the place and then, suddenly, his finger stopped, almost without his being aware, on an entry that read: Samuelson, John. Navvy, Smith, Annabelle June fourth, 1830.
Witnesses: Ivy Murchison and Hillary Prendergast.

Richard could hardly believe his eyes. But the longer he looked at the entry, the more convinced he was that it was what he sought. The names of the witnesses were something he had never even considered. They could be a tremendously valuable source of information. Here were two people who had been present at the marriage, and who might still be living in the parish. With a trembling hand, he took out a sheet of paper from his pocketbook and made a memorandum of the names and date. Uncertain of his way out of the cellars, Richard now waited for the attorney with an impatience he would not have thought possible just a few minutes before. If anyone would know the whereabouts of the two witnesses, it would probably be the attorney whose character was such that he would use his position as a license to gossip and know all the details of the church's members.
The the darkness and oppressive air of the small room seemed to add to the slowness of time's passage. Finally, the rotund shadow of the solicitor appeared in the doorway.

"Mr. Paggett," Richard said, rushing over to the solicitor. "Do you, by any chance, know either of these ladies?"

"Oh, yes. Certainly. One is gone now. But the other is still alive. In her nineties. Our oldest parishioner, in fact."

"Is she lucid. I mean, could she answer some questions about this marriage?"

"I should say that Ivy Muchison would be delighted to have the attention, sir. She is a dear old thing. A little odd, but I should say, lucid. Then, this is the name you sought?"

"Yes, Samuelson."

"Is that any relation to the famous railway builder?" the attorney asked.

"I could not say for certain, sir," Richard said evasively. "How would I find this lady?"

"I have the addresses of all our parishioners back at my chambers. But I am not due there until tomorrow."

"Sir, could I persuade you, for a small gratuity to return now with me?"

"Oh, well, sir," the solicitor said. "If the matter is urgent of course I shall go back now. I am paid by the parish, sir. Is it really an emergency?" Richard realized that he would have to pay with gossip rather than cash if he wanted the solicitor to get the address right away.

Saying the first plausible thing that came into his mind, Richard confided, "There is a bequest for my aunt Annabelle, whom I have not seen in years. If I could speak to this marriage witness and she could be identified and traced, it would be a great service to the family. The bequest, I understand is a large one."

"You know, sir," the solicitor said, growing even more confidential in his tone, "I have found that nearly all urgency in human life is associated with money. The larger the sum, the greater the urgency."

"I cannot disagree, sir," Richard replied.

Within half and hour of leaving the solicitor's office, Richard was knocking at the shiny door of a new terrace house, situated on the edge of the city where the homes of poorer middle-class people stood. The whole street had been recently and poorly built. It was quite respectable and literally filled in the gap between the poor people of the city and the suburban homes of the well-to-do. It was near dinner hour so Richard had reason to hope that the elderly lady would be at home.

A white-haired woman opened the door. She was short, wore a mob cap and was obviously near-sighted. She peered up at Richard.

"Yes?"

"Miss Murchison?"

"Oh, no. Ivey is still having her nap."

"Will she be awake soon?"

"Probably. We have trifle tonight and Ivey never misses my trifle."

"There is something I need to consult her about. I got her address from the Vestry Clerk for the Cathedral. When might I return to see her?"

"Dorothea," a brittle sounding voice called from inside.

"Oh, there she is now," the woman said to Richard. "Come through. Go to your left into the parlour."

"Coming Ivey," Dorothea called slipping into the house. "You have a visitor. A young man. Well, I don't know who he is, dear. Come and say, good afternoon. We're having trifle. Yes."

Inside the little parlour, everything was fresh and new but very poorly made. There were bumps in the plaster; the shiny new floor was uneven and the glass in the windows had a green cast and distorted the world outside. The furniture, however, was old and sturdy. Mahogany predominated, the pieces seeming too large for the little room. An embroidery frame held a piece of elegant stitchery with the words "God Bless Our Home" worked into leaves and floral shapes.

In a few moments, Dorothea reappeared with a tiny woman, whose skin was so white as to seem transparent. Her hair was also unusually white. Her features were fine and well shaped with a pair of gentle but wide awake blue eyes dominating her face. She was so tiny and finely made, she appeared to belong to another race, like a character from a children's tale. She looked at Richard inquisitively.

"I am certain I do not know you, sir," she said after a few moments of studying Richard's face.

"No, Mrs. Murchison. I got your address from Mr. Paggett at the Cathedral."

"Ah," she said. "I do not think he is really a good Christian."

"Be that as it may, Mrs. Muchison, he is the Vestry Clerk and my business has to do with the church registry."

"Does it? How interesting. You must have some tea, first. And some of Dorothea's trifle. Do please sit down."

Richard sat on the hard old empire sofa. He had the odd feeling that Ivey Murchison was looking him over carefully with her clear, startlingly sharp blue eyes.

Feeling ill at ease, Richard tried once more to enter into the reason for his business.

"There will be time for that later, Mr. Darrow. You must slow down your aura for us to communicate properly."

"I don't understand," Richard said.

"Ivey is a believer in the unseen," Dorothea explained in a stage whisper.

"My belief has nothing to do with it," Ivey said. "Mr. Darrow's mind is so fixed on what he wants that he is likely to miss something useful."

"What do you mean, Mrs. Murchison?" Richard asked.

"Just that," she said simply, as though it explained everything.

The silence stretched into long moments as they waited for tea. Finally, Richard noticed two very fine, small portraits on the side table. A lovely blonde girl smiled out of one frame and a fine looking dark haired man looked out from the other.

"Those are very nicely drawn," he said.

"That is Mr. Murchison," Ivey said. "He was from Ireland and it was he who introduced me to the Folk."

"The folk?"

"The first people," Dorothea explained in another stage whisper. "Ivey sees and talks to them."

"Now, Dorothea, you know I do not like you telling that to new acquaintances.

As it happens, it is all right in Mr. Darrow's case. But you were not to know that. Do, please, be more careful in future."

"I beg your pardon, Ivey. You already told him, yourself."

"There, there, no harm done." Then Ivey turned back to Richard. "Rhiannon is telling me that you want to know about a marriage I witnessed many years ago."

"Rhiannon?" Richard repeated startled at the little lady knowing his reason for visiting her.

"Yes, she is often with me at this time of day. Do you not see her over in the corner, a tall, beautiful girl with very fine features and long auburn hair?"

"No," said Richard looking quickly into the empty corner. Perhaps the old lady is well and truly mad, he thought.

"No," Ivey said in answer to Richard's unspoken thoughts. "I am not mad. Rhiannon is there. I thought you might be able to see her."

Richard had begun to feel quite peculiar. He felt oddly relaxed and happy, sitting in the little parlour with the strange, tiny lady.

"That is good, Mr. Darrow. You are getting into the right vibration, now," Ivey said. "Rhiannon says that one day you may be able to see her people."

A young woman servant came in with a tray bearing the tea and trifle.

"Just put it down and leave us, Melody," Ivey said to the girl.

The trifle was delicious, Richard thought as he took his first bite.

"Yes," Ivey remarked, "Rhiannon always enjoys it when we have it. She can taste it through me, you see."

"And is she the one who tells you what is passing in my mind?" Richard asked.

"In a sense."

"Then do you know all about why I am here?"

"Yes and no. That is, I know you want to find out about someone you are afraid of, but I do not yet know his name."

"The name was Samuelson," Richard said.

"Oh," Ivey said, frowning for the first time.

"You remember?" Richard asked.

"Certainly, I remember. I almost refused to witness the ceremony, but in the end I let Hillary Prendergast talk me into it. She did so want the sovereign he offered us."

"Then why did you almost refuse to witness the marriage. Was there something wrong with it?" Richard asked eagerly.

"More something wrong with them."

"Who?"

"The bride and groom."

"A very tall, dark-haired woman and a very big man?" Richard asked.

"Yes, Mr Darrow. Now do not get excited, you will make it harder for yourself. Just calm yourself, as you were a little while ago."

"What was wrong with them?" Richard asked, more quietly.

"Well, it was very odd. It was as if they were already married, not married, but profoundly connected. Not just that they lived together as man and wife. I should have thought they had known each other for years, yet they were getting married to hide the fact of their closeness, instead of getting married because of their closeness. It was very odd, and I have witnessed many weddings in the parish, Mr. Darrow. This one was very odd. She was with child. But that wasn't unusual."

"They told you?"

"No. Rhiannon did. But after the ceremony, they said they were going to the highlands in Scotland. That seemed wrong, too. Why go to such a remote difficult to reach place for a confinement?"

"But they didn't know you knew about the child?"

"No, of course not. I never talk about what Rhiannon tells me, unless someone asks and Rhiannon says it is all right."

"Did they say where they were going, Mrs. Muchison?"

"No. But some weeks later the bride sent me a note. It might have had an address on it. I can't remember. Oh, perhaps it's still in my album. I have some very old things in there. Even a lock of Mr. Murchison's hair. Dorothea, would you get it? Of course it may have only been a holiday place, but that would seem very awkward for a confinement."

While Dorothea went out of the room for the album, Ivey sat quietly but wore a look of sharp concentration. Then she looked up at Richard, and spoke. Her voice had an odd ring to it and a slight Irish lilt, "Rhiannon says that if you go to this place you should be very careful. There is great danger there— and violence. Oh, yes. Thank you, Dorothea," Ivey said taking a big leather bound volume that was fastened with two clasps. She opened it and inside, between the thick vellum leaves, were pressed old letters, pictures, cards, two flowers, Mr. Murchison's hair, the memoranda of a lifetime. She looked through these for what seemed a long time to Richard. He began feeling restless again. What if the letter was not there? Then the trail would end here in the quaint parlour of the two elderly ladies. What then? he wondered.

"Oh, here it is," Mrs. Murchison said. Richard's heart gave a bound. "The return address is Dardoch Cottage, Arrdaroch, Scotland. Here are the directions."

Richard hastily copied the address into his pocketbook.

"Thank you, so much, Mrs. Murchison. Can you tell me anything else?" Richard asked.

"No. I don't believe I can." She gave Richard a look that made him understand that the interview was over. He rose and she walked to the door on his arm.

"Thank you, Mrs. Muchison. You've been very helpful."

"I am truly happy I could be of use, Mr. Darrow. Please remember Rhiannon's warning. She never speaks, idly."

"I shall."

Stepping out from the little house back into the thin watery sunlight of the late afternoon was a strange kind of shock to Richard. He could not say why. But the odd little woman literally carried a special kind of air with her. Once outside, Richard realized, the sulphurous fumes in the town had not existed in the little house, though they were present in every other place in the city, even in the depths of the Cathedral. At least, the curious interview had shown him where he might turn next. It had also provoked a suspicion in Richard's mind of yet another crime committed by Mighty Jack.

If he was right, and if the secret could still be recovered and proved, it was probably to be found in the neighbourhood of this remote cottage in the Scottish Highlands. He had to try this last desperate chance to see if Mighty Jack's villainy could be legally demonstrated. It was the one last hope of a weapon that could be used to protect himself, Sally and Emily from the railway king. Richard now believed that the crime Mighty Jack had committed in the Scottish highlands was one universally abhorred by all civilized societies, and abhorred by God.

If his surmises were correct, Richard knew that from here on, he would have to be on the watch for ruffians in the pay of Samuelson. If there were such a secret with clear proofs that could be discovered, Samuelson would spare nothing to stop Richard from finding it. No one had molested Richard in Manchester, but how close could he get to a remote highland cottage without some sentinel alerting Jack Samuelson that his secret was in danger? Also, Collins was going to tell Samuelson that Richard had gone to Manchester. Someone could be watching him at this very moment. Perhaps the too-confiding vestry clerk was in his pay. The journey to the remote and wild country of the Scottish highlands where this cottage lay would provide ample opportunity for paid villains to waylay him on the road. Or would the secret crime be hidden so well that none could uncover and prove it?

After visiting Samson, Richard returned to his lodging house where, he decided, that he must write to Sally. It might be that he would never return from the lonely road he would now travel. Collins had told him that he would tell Jack Samuelson what Richard knew of Mighty Jack, and the rest of Charles Wilney's tale. This, the spy hoped, would make Samuelson act. It also made it more likely than ever that the man or his minions would follow Richard and catch him up somewhere on the remote highland roads. He did not know if Collins would be watching and waiting to help or not. If there were a secret in the distant hills that needed guarding, Richard welcomed the danger, for then he would know that Mighty Jack was vulnerable and frightened. On the other hand, Richard had to survive the attack, whatever form it took. With these grim thoughts in his mind, Richard took up his pen to tell Sally of his plans, the possible risks and re-affirm his love while he had the opportunity. He also had to explain that with the coming of winter, he might be unable to return from the highlands before spring if he was detained for any length of time.

When Richard visited the great warhorse in his stable outside the town, the blacksmith, who was an unusually well-traveled man, told him that the snow in the higher passes could block access to the lonely, mountainous area where he would go to continue his pursuit. As Richard described what he knew of this road to Sally, he saw it in his mind's eye, stretching into the dark, perilous distances of the Highlands. The future appeared ever more uncertain, but at least now, with the unlikely help of Mrs. Murchison, the strange little lady who talked to the fair folk, there was perhaps some chance to clear away the shadow of Jack Samuelson from their lives.

Chapter 39

Fortunately, Richard's letter to Sally arrived from Manchester during the afternoon, when Emily was out at the park with Anne, who, since the trip to the zoo, had been kind enough to call for the child on a fairly regular basis. Anne now had her own little gig and certainly enjoyed driving in it with Emily. She and the little girl were good company for each other.

Reading the letter made Sally fretful. Richard sounded so worried and alone. How she wished she could go to him. It put a lump in her throat to think of him making his way through the wilds of Scotland by himself. She wondered, too, if Collins would be there to help protect him. Almost as the thought formed in her mind there was a sharp tapping at the door. Sally opened it and was dismayed to see Collins. The old soldier would not be in the Highlands with Richard! His manner was brusque. Sally could see that the man laboured to suppress some deeply felt emotion.

"Mrs. Darrow, I called to ask how your young friend at #14 Warwick Square is getting on."

When Sally thought of Richard's isolation, tears formed in her eyes.

"What? What have I said, Mrs. Darrow?"

"Oh, why are you here instead of there?" she replied.

"Where?" he asked.

Sally handed him Richard's letter.

"I see," the spy said as he finished the letter and handed it back to her. "Perhaps my business in London can be concluded tonight and I can start for the Highlands. If I ride all night and the next day, I may still catch him up before he had gone too far from Manchester. And don't forget, Mrs. Darrow, he is riding Samson."

"A horse? What does that signify?"

"Samson is a warrior, Mrs. Darrow."

Sally sniffed. "I am sorry, sir, that he does not have your protection, as well. A horse seems a poor defender."

"Well, you are wrong, but I shall do what I can, too, Mrs. Darrow, but I have some business to conclude here in London first. So tell me, how is the girl you found? Does she progress toward a better life?"

"Oh, Anne is doing much better. In fact, Emily is with her right now. They are riding in Anne's new gig."

"A new gig?"

"Fanny, that is, Mr. Darrow's sister got a large sum of money for her from, from the wife of that man."

"Yes, I know something of it. But not all," Collins said.

Setting aside her own feelings for the moment, Sally gave a full account of the scene between Fanny and Elspeth.

"Mon dieu," Collins said when Sally had finished. "She is a lioness, this Fanny. I knew of the money but not how it had been gotten."

"Are you now certain, sir, that this girl is your daughter?" Sally asked.

Collins lowered his sharp black eyes for a moment. "Yes, she is my own dear little one whom I held in my arms. It made me want to weep when I learned what she has suffered."

"How do you know about her life, sir? How did you learn about it?"

"Knowing where and when my wife took my child and knowing where this girl now was, I traced all her movements from that time to this. It is a terrible story. You were right to forbid my seeing her right away. How do you judge her condition now?"

"She is better, sir. Much more well regulated in her habits. She has a good maid and cook who look after her now and Fanny and I or Emily see her nearly every day."

Collins bowed deeply to Sally and took her hand and kissed it.

"Merci beaucoup," you and your friend have been good friends for my poor little one. I shall do everything I possibly can to help Mr. Darrow. But first, I must settle this monster who has been treating my little one so viciously."

"Bradley?" Sally asked.

"That is the name," Collins said.

"I wish you would go to Richard straight away. You men. Cannot your anger wait?"

"But if I remove Bradley, it will also hurt Mr. Darrow's enemy, Samuelson, Mrs. Darrow."

"But not soon enough," she said. "Oh, please go now."

"Madame, I cannot. I will tell you why. I have in my employ a footman at this Bradley's house. From him I learned that this Bradley, being a greedy man, wants back the money his wife settled on my daughter. He means to get it from her by any method he can. I am sorry, but I must protect my little one, first. Honestly, now that you tell me our two children are together, I am concerned for them both."

"You think Emily at risk?"

"Yes, the brilliant child."

"Good lord, what do you mean?"

"You say she is with my Anne. This Bradley...I do not know what kind of thugs he would employ. It is already growing dark outside."

"What do you think he will do," Sally said biting her lips in vexation.

"Ransom them both to get his money back."

"But that means he will abduct them."

"Not him, Mrs. Darrow. He has no courage, that one. But those whom he hires. I am afraid the people he employs will be as crude as he himself is. Should that occur..."

"Leave," Sally said suddenly. "Go and find them this instant, sir. Now, both our children are at risk. I am so sorry Fanny took money from that man."

"It was well-intentioned, Mrs. Darrow. And he does not have it back, yet. Nor shall he, if I can help it."

"Go," Sally said, peremptorily, pointing at the door. A moment later she was alone.

She began pacing back and forth in the small rooms. She wished she could do something more active, but she was afraid to leave for fear that perhaps the girls would return. Perhaps all would be well, she thought, calming herself. At least, they could not have a better ally in this crisis than Collins. But perhaps, maybe, that is, she hoped that perhaps there was no crisis at all. But Collins would not be wrong about something like this, she told herself. If anything, he would have said less than he knew, so as not to alarm her. Good lord, what would a man like Bradley do with the two young girls. "If he touches Emily," she said out loud, "God help me, I shall scratch his eyes out." But perhaps everything would be all right. She tried to slow her pacing.

Back and forth she went from fearing the worst to hoping all was well. How long she paced back and forth in her mind and in the little apartment, she did not know, but when there was a tapping on the downstairs door, she flew down the stairs and flung open the door. Fanny stood under in the flickering light of the street lamp. It was dark out and the gas had been lit.

"Oh, Fanny," Sally said, throwing her arms around her friend.

"Sally, you so hot? I am the one with the fiery temper. What has happened?"

"Come in and I shall tell you."

As one would expect, the two women calmed themselves by making tea, while Sally shared her concerns for Anne and Emily.

"Good lord," Fanny exclaimed. "This is my fault. If I hadn't been so greedy on Anne's behalf, perhaps this wouldn't have happened."

"Nothing has happened, yet," Sally said, feeling soothed at being able to soothe Fanny.

"But this man, this Collins. You say he is to be relied upon in a matter such as this?"

"Yes, but even he said only that he was concerned. The girls may be simply gawking at shop windows."

"Getting rather late for that," Fanny said."The gas is lit."

"But some shops will be open."

"Yes."

"Perhaps one of us should go out and look up and down the nearby streets?" Fanny said. "The other could stay here and wait."

In the end the two women could not decide who was to stay and who was to go, so they both stayed and waited. As the minutes dragged on, each knew that the chances of their fears becoming facts increased.

"Perhaps we should go to the police," Fanny said, finally.

"My own belief is that Collins can do more than the entire Metropolitan Force. I think he has confederates all over the city. Even in places the police could not go. He heard about all this from one of Bradley's servants. He may have been to the police, already."

"Very well. But I should like to do something. I am feeling quite breathless with anticipation."

"I know," Sally said. "I am also worried to death. And poor Richard. Oh, I am glad he is not here. He would be quite mad with worry if he felt Emily in danger."

Both women were quiet for some time. Then Sally said, "Fanny, how did you happen to come here, now? Was there any special reason for your visit?"

"Sally," Fanny said suddenly in a changed tone, "I think that Paul has left me."

"What? Why do you think that?"

"He is going off with his father somewhere, somewhere distant, I believe. He's told me he didn't know when he would be back. I think he may just be trying to get away from me. It would be as well. I could not pretend with him that I was sad to see him go."

Sally sighed deeply, "No, Fanny, I do not think so. I think he goes with his father to pursue Richard to Scotland."

"No, I am sure not. His father has already left London."

"What? Are you certain?"

"Yes, as certain as I can be without the evidence of my own senses."

Sally jumped to her feet and began pacing again. "Oh lord, why are we so afflicted? Richard far away and Emily here." She began pacing again.

By the time the bells were tolling midnight, both women were exhausted with worry. Sally had mercifully fallen asleep on the sofa in their little sitting room next to the kitchen. Fanny watched her affectionately.

"How good it is to have such a sister," she thought. "But dear little Emily...and Anne. What will come of this, she wondered?"

* * *

The man known in these pages as Collins had many names and many professions: soldier, solicitor, actor, spy. He had served so many nations and masters that he no longer had any allegiance, except to the child who had been stolen from him. He had sought her so long and in so many places that she had become more of an idea, more a part of his own mind, than a real person, but she was his reason to go on living, the mainspring of all his actions. When she had been identified by the jewel given to Richard and by her unusual colouring, Collins had wept and then carefully checked her identity in every way he could. Satisfied at last that she was his own, he promised himself revenge on those who had used her so monstrously. In his investigations, he had learned whose creature Bradley was. He had learned that Samuelson knew of her whereabouts in the brothel, even when he had promised Collins that he would use his immense wealth and influence to help find the girl. For years Samuelson had utilized the unique resources of the master spy to help build his empire of iron roads, just as Napoleon had used him to build his political and military empire. Now that Collins knew of Samuelson's treachery and the extra years of suffering it had bought for his child, he promised himself that the railway king would pay a heavy price. That night, when Sally told him that Anne was healing and was ready to meet her estranged father, Collins decided it was time to change *les regles de jeu*. First, Bradley and then Samuelson would die. Then he would take Anne back to the sunny beaches of southern France and disappear into the quiet life of the small fishing village where he had been born decades before. This was his settled purpose when he crossed the city and approached Bradley's house after leaving Sally. Getting Bradley in his grasp would be the quickest and surest way to find out if the girls were in any danger.

He waited patiently on the street outside Bradley's house, watching as one light after another was turned off in the house. He did not even feel the cold or wet of the gray, fogbound night. He did not allow himself the luxury of becoming angry at Bradley. It was a question of winning the engagement. Anger would make him less effective. An enemy strikes a terrible blow, he is then to be taken off the field of engagement, calmly and quickly. He watched the Bradley house go to sleep with as much feeling as the iron lamp stand that stood across from Bradley's door. He would not use the footman in his pay to let him into the building, for then the servant would know of Collins' presence and would have to die as well. The bells of St. George's tolled midnight, one o'clock and two. During the hours he waited, Collins carefully observed the intervals of the policeman's passage on his rounds and knew to a heartbeat how long he had before the constable's next appearance.

Once all the windows were dark, Collins approached the locked gate of the area at the side of the house. With a small oddly twisted piece of metal, he gently and silently opened the lock and disappeared into the shadow fringes of the street lamps. Once covered by darkness, he took another small implement from his pocket and cut a perfectly round circle of glass from one of the windows. He reached inside, opened the latch and then raised the window. He knew the window would let him into the kitchen pantry, far from anyone's sleeping quarters. From the reports of the footman, Collins had drawn a map of the house's interior. Then, he had memorised and destroyed it. Inside, he could find his way as surely as Bradley himself. He paused in the darkness of the interior, waiting for his eyes to grow accustomed to the reduced light. Then, he opened the pantry door and stepped out, moving as silently as one of the shadows cast through the windows by the lamps on the passing carriages. He quickly moved through the kitchen, the servants dining hall and ascended to the main floor. His only hazard here was a chance encounter with a restless servant. The bells of St. George's were tolling three when he paused before climbing the stairs to the family's bedrooms on the second floor. Bradley would be alone in his room, the third one on the left from the top of the stairs. Bradley and his wife always slept separately, Collins had learned. With as much noise as the family cat, Collins rose to the second floor, found Bradley's door and stood listening for a moment before taking hold of the handle. After a moment of reassuring silence, Collins entered the room. Bradley was sprawled on his bed, breathing stertorously. Had he wakened at that moment, he would only have seen a dark shape moving toward him with a flickering light in the center of it. The light was the small, razor sharp stiletto Collins held, which reflected the light from the window.

A moment later and Bradley woke to a nightmare. He could not breath. Then he heard a soft voice that said, "If you make one sound, monsieur, you will die immediately. Do you understand?"

For a moment, Bradley tried to move away from the hand clamped over his face, but the sharp prick of the knife against his throat quickly dissuaded him.

"Do you understand, now?" the voice repeated.

This time Bradley nodded.

"You will dress," the voice continued. "Then you will take me to the place where you have had the two children taken. Do you understand?"

Some grunts of protestation were quickly stopped by an iron grip shutting off Bradley's breath.

"I know you have them," the voice whispered. "You will take me there, now. If you make any sound, you will die immediately."

Bradley shook his head affirmatively. He was encouraged to sit up by the knife,whose pressure never left his throat. Even as Bradley dressed and walked down the stairs there was not one moment when he did not feel the cold metal against his neck.

The two men silently left the house by the servants' entrance, which let them out to the area which adjoined a lane behind the building. Here, Collins had left his carriage. At knife point, he led Bradley into the landau and manacled him to the iron rail in front of the seats. He placed a small rug over Bradley's lap to hide the manacles. Then, Collins turned to his prisoner.

"Now, monsieur, you will tell me where we are going. If you make any attempt to attract attention to us, I will kill you instantly. Do you understand?"

"Yes," Bradley's face was pale with fear and resentment. "But if I do as you ask..."

Bradley started to say.

Until that moment, Collins had not been entirely sure that the girls had been abducted. It was almost a relief to be certain. "Ask nothing of me, monsieur, until I have the two children. I will only say that if they are harmed, you will die quickly. That is the only promise I will make to you. Now, where are we going? Just give me the address. I shall find it."

"Number 78 Throgmorton Street. Go to the lane behind the house."

"Ah, that is the brothel where you ill used one of the children, is it not?" "The girls are in the basement," Bradley replied sulkily.

"With how many men?"

"Only one," Bradley answered. He suddenly felt the sharp point of the knife pressed against his throat.

"You are lying, monsieur. Even a fool like you would not send a single man on such an errand."

"There are two," Bradley said hoarsely.

Collins nodded and took up the reins.

"Remember, monsieur, one word and you are a dead man." With that final remark, the carriage began to move.

In spite of the elegant trade to which it catered, the brothel was not in a respectable residential neighbourhood. It was surrounded by commercial establishments and the streets near the brothel were narrow and dark, helping to preserve the anonymity of the men who frequented the house. This was not the luxurious brothel where Bradley had met Anne. This was a house that specialized in perversions of all sorts. Anonymity was essential to the clients. The fog, the late hour and the location insured that Collins' carriage would probably pass unseen. The only sound Bradley heard as they drove was the muted clatter of their passage echoing from the shuttered warehouses that lined the warren of narrow lanes Collins used in preference to the larger thoroughfares. Collins unerringly found the alley behind the building from a direction Bradley did not know.

In fact, Bradley's fear, the fog girt darkness and the unfamiliar route left him completely disoriented. His only hope, he felt, was in the third man whose presence he had withheld from Collins. Surely, the three men with an element of surprise would be able to disarm his abductor, who was by no means, young.

The carriage wheels scraped to a stop on the wet cobblestone as Collins tied the reins to the brake.

"Which door?"

"That one, I believe," Bradley said nodding toward his right. "I have only been here once, and it was day time then."

"And the children?"

"Are in a small room at the bottom of a flight of stairs."

His words had barely died away when Bradley felt a cloth stuffed into his mouth so tightly that he could hardly breath. He tried to grunt a protest and could not even manage that. Then, a band of leather was fastened across his mouth and around his head. A moment later, he was alone. When he tried to move, he found that the band around his mouth was secured to something so that he could not even move his head. His hands were numb with the pressure of the cold iron of the manacles. Feeling his utter helplessness, he subsided and waited, terrified.

Collins found the door to the dark entrance barred from within. No lock pick would answer here. Instead, he drew out a long, flexible piece of metal that was hooked at one end. Slipping this device between the door and jamb, he felt his way with the hook, caught it on the bar inside and lifted it, but was unable to keep it from falling with a thud against the interior wall. The possibility that the sound had given an alarm to the men below made him move more quickly. He took up his dark lantern and opened it to give him a thin wedge of yellow light on the stairs. It showed him a dusty, little-used stair pitching steeply down into the cobwebbed darkness of the cellar. The smells of earth, rotting wood and mould prevailed. He shut the lantern and from memory, quickly but silently made his way down the steps. He felt the wood of the staircase give under his feet, but fortunately, none of the treads broke. Finally, he felt that he was standing on stone at the bottom. It was utterly black. He again risked some light for a moment and saw a tunnel-like hallway in front of him that seemed to end in a blank wall. Once he traversed the hall, however, he saw a faint light emanating from another corridor on the right. He felt certain that this must be where the girls were held. The walls here were earth and the odors of mould and decay stronger.

"How frightened the children must be," he thought, moving silently as his own shadow toward the faint light.

The faint, flickering glow began to take on the ruddy colour of an oil lamp, which radiated from a passage or chamber to his right.

"There must be a sentry posted there," Collins thought. Very slowly, he moved his head so he could see around the edge of the opening. He saw a small chamber of stone with an oil lamp flickering on a rude table. A sleeping man was slumped forward onto the table next to a bottle of spirits. Beyond, there was another door. In two quick steps, Collins reached the man and slipped his small blade into the man's neck and up into his brain before he could sit up. There had been no sound and there was little blood. Collins paused, looking hard at the thick wooden door in front of him. Here was danger. The children could be inside with the other guard or guards. The hinges told him that, fortunately, the door opened out. He hoped that it was not barred. He could only see a latch handle. Very slowly, he pressed down on the latch. There was a metallic click and the door began to swing open by its own weight. He stood to one side, not knowing what would emerge from the darkness. Then very slowly, he bent forward and looked within what must have once been a root cellar. The air was dank and cold. From the light of the lamp in the outer room, he could see that the only figures in the closet-sized room were the two children huddled together in a pile of rags.

Any other guards must have retired to some more hospitable place, but Collins remained alert for sounds of their return. He gently put his hands over the mouths of the two sleeping children and shook them softly. Emily woke first.

"Do you know me, little one?" Collins whispered, loosening his grip.

"Mr. Collins?" the little girl answered in a loud whisper.

"Yes."

"Anne," Emily said shaking her friend, "wake up. We're going home, now. You shall be safe."

The other, older girl woke much more slowly. She started when she first saw Collins bending over them.

"It is all right," Emily said in a whisper. "He is a friend. He will help us get home. I'm certain he will."

"The little one understands so quickly," Collins thought. His own child still looked fearful, the vestiges of sleep clung to her countenance.

"It is all right, *mon enfant*. What Emily says is true. Come with me now."

Anne tried to stand and at the same time hold the ragged blanket around her, but the two movements were incompatible. The rags fell away and Collins could see that she was naked below the waist. There was a little blood smeared on her thighs.

"Betes," he growled. Then he wrapped Anne in the ragged blanket and picked her up and carried her. The joy he would have felt to have his daughter in his arms after more than a decade, was tempered by her fear and the injury that had been done to her. He took the girls quickly back the way he had come. Finally, the three emerged into the fresher air and greater chill of the outer air in the lane.

In a few quick movements, Collins unlocked Bradley's cuffs and leather strap, and killed him so deftly with the sharp little knife that to the girls it looked as if he had simply taken the man out of the carriage so they would have a place to sit. The children did not have time to see the open, staring eyes of John Bradley, MP, reflecting the light from the carriage lanterns as Collins drove away. Collins threw one backward glance at the chubby figure sitting in a pool of fetid water.

"Walk on, *mes amis*," he said to his horses.

Even apart from the outrage committed on Anne, Collins had known he could not leave Bradley to harass Anne or Emily again, especially with Richard gone from London and needing help. Bradley's own actions had made his death a necessity. The fact that his removal would hurt Samuelson's parliamentary stratagems did not even occur to Collins, nor would it have mattered to him.

In a short time, the two girls were being put to bed by Sally and Fanny. Emily fell asleep immediately after a kiss from her adopted mother, but Fanny held Anne and rocked her for a long time before the older girl slept.

409

Collins waited in the kitchen until Sally returned from the girls' room. He stood as soon as she entered.

"Emily is well?" he asked. "My own daughter...they,"

"I know," Sally said. "Fanny told me. We will send for the doctor and take care of her."

"Thank you, dear lady."

"God bless and keep you, sir."

"I waited only to tell you that I leave for Scotland within the hour."

"After this, you will ride all night? I am grateful, but..."

Collins put on his hat. "One learns on the battlefield, Mrs. Darrow, that fatigue is mostly a thing of the mind. Madame, I owe your husband a great debt. You have made it even greater. Good night."

Chapter 40

The days after Cynthia's death and Collins' departure for Scotland were painfully slow for Sally. Anne was more frightened than injured, the doctor said.

Cynthia's funeral was a strange affair with Fisk describing the angels who hovered around Cynthia's grave, disporting themselves happily in the air. The Non-Conformist minister was scandalized and the working women who had been Cynthia's friends were convinced of Fisk's madness when he stood by the grave side, called the angels by name and gave them each messages to take to the dead woman. Even Sally looked askance at Fisk. The only one who was not perturbed in the least, was Fanny, who acted as if Fisk's behaviour were perfectly commonplace.

Afterwards, as Sally and Fanny returned to the Darrow's lodgings from the churchyard Sally said, "That must be one of the strangest days I have ever spent."

"Why so, sister?" Fanny asked.

"Fisk and his angels. How strange it all was."

"I do not see why. So many say they believe in God and his angels, yet when there is a man who is actually able to see and talk to them, people act as if he were mad. Why should he not see them? At first I found the idea odd, but that was mostly because I have known Fisk for so many years. But after listening to him today, I think it is a wonder that we don't all see angels and demons, if the Bible is true. I was comforted by his words and I know Cynthia should have been, too."

Sally was silent for a long time and then said, "You are right, Fanny. It is my bias toward commonly held views that made me think that way I did. I shall do better with Fisk and his angels."

***

Soon after the funeral came the onset of winter which brought rain, slate coloured skies and terrible oily fogs but no news of Richard or Collins. Fisk sat as though carved of stone in a corner of Sally's kitchen staring at the floor. When spoken to, he would only say he was not unhappy. He knew Cynthia was with the Lord.

Anne, who had no other friends but Sally and Fanny, had become a fixture in the sitting room. She was in shock from the murder of Bradley, "by person or persons unknown," the newspapers said. The story lingered on the front pages of nearly every paper in London for days. Mercifully, Anne had no idea that she had witnessed Bradley's death.

Finally one morning, Fanny, who could see Sally's worry about Richard become more acute with each passing day, insisted on taking Fisk out to Greenwich with Emily and Anne. It was some four weeks since Richard had mailed his last letter from Manchester.

Fisk sat distracted in the cab that carried them out to the Isle of Dogs to the Greenwich ferry. He looked out the window and saw nothing. Anne and Emily looked out the other side and saw and remarked on everything, especially the women's clothing and parasols.

"Mr. Fisk," Fanny said abruptly as she took his arm coquettishly, "I thought you used to like me, sir. Here you have me for a whole day and all you can do is be dull and look out the window."

Fisk seemed to wake from a dream of some kind. He smiled and blushed at the same time.

"Please excuse me, Miss Darrow. I shall do better."

"Well," Fanny said in mock offense, "if I am only forcing myself on you, sir..."

"No. No, Miss Darrow," he said patting her arm. "I do like you. I mean, I have always liked your company, ever since you were a little girl." "And now that I am no longer little?"

Fisk broke out laughing and Fanny joined him.

"You are right, Miss Darrow," Fisk said, smiling, "What man wouldn't be charmed and delighted to have you by him. I cannot think what has been wrong with me."

As Fisk, Fanny and the two girls rolled west, back at Sally's lodging, there was a sharp tap on the door. Sally's heart skipped a beat and she sprang to her feet. She had been sitting at the table, trying to quiet herself end enjoy the stillness of the rooms without people in them.

As she had hoped, it was the post and it brought and envelope postmarked in Scotland, the long-sought letter from Richard. Her fingers were trembling as she tore open the paper.

"Dearest Sally, First let me assure you that I am well."

Sally exhaled a long breath of relief and began to cry, softly, dashing away the tears so she could continue reading:

"I am sorry it has been so long since my last letter but events have rushed in upon me so quickly that I have not had the leisure to write before now. My news is essentially good, however, there have been some grisly, horrible incidents here. I think the best way to proceed is to arrange events in the order they occurred. Then, as much as possible, we shall share all the experiences I have had in these last weeks.

The ride up through the Cotswolds to the border was uneventful, except for the fact that there was some early snow before we even reached Scotland. (When I say "we", my dear, I am referring to Samson, the wonderful horse Collins let me ride. He has an intelligence that astonishes me. If not for him, I should not be writing to you now.)

The skies were sunny even during heavy snow showers, and the white covering on the ground glinted like gems in the sun. The brilliance of the light and air here is not to be credited by a London dweller. The wind that blows from the North Sea or down from the mountains is often of gale force. Even before I was in any truly wild place I had to put on the cloak of sheepskins I bought in Jedburgh in order to stay warm.

In the border area of Scotland, I crossed beautiful lush meadows dusted with snow, skirted rich farmland and rode through heavily timbered forests. My route followed the old Roman road that is still in use there. I often thought of my friends Charles Wilney and Reverend Franklyn while in this region, for there are many sites of enormous antiquarian interest, not least of which is the Abbey of Melrose, recently restored by Walter Scott, where the heart of Robert the Bruce is said to be buried. But more than antiquarian interests, I felt as I entered Scotland, that I might be closing in on the man who had foully murdered Charles and who continues to persecute us. With every step, I felt more certain that he had sequestered himself and his family in this rugged, wild country to hide a guilty secret, a secret that had to do with his marriage or the birth of his child. What other reason could there be for coming so far, across such difficult terrain when Annabelle was expecting a child? However, I must confess, that at other times my chain of surmises looked flimsy and insubstantial.

The early part of the journey through the border region was tame as an excursion to Greenwich compared to what we encountered once we passed Inverness and entered the wilderness of the Highland realm. This is where the vicissitudes of the trip truly began. We had to walk over mountainous passes, some of which were already choked with snow. If not for Samson's tremendous strength, I don't think we could have crossed. There are easier routes, but I wanted to make haste and took the shortest way. I knew that if Collins' warning about my knowledge of Mighty Jack had moved Samuelson, he might be ahead of me or behind, racing to hide his secret in the place where he had once thought it safe. These considerations drew me on to cross through the mountain fastnesses and deep valleys as quickly as possible.

We rode southwest from Inverness, usually finding shelter in the stone barn of some crofter. The weather was inclement, and my goal was far off when we left the highland capitol. Though, I was told that once we crossed the mountains and got into the neighbourhood of the cottage where Samuelson had gone with his expectant wife, I would find the air quite mild due to a warming current in the ocean that swept close to the coast. With every struggling step we took through the deep snow of the high passes, my hopes rose, for this was the same time of year when Mighty Jack had taken a pregnant woman over this same country. As I experienced the difficulties of the trip firsthand, it seemed more and more likely that he came to this remote country for a very pressing reason.

On the heights, we passed through great drifts of snow, but at lower elevations the climate was much milder with only a light dusting of silvery flakes. I saw great white hares the size of small dogs and huge, shaggy deer with enormous antlers. I often thought how much Emily would enjoy seeing these unusual beasts. Even the small cattle of the Highlands were savage in their appearance, with thick coats of long hair and long, sharp horns. We passed through wild places with such odd names as Achnasheen, Sheildaig and Strathcarron, going from greenery underfoot to the cleanest, most brilliantly white snow I have ever seen. Through the kindness of Providence, we always found shelter. Often, we were quartered in stone barns with Samson's kind, or a crush of woolly sheep. At other times, I was fortunate enough to find a farmer who would rent me a spare room for the night. Had we been less fortunate, I believe that at the higher elevations, one night outside in the cold, blowing snow would have killed us both. But once we descended into the long valley overlooked by the great mountain of the region, Sgorr Ruadh, the snow was less and in places I could hear water rushing past somewhere under the snow and ice.

The air grew remarkably warm as we descended and drew nearer the sea. Yet, never have I been so cold as I was on the heights, but what a beautiful land! Over one hundred miles as the crow flies from Fort William to Dardoch Cottage, we traveled, and against all likelihood, we survived through the Lord's mercy. But I thought continually of what the trip would have been like for Mighty Jack and his pregnant wife.

Just before we began our descent from the high mountain pass into the narrow river valley above Loch Carron, snow began falling thickly. The twilight closed in on us very rapidly. Huge fluffy flakes made a wall of white just a few feet ahead of Samson's head. No matter which way I turned it was difficult to see anything except the snow.

We were caught in a blizzard with no sign of shelter, and were crossing the worst part of the pass. Suddenly, Samson showed me that something out of the ordinary was ahead of us. He stopped, shook his head, stamped his right foot several times and turned to look at me with a glance that seemed to say, "something untoward lies this way." Then he quickened his pace. As we breasted the top of the rise, the wind howled and shrieked around us, but never once did Samson show any sign of fear. Through the lashing snow, I first saw a tumble-down stone shelter, a shed, probably built for shepherds in the milder season. Then, not far from the open door of the building I saw a dark shape on the ground, which the blowing snow had partially obscured. A moment later I realized it was a man in a dark cloak.

I slid off Samson and bent over the still form. The man's head was badly injured. Imagine my shock when I finally realized that the figure was Colling, barely recognizable for all the blood marks on his face and the stinging snow that burned my eyes. I grabbed him under his arms and dragged him into the shelter of the shed. Samson watched me and pawed restlessly at the ground. Again, I had to thank God: there was dry firewood laid by inside and I soon had a crackling source of warmth going for the injured man, for he was not yet dead and groaned slightly when I moved him.

After making him as comfortable as I could, I went outside to care for Samson. He, however, was no longer standing where I had left him. For a moment, I was afraid he had wandered off, but then I heard a banging sound coming from behind the cottage on slightly lower ground. I followed the noise around the back of the cottage and found Samson inside a barn that was larger and in better repair than the shed where Collins and I were billeted. Its open door banged intermittently against the stone of the jamb. Inside, there was hay in a loft overhead. Some had fallen on the ground and Samson was having his supper. I again thanked the Lord for taking care of us. I removed the horse's saddle, patted him and gave him a handful of the sweet dried fruit I had brought as a treat for us both. Then, I made sure the door to the barn was closed and secured. I then returned to the shed and fed the fire, grateful that the dry wood was piled to the ceiling. Outside, the wind howled like the Furies. Leaning against the firewood, I huddled into my sheepskin cloak and almost immediately dropped into the deep sleep of exhaustion.

***

I was wakened by a sudden noise outside. The wind had died down, which made the eerie cry which woke me that much more penetrating. Though I'd never heard anything like it, I assumed it must be the cry of a wolf. The cry was soon answered by several other similar voices. Their long wails echoed from the surrounding rocks and hills and seemed to rise and fall on all sides of the shed. I staggered to my feet, took up a heavy piece of burning wood from the fire and went outside to make certain that the barn door was still fastened and that Samson was safe.

Just beyond the clearing, between the shed and barn, I saw two pairs of glowing eyes, reflecting the fire I carried. They followed me with interest. I could not know what the beasts would do, so I tried to move slowly and deliberately. When I got to the barn, I did not see any possibility that the bar across the barn door could be dislodged so I turned and went back to the shed. I found Collins conscious. His eyes were half open. He tried to speak. Not knowing what else to do, I gave him some of the snow I had melted earlier. He drank greedily and then coughed and moaned.

"Collins, can you speak?" I asked.

"Perhaps. Is it you, Darrow? Or my death swoon?"

"It is I, Collins. Can you speak and tell me what happened?"

"I found Samuelson."

"He did this?"

"Yes, though he is wounded too, but not as badly."

My heart gave a leap. For surely, if Samuelson was once again taking this difficult road, my surmises were correct. Somewhere in the neighbourhood of Dardoch Cottage, the secret could be found and exposed!

"Did you speak? Did you learn anything?" I asked eagerly, forgetting his injuries for the moment. "How did you come to fight with such violence?"

"When I approached the shed, looking for shelter, he was already inside."

'What, you, Collins? he said, when he saw me. 'I knew the teacher would come this way, but not you. What are you doing here?'

'You have known where my daughter was for the last two years, villain,' I said. 'But you told me nothing. You used my services, baiting me with the promise that you would find her in future. And all the time you knew how she was being used. How dare you do such a thing?'

'It did not suit my plans for you to find her, yet, Collins,' he said, unmoved.

'You will make no more plans,' I raged. I drew my sword.

"He took up a thick piece of wood and deflected my first blow, but my next one bit into his arm. As his hot blood steamed in the cold, he lashed out at me with his stick. He missed, but he smiled at me, a cruel smile."

'You are a fool, Collins. I will kill you and then your daughter will be no better off.'

'How could you let her suffer as you have?' I shouted at him.

'One child or ten must not stand in the way of the future, Collins.'

"We exchanged another series of blows, none of which left either of us worse off. I kept waiting for him to weaken as the blood flowed out of his arm. But he never tired."

'If nothing can stop you," I said "Why are you here? '

"My question drove him into an utter frenzy and he suddenly charged at me with such fury that he broke my sword, beat me senseless and left me for dead."

"And this was how long ago?" I asked.

"I do not know, Darrow. I have been in no condition to consult my pocket watch," he laughed softly and a spasm of pain shot across his face. "I think he must be very eager to get to the cottage ahead of you, Darrow, otherwise, he would have taken the time for the *coup de grâce* and made sure of me. It was early in the day when I came here. It is dark now. That is all I can tell."

I was sorry that Samuelson knew I was near, but now I knew with absolute certainty that there was a secret and something at Dardoch Cottage that could reveal it. But the urgency Samuelson now felt could work against me. If there were documents to destroy or other evidence, he would do it now before I could reach him. I could not decide whether to leave Collins and press on in the dark or wait for morning. While I was weighing the alternatives, the wailing of the wolves broke in on my thoughts and decided my actions for me. I dared not risk Samson on a such a dangerous descent, down into the valley below with wolves at his heels. Not only could I lose my mount and possibly be killed, if anything happened to Samson, I would also lose a friend.

Seeming to read my inmost thoughts Collins said, "Yes, it is better if you wait until morning, Darrow."

"Then, can I do anything more to make you comfortable before I sleep?" I asked.

"No. I am a tough old man and have lain on more than one battlefield with wounds worse than these. I would have frozen, though, if you had not brought me inside. Good night, Darrow. But before we sleep, I wish to thank you for finding my daughter."

"What do you mean?" I asked.

"The girl you met in London on the street who gave you the cameo is my daughter. I have been searching for her for many years."

"I did not understand what that reference to children was when you were telling me about your encounter with Samuelson. Now I see. I understand the violence of your feelings toward him. I know how I would feel if someone used Emily the way Anne has been used."

"Sleep now, Darrow. You will need your strength tomorrow, I know. Tomorrow, we will kill this *bête*, this beast."

I leaned back once more against the firewood piled at my back and fell asleep quickly. I heard only moments of the crackling fire and the voices of the howling wolves.

The following morning, a shaft of brilliant sunlight woke me. It entered the shed through some large chinks in the wall. I jumped to my feet when I realized that Collins was no longer lying nearby. I pulled open the door and was met by intensely brilliant sunlight reflected off the new, powdery snow. The sky was radiant. The snow that had gathered across the threshold during the night had been pushed into a high fluffy mound when Collins had opened the door. His tracks led to the barn. I have never learned the French language, but I was sure that was the language I heard coming from the barn as I walked toward it. When I stepped inside, I found Collins talking to the great horse. As I entered, he turned to face me. I could see that he moved stiffly and limped.

'I was just explaining to Samson that today he will have to carry both of us down the steep rocks into the valley.'

In spite of his injuries, Collins quickly and expertly saddled Samson and adjusted his bridle.

'Get into the saddle, Darrow, and leave the reins in your lap. Samson knows his footing better than either of us. I shall ride behind you.'

A few moments later and we were riding through the soft deep snow of the mountain trail. I did not direct the horse at all. Collins merely spoke to him.

'*Lentment, mon ami,*' Collins would call to the horse when the trail became even more sharply inclined.

'I think I could walk, Collins,' I said.

'There is no need for now. If the footing becomes too treacherous, Samson will stop and tell us to get down.'

Hour after hour we crawled down the steep, badly marked trail. The sun disappeared behind thick, dark clouds that seemed to hover just above our heads. At times, there were chasms on either side of us. Waterfalls fell from these heights once they reached the warm weather below but at these elevations, the water had frozen against the rock. The ice that formed here was knotted in strange, twisted shapes, some like the roots of crystalline trees, some like wild goblins that looked as if they would come alive when the moon rose again. But as we descended, we left these dramatic crags behind. I could feel the air become warmer.

The snowy mantle diminished until at mid day only a couple of inches of fluffy whiteness covered the way ahead. One or two houses of whitewashed stone appeared along what might now be called a road. The country became less and less wild until, in the distance I saw my first Scottish loch, or lake.

Long and narrow, Lochcarron nestled between rugged peaks that sloped down almost to the water's edge. Steep hills covered with snowy ever-green trees and heather surrounded the loch. The fishing village of Strathcar-ron was stretched out alongside the narrow portion of the loch, with all doors facing the single thoroughfare of the town. Great masses of dark gray clouds lowered over the loch and village, dwarfing them, alternately hiding and revealing different parts of the folded, snow covered mountain heights that towered above. All the village buildings were of whitewashed or dark brown stone and seemed to grow directly out of the base of the looming hills. The waters of the loch itself were gray and sluggish-looking, the colour and texture of slate. It was a wild, brooding place, magnificent in its way, though, to my mind, cold and uninviting. It was a landscape that made me think of the man we were pursuing: remote, devoid of warmth or human sentiment.

During our descent, Collins explained how he happened to be on the trail where I met him, for I was quite astonished to see him in this remote, distant land. He told me about your meetings and the extraordinary chance of Anne being his daughter. Had she not given me that jewel, she might still be lost to him and we would not have had Collins' aid. How can anyone not believe in God's grace when such things happen?

I had elaborated to Collins on the way I thought to proceed against Samuelson.

For the most part, he agreed with my plan. The first thing I had to do was ascertain if there were a church or place where records might be kept that was even closer to Dardoch Cottage than Strathcarron. This I would do by making inquiries in any public place in the town.

As we entered Strathcarron we both saw a small inn in the centre of the single row of buildings, which constituted the entire village. After our ride down the icy fells, I looked forward to a warming drink and assumed that Collins would as well. In addition to enquiring about the location of parish records, we would also need to be directed to Dardoch Cottage. The directions given on the envelope, which I had written down at Mrs. Muchison's assumed a knowledge of the environs which neither I nor Collins possessed. When we drew up in front of the tiny hostelry, Collins refused to join me inside.

"Should Samuelson make enquiries or have anyone watching this route," he said, "it is better if he thinks you are alone. Let him think he killed me," he said. "This preserves the advantage of surprise for us."

Inside, there were seven or eight men who were so obviously unfriendly and suspicious of strangers, I decided to forego my questions here. Collins and I would have to look elsewhere for help. When I went outside and told him, he said,

"Your thought is a good one, Darrow. Who knows how many of these people are in the great man's pay? He could buy the whole town. We need information, but we shall have to be circumspect as to how we get it. We have no idea which hands may be turned against us here."

So we rode back the way we had come, making for the place where the loch was fed by a narrow, shallow salt river only a few inches deep at low tide. We knew it was salt because Samson wouldn't drink it. Then we tasted it and knew that the narrow bar of water would probably swell to a flood at high tide. It lay right at the bottom of the mountain trail we had come down. We had just reached the water and were about to start across when we heard a horse galloping dangerously fast, coming down from the heights. Collins immediately hid us behind a wall of piled brown stone. As we huddled down it began to snow again. In just seconds it began falling thickly. When the rider galloped by us, I saw Paul Samuelson riding at breakneck speed into the shallow salt water of the, tidal river.

"We are in luck," Collins muttered. "Now,"Collins commented, as Paul rode past our hiding place, "we have a guide. The snow is fresh and if we stay close to him but out of sight, we shall have an easy trail to on the other side of the water. We should be able to follow it all the way to the cottage. Once we have found our way there, we can return here or go to other villages to search for parish records."

Neither of us had any way of knowing that the grisly climax of our mad dash through the mountains and snow would make written evidence meaningless.

Once again, I felt that the mightiest of hands was pointing the way to the heart of the secret that Samuelson had tried to bury in this remote place. The Lord's hand was reaching out to expose him. Even as the sun went down, a full moon was rising, giving us ample light to see the rider's marks in the snow. His trail was as easy to read as handwriting. As we crossed the shallow water to the other side of the loch, I saw a ruined stone tower outlined grimly against the clear sky. It looked like a great arm and hand, pointing up at the heavens. At its top was a structure that really did seem to have the shape of a hand. It pointed upward, into the vastness of God's heavens.

The cold, clear air rushed against my face. Nature itself was removing the barriers that hid Samuelson's secret refuge. What form the evidence of the secret would come in, I did not know, but I was convinced that a just and all-powerful God had brought us this far and would lead us to the final exposure of crime. It simply could not be that I could come all this way not to find that which would free us from this dangerous man.

You have told me, dearest, on various occasions, that my faith in a just Providence is the best part of my character. Your words are true: I look back now over this journey in the twilight and wonder myself that failure seemed an impossibility to me, as we dashed along. When I think back now on how vague were the indications on which I had pinned our hopes, I am astonished at my certainty that night, as we followed the dark streaks of the tracks in the snow.

Samuelson had taken his wife to this remote place when she was expecting a child, and there were some oblique references in Charles' document suggested the possibility of a secret and terrible crime. How insubstantial it seems now, but then, I felt that the railway king could not possibly escape us. Of course, I could never have guessed the horrifying way the crisis of our lives was to be resolved, only that somehow, Mighty Jack would fall.

After crossing the water, we were able to follow the trail with little or no difficulty. As the moon rose, it became brighter and brighter and the snow reflected the light into every corner. We came around a tight bend in the road and suddenly, we were flying by the lit windows of a cottage set back from the road but within sight of the large loch whose banks we had been following. There were no longer any tracks ahead of us. It could only mean that we had reached our destination, Dardoch Cottage.

Collins turned Samson around, and we dismounted behind a storage building that formed one of the boundaries of the yard and hid us from view of the house windows. We could see the fresh tracks leading into the drive. Collins and I both understood without words that we must approach the cottage with the greatest possible stealth.

The yard of the gabled cottage was formed by a low stone wall, a stone barn and the low hay storage shed, which we used as cover for Samson. The drive lay between the shed and the wall. The house faced the wall across the yard and stood perpendicular to the barn and shed which were attached. The only way to approach the house from the front was through the drive which led to the small yard directly in view of the windows. In the bright moonlight we would be utterly exposed if we tried to approach this way. From the road, we could see Paul's riderless horse standing in the yard. There were, of course, no servants about. One would not have servants about if one's business were to hide a fatal secret.

We tramped through the new snow drifts behind the shed and barn, the new dry snow crunching noisily under our feet and, hidden by the buildings, made our way to the back of the house. The moonlight on the snow was so bright that it might as well have been broad daylight. Fortunately, there were no windows in the house on the end that faced the barn, so we were able to slip from behind the barn into the pine trees that lay between the shore of the loch and the back of the house without any possibility of being seen. Under cover of the dark trees, we were able to see easily into the brightly lit interior of the house.

From the abrupt gestures of the two men, It was apparent that an argument was in progress between father and son, though we were too far away to hear what was being said. I decided to leave the cover of the trees and, by crawling through the snow below the windows to avoid detection, overhear what was being said. I made a sign to Collins to signify my intention. He nodded affirmatively.

I waited for a moment when the two men's backs were turned to the window, then I bent low and began creeping through the snow to the building. I ended by squatting just below the window of the parlour where the two men were shouting at each other. There was a fire in the grate and I could see heaps of fluffy ashes in the fireplace that had obviously been paper. My heart sank, but then my attention was caught by the voices of father and son.

'You were the one who was enough of an idiot to lose her regard," Samuelson said. The big man's arm was bandaged. His face was red, flushed with drink and anger.

"So now you make her an offer yourself so that I will get no money," Paul answered angrily.

"Obviously, you fool, if you don't marry her, you will not get any settlement."

"And where does that leave me and..."

"And your whore,' Samuelson bellowed. "I don't care what happens to either of you. I have a son who is a fool, who is not capable of curbing himself even for a short time. You will never be of use to me or anyone. I should have ended your life right here in this cottage when Annabelle had you."

"Why speak of her, now?' Paul asked, furiously. 'You made her miserable enough when she was alive."

"A ghastly mistake, both of you. And you the worst."

"Are you saying you regret my existence?" the son shouted angrily.

"I am saying I regret the existence of a bastard I got on my sister." Samuelson shouted back. "An unholy piece of filth that never should have been allowed to survive."

Paul suddenly stood as though he had been turned to stone. He faced his father motionless for a long moment and then spoke, "What? What are you saying about a sister?"

I could see that the son's flow of feelings was stopped and suddenly frozen in mid-course. My heart leapt at Samuelson's admission, which was what I suspected from my knowledge of the railway camps and from my conversation with Mrs. Murchison. It
was so horrifying a secret for the son that Paul had barely been able to grasp it.

Looking through the window, I saw for the first time the cruel smile that Charles had written of when Samuelson beat a man to death in the boxing ring.

"That must be why you are such an inferior idiot," Samuelson said.

"What, what are you saying, father?" Paul said in a high-pitched, suddenly childish voice. "What are you saying about my mother?"

"She was a good woman." Samuelson said moving to a cabinet and pouring another drink. "Strong. She and I were both strong. We had to be to do what we did. But you, you are a weak idiot," Samuelson bellowed out the last word as he held his contemptuous face only inches from his son's.

"What are you saying about my mother?" Paul growled at his father.

The cruel smirk appeared across Samuelson's face once more.
"Too stupid to hear anything but the plainest words? All right then, Annabelle, your mother, was my sister. We were inseparable as children and once we were older...well, you of all people should know about uncontrollable passion."

The younger man blinked a few times as if waking. Then he screamed at his father, "You are a liar. You are disgusting."

The same cruel smirk spread across the older man's face. He turned his back on his son's rage and said, "Screaming at me won't make things any different. I was afraid when she had you that you would be deformed. I brought you to this God forsaken place so I could get rid of you if you had two heads or an extra foot the way farm animals sometimes do. I was relieved to see you were whole. But you weren't, really. You poor excuse for a man."

"I don't believe you," Paul screamed.

"Come, son, I give you my hand on it," and the railway king turned away chuckling while Paul stood absolutely still for a moment, frozen like a carved likeness.

Then, suddenly, he sprang forward, seized the poker from the hearth and stuck his father across the back of the head before the big man could turn around. As Samuelson did slowly turn toward his son and the window where I watched, I could see a strange look of surprise spread across the big man's face. He swayed stiffly for a second like a tree being felled. When he did fall, Paul jumped on his chest and kept hitting his face with the poker over and over again. In moments, blood and brains were everywhere. It was a sickening sight. Then, as if waking from a dream, Paul dropped the poker and screamed, a scream I shall hear in my dreams for the rest of my life. He threw down the poker and ran out the front door of the house.

I rushed around to the door and Collins followed me, coming out from under the trees. But Paul was too quick. By the time I got around the house, he was galloping away.

'Collins, I must go after him. Samuelson is dead inside,' so saying, I ran out of the yard, grabbed Samson by his reins and jumped onto his back. Moments later we were flying over the same ground, returning the way we had come.

The moon had started to set, but the way was still bright. I could see the rider ahead of me. Paul galloped at top speed until he reached the water, which was now much higher. Near the water's edge, I could just see him as he dismounted and ran into the ruined tower I had noticed before. I suppose he thought he his horse could not cross. We shall never know what his intent was, or even if he knew, himself. By the time I drew up to the ancient tower, Paul was nowhere in sight, though his horse stood nearby.

I entered the ruined tower. The setting moon was still bright and shone onto the stones through the broken roof and the damaged walls. The dislocated stones and beams of the tower cast strange shadows everywhere. For some moments it was hard to get my bearings among the eerie shapes and the contrasts of bright moonlight and deep shadow. Then, I saw a winding stair, which was built right into the curving wall of the tower, running up to the broken roof above like a giant corkscrew.

Steps in the corkscrew were missing in places and I heard and then saw Paul make a wild leap over one of these gaps. Without thinking, I dashed onto the stair and went after him. When I got halfway up, I glanced down onto the circular floor beneath me where the moonlight was brightest, coming in unobstructed through the centre of the ruined roof. In just that moment when I looked away from him, Paul must have missed his footing, or jumped, for an instant later I saw him falling through the shafts of moonlight and onto the stone floor below, landing with a terrible, indescribable noise.

For the longest moment of my life, everything was still, including my own breath. He lay unmoving, a dark shape no longer human, but strangely twisted and broken. The horror of the scenes I had witnessed gripped me and my teeth chattered in my head. For some moments, even after I began breathing again, I could not move for the shaking of my legs. Then, very, very slowly, I made my way down the ruined stair, weak and shaking in all my limbs.

I went over to Paul to be absolutely certain that I could do nothing. When I turned him over, the moon showed me his terrible, shattered face. More dead than alive, myself, I crept out of the horrible tower and sat on a stone, lost in the horror of what I had witnessed. How long I sat beneath the darkening sky of the setting moon, I do not know, but by the time I stood up the only light left was on the snow and the white, foamy edges of the surf that had risen even higher in the in the tidal river.

As if understanding that I needed some contact with the living,

Samson moved close to me and nuzzled me with his warm face. A short time later, I was enough myself to climb on him and start back to Dardoch Cottage.

I rode slowly thinking of the dark road I had taken, and could not help remembering what Charles had said in his letter to me: Revenge was reserved for the Lord, not for man. How much more terrible an end than anyone could have imagined, had come on the railway king. I felt that in the cottage and in that grisly tower I had seen retribution for human evil that was like a foretaste of hell itself. What human hand could have avenged Charles as completely as the events I had witnessed? I shall never forget that night. Collins and I cleaned up the mess in the cottage. We agreed not to notify anyone.

Father and son, victims of each other were both dead. Let their deaths be a mystery to the local authorities. No one would be the worse for it. The Lord's hand had done His work more thoroughly than any human agency could have done it. Father and son were both avenged and both punished.

"That is our tale, Sally. As I write this, I am once more back in Manchester with Collins. We shall be home soon, dearest. I cannot wait to hold you in my arms. I believe that with Samuelson dead, we shall be free of persecution in future. You, Emily and I will be free to live our lives, darling. I shall see you soon. Your loving husband, Richard."

As soon as she finished reading, Sally burst into tears: Tears of relief, of happiness and of sorrow for the horrible deaths. She immediately claimed for herself the difficult duty of telling the story of Paul's death to Fanny.

Chapter 41

In the months after Richard and Collins returned to London. The mood in the metropolis was uneasy. But in the north, in the vicinity of Manchester, the mood was more uneasy, yet. The authorities feared there would be a rising by the millions of people who had signed the petition calling for the Charter. Especially after Feargus O'Conner addressed a crowd of over forty-thousand at Rochdale. What the result of all the agitation would be, no one knew. No matter what happened, it would mean unrest. There was already much anxiety about the rebellious attitude of the poor and labouring classes. The questions being asked in every quarter were these: Would there be an armed uprising if the Charter were not made law, and if so, how large would it be? But the meeting in Rochdale was actually the death throe of Chartism. After that gathering, the Chartist cause faded away.

During the time leading up to the final Chartist gathering, Fisk continued to write what were regarded as inflammatory pamphlets, and the authorities tried to suppress them in spite of their largely metaphysical contents. In order to avoid arrest, he kept moving from place to place. It was during this time that he published his infamous *Angelic Prophecies* which, according to the established Church, blasphemously purported to be a vision of man's future as described by the greatest angels of heaven. These prophecies told of a time only two hundred years hence when man's greed and the inequality between the rich and poor of all nations would destroy the world. They predicted terrible storms, poisoned air and water, the very death of nature itself. This, the prophecies said, would come about through the worship of the Beast and his machines. Love, kindness, Man and God, Himself, would be forgotten in the frenzied race for the wealth that the offspring of the Beast, the Beast's machines promised.

"In our own age," Fisk wrote, "We are creating this terrible future. We have given birth to the Iron Beast, now, today, in the 19th Century, in our age of "progress". Let all men of good will make certain that the offspring of the Beast serves, not merely the wealthy, but God and the poor as well. Let us harness the Iron Beast with Love and Charity, not in words only, but in actions, so that the high are lowered and the low are raised up. Then and only then shall we all see the advent of the New Jerusalem. Now that the Beast roams the world clad in the power of steam and iron and will one day even fly in the heavens, we must learn to live in true charity or we shall not live at all."

When *The Angelic Prophecies* was published, the authorities became so determined in their pursuit of the carpenter, he began to feel he had no choice but to be arrested or leave the country. It was a period of crisis in his life for more than one reason. After Cynthia's death, and Richard's return, Fisk had spent more and more time with the teacher and his family. As a consequence, he also found himself much better acquainted with Fanny. He had always greatly admired her, from the time she had first grown out of short frocks. Now, he learned to appreciate her laughter and her complete acceptance of all people and creatures. What many, including Richard, had construed as a light character was really a very open and loving one which could accept all God's creation with and love. Fanny did not strive for anything. She was content with herself and others. This, Fisk decided, was the true key to her character.

He watched her one day as she stood on the street talking to Maudie, the old mudlark, still in her filthy rags in spite of the coat Richard had bought her. Fanny put her arm around the mudlark's sooty shoulder as she would with any old friend, and kissed her dirty cheek when they parted.

After the old lady shuffled off, Fisk went to Fanny and told her, "You have the attitude of true charity. You judge no one. You are kind to all."

"How could I judge anyone," she replied. "I have not the right."

"No one does, but God," Fisk said."But few of us seem able to remember it."

Could he ask her, he wondered to go into exile with him to America? Could he ask her to leave her brother's family, perhaps for the rest of her life? He would have to decide soon, for the police had already come within a hair's breadth of arresting him on several occasions. It was only because of Fanny that he postponed his departure. He had already had an offer from the New Jerusalem Church, recently established in Pennsylvania in North America, to be a paid lecturer. It was a fine opportunity and, he would be able to write and say what he wanted without the threat of arrest.

In spite of being preoccupied with his own thoughts during these weeks, Richard could guess what his friend was thinking about, but said nothing. Since he and Collins had returned from Scotland, he spoke less and kept his own counsel more often. It was tacit with his friends that Samuelson was a topic not to be discussed with anyone, even after the deaths became public knowledge. Given Samuelson's financial prominence and the dangerous mood of the population, the police would be bound to act on even the mildest gossip about the railway king's death. Collins, fortunately, was gone, having taken Anne back to France to some obscure coastal town where they might live quietly in undisturbed seclusion. Apart from stockholders, there was really no one to be interested in Samuelson's death. The authorities had decided that it was a horrible family quarrel that had ended in murder and suicide. The matter had been completely laid to rest.

Richard did get a note from Pamela saying that she had recovered some of her wealth, thanks to the assiduity of Mr. Barnes, after Samuelson's death. She reiterated her invitation to visit Blackdale with Emily and his wife at any time. She would soon be leaving on a concert tour that would take her to every corner of Europe. With each of his friends well situated in life, but Fisk, all of Richard's energy could now be directed to securing a good future for himself and his family. He kept one watchful eye on Fisk and Fanny, waiting to see what would happen.

The danger and uncertainty of Fisk's situation was approaching a crisis when the Chartist meeting in Rochdale took place. The conflict between rich and poor, the masters and the labourers was at a white heat. So, when Richard received a letter from Vicar Franklyn in early June which offered him the position of headmaster at a new school that was being built in the village, it indirectly affected Fisk as well. Richard, Sally and Emily would be able to remove to the cottage that had once belonged to Charles Wilney. Fanny would have to find a place in Dorsetshire, near Richard's new home, or return to the streets as a coster, or find some other mode of life.

Richard told Fisk of his opportunity and the carpenter spoke to Fanny soon afterward.

"Fanny, what will you do when your brother removes to Dorset? Will you go as well?" the carpenter asked.

"I have not decided, yet, Mr. Fisk. I do not think I am exactly suited to country living. Richard is going to be living in the woods."

"So you would stay here and find some kind of work? I do not seek to surprise your private plans, but I do have a settled purpose in asking, Miss Darrow."

"Every time you call me, 'Miss Darrow', I know you are going to say something serious to me."

"Do you dislike it when I am serious?"

"No. It was just an observation. I thought that perhaps I could learn some of your seriousness, if you preferred it."

"No, Miss Darrow, not at all. In heaven, it is the heart that matters. And you have one of the best I have ever known."
Fanny looked thoughtful. "Cynthia told me exactly the same thing about heaven and...myself. I suppose if you say it, it must be true."

"It is true. And, I was wondering," he went on awkwardly, pausing for a very long time.

"Yes, Mr. Fisk. What were you wondering?"

"I was wondering if you could think America a good place to live."

"America? Why so far?"

"Well, Miss Darrow, I think I shall soon have to go there. I have been offered employment as a lecturer and the police are looking for me here. There, I should be able to speak my mind freely and write without fear of suppression."

"I had not realized you were going to emigrate." She looked at him quite solemnly.

"Yes, I fear I have to." Then he blurted out, "I know I am rather older than you, Miss Darrow, but I have always liked and admired you and now I can say I know you enough to respect you as well."

"Yes?" she said, her face still solemn.

"Well, I was wondering, Miss Darrow, if you would consider, coming with me to America."

"Coming with you?" she said looking surprised."

"Well, I wondered if you would consider marrying me, Miss Darrow?"

"Thank goodness," Fanny exclaimed. "I was beginning to think I was going to have to do something immoral before you would make an offer."

"Really? You mean, you want to?"

"Why would I not? You are a handsome man, Fisk and one of the kindest and most gentle I have ever known."

"I thought Paul's death..." he left the words unfinished.

"That was very sad," Fanny said. "Not for me, particularly. But in itself. That he and his father should have hated each other so much. We had little together, Paul and I," she said, looking more grim than he had ever seen her "—except lust. We both needed each other when we met. He to escape his father and me because I had no sense of any great object in my life. But knowing you and having friends...I feel differently, now." She glanced at Fisk to watch his response to her words.

He moved close to her and slipped his arm around her waist.

"Dearest Fanny. Could you like me as a husband, do you think?" he asked.

"With the gray hairs in my beard?"

"I think I could do more, Fisk. I believe I could honour and love you."

"You feel certain of that?"

"Yes."

"I have wondered about your feelings almost continually these past weeks. I thought, perhaps you were just trying console me after Cynthia's passing."

"I was. Cynthia wanted me to, but then I wanted to."

"Did she? You spoke of this?"

"She asked me to look after you. I do not know how well I shall do it, but I know I should prefer not to be parted from you."

He kissed her very gently on the mouth.

At just that moment, Sally and Richard opened the door. Fanny and Fisk both jumped in surprise.

"What is going on here?" Richard said smiling.

"Mr. Fisk has just made me an offer. And I have accepted it, brother. That's what is going on."

"Oh, that is wonderful," Sally said.

"It certainly is," Richard added. "I was starting to think we were going to have to tie you up, Fisk."

"What?"

"Well, I have known for years that you more than liked Fanny. I cannot understand why it has taken so many years to force an offer out of you."

"I, suppose that I just did not think she would have me," Fisk answered smiling at Fanny.

"I think it just as well that it took so long," Fanny said.

"Why?" Richard asked.

"You know, better than anyone, Richard, I have had some difficult lessons to learn...to, to make me worthy of him." She looked over at Fisk with a soft light in her eyes.

"When is the wedding?" Emily asked running in with Hilf from the other room.

"Where did you come from, scamp," Fisk asked.

"Just behind the door. I was waiting for you to finish."

"Gracious," Fisk said, smiling. "It's been a conspiracy and I knew nothing about it."

"Well, it is too late, now, sir," Fanny said. "Conspiracy or no. I have witnesses," she added putting her hands on Emily's shoulders.

Richard leaned over and kissed his sister on the cheek.

"Really Fan, I am so happy for you, both. He is the best man I know,"

"I agree," Fanny said, taking Fisk's arm. "Charles, I shall do everything in my power to make you a good wife. I know I have not been a very go..."

Her mouth was suddenly stopped by a kiss. This time, he kissed her deeply.

Afterwards he said, "Fanny, I feel gratitude for being accepted. You are more than worthy of me."

"Well," Sally said, "this calls for a celebration."

"Let's go to the giraffes at the zoological gardens," Emily called out.

"I was thinking of something more like a nice dinner, little captain," Sally said.

"Good. Let us have a wedding feast," Richard said. "I shall go out and order one and have it sent. There is nothing wanting now for our happiness."

* * *

But it was still to be some years before reform came and the poor had the vote. What is more unfortunate, even when reform did come, the appetite of the Iron Beast would remain the driving force behind society. The

429

railway corporations would become the largest and richest corporate bodies the world had ever seen, preparing the way for a future of unbridled greed, which went by the name of capitalism. The race for wealth would continue unabated and move faster and faster.

The richest nations sought to hide their greed from each other and from God by offering the Beast obscure, poor nations to consume. The people of those nations became the slaves of the Beast. And this was applauded by all mankind.

Now, we are closer than ever to worship of the Beast, and closer than ever to the consequences of that worship.

The End

A NOTE ABOUT ALAN MCKEE

Alan lives with his family in Toronto but spends time writing at his second home in Nova Scotia. He studied violin in New York City for ten years. His special interests are British history and nineteenth century literature. He has been inspired by E.P. Thompson and Eric Hobsbawn, both great British historians.

OTHER TITLES

The Minotaur's Children
Shadows of Empire

www.hudsonhousemysteries.com